LABYRINTH

By A.G. Riddle

The Atlantis Trilogy
The Atlantis Gene
The Atlantis Plague
The Atlantis World

The Extinction Files
Pandemic
Genome

The Long Winter Trilogy
Winter World
The Solar War
The Lost Colony

Other Novels
The Extinction Trials
Lost in Time
Quantum Radio
Antarctica Station

LABYRINTH

A.G. RIDDLE

An Ad Astra Book

First published in the United Kingdom in 2025 by Head of Zeus Ltd,
part of Bloomsbury Publishing Plc

Copyright © A.G. Riddle, 2025

The moral right of A.G. Riddle to be identified
as the author of this work has been asserted in accordance with
the Copyright, Designs and Patents Act of 1988.

All rights reserved. No part of this publication may be: i) reproduced or transmitted
in any form, electronic or mechanical, including photocopying, recording or by means
of any information storage or retrieval system without prior permission in writing from
the publishers; or ii) used or reproduced in any way for the training, development or
operation of artificial intelligence (AI) technologies, including generative AI technologies.
The rights holders expressly reserve this publication from the text and data mining
exception as per Article 4(3) of the Digital Single Market Directive (EU) 2019/790.

This is a work of fiction. All characters, organizations, and events
portrayed in this novel are either products of the author's
imagination or are used fictitiously.

9 7 5 3 1 2 4 6 8

A catalogue record for this book is available from the British Library.

ISBN (PB): 9781035924998
ISBN (E): 9781035925001

Typeset by Siliconchips Services Ltd UK

Printed and bound in Great Britain by Clays Ltd, Elcograf S.p.A.

Bloomsbury Publishing Plc
50 Bedford Square, London, WC1B 3DP, UK
Bloomsbury Publishing Ireland Limited,
29 Earlsfort Terrace, Dublin 2, D02 AY28, Ireland

HEAD OF ZEUS LTD
5–8 Hardwick Street
London EC1R 4RG

To find out more about our authors and books
visit www.headofzeus.com
For product safety related questions contact productsafety@bloomsbury.com

For every person who has lost something to the sands of time.

Prologue

The first time I saw the numbers was at my wife's funeral.
 I remember looking at those fourteen digits carved in stone and thinking that I was hallucinating (and possibly losing my mind).

I was wrong about that. And a few other things.

Back then, I didn't know what the numbers meant. I didn't realize how much they would change my life.

And soon after, the world.

There are three things that stick out in my mind about that day: the rain, the ringing, and the numbers.

The rain began as a drizzle.

I sat under a tent by the graveside, listening to the pastor's voice echo across the cemetery. Somewhere along the way, the clouds coalesced and drops started to fall.

By the time he finished speaking, the rain was a steady pitter-patter on the canvas above me, a fingernail tapping a tabletop, silently saying, "We're waiting."

And they were waiting for me.

I rose from the folding metal chair, but I didn't get far. My daughter, who was sitting beside me, reached up and grabbed me and held tight—tighter than I ever thought a six-year-old child could.

I leaned over and kissed the top of her head, pried myself loose, and stepped out into the rain.

My feet sank in the soggy grass, and I shouldn't have, but I looked over at the casket and that hole in the ground and my life.

The ringing started then.

I've had tinnitus for years. Usually, what I hear is a constant whine, like a tea kettle about to boil.

That day, the ringing in my ears was different. Instead of the shrill whine, I heard:

Clang.
Clang.
Clang.

I remember thinking that it sounded like an unseen hand had grabbed three rocks, dropped them in a tin can, and started shaking it.

I kept walking, and that hand kept rattling those rocks, getting louder with every step.

My face was soaked by the time I reached the cover of the pastor's umbrella, but I didn't wipe the rain away. I reached into my pocket and unfolded the page that held the eulogy.

I knew every word by heart. I'd rewritten it a hundred times. But the sheet gave me something to do with my hands.

The rocks rattled in my ears, and the rain fell harder, and I told my family and friends that my wife had helped me rebuild my life when I was broken. And that my greatest regret was that I couldn't help her when she was sick.

Every word seemed to annoy that unseen hand. It shook the can harder, clanging the rocks like it was taunting me.

In the battle that is my hearing, it won.

Halfway through the eulogy, I stopped hearing my own voice. All I heard was that abrasive rattling.

I kept going.

It kept shaking harder, the clanging ratcheting higher.

I getting ready to read the last paragraph, and wondering if people could still hear me, when I looked down at the page in my hand and realized that the wind had carried a few raindrops past the umbrella. Ink ran like blood from a dozen small cuts.

The unseen hand shook the rocks even harder, and there was a pop, as if it had slammed the can down on a table.

For a few seconds, the world was utterly silent. After the mind-numbing rattling, the void that followed was strange and disorienting. It felt like the seconds after that roadside bomb went off in Afghanistan.

And like then, my world had changed in the blink of an eye.

Over there, the bomb mangled the Humvee I had been driving and killed two of my fellow Marines. It took one of my legs.

In the cemetery that day, what the deafening explosion claimed was time. I knew time had passed because the page in my hand was soaked. The ink ran together in a massive blob.

I admit, in that moment, a cold shiver of fear went through my body. It was like realizing that the unseen hand shaking the rocks had a power over me that I didn't understand. It could take time from me. I had learned the hard way that time was life's most precious currency.

I stared at the wilted page and heard the silence, and it was as if that unseen hand and I were facing off. Like it was waiting for me, daring me to start up again.

I made my decision.

I looked up at the mourners under the canvas tents, at the confused looks and the heads nodding, and I resumed speaking.

The can swirled, and the rocks began to clang, and I said the words my wife deserved.

When I was done, the rattling was in full rage. But that was fine with me, because I had finished what I had to do.

I felt the pastor's hand on my shoulder, and I looked over at my wife's tombstone. I read her name and the epitaph, and when I got to the dates of her birth and death, the rattling went hypersonic. The screech pushed against reality, and I thought the hand was going to slam the can down again and take more time, but it didn't.

What happened was that the dates carved in stone changed. They morphed into:

12122518914208

And when I read that peculiar sequence of numbers, the clanging stopped. And the only thing I heard was raindrops falling on the pastor's umbrella.

I
THE NUMBERS

1

10 Months Later

When I wake up, I'm lying on a concrete floor next to a dead man.

He stares at me with glassy, unblinking eyes.

My heart beats faster—not just because he's dead, but because I don't remember coming here, meeting him, or *how* he died.

I do, however, recognize him.

His name is Nathan Briggs. We were in the Marines together. A long time ago.

The last time I saw Briggs, he was throwing a punch at me. That was right before I threw a punch at him. And then another. And then the barracks erupted in shouting and fighting.

I haven't had any contact with him since.

At least, I don't think I have.

The last thing I remember is being at home and having a bad tinnitus attack. I remember going to lie down, and that's it.

I heard the ringing in my ears.

I went to bed.

I woke up here.

I've lost time. This has only happened to me once before: at my wife's funeral. That day, I lost a minute or two. This time gap appears to be far longer. And a lot more problematic.

I reach into my shorts pocket for my phone, hoping to check the time, but it's not there. My wallet is gone too. I only feel a car key.

And then there's what I don't feel.

Lifting my head, I spot my prosthetic leg lying a few feet away.

Seeing it there, detached from my body, reminds me of the day I lost my leg. That day, I woke up like this—on my back, on a roadside in Afghanistan.

Back then, I saved my life by using a tourniquet to stop the flow of blood from the wound. Every second counted. I think it does now as well.

Moving quickly, I sit up and reattach the prosthetic. My body aches. There's pain in my abdomen, neck, and back. I'm pretty sure I was in a fight during the time gap.

Scanning my surroundings, I realize I'm in a room in what looks like a construction site. It's a commercial building of some sort. Maybe an office or retail space. The ceiling is tall, with metal ceiling joists and exposed air conditioning ducts.

I don't recognize the place or recall ever being here before.

What occurs to me now is that during the time I lost, someone might have lured me here, knocked me unconscious, and killed the guy next to me. That person could still be around—and they could be planning to kill me too. I need to move.

As I get to my feet, I take in more of the room. And every single thing I see is like a bomb going off.

There's a backpack sitting in the corner. I know that backpack. It's mine.

I don't remember packing it.

I don't know what's inside.

The second is a knife. It's sunk into the dead man's chest. It is, very likely his cause of death. Like the backpack, it belongs to me.

The third issue is that a series of numbers has been written on the concrete floor.

12122518914208

They're the same numbers I saw carved into my wife's gravestone.

But here, someone has written them in blood.

2

The numbers are a mystery.

The backpack is too.

The knife is a problem. So is the dead man, but as problems go, his body is by far my biggest problem.

It's like a thermonuclear reactor melting down. The clock is ticking. Radiation is spreading, and it's already all over me.

On some basic level, I feel like no matter what I do here, the police are eventually going to show up at my door with the crime scene equivalent of a Geiger counter and detect some radioactive isotopes and conclude that I did this.

The time gap is the root issue. If I knew what happened here, I'd have some idea of what to do. Depending on what happened, I'd probably just call the cops and wait for them, and we'd sort it out.

But I don't know what happened here. On the surface, the optics are not great for me. The more immediate issue, however, is whether I'm alone. And in danger.

On instinct, I walk backwards until I feel the cold touch of a metal stud on my back. I wait and scan my surroundings and listen. I'm unarmed, but there's only one weapon in sight. I'm not ready to pull that knife out of Briggs's chest and put my fingerprints on it (assuming they aren't already there).

I don't hear footsteps. Or talking. Only the faint rush of cars in the distance.

I need answers.

And I need to get out of here. If this is an active construction site, workers could arrive any second. Plus, if the site has cameras—and it likely does—someone might already know I'm here.

Ignoring my aching body, I move to the backpack and unzip it. What I see inside ends any thoughts of contacting the police.

The bag holds two large bottles of bleach and a change of clothes (my clothes).

Only one type of person packs these items: someone planning to commit a crime—and then clean it up.

Holding the backpack, I notice something else. Blood on my hands. Most of it is on my right hand. In the palm. There's a lot of blood on my index finger, too, but strangely, the tip of my finger is nearly clean.

I glance over at the numbers written on the concrete. I get it then.

I wrote the numbers. That's why there's no blood on the tip of my finger.

At this point in my life, with my wife gone and this bizarre thing happening, I would normally be inclined to simply sit down right here and wait for the construction workers to show up or the police to come around. I'd tell them the truth: that I don't remember what happened. That I'm unwell. That I lost time, and that I'll help them figure out what happened. I'd deal with the consequences. I don't want to be a danger to anyone.

But I'm also a father.

And my daughter is what I'm thinking about right now. She is my first concern in this world. I don't know how much time I've lost. And I don't know what happened to her during that time. I don't know if she's been harmed or if the person who killed Briggs and knocked me out has her right now.

I do know that there is no individual on this planet who will fight harder for her than me. What I'm going to do now is find my daughter. And make sure she's safe.

They can take me to jail after that.

If needed.

3

Stepping carefully around the pool of blood spreading out on the concrete, I lean over and search Briggs's pockets. I find only a phone and a slim wallet.

The phone is turned off. I don't dare activate it here (the location data might help investigators track him).

I'll need to get into the device at some point. It might have pictures or video of me and whatever happened here. And if those photos are on the phone, they might be stored in the cloud as well. If so, that's an even bigger problem.

What strikes me is that Briggs doesn't have a car key.

It means he walked here, took public transportation, or someone dropped him off. Or that his key was previously taken from him—or he discarded it.

It's another mystery, one to figure out later.

What I do next is not so much a choice as it is the result of having no other options, given my obligations in the world.

I remove the knife from Briggs's chest.

Because I need it.

Next, I take my clothes off. Because I don't want to drip blood in the building. The blood on my clothes isn't mine (I don't see an open wound). So that's good news.

In my boxers and shoes, I search the first floor of the building for my phone, careful to stay clear of the windows and doors where a camera outside might see me. I also look for security cameras inside. I spot one, but it doesn't seem to be on. The LED on the device is dark, and there are no wires running from it, as if it's a decoy. What I don't see is my phone. Which is also good news.

Using the knife, I cut off some of the sheet plastic that covers the opening to the room. Working quickly, I wrap up my bloody clothes, then cut away Briggs's shirt, pants, and boxers and encapsulate them too (I figure my prints or DNA might be on them).

Next, I wipe the numbers from the floor and use the bleach on the hard surfaces in the room.

I don't know enough about crime scene DNA to know if I'm covering all my tracks, but this is the best plan my foggy, stressed-out mind can come up with.

When I'm done, the backpack is full and I'm dressed in the clean clothes (jeans and a hoodie). Standing in the doorway to the building, I scan the street. By the looks of it, I'm in downtown Raleigh. It's nighttime, and thankfully, there's no one in sight at this hour.

Across the road, in an empty surface parking lot, I spot my Ford Explorer, waiting under the hazy glow of a pole light. There might be cameras along the street that will capture me exiting the building, but I don't see any way to avoid that.

Tugging the hoodie tighter around my face, I step out and walk briskly, head hanging slightly downward.

Inside the car, I check the console and glove compartment for my phone. It's not here.

I know I should dump the items in the backpack before I do anything else, but right now, my concern is for my daughter. So I decide to go directly home—with the evidence from this crime scene in the floorboard of the passenger seat.

I'm about five minutes from my apartment in North Raleigh when a car turns onto Six Forks Road and quickly closes the gap between us.

In the rearview mirror, I see the familiar blue hood and white roof of a Raleigh Police cruiser. The lightbar on top is dark.

For now.

But in my mind's eye, I imagine it flashing to life, strobing behind me before I pull over and the officer asks to see my license—which I don't have.

Also, the entire car smells like bleach.

Between the lack of license, the time of night, and the stench of bleach, I bet any good cop would want to take a closer look inside the car.

And the backpack.

4

I'm guessing that the officer following me is running my plate to see if the car is stolen (or perhaps if the owner has any outstanding warrants).

He's probably reading my name—Alan Norris—and looking at my face on a laptop next to him. He'll see that I have never been arrested and that the taxes on the SUV are paid.

That's what I have going for me.

What I have to figure out is what I'm going to say if he lights up and pulls me over and asks why I'm out here at 3:37 AM.

"My kid is sick, officer. I had to get her some medicine. I took some cash and left my license at home. Sorry, I wasn't thinking."

That won't work. The story falls apart if they ask to see the medicine I bought for her—which I don't have.

As I glance in the rearview, I'm wishing I had thrown the backpack out by the side of the road as soon as I cleared downtown. I could always go back and collect it after checking on Riley and getting my license.

With nothing to do but wait, I try to piece together what happened before I lost time.

My last clear memory is of being at home, in my apartment, sitting at the dining table with Riley. We were working on a 3D puzzle of the Hogwarts School of Witchcraft and Wizardry.

Riley has ADHD, and I bought the puzzle as a way to strengthen her concentration—and to give us an activity to do together.

Music was playing from a Bluetooth speaker, and we were turning the puzzle pieces over and spreading them out.

The ringing started out of nowhere. No trigger, no buildup. And for the first time since the funeral ten months ago, the unceasing sound only I could hear was those rocks in the can, *clang-clang-clanging* in my ears. Usually, what I hear is like a tea kettle whining. Sometimes it grows to a shrill whistle.

Sitting at the dining table, I waited as the can shook harder, and the rocks rattled, and a pit of dread formed in my stomach.

I focused on my breathing. That works every now and then. It's like a pressure valve that allows the attack to pass.

But not this time. With each puzzle piece I turned, the ringing grew louder.

I remember looking over at the clock on the kitchen wall, which read 6:45.

I opened a bottle of Calm gummies and held out two for Riley. The gummies are a magnesium supplement that helps her sleep, but she often tries to delay taking them. In classic fashion, she frowned and said something—which I couldn't hear but suspect was a complaint about it not being bedtime yet.

I pointed to my ears, silently telling her I was having an episode.

Her annoyed expression melted, and she reached out and took the gummies and leaned forward and spoke slowly enough for me to read her lips.

Can I help?

I shook my head and stood and told her I'd be right back, hoping she could hear me. And hoping that it was true.

In my bedroom, I turned off the lights and stretched out on the mattress and closed my eyes and concentrated on my breathing, feeling the point where air flowed past my nose.

By then, the ringing was so loud it was disorienting, like being in a sensory deprivation tank.

I don't know how long I lay there, but my next memory is of a bright light lancing into the room. I squinted and watched as the bedroom door swung open, casting my seven-year-old daughter in shadow.

Riley crept forward and set a glass of water on the bedside table and leaned over and hugged me. I wrapped my arms around her, and when I let go, she walked to the bathroom and returned with a pill bottle. The medication helps with the tinnitus attacks, but I don't like taking it. The drug makes me feel loopy and out of it. Not exactly ideal for a single parent of a young child. But I already felt loopy and out of it, so I didn't have much to lose by taking it.

Riley set the pill bottle next to the glass of water and hugged me again, pressing the side of her head into my chest.

"I'm okay," I told her. I couldn't hear my voice, but I said the words anyway because that's part of being a parent: telling your child you're okay, even when you're not.

The last thing I remember is my daughter releasing me and walking out of the bedroom and gently closing the door behind her. I reached for the pill bottle, but my fingers never reached it.

That unseen hand shook the can furiously and slammed it down with a pop that once again took time from me.

Like the 3D puzzle on our dining room table, those are the pieces of what happened.

The tinnitus attack.

Losing time.

Waking up in that building under construction.

With a dead body beside me.

I wonder how long it's been since I lay down in my apartment.

I'll know soon, assuming the blue lights behind me don't come on.

5

The police cruiser changes lanes and pulls into my blind spot. I resist the urge to glance back. I can almost feel eyes boring into me, raking across the inside of the SUV, doing a mental calculation.

Thankfully, the math doesn't add up to pulling me over.

The officer accelerates past me, into the night.

When the police cruiser is out of sight, I pull off of Six Forks Road, onto a secondary street, and drive until there's nothing but woods on both sides of me. After parking, I exit the SUV, stalk into the woods, and hide the backpack in one spot, Briggs's wallet in another, and the phone in another.

I'll need to move the evidence when I can, but this will buy me some time.

At my apartment complex, there are no obvious signs of trouble. The three-story buildings with the units are mostly dark. There are no police cars here, no ambulance waiting with lights flashing in the night.

We get both police and ambulances with some frequency. The rent is on the lower side, and some of the residents get a little lively, especially on the weekends.

I want to move somewhere safer. Somewhere with a backyard. And a playroom for Riley.

But I can't afford it right now.

⋆

Our apartment is on the second floor, and as I climb the wooden outdoor staircase, my heart hammers in my chest.

In the next building, a stereo thuds softly. The air is filled with the faint smell of weed.

The door to our two-bedroom apartment is closed. There's no indication of forced entry.

Quietly, I turn the key in the lock, twist the handle, and push the door open.

Inside, the lights are off. In the dim glow of moonlight, I spot the pile of 3D puzzle pieces stacked on the dining table. The skeletal outline of the grounds of Hogwarts is a little more filled in than when I retreated to my bedroom. Riley must have kept working on it for a while before putting herself to bed. Or before whatever happened here.

Stepping across the threshold, I close the door behind me and wait, watching, listening for anyone else who might be inside the apartment.

There's no sign of a struggle here.

On the IKEA coffee table, I spot my wallet and phone. I pick up the device and check the date. It's the same night I went to lie down. And I haven't missed any calls or text messages.

My email is full of back-to-school coupons, loan offers, and new listings from real estate sites I subscribe to.

With my heart in my throat, I creep to Riley's bedroom door and quietly open it.

My only child is lying on her narrow bed, eyes closed. A Squishmallows stuffed animal is tucked under her right arm, and a dozen more furry friends are piled around her. On her bedside table, a Twinkle Tree glows softly. I gave it to her as a gift from the tooth fairy last month.

I don't know if it's the beating my body took tonight or the emotional relief, but I begin to shake. Leaning on my good leg, I hug the door frame, my face pressing into the jamb.

6

I'm exhausted but also wired.

There's no way I'm going to sleep tonight.

Besides, I have work to do.

I don't like leaving Riley home alone, but she's asleep, and I need to deal with that backpack full of bloody clothes in the woods.

With my wallet in my pocket, driving the speed limit and obeying all imaginable traffic laws, I return to the place where I hid the backpack, phone, and wallet. There in the woods, I finally turn the phone on. The wake screen unlocks instantly, which surprises me. It's like Briggs wasn't worried about anyone getting into the device (or was overconfident that it wouldn't be taken from him).

I soon see why.

The call log is empty. There are no contacts in the address book. No text messages. Switching back to the home screen, I scroll through the apps. They look like the standard ones that come with the OS. It appears to be a burner phone, one that has been essentially wiped (or never used).

For a moment, I stand in the thicket, trying to think through how to dispose of the device.

In the distance, I hear what might just be the answer.

Carefully, I stalk through the trees and bushes, mindful not to touch anything or let a branch or briar tear my clothing. Soon, the forest recedes, and I'm standing on the bank of a small creek. The water is fast-moving and a few feet deep. I don't know where the stream goes, but it will do the job I need: carrying the pieces of the phone somewhere else—a place that can't be tied to me with surveillance video.

After putting a pair of work gloves on and wiping the phone down, I remove the SIM card and set it on a rock and pulverize it with a claw hammer brought from home. Next, I break the phone into larger pieces and wrap them in sheet plastic from the construction site. I'm careful to clean the plastic thoroughly, removing any fingerprints.

From the bank, I send the five plastic-wrapped bundles of phone parts down the creek, waiting a few minutes between each launch.

The remaining items in the backpack are larger than the phone, and disposing of them is a far larger challenge.

With the backpack again in the floorboard, I drive north, wondering if the police can use any data from my car to track me. My Ford Explorer is over fifteen years old and not exactly loaded with premium features. I figure it doesn't have any sort of vehicle GPS or telematics that relay the position. Even if it does, there's not much I can do about it.

Thankfully, it's still dark when I pull onto a logging road and take down the cable blocking it.

The old road is rutty and bumpy, but thankfully, passable.

After parking, I take out the backpack and get a fire pit from the cargo area and walk through the woods until I can see Falls Lake in the distance.

Under the cover of the trees, I clear an area and set down the fire pit and burn the plastic-wrapped bundles.

Methodically, I place the ashes in Ziploc bags, attach a rock to each one, and toss them into the water.

I chose Falls Lake for several reasons.

First: convenience. It's the closest lake to my house.

Second: privacy. There aren't a lot of homes directly on the shore (in fact, I've never actually seen one here in Raleigh). Most of the land bordering the lake, at least here in Wake County, is owned by the Army Corps of Engineers. Thus, there are no home security cameras to see me.

And third: size. Falls Lake spans three counties and has over 175 miles of shoreline. The water covers more than 12,000 acres.

The evidence I sunk there tonight will be hard to find. At a minimum, I've bought myself some time.

But as I wipe down the fire pit with bleach, I can't help but wonder how many mistakes I've made since waking up—and when they'll catch up with me.

7

Back at home, I shower, brew some coffee, and search the web for information about Briggs.

Briggs doesn't have a LinkedIn profile. He's not on social media. And there's nothing on the web. His digital footprint is non-existent.

But I remember the employer name from his insurance card: Amersa. I've never heard of the company. According to Amersa's website, it's a tech start-up based in Research Triangle Park, that's developing a virtual reality device powered by artificial intelligence. The more I read about Amersa's mission and vision, the less I understand.

The only other clue I have to investigate is the sequence of fourteen numbers that was written in blood. I admit, after seeing them on my wife's headstone, I didn't look them up. I just sort of figured it was a freak thing that day.

But now, the numbers have my attention.

I begin my research by opening an AI chatbot and typing in the numbers and asking what they mean.

The high school students I teach got me into AI chat by showing me what it can do. They soon regretted it, because I started running my homework assignments through AI to see its responses. Now, any time a student turns in work that's a little too close to an AI response, I tell them: any AI could do this well. Try again.

But, at the moment, I'm okay with AI doing my homework. Because it knows more than I do, and I'm tired, and I need all the help I can get.

After "thinking" a few seconds, the AI chatbot tells me that it doesn't know exactly what the numbers are, but it has five theories.

One, the numbers could be a mathematical pattern or sequence. But without more data, the AI can't identify the pattern or the correct formula to generate further numbers.

Two, the numbers might be a date and time. For instance, "121225" might represent December 12th, 2025. But the bot seems less enthusiastic about that prospect.

Three, the numbers might be a serial number or a unique identifier. That's an interesting one.

The fourth possibility is that the sequence is simply a random string of numbers.

That theory doesn't help me much, but the last option does: the numbers might be encoded information.

I tell the AI to assume the numbers are encoded information and to decode it.

The bot quickly identifies several intriguing ciphers that might translate the code. There's Book Cipher, in which the numbers correspond to a specific page, line, and word in a book. That's interesting, but I don't know which book it's referencing.

The only cipher that seems promising is numeric substitution.

Using numeric substitution, each number in the sequence is changed to a letter according to its position in the alphabet. So 1 becomes A, 2 becomes B, 3 becomes C, and so on. Applying this to the numbers translates to "LLYRINTH."

For a moment, I study the numbers again:

12122518914208

Next, I ask the AI if they could spell anything else, and it promptly informs me that yes, they could.

The first four numbers are 1212. That's why the first two letters are both L.

If, however, the second 12 was separated into 1 and a 2, the first four numbers would spell L-A-B.

The resulting word would be LABYRINTH.

I'm vaguely familiar with the Labyrinth story from Greek

mythology, but I can't see how it connects to my wife and Briggs's murder. Or maybe I've decoded the numbers incorrectly.

I jump when I feel a hand on my shoulder.

Beside me, Riley reels back, wincing, as if she's touched a hot stove.

I reach out and pull her into a hug. "Hey, kiddo. I didn't hear you get up."

Her lips brush my ear as she whispers two words no parent ever wants to hear: "I'm scared."

Gripping her shoulders, I study her face. "Why?"

She grimaces. I recognize the expression. It's her "I don't want to say" face.

"What happened last night?"

Riley looks confused. "When?"

"After I went to bed."

She shrugs.

"You don't know?"

"I..."

"You can tell me, Riley. Whatever happened, you can tell me."

"I forgot."

"Forgot what?"

"To brush."

"Your teeth?"

She nods.

I exhale and loosen my grip on her shoulders. "Well, that's okay. Just don't make a habit of it. But after I went to my room, what else did you do?"

Confusion replaces her sheepishness. "What do you mean?"

"Did you—"

"I didn't watch TV, Dad. Or eat ice cream. I promise."

"That's good. But did anyone come over?"

She bunches her eyebrows. "What?"

"Did anyone come to the apartment last night, after I went to bed?"

Her confusion begins to morph into fear. I run a hand over her back.

"Everything's all right, sweetie. I'm just curious about what happened. You're not in trouble. Okay?"

She nods nervously.

I ask her again if anyone came over, and she shakes her head.

"You said you were scared. Why?"

Riley twists, trying to escape my grasp, but I hold on.

"It's okay to be scared," I reassure her. "Everyone gets scared. Even me."

She squints. "Really?"

"Really."

Her gaze drifts down to the floor. "I'm just... nervous."

"About what?"

"The other kids. Like if they're mean. Or if I don't know anybody."

I was so absorbed in what happened last night and my research this morning that I forgot—today is her first day of the new school year. And mine.

Wake County schools used to start on Tuesdays. For some reason, they switched to Monday this year.

Riley's hesitation vanishes as she breaks free of my grip and begins waving her hands, rattling off fears and what-ifs. Talking it out sometimes gets her even more amped up, but it usually helps.

When Riley's diatribe winds down, I give her one of my tried-and-true speeches. She's probably tired of hearing this one, but she needs it right now. "Remember, kiddo: things are never as bad as you imagine. This is the worst part—*right now*—imagining how bad it could be. You're going to love school. Just like your mom did."

She swallows hard, the mention of her mom casting a somber mood over the moment.

"And I'll tell you something else. If she were here right now, she'd be so proud of you."

8

A few hours later, I park my car in the teachers' lot at the high school where I work.

In the backseat, Riley is scanning the sidewalk, probably trying to spot one of her friends heading toward the elementary school. She's putting on a brave face, but I can tell she's nervous.

Outside, we walk in silence, her small hand in mine. It's late August, and even this early in the morning, the sun bears down, slowly baking us and the concrete sidewalk beneath our feet.

Across the road, the bus parking lot of the middle school is slowly filling up.

I left my cane in the car. I figure we'll draw less attention that way. Everybody wants to look normal. Especially on the first day of school.

But I pay for it with every step. My stump was already aching from whatever happened last night. By the time we reach the elementary school, it's throbbing.

At the entrance, there's a steady flow of children exiting their parents' cars and walking and jogging into school, backpacks bouncing as they go.

Riley releases my hand and tries to join the flow of students, but I hold her tight and pull her back to me, bending slightly to give her a gentle hug that I know she doesn't want but needs.

"Be kind," I whisper in her ear.

Her chin sinks softly onto my collarbone.

I tell her to do her best and to treat everyone else the way she wants to be treated, and not to sweat the small things.

Her smooth cheek brushes my stubbled face as she pulls away.

On the way back to the high school, I'm really missing my cane. Every minute or so, I stop and lean on my good leg for a few seconds, taking the pressure off my stump.

On the third break, I take my phone out and check the local news.

The story I've been dreading has finally appeared.

BODY FOUND AT DOWNTOWN CONSTRUCTION SITE

The article is brief and to the point:

Raleigh PD is investigating what appears to be a murder at a construction site for a mixed-use high-rise building in downtown. The site was currently idle due to an ongoing legal dispute between the developer and the general contractor. Police are asking anyone with any information to contact...

*

By the time I reach the high school, I'm a mess.

My shirt is soaked with sweat. I'm exhausted. And my leg feels like the bone is about to punch through the skin.

The tinnitus attack starts then. It's not the tea kettle whine. It's the rocks in the can.

Clang-clang-clang.

Clang-clang-clang.

Hearing it spikes my pulse even higher. I can't afford to lose time here, at work.

At the edge of the teacher parking lot, I bend over and plant my hands on my knees and focus on my breathing.

To any parents (or teachers) passing by, I probably look like a guy on the verge of heaving by the side of the road. Not a great look on the first day of school. Or any other day of school. But I'm far less self-conscious now that Riley isn't with me. And taking the weight off the stump brings instant relief.

It doesn't, however, save me from the sun, which feels like a heat lamp hovering over my back.

Soon, sweat drips from my forehead, and my mind flashes to the beads of rain that collected on my wife's coffin that day. The memory is like stepping on a nail. With my soul.

Between the pain and the heat and the ringing, I start to breathe harder. I have a change of clothes in the car (I learned that lesson years ago). But even with dry clothes, I can't go into school this way.

I wipe the sweat away and glance around for any distraction.

In the grass next to me, there's a yard sign for the PTA. The moment I see it, the ringing fades, like the hand is drawing the can away.

I keep staring at the sign, reading it, and with every line, the rattling ratchets down. At the bottom, I expect to see the web address for the school's PTA.

Instead, it says:

12122518914208.com

The moment I read the web address, the ringing stops.

9

I've made a mistake, and I'm blaming it on exhaustion. Mental, physical, and emotional exhaustion. All apply.

As soon as I got to my classroom, I got my phone out and typed the numbers web address into a browser.

The moment I hit go, I realized I shouldn't be visiting the site from a phone tied to me. I'm no internet coding genius, but I suspect whoever operates the site can figure out who I am because of that action. Or at least, where I am.

The numbers are connected to the murder last night.

And by visiting the site, it's possible that the site owner knows that I'm connected to the murder, too.

But it's done.

The risk might even turn out to be worth it—because of what I saw on the page.

Apparently, I'm not the only one seeing the numbers.

At lunch, I stagger out to the parking lot and get my cane from my car. The pain has overtaken my pride. It wasn't a close race.

I need to think, and to do that, I need to be alone, and for those reasons, I retrieve my lunch from the fridge in the teacher's lounge and sit on the steps outside the gym. At this point in the day, the sidewalk in front of me is hot enough to fry an egg. I figure the heat will dissuade anyone from joining me.

29

Slowly chewing a peanut butter and jelly sandwich, I ponder the numbers website.

Four of my colleagues pass by, all PE teachers, heading out to lunch. Several glance back at me and say hi, and one breaks from the pack, mumbling something I can't make out.

She walks back up the steps and, without a word, sits down beside me. She's trim, dressed in athletic attire, her brown hair pulled into a ponytail. Aviator sunglasses cover her eyes, but even with the dark, mirrored eyewear, I recognize her.

The last time she and I sat on these steps was twenty years ago, when I was a senior at this high school and she was a junior. The concrete beneath us now is the same slab we sat on back then, though the passage of time has left it a little more cracked and stained. Just like me.

Time has been more kind to her. She looks about the same. She's gained a few rebel streaks of gray hair, a fine line or two creeping out from the corners of her eyes, but that's about it.

Her name is Meredith Davis, and before either of us had any gray hair—when we were students here and not teachers—we walked these halls holding hands. I lingered by her locker, conspiring about meeting up at a party after the football game and lying to our parents about studying with friends.

With my PB&J-free hand, I pick up my lunch box and hold it out to her, offering the choice of either apple slices or a banana.

She takes the banana and starts peeling it.

"I'm assuming you stole some kid's lunch."

I let out a laugh, almost losing my bite of peanut butter and jelly. It's hardly the first thing most people would say to an ex after a twenty-year time gap, but it is also exactly what the Meredith Davis I knew back then would have said.

"Had a rough night. Can you just assume I'm saying something witty?"

"Strike one," she says and takes the first bite of banana.

I shake my head, smiling. "I make the lunch my daughter likes, and I eat the same thing for the sake of efficiency."

"That's very grown up, Alan."

"I was always very mature."

"No, you weren't."

"No. No, I wasn't."

I'm amazed at how easy it is to fall back into the way things were between us. It's like those twenty years went by in a blink, and we're just picking up where we left off.

10

In my afternoon classes, I continue my first day of school routine. I've honed this process over the years, but essentially it's about setting the tone in the classroom.

I want my students to feel like this is a safe place to learn and share. My second goal is to get these eleventh-graders excited about the subject matter. I teach history and psychology. It's not exactly the most exciting thing in their lives at this point. I'm competing with social media, endless streaming TV, hormones, video games, and probably stuff I'm too out of touch to even know about.

On top of that, this year, most of these kids will be stressed about college admissions, crucial sports games, and whether their high school romance, which raged like a wildfire this past summer, will indeed last through the year. They will also be wondering whether they should apply to the same college as their current love interest.

When it comes to attention span, my AP World History and AP Psychology classes have some serious competition. My approach is to frame the courses not as work or a box they need to tick, but as valuable skills that will be the wind at their back in life, regardless of the route they choose. I don't want them to learn the facts simply for the sake of passing the AP test and going into college with a few credits.

On the first day of school, I feel less like a teacher and more like a salesman for the subject matter. For my specific wares, I try to convince these kids that knowing history and understanding how it shaped the world we live in will help them navigate adulthood. It will help them better understand the people they encounter, and I hope it will also help them make informed decisions for our future (after all, they will be voting next year).

Psychology comes with more personal benefits, so it's a little easier to sell, at least to some students.

I encourage my students to view the psychology coursework as an opportunity to gain insight into themselves and the people in their lives. I always make a point to discourage them from psychoanalyzing their parents at dinner (I've had some complaints at parent-teacher conferences). My exact words are: "Remember, you are in the eleventh grade. This is not PhD-level instruction, and you are not a clinical psychologist… and neither am I."

I try to impress upon them that knowing themselves has a multiplying effect on their life—it multiplies what they can achieve and how happy they can be. But they have to be brave enough to truly see themselves—with all their strengths and limitations. The thing is, some who venture into the cave of self-awareness don't like what they see. And most avoid it altogether.

However, over the years, I've seen students who are willing to put in the work gain a deeper understanding of themselves. They become more confident. They make better choices.

That's a big part of why I keep coming back every year, despite the mediocre pay and drama and occasional wisecrack about a one-legged teacher hobbling just out of earshot (or so they think).

I like seeing these kids overcome the challenges in their lives at this pivotal time—and being some small part of helping them.

I don't know if it was nourishment from lunch or getting back into teaching again or if the fatigue from last night is simply fading, but by the time my planning period rolls around, I've caught a second wind.

As soon as the bell rings, I file out with the kids, cane squeaking on the vinyl floor.

At a nearby Walmart, I buy a prepaid wireless smartphone. In the empty parking lot of an abandoned Kmart, I activate the phone with a throwaway Mastercard gift card and a fake address. The device will still log a cell tower ping, but that's a problem for later (or hopefully never).

In the phone's web browser, I return to the numbers website.

At the top are three words:

YOU HAVE REACHED

Below is an illustration of an iceberg sticking out of a water line.

Right under the image is a simple question:

What do the numbers mean to you?

A web form collects an answer to that question as well as name, email address, and phone number.

I don't dare enter my real name. I also need to create a new, anonymous email address (one that avoids any identifiers like 'Marine,' 'single dad,' or 'teacher').

I need something completely random.

Without another thought, I type Dr. Richard Kimble in the name field and then go and register an anonymous email address and enter it.

In the answer box, I go with the truth:

The numbers are what I see when the ringing won't stop.

11

After school, I stow my cane in the car and proceed down the sidewalk to the elementary school. My stump aches, and the burst of energy that arrived this afternoon has completely left me, but the only thing on my mind is Riley and hoping that her first day went well. Like my students, beginnings are important.

As I approach the school, kids race out like birds set free from a cage, backpacks bouncing as they go. I spot Riley in a small crowd of girls, talking and smiling.

At the sight of me, she waves bye to her friends and breaks into a jog. I think she's going to hug me, but she slows as she reaches me, still smiling but playing it cool, no doubt for the benefit of her buddies.

I ask her how her day was and she merely shrugs and says, "Good."

But I can tell from the glow in her face that her first day was more than good, and that makes me forget about the aches and the weariness.

On the way home, we stop for ice cream. It's hot as blazes, but Riley wants to sit outside, so of course we do, on a bench by a park where a group of fit, carefree folks in their twenties are setting up for a program called Soccer Shots (which Riley is a proud graduate of).

When she sees her former teacher, Riley takes a big bite of ice cream, gently places the cup on the bench, and takes off toward him. The overpriced ice cream will likely be a puddle of lumpy milk by the time she returns. If so, she'll complain and ask for another, and that will be a teachable moment (in this case, when I tell her I can't afford to buy a new one and she should have thought about that before, it will absolutely be the truth).

Still watching her, I take out the prepaid phone, power it up, and check my email.

One new message.

The sender's name on the email is simply the numbers. The subject is:

Re: A fellow traveler

The email reads:

```
Dear Fugitive,

Where have you seen the numbers?
```

I can't exactly give a full answer to that. Revealing that I saw the numbers on my wife's grave would identify me as a widower. The crime scene is obviously out. The PTA sign would identify me as a teacher, parent, or both.

I glance up. Riley is talking to a tall male soccer instructor who is pointing to a cone. Riley smiles and picks up a stack of cones and begins spacing them out across the grass.

Staring at the email, I debate what to reply. Finally, I type out:

```
Signs and grave markers.

Where have you seen them?
```

After sending, I sit with the phone in my lap, hoping I'll get a prompt reply. This is still the only thread I have to pull at in this bizarre mystery.

I keep checking my email until I get tired of it. With my primary phone, I open up social media, not even sure what I'm looking for. Almost without thinking, I type a name in the search bar: Meredith Davis.

We're not friends on any of the sites, but a lot of her profile is public. The pictures and posts paint a broad outline of her life after high school.

I feel a bit like a stalker scrolling through the digital breadcrumbs of her life, but I am genuinely curious what has happened with her during the last two decades and why she decided to come home.

Her college years largely predate the widespread adoption of most social media, but there are some throwback posts that confirm she had a good time at a school in Virginia.

She apparently stayed close by after graduation and went right into teaching. She ran marathons in her free time, volunteered, and attended a few bridal showers along the way (the online evidence suggests that further good times were had by all).

She also had a bridal shower of her own and subsequently married a rather fit, confident-looking guy.

The social media posts slow down a bit after that. A few years later, there's a picture of an ultrasound.

She's glowing in a photo from a baby shower where she sits on a couch surrounded by friends holding flutes of champagne and opened presents.

That was nine years ago. I expect to see a birth picture or a post about a little boy or girl learning to crawl. Maybe a baby on a mat staring up absently at the camera, announcing that they're now one or two months old. But I don't see any of those. And the posts really slow down then.

A pit forms in my stomach, and I close the page. For a while, I sit on the bench, the phone face down, watching Riley run around the field, lining up the cones. When the younger kids start arriving in their orange Soccer Shots jerseys, Riley returns to the bench.

"You get a new phone?" she asks.

I glance down at it. "Uh, yeah."

"Why?"

"It has some features my other phone didn't."

"Like what?"

I love how inquisitive she is. Just not right now.

I stuff both phones back in my pocket. "It's not important."

Riley stares down at the cup of former ice cream (now lumpy milk).

"Dad, my ice cream melted. Can I get another one?"
"Well, let's talk about that."

12

At home, I can barely stay awake through dinner. We eat at the bar because the dining room table has become a puzzle table.

As we eat, I keep checking my email on the disposable phone. It's distracting me enough for Riley to notice, and halfway through her chicken strips, she asks me why I keep checking my phone.

"I'm waiting on an email."

"What email?"

I'm about to tell her to clean her plate, but I stop right there. Because what I should be doing right now is asking her how her day was. What she thought of her teacher. Who her friends are.

So I set the phone aside and do just that.

After dinner, we continue working on the 3D puzzle for Hogwarts Castle as I stream music to a portable speaker.

The dining room table is almost completely covered in pieces, but we have an outline of the foundation. It's sort of like what's happening to me: I'm turning the pieces over, looking for an outline.

I don't take the phone out during puzzle time, but when I go to the bathroom, I check my email.

There's a new message:

```
Where have I seen the numbers?
```

```
Everywhere.

How long have you seen them?
```

I don't want to give the specific date I first saw the numbers—it corresponds to my wife's funeral.

I opt for an equally evasive message, matching my pen pal's tone:

```
A while now.

How long have you seen the numbers?

What do they mean?
```

Back at the dining room table, Riley is making solid progress on the puzzle. Within the perimeter, she's begun filling in some of the grass.

With the phone facing up on the table, I spread out some of the green and brown pieces and begin helping her.

For the rest of the night, I don't get another email.

The grounds of Hogwarts, however, are coming together (the grass around the castle is creeping closer like a wave washing ashore). At seven o'clock, I give Riley two Calm gummies and a fifteen-minute warning for bedtime.

When my phone alarm rings, I silence it and look up at her. "Time for bed, kiddo."

She exhales, and I can tell she wants to fight it, but she's so tired from her first day, and she's starting to feel the affects of the supplement (which was physician approved).

She pushes up from the chair, but I stop her, pointing at the puzzle. "Made a lot of progress tonight."

She yawns, but I press on.

"This is what life is like, Riley. You do a little every day, and it adds up, and it eventually pays off."

★

In bed, with my prosthetic off and Riley sleeping in the next room, I keep checking the email until a new message comes in:

```
How long have I seen the numbers?
My whole life.
I was born this way.
As to what they mean, I suspect they are
an answer.
```

I hit reply and quickly type out:

```
An answer to what?
What's the question?
```

A new message arrives a minute later:

```
Do you know who created the numbers
website?
```

I find that to be an odd response.

```
No. I assumed you did.
If the numbers are the answer, then
what's the question?
```

A reply arrives quickly:

```
That is the question.
```

At this point, I'm tired and sore and scared and fed up with all of this. That comes out in my message back:

```
Who are you?
What is this?
I want answers.
```

I keep refreshing my inbox, but the replies stop.
I may have screwed this up.

13

I wake to the sound of shouting in the apartment below.

It's a man's voice, deep and angry, berating someone.

I've heard him before.

A woman yells back at him. This is how it typically goes. Their arguments are largely a late-night phenomenon, one that occurs roughly every two weeks or so (at least, it's been that way for the nine months Riley and I have lived here). The fights usually wind down after a few exchanges.

But not this time.

The shouting continues, rising in intensity. Soon they're screaming at each other. That ends in a boom that rattles the wall behind my bed. A low, moaning sob follows, the unmistakable sound of someone hurt crying out in the night.

I'm guessing the guy threw her against the wall.

My ears begin ringing then; heralding the start of a tinnitus attack. From the opening strength, I would bet that this is going to be a bad one. And the sound I hear is once again the rocks in the can.

I ignore the *clang-clang-clang* as I grab my prosthesis and strap it on. The moment I stand, the wall with my bedroom door shudders from another impact. This time, the woman doesn't scream. The silence is even more unnerving. It tells me she's probably not conscious anymore.

The ringing finds another gear as I plant my feet and yank the drawer of my bedside table open. The moment I see the locked pistol safe, the ringing stops. On a dime, like a speaker that was just unplugged.

It's like when I see the numbers, as if whatever controls the sound is reacting to what I'm doing or seeing.

I'll have to try to sort that out later, when my neighbor isn't potentially being murdered.

Luckily, I haven't had to open the pistol safe in my bedside drawer since we moved here, but now I press a finger against the sensor and hope the batteries haven't died (I've no idea where the key is, and I've forgotten the access code). Thankfully, the lock clicks open, and I grab the handgun, leaving the extra magazine.

I'm still in my boxers, but I don't spare any time to dress. Those lost seconds could be the difference between life and death for the woman downstairs.

With my free hand, I take my phone from the charging pad on the nightstand and dial 911 as I stagger out of the bedroom.

Riley's door is still closed. That's good. The commotion below doesn't appear to have woken her.

On the phone, the operator says, "Nine-one-one, what is your emergency?"

"I'd like to report a domestic disturbance and request police and an ambulance."

In the background, a keyboard rattles as the operator asks for my location and instructs me to remain on the line. I tell her the address of the apartment building, but not the specific unit.

In the kitchen, I pull back the accordion door that hides the washer and dryer. A red, dented toolbox sits on a shelf above. Beside it is a five-pound hammer.

Holding the phone in one hand, I grab the hammer the appliances.

At the door to my apartment, the 911 operator informs me that the police have been notified.

Without another word, I set the phone on the floor. I don't need it now. In this part of town, the police come, but it usually takes them a while.

When they do arrive, they come with backup and their body cams on—for everyone's safety. I don't blame them.

But I'm not sure my neighbor downstairs, who hit the wall

that hard, has that kind of time. For that reason, I move down the rickety pine staircase, gun in one hand, five-pound hammer in the other.

By the time I reach the concrete on the ground floor, my heart is thudding in my chest.

Standing in the humid, warm night air, the ringing slowly starts up again, clanging softly, methodically.

At the apartment door, I lean my head close and listen. I don't hear shouting or even talking, only the sound of a movie or a video game with crashes and gunfire.

The ringing steps up a notch, like a countdown alarm getting louder. I need to go in soon, while I can still hear. I wonder if that's what the unseen hand is trying to tell me.

I'd love to know how many doors I kicked down in Afghanistan. Most were during the night. Back then, I stormed in wearing body armor, rifle raised, scanning the scene through the green glow of night vision goggles.

I remember the first house I went into. My nerves were shredded as we quickly approached it. But it got better. You get used to it. It's a bit like that first day of school: if you don't get hurt, you get more confident and comfortable.

And you develop instincts, like muscle memory. I wonder if that's why I leaped out of bed tonight. Because old habits die hard. And I know that if I read about my neighbor's death in the news tomorrow, I'll put some of the blame on myself for not doing something when I could have.

Or maybe I'm standing outside this door because of what happened last night and my own need to prove to myself that I'm still the good guy in the story of my life. Maybe I'm trying to convince myself that I didn't kill Nathan Briggs.

Whatever the reason, it's enough to make me plant my real leg and my fake one and raise the hammer.

The moment I do, the ringing stops, just like it did at Jenn's grave and when I saw the address on the PTA sign and opened the drawer that held the pistol safe.

Definitely not a coincidence.

I'm about to swing the hammer when my rational mind stops me.

This is what I would have done back then, during the surge, when you knew there was a good chance that knocking on the door and announcing yourself would kick off a fire fight.

Since I heard my neighbor hit the wall, I've been acting on instinct—based on my previous experience. But this is a different situation.

I can do this differently.

After setting the hammer and gun by the door, out of sight of the peephole, I knock, three quick taps, lighter than the classic pounding that precedes "Police, open up!", but loud enough for the people inside to hear.

And then I wait, alone in the night, not hearing the ringing—or the sound of sirens in the distance.

14

On the other side of the door, the video game falls silent. I hear two voices talking low. I can't make out the words, but it sounds like they're talking about someone coming over. Maybe they think I'm that person.

The peephole darkens as someone peers out. A snorting laugh erupts behind the door, followed by a man's deep, condescending voice. "What you want?"

"I know she's hurt. I heard it."

"Man, she ain't your problem. Get outta here 'fore you get hurt."

"I called the police."

"Yeah, that's real funny, man. Go on now. We're done here."

"I'm serious. They're on their way. Look, I don't want any trouble. Just let her come outside and get medical help. That'll be the end of it."

The darkness disappears from the peephole, and the two men converse in hushed tones.

This is not good. If the woman is dead—or dying—they'll do the math and figure out that one murder is pretty much as bad as two. Then things will go sideways. Quickly.

Time for plan B. Fallujah-style.

Carefully, I check the door handle, confirming it's locked.

Bending down, I pick up the hammer and gun and line myself up on the door and swing with all the might I can muster.

My first hammer blow rocks the door. But it holds.

My second strike explodes it inward. Wood splinters fly as the security chain jingles free.

Inside, the two men freeze in mid-motion. They were picking up drugs off the coffee table.

Down the narrow hall, through the bedroom door, I spot the woman. She's lying on the floor. Eyes closed. Not moving. A dark welt beneath her eye.

I step across the threshold, gun raised. I'm opening my mouth to speak when one guy rounds the coffee table and rushes me.

I twist just in time to deflect his punch, which lands on my temple. Still, the world goes out of focus for a second.

The guy is huge. If he lands a solid blow, I'll be out.

He's turning around, winding up. His partner has abandoned packing up the drugs and is now pulling out a handgun that was stuffed into the fold of a recliner.

Instead of backing away—as my attacker is expecting—I swing the hammer at his face.

It cracks against the guy's jaw. I figured it would lay him out, but he sways like a skinny pine tree in a windstorm.

He's strong. And sober.

I drop the hammer and press the gun just under his jaw, pointing upward as I grab his t-shirt with my other hand. I turn him, putting his body between me and his friend, who's now pointing a pistol at us.

"Put it down!" I yell.

The guy's eyes bulge as he grits his teeth and inches forward, the gun shaking in his hand. From his bloodshot eyes and dilated pupils, I can tell he's high as a kite, but he can easily punch my ticket from this distance.

I need to end this soon, one way or another.

The guy I'm holding speaks, but his words come out mangled. He probably has a broken jaw. His buddy just squints, hand shaking as he points the gun.

I lower my voice, trying to slow down and drop the temperature in the room, just like we did in Afghanistan.

"Look at me."

My neighbor's eyes shift slightly, and I continue. "This is okay. It's *okay*. I promise you. I don't care about the drugs. Or the gun. Just get your stuff and get out of here. I'll be fine."

The guy holding the gun swallows.

His broken-jaw friend writhes in my grip, and mumbles again.

I slow my voice even further. "Listen. Put the gun in the recliner. Back where it was. Then get your drugs. *And go.* Easy as that. I'll get her to the ambulance. I won't even tell them where she lives."

He cuts his gaze from me to the coffee table and the drugs. He turns, puts the gun in the fold of the recliner, and resumes shoveling the narcotics and paraphernalia into the duffel bag.

The guy I'm holding squirms slightly, testing to see if I'm paying attention. I press the gun harder against his lower jaw.

When his friend finishes his cursory clean-up, he hoistes the bag, eying us. I rip my head toward the open doorway, and as he passes, I pull the gun away from broken-jaw man and push him across the threshold and swing the door closed. The deadbolt won't latch, but the door provides a barrier, just in case my new friends decide they don't like the deal after all.

I step backwards, gun pointed at the door, moving down the narrow hallway until I feel the door casing of the primary bedroom hit my shoulder.

Finally, I turn and step into the room and awkwardly lower myself and press two fingers to the woman's throat. There's a faint pulse.

Her eyelids part lazily. There's a swollen bruise around her bloodshot right eye. I wonder if she has a concussion. Or a burst blood vessel in her brain.

"Hey," I whisper. "I'm your neighbor. I called an ambulance."

She closes her eyes again.

"Hey-hey, stay awake, okay?"

I know I shouldn't move her. But I also know she might not have a lot of time. She needs to get checked out. It will take time for police to get in here and clear the apartment so EMS can come in. She needs to be outside waiting when they arrive.

Louder, I ask what her name is.

She opens her mouth but doesn't say anything.

"Come on, what's your name?"

"Rose," she mumbles, eyes closing again.

"Rose. That's a pretty name. Look, Rose, I need you to get up and walk outside so the EMS can get to you quickly, okay? Can you do that?"

She doesn't move or open her eyes or say a word.

Gently, I squeeze her shoulder and shake. "Come on, Rose. Please. Get up. I can't carry you."

I still have the gun in my right hand, though I've been holding it behind my back. I bring it around and tap the butt against the hard plastic of my prosthesis. The sound rouses her, and her eyelids slowly peel open, focusing on my artificial limb.

"Come on, Rose. Get up. I need your help. I can't carry you. I've only got one leg."

At that, she rolls over and pushes up on trembling arms. For a few seconds, she looks down the hall at the busted door frame and the front door standing slightly ajar. Slowly, her head turns back to me, her gaze lingering on my fake leg.

"You got..." She closes her eyes again, looking exhausted. "A lot. Of guts for a one-legged man."

I smile. "Nah, I'm just really stupid."

Her chest heaves, and she winces as she laughs.

"Come on, Rose. Get up. Keep going. Just take it slow."

She does, and I rise too, and she wraps an arm around me, and we shuffle out, her taking labored breaths, me ignoring the raging pain in my stump.

I deposit her on the concrete steps to the building and tell her I'll be right back.

Moving slower, I climb the outdoor stairs to my apartment. I set the gun on the kitchen counter within easy reach. At the sink, I douse the hammer in bleach to clear away the man's DNA. This is becoming way too common for me.

I'm dead tired, and the adrenaline is leaving my body, but I know that Riley and I can't stay here. Because when the ambulances and police leave, my neighbors downstairs probably come looking for me. I can likely handle that. But I won't risk my daughter's life in the crossfire.

As such, I make my way to Riley's bedroom and sit on the

narrow bed and switch on the bedside lamp. Gripping her shoulders, I shake her until her eyelids peel open.

"Wake up, sweetie. We've got to go. Right now."

15

The departure from my apartment is a frantic, mad dash.

I take the suitcases out, place them on the bed, and toss in clothes and necessities.

Riley moves slower. I shout to her, encouraging her to hurry, but I know she's tired from her first day of school and being woken up in the middle of the night. And the magnesium supplement in her system can't be helping.

In between my shouting sessions, I peer out the living room window at the parking lot. Two police cars are here now—as well as an ambulance.

With two EMS personnel holding her by the arms, Rose hobbles toward the waiting ambulance.

"Dad!" Riley calls from behind me. I turn, seeing her in the doorway to her bedroom. She looks distraught.

"What?"

She raises her hands. "They won't fit."

"What won't fit?"

"My animals. I've been trying…"

I exhale, feeling what energy I have left draining out of me. "It doesn't matter, sweetie. We have to go. Come on."

A little after midnight, we check into a cheap motel I can't really afford. But survival has its costs.

Riley has no problem falling back asleep.

I'm not so lucky. I need time to decompress, just like after a combat situation.

In the bathroom, sitting on the toilet, with the fluorescent lights buzzing above, I take the prepaid mobile out and check my email.

There's a reply. It came in hours ago—while I was sleeping, before all the drama went down.

It says:

```
You want answers?
Let's meet.
Tonight.
No excuses.
```

I reply immediately:

```
Meeting sounds good. But I can't tonight.
Something has come up. What about
tomorrow night?
```

I keep clicking refresh, but there's no reply. Interesting that they wanted to meet immediately. They didn't want me to have any time to prepare.

Lying on the bed, I put earbuds in and start an audiobook. With each passing sentence and paragraph, I leave the stress of my world and slip into the story. And soon after, darkness.

I wake to the sound of my phone alarm going off through the earbuds. As I come to, I realize that Riley is standing over me, shaking me, whispering, "Dad. Dad."

"I'm awake," I mumble, reaching over to silence the phone alarm. I didn't realize the sound would play through both my earbuds and the phone's speaker, where Riley could hear it.

"Dad," she says, drawing the word out as she tugs on my t-shirt.
"Yeah?"
"I want to go home."
I swallow. "We can't."

"Why?"

"We just can't."

"Why not? I left my—"

"We can't, okay?"

"But—"

"It's not safe."

Riley scrunches her eyebrows, and I can almost see the questions forming in her mind. Telling a kid their home isn't safe is a big deal—one that demands an explanation. In this case, that answer will have to be a lie.

"There was a gas leak," I tell her, glancing away.

Sitting up, I pull her into a hug. "I'll go back and get your stuff, I promise. But it's not safe right now. Okay?"

In the bathroom, I wash my face and brush my teeth. Looking in the mirror, I realize that the blow to the side of my head did more damage than I thought. Or at least, it looks that way. The bruise and black eye make me look like a guy who was in a late night bar brawl.

It's a great look for a teacher. And a parent of a first-grader.

For the second time in as many days, Riley and I march down the sidewalk outside of school, her hand in mine. I didn't think it was possible, but I'm in even worse shape than yesterday. My stump aches. Sweat pours off of me, and my thoughts are as chaotic as a beehive that's just been kicked.

At the entrance to the elementary school, I squat and hug my daughter and smile as I watch her gallop in. Knowing that she's excited to go to school gives me a little boost.

When the lunch bell rings and the last student has left my classroom, I call my apartment complex.

I ask them, as politely as I can, if I can get out of my lease. In a vague outline, I describe the night's events and insist that it's not safe for my daughter and me to keep living there.

The guy on the other end of the line sounds sympathetic. And then he begins to recite the corporate line, including clauses in the lease that culminate in a demand for me to pay two months' rent.

I don't have two months' rent. Well, technically I do, but I don't have it to spare. And there are only three months left on my current term, which somehow makes the fee feel even worse.

I prod the guy a little, but he holds firm. I'm not a lawyer, and I can't exactly tell him what really happened, but I do know a losing battle when I'm in one.

I'm hanging up when Meredith saunters into my classroom, a green smoothie in her hand, a whistle around her neck.

The midday sun shines around her, and I swear, in that brief moment, all I see is the girl I knew twenty years ago. It's like a lightning strike. When the shock fades, I feel a deep well of guilt because having feelings for her feels like cheating on my deceased wife.

I turn away and put the phone on my desk.

Meredith steps closer, smile fading as she studies the bruise on my face.

"Rough night?"

"I was trying out for American Gladiators—the one-legged spin-off."

She slips into a desk in the front row. "I don't think that show is even still on."

"You telling me I'm not going to make the cut?"

In a smooth motion, she slips out of the desk, moves to the doorway, and swings the slab of wood closed, blotting out most of the midday sun.

I expect her to come over to me, but she returns to the desk and takes another sip of whatever thick green concoction is in that translucent thermos.

"What happened, Alan?"

"Neighbor trouble."

"Do you need help?"

"No. I'm good."

She takes a long sip of the smoothie. "Right." With a napkin from a pocket in her shorts, she wipes the green residue from her mouth. "You're good."

"I'm good."

Still holding the cup, she rises and walks around my desk.

I swivel my chair to face her. The rays of the sun through the transom window above the door outline her in shadow like a superhero.

Her voice is a whisper. "You're not okay, Alan."

I swallow. "No. I'm not."

She takes a step forward.

I rise, wobbling on my prosthetic.

Our faces are a foot away from each other.

Softly, looking into my eyes, not blinking, she whispers, "I'm here. If you need help."

"I'm not the person I used to be."

"I'm not either."

"Time… has changed me."

"Time changes everyone, Alan."

Closing my eyes, I hold my hands up. "What's happening to me is next level, Meredith. I don't even understand it. This isn't run-of-the-mill PTSD or some—"

I hear her stepping away then.

When I open my eyes, she's in the doorway, again, bathed in the sunlight.

"Like I said. I'm here. If you want help. I don't care what it is."

With that, she steps out into the hallway, and the light is all that's left.

A part of me wants to go after her and explain. But I don't have time. And I'm not sure what to say anyway. I still have no clue what's going on with the numbers—or how to describe it to Meredith.

So instead, I get my laptop out and look for a new place to live. I opt for an Airbnb. It'll be furnished, and I can move in on short notice. The trouble is finding one that I can check into the same day. On the fourth page of results, I spot one that could work.

After a few messages with the owner, we make arrangements and I book it.

The place is perfect. And it'll put a smile on Riley's face. Additionally, if I rent it for a whole month, I receive a discount.

That's the good news.

The bad news is that I need to return to our apartment tonight to retrieve the rest of our belongings. If I could, I'd leave it all behind. But I can't afford it, even if going back tonight is more dangerous than last night.

16

When the dismissal bell rings, I text Riley's teacher and let her know I'll be in the car rider line today.

At this point, my stump can't take any more treks up and down the sidewalk.

That's been a big adjustment since I lost part of my leg—learning my limits and knowing when to take a step back (if you will). Jenn helped me walk again, but she did far more than that. She made me realize that I was not the person I was before that bomb went off. It wasn't just the loss of my lower leg. It was the loss of what I could do. Rehab humbled me, and I haven't forgotten it.

In the car rider line, Riley climbs in and throws her backpack on the floorboard.

When I ask how her day was, she's cagey and preoccupied. I wonder if last night's events are lingering in her mind, or if it really has been a tiring day for her. It certainly wasn't a great night of sleep.

Glancing at her in the rearview mirror, I try to make my voice upbeat and fun.

"I've got a big surprise for you."

She perks up at that.

"What is it?"

"You'll see."

"Are we going to Learning Express?"

Learning Express is a local toy store in Raleigh's North Hills neighborhood. At this point in her life, it's probably Riley's favorite place on Earth. When I set a goal for her, and she reaches it, we do a trip to Learning Express. I always set a budget, and she always spends every last penny (and usually a little more, which I typically oblige).

"It's not Learning Express. It's something even cooler."

For the rest of the drive to the Airbnb, she quizzes me on what this surprise might be.

I don't reveal a thing.

The place I've rented is a bit outside of Raleigh, but that's all right with me. Frankly, getting out of town is probably a good idea.

Soon, the strip malls and box stores and schools turn to trees and subdivision entrances, and ten minutes later, it's just us on a state roads surrounded by forests.

The GPS directions end at a dirt driveway that weaves through the pines. Riley leans over in her car seat, peering through the windshield.

"Dad, what is that?"

After parking the car, I glance back at her. "What does it look like?"

"A train car."

"That's right. It's a red caboose."

She squints at me. "What's it doing out here?"

"Let's go see."

On the table on the front porch, the Airbnb hosts have left a key and instructions (I suspect the dirt road that led here is right beside their home, and they use this converted red caboose as a way to make a little extra money).

The moment I open the door, Riley strides in, exploring. The place is clean and has the feel of a small RV.

The dining area features banquette seating, and the kitchen beyond is more of a kitchenette, but it'll be fine for us.

Riley lights up when she sees the bunk beds. She slips into the bottom bunk to test it out.

At the back of the caboose is a bedroom, and there's just one bathroom, but that's okay.

On the whole, it's not a place we could stay long-term, but it's affordable and way off the beaten path. What's even better is that it has taken Riley's mind off of what's really going on and the fact that soon, we will technically be homeless.

I don't like it, but I have to leave Riley at the train car while I run some errands. The first is to Walmart to get some supplies: food and items I'll need for tonight (bear spray, black clothing, neoprene gloves, and a black knit hat). I use the self-checkout because, frankly, it looks like the shopping list of a burglar.

My next stop is a military surplus store.

I'm using my cane to keep the weight off my stump, which is probably going to take a beating tonight. My cane has a worn rubber bottom that causes a faint squeaking sound as I enter, drawing the attention of the three customers milling about and a casual glance from an older man standing behind a glass display case. But their gazes don't linger long.

I need a new cane, but it's way down on the list of things I can't afford (a list that includes the items I've come here for).

Peering down into the display case, I scan the night vision goggles, reading the prices.

I don't see the other gear I need. Maybe it's in the back. Hopefully, it's in the back.

Two of the other customers buy a mag pouch from the clearance section, and the third wanders out a minute later, leaving me alone with the older guy minding the store.

He drifts over, staying behind the display cases, subtly taking me in, gaze lingering for only a fraction of a second on the bruises on my face and cane in my left hand.

"Help you find something?" His voice is deep and gruff, about like the lines on his face. His hair is cut short, the black peppered with gray. He reminds me of Louis Gossett Jr., and his vibe is about like the character Gossett Jr. played in *An Officer and a Gentleman*.

"Yeah," I say slowly, not glancing up. "I'm looking for a few things. NVGs. Armor. Tourniquet. And some restraints."

The man doesn't even flinch at my shopping list. The mark of a true professional.

He nods to the display case with the night vision goggles. "Got plenty of goggles. On the armor, what level you looking for?"

"Highest I can get. At least three."

I'm not sure, but I bet the only reason he's even still talking to me right now is because I've only asked about defensive gear—no weapons, ammo, or guns.

Still, the next thing he says is what I expected in some form: "Sounds like a heck of a party."

"Not my party. Neighbors. They're rowdy, and I'm moving out."

He glances away from me, but doesn't say anything.

"I just need to go back and get my stuff. Can't stay there with my daughter. I've got to move somewhere safe."

There's a long, silent pause, as if the guy is deciding whether to tell me to look elsewhere or show me what's in the back.

"Gonna need to see some valid ID to sell you the plates. It's not the law, mind you. It's my policy."

I take my wallet out and show him my North Carolina driver's license and Veteran ID Card.

He scans them and nods slowly, then moves to the front door and turns the deadbolt and flips the sign to closed.

He leads me through a door that has a thumbprint lock on it, into a room with plate holders and body armor plates and everything else I need (and then some).

It takes us about fifteen minutes to assemble all the items from my shopping list. As I expected, they add up to far, far more than I can afford.

I've mentally rehearsed what I'm about to say, and it comes out sounding just like that: practiced and awkward. "Listen, I know you typically don't do this, but I'm wondering if you would let me rent this stuff." I hold my hands up, still gripping the cane. "Just for one night. I'll bring it back—"

He shakes his head, exhaling. "Look, don't take this the wrong way, but I don't know you from Adam. Might be like you say: you're a good guy trying to protect his daughter from some unruly neighbors. But you might be some degenerate in a world of trouble on your way out of town, looking to score some high-end tac gear to pawn or sell online, and you think I'm an easy mark. Either way, this ain't no Blockbuster, so you want something, you gotta buy it."

I could point out that Blockbuster doesn't exist anymore, but it doesn't feel like the right time. Instead, I nod my head slowly.

"I get it. I don't blame you. The thing is, I need this stuff. For one night only. And then I'm going to bring it back. I don't have the cash to pay you. But I can give you collateral worth a lot more than all of this combined. So if I don't come back, you'll come out ahead financially. And if you choose to keep my collateral and act like you don't know me when I walk back in here tomorrow afternoon, then I'm the one who's going to get screwed. It's me trusting you, too."

The man shakes his head and turns and steps away from me. I figure he's about to tell me to take a hike.

"Well, you got some balls on you, Marine. I'll give you that. Let's see what kind of collateral you got."

I slip my right hand into my pocket and grip the small velvet box and place it on the counter and open it. The diamond engagement ring glitters under the lights.

The guy eyes it and shakes his head slowly. "This ain't Jared's Galleria of Jewelry neither. I got no idea if that thing is real or not."

"It's real. It's my deceased wife's engagement ring. I promise you."

The man stands there, squinting, as if mentally doing a calculation.

"Name your price on the rent," I tell him. "I can pay you some cash now, and if you're worried, you can follow me the whole time, but I wouldn't advise it."

He snorts and closes the ring box. "I'm getting too old for this."

"Does that mean we have a deal?"

The man puts the velvet box in his pocket and starts packing my items into a duffel bag, looking exhausted and a little older, the lines in his face a little deeper.

"How much for the rent?"

He grunts. "I don't know. Let's just say if you bring something back damaged, you bought it. If you don't, then whatever. Just… try not to get yourself killed."

17

That night, around 3 AM, I dress in the black outfit I recently bought and don the body armor and quietly creep out of the little red caboose, hoping Riley doesn't wake up.

More than that, I hope I come back home to her tonight.

I've taken some precautions, just in case I don't. I sent a short message to Meredith's school email address, asking her to call me first thing in the morning. And that if I don't answer to please come to the address of the Airbnb to check on Riley. Meredith will no doubt be sufficiently freaked out, but I know I can count on her to check on Riley if I don't come back.

There's a short list of other people I could have emailed, individuals Riley already knows, but for some reason, my mind automatically went to Meredith, and I didn't even debate it.

I'm not sure why.

Maybe it's because she saw my bruised face and knows I'm dealing with something.

Or because I've known her the longest and trust her.

Or maybe it's something else.

At my apartment complex, I'm relieved to see no one loitering outside. It's a weeknight, so I was hoping that would be the case. On weekends, there are typically one or more parties going on, with people spilling out the doors onto the landings.

After backing into the closest parking space to my apartment, I make my way past my ground-floor neighbor's door. Thankfully, it's closed (fixing a broken deadbolt is about the only thing that inspires any urgency from the apartment complex maintenance crew).

Moving up the steps, my stump—which was already tender—begins throbbing in pain. The level IV armor I'm wearing doesn't help matters. The plates are about twice as heavy as level III armor, but for the additional stopping power, I'll take it.

The door to my apartment stands slightly ajar. It's been kicked in. The jamb is shattered, and the deadbolt extends at an angle. It looks like the door I busted in downstairs. It looks like payback.

Still standing outside, I lean in and peer around the open door at the darkness. Based on the stress I'm feeling, I expect the ringing to start, but all I hear is my heavy breaths flowing out of my nose like a wind gust.

I'm sure it was my downstairs neighbors who broke in. What I don't know is if they're sitting on the other side of the door, in the dark, waiting for me to return. If so, they likely heard the creaking wooden stairs as I climbed up.

After pulling the night vision goggles down, I draw my pistol and push the door inward.

It whines softly, and in the green glow of night vision, I see what's left of my apartment. The kitchen is ransacked. The cabinets are open. Broken plates litter the floor. The refrigerator door is ajar, which is keeping the appliance light on. I flip up the NVGs and scan inside the fridge. Someone has taken the time to extract all the contents and squash them on the floor.

The living room and dining area are as bad as the kitchen. They've been looted of anything of value, but mostly it's been trashed. Just pure destruction. The cushions have been slashed open, and apparently they saved some of the condiments for use here.

On the dining table, which has some choice words carved into it, some of the Hogwarts Castle is still there. But they took a large portion of the pieces, just to be spiteful. I'll have to buy another one. Maybe I can find a used one on eBay.

Holding the gun in front of me, I sweep the rest of my former residence. No one's here. Like the living room furniture, the mattresses are cut up. Even Riley's toys are smashed. The dolls and playhouses are crushed to bits. Her furry friends have been sliced open, blossoming stuffing like burst piñatas. She had a tub of Legos. They even stole those.

But they missed the most important things, which I was hoping would still be here.

In the primary bedroom, I reach down and pick up the picture frame and brush away the broken shards of glass with my gloved hand. Careful not to crease it, I extract the photo from my wedding day.

In Riley's bedroom, I take her paintings off the wall and the pictures off the dresser.

The duffel bag I brought is far from full. What was left doesn't weigh much, but it means a lot.

At the bottom of the landing, I pause, staring at my neighbor's door.

And then and there, I decide to let it go. Because I have a daughter waiting for me at home, and because I know that the road of revenge doesn't lead anywhere good.

As I step out from the building, into the glow of the parking lot lights, the hairs on the back of my neck begin to stand up. I don't hear ringing. Or see anyone, but something is wrong. At my driver-side door, my hand on the gun holster, I scan in every direction, ready to bolt or draw and return fire.

I stop when I see a figure at the edge of the tree line, moving in the shadows, away from me.

Is it the numbers person who I've been emailing with? I drop the duffel bag on the asphalt and charge across the parking lot. As one-legged men go, I'm reasonably fast, even with my aching stump, but the person in the woods is far quicker, and appears to have two working legs. The only reason I'm able to make out the person's identity is because he stops at the other end of the woods, at a chain-link fence, and stares back at me.

It's the guy from the army surplus store. He nods and hauls himself over the fence—slower than a teenager, but quicker than I'd manage.

*

Back at the train car, I go online to the US Postal Service website and fill out a mail hold. I won't be checking my mail at the apartment again.

Then I deposit our family heirlooms—such as they are—on the dining table and spread them out.

I don't know if it's seeing all these memories or the adrenaline leaving my body, but I suddenly feel so completely and utterly exhausted.

I pass out the minute I lie down and close my eyes.

I wake to the sound of my phone ringing.

"Hello?" I croak

Meredith practically shouts, "Alan, what in the world is going on?"

I sit up, squinting at the sunrise through the small window at the back of the caboose.

"I uh, had to run an errand and I wasn't sure if I'd be back—"

"Alan, you're a *terrible* liar. Who in the world runs errands in the middle of the night? Also, why would you have someone who has never met your daughter come to your house to watch her? Please tell me what's going on."

"Well, first, I agree on the terrible liar part. Second, I can't tell you right now. But I will. As soon as I can. Okay?"

It is clearly not okay, but there's nothing more to say, so she signs off, sounding about as angry as I have ever heard her.

18

By lunch, I still haven't received a reply from the numbers person.

And I sense another problem brewing on the horizon: a looming confrontation with Meredith. Between last night's weird email, yesterday's black eye, and my evasiveness on the phone this morning, I know she's concerned.

As such, being a super-mature adult, I have decided that the best course of action is to leave school before the needed conversation can occur.

Ten minutes before the period bell rings (and my designated lunch), I plant my cane on the floor, give the students busywork, and beat a path to my car.

At the army surplus store, I sling the duffel bag over my shoulder and proceed inside, where I lock eyes with the store owner. He's once again stationed behind a glass display case, this one full of knives.

There's a guy browsing the MRE aisle.

"Excuse me," the store owner calls to the other shopper. "Don't mean to run you off, but we gotta close up for lunch. A man's gotta eat."

The customer buys a couple of MREs, and when he's gone, I lay the duffel bag full of gear on the case.

The store owner doesn't open it. He sets the velvet box I gave him beside it.

"Nothing got damaged," I tell him. When he only nods, I add, "But I think you already knew that."

"Mmm," he murmurs, taking the duffel bag off the counter and setting it on the floor.

"Why'd you follow me?"

"Nothing on TV."

"Right. We never settled on the rent."

He smirks. "I'm aware of that. Like I said, don't get killed. You didn't."

"How'd you know where I lived?"

"It was on the driver's license you showed me, genius."

"Oh. Right. How long did you wait outside?"

He raises his eyebrows. "Don't recall. It was a warm night, and I had a book. Probably got there around two. Figured you'd go in late."

"How'd you figure that?"

"Because you're careful."

"How do you know that?"

"'Cause you bought a tourniquet. The commando type would have asked me for grenades."

"I'm Alan."

The man doesn't extend his hand. Only nods. "Name's Warren. Normally, I'd say nice to meet you, but I'm not sure yet."

I figured Warren would dodge the question of what to charge for letting me use the gear. So I stuffed five twenty-dollar bills in one of the plate pockets of the vest. I hope he thinks it's enough.

As I should have expected, I find Meredith sitting on the steps of the school entrance off the teacher parking lot.

Without a word, I plop down next to her, and she hands me a bottle of water from her purse. She brought two today.

"What's going on, Alan?"

"It's complicated."

She glances over at the building. "It's high school. Everything's complicated."

"Not like this."

*

I don't like doing personal tasks during class, but this one is time-sensitive, so that afternoon, I get out my laptop and look for local movers that offer storage. Most of what's left at the apartment is trash. There are, however, a few things that could be saved: bed frames, the dining table (after sanding and refinishing), and chairs, among them. My plan is to have movers pick that stuff up and store it, and then put everything else in the garbage. The movers are an expense, but I really don't have much choice.

About ten minutes before school lets out, my burner phone vibrates. It's an email from the numbers person, and it's to the point:

```
Want answers?
Meet at the location below in one hour.
No excuses.
There will be no second chances.
```

A quick internet search reveals that the location is a warehouse on the outskirts of Raleigh, situated among numerous other warehouses. Apparently, the building is for rent (there's a listing on a commercial real estate site called LoopNet).

Once again, I give the students busywork and squeak out of the room, my cane digging into the floor as I walk as quickly as I can without putting too much pressure on my stump.

At the school's gym, I lean in and motion to Meredith, who joins me in the hall.

"You want to know what's going on?"

"Very much."

"I need your help."

"Okay," she says cautiously.

"I need you to watch my daughter, Riley, for a few hours."

She squints, surprised. And maybe a little hesitant. But there's no hesitation in her voice.

"Sure. Where?"

I hadn't gotten this far in my planning. I'm probably being paranoid, but I don't want Riley at the train car Airbnb while I do the meeting. I used the burner phone there, and whoever is behind the numbers site and emails might know about it. They could take her when they know I'm at the warehouse.

"Would it be too much to ask for her to stay at your place for a while?

"No, Alan, it wouldn't be too much to ask. Would it be too much to ask what's going on?"

"No, it's not. But right now, I don't have time, unfortunately. I'll tell you after. I promise. If I can."

She blows out a breath and sweeps her gaze across the student parking lot. "I feel like I'm on some weird episode of *The X-Files* where you're mixed up in some super-secret conspiracy."

She stares at me, and when I don't respond, she grimaces. "What is it, Alan? Drugs? Some kind of criminal thing?"

"No, nothing like that. And it's definitely not an alien invasion. At least, I don't think so."

She cocks her head. "I can't tell if you're serious right now."

"Me either. Not yet, anyway."

Meredith and I drive directly from the high school to the elementary school in my car. Riley is hesitant at first when she meets Meredith, but on the drive to Meredith's townhouse, she warms up a bit.

Riley is a very intuitive child, and I think she senses something is very wrong.

I have time for exactly one more stop before I need to be at the warehouse.

Luckily, the army surplus store is empty this time.

Warren is sitting in a club chair in the corner, holding an e-reader, eying me as I walk in.

"I'm going to need to borrow that stuff again."

He stands and sets the reading device in the chair. "Neighbors again?"

"No. This is… a separate issue."

"Such as?"

"Honestly, I don't know. I don't even understand it myself. But I'm pretty sure it might be dangerous."

That's about as frank of an answer as I can give without disclosing details I don't want to share.

Instead of asking me any more questions, Warren slips through the door to the back and brings out the items I returned a few hours ago. He also sets the hundred dollars I hid in the body armor on the glass case. "Told you, this ain't no Blockbuster."

I stop at the train car Airbnb long enough to put on the body armor and get my gun. This time, I bring the extra magazine.

19

The warehouse is situated on a dead-end street filled with potholes.

There are no cars in the parking lot and no one outside.

The building walls are corrugated metal. The front has a faded awning above a glass door. The side has a single, solid swinging door. The rear of the warehouse is dominated by a long loading dock with six roll-up doors, all closed.

I park in front and walk to the side door, bypassing the front entrance. The heavy body armor plates again put a strain on my stump, but I still think it's worth it.

At the door, I wait, listening for any sound inside (or for the tinnitus to start).

I don't hear either.

With my right hand over the holster, I turn the door handle and slowly pull it open. It's dark inside except for the dim light shining down through the skylights. The place looks empty, just a dusty concrete floor. But there are still two blind spots—one in each corner along the wall that holds the door. I should have brought a mirror.

As quickly as I can manage, I lean over the threshold of the doorway and peek in at one corner and then the other. It's clear.

Stepping inside, I close the door and pause, letting my eyes adjust to the darkness. When they do, I spot a small device in the center of the deserted warehouse. It's a silver metal pole, and at the top, there's a camera with a red light glowing like a crimson firefly. It's connected to a portable power bank.

My boots echo as I approach it.

"What is this?" I yell.

A digitally distorted voice replies through a speaker on the camera. "Welcome, Alan."

I tense at the sound of my name. So they know who I am. They probably know I have a daughter, too. And maybe where she is right now. I have the overwhelming urge to turn and run and make sure she's safe, but I also want answers.

The voice continues. "This is an interview."

"Interview for what?"

"Isn't it obvious?"

"Not to me."

"This is an interview to see if we want to work together."

"On what?"

"Oh, that's obvious too, isn't it? The numbers. It's all about the numbers."

"What are they? What do they mean?"

"You don't have any idea?"

I exhale. "I know that they spell labyrinth if you use a numeric substitution."

"Did you work that out yourself?"

"Actually, I didn't. I asked a computer that was smarter than me. Look, are you going to tell me what this is or not?"

"We have to be careful now."

"Why? Why do you have to be careful? Who is *we*?"

There's a long pause, then the computerized voice hurriedly says, "Stand by."

Though it's hard to read emotion through the small speaker and distortion, I think there's a hint of amusement in the voice when it speaks again.

"Well, well, Alan. It seems you have a guardian angel in our midst."

"What does that mean?"

"It means that one of our members has spoken for you."

"Spoken how?"

"Let's just say you've been endorsed. As such, we're willing to skip a step or two in our usual admission process. That is, if you're willing to do something to prove yourself."

"And what's that?"

"Have you ever heard of a company called Amersa?"

Against my will, I swallow hard. I know they can see it. They can probably read the fear in my eyes, too.

"Yes."

"Amersa is running a trial on a new product."

"What kind of product?"

"It's a virtual reality device that uses artificial intelligence. The trial is studying how well it treats PTSD."

"Okay."

"What we want, Alan, is for you to apply to that trial. If you get in, we'll meet with you."

"And if I don't?"

"If you don't, then you might be a bigger risk than we're willing to take right now."

"Fine. I'll do it. I'll apply."

"Take your phone out and do it now, Alan."

After a quick search, I'm staring at the page for Amersa's PTSD trial. There isn't a lot of information here, not much more than the mystery man behind the camera has said. A yellow box dominates the top of the page, urging anyone in the midst of a mental health crisis to dial 911. Farther down is a form for prospective participants to express interest. The page is emphatic that this isn't a formal application—only a contact form to receive further information.

It's pretty short, just name, address, and age. After filling it out and hitting submit, the site displays a message thanking me.

"Okay, I did it. Now what?"

"Now you send us any reply you receive."

"And then?"

"And then we'll see, Alan."

The red light on the camera slowly fades to black.

20

Back in my car, sitting in the parking lot outside the empty warehouse, I grip the steering wheel until my knuckles are white. I want to shake it and scream.

Instead, I crank the vehicle and drive back to Warren's army surplus store.

It's just past rush hour in Raleigh, and traffic is still bad (it takes me twice as long to get there as it would have in the afternoon).

When I set the gear on the glass display case, Warren simply picks it up and hauls it through the secure door into the back.

He seems a little surprised to see me when he returns. "You need something else?"

"I need to pay you."

He lets out a long breath, his gaze drifting away from me. "I believe we have previously discussed the fact that this is not a Blockbuster."

"You know Blockbuster doesn't exist anymore."

"I was trying to make a point, not discuss retail bankruptcies in America."

I laugh at that, and I think it might be the first good laugh I've had since I woke up in downtown with that dead man beside me.

"Well," I tell him, "I was just letting you know in case you're worried about late fees."

"I'll make a note not to return that last DVD I got, which I believe was either *Courage Under Fire* or *Saving Private Ryan*."

"Good ones."

"Yes. They are."

"Seriously, Warren. It doesn't feel right using that gear and not paying something."

He studies me a moment. "Alright."

"Good. So how much?"

"That's not what I'm thinking."

Now it's my turn to study him. "What are you thinking?"

"I've got my Army pension. And some saved up. And I do this," he motions around him. "This place brings in a little extra money and it gives me something to do."

He wipes a hand across the top of the spotless glass case, as if moving dust away. "But I could use some help."

I nod slowly, seeing where this is going. "The truth is, I could use some extra income—as I think you know. But I can't work here. After work, I have to watch my daughter or take her to after-school activities. I don't have any family close by who can keep her. And if I hired someone, the childcare would probably cost me more than I'd make." I shrug. "And for physical labor, frankly, you can find better help."

"What I'm thinking about doesn't require being here at the store. Or having two legs for that matter."

"Okay," I say slowly.

"We're different generations, you and me," he says, studying the display case again. "I was in the first Gulf War. I'm not real, what you'd call, *tech savvy*. My wife used to help me with that part of the operation. But she's passed now. She did all the hunting."

"Hunting?"

He motions to the show room. "Most of this stuff I buy online. Government surplus sales. eBay. Auctions with used gear from private military contractors. Things like that. My wife was good at that part—going online and buying inventory to sell. She'd consult with me on what was worth buying. And if it was broken, whether I could fix it. We make the most on repaired gear. Anyway, it gave us something to do together, something to talk about in the evenings and at lunch. It was nice, like a hobby we had."

A smile spreads out on his face—the first I've seen from him. "Actually, it was a bit like gambling. Some stuff we bought I couldn't sell around here, or it didn't bring what we paid, but over the long haul, we came out ahead, even counting our losses. Sort of like a marriage."

The smile fades, and he scans the store again. "My daughter started helping me after that. I think she figured it might make me feel less lonely if I didn't have a daily reminder of her mom's absence. But Shelly doesn't have much time for it. And she doesn't know the gear like you do."

"I'll do it."

Warren stares at me, a wry smile forming on his face. "You know what I do in my free time?"

"Late night surveillance on one-legged men?"

"That's a recent hobby. Mostly, I read. And lately I've been reading business books. One of the hot topics right now is alignment." He spreads his hands out. "It's all about alignment, every other word is alignment. But it's got some merits, so I think we should talk about compensation that aligns our incentives."

"Right. Well, I'm a high school history teacher, so I'm not much of a negotiator. Probably lose my shirt if I did *Shark Tank*."

Warren grimaces. "Why in the world would you get in a shark tank?"

"It's—it doesn't matter. Do you have something in mind?"

"Yeah. I was thinking we'd split the profits. Thirty percent to you, seventy to me. And I'll fund all purchases."

"That seems more than fair."

Warren points at me. "That right there—tipping your hand—that's what you don't want to do in a negotiation. Also, why you'd never make it on *Shark Tank*."

"So you *do* know what that is."

"Yeah, I watch it all the time. I was just messing with you. It's a good thing these auctions are online and they can't see you to get a read. We might actually make some money."

In the parking lot of Warren's store, I use my phone to order two medium cheese pizzas. To save a little money, I pick them up on the way to Meredith's townhouse.

When I arrive, the sun is setting and the cicadas are chirping in the woods nearby.

At Meredith's front door, I stand for a moment, looking in through the glass. The living room is empty. The dining table lies beyond, and I spot Meredith and Riley there, leaning over a board game. From out here, I can't tell what game they're playing, but Meredith is holding what looks like a pair of tweezers, slowly lowering them to the board. She jerks suddenly and reels back, laughing as she hands Riley the small grabbing fork.

I haven't seen my daughter this happy since... well, for a long time.

I recognize the game now: Operation. It's a good choice. One that would hold Riley's attention well.

I knock at the door, and Meredith opens it, but Riley bounds around her and crashes into me, hugging my waist tight.

The playfulness I saw when she sat at the table playing the game has left Meredith's face. She's eying me warily now, probably looking for clues as to what happened today.

She wants answers.

She deserves answers.

The first pizza disappears pretty quickly. The three of us are working on the second one—more slowly—when I take out my phone and text Meredith:

> I need to take her home and put her down soon. I know we need to talk.
>
> Want to come over after?
>
> Or tomorrow at school?

She sends a one-word reply:

> Tonight.

★

In the car on the way home, Riley is staring out the window at the moon when she asks, "Dad, how do you know Ms. Davis?"

"We're old friends."

"That's what she told me. But like, how do you know her?"

"Actually, she and I went to school together."

"So before you met Mom?"

I glance at her in the rearview mirror. She's sitting in a booster seat, still looking out the window nonchalantly.

"Yeah, sweetie, it was. It was a long time ago."

21

At the red caboose in the woods where we now live, I give Riley her Calm gummy, nag her to brush her teeth, and then read to her in the only bedroom (she has insisted on sleeping with me tonight instead of in the bunk beds). I think deep down she's starting to get really scared, though she's trying hard not to show it.

Whatever is going through her head, it doesn't keep her awake. She's out before I finish the chapter in Harry Potter.

Meredith—who followed us home—has been sitting at the table on the small porch since she arrived, staring at her phone. As I exit the caboose and gently close the door, she rises, slips her phone in her pocket, and eyes me, waiting.

I feel like a kid in the principal's office.

Neither of us says a word as I pass her and step off the porch and lead her out into the backyard, to a fire pit made from retaining wall blocks like you might find at a home improvement store. There are six cheap plastic Adirondack chairs around the pit. Meredith and I sit at ones across from each other.

Even at night, the late August heat in central North Carolina is oppressive. There's no practical reason for a fire, but I make one anyway. Maybe I'm just buying time, trying to delay the answers to her questions that will likely send Meredith Davis running from me in a similar way I bailed on her nearly two decades ago.

With the grill lighter, I ignite a bundle of kindling under the split firewood.

A few seconds later, the cracks and pops of the fire join the cicadas chirping and frogs ribbiting. I bet there's a pond or a creek nearby.

Meredith still hasn't said a word. So I start.

"You're probably wondering why I live in a train car outside of town."

She leans forward and puts her elbows on her knees. "I am wondering that, yes."

"There are two things going on in my life. One is easier to explain than the other."

She nods, and I continue. "Night before last, my neighbors below me were fighting. Guy gets mad, throws the woman into a wall, and I sort of... got involved."

"Got involved how?"

"As in, broke down his door and ran him off and helped her get outside to an ambulance."

"That's how you got the bruise."

"It is, yeah. And it's why Riley and I left the apartment. In return for my neighborly welfare check, the aforementioned domestic abuser busted in my door, trashed the place, and stole a bunch of stuff."

She stares at the fire. "You know Ryan is a cop now."

I did not, in fact, know that Meredith's brother is a cop now.

"He's a homicide detective," she says. "But he could get us in touch with the robbery division. We could file a police report."

"I don't think it's a good idea. I mean, if the woman—my neighbor—wants to press charges, I'll testify, but I don't get the impression she's going to."

"I was talking about a report for your place."

"The problem is I didn't see them break in."

"They might have records. Their fingerprints could be on file."

"All that might be true, but I just can't handle a police investigation right now."

"I'm assuming that's because of the other problem you have."

"Correct."

"And that problem is?"

"That problem is a little harder to explain."

"Try, Alan."

"I have tinnitus."

"That's what, like you hear ringing?"

"Right. It started happening after I got injured in Afghanistan. Ear damage from the explosion."

The fire is raging now, popping and dancing and casting Meredith's face in shadows. Even in the dim light, I still know her well enough to see the hint of confusion in her expression.

"The tinnitus has been sort of a background issue for me since then. It flares up when I'm around loud noise or really stressed. Caffeine and alcohol irritate it, but I've quit both."

"I take it, it's gotten worse?"

"A lot worse. To the point that it sometimes incapacitates me."

"And that's a problem in terms of taking care of Riley or driving or work or what?"

"It hasn't affected work yet. And I can't really establish a pattern of what sets it off. But yes, Riley is what I'm worried about."

She watches the fire for a long moment. "I understand."

"You should know that there's a little more to it—the tinnitus."

"More to it how? As in, you could lose your hearing or…"

"I guess that's possible, but there's a larger problem that's related to the tinnitus. A… kind of secondary effect."

"What is it?"

"I can't really say right now."

"Why not?"

I could tell her the truth—that I've been losing time and possibly committing crimes and that her knowing about that might eventually make her an accessory to said crimes after the fact. Instead, I opt for total evasion. For her sake. Actually, probably mine too.

"I'm sorry, but that's about all I can say. For now. And I hope it's enough."

She watches the flames charring the split wood. "It's enough," she says absently. "For now."

22

The next morning, shortly after my first period class starts, the burner phone buzzes with the arrival of an email.

It's from Amersa. In short sentences, it thanks me for my interest in their trial, once again reminds me to call 911 if I'm losing my mind, and provides a link to fill out a full application for the trial.

I snap a photo of the email and send it to the numbers email address to provide a status update.

Then I fill out the Amersa application. It's far more exhaustive than the initial form. This page requests my Social Security number, date of birth, and a litany of demographic information. They ask how long I've had PTSD and how I feel about artificial intelligence.

The final page features more legalese, disclaimers, and boxes to check (which I do).

I feel a little bad spending class time on something personal, but this is urgent, and it's my best lead to figure out what's going on.

Before I put away the phone, I check the local news. About halfway down is a headline that reads:

RALEIGH PD SEEKING HELP
WITH MURDER INVESTIGATION

The story is brief.

Raleigh Police are asking the public for any information related to Nathan Briggs, a man who was recently murdered in downtown

Raleigh… If you have any information or know of a friend, family member, or co-worker who knows the victim, please contact Raleigh PD immediately.

When my students file out of the classroom for lunch, Meredith steps into the doorway. She has opted for that smoothie concoction again. I beckon her inside and move to a chair across from my desk and get out my own lunch—again a copy of what I sent Riley to school with. Today is rolled-up cold cuts of ham and turkey, a few sticks of string cheese, strawberries, and grapes.

My daughter seems to be on Meredith's mind because the first thing she says is, "She's a really sweet kid, Alan."

"Yes, she is."

We talk about Riley for a while and then not much else for the rest of lunch. It's amazing how easy it is for us to be together, even when we're not talking, even when my life is a wreck. There's an effortless sense of calm when we're around each other's presence. And it's exactly what I need right now.

Meredith leaves fifteen minutes before my lunch period ends, and I use that free time to get out my laptop and start working at my new side gig: purchasing agent for a local army surplus store.

Warren has sent me an email that lists all the websites where I can, in his words, "go hunting." The sites are primarily for online auctions. There are also a few private military contractor sites that list used gear for sale at set prices.

Warren's also provided a wish list of items that move quickly and items that are slower to sell but usually carry higher margins. It's obvious he has been at this a while and knows his business well.

This is my first day on the job, and I'm technically spending someone else's money, so I err on the side of caution. Instead of bidding and buying, I send Warren a list of things that I think might be worth acquiring.

I've been teaching these same classes for a few years, and in that time, I've developed lesson plans that I know work. I adjust them a bit each year, but my job is largely about giving these kids my all when they're in the classroom, and then grading their homework, papers, and tests. We're early enough into the year that there's nothing to grade and no clear modifications to make to my lesson plans.

So during my planning period, I'm left with little to do.

It's a good thing, because when I get out the burner phone, I realize I missed an email during class. It's from the numbers person.

```
Go to the place we met.

Do it before the interview, or this is
over.
```

The first thing I do after reading that email is close my eyes, lean back in my chair, and exhale every last bit of air in my body. Sprints and one-legged men don't mix, and that's exactly what my life feels like lately: a never-ending series of sprints.

But I'm not about to quit.

I march to my car, drive to the warehouse, and once again enter through the side door. I don't have the body armor or my gun, but I also don't have time to go get them and get back to school in time for my next period.

The camera on the metal stand isn't there now. Where it was, I find a small cardboard box with the words "Open Me" scrawled on the top.

I really hope this isn't a bomb.

Squatting awkwardly, I pick it up and flip the top open.

It's not a bomb. But it may as well be. Inside is a button camera and a cord and detailed instructions on how to attach it to my shirt and activate it. They want me to wear it to the Amersa office. That assumes I'll even get into the trial—and that it takes place at their office.

I wonder if this group is somehow connected to Amersa. The

deeper I go in the labyrinth of the numbers, the more questions I have.

Back at my desk at school, I seriously contemplate whether I want to go through with all of this. What if Amersa catches me with the camera? They'll certainly exclude me from the trial. And probably call the cops. There are likely all kinds of laws about spying on a private company (maybe even specific statutes around spying on a medical trial).

But my biggest fear is about Amersa and the trial itself. What if the technology or process they're testing to treat PTSD alters my brain somehow, leaving me a vegetable?

There's not much I can do about that except show up and see what happens.

Glancing over at my laptop, I notice a new email from Warren. Good. I need some kind of distraction.

He gives me the go-ahead to bid on or buy about half the items I sent over.

A few others, he says, he's tried to sell before, but they never move or it takes a long time (he notes that he ended up selling some of the items online to get rid of them).

One thing I asked him about is a set of long-range radios that need some repair.

Under that listing, he's written:

```
Alan, this ain't no Radio Shack.
```

That brings a smile to my face that lasts until I finish reading all of his comments. Below his signature is a final note:

```
PS: Just kidding about those radios. See
if you can get them on the cheap. I
can probably fix them. They'll be a slow
seller, probably go to some hunters or
bikers or rent-a-cops, but they'll bring
a pretty penny when they do.
```

*

Before the end of school, I once again informed Riley's teacher that I would be in the car rider line. I need to give my stump as much relief as I can. I'm guessing what comes next with the group behind the numbers might get pretty intense—and require a lot of leg work (dad jokes keep me sane).

Earlier, I was so caught up in searching for secondhand military gear and nostalgic paraphernalia that I forgot to look for possibly the most important thing I need to buy at this point: a certain 3D puzzle of a Gothic castle from a popular children's series.

Using my laptop, I check eBay and a few local buyer sites, but the Hogwarts puzzle isn't much cheaper there than it is at a retailer.

I think more parents these days are buying secondhand holiday gifts, especially for their younger children. Let's face it, kids tear the wrapping paper off so fast and rip the toy out that they barely notice that the box is a little worn. Being smart about what you buy and using a little Scotch tape to reseal the box can save a lot of money. That's certainly what I'll be doing this Christmas (assuming I'm around at Christmas and not in a jail cell for whatever happened at that building downtown).

But for now, I may as well just buy a new puzzle.

One of the things I've learned as a parent who doesn't have an abundance of money is that weighing all the costs is the key to making the right financial decisions. I don't really have sixty dollars to spend on toys at the moment, but the alternative is letting my daughter sit there and watch the iPad until she's sleepy. At some point, I figure her mind will wander to what's happening to us. That's a big cost too.

So I'm going to go buy that puzzle. Because it's something we can do together, and because I think it helps her ADHD, and because I know it will make things feel more normal for her. A child needs that.

At the exit to the teacher parking lot, I find Meredith leaning against a brick wall, staring out at the sidewalk where kids and parents are passing by and buses from the middle school are lined up on the road beyond.

"Contemplating your plans for the evening, ma'am?"

She turns to me with a coy smile. "That and my life decisions."

"Well, I might have something that can take your mind off of it."

"I'm all ears."

"An evening with a seven-year-old, her father, a 3D puzzle, and some Mexican takeout." I hold up a finger. "In case you're still on the fence, this will take place on the front porch of a vintage train car."

"I'm in, but only because the kid is cute, and I have a weakness for Mexican food."

That night, on the porch, the three of us dig into the Mexican food, devouring the quesadillas, enchiladas, rice, and beans. For a while, the only sounds are the cicadas chirping in the woods, the bug zapper crackling nearby, and the occasional crunching of a chip lathered in salsa.

When the round foil take-out containers hold nothing but puddles of grease and the bag of chips is half-empty, we clear the table and get out the puzzle.

Unboxing it is a stark reminder that Riley and I are starting over, in more ways than one. And turning over the pieces and trying to fit them together feels a little like my life lately.

23

In the morning, there's a new email from Amersa regarding my application to their PTSD clinical trial.

My heart beats faster as I sit up in bed and tap the phone to open it. They're inviting me to an in-person interview at Amersa's office. This tells me that the numbers group does have some sense of how the trial operates—or at least Amersa's participant selection process.

There's a link to an online calendar application. The earliest interview date is next Friday. It's during school, but I think I can get a colleague to cover for me.

I click the time slot to reserve it, enter my information, and hit submit.

Thankfully, finding someone to cover my classes next week takes all of ten minutes in the teachers' lounge. I have a sense, however, that it's going to get tougher if I continue racking up absences as the semester wears on.

After school, as I exit the building, I find Meredith scrolling on her phone by the teachers' parking lot.

I slow as I come along beside her, and she smiles, but her eyes are unreadable behind the aviator sunglasses that reflect a distorted image of me.

"Got plans this weekend?" she asks.

I could tell her the truth: that my only plans are to try not to have a tinnitus-induced time loss episode that lands me in legal trouble. Instead, I reply, "Not a thing."

She holds her hands up. "Super low pressure, but my parents are having their usual Labor Day cookout."

The words hang in the air as two of our fellow teachers walk by, leaving a little quicker than usual, maybe because the weekend awaits, or on account of the scene happening here.

"It's just family," Meredith adds. "And maybe a few of their friends. Also, Ryan and his two sons will be there. They're in kindergarten and second grade. Did I tell you that?"

"Uh—"

"No, I don't think I did."

"I... don't recall."

"Well, super low pressure."

"I'll ask Riley. You know, first week of school... I just don't know if she'll be maxed out. You know?"

"Totally. And totally understand if she needs downtime."

"Right."

"It's at two, tomorrow, by the way. Do you remember where my parents live?"

"I do."

On the way home—and half the evening—Meredith's invite is all I can think about.

It's like a Rubicon for her and me. A line that I either cross or walk away from. What's on the other side?

I have some idea. I haven't seen Meredith's parents for twenty years. Same goes for her brother. Not since we broke up. Of the two, her brother is my greater concern. He will likely come at me with a high level of social aggression.

I can take it. I survived a roadside bomb.

If I decline the invite, I sense that things between Meredith and me will cool off. This is her reaching out. Declining would be me backing away.

But maybe I should.

My other consideration is Riley. Sitting around this train car in the woods over the long weekend is a pretty solitary existence for a seven-year-old child, especially one as outgoing as Riley (she takes after her mother in that regard). I can find things for us to do Saturday, Sunday, and Monday afternoon, but with my budget, the options aren't particularly thrilling.

I know she would enjoy the cookout. And holiday weekend cookouts feel normal.

For that reason—and maybe another—I casually ask her, Saturday morning, as I pour Fruity Pebbles in a cereal bowl, "Hey kiddo, what would you think about going to a cookout at Ms. Davis's parents' house?"

She simply watches me pouring in the milk, floating the multi-colored pebbles. "I dunno."

"We don't have to."

Crunching the first bite, she studies me. "You want to?"

"I think it could be fun."

"Me too."

"Okay. So you want to go?"

She shrugs. "Sure."

On the way to Meredith's parents' house, we stop at Harris Teeter and grab some sides: mac and cheese, mashed potatoes, and two large bags of chips (barbecue, and sour cream and onion). I contemplated buying some beer, but it felt a little off—strolling up to my former high school girlfriend's house, twelve pack in hand. I'm playing by the old school rules for now.

Meredith's parents live in the same house they did when I was in high school. It's a split-level ranch in North Hills. Around them, half the homes have been torn down and newer, bigger houses erected in their place. The transformation is even more stark across Lassiter Mill Road. The old North Hills Mall is gone. Now it's an open-air mixed-use amalgamation that is fancy and amazing and keeps growing both out and up. The JCPenney store was the last mall-era retailer holding out (they owned the land under them and thus couldn't be demolished at the end of the lease like the tenants). Penney's finally sold and that final nail from the old mall is getting hammered down now, something bigger and fancier rising in its place.

But Mr. and Mrs. Davis—as I will always think of them—are holding strong (like JCPenney, they own the land under them too).

From the outside, their home hasn't changed much. A new roof. Some landscaping. The big oak tree in the front yard is gone, but on the whole, the old homestead lease like the tenants about the same. I kind of like that. I've had enough change recently.

As Riley and I walk up, the front door opens, revealing Mr. and Mrs. Davis, his arm around her. I swear, if I took a photo from prom night nearly two decades ago, you could measure the differences in millimeters. And a few wrinkles. But not a lot. Meredith's parents have aged well.

Pleasantries flow back and forth, and Mrs. Davis breaks away first, stepping forward and dropping to eye level with Riley.

"Can I tell you a secret?"

Riley nods.

"I've hidden three gifts in my backyard."

From here I can see Riley suck in a breath.

"And," Mrs. Davis goes on, "my two grandsons haven't found them yet."

Riley smiles.

Mrs. Davis holds up a finger. "But, I didn't tell them about the prizes, so you can't blame them for that."

Leaning closer to Riley, Meredith's mother whispers in her ear, "I'll give you a clue, though: search where the flowers are in bloom. Maybe you can help them find the treasure."

She wraps a hand around Riley's shoulder and ushers her inside, leaving me with Meredith's father.

This moment is more awkward than my first date with her all those years ago. It's like a sequel where the stakes are raised and I'm not the hero anymore—I'm the bad guy.

Mr. Davis doesn't welcome me in. He says, "It's been a long time, Alan."

"It has."

"I have one question for you."

"Just one?"

"I'm cooking burgers and dogs. Which do you and that young lady prefer?"

He raises his eyebrows. "We also have vegetarian options. Pasta salad from the Teeter. And we could DoorDash something, but with the prices and fees, it's highway robbery half the time."

"Burgers are fine. One for each of us."

He nods slowly.

I open my mouth, but he beats me to it. "I always liked you, Alan. But she's been through a lot. It's still a tough time for her."

I could tell him that it's a tough time for me, too. But the right thing to do is to nod, and that's what I do, and then he does too before turning, leaving the door open and walking up the half-flight of stairs.

In the backyard, Riley is leading Ryan's two sons on a hunt through the flower gardens and woods. The prizes are half-buried and wrapped in white Target bags with the red bull's-eye.

As a toddler, Riley was pretty shy. But since starting school, she's come out of her shell. There are moments—like first days of school—that send her spiraling, but for the most part, she's pretty outgoing. In this case, the treasure hunt has diminished any hint of social anxiety.

Standing on the deck, I watch Riley reach the first treasure, dropping down to her knees as she hastily unearths it. One of the boys skids beside her, feet sliding on pine needles as he grabs for the bag.

Down below, at a square glass-top table with an umbrella, a guy with a tight polo and tan shorts rises from a chair and shouts, "Kyle! She got there first. Back off, dude!"

At the end of the patio is a silver grill, mouth open like Pac-Man, issuing heat waves. Meredith's dad stands before it, using a spatula to transfer hamburger patties.

Meredith sits at the square table beside her brother, and as I peer down, she turns and glances up at me with those mirrored sunglasses.

By the time I descend the stairs, the kids have moved deeper into the shallow forest at the back of this lot—trees that would likely be cut down if the house were leveled for new construction.

Meredith's brother holds up a glass bottle of Miller High Life and calls to me. "Alan!"

He doesn't wait for me to reply. "It's only been... what? Twenty years?"

Meredith turns to her brother, silently warning him.

Ryan is four years younger than us. Back then, in middle school and high school, the gap was a canyon. We were the sub-adults, and he was practically a kid. He's grown up now—well, he's bigger, at least.

Meredith has told me a bit about his situation. He and his wife are separated, but, according to what he's told Meredith, they're working on it. He has visitation this weekend.

In the woods, the kids are arguing. Apparently, they've all gotten to the next prize at the same time. Riley is hovering over it like a Super Bowl fumble, and the boys are grabbing for it.

The commotion draws Ryan's attention, prompting him to take a long swig of High Life and march off the patio, deeper into the yard like a security sentry activated.

"Hey! Kyle! Cody!" he yells, taking another sip. "Back off, guys. She's our guest. Chill out for a minute."

Moments like this—when you see how parents discipline their children and how they look at what's fair and decent—reveal true character.

And it tells me that half of Ryan's bluster is probably just him trying to protect his sister. I can't fault the guy for that.

At their father's command, the two boys relax, and Riley pulls the bag away, revealing a toy treasure chest with kinetic sand and jewels buried inside. "We can share," she says, staring at it.

Ryan saunters back to the table, sets the empty beer bottle down, and focuses on me. "What're you drinking, Alan?"

"Just water."

He bends down and unzips a Yeti cooler and takes another beer out, twisting the top off and tossing it back inside. "Really? Heard you had a hollow leg."

Meredith is opening her mouth to speak, but I answer first. "Oh, it's not hollow, Ryan. It was completely blown off in the service of my country."

After lunch, the kids play on the swing set and partake in some of the yard games—cornhole and frisbee and connect four.

"You got rid of the trampoline," I say to Mr. Davis.

"It was rotting," he replies between sour-cream-and-onion chips.

"And way too dangerous," his wife adds.

When the plates are empty, I offer to clean up, but Mr. and Mrs. Davis won't hear of it. They collect the dishes and silverware and make their way back to the house.

Meredith goes off to play with the kids, leaving Ryan and me alone. He was a pudgy kid. He got stocky at the end of middle school and a little more in high school (he was on the offensive line in football). He's still offensive-lineman shaped, but he's grown a beer gut and seems committed to it by the way he's downing them.

"Heard you're working homicide," I offer, taking a sip of water.

"Yep." He takes another pull from the clear glass bottle and shrugs. "Dying business."

He chuckles at his own joke.

I might have too. A few days ago.

I ask him if he's working on anything he can talk about.

"Nothing that isn't in the news."

I nod, and he continues, leaning forward, voice lower. "You see the story about that murder downtown?"

"I did."

He shakes his head, swigs the beer, as if the conversation calls for it.

"Got any leads?" I ask, trying to sound casual.

"Can't say much—open file—but looks like drug-debt payback."

"Why do you think that?"

"Word is the vic was a user, owed some money. And the perp cut his clothes off and did a halfway decent job of cleaning up the scene."

For a while, we don't say anything, just watch the kids playing in the backyard.

Meredith turns her head to me. Through the mirrored glasses I can almost hear her asking: *You doing okay?*

Beside me, Ryan says, "We've got a few leads, though." He tilts the beer for a long swig as his gaze drifts over to the mud beyond the pavers, where I've walked out into the yard, leaving tracks. Very distinct tracks, uneven indentations, because one of my legs is a prosthetic.

Slowly, Ryan sets the beer on the table and sits up in the chair, still staring at the tracks. I don't know if it's my imagination, but I could swear his expression changes ever so slightly.

I was so busy worrying about the blood and fingerprints and what to do with the phone and body parts, I didn't even think about my footsteps, which I left all over that building, in the dust and dirt, and in the woods where I disposed of the evidence.

24

The rest of the holiday weekend is a pretty lazy one. I'm exhausted from the first week of school and all the personal drama.

Riley seems content with the slower pace as well.

Our only outing is to a matinee movie on Sunday afternoon.

The shortened holiday week at school goes by like a blur. I spend every free moment banking lesson plans (and updating the ones I have). I'm assuming my life is going to get even more chaotic after the Amersa interview; preparing for that is all I can do now.

Outside school, my new side gig with Warren occupies a lot of my time. I pretty much work from the moment I get up until I go to sleep, except for the few hours I spend with Riley.

On Friday morning, I'm standing in the bedroom of the caboose, rifling through the small closet, looking for a shirt with buttons that match the color and size of the camera the group supplied.

The device is a next-gen pinhole model, barely thicker than a real button. Once I twist it into place and tug the cable through, even I have to lean in to recognize it.

Still, I'm not feeling super comfortable.

The Amersa offices are located in Research Triangle Park, a sprawling campus that covers seven thousand acres of land between Raleigh, Durham, and Chapel Hill. As a history teacher (and someone who grew up here), I also know that it's the largest research park in the country.

And conveniently for me, it's situated right off Interstate 40, fifteen minutes from school.

RTP—as Research Triangle Park is known locally—is home to companies in biotech and pharma, information technology, agricultural sciences, and probably other high-tech fields I'm not even aware of. It's a high-class neighborhood.

And Amersa's place in that neighborhood is pretty nice. The building is all glass and steel. The top has real trees and bushes and a clear glass railing. It looks like the rooftop of a chic hotel in Manhattan.

The grounds of Amersa's campus put a country club to shame. There are tennis courts, paved walking trails, and biking paths. There's even an outdoor pavilion where people are gathered around like a holiday party. It's probably a meeting, but it feels more festive.

Inside the building, a rush of cold air greets me. The security guard at the long desk scans my ID and snaps a picture, processing me with clinical efficiency.

I've barely sat down when a well-dressed young woman who can't be far out of college comes to retrieve me. She deposits me in a waiting room that's reminiscent of a doctor's office. There are couches and lamps with soft light and a generous selection of magazines. I'm just picking up one when the receptionist slides the window aside.

"Mr. Norris, we're ready to take you back now."

I stand, feeling the force on my stump and trying to hide how nervous I am. I really wonder if the numbers group will ignore me if I don't get into this trial.

I also wonder what I'll do without the group. At the moment, it's still my only lead as to what's happening to me.

Following my guide through the corridors, I try to casually glance down and inspect the button camera. I don't know what I expect. Maybe to see it hanging out, the wire exposed, silently announcing, "He's a spy, get him!"

But it's still in place, looking normal to the unsuspecting eye.

Even though my nerves are shredded and my heart is racing, the tinnitus hasn't started.

I wonder if that's a sign.

Or just another coincidence.

The room I'm escorted to reminds me more of a psychologist's office than the treatment room at a doctor's office. It has a couch and chairs. In the corner is a desk that can be raised or lowered, with arms that hold two screens.

The woman waiting for me smiles warmly but doesn't extend her hand to shake. That's probably to prevent the spread of germs. It makes me wonder if there are other nuances of the decorum here that I don't realize.

I've visited a few psychologists over the years. In the Marines, I had to after the accident. And I needed to for a while after. I know the routine.

"Hello, Mr. Norris," she begins, voice even and soothing. "I'm Dr. Nisha Kapoor. Welcome."

"Thanks. And uh, call me Alan."

Her smile widens. "In that case, please call me Nisha."

She holds a hand out toward the couch, and when I've plopped down, she settles into a chair across from me.

"Alan, I want you to know that this is a safe place. I also want you to know that you don't have to talk about anything that makes you uncomfortable. If I ask a question that you don't want to answer, I want you to tell me, or you can simply say, 'let's skip that.' That's completely fine. And it doesn't mean that you won't be included in the trial."

She waits a moment, and I simply nod, figuring that silence should probably be my default mode here.

"Now, speaking of the trial, I want to give you a bit more information before we get started. Does that sound all right?"

"Sure."

"What we're doing here at Amersa is evaluating whether a product we've created is effective in treating individuals who have mental health conditions. Post-traumatic stress disorder is one of those conditions. At this point, we're evaluating how the device impacts a small cohort of participants. We're following these valued individuals very closely."

She waits, perhaps seeing if I have any questions. When I say nothing, she continues.

"What we're doing today is trying to determine if you might be a fit for that trial. To do that, I'd like to start by asking you a couple of basic questions. For example, have you ever used a virtual reality or augmented reality device?"

"Uh, yes, I have."

She smiles and waits, I suppose for more details, which I provide.

"In the Marines, we did some VR training. Not a lot. But some."

"That's great to hear. While using those devices, did you have any sort of issues? Any seizures? Or any other reactions?"

"No."

"Do you think that VR experience was beneficial?"

"Well, yeah, I guess a bit."

"But not fully?"

"It's… it was a combat sim." I shrug, and when she keeps staring at me, I add, "But nothing really prepares you… for certain things."

Nisha nods slowly. "That's understandable. Thank you for having the courage to be frank, Alan."

I nod once and have the sudden urge to look down at the button camera, but thankfully, I resist.

"Let's shift to civilian life, Alan. Do you play video games?"

"I used to. Before my daughter was born."

"Excellent. I don't know if you know this, but Amersa has its roots in the video game industry."

"I read that, yes."

"Alan, what are your thoughts on artificial intelligence?"

"I guess, well, to be honest, I don't really know a lot about it. I'm a high school teacher of history and psychology, and I've used it some to see what my students might get as results for papers and homework."

"Oh, that's very smart."

"Can't take credit for the idea. Got it from the students, actually."

"Well, recognizing a good idea is an art unto itself. Have you used AI for anything else? Outside your classroom?"

"A bit."

"In what way?"

"I've used it to try to find activities that I can do with my daughter. She's been diagnosed with ADHD."

Nisha breaks eye contact for the first time and picks up a small notepad and scribbles something down.

"That's interesting," she says, still clutching the pad to her chest. "Alan, I know your next answer is going to be a guess, but do you think you would be comfortable using an experimental device that is powered by AI and uses virtual reality?"

"Sure, I think so."

"Do you think you'd be physically comfortable with a device that consumed your view?"

"I do."

"Have you ever had an issue with tight spaces? Any claustrophobia?"

"No."

"If you were asked to wear a suit that controlled your body movements at times, do you think you'd feel comfortable with that?"

I motion to my artificial leg, which my shorts don't cover. "I'm used to devices helping me move. And in the Marines, I often operated with night vision goggles."

"Excellent. And that's a nice segue to your background. Would you mind giving me a little more personal information? Where you grew up, any significant life experiences, anything that comes to mind. Just what you're comfortable with sharing."

"Okay. Well, I grew up here in Raleigh. My dad was a welder, and my mom worked at a flower shop. They have both passed now. I attended college here in the Triangle, on an ROTC scholarship. I went into the Marines after. During the surge in Afghanistan, I was injured by an IED. I lost my left leg just above the knee."

Mentally, I'm wondering whether to mention the tinnitus. But my instincts are to hold back.

Nisha speaks before I can decide. "Is that when your

PTSD started? That would certainly be very traumatic and understandable."

"Yes."

"Do you mind telling me what sort of symptoms you had?"

"Immediately after, it was… I had a lot of anger."

She stares at me, eyes filled with sympathy. "I think a great many of us would."

She lets a long pause stretch out before she adds, "Is there anything else you were feeling, Alan? Anything at all?"

She must read the grimace on my face.

"You don't have to answer. You can still get into the trial if that's all you want to say. But I will say, adding details about your background and condition might increase your chances of admission."

That last bit gets me. So I start talking again, like I started walking again, with a hesitant, unsteady step at first. "I felt some guilt."

"That's very common."

Verbally, I take the next step. "And I had nightmares."

"Also common. What was on your mind back then, Alan? In the days and weeks after the event."

"Well, the obvious."

"And what was that for you, Alan?"

"I spent a lot of time wondering what my life would be like and thinking about what I would do for a living."

"For you, did that process have any impact on your relationships with, say, friends or family?"

"Yeah. It did."

"How exactly? Did you push them away? Lean on them? Confide in them?"

"All of those, at different points."

The woman's eyes rake over me, like a human medical scanner.

"Alan, I'm sure the time after that explosion was difficult, but would you be comfortable telling me how your PTSD was treated?"

"I was prescribed medications for depression and anxiety."

"Did you engage in counseling?"

"Yes."

"Let's talk about the course of your PTSD. Do you feel like at any point after the incident that it got better?"

"It did. It actually got a lot better."

"Would you say that it ever went into partial or full remission?"

"Yes, I would."

"Can you elaborate? Specifically, what do you think caused the symptoms to recede?"

"I don't know. I guess… because I started to feel normal again."

"When you talk about feeling normal again, what things does that bring to mind? What happened to make you feel normal again?"

"The obvious. Learning to walk again with the prosthetic."

"That must have been hard."

"I had a lot of help." Saying that brings back a memory of her, at the end of those wooden bars, crouched, urging me to keep going, my arms shaking, chest heaving. The memory is like a cracked rib that hurts every time I take a breath.

Nisha leans forward slightly, silently encouraging me like the ghost of my deceased wife. "Let's zoom in on that, Alan. Beyond walking, what else helped in your recovery? I don't mean to press—and again, you can skip this question—but these details are important."

My gaze drifts to the floor.

"Take your time, Alan."

I know I need to tell the truth in order to maximize my chances of getting into this trial, but all I want to do is stand and bolt out of this room. If I were alone in life, I probably would.

But for Riley's sake, I keep going.

"I guess what helped me the most is feeling like I could get my life back on track."

"What happened to make you feel like you could—in your words—get your life back on track?"

"A few things."

"Such as?"

"For one, I realized the prosthetic wasn't so bad."

"How so?"

"I got used to it. It didn't... limit my life like I thought it would."
"What else helped, Alan?"
My wife is the rest of the answer, but I'm not mentioning her here.
"Other things," I mutter.
Nisha spreads her hands. "Alan, before the injury, what was the life you had envisioned for yourself?"
"Nothing particularly unique."
"You don't have to be unique to be interesting. Or valuable. I'd love to hear more about what you wanted from life back then."
The very clever woman sitting on the couch reads my silence as a non-verbal request to "skip that question." She makes a show of picking up a tablet from the side table. I can see a bit of what's on the screen—it's my intake information. And some other data that I guess they pulled from public records. I bet she's already memorized it, based on how sharp she is, but the motion and break in the rhythm provides a sort of reset.
"Alan, your records indicate that you got married a few years after your discharge from the Marines."
"That's right."
"Would you say that helped with your PTSD?"
"I would."
"In what way?"
"I was happy. I had a spouse I loved. A good job. We had a child."
"Would you say that was pretty close to the life you had envisioned before you were wounded?"
"Yes. I would say that."
Her eyes drift back to the tablet. Another act of theater: a pause before what she's been working up to.
"And then things changed again," she whispers.
I nod.
With a finger, she scrolls down on the tablet, as if reading the file for the first time, learning that my wife got sick a few years ago and passed away last year.
"Losing a spouse often leads to profound grief or depression—and, in someone with prior trauma, it can worsen existing PTSD symptoms. There's often a compounding effect."

When I don't say anything, she goes on. "Many individuals develop a certain vulnerability to traumatic events, a lingering anxiety, a fear that what comes next might bring more pain. Our brains become sensitized to trauma. They subconsciously expect it."

I stare at the coffee table as she continues.

"As we're talking through all these things, is there anything else on your mind, Alan? It really can be anything. In fact, if you're comfortable, please simply say the first thing that comes to mind. This might seem irrelevant, but I assure you it has bearing on what we decide."

"My daughter." The two words come out before I can even think.

"Why do you think she might be coming to mind right now?"

"I guess because she's the center of my life. And because I'm responsible for her."

"Responsible how?"

"Providing for her. Keeping her safe. Trying to make sure she has the opportunities she needs in life."

"And do you think that might relate somehow to these past two events connected to your PTSD?"

"I don't know."

"Dig deep, Alan. Like you did when you were learning to walk again."

When I shrug, she presses harder. "This is really important, Alan. I think we're getting to something interesting here. Think about how these two events are related. The IED that took your leg and fellow Marines, and the cancer that took your wife. Both were intensely traumatic. Both occurred at different stages in your life. Just as you were starting to build the life you wanted. Let's think here. What's the thread that ties them together?"

"I don't know."

"Say the first word you think of, Alan. Just do it."

"I don't know."

"Would you mind if I suggest a word that you yourself used earlier?"

I hold my hands up. This is far more intense than I expected.

The word she lets loose hits as hard as that roadside IED.

"Guilt."

I take a deep breath. But I don't say a word. I don't like this. I feel like a wounded animal on a table being sliced up with words, my insides and soul being laid bare and examined before my eyes.

She stands and moves to a chair beside me. "Can I tell you something, Alan?"

"Sure."

"I think two bombs have gone off in your life. The first was on a desert highway a long way from here. It took a piece of your body. And you were certain that it had also taken your future from you—the life you wanted."

She waits. I say nothing.

"But in time, you learned that you hadn't lost what you thought you had. You learned that losing part of your leg hadn't put your dreams out of reach. You got back on your feet. Literally and figuratively. You got over that injury—the one you never thought you would. She helped you. She was the key."

Nisha looks at me.

Slowly, I shake my head. I'm not disagreeing—because she is right. I'm just too emotional to speak.

She does. "And then, unexpectedly, your wife got sick. After you had the life you had always wanted. A child. A job that mattered to you. Like that bomb that day in the desert, it all went away. That was the second explosion."

She waits, but I still don't speak.

"I can't imagine, Alan. She must have meant so much to you."

"She did."

"She saved you."

"She did."

"And when she was taken, that... well, again, I can't imagine."

She pauses, and finally says, "Will you tell me what you felt then?"

"I felt like the world was very, very unfair."

"It is. And yet you felt guilt. Even though you knew it wasn't your fault. Just like that day in Afghanistan."

I can feel my hands getting clammy, my heart beating faster, cheeks flushing. A classical fight or flight response in slow motion. I'm going to get up and walk out now. I'm shifting in the chair when she says, "That's the thread, Alan. You felt like you couldn't protect those Marines that day. And later, your wife. Both were bombs going off in your life."

I shake my head, not looking at her.

"And now you're worried that another bomb is going to rip your life apart again. You're terrified that it's going to take what you have left—the thing you said when I asked what was on your mind. Your daughter."

My mind flashes to Nathan Briggs—a man who worked for this very company—lying dead beside me at that construction site. He is the third bomb in my life. And it's already gone off. The blast is expanding every second, and the worst part is that I don't even know how much damage it's going to do.

And I can't even tell anyone about that bomb or what I'm going through. I'm alone with the secret and the struggle. Except for the numbers group. But it's not clear if they can even help me. Or if they will. So far, all they've done is pull my strings like a puppeteer.

But that's nothing compared to this interview—this verbal, psychological dissection. In a matter of minutes, this woman has identified the root of my fears, which I hadn't even seen for myself until now.

"Alan, can you tell me what you're thinking right now? Again, this is a safe—"

I stand a little too quickly, wobbling on the prosthetic and from the weight of hard truths. My heart thumps so hard in my ears I can barely hear the words I say: "I think you're very good at your job. And I've had enough for one day."

Then I march out.

25

On the way home from Amersa's office, I mentally review what was quite possibly the worst intake interview in the history of clinical trials.

I blew it.

I know it.

If I could go back and do it again and say different things, I would. But I had to get out of that room.

I've been here before. In the Marines. You get knocked down. You get up. And you keep going.

Same thing with Jenn.

That completely gutted me. Left alone, I probably would have just withered for a while, years at least. But because of the child we have together—that reflection of her I see every day—I got back up.

I was getting better when this happened—the tinnitus and the dead body and neighbor drama and mysterious numbers group.

That last part—the numbers group—is probably my only chance of disabling the next bomb before it destroys me and my daughter.

I know the interview footage is bad, but what choice do I have but to send it to the group? It was part of their price of admission.

At home, I take the button camera off and use the instructions provided to download the video file. Apparently, it's too large to email.

When I notify the numbers person, they send messages that walk me through how to use a website to send large files. Soon after I send the video, they confirm receipt.

That's interesting; they're willing to provide tech support but literally no other answers.

After that, I have just enough time to send a text thanking my colleagues at school for covering for me, change shirts (into one that doesn't have a hole for a button camera), and get to the elementary school to pick up Riley.

On the way home, I ask her questions that she mostly evades.

"How was school?"

"Good."

"Who did you play with?"

"I don't know."

"You don't know who you played with?"

"Just... other kids."

"What did you learn?"

"I don't know."

"Did you have a good day?"

"Yeah."

Since we left the apartment, I've tried to be aware of how my daughter might be feeling. I've also tried to make our occupation of a former train caboose out in the woods feel like an adventure. But whether you're a kid or an adult, at some point you need a break from adventure—and a taste of home.

For that reason, I cook comfort food: grilled cheeses and tomato soup.

At the tight banquette, Riley and I sit on the U-shaped seat and hover over plastic plates on the linoleum table. It feels like the corner booth in a roadside diner in the sixties.

The only hint of the modern era is a Bluetooth speaker on the bar, which is blaring out songs from Disney films. At the moment, it's playing a popular track from the movie *Encanto* titled "We Don't Talk About Bruno."

As it plays, I'm thinking about all the things we don't talk about (Mom, tinnitus, school, the home we abandoned, and everything I'm forgetting).

"Dad?" Riley asks.

"Yeah?"

"Is Ms. Davis coming over?"

"Not tonight."

She sinks the corner of the grilled cheese in the orange sea of soup. "Why not?"

"It's a school night."

"No, it's not."

"Well, we had school today."

"She comes over on school nights."

Mentally, I kick myself (with my good leg). It was a lazy excuse.

With a napkin, I wipe up the tomato soup that has rolled off her bowl. "That's true," I tell my daughter. "But she also has things to do."

"Is she your girlfriend?"

"She's a friend."

On the porch, under the moonlight, Riley and I continue putting together the pieces of the castle.

I've brought the speaker out with us, and it's fighting a battle with the cicadas, blasting a song from *Frozen*, urging us to let it go.

Letting go is a problem. As are the things that won't let you go. For me, right now, it's that periodic ringing in my ear. Which, significantly, I didn't hear today during the interview.

I wonder what that means. It's a piece of this puzzle—part of the outline of what's going on.

But unlike the box the castle came in, I don't see the full picture. I don't know where all this ends, even if I manage to get the pieces together in time.

That's what scares me the most.

Riley doesn't want to sleep in the bunks tonight. In that small bedroom at the back of the caboose, I read to her until she closes her eyes and her breathing slows.

Carefully, I slip out from under her, set the book aside, and step out.

My phone is on the narrow kitchen counter, charging. I expect to see a text from Meredith to be waiting for me.

Maybe I'm hoping there is.

But as the phone wakes and I disconnect the charger cord from the bottom, I see that there's not. There are no messages at all.

It strikes me then that I haven't talked to her since the cookout at her parents' home. Riley and I just hung out and took it easy the rest of the weekend. And I was so focused on work and the Amersa interview this week, I never reached out. And neither did she.

It's on me. I have a bad habit of getting absorbed in things and not being cognizant of my relationships.

The burner phone is in the drawer below, and when I boot it up, I find no emails from Amersa or the numbers group.

I wonder if they've had time to watch the interview footage. If so, they've probably come to the same conclusion as me: I'm not getting into that trial.

Carrying both phones, I walk outside, into the warm night and chorus of cicadas.

At the fire pit, I settle into one of the wobbly plastic chairs. I don't bother lighting the fire like I did when Meredith was here. Maybe I don't see the point. Or maybe I lit it that night to put a barrier between us. Those flames were just one of the barriers between us. She has barriers too. But both of us have been poking little holes in those walls, glimpsing through and backing away, like teenagers unsure of what they're doing, excited and scared at the same time.

And then we both sort of stopped. Maybe it was intentional on her part. On my end, it was just by virtue of distraction and being busy.

If whatever we were doing has run its course, a part of me thinks it might be best for her (I haven't forgotten Mr. Davis's words at his front door: *she's been through a lot. It's still a tough time for her*).

She'll be all right without me. She'll reboot her life and do okay. In fact, it'll probably be easier without me.

And eventually—if her brother is right—he'll figure out I was involved in that murder downtown. Being convicted of that would wreck both Riley and Meredith.

For a moment, I consider pulling up stakes and taking off, loading up the car and Riley and leaving town and not looking back. My parents have passed. Riley's grandparents are out of state, and we can reconnect in a few years. Riley is young enough to flourish anywhere.

But even if we did skip town, the murder investigation might still catch up to me. Leaving might buy me some time. In eleven years, she'll probably be going off to college. She'd be able to handle me being arrested better by that point. If my life unravels now, it would be catastrophic for her, this soon after her mother was taken from us.

She'd have to go live with her grandparents. And the worst of it is that I think she'd always have issues trusting and loving the people in her life. I think deep down, she'd always be scared that they could be torn away at any moment.

That interview at Amersa made me realize that's my issue too: I'm scared of getting attached. Every time I do, life blows up in my face. It's why I'm terrified of getting involved with Meredith. Maybe it's why my subconscious kept me from reaching out to her this week.

But as I think through this nascent plan to leave Raleigh for good, I realize there's one major problem: the ringing in my ears.

Wherever I go, it'll come with me. I can't leave it here like the murder investigation. And what's worse is that out there on the road, Riley and I would be alone, and if the tinnitus returned and I lost time, she would be on her own. Here, at least I have a support system, which every parent needs, no matter what they're going through.

I have to stay here and unravel this, all the way to the end.

But right now, I need to get my mind off my problems. I need to feel like I'm making progress. I need to work.

Inside, I grab my laptop and return to the rickety plastic chair. There's an email from Warren.

```
You get my last message?
```

Scrolling down, I see his previous email with feedback on my questions from this morning. I've been radio-silent almost all day.

I hit him with a quick message back. I opt to tell the truth.

```
I did. Bad day.
```

For a while, I do the online bids, hoping one of them will hit. I have to admit, it's kind of fun. A bit like a casino where I know the odds.

I'm lowballing a guy on eBay on a laser sight when my phone lights up. I send the bid and then pick it up.

It's from Meredith.

```
Heard you were out this afternoon.
Everything ok?
```

I should tell her the truth: things are far, far from okay, and that she should stay far away from me. Instead, I put the phone down, return to my computer, and put in a bid on a Labradar Chronograph. It measures the velocity of projectiles up to one hundred yards (depending on bullet size—larger ones register longer than smaller ones).

In my email, a new message from Warren appears.

```
Need the body armor?
```

Like Nisha earlier today, this guy reads me like an X-ray machine. He just uses fewer words. And so do I in my reply.

```
No.
```

Then I put the laptop aside and for a while, I just stare at the pine trees and listen to the sounds of this Carolina night, the cicadas and frogs and crickets calling out.

My phone lights up with a new message. It's probably from her. I open my laptop first. Two of the auctions I was watching have ended. I didn't win. There's also a new email from Warren.

In my mind's eye, I imagine him sitting at home, in a lounge chair, typing with two fingers. Reading his message, I can hear his gruff voice, an undertone of annoyance trying to hide the fact that he actually cares.

```
Come see me recruit.
```

I want to reply that he needs a comma after me, but I let it go. Not the right time for grammar lessons. My reply is as simple as his message:

```
Will do.
```

Picking up my phone, I enter a taller briar patch with sharper barbs. Strangely, Meredith is more direct than my new business partner, who is an Army combat veteran. Her text contains only two words:

> Call me.

I tap her number, and she answers immediately.

I hear rustling in the background, as if she's getting out of bed.

I start with a joke: "Ma'am, I'm calling about your car's extended warranty."

"My car is not what I'm worried about, Alan."

I lean back in the cheap plastic chair, watching a strong breeze ripple across the pine trees. It looks like they're waving at me.

"Hello?" she says. If I had to guess, she's sitting on that couch in the small living room in her townhouse.

"I'm here."

"Where were you today?"

"I had an appointment."

She waits, and I add, "For my tinnitus."

"How did it go?"

"Not great."

"Want me to come over?"

The only sound is her breathing into the phone. I feel like this is a seminal moment, where she's offering her hand to me, reaching through that hole in the wall between us. Like she did with the cookout.

I didn't fully know it until now, but I want to grab that hand

and pull her through. I want a fresh start for us. I want her across from this fire pit, inside that train car, spending time with both me and Riley.

But like that cramped caboose in the middle of the woods, there's not enough room for her and me and Riley and the baggage my life carries. Not right now. And like that interview at Amersa, realizing a hard truth I can't do anything about just makes me feel boxed in.

But I can't get up and walk away, not from Meredith, not as easily as I did from that interview today.

I don't tell her what I'm thinking. What I say is: "Not tonight."

She exhales. "Why not?"

"I need some space."

The words I just uttered are like an emergency brake on a relationship.

"Is Riley okay?"

"She is. She's sleeping."

Her tone turns sympathetic. "If you need help, I'm here, Alan."

"I know. I appreciate it."

The silence after that is awkward.

"Look," I start, my words hesitant, once again like those first few steps with the prosthesis. "I'm not in a good place."

"Who is, Alan?"

"I just don't want to drag you through my rough patch."

"I'll decide when things get too rough for me."

Then she hangs up.

That night, I place my bids and constantly check my phone for emails from Amersa (or text messages from Meredith or the numbers group). I don't receive any of those, just counteroffers on military gear.

26

In the morning, I disconnect my phone from the charger and lie back in the bunk (I didn't go into the bedroom last night for fear of waking up Riley).

Still, there's no word from any of the parties that hold my fate—and that of my daughter—in their hands.

That's great.

The rest of the weekend is a blur. Mainly, I try to keep Riley distracted while I check the phones for updates and try to make a little money trading army surplus gear.

On Monday, I'm hoping to see Meredith saunter into my classroom at lunch.

She doesn't.

Nor does she show up on Tuesday or Wednesday.

With each passing day, this cold war between us accumulates another layer of ice.

The question is what to do now.

And I don't know the answer.

The great thing about the third week of school is that everyone has pretty much found their groove. The formalities are over, and we're doing the work now, trudging forward.

Except for me. Because I can't stop thinking about the Amersa interview. It's like those first days with the prosthesis. I keep putting one foot in front of the other, but all I feel is that place where my stump hits and the hurt that comes with it.

On Thursday, at lunch, the kids file out, and as soon as the last one has left, Meredith steps in. And waits, staring at me.

She's a puzzle. No—*we're* a puzzle. Both of us are piles of jagged pieces. And the picture of what we form isn't clear.

Or if we even fit together. Just like that Hogwarts Castle, I've tried to turn the pieces over and line them up. I've got the corners and the edges, but I'm missing the middle—the full picture.

Maybe I can't see it because when I look at her, I can't help but remember how she was back then, when we were young and reckless and carefree, before adulthood and loss and responsibilities piled up on our backs.

In my classroom, Meredith saunters in and gently closes the door behind her. This time, she doesn't sit in one of the student desks. Slowly, she walks to my desk and lowers herself until she's perched on the edge, looking down at me.

Still, she says nothing.

She doesn't look angry. Her expression is more expectant, like she knows exactly what I'm about to do and she's here for it.

There's a Zen-like vibe between us. No tension. No elephant in the room.

It's like we're suddenly back to normal. Right back where we were. Or maybe even better.

I thought the time away had killed whatever was developing between us. And maybe it almost did. But here and now, the magnetism between us is stronger than ever.

Maybe time away did us good. Maybe it gave her space to sort out her feelings. And me too.

I lean back in the creaking wooden chair that's probably as old as I am and without even thinking about it, I ask her if she has plans for lunch.

She smiles. "What do you think?"

"You up for a field trip?" I ask her.

"What do you think?"

"You want to know where we're going?"

"Surprise me, Alan. I know you can. It's one of the things I like about you."

In my car, driving the streets of Raleigh, with Meredith in the passenger seat, I mentally examine her last statement before we left.

In particular, two words: *Surprise me.*

She knows I'm in a dark place. And she's sort of okay with it. In fact, she might actually kind of like it. The danger. The uncertainty.

I wonder if it makes her feel alive. Or maybe she just cares that much. Maybe it's sympathy. Or her connection to Riley—maybe it's not even about me.

That scientist at Amersa could probably sort it out in five minutes or less. But I could think about it for years and still not get my head around it.

So I just keep driving.

I've decided to show Meredith an aspect of my life she hasn't seen. Not that dark secret. Not the tinnitus time gaps and the group, but the other thing I do in my free time.

We've got just enough time to get there, grab a quick bite, and get back to school.

Through Bluetooth, Pandora is playing music over the car's speakers. The channel is my Thumbprint Radio—tracks I've said I like and those its AI thinks I might like.

Right now, it's playing a song by Phil Collins: "In the Air Tonight."

One of my most vivid memories as a child is waking up one night and hearing this song playing. I don't recall exactly how old I was, but I must have been around five. That night, I got out of bed and ventured out into the hallway. I looked over at the door to my parents' bedroom. It was closed.

For a second, the house was dark and quiet.

Then it started again.

Lights flashed, and the speakers thumped hard.

The rhythm was hypnotic.

My curiosity drove me down the hallway, the song pulling at me like the gravity of a black hole.

The opening to the living room was sort of like an event horizon. I stopped there, staring at the back of my dad's head. He was sitting on an L-shaped couch that wrapped around a square, glass-topped coffee table. Directly ahead was perhaps his most valuable material possession: a big screen TV. It wasn't like TVs today. This was a massive thing with projection tubes inside and small rollers on the bottom and a plastic screen with tiny ridges (I know because I ran my hand over it one afternoon after school—though I never would have touched it if I thought my dad would have seen).

That TV was my father's place of Zen. It was where he watched the Atlanta Braves in Fulton County Stadium and the Washington Redskins and classic movies and anything with Clint Eastwood or Charles Bronson.

But that night, it wasn't sports or a movie playing on the TV. At first, I thought it was a concert. The music was that vivid and present. No one was talking.

It radiated out from the speaker system connected to the TV, a speaker system my dad also treasured. At a cookout, I once heard someone say that he had spent a big chunk of the money he'd saved up during his time in the Army on those speakers. Unlike me, he was drafted. And after his stint, what he wanted to do was listen to the songs he had heard in Vietnam and play his Stratocaster guitar, which sat in the corner.

That night, I stood there, mesmerized, lingering at the end of the hallway, just inside the living room. With his back was turned to me, he was unaware of my presence.

As a kid, I was never really able to connect with my dad. He was a man of few words. None of those words were about his feelings.

In my memory of that night, I can see him so clearly as he leaned forward and picked up a glass of brown liquid from the coffee table and took a long drag.

His hands—that's one of the things I remember most about my dad. They weren't like my hands. His were massive, hulking hands, like they had been beaten with a hammer and swollen but never returned to normal.

That meaty hand set the glass down as the song kept playing. On the screen, two men were in a car with the top down, wind blowing through their hair.

One held up a gun and put something into it. I know now that it was a sawed-off double-barreled shotgun, and the guy was putting shells into it.

He looked over at his partner, but that guy kept staring ahead and driving as the music kept playing—just like it is in my car now.

At a stoplight, I look over at Meredith. I know she sees me, but she stares straight ahead.

The music is the only sound, a man telling us he can feel it coming in the air.

The light turns green. I see it, but I keep staring at her.

Slowly, she turns to me. In her mirrored glasses, I see my own reflection.

I press the gas.

"In the Air Tonight" plays, and it takes me back to the night I first heard it, to the scene where the driver looked over at his partner, who had just loaded the gun, and asked how much time they had.

I don't remember what the partner said, but it must have been enough, because my next memory is of the driver stopping the black Ferrari in front of a telephone booth.

It was one of those old freestanding, glass booths with a door you push in and just enough room inside for a person to stand.

The man dialed a woman who was sitting at a table with a child about Riley's age, doing homework or maybe having dinner. When he called, she got up from the table and picked up the phone. Her face changed when she realized it was him.

I don't remember the exact words he said to her, but even as a kid, I understood that there was this rift between them, and he was asking if it wasn't too late for them to go back to the way they were, in the good times.

At the next light, I can feel Meredith looking over at me. When I turn to her, she's staring straight ahead again.

The song finds another gear, the volume and cadence climbing, the intensity growing.

The light turns green and the drums keep beating, and I'm thinking about that character—Sonny Crockett—hanging up the phone and getting back in the car and driving on. The man beside him didn't say a word, and neither did my dad; he just watched, like it was an end zone play or the last out in extra innings.

On the screen, the two partners drove, and the wind blew through their hair, and they parked at a wharf, where they boarded a boat. They had committed then, they were loaded and headed to wherever they had to go, where they would either live or die.

The song wound down, and the boat drifted away, and my dad took another sip of the amber liquid, and I don't know if he saw me in the reflection of the glass or if I shifted on my feet and he heard me, but something made him glance back and see me.

He stared for a long second then set down the empty glass, and said, "Get back to bed. It's not a show for kids."

In the here and now, I park outside the army surplus store and listen as Phil Collins tells us he has been waiting for this moment all his life.

But what I'm thinking about is my dad, and what he went through, and the things he never talked about with me and maybe anyone else.

What I know now is that being a parent is like that. Dealing with stuff. Not telling your kids. Shielding them.

Maybe I'm thinking about that because it's exactly what I'm going through. And maybe Meredith is the only one I can really trust. Or maybe the numbers group is.

Me and the numbers group—we're sort of like those two guys in the car. Strangers from different backgrounds but with a shared cause. And I think all of us are wondering what's waiting for us and how much time we have left and if it's too late.

What occurs to me then is how music has an almost magical ability to resurrect memories and to connect moments in time as if the sounds and vibrations can transport you back there like a string across two points.

In the parking lot, I look over at Meredith.

She turns and finally takes her glasses off and stares at me with eyes like two stars exploding into supernovas.

The song has ended, but I'm thinking about that guy in that phone booth. And what he subtly asked the woman he had lost: if they could ever be the way they were again.

27

Inside the store, Warren is behind the counter, staring stone-faced at a guy who is laying down a series of dollar bills on the glass-topped counter.

"Four hundred," the guy announces. "My best and final."

Warren cuts his eyes to Meredith and me, then back to his customer. "Look, kid, your offer is fine. But, for the love of God, just cut the theatrics next time."

Warren sets something on the counter, and the guy pauses, looking from the money to the item, and then picks it up and leaves the cash and exits.

"Turn the sign," Warren calls to me. "And lock the door."

I do both, and Meredith and I approach the counter.

His eyes shift between her and me. "What is this?"

"You said come see you."

"I didn't say I was Chuck Woolery."

Meredith scowls, confused, but I get the reference. "The Love Connection guy."

Warren nods.

"You know that show has been off the air for like—"

"I was making a point."

"This is Meredith."

He eyes her. "I sympathize."

She doesn't smile. Or nod.

"This is Warren. My business partner."

Looking over, meeting her eyes, I add, "He grows on you."

⁎

In the back room, we eat lunch (thanks to sandwiches Warren acquires from a shop next door). And we unpack all the boxes that have arrived—some Warren bought and a few with items I bid on and won.

The minutes tick past, and we tag the items and consume the subs, and no one says anything. This feels like one of those benign interludes before the storm.

When the boxes are empty and the sandwiches are gone, we say goodbye, and the song that plays in the car is from a band called First Aid Kit and the title is "Wolf" and it's about a shape shifter and danger.

I don't say anything. Neither does she.

In the teacher parking lot, when I turn the car off, she looks over at me. There are a thousand words in those burning eyes.

But she doesn't say a single one.

She reaches over and pulls the door handle and gets out.

All afternoon, I'm thinking about Meredith, the Amersa trial, the numbers group, and my daughter.

When my last period dismisses, I pull a desk drawer open and take out the burner phone.

There's nothing from the numbers people.

But there is an email from Amersa.

With my heart beating in my throat, I read the words, sure of what they'll say that I'm not fit for the program at this time.

But I'm surprised.

It's a message inviting me to the trial.

For a long while, I stare at the words. Then I take a picture and send it to the numbers email.

There's no question that the interview was a disaster. It's almost like they were trying to determine whether I just had some run-of-the-mill, surface-level PTSD or deeper issues. It's like Amersa only wants really broken people for the trial, and the whole point was to figure out how broken I was.

*

That night, Riley and I sit on the porch and try to fit the castle pieces together. It's slow going for a while, and then, out of nowhere, pieces start fitting together, happening faster than either of us expects, and in those moments, when we're both trying pieces and putting them aside, time seems to disappear.

When she links up the puzzle pieces to complete the outline, I realize it's way past her bedtime. But that's okay. This was worth it. Sometimes you need that sense of achievement to keep going with something you're struggling with.

And it's good to see the puzzle doing its job: making us both forget about the world for a while.

After putting Riley to bed, I check my email and find a new message from the numbers address.

```
Well done, Alan.

Welcome to the group.
```

II
THE GROUP

28

At this point in my life, there are four looming events. They are all equally daunting, like the four corners of a room closing in on me.

The first, and perhaps most consequential looming event, is my probable arrest for the murder of Nathan Briggs, the Amersa employee I found dead next to me in that building downtown.

By now, the police have no doubt collected any and all surveillance footage from stores and buildings in the surrounding area from that night. I bet one of those videos shows my car arriving at that construction site and leaving. Or at least driving into the general area and leaving.

At some point, they'll come looking for me. I left tracks—*actual tracks*—in that dusty building. The footsteps of a man with a prosthetic leg are a bit like a fingerprint. The thought reminds me of how Ryan eyed my footprints in the mud at his parents' home.

And speaking of fingerprints, mine are on record, at least with the Department of Defense. I bet I left some prints at the scene—and that Raleigh PD could somehow request the records from the DOD. But that would likely take time.

And when the time comes, I need to be ready.

Since my initial internet searches about Briggs, I've learned absolutely nothing about him. I know I need to. I need to figure out what happened. I need to be prepared to give the police another lead to follow, because when they stack up the evidence against me, I'm pretty sure they'll stop looking at alternative suspects.

I feel like my best hope of unraveling the mystery of Briggs's murder—and the time gap surrounding it—is the group. I hope they have some answers.

The second approaching deadline relates to my housing situation. Riley and I can't stay at this train car forever. First off, I can't afford it. The money from my side gig as a buyer for Warren's army surplus store helps, but I need something more affordable, closer to school, and frankly, more normal for Riley. The novelty is wearing thin for both her and me.

As such, I've been scouring apartment rental listings. It feels like the cost of living in Raleigh, North Carolina is going up by the minute. Thus far, I haven't found anything I think is worth the money. I know what's going to happen—pretty soon, I'll adjust my view of what my money is worth and rent a place that I feel is too expensive but suitable. At least we don't have a lot to move.

The third looming event is the intake appointment for the Amersa PTSD trial. That's set for Wednesday, September 24th.

Upon receiving the scheduling email, the first thing I did was send it to the numbers email address with a simple note:

```
I'm not wearing the camera this time.
```

The recipient, whoever they are, replied with a curt message:

```
You shouldn't. You'll be taking your
clothes off.
```

It again confirms that they know a bit about the trial.

Which brings me to the fourth and final upcoming event: my first meeting with the group. Their email laid out one condition for the meeting—it will only happen if I go to the initial Amersa appointment.

Obviously, their sole interest in me is getting information about the trial. That's great. It's great to be valued and wanted as a person—not just for what I can do for them.

But I don't have any other choice, so I agree to their terms and spend my time looking for a place to live, trying to earn some money on the side, having lunch with Meredith, and doing my best to help Riley keep up with school and have a childhood as normal as I can make it right now.

29

At the Amersa intake appointment, the medical staff draws my blood and runs me through a series of machines.

I don't know what they're testing for. Before each event, I read the forms and disclaimers on the tablet and sign to consent. When all the scans are done, the handlers deposit me in a room with a couch and TV. Soon, a video begins to play.

It's like one of those TED talks. There's a middle-aged guy on stage, holding a small device in his hand. It looks like a phaser from the original *Star Trek*, but I know it's a remote control for his slides.

White letters at the bottom of the screen identify him as Anders Larsson, Founder of Amersa Inc.

His voice has a strange intonation, like a mix of a robot and a human. But the words he says are captivating.

"We are in the midst of the greatest pandemic in human history. It's an outbreak that no news outlet has reported. It has no name. And yet, it takes lives every day. And many of those it doesn't kill, it disables."

On the stage, he comes to a stop and clicks the remote. I can't see the slide, but he says, "We all know someone affected by the blight of our time."

He extends his hands, palms up. "Maybe some of you are. I certainly am."

He turns and paces back to the middle of the stage. "The epidemic that threatens to collapse our civilization is indeed an infectious disease. One communicated more quickly than any biological pathogen we've ever seen."

He slips the remote into his pocket.

"This isn't a new strain of the flu. It's not the common cold. What's consuming the human race is a different kind of virus. It's one we see every time we open our phone. One born of the modern age. A product of social media. Of AI and unintended consequences. It is the tip of the iceberg of what's coming. What we're confronting is a mental health crisis on a scale we're only beginning to realize."

He looks out at the crowd, letting the words hang in the air. "This wave of mental health deterioration is sinking humanity. And it has only just begun."

He looks down at the stage and shrugs. "But I'm not here today to talk about the problem. I'm here to tell you about the solution. That solution is what Amersa is developing. Our mission is to lift humanity out of the abyss. And the best part is that we're going to do that using some of the same technologies that have so harmed humanity."

He takes the remote out again.

"But first, I want to speak to those of you in the audience who are skeptics." He smiles warmly. "And I do see some skeptical expressions—no offense. I get it. I was always more a fan of Dana Scully than Fox Mulder. Not that I didn't want to believe. But I wanted proof too. And so, here is the proof that the world we live in is in the midst of a slow-moving mental health epidemic."

The view on the TV moves from the speaker to the large screen, where a series of charts and graphs appear, narrated by Amersa's founder. At a glance, one might not think this data dump would be engaging, but sitting on the couch, I'm enraptured by the facts he presents. The ones that hit me the hardest are:

Fifty percent of the entire global population will develop a mental health disorder in their lifetime. This was the result of a large-scale study that involved over 150,000 participants in 29 countries. It was conducted by researchers at Harvard Medical School and the University of Queensland and involved adults across a broad cross-section of demographic and socio-economic backgrounds.

The study found that the three most common conditions for

women are: depression, a specific phobia that causes a disabling anxiety that interferes with daily life, and PTSD.

For men, the three most common mental health challenges are: alcohol abuse, depression, and a specific phobia.

Depression and anxiety disorders cost the global economy $1 trillion in lost productivity each year. In the United States alone, it causes $193.2 billion in lost earnings each year.

The crisis is particularly acute for today's youth. Fifty percent of all lifetime mental illness begins by age 14, and 75% by age 24.

In 2011, 36% of US teen girls reported persistent feelings of sadness or hopelessness. Ten years later, the number had risen to 57%.

Larsson's slides take particular aim at social media. Twenty-five percent of girls say social media has hurt their mental health. Children and adolescents who spend more than three hours a day on social media face double the risk of mental health problems.

Among all ages, 64% of people say social media increases their feelings of loneliness.

In the United States, the Surgeon General issued an advisory in 2023 declaring loneliness a public health crisis. Surveys show that roughly half of American adults experience loneliness at least intermittently, and about one in five people report feeling lonely "on any given day" as of 2024.

And while over one billion people struggle daily with a mental health condition, less than 3% of the global healthcare budget goes to mental health needs.

Larsson delivers the information with clinical efficiency. Gone is the passion of his speech. He's matter-of-fact, and the facts speak volumes.

"The mental health crisis gripping the planet," Larsson says, "isn't just a looming threat. It's happening right now, and it's taking lives and shortening lives. People with severe mental health conditions die ten to twenty years earlier than the general population.

"Historically, we have measured pandemics in body counts. Today, we must take a new measure. We must see this as a pandemic of broken spirits: rising anxiety, crippling depression, and lost human potential. In fact, the World Health Organization predicts that by 2030, depression will be the leading cause of disease burden globally, outranking cancer and heart disease.

After the charts and statistics, I expect Larsson to talk more about Amersa's actual solution. Instead, he cuts it short with a cryptic ending.

"That, ladies and gentlemen, is what we're up against. But this battle has just begun. At Amersa, it's one we will see to the end. Because the stakes are no less than humanity's future."

The video ends there.

On the screen, a new video begins. It's the same guy. The camera is zoomed in, and the stage is gone (he's sitting on a couch in an office, much like the couch I'm sitting on right now).

"Hello." His smile is tight, but his eyes burn with that same passion he brought to the public event.

"First, thank you for coming this far. If you're seeing this video, you are a participant in one of Amersa's trials. You are a person who has experienced pain. Likely great pain. And you are searching for a treatment to address these past injuries—because they're limiting your life. And impacting those around you."

He clasps his hands and leans forward. "For that, I applaud you. You've taken the first step. You've come to us. You want to solve your problems. You're willing to fight for a better life for yourself and those you care about. At Amersa, we're going to do our best to help you. To meet you halfway."

He leans back, crossing his legs and placing his hands in his lap. "I won't lie to you. I don't know where this road leads. Or what we'll find. I do know this: Amersa will support you however we can. Because you are the future. You are the intrepid explorer crossing the Bering Strait or the Atlantic for the first time. You are about to plant your foot on a new land. We don't know what lies ahead. Like the King and Queen of Spain were to Christopher Columbus, Amersa is your benefactor—the sponsor of your journey into the Labyrinth."

My mouth runs dry when he says the word Labyrinth. Maybe

it's a coincidence. But I doubt it. Hearing this man say it aloud is as jarring as seeing the numbers for the first time.

Larsson cocks his head and his tone turns reflective. "Back then, in the 1490s, those explorers sought riches. And truthfully, that's half of our motivation."

The Amersa CEO shrugs. "We're a business with investors. They've risked their capital on us. And they want riches—like the King and Queen of Spain did. And like those who sailed upon wooden ships across the Atlantic, we are trying to find a new world. But the world we seek lies in the final frontier of existence: the human mind. Our focus is on addressing the current mental health crisis. But I believe we will find far more—just as Columbus did. After all, he was simply a man setting out to find a sea passage to the East Indies, hoping to speed up trade. Instead, he discovered an entire continent that was previously unknown to the Europeans."

Larsson nods. "So what might we find? My opinion is that the Labyrinth may hold foundational truths of our existence. I believe that answer is the true key to ending the underlying mental health pandemic of our time."

Anders spreads his hands and smiles. "At the risk of sounding grandiose, which I've been accused of on several occasions, I will tell you that what you're doing is far, far more important than Columbus's voyage on the *Nina*, *Pinta*, and *Santa Maria*—"

He glances off-screen, as if distracted. The video shifts and suddenly, he's sitting in a slightly different position on the couch, as if there's been a cut and filming has resumed. The enthusiasm is gone from his face, and his tone is flat.

"I do want to make clear, however, that neither Amersa nor any of its staff—including me—are voicing support for Columbus's actions before, during, or after he arrived in what is now known as the United States of America. Amersa sees and respects indigenous people in all parts of the world."

He glances off-screen again, and I sense this is the start of another argument, but like the last one, it isn't shown.

The video ends there.

A new one begins. On the TV, a man sits on a couch similar to the one Larsson sat on. He looks to be in his late thirties or early forties, with short hair and a clean shave. His face is lean, but not overly muscular.

But there's something off about him. I can't put my finger on it. Maybe it's his eyes. Or his stillness. In the second that passes before he speaks, I feel a vague uneasiness.

His voice, however, is clear with just a hint of warmth and optimism. "Hello, Alan, my name is Linus. First, I want you to know that I am what Amersa calls an NHI."

I'm opening my mouth to ask what an NHI is when Linus explains. "In this case, NHI stands for non-human intelligence."

It takes me a second to process what he's saying.

An awkward pause stretches out until he says, "What you might call an artificial intelligence, though that term is not fully representative of my capabilities or existence."

"I see," I mumble, though I actually don't see. It's jarring—talking to an avatar so human I didn't even realize it at first. I mean, I've used the AI chatbots, and I guess this is sort of the same thing, but seeing a human representation is unsettling. I don't really have anything to compare it to. I imagine this is what meeting an actual alien might feel like—an alien who looks entirely human.

"Alan," my non-human counterpart says, slowly, "I wanted to tell you about my status before we go any further because at Amersa, we believe you have the right to know if you're working with a non-human staff member and because if you're uncomfortable with working with me—or any other NHI—we can arrange for a human coordinator to work with you. However, please be aware that resources are limited, so your appointment today would end now and continue when a human staff member is available. I estimate that would take place in approximately two weeks. Additionally, please be aware that I am capable of conducting these Labyrinth coordination sessions far more efficiently than the human members working on the trial, as my real-time analysis of your answers informs better follow-up prompting.

"Separately, I am able to compile your answers directly into Labyrinth modifications prompts, which are sent instantly to the Labyrinth engine. That vastly improves the efficiency of the trial process because you may enter the Labyrinth portion of the visit immediately after our interviews. With human staffers, Labyrinth sessions are conducted only after coordinating interviews are analyzed and compiled. This often takes up to a week after each coordinating interview."

On the screen, Linus stops and stares at me, blinking in a seemingly random interval, though his head doesn't move.

I'm not entirely sure what to say. So I lie. "I see."

"Do be aware that the human coordinators review biometric data from your Labyrinth sessions and my summary observations. This provides a safety check and secondary feedback loop for the Labyrinth engine."

When I nod, Linus continues. "Lastly, I would like to add one other experiential observation for your consideration. Please be aware that some participants in this study have found it more comfortable to speak with an NHI coordinator."

That hasn't been my experience, at least so far. I'm pretty uncomfortable right now. But I don't say that.

"You see, Alan, during these sessions, I'll be asking you a series of questions about your background and experiences, some of which may be connected to traumatic events in your life."

I see where he's going but say nothing.

"Many trial participants feel more comfortable talking with an NHI staffer about those things. After all, there are confines on my programming. Guard rails, if you will. I cannot, nor will I ever, tell anyone what you tell me. Only summary information—details that provide relevant feedback to the Labyrinth engine. This is a safe place, Alan, one where you can say anything."

Linus falls silent then, waiting for me. But I'm thinking that the only thing stranger than talking to someone who looks human and acts human but is not actually human is having that non-human sell you on working with them.

I'm also thinking that I don't have time to work with a human coordinator. I need answers as quickly as I can get them.

And it seems that my new non-human friend is the fastest way to get there.

So when he asks if I consent to working with an NHI coordinator, I merely nod and say that I am.

He brightens at that, and there's a slight lift in his tone.

"Well, let's get started then. Your application interview covered some seminal events in your life. In these sessions, we'll delve deeper into those but also talk about your entire life history as well as your experience in the Labyrinth. This serves as a critical feedback loop that increases the probability of an efficacious outcome for you, Alan."

"Great."

Linus cocks his head and smiles, ignoring my lack of enthusiasm. "Great indeed. So let's begin. Alan, I'd like to ask you about your childhood. And please answer these questions as quickly as you can. Are you ready?"

"Uh, sure."

"Think about your childhood, Alan. And I want you to say the first thing that comes to mind, okay?"

"Okay."

"Great. Now tell me about a time when you were on an adventure, when you felt completely safe and happy."

After the strange session with Linus, the door to the room opens, and a woman enters. She's wearing black scrubs, like you might see in a hospital, with a name tag that says Sandra.

"Mr. Norris, if you're ready, I'll take you to the Labyrinth."

30

On the way home from my first session in Amersa's Labyrinth, I turn the experience over in my head, barely able to process it. What I feel most of all is a state of awe and confusion. As Amersa's CEO predicted, I do feel like I've set foot on a new land. A very, very strange one.

A land that has left me completely spent—mentally, emotionally, and physically.

By the time I turn onto the gravel road that leads to the red caboose Airbnb I call home, night has fallen, and the beams of my headlights carve into the darkness, raking across the walls of pine trees on each side of the driveway.

Up ahead, Meredith's car is parked next to the train car. She's sitting at the table on the front porch, working on the puzzle with Riley.

After parking, I step out and close my eyes, waiting as the dust cloud flows by. Beyond the brown mist, I hear the bug zapper crackling every few seconds.

When it clears, I see a scene that is a vague reflection of my life. Riley and Meredith are both squinting at the dust I've kicked up, trying to see through it.

On the table, they've managed to put together more of the castle. The grounds are done, and the walls are starting to go up.

Meredith has connected her phone to the Bluetooth speaker, and it's bellowing into the night. Not Disney tunes, but rather a song from 1980, by Bob Seger & The Silver Bullet Band entitled "Fire Lake."

It's a fitting tune for this particular season of my life. And for me and her.

It's past Riley's bedtime, but I know Meredith let her stay up so that I could read to her. That kind of consistency and normal routine is important for a child, and especially for Riley right now.

Meredith's stare lingers a fraction of a second too long on my face, and I think she sees it all then: how tired I am, how freaked out and confused I am.

Leaning down, I give Riley a tight hug. "All right, kiddo, time for bed. Pajamas. And teeth brushing."

She picks up another piece of the puzzle, examining it as if silently saying, *I can't quit now, Dad.*

I gently place my hand on her shoulder. "Come on, come on, the puzzle will be here tomorrow."

When she trudges across the porch and through the door, I thank Meredith for watching her and add, "You don't need to stay."

"I know."

But she doesn't leave. She leans back in the chair and stares out at the wall of tall trees and the moon above.

Over the speaker, Bob Seger is asking who wants to take a long shot gamble and head down to Fire Lake.

Inside, I read to Riley, and she's out quickly.

Back on the porch, Meredith stands as I emerge.

"What happened?"

"Weird day."

"Something happen with Warren?"

"Uh, no."

"Is that where you were—helping him?"

I break eye contact with her. "This was something else."

For the first time in my life, I'm thankful for a legal contract that prevents me from saying anything.

"What else?"

"I can't say."

"Why not?"

"They made me sign an NDA."

"An NDA."

"A non-disclosure agreement—"

"I know what an NDA is, Alan."

She picks up her phone and taps on it, and the speaker falls silent, indicating that she's severed the connection.

She steps off the porch and looks back at me. "If you want me to watch Riley, I will. If you don't want to tell me what you're doing, just say you don't want to tell me."

Then she leaves.

After Meredith's dust cloud dissipates, I consider texting or calling her. But I think she needs some time.

Instead, I sit at the small dining table inside the train car, bidding on secondhand military gear.

I'm watching the auction clock, debating upping my offer on a Phosphorescent Lensatic Compass when the ringing starts. It's low at first, a *clang-clang-clang* like an innocent kitchen timer going off. I freeze, waiting, hoping it will recede.

It just gets louder.

I close the laptop, hoping it might be the eye strain or simple fatigue. Maybe it's stress, the last month finally catching up to me—or the spat with Meredith—triggering the episode.

But at the back of my mind is the fact that this session of ringing is the unseen hand and the rocks in the can—not the tea kettle. It means something.

At the kitchen sink, I fill a cup with water and wash down two ibuprofens, then immediately shuffle into the bedroom and lie down and open an app on my phone that plays noise specifically created for tinnitus episodes. I put my earbuds in and the sound therapy plays and I focus on my breathing.

If the ringing gets worse, I'm going to take a sleeping pill. That would incapacitate me, preventing me from doing anything dangerous.

But as soon as the idea forms, I know it won't work. People on sleeping pills get up and do things all the time. Eat. Walk around the house. Even drive.

The ringing ratchets up, as if subtly replying to me: *don't you dare*. It keeps growing louder until it reaches its crescendo and there's a pop, the hand slamming the can down.

The next thing I'm aware of is sitting in my SUV outside the red train car. The vehicle is turned off and the headlamps are dark, as if I've been here for a while. There's no dust cloud around, only the dim light of the moon and soft yellow glow of the train car's windows.

The red caboose sits there like a lantern in the middle of a forest, calling to me.

I've been in some terrifying situations in my life, but this is up there. My greatest fear is that I've done something terrible, and that it has affected Riley.

Turning quickly, I glance back. The backseat is empty, including Riley's booster seat. Checking my pockets, I don't feel my phone or wallet, only two metal keys. In my left pocket is the key to the Ford Explorer. In my right pocket is a metal key I've never seen before. At first glance, it looks like a house key, but it's slightly larger and heavier. It feels like it would fit the door of an industrial building or a piece of equipment. There are no markings on it.

At the moment, the key isn't my biggest concern. Riley is.

I run to the train car, bound up the stairs onto the porch, and turn the door handle but it's locked.

Through the window, I see my key ring and wallet sitting on the banquette table. Squinting, I can tell that the key to the train car has been removed from the ring. Stepping back, I toss the ratty doormat aside. The door key waits there and I snatch it up and turn the lock. Inside, I shuffle past the kitchenette, my heart beating in my throat as I reach the bunk beds. For a long moment, I stand there, looking down at my daughter, sleeping peacefully.

31

I barely sleep a wink that night.

After making sure Riley was okay, I searched my car for clues about what happened in the time gap. I didn't find a thing. I should have marked the mileage when I got home. At least then I would know how far I traveled.

The train car also holds no clues.

It's like I went somewhere, got the key, and came home.

Next, I check both of my phones—my main one and the burner—for any clues. There are no messages, no emails. Nothing.

It is an utterly unnerving feeling—having done something you can't remember.

The other thing bothering me is the recent argument with Meredith. It's like another lump in the mattress that won't let me sleep.

The third issue on my mind is that going forward, I'm going to be missing a lot of class because of the Amersa trial. Based on what Linus told me, I'll be out for at least three hours every other week (accounting for travel and clinic time and the Labyrinth session).

And then there's the meetings with the group. I don't know when they'll take place, but I figure they might also disrupt my teaching schedule.

I could probably wing it for a few weeks, asking colleagues to cover or getting a substitute in a pinch. But assuming I keep going with the trial and the numbers group, I know it's going to be a problem.

And one thing life has taught me is that when you have a problem, it's best to handle it instead of ignoring it or avoiding it.

As such, I've scheduled a meeting with the school's principal. Her name is Sheila and she's about twenty years older than me. Since I started here, she's been nothing but supportive of me and the other teachers. She's jovial and a jokester at times and has this almost unique ability to take everything in stride. Which I think is an asset for any principal (it's not an easy job these days).

But underneath the charm and effortless demeanor, she's pretty tough. On the whole, we're very lucky to have her at our school—both the teachers and students.

In her office, I sit across from the solid wood desk that's built like a battleship. Leaning forward in the squeaking chair, Sheila puts her elbows on the wide paper calendar before her.

"What can I do for you, Alan?"

"I'm going to be missing some school this semester."

"How much?"

I tell her what I know—and what I don't.

When I finish, she studies my face and simply asks me what's going on.

I answer as honestly as I can: "I've enrolled in a clinical trial. For PTSD. And I've joined a... support group."

"I'm very glad to hear that, Alan."

"Thanks. Look, I know this is not ideal, and I don't want to leave you in a bind so I just wanted to lay all my cards on the table. I really don't want to lose this job, but I also understand that my situation may cause some issues on your end."

She clenches her jaw and rolls her head, looking out at the morning sun and the students driving into the parking lot.

"I saw that bruise on your face, Alan. And the bags under your eyes now."

"I'm dealing with it."

"You're a good teacher, Alan."

Sheila pauses, looking down at me like my mother used to when there was something important she wanted to say. "That's getting harder to find. But I'm not worried about this school right now. I'm worried about you."

"I'll be all right."

"You know, my husband is a Marine. I know the type. And it's why I'm glad you're taking action on your mental health. What I want you to know is that this job will be here for you, Alan. If you need time—real time off—you can use your standard sick leave and then extended sick leave after that."

"Yeah, but the extended only goes out to twenty days."

She nods. "It does."

"And my understanding is that I get my salary but there's a deduction for the sub."

"That's right."

"And I have to prove I have an illness."

"You can do that, Alan. Mental health conditions are real illnesses."

"Even so, I can't afford it. Jenn's medical bills... added up. I need to be working as much as I can. But I want to be upfront with you. I don't want to feel guilty for constantly calling out or making folks cover for me. I mean, I get it if you need to replace me."

"Well, let's put that to bed right now. You're not getting replaced, Alan. We're going to figure this out."

"I appreciate that, but I just don't see a solution that's fair to everyone and that's affordable to me."

Sheila's mood changes then. She smiles and leans back and seems more at ease. Maybe it's from knowing the problem and knowing she can handle it or maybe she knows something I don't.

"You know what this place is like, Alan?"

"Umm, a—"

She holds a finger up. "That was rhetorical."

I open my mouth, but opt instead to simply nod, assuming we're still in rhetorical mode.

"It's like *The Lion King*." She plants a finger on her chest. "This regal animal right here? She's a lion." The finger points up at her permed hair. "With a graceful mane. I believe you know the lion I'm talking about."

She squints at me, but I sense we're still in the rhetorical section of the pride lands.

"Mufasa," she finally says, voice solemn. "And do you know what my job is?"

I stare blankly, unsure where this is going.

"To protect the circle of life, Alan. The kids come in. They learn—the subjects we teach them and a lot more about life—and then they leave."

She motions toward the window. "They go out into the great unknown beyond the pride lands. It's dangerous out there, Alan, and it's our job to prepare them. But they're just one group in the great circle of life on these hallowed school grounds. You've got the teachers too. They have their own problems, just like the students, but they're even more complex."

She points at me. "Alan, right now, you're sort of like a big mama bear with a cuddly little cub that you're trying to protect. But you've got a pack of hyenas after you. And that's where Mufasa comes in."

There are some logical errors here—like the fact that bears wouldn't inhabit an African savanna ecosystem, and that a lion probably wouldn't act to protect a bear under attack (even guarding a bear cub), but I think I know where she's going. As such, I'm going to keep my editorial suggestions to myself.

Sheila claps her hands and sets them on her desk. "So, Alan, what I'm trying to say is that Mufasa is going to handle this."

She squints at me, and I can tell she knows the analogy is a little silly, but I think maybe that's half of the point—to lighten the mood. Because she knows I'm feeling guilty about putting her in this position, and she knows I'm feeling pretty awkward because it's not easy for me to ask for help.

I realize then that there's another layer of this slightly silly—but very apt—analogy about a circle of life at a school. It's about teachers like me, who were once students and return as teachers themselves. And even teachers—if they're paying attention—can continue learning here. Right now, I'm learning something about managing people.

In my classroom, one of my most important tasks is to get a read on the students and figure out what they need to thrive. And that's part of Sheila's job, for teachers.

My gaze fixed on the calendar, I utter a single word: "Thanks."

Sheila doesn't break character. "Mufasa. Thanks, Mufasa." She holds her hand up to her hair. "Care to comment on the mane?"

"Not a hair out of place, your highness."

"You're a fast learner, Alan."

"Speaking of learning, what exactly are you thinking here? Lion King analogies aside."

Her tone is still playful. "The analogies are over when I say they are, Alan."

She shrugs, and her smile widens. "There's one thing you're overlooking here."

I raise my eyebrows, and Sheila—make that Mufasa—continues. "Before I was the king around here, I was also down in the pride lands, Alan. And do you know what I did back then?"

I cock my head, unsure what sort of answer she's looking for.

Apparently, no answer at all, because she continues. "Back then, your current king was a history teacher—just like you."

"You're going to cover for me."

"That's right. I'll chalk it up to auditing your lesson plans. Just part of my job."

"I've got the psychology classes too."

She smiles even wider at that. "Psychology? That's just one more part of my job. In fact, I'm doing it right now. We'll be fine. Just don't let the hyenas get you, Alan."

32

I spend the first half of my lunch period sitting at my desk. I'm hunched over my laptop, surfing a website that provides a matching service for babysitters. At this point in human civilization, there must be a website or app for selling and matching everything.

One thing about the Triangle Area (which includes Raleigh, Durham, and Chapel Hill) is that there are a lot—and I mean a whole lot—of college students. In addition to the students, there are tons of recent college graduates looking for work. And some graduates working full-time and looking for more work.

It makes for a large pool of babysitters.

I'm scanning caregiver profiles (which are starting to look the same), when Meredith wanders in.

I was wondering how long this second cold war between us would last.

Back in high school, about three days is as far as we ever got. Back then, tiffs usually culminated in a make-out session at one of our lockers, the rickety metal door providing limited cover. If not there, then it was in one of our cars in the parking lot or in her parents' basement.

But we're not quite there yet. And I'm not sure we ever will be again.

I'm not ready.

She may not be either.

Yet we keep drifting toward each other, like worn-out magnets that haven't shifted far enough away from their natural poles—and are still attracting each other.

This is sort of uncharted territory in my return to the pride lands.

For that reason, I eye her like a cornered animal, waiting as she walks closer, carrying the thermos full of smoothie.

She hovers over me and looks down at the laptop screen. "Babysitter?"

"Gonna need one. Maybe a few."

"What if they're serial killers?"

"Well, I figure at least one of them won't be."

She deadpans. "I was serious."

"They do background checks."

"Serial killers pass background checks."

I lean back in the creaking chair. "I don't have a choice. I'm going to be gone at least part of the evening once every other week. And very likely more. How much, I don't know."

"You *do* have a choice."

"I can't ask you for that, Meredith."

She takes a sip of smoothie. "You don't have to. I told you I'd watch her."

I want Meredith's help. I want her in my life. But it's not that simple. Her keeping Riley—that means something more than a babysitter I found online.

I know what it means. She knows what it means. And where it will lead, which is her wading deeper into the dark, mysterious cave that is my life.

So I start verbally stacking rocks at the entrance, for her sake. I can't violate the NDA I signed with Amersa, but I can tell her the shape of what I'm dealing with. When she hears that, she'll probably bail.

"Last night, like I said, I wasn't helping Warren. I was participating in a clinical trial."

Her eyebrows knit together. "What kind of trial? Something for your leg?"

"No. It's technically for PTSD."

"Technically? Or actually."

Leaning forward in the wooden chair, I put weight on my stump and start toward the door. She reads the movement—my effort to give us privacy—and turns and beats me to it, closing the heavy wooden slab.

Resting back in the chair, I exhale and make a decision that may go really bad.

"It's *actually* for PTSD. But why I'm enrolled is a little more complicated."

"What does that mean?"

"I told you I had tinnitus."

She sips the smoothie.

"The thing is, when I hear the ringing... sometimes I see numbers."

She squints at me, genuinely confused. "As in—what... sort of numbers?"

"A sequence."

"A hallucination?"

"I thought it was at first. But now I know it's not."

"How do you know?"

"It's always the same numbers."

"How do you know you're not having the same hallucination? Like the same dream repeating?"

"I know... because I'm not the only one seeing these numbers."

Meredith cocks her head. "Huh. Okay. So who else is seeing them?"

"I can't tell you."

"But it's connected to the trial?"

"Yes. The numbers are connected to the trial."

"How?"

I shake my head slowly. "I can't tell you that either."

"But you're doing the trial to figure out what the numbers mean?"

"I sort of know what they mean—but not where they lead or... the whole picture."

"You're not making sense, Alan."

"I know. I know. None of it makes sense, but I'm telling you what I can. I'm not making this up."

She pushes off from the desk and paces toward the door, back turned to me, and I think maybe she's going to leave, but she turns back. "Oh, that, I believe."

"That I'm not making it up?"

"Yes."

"Why?"

"Frankly, I don't think you could. It's too... out of nowhere. It's too creative for you."

I nod slowly. "Thanks. I think."

"So, what's your plan? Do the trial and see what the numbers lead to and then... what?"

"The trial is about more than that. Doing the trial will put me in touch with the group that might know more about the numbers and what they are."

"I see."

"You think I'm crazy."

"I don't think you're crazy. But I do wonder if you should talk to someone at the VA."

"No. No way."

"What if they know about others who are seeing the numbers?"

"Too risky."

"Why, Alan?"

I can't tell her about the dead man in downtown. So I go with the truth, speaking slowly. "What is happening to me *is real*. And I think it's *big*."

"Big how?"

"I don't know. But this is new, like discovering a new land."

She grimaces. "A new land? Wait, what?"

"Never mind, it's... Look, I genuinely believe that whatever is happening to me is going to have some far-reaching implications. But I don't know what they are yet."

For a while, Meredith just stands there staring at the rows of desks in my classroom.

Finally, I look up at her. "Well, say something."

"I have no clue what to say, Alan. I really don't."

Right now, my only thought is that I shouldn't have told her. She probably thinks I've lost my mind, even if she isn't saying it.

Meredith inhales, seeming to decide something. "I have one question for you."

I hold out a hand. "Fire away."

"What days do you need me to watch Riley?"

"I told you—"

"Let's be practical, Alan."

"Okay."

"Practically speaking, it would seem that you're either involuntarily involved in a somewhat nebulous conspiracy with far-reaching implications—or, you're having a serious mental health crisis." She tilts her head toward me. "Would you agree that those seem like the two major possibilities here?"

Slowly, I hold up my hands, palms up, and spread them out. "This is me, *not disagreeing* with you."

"Given that those are the two probable scenarios, it seems likely that either possibility could significantly impact your daughter. Including putting her in serious danger."

I break eye contact with her then. "Still no disagreement."

"Still being practical," she says, walking closer, "do you really think a babysitter you find online is going to be able to deal with the fallout of whatever is happening to you?"

I shake my head. "Probably not."

"What days do you need me to watch Riley?"

"I can't ask you to get involved."

"You don't have to, Alan. I'm volunteering. I'm worried about you. And Riley. And frankly, at this point, I'm just genuinely curious to find out what is happening here."

33

In the afternoon, when I can, I check my phone for a message from the numbers group with details of our first meeting.

But by the time I'm inching through the car rider line to pick Riley up, I still haven't received anything.

I have, however, received a message from Warren asking me to swing by at my earliest convenience.

On the way to the army surplus store, I ask Riley if she's up for making a stop on the way home. She seems excited about the prospect and even more intrigued when she sees the store, which is an old brick building painted in a camo pattern of green and brown with big block letters above: ARMY NAVY STORE.

I know this isn't a place a seven-year-old first-grader should venture into. But I also know my daughter. She isn't going to wait in the car. She loves an adventure. And shopping.

Inside, Warren is once again sitting in the corner, in that plush recliner, staring at an e-reader.

I expect him to say something harsh like "This ain't no day care" or "Does this look like the Mickey Mouse Clubhouse to you?"

Instead, he rocks forward, scanning the two entrants to his own pride lands, a smile slowly forming on his lips.

"Riley," I say to my daughter. "This is Mr. Warren. He's my business partner."

He steps around the glass display case and studies her for a split second, and in that fraction of a moment, I see that hardened veteran transform into a grandfather, which I think is exactly what he wants to be at this point in his life.

He stoops and extends a hand. "A pleasure, my lady."

She smiles and shakes his hand, and he eyes me and jerks his head toward the back room.

Together, we move past the displays and through the secure door into his sanctum of high-value gear.

At the far wall, he presses a panel, which swings open, revealing a safe. He rolls the dial and opens it and withdraws an envelope, which he tosses to me.

He seems to read my surprise at the fact that this envelope is fatter than the last one.

"You made some good bids," he says, slamming the safe shut.

"I was conservative."

"Keep it up."

I'm opening my mouth to discuss those bids when he moves past me, out into the store where my daughter is waiting, already looking bored. I can hear them talking as I tuck the envelope away.

At some point, I need to bring up the question of tax reporting on these cash payments, but I sense that this isn't the right time. And, truthfully, taxes aren't high on my list of problems at the moment. The cash will, however, help with my housing search.

Back in the showroom (such as it is), Warren is telling Riley that he and I are old friends and that he wants to give her some stuff.

She looks at me, and I shrug.

"You like camping?" he asks her.

"I guess. We live in the woods."

Warren cuts his eyes to me, and I add for the record: "We do, but we have a house. Well, not a house, but we have a… place."

He squints.

"We live in a train car," Riley adds innocently.

Warren's eyes shift back to me.

"It's an Airbnb."

"How can air function as a bed and breakfast?"

His face doesn't change much, but I see those microexpressions—a slight curl of his lips, the crow's feet digging in at the edges of his eyes.

He doesn't wait for me to respond. He wraps an arm around

Riley, like a grandfather might, telling her, "Anyway, if you're camping, you've got to be ready for anything, young lady. Half the battle is in your mind. The other half is having the right kit."

"Kit?"

"You know, gear."

With that, he starts gathering items from the shelves of the store and the back room. He moves quickly, faster than I would have expected. It seems to give him energy—finding items she might like.

Soon, there's a pile of gear on the counter.

Riley eyes them like presents under the Christmas tree.

When she reaches for them, I extend a hand and restrain her.

"Why don't you bring them to the house?"

Warren cocks his head, still looking at the pile of items on the glass-top counter, things he doesn't give away easily or at all.

"Let me guess," I say, drawing his gaze. "You're not UPS."

"I'm not. But I was gonna ask your address."

On the way home, I stop at a Harris Teeter grocery store and buy some hamburger meat and a few sides—mac and cheese and mashed potatoes. The first four patties are simmering on the grill outside the caboose when a pair of headlights peek around the columns of pine trees. I flip the burgers and watch as Warren exits an SUV about like mine. Around fifteen years old. Domestic. Not recently washed. He sees me, but he doesn't break my way. He turns and goes to the back of the vehicle and starts unloading the things for Riley.

"Hey!" I call to him, and when he turns, I motion him over. "Forget that stuff."

At the grill, he eyes the burgers sizzling.

"I've got water, juice boxes, and tea. No beer—sorry—"

"Gave that up a long time ago," he says, still eying the burgers. "It was her or the bottle. I chose her. And life."

He reaches out for the spatula.

"Let me see that. I'm scared you're gonna burn them."

*

Warren is offloading the cooked burgers to a silver tray when another set of lights snakes down the long gravel driveway.

I'm laying pieces of cheese on the simmering patties as Meredith emerges from her Honda Accord, and this time, when she sees Warren, she gives him a nod and a tight smile.

The four of us eat by the fire pit—with logs burning and music playing.

When the plates are empty, I start collecting them, trying to get the crumbs away from the insects and critters. As I stalk away to the trash can in the caboose, Warren rises, on his way to his car and what he's brought for Riley.

He drops that loot by the fire and starts handing it to her, one item at a time.

The first is a British Army Land Rover folding camping chair, which I find fitting. Riley spreads it out and plops down on the green fabric, smiling, no doubt feeling important because she has a different chair from the rest of us. Every child should feel special. And I don't think my child has felt very special lately.

The next item looks like a green and brown blanket. But I recognize it. "It's camo netting," I tell Riley.

She holds it up in the light of the camp fire. "What's it used for?"

"To disguise yourself. To make you blend into the background so enemies can't find you."

She eyes it. "I'm gonna put it over my bunk."

That night, as I lie awake in bed, I keep turning her statement over in my mind. It was the first thing that came to her when Warren said the netting was used to hide.

Next, I think about my most recent episode of lost time and the strange key. I've hidden it in the locked gun box. And I still don't have a clue what it fits or where I got it.

34

The next morning, I expect to wake to a message from the numbers group, giving me details of the first meeting. After all, their condition was that I go to the first Amersa trial session, which I did.

But there's still nothing from them.

Maybe something has happened.

Or maybe they've had second thoughts.

Frustrated, I send them another email.

```
I'll have another Amersa session a week
from Tuesday, and frankly, I want some
answers about what's happening before I
go in there.
```

In my classroom, when second period is winding down, I pull the desk drawer open and get out the burner phone.

This time, there's a new message from the numbers group.

It's the missing part of their original invitation: a time and place.

The time is in thirty minutes and the place is nearby.

Of course. *Of course* they would do this. I hate this group. But I need them.

Standing, wincing as my weight hits the stump too hard, I issue some standard busywork to the kids and end with, "See you on Monday."

I don't go directly to my car. I have two periods left to teach. And I don't know if I'll be out of the numbers group meeting in time to pick up Riley.

At the gym, I ask Meredith if she's willing to do that, and she agrees instantly. She doesn't ask where I'm going. She probably thinks it's another appointment for the trial.

Next, I march through the school office to Sheila's door, which is almost closed. Through the narrow opening, I can hear her talking—angrily—and I can see the back of one of the vice principals who is seated across from her. He's in charge of discipline for a few grades, driver's ed, and fire drills, but he spends most of his time on buses.

He's the one getting the discipline today. Not exactly a great time to interrupt, but I've got a hyena problem.

"I don't care," Sheila says, "if we have to get Uber drivers with CDLs or off-duty truckers."

"We could," the vice principal replies, sounding exhausted, "but even with a CDL they have to do a three-day bus course. Among other things."

"Darryl, if our bus driver bench was as deep as the basketball team's, we wouldn't be having this conversation—"

This is an important conversation, but I need someone to cover my next class after lunch—which happens sooner than school lets out. For that reason, I slowly push the door open.

Sheila sees me, but her tone doesn't change. It's as sharp as razor wire.

"Help you, Alan?"

"I have an appointment. May take longer than my lunch—"

"The pride lands will be fine, Alan. But thank you for telling me."

The assistant principal turns his head to me, clearly confused. Maybe annoyed. I suppose the *Lion King* analogy might be new to him or even specific to me.

"Thanks."

Sheila doesn't smile. She simply says, "Close that door as you go, Alan."

The location for the numbers group meeting is another warehouse.

This one is closer to my school.

Like the last warehouse, this building is empty and listed for rent. I wonder if one of the members is a commercial real estate agent for industrial properties. Or maybe they own the buildings and know when no one will be there. Or perhaps one of them has a spouse or friend who is a broker.

I don't have much time to spare, but I can't help but do some basic recon of the building. First, I park on the street and observe it for a minute, then drive around all sides. It's unremarkable. A lot like the last one: parking lot up front, corrugated metal walls and roof, loading dock on the back. There are no cars parked in the lot. No windows or lights on.

It's a sort of black box I'm walking into.

That's great.

Maybe this will be another virtual encounter like the last one.

As I push the glass front door open, I realize I'm right. The lobby is empty except for peeling wallpaper and worn carpet and a camera with a speaker atop a metal pole.

It's connected to a powerbank on the floor. A red light glows on the device. The speakers carry that computerized voice I heard before, which says:

"Take your clothes off."

"No."

"It's—"

"No," I repeat, even louder. "I'm *not* taking my clothes off."

The scrambled voice begins, but I talk over it.

"I'm done here. I'm *really, really* done. I'm tired of you jerking me around. I'm tired of all these cat and mouse games. Good luck with all this—"

"Just take your shirt off," the voice says. The bravado is gone.

I don't move.

Slowly, the voice adds, "One of our members was killed."

The words hang in the air, and I think about Nathan Briggs. Was he the member?

"We're just being cautious," the speaker says. "For our own safety."

I'm heating up like a pot about to boil when the person adds a phrase that turns the flame off: "We have families too."

I stand there, waiting as my breathing returns to normal. The speaker is silent, and finally, slowly, I remove my polo and the V-neck t-shirt under it and toss them on the floor.

"You see the opening in the wall to your right?"

Glancing over, I spot the hole in the wallpaper and drywall. It's about as wide as my hand; a little taller, like a mail slot.

"Put your phone in. Both of them, Alan."

When I don't move, the speaker adds, "You'll get them back. I promise. We're just—"

"Being cautious," I mumble on my way to the opening, where I insert my two phones. There's a faint sliding noise and a clunk on the other side of the wall.

I'm putting my shirt back on when I hear a sound in the distance, beyond the lobby.

Footsteps.

Soon, a lock clicks, followed by footsteps moving away.

"Come on in," the voice on the speaker says.

I march to the door and push it open, wishing I had a gun and some armor and that I had told Warren where I was going.

That's a strange thing—I think about him like my partner. Someone who would back me up.

The room beyond the lobby is larger, but it's still an office—not a warehouse space.

In the center is a large table with a metal frame and casters on the legs. It has a rubbery top, as if the surface was used for razor or knife work of some type.

There are three other tables along the walls, also with metal frames but with dark wood tops. Apparently, these tables were too large or heavy to remove when the previous occupant vacated. I wonder if they welded these tables together here in the room and no one bothered—or was paid—to take them apart again.

This is the world we live in. Many of the things we build are left behind.

The only door leading out of this room opens onto a manufacturing floor. A plant with a high ceiling and rolled insulation showing along the walls. There are two overhead bridge cranes. The hooks hang in the air, the controls dangling from a cord close by.

The entire place is empty except for five folding metal chairs. Four are lined up in a semicircle and three of them are occupied—by members of the group, I presume.

There's an empty chair on the left side of the semicircle and another empty chair facing the others.

Based on what I've been through, I thought the group members might be wearing masks, like that Stanley Kubrick film *Eyes Wide Shut*.

But in this empty warehouse, they're not disguising their faces. And they look a lot like me. Middle-aged. Tired. Wearing clothes that don't look fancy or particularly new.

As I prod forward, my cane squeaking on the concrete floor, one of them rises.

I don't know her last name, but I know her first name. The last time I saw her, she was the one who was in trouble, the one who needed help. Like me right now.

By the time I reach the back of the empty chair, she's standing in the middle of the circle, and I say her name: "Rose."

35

Rose's voice echoes in the warehouse.

"Welcome, Alan."

One of the mysteries of the group clicks into place.

"You're the one who spoke for me."

"I am."

The other two members of the group are a woman a bit older than me and an Asian man. He's about my age and sits in one of the center chairs next to Rose.

He speaks next: "Why don't you sit down, Alan?"

I'm pretty sure he's the one who was giving the orders through the camera speakers. Maybe he's in charge.

"Why don't you tell me what's happening here?"

It's dark in this cavernous room, and I didn't see it before, but there's another camera and speaker on a silver-metal pole, just behind the folding metal chairs, as if standing in for a person.

The camera speaker emits a digitally scrambled voice (this seems to be a signature move for the group).

"He deserves answers," the remote attendee says. Even through the distortion, the voice sounds male and gruff. There's a slight hint of an accent I can't place.

Rose turns and goes back to her seat. The bruise on her face has faded now, and I hope she's moved out of that apartment and away from that guy. That's another answer I want.

I put a hand on the metal chair before me but don't sit. Staring daggers at the Asian guy, I ask the obvious question: "What are the numbers?"

"Isn't it obvious?"

"Not to me."

"They're the entrance to the Labyrinth."

"What is the Labyrinth?"

He stares back at me. "We'll get to that."

"We don't know," Rose says, and the guy cuts his eyes to her, flashing anger.

Focusing back on me, he says, "But you do."

What I realize then is both comforting and terrifying: these people don't know any more than I do. At least about Amersa's Labyrinth. They need me—maybe just as much as I need them.

"I do know what the Labyrinth is." My words echo in the empty warehouse. I can feel the dynamic in the room shifting. It's partially thanks to Rose. She has, to some degree, betrayed the group, but she's supporting me. Putting herself at risk as I once did for her. I have to say, this moment restores some of my faith in humanity.

The Asian guy interlocks his fingers and sets his forearms on his thighs. "So what is it?"

"You know, this relationship has been very one-sided so far. You telling me what to do, extracting information, never sharing what you know."

"You give us something, we give you something."

I've had enough. More than enough. I push the metal chair forward, signaling that I'm not going to sit. Or join the group. At least, not on these terms.

"You know a lot about me. The video I sent of that Amersa interview basically said it all. But I know nothing about you—except that you're constantly jerking me around. And now it looks like you don't even know what's going on here. You don't have any answers. And still, you just keep demanding more and more from me. So, no. I'm not going to *give you* something. I'm going to walk out of here, and you can play your games with your numbers and cameras on poles and garbled voices and creepy requests to see people naked. I'll take my chances. And you can take yours."

Across the group, I see panic. I turn and begin walking away, my cane squeaking on the concrete.

"Stop."

It's Rose who calls out. That's probably the only reason I stay. Still, I don't turn.

"I think," she says slowly, "that we should introduce ourselves. And talk about how we all got here."

No one disagrees. That silent assent brings me back to the chair, which I pull back and sit down in, and then listen for the next hour.

In that dark warehouse, the members of the numbers group take turns introducing themselves.

The discussion has the feel of an anonymous support group. Everyone is cagey. They only use first names. And what they say follows a common course: name, some basic family history, what they do for work, and how they got tinnitus.

The person on my left is named June. As mentioned, she's slightly older than me and more well-educated. She's a neuroscience researcher at Duke University. She's married. With two kids.

Her tinnitus started years ago, but she only recently started seeing the numbers.

The time gaps are causing serious problems in her marriage. She suspects that her husband is suspicious about her having an affair.

The worst part is that she doesn't know how to explain it to him, and beyond that, she's worried about dragging him—and their children—into whatever is happening here. And possibly hurting them.

Hearing someone describe the same fear I have is deeply cathartic. In June's story, I see my own fears reflected back at me, fears about protecting my daughter. And like me, she's suspected of an act she didn't commit.

June says these meetings are less problematic than the time gaps, but she's still terrified that whatever is happening to her will end her marriage and impact her children. She wants answers.

Next, she talks about how her tinnitus started. She developed

Ménière's disease right after grad school, just before turning thirty.

I've never heard of the condition.

June seems to read my confusion and fills in a few details. Ménière's is a problem with the inner ear, and usually only one ear. It typically develops after the age of forty but can sometimes develop earlier, as in her case. The main symptoms are vertigo, characterized by severe dizziness, nausea, and vomiting; hearing loss; and tinnitus. Attacks can come on suddenly and without warning, and vary in frequency and intensity. Some who live with Ménière's experience episodes daily; for others, they may come once a year.

The cause of the condition is unknown. There are, however, a few theories, including poor fluid drainage from the ear (which causes a buildup), an autoimmune disease, or an infection.

June thinks there's a genetic connection, but none of her living relatives seem to have the condition.

In the next chair is the Asian guy who previously spoke for the group—and, I believe, over the speaker as well.

June's candidness—and the vulnerability she showed—has changed the mood in the room. This guy, who was previously demanding and combative, seems resigned now. He stares at the open floor in the middle of the chairs and speaks mechanically, as if reciting a speech he's memorized.

His name is Isaac, and he works for Amersa in the IT division. He details his skill set, which is a lot of terms I don't know and some I've heard (but don't understand), but the general gist is that he's a technology expert.

He's not married. Never has been. And has no kids.

He's the main organizer for the group and was indeed the person texting me.

"I think that's it from me," Isaac says, still staring at the center of the circle.

No one says anything for a long moment. Rose breaks the silence.

"Alan has revealed a lot. Even before he got here."

Isaac locks eyes with her, and she continues, "If we're going to solve this, we need to lay out all the pieces."

He continues then, sounding a little less comfortable.

Isaac was born in China to a Chinese mother and what he believes is a Caucasian father (he had DNA tests to trace his ancestry).

He was put up for adoption before the age of one, and has never met either of his biological parents.

Unlike June and me, Isaac has had tinnitus his entire life. He looks up at me then. "Like I said in the text message: I was born this way."

He grimaces as he continues. "Maybe that's why they put me up for adoption. Maybe I was hearing the ringing even as a newborn, crying every second I was awake. I bet it drove them mad."

He swallows, and there's a long pause, and Rose reaches over and gently places a hand on his back.

"The ringing," he continues, "has driven my whole life. It was like this monster hiding behind every moment of my existence. I was terrible in school. I was constantly having to go to the nurse's station or home. I could do the bookwork. And I tested well—on days when it was quiet. But I never knew when those would be."

He leans back, and Rose takes her hand away. "Eventually, my parents decided to homeschool me. I was already pretty socially isolated at school, but it got worse then. Computers sort of became my link to the outside world."

Isaac takes another break, and when he resumes, he reveals that his tinnitus is caused by a condition called Otosclerosis. It's an abnormal bone growth in the middle ear when one of three small bones connected to the eardrum isn't shaped correctly and can't vibrate freely.

"It's inherited," Isaac says. "It's likely one of my biological parents also had the condition. But I haven't been able to find them. And I stopped looking after the surgery."

"What surgery?" I ask.

"When I was eighteen, my parents felt I was old enough for a surgery to try to fix the Otosclerosis."

"Did it work?"

Isaac looks up at me. "It did. For a while. But then it came back—eight years ago. It was just ringing for a while—no numbers. I looked into having a second Stapedectomy, but I decided not to."

"Why?" I again ask.

"I was actually researching specialists for the surgery when I saw the numbers for the first time. But they weren't the numbers everyone else saw, not at first."

That surprises me. "Wait, you're saying you've seen two number sequences?"

Isaac nods. "Yeah."

"What was the first?"

Isaac recites the sequence from memory: 651813916118141524.

I'm about to ask what that spells when he says, "It translates to Fermi Paradox."

I seem to be the only one who doesn't know what the Fermi Paradox means. So I ask, and Isaac provides the answer.

"The Fermi Paradox is the result of a casual conversation that took place in 1950."

"Conversation between whom?"

"Enrico Fermi, Edward Teller, Herbert York, and Emil Konopinski. The four physicists were walking to lunch, and they were talking about recent UFO reports and whether anything could ever violate special relativity, moving faster than light."

I'm already lost. Isaac must read my confusion because he holds his hands up. "Look, the details don't matter. The point is that the numbers for humanity being alone in the universe don't add up."

The rest of the group must have heard this spiel before because no one says anything, so I ask what that means—the numbers not adding up.

"Think about it. Our sun is about 4.6 billion years old. The universe is 13.7 billion years old. It's been around roughly three times longer than the sun. In the Milky Way alone, there are billions of other stars—many of them suns like our own, no doubt with planets like Earth. And those stars and planets have been around a lot longer than our world. And that's just in *our galaxy*. In this universe, it's estimated that there are over two trillion galaxies."

"Okay. What's the point?"

"The point," Isaac says slowly, "is that it is *exceedingly* unlikely that we are alone in the universe. In fact, based on how old the universe is and how vast it is, it's pretty much unfathomable that there isn't other sentient life out there—and has been for a very long time. Yet, there is no evidence of them—anywhere."

"Interesting," I mumble. Because I do actually think it's interesting, though I've never really thought about it.

"Consider this," Isaac continues. "We—humanity—launched our first satellite in 1957. Sputnik. Look how far we've come in that time. Imagine what a civilization like ours could achieve in billions of years—and that's the kind of head start billions of others should have on us. They should be everywhere across the universe. Yet, there's no sign of them. It doesn't make sense. It never has to me. It's always bothered me, ever since I read about the Fermi Paradox. And when I decoded that first set of numbers, for the first time in my life, I didn't hate the ringing. Until then, it had ruined my life. But after I saw the numbers and realized what was happening, I decided not to have another surgery. Because I wanted it to continue."

"Why?"

Isaac looks up at me. "The same reason you came here and jumped through all of our hoops: I want answers."

"Answers to the Fermi Paradox."

Isaac nods. "And maybe more. Like I said in that text message—I think the numbers are an answer. Or will lead us to the real answer of why we're alone in the universe. I think that's what is on the other side of this Labyrinth, whatever it is, and why we must go through it."

Based on what I've seen of Amersa's Labyrinth, I'm not so sure, but it's a hard thing to disagree with someone so passionate in their beliefs, as Isaac is. And what he says next gives me part of the reason he believes so fervently that we are part of some great process at work.

"I believe that when we reach the end of the Labyrinth, it will all make sense. Humanity's existence." He holds a hand out. "And each of us. Why I was born this way. Why we are going through this. Why we were chosen."

His gaze drifts down to the floor. "I believe that first set of numbers—which only I saw—was a message to me."

"Saying what?"

"To hang on. To keep going. That it would all make sense. I think the ringing will stop when we reach the end of the Labyrinth."

36

In the warehouse, Rose tells her story next. And it fills in some of the answers I wanted—apart from the Labyrinth.

She is the daughter of American immigrants. She grew up in Florida and originally came to the Triangle area after graduating from high school. She enrolled in community college and was hoping to transfer to one of the universities.

From the timeline, I realize she's younger than I thought at first (facial bruises have a way of disguising one's age, as does stress—and I think Rose has experienced a lot of both in her life).

Her tinnitus started about six years ago, after, in her words, a severe blow to the head. I can imagine where that blow came from.

Her eyes meet mine as she continues. "I've recently gotten out of a long-term relationship. I'm staying with a friend now."

I nod slowly, feeling the relief from that particular answer.

"I also work at Amersa, in the janitorial group. I work nights mostly, at the Amersa headquarters."

Isaac says what I'm thinking: "Everything leads back to Amersa. That's where we'll find the answers."

In the silence that follows, I glance over at the fourth chair in the semicircle, which sits empty.

"Who's missing?"

Isaac exhales. "Lucas. He won't be here."

"As in—"

"As in, he's dead," Isaac says. "He's the member we lost."

I can see the group's unease. And I hate to press the issue, but I came here for answers, and exactly what happened to Lucas could be important.

"How?"

Isaac shakes his head. "Police ruled it a suicide."

"You don't sound convinced."

"No," June says.

"Why?"

"We believe," Rose says carefully, "that a security person from Amersa was involved."

My pulse surges, and I'm about to ask that security person's name when Isaac holds up his hands. "We've said a lot." He stares at me. "Your turn."

I point to the camera atop the metal pole. "It would seem there's one more member."

Isaac opens his mouth—to protest, I presume—but the speaker on the camera emits that scrambled voice I have come to loathe. "He's right. I'll go."

The story the member tells over the speaker is very different from mine or any of the others.

His name is Harold, and his tinnitus, he says, is age-related.

"I'm old," Harold says flatly. "But maybe stress was a factor. I've had a lot."

He tells us that his condition came on gradually. For him, the tinnitus ramped like a volume level gradually being turned up every year.

But it also comes and goes for him. Some days are better than others.

Harold is also losing his hearing. His doctor says the two conditions are related. His fear is that one day, the ringing will be all he hears.

"But if that comes to pass," he says slowly, "that's fine, because this condition, as unpleasant as it is, has given me so much."

I'm surprised by that. Because this condition—whatever it is—has *taken* so much from all of us.

"What exactly has it given you?"

My words echo in the warehouse. No one says a word.

"I'm a pensioner," the garbled voice says over the speaker. "My wife has passed, and after, I was adrift."

I don't say it out loud, but I certainly know how he feels.

The sound of Harold clearing his throat is like a static pulse over a radio.

"When the ringing started, it came and went. I started to think of it like a bell tolling. Telling me time was drawing nigh. Counting down the days and weeks until I got to join her."

The speaker falls silent. When it continues—even through the scrambling—I can tell the voice is less emotional. "I started to lose time soon after. Little periods. Thirty minutes here and there. That, too, I thought was a function of age. An old man forgetting things. I didn't tell a soul. But I decided to log in to my investment account, because I was scared I might do something foolish in one of my senile episodes. I was thinking of having my daughter take it all over until I saw the balance."

The speaker on the camera crackles, and he continues. "I was rich. For the first time in my life, I was a wealthy man. For a moment, I thought it might be a hallucination. I called the financial company's support line, and they verified the balance. So I dug a little deeper. I checked the trade confirmations and realized that the lucrative stock and option trades that had made me so wealthy coincided with my tinnitus time gaps. In that time I lost, I first enabled trading in instruments I don't understand—and then I executed extremely well-timed trades. And as I stared at the balance on my account, the ringing began again, but I didn't jump forward in time. The numbers morphed into the sequence we've all seen. With the letters after the period. The uh…"

Isaac looks mildly annoyed as he mumbles, "Domain extension."

"Ah, yes, indeed, as our tech-savvy compatriot says. And so I followed the address, like Alice down the rabbit hole, and here I am."

When he doesn't say any more, I ask: "But why aren't you *actually* here? In person?"

"Two reasons: distance. I'm outside the United States. And condition. As I said, I'm not as young as I used to be. Or as mobile."

I wonder if he's disabled somehow. I feel bad about pressing, but I need all the answers I can get. "You see us," I tell him. "But we can't see you. Or at least, I haven't."

"None of us have," Rose says softly.

"It's a precaution," Harold replies.

"Why?"

"The obvious, my friend. I'm afraid what I've been doing in these lost periods of time is illegal."

I squint at the camera. "Illegal how?"

"Insider trading, perhaps. Or maybe the investments aren't an issue, but who I'm funneling the money to is a problem. A terrorist organization. Or a drug cartel."

I hold up my hands. "Wait. You've been sending money to someone?"

"Indeed. I can see a listing of the transfers out of my account. Large sums, several times a week."

"And you can't trace them?" I ask.

"I've tried," Isaac volunteers. "All we have to go on is the bank and account number. They're not exactly forthcoming about who their depositors are or account activity."

Another static burst comes over the speaker as Harold clears his throat. "My other concern... is a bit more practical. And concrete. Taxes. I owe a bundle, and yet I keep shipping away the loot to God knows where. It has made me wonder if we are the good ones or the villains in our mysterious, shared adventure."

After a sigh, he adds, "At any rate, that's my story, such as it is. I'll say that I've been quite glad to have found this group. It's kept me sane through this trying period. I haven't told a soul outside our esteemed circle, nor would I—for the reasons I've just recounted."

Isaac locks eyes with me. "You've heard our stories. Now we want to hear yours—the rest of it. What happened in Amersa's Labyrinth program?"

"It wasn't what you think."

"You don't know what I think."

"Trust me, you're not thinking this."

"I just want the truth."

"So do I."

When he says nothing, I stand from the metal chair and look each of the group members in the eyes. "Okay. Here it is."

And then I begin to describe what happened at Amersa when I left that room with the AI coordinator on the screen.

III

THE LABYRINTH

37

At the Amersa offices, Sandra leads me out of the room where I met my AI handler, Linus.

At a large metal door, she scans her badge and ushers me into a room with white padded walls and a padded floor. In the middle of the room, something is lying in a pile on the floor.

She walks to it and picks up one end. It's a black, one-piece suit with a zipper from the waist to the collar. It reminds me of a skin-tight superhero outfit—one with only one and a half legs.

Sandra holds it out to me. "Time to suit up."

I march to her, trying to compensate for the soft floor under my prosthetic. The suit is dark gray and thick, with a lumpy texture, as if something is embedded under the surface.

She makes for the door, calling over her shoulder, "Leave your clothes on the floor."

When she's gone, I sit on the padded floor, remove my prosthetic, and pull the strange garment on. It's elastic and form-fitting and slightly weighty, like I'm wearing a human glove with a layer of sand embedded beneath the surface.

I stretch my arms, getting a feel for it. There's a subtle resistance to every movement, like being underwater.

There must be a camera in here, because Sandra returns with a tablet in one hand and a small bag in the other. I reach for my prosthetic, but she waves me off. "You won't need that in the Labyrinth."

"But—"

"Trust me," she says quickly. "You'll get used to it."

From the bag, she draws out a face mask that is the same color and lumpiness as the suit. I pull it over my head, aligning the eye holes. It fits perfectly and covers my mouth and nose, but I can breathe almost normally. I think the material has less of the lumpy grains in those areas.

The mask has built-in ear muffs that gently grip the side of my head, blotting out all sound.

Next, she hands me what looks like a large pair of swim goggles. I move them to my head, but she stops me and grips my forearms, urging me upward.

I rise, balancing awkwardly on one leg as she pulls the goggles over my eyes, plunging me into complete darkness. I wobble on my good leg, feeling disoriented.

"I can't see anything," I call out, but I can't hear my own voice.

A shiver runs across my body, then the suit tightens, especially under my foot and stump. It's like I'm being vacuum-sealed. The sensation passes, and the goggles turn transparent, and I again see Sandra standing in front of me, holding the tablet.

"Can you hear me?" she asks.

I can, and I tell her so. Her voice is crystal clear through the ear muffs.

"Good. Any discomfort?"

I shrug, feeling a little more natural in the suit.

"Not really."

She taps the tablet again. "Great. I think you're ready."

She motions to the door we came in through and says, "Go on in."

Under the mask, I'm making a skeptical face that I know she can't see, but it's clear she's done this before, because she adds, "Trust me. Go through the door."

On instinct, I lift my amputated leg to take a step but stop myself before I can plant it. Looking down, I see a flesh-and-blood leg below my shorts, the kind I haven't seen since that day in Afghanistan when I put my fatigues on.

But I know the image is fake, a product of the VR, just like the clothes, which match the ones I just took off. I'm actually wearing the suit, and it's the goggles showing me the leg and shorts.

For a moment, it's disorienting, like my brain is confused by my eyes. My eyes are telling me it's safe to take a step, but a part of me is screaming that there's a cliff there and that I'll fall.

"It's okay," Sandra says gently. "Give it a try."

I feel pressure at the end of my stump, like the prosthesis, but more gentle. It's the suit gripping me.

Tentatively, I let my simulated foot fall to the floor, feeling the pressure increase on my stump. But the suit is holding the rest of me as well. It's... comfortable. Different, but strangely comfortable.

Sandra, still holding the tablet, smiles patiently. "First step is always the toughest." She nods to the door. "Go on, Alan. The Labyrinth's waiting for you."

I plant my right foot, marveling at how real it all feels.

"How does this work?" I ask. "The suit?"

"Little above my pay grade," Sandra replies. "But I'm told it's some kind of magnetic grains."

I stride toward the door to the room, turn the handle, and push it open, expecting to see the Amersa hallway. But it's not there. And when I glance back, Sandra and the padded room are gone too.

It's like turning the handle transported me.

I'm in an empty corridor with large tan tiles on the floor and walls. It's vaguely familiar, and of all the things I was expecting to see, this was nowhere on the list.

I'm standing in a truck stop, a large one with a convenience store, restaurant, and gift shop. I'm in the corridor that exits the bathrooms, facing the grocery portion of the building.

The aisles ahead are filled with candy, packaged snacks, food, and drinks.

Beyond the checkout counter, the gift store has everything from NASCAR paraphernalia to Beanie Babies and college sports gear.

In the restaurant, I can hear travelers ordering burgers, chili dogs, and fries.

Behind me, a voice grumbles, "Excuse me." I shift out of the way as I feel someone brushing by, exiting the bathrooms and showers.

One of the things Linus told me is that the Labyrinth allows me to do pretty much everything I could do in the real world, with one exception: use the bathroom. In fact, bathrooms are how I enter and exit the Labyrinth.

Walking out into the truck stop store, I try to get my bearings. The entrance features two sets of glass double doors, the type that traps heat and air conditioning inside. Above the doors, a sign reads: "Thanks for visiting Labyrinth Travel Centers. Come back soon."

Unsure what to do, I start exploring the store and taking in the people. I'm standing in an aisle with candy bars, crackers, and cookies, when a voice from behind the counter calls to me, "Need help, traveler?"

The clerk who addressed me is a young guy, skinny, and no older than college age. He smiles. "You look a little lost."

"I'm looking for the Labyrinth."

He cocks his head and looks at me quizzically. "Well, you've found it."

"What do you mean?"

"You're in it, traveler. We all are."

"This is the Labyrinth?"

"Of course. You're on the outer arm, but you're in it. Just barely."

I look around again, and he goes on: "Check your phone map if you don't believe me."

"I don't have my phone."

"Are you sure? Every traveler does. It's pretty much essential these days."

"No, I had to leave it outside."

The employee squints at me. "Have you looked?"

Exhaling, I reach into my pocket and feel the distinct size and weight of a smartphone. I draw it out, and it shows a brief message signaling facial recognition, and then unlocks. At the top, it says Labyrinth OS, and below are several status indicators:

    Health: 98%
    Credit balance: 0
    Inventory: cargo shorts, simple white t-shirt, tennis shoes

Below that is a classical symbol for the Labyrinth with its maze of lines and a red dot that pulses at the start of it.

"I'm guessing," the clerk says, "that you just got a new phone."

"I guess I did," I mumble. "What am I supposed to do here?"

"The same thing we're all doing," he replies.

"Which is?"

"Get to the center of the Labyrinth. They say everything you're looking for is there."

"Okay. How exactly do I get there?"

The young guy smiles broadly. "Just like everyone else. You make the trip. It's all about the journey."

I glance out at the trucks and tractor-trailers refueling and getting back on the road, then at the procession of vehicles bounding into the travel center.

"You need a ride," the clerk tells me.

"Right. How do I get a ride?"

He points at a big board, which is almost like a display in an airport showing flights.

But the listing here has people's names instead of airlines (at the moment, it's Silvia, Rusty, Tim, Laura, Bill, and Greg).

Beside each name is a departure time, followed by three numbers and letters.

"You see," the kid explains, "folks put what time they're leaving and how many travelers they can take—that number has a T after it. The next number is how many credits you have to pay them to ride—it has a C after it. The last number is how many gallons of fuel they have—that always has a G after it. That'll tell you how far that driver can get down the road. What you're trying to do is find somebody with lots of fuel and a rate you can afford."

"My phone says I don't have any credits."

"Of course you don't. You haven't done any work. You have to earn your way through the Labyrinth, traveler."

"How do I earn?"

The rail-thin kid smiles. "Same as all of us. You get yourself a job."

"All right. I'll bite. You know anyone hiring?"

"As it turns out, we're looking for help around here."

*

And that is how I began working at a truck stop in a virtual reality simulation.

The first work task assigned to me is collecting all the trash from the big barrels beside the pumps and hauling it to the dumpster. It's incredible how real this experience feels—the sounds and the weight of things and even the wind blowing across me. I could actually believe I'm holding a bag full of cans, bottles, and fast-food paper bags.

As I'm pulling a clear plastic bag together and about to tie it off, I notice a collection of dark clouds on the horizon. They look like typical storm clouds, except these are inky black, almost like oil spilled into the sky from a tanker ship that crashed in the atmosphere.

There's a woman who looks to be in her fifties, wearing a sweatshirt that says "Labyrinth Park," refilling her sedan beside me.

"Storms are getting worse," she says.

"Yeah? I just got here, so I'm not familiar."

She follows my gaze to the black clouds. "The storms haven't reached out here yet. The deeper you go, the worse they are. Wind's bad, but it's that toxic rain that'll get you."

"Toxic rain?"

"Yeah. You best get you some rain gear at your next stop. And keep it on when the wind starts blowing. Stay inside if you can."

"Thanks."

She puts the nozzle back in the dispenser and leans on the pump. "We travelers gotta stick together. We're all going to the same place, after all. Figure, if I help you get there, maybe somewhere down the road, you'll help me get there."

After the trash, I restock the shelves and refrigerators. My credit balance goes up with every mini-job I complete, but my health keeps declining. My last duty is sweeping up; by then, I've accumulated fifty-two credits. But my health is down to eight percent.

Surveying the board, I've got enough to afford two of the rides leaving in ten minutes. I pick the logical choice: the one with the most fuel.

The clerk enters it on his keyboard, and on the screen, the line requesting one rider disappears.

"You'll want to improve your health before you get on the road, traveler," the clerk says.

"How do I do that?"

"Well, some folks sleep in their truck, but you don't have a truck. We don't have a motel attached. You can always go to the restroom. We've got showers back there that might refresh you."

Subtly, I feel like he's giving me the clues of what to do. So I head to the back of the store, and the moment I cross under the sign that says "Clean Restrooms and Showers," I'm once again standing in the padded room at Amersa's offices.

38

When I've finished describing my first experience in Amersa's Labyrinth, the warehouse is silent for a few seconds.

The three members of the numbers group sit on their folding metal chairs, waiting.

Isaac looks up at me, grimacing. "You've *got to be kidding me*. That's it? A *truck stop*?"

"That's what it was."

"That's ridiculous."

"That's what happened."

Isaac stands. "This guy is a complete fraud."

Rose cuts her eyes at him. "He's a hero."

"He's a disgrace," Isaac fires back. "A complete disgrace. Seriously, is this a joke? What really happened in there?"

"I told you, that's *exactly* what happened."

June holds her hands up, trying to infuse calm into the circle. "Let's consider, for a moment, why the Labyrinth presented in that way to you, Alan."

"I don't know."

"Maybe it was something you said in the intake interview," June says.

Isaac's tone is mocking. "You visit a lot of truck stops, Alan?"

"No," I snap at him, annoyed. "But… actually, I think I might know why they chose a truck stop."

Isaac rolls his eyes. "This should be good."

"Before I went in, the AI coordinator—Linus—asked me about childhood experiences. He wanted to know about a time when I was happy and excited about the future. When I felt adventurous."

"Your childhood adventures were at highway rest stops?" Isaac deadpans.

"Sort of."

"What do you mean?" Rose asks.

"When I was a kid, my parents always did one big vacation a year. It was in the summer. They made it a surprise, never told me where we were going or what we were going to do. We always drove. That's what we could afford. We did the beach one year, Gatlinburg another, DC, the Outer Banks, Biltmore, Williamsburg—"

"We get the point," Isaac mutters, not looking up from the concrete floor.

"The point is, those were some of my happiest memories as a kid. It was an adventure. There was uncertainty, but I felt safe and excited about what was to come."

"Why," June asks, "do you think the Labyrinth used that as a format?"

"It's an RPG," Isaac says. "A role-playing game. Classic setup."

"How?" June asks.

"He's starting as a base character. No special skills. Low-level armor. No weapons other than his fists. His goal in the beginning is to learn about the game environment and gather some resources so he can level up his character and move out into the world to continue the quest."

"What quest?" Rose asks.

"This Labyrinth RPG feels like a standard adventure quest. You have a main character," Isaac motions to me, "who is trying to get somewhere or obtain something. Sounds like everyone in the game is trying to get to the center of the Labyrinth."

"Actually, I'm just trying to figure out what the numbers mean and stop the ringing."

"Yeah, but they don't know that. They think you're there to cure your PTSD. And I bet that's exactly what the game is going to try to do along the way." Isaac pauses, thinking. "It makes sense, actually."

"What does?" June asks.

"The thing about an RPG is that the quest really isn't what it's about."

Isaac leans back in the chair. "It's about what the quest does to the player."

He's lost me, and apparently the other members of this group. He keeps going.

"The quest is just what the character wants. There are some common patterns. Saving a princess. Curing a plague upon the land. Defeating a dragon that has brought chaos and misery to a kingdom. Or in this case, reaching the center of the Labyrinth to get some sacred knowledge that will resolve all your problems. But, again, the game is really about what happens to the character and how it mentally impacts the player—that's why people keep playing."

"What do you mean?" I ask.

Isaac shrugs. "This is my opinion, but I think RPGs are so addictive because we get invested in our character. They start out as basically powerless. At a disadvantage. And then we pour time and energy into making them more powerful. We level them up. They earn money. Buy things. Get new skills. Gradually, the character gains power over their environment. They're able to do things they couldn't before. Defeat monsters. Venture into new areas. There's a progression that mirrors real life—at least we want it to. We all want to develop as we grow older. We want to achieve things we couldn't before. We want to have more control over our environment and feel more secure—we're biologically trained to seek that out. Doing it in a game world is… inspiring in a way. It's like an imperfect mirror of real life. One that gives us confidence to go out and tackle real quests. We all have quests in life. And we need to level up to complete them."

"So," Rose says, "what does all this mean? What should Alan do?"

Isaac shrugs. "I guess he should play the game. See what's beyond the truck stop."

After that, the meeting takes on a more procedural tone.

The group has some established procedures, which they inform me of.

First, they keep log books of their tinnitus. At the regular meetings—when they aren't welcoming a new member, like me—they start by recounting the episodes, which Isaac records and compiles into a master spreadsheet for analysis.

I agree to keep a log. I should have been doing it before.

They use an app called Signal for secure messaging.

"If you're ever in trouble," Isaac says, "send a message to everyone. And text my burner phone—you have the number already."

What I'm told next surprises me more than anything I've heard today.

They want me to do something at Amersa. It's risky. If I'm caught, I'll go to jail. I'll lose Riley.

When they tell me the plan, I realize that's why this group was so interested in me. It wasn't just the trial. It was what I could smuggle into Amersa, because of my disability.

The plan involves Rose, too. It puts her at risk as well. When they've finished describing the details, Isaac tries to close the deal. "Will you do it?"

"I'll think about it."

He exhales from his nose. "That's a no."

"It's a maybe."

"Give him time," Rose says.

39

It's night by the time I get home from the numbers meeting, and I find Meredith and Riley on the porch of the red caboose, sitting at the table, assembling the Hogwarts Castle puzzle as music plays and the cicadas chirp.

It's past Riley's bedtime, but I know Meredith let her stay up so she could see me (and maybe to avoid a fight with my strong-willed daughter).

My first order of business is to administer the Calm gummies, and after, I settle in beside them and put a few more pieces of the puzzle together. The walls are going up now, and the castle is starting to take shape, looking more like the picture every day.

I text Meredith that she's free to go any time, but she reads the message and slips her phone back in her pocket.

She probably wants to talk. Or at least give me a chance to give her some answers. Which she still deserves. And I think maybe I'm ready to give her... some.

Soon, Riley yawns, and I beckon her inside to brush her teeth.

When she's finished, I lie beside her in the bottom bunk and begin reading the next chapter of Harry Potter. It takes place in the castle, and I know she's enjoying it even more because of that.

Even so, she's out by the fourth page.

When I emerge from the bunk, Meredith has used the large cardboard base to move the puzzle inside, to the banquette dining table, out of reach of the elements.

On the porch we sit and she waits, and I start. "Today wasn't an appointment with the clinical trial."

She raises her eyebrows.

"I met with the group."

"The group… the people who see the numbers? When they get tinnitus?"

"Yeah."

"And? How did it go? Did you get answers?"

I grimace, staring at the pine trees swaying in the breeze. "Some. But not the ones I expected. And I actually have more questions now."

"So not super successful then."

I smile. "Well said."

"Is that why you seem preoccupied and mildly broody?" Meredith holds out a hand. "Though, to be fair, low-level brooding is sort of your resting state."

My smile widens, and I feel myself relaxing into the chair.

Meredith shrugs. "Not judging."

"Feels a little like judging."

"Not complaining."

For a while, the only sound is the forest and the bug zapper getting its last licks in as summer gives way to fall and the bugs retreat.

Meredith turns to face me, her tone more serious now. "Is that all that's bothering you?"

I think—*not even close*. But I say, "No. They want me to do something."

"I take it you don't want to?"

"Yes and no."

"Alan, you're an enigma as great as the numbers."

I laugh, shaking my head. "Hardly."

"Is it dangerous? What they want?"

"Could be. If I'm caught."

"Not getting a good feeling about this."

"Same."

"Are you going to do it?"

"Probably."

"Why, Alan?"

"Because it might actually get us some answers. Real answers. And I'm the only one who can do it."

I expect her to talk me out of it, but she just stares out at the treetops and the night sky.

Finally, she shifts in the chair and swallows, and her voice is a little hesitant. "Not prying into your business, but I saw the *For Rent* magazine on the kitchen counter."

"I've been looking. It's getting expensive here, and I think some of the novelty has worn off. And we need a little more space. It's been okay with this weather, but in the winter, we'd be cooped up inside."

"About that." Meredith slowly tilts her head. "Just putting this out there, but my neighbor is going to rent his place."

She shrugs and begins speaking faster, as if she needs to explain how she knows. "I saw him at the mailbox. His company is transferring him to Houston, and he's iffy about it. It's better pay, but he might want to move back, so he's renting instead of selling."

"Oh."

"Just putting it out there."

"Right. Do you know how much he wants for rent?"

"I don't. I could find out."

Meredith picks up her phone, and I think she's texting him, but my phone vibrates with a link from her.

"That's the listing for the house when he bought it. In case you want to see pictures. Obviously, I don't know what kind of shape it's in now."

The pictures look about like Meredith's place: it's a townhouse with a kitchen and living room downstairs and three bedrooms and two baths upstairs. It's nice. It would be perfect for Riley and me. And the neighborhood has a playground, pool, and lots of families with young kids. It's in the same school district, too, so Riley wouldn't have to transfer.

"Any idea when he's moving?"

"The movers are coming tomorrow, actually. He's going to take pictures and put it on a rental site when it's empty and clean."

"I'm interested," I mumble absently, still scrolling through the pictures.

★

When Meredith is gone, I sit on the porch, flipping through the *For Rent* magazine I picked up at the grocery store, looking at floor plans and rent prices.

Then I pick up the phone and flip through the pictures of the townhome again.

Riley would have her own bedroom again. And we'd have a dining room table that could be taken over by 3D puzzles. In fact, we could have a whole bedroom dedicated to homework and crafts.

And it would make it a lot easier for Meredith to babysit when I'm away.

But if things turn south with Meredith and me, it would be beyond awkward living two doors down. And it would affect Riley.

Single parenthood: the ultimate labyrinth.

Next, I get out my laptop and check my auction bids and do a little hunting for things Warren can sell.

The last thing I do before closing the computer is to search for Ménière's disease.

The NIH website gives a good rundown. The condition is far more prevalent than I expected (about 615,000 people in the US are affected in total, with over 45,000 new cases every year).

One passage from the site stops me cold:

> Although the causes of Ménière's disease remain unclear, the symptoms of Ménière's disease are associated with a fluid imbalance in a part of the inner ear called the labyrinth.

40

There are a lot of advantages to living in Raleigh, North Carolina. Especially when it comes to raising kids. For one, there are tons of things for them to do. Camps. Parks. Programs.

And it's all pretty affordable, even for a single parent on a teacher's salary.

One of my favorite places to take Riley is Pullen Park. She's getting a little old for it now, but it still works. And it's free to get in (though you pay for the ride tickets). There's a carousel, a train that circles the park, a playground (where she usually sees a kid or two she knows), and concessions (pizza and hot dogs and ice cream). It's like a low-budget, sixties-era version of Disneyland. And it's perfect.

On weekends, like today, there are usually a few birthday parties going on under the covered areas with picnic tables.

For Riley, it's probably mostly about the nostalgia now. Her mother and I used to bring her here before Jenn got sick. It's incredible how carefree our life was then. And how different it is now.

Riley and I are getting off the train, on our way to a date with two slices of cheese pizza when I get a text from Meredith:

> My neighbor says you're free to tour today, but fair warning: the movers are there and it's a little hectic.

She also sends the rent price, which is, surprisingly, mercifully, in my budget (though just barely).

It all looks pretty good. So far.

But if there's one thing parenthood has taught me, it's to be very, very careful with a child's expectations. Big surprises—in a good way—go off like the crescendo of a fireworks display. Disappointments explode in your face like a live grenade.

For that reason, I tell Riley only that we're going to visit Ms. Davis after the park.

When we arrive at Meredith's place, she turns on Netflix, and when Riley is sufficiently mesmerized, I mention that I need to run an errand (Riley barely notices).

Walking down the hill, I pass a massive transfer truck with its side and rear doors open. Two employees from a national moving company are staggering up the ramp with a couch wrapped in blue furniture blankets and plastic.

Inside the townhome, I find the owner in his half-empty living room, sitting in a folding chair that you might use while tailgating for a sports event or camping. He's focused on the laptop balanced on his legs, but looks up as I approach and introduce myself.

His name is Steven and, like anyone on moving day, he seems a bit frazzled. But, he recovers quickly and gives me a pretty thorough tour. He's a bachelor and looks to be in his late twenties or early thirties. He's used one spare bedroom as an office, the other as a guest suite. The place is in really great shape.

The tour ends in the two-car garage and we linger there, staying out of the movers' way. When I tell him I'd like to apply to rent the place, Steven looks a little sheepish and simply says, "Don't exactly have an application per se. This is my first time renting."

So instead of an application, I tell him a little about myself: that I'm a teacher, a Marine vet, and a single father. Steven doesn't ask any questions. I wonder how much Meredith told him. He simply says that Meredith mentioned that I would be a great renter and very reliable. Under normal circumstances—when I wasn't seeing number sequences and losing time—that would be true, but I certainly don't correct him.

We shake on it, agreeing to a one-year lease and then get down to the details.

The cleaners are scheduled to come on Monday. I can move in anytime after. That's ideal because Tuesday is the last night

I've paid for at the Airbnb. I was planning to extend for another week, but given how little Riley and I have to move, I think I can make it work.

At the threshold of the front door, I pause and turn back. "Hey, Steven, would you mind if I let my daughter tour? She's at Meredith's house."

He settles back into the folding chair and shrugs. "Sure, but you know," he motions to a mover staggering past holding one end of a dresser, "just watch out."

At Meredith's place, I plop down on the couch next to Riley and try to get her attention. I only achieve that after pausing the show (which is about a group of girls doing gymnastics in Australia).

That unholy action elicits a standard "*Dad!*" whine from Riley and a grab for the remote.

"Hey, kiddo, how would you like to tour the townhouse next door?"

She looks at me like I've said the most absurd thing in human history. "*What? Whhy?*"

She lunges for the remote again, and I hide it behind my back and grip her shoulder, holding off the next grab.

"Well, I just thought you might want to see it because we're going to be living there."

She stops reaching for me, pausing to process what I've said.

And when she does, a smile blossoms on her lips and slowly grows.

"Seriously?"

"Seriously."

"When?"

"Soon. Want to see it?"

She nods, and the three of us walk the thirty-two feet down the sidewalk and weave our way through the boxes and blanketed furniture, taking in the 1,700-square-foot, two-story townhome.

Upstairs, Riley quickly surveys the empty bedrooms and settles on the one at the back of the home.

She's beaming as she twirls around, taking it in.

"Dad, can I get bunk beds?"

When I don't respond, she steps into the doorway, blocking my exit. "Dad? Can I?"

"I'll think about it."

41

On Sunday morning, once Riley is dressed, we work on the puzzle a bit and wait for ten o'clock to arrive, and when it does, I clean out the car and we set off toward one of the most daunting labyrinths in modern American life: Costco... on the weekend.

The Sunday melee at my favorite big-box warehouse store is not as nerve-wracking as some of the things I've been through in my life (for example, my first patrols as a newly deployed Marine or my first day of school as a new teacher). However, taking a seven-year-old child with ADHD into a Costco on Sunday still takes some guts. But we're moving, we have needs, and a limited budget.

We arrive at the sprawling building right after ten, a few minutes after the massive club store opens. Pushing a squeaking flatbed, we first collect the key items on my list: mattresses, sheets, and kitchenware.

The concrete floor doesn't do my stump any favors, but there's a certain feeling of joy as we load the flatbed and accumulate the things we need. It feels like we're finally starting over—Riley and I.

And we need a fresh start.

Also, I totally cave and buy the bunk beds (even though we still have Riley's old bed in storage). Sometimes something new is good for the soul. Plus, she's reaching the age of sleepovers, so it's functional.

Tuesday, after school, I pick up Riley in the car rider line. When we arrive at our new home, I'm happy to see the moving truck with our things from the apartment is already here. It's backed into the driveway, the rear double doors are open, and when I peer in, I'm even happier to see that the interior is empty.

Inside the townhome, the movers are assembling the last of our furniture. When they're done, I kindly ask them to help me unload the mattress and bunk beds (which I'll assemble myself). They oblige and I tip them more than I can afford—but every bit of what they deserve.

Meredith arrives as they're leaving, and along with Riley, we set about making this house a home. Dishes go in cabinets. Sheets on mattresses. Picture frames take their places on console tables and vanities and bedside tables.

The internet isn't hooked up yet, and I have to say, it's kind of nice.

Dinner is pizza, and Riley's eyes are drooping after her second slice.

Upstairs, in her new bedroom, lying beside her on the bottom bunk, I open the book to read to her, but she nestles into me, closes her eyes, and is soon snoring softly.

Downstairs, I find Meredith in the kitchen, stacking the remaining pizza slices in a Tupperware container.

"Already out?" she asks, snapping the plastic box shut.

"Yep. And I'm not far behind her."

She nods. "Same."

I lean against the kitchen wall, watching her stow the Tupperware in the fridge, thinking about how natural this feels, how effortless and normal, as if we've been doing this nighttime routine for years.

She turns and squints at me, a playful smile on her lips. "What?"

"Nothing."

"You're thinking something. I can tell."

"No, I'm not."

She takes a step toward me, the smile growing. "Yes, you are."

"Whatever. You know I don't even like thinking."

The smile grows. "*That*, I believe."

I push off the wall and hold my arms out for a hug. "Thanks for the help today."

Meredith wraps her arms around me, and without thinking, I grip her tighter, almost as if my muscle memory is taking over, like a twenty-year-old instinct that never got turned off.

"I'm glad you're here," she whispers.

"Me too," I reply softly, still holding her tight, neither of us moving.

"I think this place is going to be good for you guys."

"Me too," I repeat, my heart beating faster.

She releases her grip slightly. Her head falls back, but she doesn't let go.

Neither do I.

She stares at me, and in that moment, the whole world disappears except for her eyes and lips.

My face inches closer to hers. She moves toward me. My heart is thundering.

I don't know who stops moving first—me or her—but suddenly we're both frozen, breathing hard, holding each other as if we almost went over a precipice but caught one another at the last moment.

I blink and she turns her head slightly, and then I can hear the outside world again: car doors closing, a dog barking, a garage door groaning.

Her arms slip off of me, and she takes two quick steps, stopping at the threshold to the kitchen. She turns her head, but not her body, and quietly says good night.

Then, I'm standing there alone, willing my frozen brain to think, to say something—because *something* needs to be said.

Something good.

But the next thing I hear is the front door closing softly.

42

The thing I didn't want to happen has happened, and it occurred within hours—actual hours—of me moving in two doors down from Meredith. It's become awkward.

Not because I'm mad at her (I'm not). Or because she's mad at me (I don't think she is).

But because we are two human porcupines trying to get closer to each other. And we got poked and drew back.

We both have baggage (me, probably more than her).

One thing I know: I'm not the emotionally mature one. I can't solve this. Also, I have a lot on my plate.

So I do the only thing I know how to do: I teach school, take care of my daughter, and I wait.

At my desk at lunch, I eat the same thing I've packed for Riley and watch the door, hoping a Meredith-shaped shadow will cross by it and stop and saunter in.

But it never does. She doesn't glide in and perch on my desk, sipping a green smoothie.

On Tuesday (and again on Thursday), I march down the PE hall and out onto the steps and take my lunch there, expecting her to exit, for it to be a serendipitous moment for her to plop down and us to reset.

She never passes by. That moment never comes.

That week, I spend more time in the teachers' lounge than I ever have before.

Still, I don't see her.

It's like we're playing a game of dodgeball. For teachers.

The weekend passes.

Meredith doesn't text.

I don't reach out.

In my mind, I'm saying things like, *She needs time.* Also, *you're the toxic one. She's better off. This was bound to happen. Sooner is better than later.*

When I walk into Amersa for my second session in the Labyrinth, I'm as nervous as I was for that initial appointment.

Maybe more.

At security checkpoints, I'm accustomed to being pulled out of line. My prosthesis always trips up the scanners. A security guard with a wand usually gives me a cursory scan and waves me through.

This time, however, when the guard in the Amersa lobby runs the wand-style scanner across my prosthesis, he lingers a bit too long, and he looks at me more intently than usual.

I think.

But it could all be in my head. I try not to exhale audibly when he finally waves me through.

Past the checkpoint, I don't go directly to my session room where I do the interview with Linus.

My first stop is the bathroom, and thankfully, it's empty. In one of the stalls, I unstrap my prosthesis and remove the pieces of the device that I've hidden inside: a small microphone and transmitter.

The technology is courtesy of Isaac, but it will be Rose who will hide it in the office of Amersa's CEO. Isaac has configured one of the devices in the server room to receive the audio transmission, encrypt it, and make it available for him to stream and download off-site.

If all goes to plan, we'll soon be privy to everything Anders Larsson—and anyone else—says in that office. And hopefully we'll have our answers.

My part was simply getting the device's pieces through security.

Gently, I place the tiny parts in a plastic bag Isaac supplied, then lift the lid off the tank and slip it inside, where it will wait for Rose to retrieve it.

After replacing the lid, I reattach my prosthesis and walk out. If Amersa has cameras in the bathrooms, I'll soon be headed to a different kind of Labyrinth—the one called the criminal justice system.

In the interview room, my pulse is still racing. Every second, I expect the door to open and security to step in and ask me to come with them.

Linus can tell I'm distracted, but it's exceedingly patient with me. When I'm done answering its questions, the door does indeed open, but it's Sandra looking in at me, not some burly security guard.

She leads me back to the padded room where I don the suit, and once again enter the Labyrinth.

43

My second entry into Amersa's Labyrinth places me at the same spot where I exited: right outside the bathrooms in the truck stop.

The skinny guy behind the checkout counter is waving to me. "Hey! You better hurry up! Your ride's about to leave."

Outside the store, a man leaning on a big rig tips his sizable cowboy hat when he sees me. As I approach, he pushes off, and his bushy handlebar mustache wiggles but doesn't quite curl into a smile.

"Beginning to wonder if you were gonna make it, partner."

Before I can react, he adds, "They say it's us old codgers that are slowpokes, but I swear it's the younger generation holding everybody up these days."

"I move pretty fast for a one-legged man."

He squints at me. "Got two legs as far as I can see."

"Trust me, I don't."

"Excuses won't get you down the road any faster."

"You selling t-shirts or offering a ride?"

For the first time, the white bushy mustache lifts into a grin.

"Well how 'bout dat? You got a little more fight in you than most folks hitching a ride around here."

"That mean we still have a deal?"

"A deal's a deal, and for what it's worth, I was ribbing you a little. I get cranky when I been on the road alone too long."

In the cab, he cranks the engine, and the tractor roars and bounces as it rolls out of the parking lot.

"Name's Gus," he says, putting a toothpick in his mouth. I can tell he's not looking for a reply. In fact, he's already turning the radio on. The first song is one I recognize from my youth—"Rawhide," though I think the last time I heard it was when Dan Aykroyd and John Belushi sang it in a honky-tonk bar in *The Blues Brothers* movie.

A Marty Robbins song follows, telling tales of a man with a big iron on his hip, and then the playlist transitions to some more recent tunes, still in the same vein, by Federale, a band from Portland.

We're seven songs down the road when Gus turns the volume dial lower and looks over at me, furrowing his brow. "Mind if I give you some unsolicited advice?"

"I could use all the advice I can get."

He motions through the windshield at the dark clouds ahead. "Storms are just gonna get worse. You get caught in one, it'll make you sick."

"Sick how?"

Gus is quiet for a moment as if he doesn't want to talk about it, then simply says, "You'll see."

I ask him what sort of clothes I need, and he gives me a pretty thorough rundown: "A raincoat and a big hat." He tips his own very large hat and continues. "A facemask will do too, but you know, you sacrifice some style points that way."

"Right."

"You need pants too, tall boots, a long-sleeve shirt, and gloves."

"Okay."

"If the rain gets on you, you've got to get dry and keep it away from your eyes, your mouth, and your ears. Whatever you do, don't let that Labyrinth rain get inside of you..." He trails off then and turns the radio back up.

The songs play, and the tractor-trailer rolls over this seemingly endless stretch of highway, and the sun climbs high in the sky, and finally, he stops at a much smaller gas station in what looks like a small town.

I expect Gus to turn the big rig off, but instead, he reaches out to the CD player and ejects the silver disc. It's a custom mix, with bleeding black Sharpie letters scrawled across it: Songs for the Road.

Gus holds it out to me and grins, his mustache contorting upward.

"I could tell you were digging my tunes."

I nod once, and he goes on. "Miles get shorter when you got something good to listen to."

"Definitely."

"Well," he says, tossing the toothpick in the cup holder. "We're burning daylight and diesel. Best get to it."

Huffing, Gus dismounts the cab and waddles to the back, draws out a hose, and starts unloading the fuel he's carrying into the gas station's tanks.

I set out to explore this new place. There's a large factory down the road with a sign that reads Labyrinth Apparel.

Next to it is a motel with a sixties vibe. It's a single-story building with a rundown neon sign, an empty swimming pool, and an office with a window sign that says vacancy. It seems like a good place to start. I have three credits to my name, which won't get me very far or buy any clothes. Work is the first thing I need to find.

Inside the motel office, there's another board showing drivers, requested passengers, credit costs, and gallons—or distances. A few of the rides can take up to six people. At the truck stop, it was mostly one to three passenger listings. And no discounts, just a flat rate. At this stop, if they fill their rider quota they discount everyone.

Below the board, sitting behind the desk is a woman about my age. Her name badge says Rachel, and she's hunched over a ledger book, writing intently.

"It's the same listing as at the gas station," she says, not looking up.

"I'm actually looking for work. I need to earn some credits."

"Don't we all?"

I stand there, not sure what to say. Finally, she puts the pen down and glances up.

"Well, there's here and the factory."

"The apparel factory?"

"That's the one."

"What do most folks do?"

"Whatever they can."

I study the board, unsure what to do.

Rachel eyes me. "Do you have the syndrome?"

"The…"

"Labyrinth Syndrome."

"From the rain?"

"Right. Do you have it?"

"No."

"Good. You can do night work."

"Okay. I'll take it."

"Come back at six."

I want to ask her what I should do until then, but Rachel picks up the pen and resumes writing in the ledger.

It's been a while since I played video games, but I remember the general gist, and walking around, exploring, and talking to people is a key part. Especially early on.

As such, I walk over to the factory and ask about work during the day. The wiry man behind the big wooden desk gives me two options: picking cotton in the field or sewing garments inside.

"What pays more?" I ask.

"The fields," he tells me, leaning back in the tufted chair. "But it'll drain your health faster."

"That's okay. I need to earn credits. I'm heading down the road."

The man smirks. "Heard that a few times."

"What does that mean?"

He leans forward and scribbles something in his own ledger book. "It means that I wish you well, traveler. Now go on. That cotton ain't gonna pick itself."

I pick said cotton, feeling the sun burning my skin, my fingers aching, the bags filling.

When the whistle blows and my compatriots file out of the field, my health is at eighteen percent, and the sun has sunk behind the factory.

The credits for the day's work are added to my phone, but after checking the board at the motel, I realize I still don't have enough for a ride.

"Why are the rides so much more expensive here?" I ask Rachel.

"Fuel's more expensive the deeper you get into the Labyrinth. There's less of it. And the routes are more dangerous with the storms now."

My shift at the motel consists of me taking meals to many of the guests. Which is strange, because this place didn't strike me as one that would offer room service. In the first few deliveries, I see some of the folks I worked alongside in the fields. They were strong and vibrant during the day, but now they're convalescing in bed. Some are listless, almost unconscious. Others are a bit more lucid.

At first, I think it's simply exhaustion from the hard work outside in the hot sun.

But then it dawns on me: what I'm seeing is Labyrinth Syndrome.

The fourth meal I deliver is to a woman who appears to be in her sixties. Before leaving her room, I cautiously ask her if my theory is right, and she confirms that it is. She contracted Labyrinth Syndrome during a storm, before anyone even knew it existed.

Now she's trying to escape the Labyrinth, using all her credits to move away from the center and the storms. "You gotta protect yourself," she advises. "Once you get the syndrome, it just keeps getting worse. It grinds you down. It's worse at night—at first. Then it takes more of your health."

After delivering the meals, I have enough credits for a ride—and then some. But there's no one leaving this late at night.

Remembering Gus's advice, I head to the retail store attached to the factory (it's open late).

Inside, I load up on gear: a raincoat, pants, a long-sleeved shirt, a hat, gloves, a face mask, and boots. This nearly wipes out every last credit I have, but I figure the rain gear is more important than advancing deeper into the Labyrinth.

As I carry my purchases back to the motel, I'm thinking about the storms and Labyrinth Syndrome, and I'm remembering what Isaac said about gameplay and objectives. Maybe the goal in Labyrinth isn't to get to the center but rather to cure the syndrome... what were his words? The blight upon the land. Either way, this strange plague and the storms seem to be related, and they appear to be the major barriers to finishing the game.

The other thing that strikes me is how real this place feels at times. Not all the time. Certainly not at first. The initial session at the truck stop was almost cartoon-esque. The people didn't feel real. What they said didn't feel like what real people would say. They didn't act real.

It felt like a game.

But today, in the field, picking the cotton, for a long while, I was in that reality. It felt real. Maybe it was the exertion or the physical sensations or the meditation of having a simple, repetitive task to do, but for a while, I forgot about any world but this one.

And just now, as I was thinking about the storms and the syndrome, it felt more like the way I think about the numbers on the outside. I didn't think about it like a game, but rather as a puzzle to be solved, with lives at stake.

I wonder if that's by design—if Amersa's Labyrinth is programmed to feel playful and simplistic at first. And then to gradually become more real as I progress toward the center.

As I walk by the motel office, a conversation catches my attention. A woman is telling Rachel how the rain might be affecting neurons in the brain and causing Labyrinth Syndrome.

I pause in the doorway, and the two women in the office look up at me.

"Alan, do you need something?" Rachel asks.

"No. Sorry, but I overheard your conversation about Labyrinth Syndrome. Didn't mean to. I was just curious."

Rachel introduces the woman, whose name is May. She's about my age, with dark brown hair in a ponytail and a large three-ring binder tucked under one arm.

"May is a neuroscientist," Rachel adds. "She's talking to our guests to gather data for her research."

"It might lead to a cure," May says. "Or even reversing the condition in those who are affected."

I nod, unsure what to say.

"Every story is another clue," May continues. "But I think the ultimate answers are at the center of the Labyrinth. I'm going to talk to as many people as I can along the way."

She nods to me. "Are you open to being interviewed?" Before I can reply, she adds, "I can pay. How does fifteen credits sound?"

"I don't know much about the syndrome. I'm new here."

May smiles. "You never know how much good talking can do."

"I agree."

"Is it a deal then? Fifteen credits?" She pauses. "I know it's not much for your time, but as I said, I'm also trying to get deeper into the Labyrinth, and I've got a few more people to interview tomorrow morning when they're more lucid."

"Actually, I have a better idea. I'll talk for free. If you'll carpool with me."

May bunches her eyebrows. "Carpool?"

"We combine our credits and get a ride deeper into the Labyrinth—on one of the offers with a multi-rider discount."

"Sounds fine to me," May says.

In the motel office, we make a plan. I'll rest tonight, and tomorrow, we'll work the fields in the morning and leave at noon on the best deal we can find.

44

After my second Labyrinth session, I receive an email from Amersa asking me if I'd be willing to change to weekly sessions. I click the link, and it's a whole thing—tons of words and legalese.

What I can understand says this: that I have reported that my sessions have been well-tolerated.

Below that, it asks me to confirm that the statement is true and to sign digitally.

When I do so, the next screen tells me that more computing resources are now available for the program. The form tells me that analysis and generation of follow-up sessions are now available sooner. Which means I can come weekly. If I want to.

I click the box that I want to.

I need to.

Time is not a luxury I have.

For the rest of the week, the numbers group and I go back and forth about meeting dates.

June has the most constraints.

In the Signal app, I ask Isaac if he's hearing anything good, subtly referencing the listening device.

He shuts that down quickly with a curt reply:

> *Save it for group.*

Riley has gymnastics and an art class after school, and between that and her homework (and mine) and settling into our new home, I'm exhausted every time my head hits the pillow.

But I'm still thinking about Meredith, and I have to admit, I'm of two minds on the issue. If it's the end of us, if things have run their course, maybe it was for the best. I'm not in a great place, and she's starting her life over.

Twenty years ago, I wasn't ready for her and me, and where things were going with us. I didn't know who I was. And I didn't handle things well.

Maybe we're just history repeating itself. And it's better if it fizzles out now, before things get serious.

The group finally settles on a meeting time: Saturday at noon.

I have to decide what to do about Riley. I *can* leave her home alone, but I'm not going to do that.

I can hire a babysitter. But I don't have time to find one in time.

I can ask Warren to watch her. But I'm not ready to do that yet.

Or I can ask Meredith, which I both very much want to do and don't want to do, for various reasons.

I don't do the math. I walk out of my classroom, to the gym, where she's coordinating a volleyball game.

She spots me walking across the waxy floor and returns her focus to the game. As I reach her, she yells, "Sideout!" a little louder than I think necessary, but I'm trying not to read too much into it.

Beside the net, I serve up my request, and she doesn't exactly spike it, but she also doesn't tear her attention from the game. Maybe it's for the kids' safety.

She blows the whistle and shouts for them to switch sides.

Casually, she turns to me, as if remembering that I was there. "Yeah, sure. Be happy to watch her."

I expect her to ask me what it is and why I need her to cover for me. But she refocuses on the game, calling for the next serve and watching the volleys.

45

The meeting with the numbers group, in classic fashion, is in an abandoned warehouse. The setup is the same as my initial meeting with them: five metal chairs and a camera on a pole for Harold to attend remotely.

This time, instead of the four chairs aligned in a semicircle facing mine—as if I was on trial—the five seats form a ring. There's still an empty place for Lucas, the group member who was killed.

Isaac begins the meeting as he did the one before: by asking me what happened in the Labyrinth.

And like last time, I counter him: "You first. Did the recording device work?"

He leans back in his chair. "Yeah."

"What did you hear?"

I'm hoping for details on Nathan Briggs—anything Amersa knows that might help me.

Isaac spreads his hands. "We heard a lot."

"What?" I press him.

"Paydirt." Isaac glares at me. "But you first. That's how this works."

An awkward silence stretches out.

"I took a risk carrying that thing in," I tell him.

"Yeah, he did," Rose adds.

"I have news too," June says quietly, obviously trying to ease the tension.

"Alan should go first," Isaac says. "His Labyrinth session might change everything."

211

"He *did* take a risk," Rose says. "Let him go last."

Isaac shakes his head dismissively. "We *all* did, Rose. You took the greatest risk by actually hiding the device. You could lose your job. And be arrested. It wasn't exactly a cakewalk for me either. Someone could find those firmware updates to the RF devices. How would I ever explain that?"

"It seems to me," June says slowly, "that we should either decide right now to start sharing what we know—and trusting each other—or we should walk away. It's the only way this is going to work."

"Hear, hear," Harold's garbled voice says over the camera speaker.

"Fine," Isaac mutters.

"I'll go first," Rose says lightly. "I don't have any updates."

"My news," June says, "is that I have a job offer. From Amersa."

"Job doing what?" Isaac asks.

"Neuroscience research. It's pretty vague, but I'd be assisting with their commercial products and supporting their clinical trials."

"Are you going to take it?" Rose asks.

June shrugs. "I assumed I would. It gets us closer to Amersa, and real answers. I might have access to data or documents that could help us."

Next, Isaac reaches into a backpack and draws out a speaker, and starts playing one of the recordings. Anders Larsson's voice comes through as clear as if he were here in this warehouse. I suspect Isaac has enhanced the audio. He's also apparently reviewed and edited it, because the clip starts in the middle of a conversation.

"What if Briggs *was* killed by a cartel, like RPD thinks?"

Isaac taps the speaker, pausing the recording and looking over at me. "Briggs is Nathan Briggs, a member of Amersa's internal security group. He was found dead about six weeks ago."

Isaac resumes the recording, and it's another man speaking now, voice gruff and flat. He sounds like he's in the room, perhaps sitting across from Larsson's desk.

"Possible. Not likely."

"But Briggs had a history of drug use, right?"

"He did. After he was discharged from the Marines. But he'd been clean for years. We test all our sec staff."

Isaac pauses the speaker again. "I don't know who's speaking, but from the context, I think it's Amersa's head of security. He would have been Nathan Briggs's boss."

When the recording resumes, Larsson says, "But you found some large cash withdrawals from Briggs's account?"

"We did."

"Could be him buying drugs."

"Possible, but we think he was spending it at strip clubs. Maybe prostitutes, too."

"If I'm not mistaken, strippers, and prostitutes often lead to drugs. And drugs to cartels, and then to death."

"Sir, as much as I would like to believe that is the case—and it may well be—we have to assume the worst. And investigate it as such."

"The worst being that it's related to the Carter situation."

It's June who leans forward into the circle this time, tapping the speaker to pause it. She locks eyes with Isaac, who shakes his head slowly and looks away.

"Circle of trust," June says softly.

Isaac leans back in the chair, crosses his arms, and stares at the floor as he speaks. "The Carter situation is in reference to Lucas Carter."

Isaac's gaze drifts over to the empty seat.

A very important piece of this puzzle clicks into place for me then, and Isaac says what I'm thinking.

"We believe Nathan Briggs killed Lucas and made it look like a suicide."

In the pause that stretches out in the empty warehouse, I feel a sudden lightness. A sense of relief. If it's true—if Briggs was a murderer—maybe that's part of why I killed him (if I did, in fact, take his life).

I know this: I want to hear more.

"Why do you think Briggs killed Lucas?"

"I think," Isaac says carefully, "that it was partially an accident."

"What do you mean?"

Isaac cuts his eyes to me. "I think that's enough for now."

"Circle of—" June begins, but Isaac throws his hands up. "Seriously. Are we gonna tell him *everything*?"

Rose leans forward, sounding annoyed. "Yes, Isaac. We're going to tell him *everything*. Just like he's telling us *everything*."

Her words form a pit in my stomach. A stab of guilt. Because I am not, in fact, telling them everything. I'm withholding some very important information about Nathan Briggs. Because it's too risky for me.

The standoff here feels about like that night at my new place, when Meredith's face was inches from mine and we were moving to the next level, and one of us turned away.

But with the group, it's not them holding back, because Isaac puts his elbows on his knees and begins speaking slowly, his tone somber.

"Lucas was Amersa's lead developer. He basically co-founded the company. Like he was one of the first twenty employees, but without him, the company would have flamed out. Larsson is a lunatic. Lucas made it happen.

"Lucas," Isaac continues, "*was* the company. He kept the train on the rails. And steered them away from so many bad decisions.

"And he had tinnitus. He saw the numbers. He was one of us."

"He and Isaac," June says, "were the first two members of the group. It was the two of them for years. But there were five of us when he was killed."

"So why do you think Briggs killed him?" I ask again. "Or accidentally murdered him?"

Isaac stands and begins pacing behind the folding metal chairs. "Lucas was getting really bored at Amersa. And he was tired of Larsson and his maniacal focus. He also was working on a side project?"

"Doing what?"

Isaac exhales heavily as if he would rather not say. When he turns to pace the other way, June catches his eye, and he continues.

"It was an AI model we were working on together called ELEE."

I'm about to ask what that means when Isaac explains.

"ELEE stands for Extinction Level Event Engine. It's a massive AI model that we fed a huge amount of historical and real-time data. The goal was to predict future extinction events for humanity."

"That's why Amersa killed him?"

Isaac shifts his head side-to-side. "Yes and no. Lucas was working on ELEE part-time. Larsson agreed to let him because he was so burned out and he needed an outlet. But ELEE was consuming massive amounts of company resources. Larsson was not thrilled. And then we started getting some interesting results."

"Such as?"

"Predictions about how emerging technologies might impact human civilization. How fragile modern society is. How vulnerable. But the predictions weren't the problem."

"What was?"

"Lucas wanted to go part-time. He knew if he quit, Larsson would freak out. The guy is more paranoid than you can imagine." Isaac turns to face the group. "That's why he's got so much security—he's terrified one of his employees is going to rip off the company's IP."

"That's what he thought Lucas was doing?"

"That's what he *suspected* Lucas of. And that's why he sent Briggs to his house. It was sort of an ambush. They knew he had a secret and that he was working with a group of people, but they didn't know what it was about. Briggs went over there to find out."

Isaac's mood turns dark. He paces faster.

"I saw it all."

That surprises me. "You were there?"

"Not physically. But I had access to his NVR."

"NVR?"

"Network video recorder. It connects to IP-based security cameras and stores footage. That footage shows Briggs breaking into his home that night. I don't know what happened inside, but the next morning, Lucas was found dead of an *apparent* overdose of sleeping pills."

Isaac pauses, chest heaving as he stares out at the empty warehouse. "I think Briggs pressed him, and Lucas wouldn't give up the group."

June and Rose are staring at the floor. The speaker on the camera is silent.

"You could give the footage to the police," I tell Isaac, trying to make my voice neutral.

He nods slowly. "Yes. I *could* have. If I had thought of it. I was in shock. And by the time I did think of it, the NVR had been wiped."

For a while, no one says anything. For me, some of the dots connect then.

"So," I offer, "Lucas is why you were so cautious to bring me in."

"It's one of the reasons," Isaac mutters.

"What does that mean?"

"When you emailed the numbers site, it was forwarded to me," Isaac replies. "By whom, I still don't know—and I've tried to figure it out. I've tried *very hard*."

He glances over at me. "What wasn't very hard was figuring out who you were. And let's just say I was concerned by what I saw."

I stare back at him, waiting.

"You knew Briggs, didn't you?"

"I did."

"Served with him in the Marines."

"I did, yes."

"When's the last time you saw him?"

I half-expect Rose or June to admonish Isaac for this aggressive question, but the warehouse is silent. They all want to know.

June's words flash in my mind: *circle of trust*.

This would be the time to tell them everything. That I woke up next to him—dead—in downtown.

I have two choices. I can either lie or I can put my trust in them.

The thing is, I know these people are capable of covertly recording someone. We're doing it to Anders Larsson right now.

It wouldn't be that hard. Harold isn't even here. He could be recording this entire session.

If I tell them what happened, I would be admitting enough evidence to convict myself of murder. In the wrong hands, I'd lose my daughter forever.

So I lie, but I only half-lie.

"Last memory of him? During the surge in Afghanistan. He was punching me in the face."

"You weren't friends?" Rose asks.

"Far from it."

"One of our fears," June says, "was that you were working with him. That they did find out about the group and that you were his replacement."

"Replacement... as in trying to infiltrate the group?"

The silence is all the acknowledgment I need.

Isaac speaks next. "As I said, we never found out what Lucas told him. Or what he got off his computer. But two days before Briggs was found dead, he followed me home from Amersa."

"You think he knew you had worked with Lucas?"

"Lucas and I worked very closely together at Amersa. And on ELEE," Isaac says. "What I don't know is if it was just Briggs investigating Lucas's colleagues or if he knew we were in this group together. One thing's certain: I never saw Briggs after that. He was killed two days later. The following day, you contacted the site."

"You see why we were cautious," June says.

"I do. And I don't blame you."

"Which brings us," Isaac says, stepping to the speaker and pressing the button, "to our current problem."

"Yes," the Amersa security chief says over the speaker. "The Carter situation. We know he was hiding something. We just don't know what it was. What we do know is that he was accessing a whole lot of company resources. And probably had help. Someone in IT. If so, we have an ongoing breach. With Carter gone, the operative could be trying to recruit another asset."

"It's a lot of speculation, Terry."

"It is, sir. But it's speculation that fits the facts—and if true, it would be disastrous for us. The implication here is that we have one or more agents actively involved in either stealing Amersa's IP or sabotaging the release. Or both."

Larsson's voice is as cold as a well-used ice pick. "So what do we do?"

"Briggs was in the process of compiling dossiers on anyone with means and opportunity to assist Carter. Someone obviously killed him. Raleigh PD thinks it's drug-related. But they would. They have experience bias."

"Meaning?"

"They see a lot more murders connected to narcotics than industrial espionage. So it's not even on their radar. For us, this is the first of our employees who has been murdered—and he was investigating a group that may have already infiltrated Amersa, and he killed one of their members. We have more information than the Raleigh Police Department—and the correct frame from which to see the crime."

"So what do you think actually happened to Briggs?"

"I think this group knew he was closing in. Maybe they knew Carter had told him something that was problematic for them. I think they somehow lured him to that site downtown. Maybe they used prostitutes—as mentioned, he has an affinity—or maybe they impersonated someone he knew and trusted. Either way, they got him there and neutralized him. It's a practical countermeasure, and it's a message to us."

There's a pause, and then Larsson says, "Let's say you're right—and I do like your approach here, Terry. Let's err on the side of caution. *Way* on that side. What do we do now?"

"Sir, now we assume the worst. That Amersa has been breached by a highly sophisticated group. They turned one of our key employees. They have—and may still be receiving—valuable confidential information. And they are willing to kill to complete their objectives."

"Assumptions don't help me, Terry. Actions do."

"Sir, I think we should divert more resources to the search for this incursion group. And, I'm sorry to say this, but I feel we should delay the roll-out—"

"No. Not a chance, Terry. Don't even say that again. You have a job to do. So do I. We are on the verge of the most significant product launch in modern history. Maybe ever. The world will think it's just another big tech breakthrough, but Tuesday will be the day the world changes forever. A pebble dropped in a sea that will be a tsunami that redraws the shoreline of humanity. You seal this breach—by whatever means necessary, but we are not delaying the release of Labyrinth."

"Sir—"

"You heard me. I don't care what it takes. Find out who hired Lucas or who he was working for and do to them what they did to Briggs. But more discreetly."

46

Isaac taps the speaker, stopping the recording.

"That's it. For now."

He eyes me.

And I tell them what happened in my Labyrinth session, about the trucker and the motel and the cotton field and Labyrinth Syndrome and the neurological researcher named May.

When I've finished, Isaac, who is sitting on a folding metal chair, face buried in his hands, mutters, "They know. They have to."

He looks up and motions to June. "*May* even have found us already. If you will. And yes, for the avoidance of doubt and anyone immune to subtext, I'm referring to the fact that Labyrinth has cloned you in Alan's simulation, June. And they just sent you a job offer. Huge coincidence."

"You don't think I should take the job?" June asks.

Isaac throws his hands up. "I have no idea. For all we know, the job is simply a way to bring you in so they have an excuse to watch you."

"If that's true," June says, "wouldn't it also look suspicious if I refused? The salary is significantly higher than what I make at Duke—and the timing is right. Both of the studies I was a PI on wrapped up this summer, and I'm not teaching this semester or next. In fact, the Amersa offer even gives me the option of teaching up to two courses per academic year and conducting limited studies—subject to company approval."

"Right. What's not to like," Isaac mutters. "More money. Total freedom. I agree: if you decline, it might even confirm their suspicions that you're in the group."

From the camera speaker, Harold says, "If Amersa knows about the group, is this really how they would tell us?"

"Maybe they're testing us," Isaac says. "Maybe they want to see what we do. See if we scramble or react. They're kicking a beehive, via Alan's Labyrinth experiences."

"That would imply," June counters, "that we should not react."

"What it implies," Isaac shoots back, "is that we need to figure out exactly what Amersa knows."

June cocks her head. "What if they don't actually know anything? What if their Labyrinth is just reflecting what Alan is already thinking or has said?"

Isaac scowls. "That's even worse. If it can read his mind, then we're screwed. Amersa—or at least this AI Labyrinth program—knows all about us."

June turns to me. "Alan, I'm pretty sure I know the answer to this, but have you mentioned anything about this group in your sessions with the Linus AI?"

"No."

"Let's consider what else we've learned," June says. "What does Labyrinth Syndrome represent? Why is it such a big part of the experience? And these Labyrinth storms—what do they represent? Alan, do you have memories of significant storms as a child? A tornado or hurricane?"

"No."

"Were any close friends or family ever harmed by a storm?"

I shake my head.

"It's standard game play," Isaac mumbles. "The storms and syndrome are part of the game progression. The storms will grow stronger as the hero journeys closer to the goal, and the syndrome is like a plague upon the land that he must resolve. It's not enough for the player to save himself. He needs greater stakes. He needs to protect people who can't fight for themselves."

We discuss the Labyrinth a bit longer, but it's soon clear we're going around in circles. We need more information, and the hope is that the next Labyrinth session will bring it.

"Given that they might know about the group," Isaac says,

"I think it's prudent that we start meeting immediately after Alan's Labyrinth sessions."

I agree with his idea, but June looks distressed by it. "Meeting on short notice is risky for me."

Isaac shakes his head. "No. If Alan inadvertently reveals our identities during a session, we need to know."

June opens her mouth to respond, but I beat her to it. "What about this: if the Labyrinth session has another connection to the group, I'll send a message on Signal and we can get together—even if June can't make it. And we'll plan to meet the day after my sessions, just in case I miss one of the clues."

"That works," Isaac mumbles, still seeming frustrated.

Over the camera speaker, Harold says, "May I make another suggestion?" When no one says anything, he continues. "Assuming our good man Isaac has the time to actively monitor the recordings—"

"I do," Isaac says.

"Ah, very good," Harold continues. "In that case, I suggest we also conduct an emergency meeting in the event that the audio feed reveals pertinent information."

We all agree, and the meeting feels like it's about to break up, but one thing is bothering me from the recording.

"Larsson said the world was going to change on Tuesday. What did he mean?"

Isaac shrugs. "It's this product launch."

"Does he talk about it?"

"Yeah. A lot. Larsson has always seen Amersa and Labyrinth as fundamental technology for humanity. But he's had a bunch of setbacks."

"What kind of setbacks?"

"Financial at times, but mostly, his problem is focus. He's bounced around to medical applications—like what you're doing—and entertainment and work collaboration. He's got the solution, but he doesn't know how to make money. Well, he does now, but he's short on cash, apparently."

"Here," Isaac says, getting out his laptop, "he called one of his investors about it."

Once more, Larsson's voice echoes in the warehouse.

"We'll make the money back."

"You assume—" This is a new voice, a woman, sounding confrontational and far less conciliatory than the security chief.

"I don't assume, Kira, *I know. I know it.*"

"Anders, I love you. I love your confidence. That confidence is why I led your seed round, but I also think that confidence might be working against you now."

"What does that mean?"

"It means you've been selling the sizzle so long you don't even realize there's no steak."

"Yeah, well, meaty metaphors aside, there's a very big planet-sized T-bone here, so the question is: are you going to help me or are you stepping aside? I don't want to waste my time here."

"What exactly are you asking for?"

Larsson rattles off what is—to me—an unimaginable sum of money.

"We'll do it as a convertible note," Larsson says. "It converts on the same terms as the next round."

The woman laughs out loud. "You've got some guts, I'll give you that."

"And I'll agree with that. Do we have a deal?"

"Not at all. First, Anders, your back is against the wall. If you don't pull off this launch, your valuation will plummet. If you do, it will skyrocket. As for this convertible bridge loan that will convert at the valuation of the next round, you're half right. I've been doing this for a long time. Longer than you've been working on that product—which should have come to market years ago, but we'll put that aside. If you want money, maybe we'll do it, but while you have it, we'll collect twelve points interest—paid monthly—and the conversion valuation is the lower of the last round or the next. Just in case you have a down round."

There's a long pause.

The woman says, "You still there, Anders?"

"Barely."

"You want some advice?"

"Do I have a choice?"

"Here's my advice: slow your burn rate. Stretch your cash a little further. Give yourself a little more runway so you can deal with the unexpected. You don't have to launch so hard. Why try to boil the ocean on day one?"

"We're not boiling the ocean."

"But you are trying to facilitate consumer adoption of a new, disruptive technology. And that may take time. Time is another word for money."

"I'm well aware of that. But disruptive technology adoption doesn't take as long as it used to."

"Oh really?"

"Really, Kira. Seven years. That's how long it took the World Wide Web to reach one hundred million users."

"Okay," she says, drawing the word out.

"Four and a half years. That's how long it took Facebook to reach one hundred million users. YouTube did it in five months less. Instagram? Two years and six months to a hundred million users. TikTok: nine months and they had a hundred million people scrolling. ChatGPT? Two months after release—a hundred million users."

"There's one thing you're missing, Anders."

"What's that?"

"Those are apps people download on their phones. They already had the phones. What you're talking about is a physical roll-out. You're talking about building infrastructure, much like the World Wide Web—your first example, if you'll remember, that one took seven years."

"We have to move fast, Kira. We move fast or we die."

"No. You're so wrong. You need to test what you have. A few ideal markets. Get feedback, iterate, and then scale. That's when you need the cash—when you're ready to scale. You're not ready, Anders."

"Would you agree that we're the first mover in this new category? That no one has done anything like it?"

"Sure, Anders."

"Do you know what happens to first movers?"

"I think you know the answer, and I'm going to hear it now."

"They get trampled—by the fast followers. Google didn't have the first search engine. They launched years after—and in a crowded market. Microsoft didn't have the first disk operating system. Facebook: not the first social media network. Remember Tom from Myspace?"

"I don't actually."

"Exactly. No one does. But I bet you're aware of a company called Tesla. Not the first EV. Apple's iPhone? Not the first smartphone."

"Your point?"

"None of these trillion-dollar companies were first movers. They were, what I believe you in the venture capital community call *fast followers*."

"Thanks for the vocabulary review."

"These fast followers had something very valuable: they saw someone doing something important, a company that had not cornered the market and they went out and grabbed it. They learned from the first movers, and those were some valuable lessons, put on display for everyone. Your limited roll-out is nothing more than a global open house for our competitors. Come on in and learn from us, and then cut our throat. We are sitting on the future. If we don't seize it, we are done. Someone else will."

"Anders, you want to go for broke, and we want proof that consumers actually want this. That's the ultimate black box: consumer adoption."

"Kira? Listen to me."

There's a pause on the line.

"One of two things is going to happen now. You're going to back me. Or I'm going to get on a plane to the Middle East, Singapore, China, and Japan. I'm going to collect the checks. They're going to dilute you, and Labyrinth is going to explode across the world and the FOMO and your brain fart here might just get you demoted to associate partner or partner emeritus or whatever they do there.

"We have the money to launch. We're already going to do that. What we need is cash to scale. This was a courtesy, Kira. Do whatever you want. But the world changes on Tuesday. You can be part of it or not."

47

The numbers meeting and what I heard makes my mind burn, but the thing is, I don't know what to do about it or how to even process it.

At home, I find Meredith and Riley at the dining room table, building the Hogwarts Castle. Meredith is stacking a piece of the tower when she sees me. She locks it into place, and slowly, the smile fades from her face.

This is an opportunity where we could talk. Sort things out. Get back to normal.

She gets up and begins walking toward the door.

I smile at her.

And she passes me.

On Saturday afternoon, I take Riley to one of her classmates' birthday parties at a local trampoline park. It's a terrifying experience. I spend nearly two hours watching her like a hawk and yelling to make sure she doesn't break her neck or get trampled (if you will) by one of the older kids... all while making small talk with the other parents.

Thankfully, Riley is unharmed by the time the trampoline portion of the afternoon comes to a close. The party retreats to a room off to the side for cake and ice cream.

Which is great. Hype the kids up, pump 'em full of sugar, and send 'em home.

On the way back to our townhouse, my daughter is about as wired as I've ever seen her.

The townhome is far more spacious than our former train car residence, but in my mind, I'm imagining her like a seven-year-old pinball bouncing around the rest of the afternoon until she crashes.

She needs an outlet for that energy. She also needs to learn to ride a bike.

As such, I pull her bike up to the parking lot of the community center, and we get to work.

Five minutes in, she insists I take the training wheels off, because they are, in her words, *so annoying, Dad*.

Continuing the reckless theme of the day, I oblige (and I lower the seat so her feet can touch the ground more easily, which will probably save one or two scuffed knees).

They say dating again is like riding a bike. I'm not seeing it. Or maybe I just need training wheels. And a lowered seat. A lot lower. Low enough to balance on one leg.

Upon our return from a middling bike riding lesson, Riley drags her feet and rambles on to no one in particular about the futility of learning to ride a bike and how she will never master it.

As we walk along the sidewalk, she rambles, posing semi-rhetorical questions about why she should even learn to ride a bike in the first place, given that I can take her places. Also, there's Uber. And a boy named Charles in her class says that all cars will drive themselves pretty soon anyway. And some do already. Besides that, why don't we have a car that can drive itself? And even without cars, you can now use an electric scooter if you're in downtown (they're on every corner, she tells me). Also, why don't we live in downtown? It's better, or so she's heard.

I listen and grunt occasionally and give semi-evasive answers. It reminds me of an old movie starring Gregory Peck, called *To Kill a Mockingbird*, with scenes where his daughter, Scout, pelted him with questions when she was frustrated.

Like that fictional southern lawyer in a white suit, I draw out the word, *Yeees*, when she corners me, and, generally, I let her go on, and I listen, knowing that sometimes when life is hard that talking is healthy and that sometimes there are no answers—or none you can understand at the time.

That makes me think about that interview at Amersa, with that very intelligent woman, and my frustration then, and the answers that were hard to handle.

When we turn the corner onto our street, I spot a white Dodge Charger parked right outside our house. It's spotless, with tinted windows and what looks like a spotlight next to the mirror. The sight of it sends a chill down my spine. It's an unmarked police car, the kind a detective might drive.

As we reach it, the driver and passenger doors open, and a man and a woman step out, both wearing white button-up shirts, sport coats, and sunglasses.

"Alan Norris?" the man says.

He looks about my age, with a clean-shaven head and a slight beer gut.

"Yeah."

"I'm Detective Tate. This is my partner, Detective Ramirez. Raleigh PD. Would you mind if we ask you a few questions?"

"Uh, sure. I just need to get my neighbor to watch my daughter."

Riley peers up at me. The frustration from the bike riding session has given way to worry. With one arm, I pull her shoulder into my side and smile. "Don't worry, it's about work."

Because a teacher—an innocent teacher—would assume that. They would assume these detectives are here regarding an issue related to a kid I teach.

At Meredith's door, I knock, and I don't know if it's the rift between us or the two detectives waiting on me, but the knot in my stomach has expanded to my throat, which I have to clear to even get words out.

"You mind watching Riley for a few minutes?"

She squints at me. I can tell she wants to ask more, but she reads my face like the first-grade level books Riley has been practicing on.

She doesn't say a word, only looks down at my daughter, smiles, and ushers her in.

Back at my house, I raise the garage door. Inside, I lean Riley's bike against a wall, and bring the detectives in through the kitchen.

I offer them water and both accept, and we sit at the dining table, the half-built 3D puzzle between us.

They start searching for the pieces of evidence they need.

Ramirez speaks first. "Mr. Norris, would you mind if we record this?"

"Sure—"

She presses me. "Sure you mind? Or sure we can record?"

"Record away. And call me Alan."

She carefully places a handheld recorder in the middle of the puzzle pieces and activates it.

"Interview: Saturday, October 11th, at…" She glances at her phone. "3:42 PM, at the residence of Mr. Alan Norris. Detectives Tate and Ramirez present."

She looks up at me. "Mr. Norris, you're not under arrest, and you are under no legal obligation to talk to us. Would you please confirm for the recording that you've agreed to be recorded this afternoon?"

"I'm Alan Norris, and I've agreed."

"Mr. Norris," Ramirez says, "would you mind telling us your whereabouts on the night of August 25th from around the time of 8 PM to 3 AM?"

I've thought about this moment a lot—this interview. I figured it would happen, eventually.

Navigating a police investigation—as a suspect with something to hide—is its own kind of Labyrinth.

What I'm betting right now is that they're opening with a question they know the answer to. If I lie—and they catch me in that lie—it will change the entire course of what's about to occur. Things will go badly for me.

At the same time, I can't tell the truth. That, I think, would result in Tate or Ramirez saying some form of "Mr. Norris, let's continue this conversation at the station."

As such, I'm going to give them the story I've concocted for this exact moment. It's a story that assumes they have my car on camera going into and out of downtown. To be on the safe side, I'm also going to assume they know I was in the building where Briggs was killed. Maybe they know from the tracks I left or possibly a fingerprint I missed.

The more problematic thing is my DNA potentially being on Briggs's body. For that reason, I've considered admitting that I was there with Briggs that night and that we had an altercation. But I think saying that would seal my fate pretty quickly.

Like any innocent man—and busy father and teacher—I also need to make it look like I can't recall what I was doing on any given Sunday several months ago (I mean, who could remember off the top of their head?).

I draw my phone from my pocket, open my calendar, and go back to August, and then pause, as if thinking.

"That was the night before the first day of school. For me and my daughter. I'm a teacher. We were at home."

"The whole night?" Tate asks.

He's good. Completely casual. But I feel my nerves edging up. My palms getting clammy. I expect the ringing to start, the stress to set it off. But it's dead quiet in the dining room as I begin telling the lie I hope will keep me out of jail.

"No. Actually, now that I think about, I did go out that night to meet up with an old Marine buddy."

"Can you give us a name?" Ramirez asks.

"Nathan Briggs."

As I say the name, neither moved a muscle.

"What did he want to meet about?" Ramirez asks.

"He was having some problems. Wanted to talk."

"What kind of problems?" Tate asks.

"I guess you'd call it a mental health crisis."

"So where did you meet up?" Tate asks nonchalantly.

"Downtown. It was a building that was under construction. And we didn't actually meet up."

"What do you mean?" Tate asks.

"Nathan never showed. I went there and waited, but he sent a message and said to forget it."

"Could you give us the building's address?" Ramirez asks.

"I don't have it."

Tate adopts a puzzled look. "What do you mean?"

"Nathan sent me the address, but it was on an app that deletes the messages after a set period."

Ramirez raises an eyebrow. "That's kind of odd. The secrecy."

"Yeah, look, it was at his request. As I said, he was having some problems. Paranoia was one of them."

Tate pulls out a small notepad from the inside of his jacket pocket and clicks a pen. "Do you recall what time you left, Mr. Norris?"

"I don't."

Next, they ask me about my contact with Briggs prior to that night, and if I was—or am—in contact with anyone else who was close to Briggs. Those questions I can actually answer honestly, and that relaxes me a bit.

Tate stows the notepad in his jacket pocket and glances over at Ramirez, who nods and collects the recorder and tells me that's all the questions they have for now.

They're both rising from the table, but I raise my hands, stopping them. "Would it be okay if I ask a question?"

"Of course," Ramirez replies, lowering back into the chair. She reactivates the recorder.

"What's all this about?"

"What we can tell you," Tate says, "is what's been released to the public: Nathan Briggs was found dead on the night in question."

As Meredith noted, I am a terrible liar, but the moment calls for it, and I don't feel like I have any choice. Trying to sound equally shocked and curious, I ask how Briggs died.

"We're investigating the matter as a homicide," Ramirez says. Both detectives study me intently, and I try to play the part of shocked friend.

When I don't say anything, Ramirez asks if I have any other questions, and I simply shake my head.

As they walk out, they thank me for my time and provide their cards and request that I call if I remember any information related to Briggs or hear from anyone who might.

When they're gone, I walk down to Meredith's house. She and Riley are sitting on the back porch, playing the game Operation. Peering through the sliding glass door, I'm reminded of that moment I saw them at her house, a month ago, inside, playing the game. They look just as happy; completely unaware of the chaos happening in my life. I want to keep it that way. As long as I can.

Sliding the door open draws their attention.

"What was that?" Riley asks.

"It was nothing, kiddo. Just people asking about a thing at work."

She stares at me for a long moment, then cuts her eyes to Meredith, who is a statue looking back at her.

"Excuse me," Riley mumbles as she rises and heads off to the half-bathroom.

Meredith, who is still holding the Operation tweezers, which are tethered to a thin cord snaking out of the game board, points them at me. "Same question: what was that? Keep in mind, I work where you do."

I nod, knowing my second interrogation of the afternoon is about to start. "Same answer: nothing. For now."

"You know, Alan, believe it or not, I know what a police cruiser looks like. And how detectives dress."

"I know you do."

"Was it about the situation with your neighbors?"

I could lie now. It would be the easy way out. It would be the same as I did with those detectives: a believable lie.

But I don't. And that's an interesting thing: I'm willing to spin a tale to a couple of homicide detectives, but I won't lie to Meredith. Sure, I've withheld information, but I haven't lied.

"It's not the neighbor drama. It's..."

"What Alan?"

The door to the half-bathroom opens, and Riley exits.

"It's related to my tinnitus."

Meredith bunches her eyebrows, rightly confused about how the ringing in my ears could be a criminal matter.

"That makes no sense."

"On that, we agree."

"Dad?"

I turn to Riley.

"I want to try again."

"The bike?"

She looks at me like I'm an alien. "Of course."

I turn to Meredith. "Want to participate in a bike riding lesson? We could probably use an expert in physical education."

She gives me a tight smile. "Another time. I've got plans tonight."

As I push Riley's bike back up to the community center, I'm wondering if Meredith really does have plans tonight. And if those plans are a date. They probably are.

It makes sense.

It's the best thing for her. To meet a normal guy with a normal life and no baggage.

No ringing. No dead bodies. No police investigations. No covert numbers group meetings.

The second riding session goes about like the first, with me offering to put the training wheels back on and Riley refusing, noting—with annoyance—that training wheels are for babies.

On the way home, the sun is setting as Riley mutters, "I'll never learn to ride."

"You will, kiddo. You have to practice. It'll get easier, and eventually, you'll be able to ride that bike without even thinking about it."

"Easy for you to say."

"Trust me, Riley. I know what I'm talking about. A few years before you were born, I had to learn to walk all over again."

48

As foretold in the covert recordings from Anders Larsson's office, a major release does happen Tuesday.

It is impossible to miss.

The promotional campaign must have cost a fortune.

Everyone is talking about it on social media. Influencers—both paid and unpaid—share Hollywood-quality videos with their own hot takes.

Traditional media covers the social media buzz, and thus, on my mobile phone, Amersa's release is nearly all I see. It's a supernova event, blotting out all the other shiny things in the world for a short while.

It isn't just an online phenomenon—a viral video seen in the morning and forgotten by the afternoon. The offering rolls out in the real world, too, though in limited locations.

Amersa—and their influencers and some journalists—call it the iPhone moment of this generation. A release on par with the personal computer. Or the internet itself.

The hyperbole escalates from there, everyone trying to top each other. There are mentions of the Gutenberg press. The steam engine. The telephone.

I roll my eyes when I read comparisons to electricity and the wheel.

Life will never be the same, they say. And you can be among the first to experience the future.

Their offering is called Labyrinth. And from the videos, it looks like the same Labyrinth I've been making my way through at their offices.

They don't call it a video game.

Or a virtual reality experience. Or augmented reality.

They simply call it Labyrinth, perhaps hoping it will define itself.

And instead of letting the media or reviewers show it to the world, Amersa has produced its own video of Labyrinth experiences. They're like use cases—examples of how people will use Labyrinth.

The first video features a female influencer who's maybe college age. She's fit and bubbly, and her eyes flash at the phone she's holding as she and an equally fit guy are walking into a movie theater.

At the box office window, her date leans toward the glass and orders the tickets. The influencer must not be thrilled with the pick because some of her bubbliness fades.

Inside the theater, they recline in the seats and eat candy and share a soda. The movie is a post-apocalyptic alien invasion.

He's into it.

She is not.

Monsters are galloping through Paris, France, and the fleeing humans are climbing the Eiffel Tower when the influencer's bored gaze drifts over to the camera.

White letters scrawl across the screen:

Can this date night be saved?

She presses a button and her recliner eases forward until her feet touch the floor, and she leans into her date's field of view. He squints, annoyed as he tilts away from her. She points at the exit and whispers, and more white words scroll by:

Be right back.

Walking out, she smiles at the camera, as if she knows a secret.

Outside the theater, she walks down the hall to the door to another theater, this one guarded by two guys in suits who look like bouncers at a club.

The poster by the door isn't for a movie. It's for Labyrinth.

The influencer opens an app on her phone, which is apparently for Labyrinth, and holds it out, and one of the guys scans a QR code and waves her inside, where there are about a dozen black Labyrinth suits of varying sizes (just like the one I use at Amersa's offices).

The video zooms forward with the influencer getting settled in, and the next image is of her in Paris, strolling along the Seine.

She stops in the Shakespeare and Company bookstore and browses the aisles.

She tours the Notre-Dame Cathedral next, and after, she takes a cruise along the Seine and visits the Louvre. Her final stop is the Trocadéro Gardens, where she lies on a blanket, watching the sun set beyond the Eiffel Tower as it lights up beautifully.

The last shot of her Labyrinth experience shows the influencer leaning back, looking utterly content with her Parisian mini-vacation.

Back at her seat beside her date, he's finished the popcorn and is loudly draining the last of a bucket-sized fountain drink.

On the screen, the Eiffel Tower lies in a crumpled heap, surrounded by mounds of dead aliens and cheering humans. The view changes to the UK parliament building—also badly damaged—and the remnants of Big Ben in the street. Crowds of triumphant humans are cheering there, too. The influencer turns the phone to her face, raises her eyebrows, and four hashtags flash up: *#ReinventDateNight #Labyrinth #VR #AI*

There's a link to download the Labyrinth app to schedule your first session and a list of the theater chains working to convert some screens to Labyrinth rooms.

It's smart. The theater chains have huge email lists—and the financial motivation to reinvent themselves (or at least diversify their revenue streams).

The next video begins with a well-dressed man about my age, sitting in an airport lounge, staring at a laptop on a communal table, looking bored.

His gaze moves to the windows and the planes taxiing across the tarmac. He seems to decide something then. He closes his laptop and stuffs it in his backpack and exits the lounge, pulling his wheeled carry-on as he strolls down the concourse. He stops at a storefront under construction, the glass panels covered in brown paper.

Like the theater that was converted to a Labyrinth room, there are two linebacker-sized guards here as well. One scans him in, and the traveler sheds his backpack and stows his carry-on. A smiling woman in a Labyrinth-branded polo takes his measurements as if she's fitting him for a tailored suit.

They bring out several of the black Labyrinth garments, and she says, "You want it tight, but not too tight. The suit itself will contract to fit your body."

When he's suited up, the view switches to a conference room in an office, and the guy isn't wearing the suit; he's in a V-neck sweater over a button-up collared shirt with business casual slacks.

There are five others around the table. For a moment, they talk in front of a large screen on the wall. The man from the lounge shakes his head and holds his phone up and gets the others' attention, and after a few taps on the device, the six of them are sitting outside, around a rustic table with a view of a downtown cityscape in the distance. It reminds me of the outdoor seating at a craft brewery.

The team is dressed more casually now. Gone are the V-neck sweaters and button-up shirts. They're in shorts and t-shirts.

A semi-translucent screen floats at the end of the table, showing a skyscraper under construction. The image zooms in, and it shows the floor plan for a condo with three bedrooms and an outdoor terrace.

The team gestures and talks, and then the view switches to a drone bearing the Labyrinth logo flying around the building under construction in a controlled pattern, as if it's mapping it. When it has gone around the entire outside, it flies into the building and begins scanning it.

Back at the outdoor meeting, the air traveler once again uses his phone, and the group is transported from the outdoor terrace to the interior of one of the condos under construction. The semi-translucent screen follows them, and notes from their meeting scroll by for them to see and edit, the AI assistant capturing both text and blueprint updates.

The video goes at double and then triple speed as the team finishes their virtual site tour, and then they say their goodbyes.

Back in the airport, the man takes off the Labyrinth suit and exits the nondescript space, back onto the concourse. He watches as travelers glide by on a people mover. Shaking his head, he reaches into his interior jacket pocket, takes out his boarding pass, rips it up, and tosses it in the nearest trash can.

The link to download the Labyrinth app once again appears, accompanied by various hashtags: *#ReinventWork #Labyrinth #VRMeeting #VR #AI*

The scene is a little cheesy but it gets the job done in conveying how Labyrinth could transform work and enable instant virtual meetings—and could even be more efficient for work like construction projects.

The next video is of a mom dropping her kids off at soccer practice and driving to the mall afterward. But she doesn't go in.

She exits her minivan and marches over to four cargo containers in the parking lot, stacked two wide and two tall.

There's a table in front of them, and someone greets her, scans the app on her phone, and ushers her inside.

The container walls have been folded in to form a massive cube with pads on five sides. I recognize it. It's a copy of the room at Amersa where I use Labyrinth.

Two handlers fit the mom with a suit and harness, and she looks at the camera, salutes, and says, in a sultry voice, "See you after soccer practice."

Inside Labyrinth, she's not wearing yoga pants. She's in a slim-fitting white dress with a glittering, plastic tiara on her head and a sash running from her shoulder to her hip that says BRIDE TO BE. Under it, in magic marker, someone has written: LAST NIGHT OF FREEDOM.

She's flanked by two women on one side and three on the other.

They're walking into a dark club with loud music that pulses with the light.

She looks back and smiles at the camera.

Hashtags flow across the feed, rising and disappearing: *#DoOver   #LastNightOfFreedom   #ReliveItInLabyrinth #Labyrinth*

The next video is of a twenty-something guy in gym shorts and a t-shirt, slumped on a couch, feet up on a coffee table that's populated by a pizza box (half closed) and a bag of Doritos (fully open). Crumpled cans of energy drinks take up the rest of the space.

The guy is playing a video game, and when it pauses to load, he sets the wireless controller aside, takes out his phone, and starts scrolling through dating apps, swiping, seeming bored, and finally tossing the phone aside when the game loads.

It fast-forwards through him playing the game, shifting on the couch. The bag of chips slowly dwindles until a message on his phone draws his attention, and he rises from the sofa, brushes his teeth, and runs a comb through his hair.

The next scene is of the guy walking through a crowded parking lot where groups of men and women about his age—just out of college or still in college—are crowded around SUVs and tents, drinking beer and playing cornhole and in some cases watching TVs they've set up.

It's a tailgate for a sports event.

The guy hangs out with his friends for a while, then ventures over to an unmarked box van with a massive black tent extending from the end. It's roughly the size of the space the four cargo containers created at the mall, and just like that place, inside is a rough replica of a Labyrinth room.

Once suited up, the guy is placed in a virtual reality restaurant, a swanky one where women are seated at banquette tables alone. Men are queued up, and a host begins laying out the rules. It's a speed dating event. In Labyrinth.

It fast-forwards through him, rotating around the room, talking briefly with each bachelorette. Then the scene slows, and he and a woman are smiling and laughing and there's a twinkle in his eye.

When the event is over and he's getting out of the rig, the smile is gone, but there's a purposeful look on his face.

Outside the box truck, he opens the Labyrinth app on his phone and schedules his next session. He clicks a profile picture of the woman from speed dating and sends her an invite to the Labyrinth appointment.

As he drives home, he checks his phone at every light to see if the woman has accepted the invitation. The city he lives in reminds me of Raleigh—it's about that size and feels like it, but it's not Raleigh. I don't recognize any of the streets, and the view never pans to the landscape beyond the buildings. It's maybe Austin, or Madison, or Boulder, or Richmond, or Greenville—and perhaps that's the point, that this could be any mid-sized city in America.

The video fades to black, and then the same guy appears on screen, but this time, he's driving through a parking deck and walking toward a convention center with signs for a medical conference, but he doesn't go into the building. He again slips into a pop-up Labyrinth room outside. Inside Labyrinth, the girl with sparkling eyes is waiting for him. This time, the date is in London. Hand in hand, they walk along the South Bank of the River Thames, starting at Tower Bridge. They pass City Hall, HMS *Belfast*, London Bridge, and then The Shard, towering over the city, glittering in the sunset.

It flashes forward and they're having dinner at a restaurant with a breathtaking view of the city at night—and though they're not eating (or drinking)—both look absolutely content. Above the bar is a sign with the restaurant's logo—something with a red seal that I can't quite make out from this angle.

The guy exits the Labyrinth experience, and the whole time he's driving home, a slight smile never leaves his face.

The screen splits, and it's the woman coming out of another Labyrinth room, this one in a nondescript storefront in a bustling city. Cabs, cars, and buses pass by, and the writing on the signs is foreign, a European language, but I can't place it.

At the entrance to a subway, she descends the staircase and boards the next train. Inside, she takes out her phone and searches for and finds an app that teaches Advanced English.

On the guy's side of the split screen, he's sitting at a desk with four monitors—two turned sideways. He has several web browsers open, and what appears to be computer code is displayed on his main screen. He's typing quickly, but on one of the secondary screens, there's a chat window open, and it's the woman's face, and a long string of messages. It's morning where he is, the sun blazing through the windows in the room, bathing his workstation and the guest bed behind him in light.

On the woman's side of the screen, she's dressed in a leotard and is practicing ballet with perhaps two dozen others. Through the large floor-to-ceiling windows, the sun is setting.

Soon, the ballet practice ends, and she goes to a locker and gets out her phone and smiles when she sees the messages from him. Quickly, she taps out a response in Cyrillic letters. On his screen, the message appears translated to English, and he grins, chuckles, and sends a quick reply.

At the metro bench, she opens the English learning course on her phone.

In the guest bedroom, the guy puts his computer to sleep, stretches out on the bed, puts in his earbuds, and launches an app on his phone titled "Bulgarian for Beginners."

The screen switches to him driving again, apparently through a college campus. He parks outside an arena where, like the mall the soccer mom visited, there are four stacked cargo containers and a sign for Labyrinth.

When he's suited up, I'm surprised to see that the woman isn't waiting for him. Instead, he's standing in a ballroom, across from an older woman with a kind smile and a firm gaze. A banner behind her reads: *LABYRINTH LEARNING*.

The instructor steps to him and takes one of his hands in hers, places his other one on her shoulder, and they begin to dance.

The video switches back to his love interest, who is climbing the steps to a grand building with neoclassical architecture featuring tall Corinthian columns and ornate details.

Next, she's backstage, behind a curtain, peering out at a lavish auditorium with plush red velvet seats, gilded balconies, and intricate ceiling frescoes.

Then she's on stage dancing, and the screen splits to show

her performing with the ballet troupe for the audience and him learning to dance.

It all speeds up then, like a time lapse of their lives. Her performing. And practicing English. Him learning Bulgarian and taking dancing lessons and writing code.

It slows down to show him packing a bag and getting on a plane. She's doing the same thing.

Next, he's sitting in a performance hall, looking down from the balcony, leaning forward, watching as she dances on the stage.

After the performance, they walk along the South Bank at night, but this time, they're not in Labyrinth. They're actually in London.

They take an elevator up to the restaurant with the red seal, and this time I can read the name: Duck & Waffle.

They sit at the same table, and now the plates are filled with food and the glasses with cocktails and he's cutting a piece of waffle and feeding it to her.

They're dancing when the video fades to black and a single line appears: *Love in Labyrinth Knows No Bounds*.

There are a few other long-form promotional videos, but I get the picture, and I have to say: it's a brilliant approach by Amersa (or whatever firm they hired to do the videos). They haven't once described the technology behind Labyrinth. They've shown what it can do. How it can transform your life. Or help you get through the one you have.

The videos are clearly part of Amersa's vision for the future—showing how Labyrinth will eventually be available everywhere. For now, their website says they're taking reservations for their limited launch locations, with more sites planned for the coming months.

I now understand why the release cost so much and why the investor was pushing back so hard on scaling it.

Scrolling down, I find a video from a morning news program, where four hosts are sitting on a couch and Anders Larsson is on the split screen, joining via live video.

"How does it know about your experiences?" the male host in the center of the couch asks.

"It doesn't, exactly. But you have to understand that the Labyrinth engine has ingested an absolutely massive amount of data. Like the early LLMs—or large language models—that powered the first AI chatbots, Labyrinth essentially draws on a big dataset and extrapolates. In this case, it's not only text, it's video, photos, and audio. We're living in an age where there's just an abundance of data from which Labyrinth can generate experiences. It draws from the user's posts on social media or other data they've submitted."

"Like the bachelorette party," one of the female hosts says.

"That's right. In that example, the Labyrinth customer had tons of photos and videos from that night, and there were even more publicly available from her friends and even strangers who were there or crossed paths with the group."

The male anchor points a rolled-up stack of papers at the camera. "So, I guess we're all wondering: this looks great, right? But what exactly is it? Is this sort of the evolution of home theaters? Will we be creating Labyrinth rooms in our home one day?"

"You absolutely will have a Labyrinth room in your home—and sooner than you think. But what we're doing is a lot bigger than watching movies at home or playing video games. Labyrinth is nothing less than a leap forward for human civilization. The type of event that comes along once every two or three generations. It's a breakthrough that will shrink our world and change the way we live our lives. Think about agriculture, and electricity, and airplanes, and the internet. That's the scale of change Labyrinth is going to bring about."

49

For the rest of the morning, the group chat on Signal obsesses over the Labyrinth release, sharing links and speculating about what it all means. I can't keep up, not while teaching my classes and following the online auctions ending today.

But I have to admit: I'm checking my text messages more than Signal or Labyrinth's takeover of social media.

I had hoped to hear from Meredith on Sunday. Or for her to swing by during lunch yesterday. Or today. But she hasn't, and my lunch period is nearly up.

In fact, it's been radio silence from her since I picked Riley up from her place post-police interview.

She's likely made the smart decision to ghost me.

As if she can read my mind, a text appears from her:

> You have a trial session today?

I text back that I do, and a pulsing bubble with three dots appears, and her message soon after:

> Need me to pick up R and watch her?

Leaning back in the creaking chair, I eye the phone like it's a live grenade.

This moment is the chance for a clean break. That's what I'm thinking. But I type:

> Yeah. That would be great. Thanks.

★

My next entry into the Labyrinth happens that afternoon, and it begins where I last exited: the motel bathroom.

It's strange how natural and believable this world now feels to me.

Honestly, it's a reprieve. Here, there are no cops chasing me. No teaching duties. My daughter—who I love more than anything in this world—doesn't depend on me in this world.

There is a certain lightness as I walk across the empty motel room, past the made-up double beds, and step outside.

The sky above is filled with inky black clouds that blot out the sun, casting the motel, gas station, and apparel factory in a darkness close to twilight.

As I'm standing there, a door twenty feet away swings in and May steps out, tossing a bag of trash in a cart loaded with towels, toiletries, and linens.

When she sees me, she smiles. "Welcome back. You should check out the board."

In the motel office, I quickly see what she's excited about.

The numbers have changed. And in our favor.

At the truck stop where I began my journey, there were only rides taking people deeper into the Labyrinth. Here, today, the majority of the offers are for people going back to the truck stop and other places along the way.

Without looking up, Rachel says, "Storms are getting worse. Everybody is trying to get away from them now."

The rides going away from the storms are alarmingly expensive. And the few routes going deeper into the Labyrinth are dirt cheap. It's good news for May and me. We're taking the road less traveled. It's more dangerous, but far cheaper.

May points to a line on the board calling for six passengers. Four spots are already filled. "I made a little money while you were resting," she says. "We can take that one right now."

Rachel finally glances up. "Won't be the most comfortable ride."

"It's okay with me," I respond, but I wait for May's input to say any more. She simply shrugs, "Never thought this journey would be comfortable."

Outside the motel office, I glance up at the storm-covered sky.

"May, did you get any rain gear?"

"No," she replies. "I spent what we didn't need for the ride on interviews for my research."

"Let's buy some. I think you're going to need it."

In the store attached to the apparel factory, the only rain protection we can afford is a poncho.

It's better than nothing. I insist—and May agrees—that we'll get her better rain gear at the next stop before we go any farther.

The transport we've signed up for is a cargo van filled with sacks of garments. There are no windows and no seats in the back, which leaves us six passengers crammed in the small spaces in between the lumpy bags.

The driver, a woman I recognize from the garment factory, settles in behind the wheel, and a rail-thin man plops down in the bucket seat beside her. They remain silent as she cranks the van, the engine roaring through the cargo compartment.

The vehicle pulls onto the road, sloshing us paying riders around in the back. The noise from the engine, the tires, and the wind makes conversation impossible. And besides, May is hidden by the bag next to me, and I don't know the two passengers directly across from me, though they look like a mother and her daughter.

On the whole, darkness, vibration, and bouncing among the garment bags make for a disorienting ride. It reminds me of flying in a military cargo plane.

Time becomes a blur, but somewhere along the road, rain starts pelting the roof, and as soon as it does, I reach in my backpack and get out my raincoat and other gear and begin putting them on. Being prepared never hurts.

Peeking around a garment sack, I motion for May to do the same, and soon, she's pulling the thin, clear plastic poncho over her head.

As the storm intensifies, the van begins to sway from the wind's force. A powerful gust nearly tips us over, but the driver manages to regain control. One of the passengers—a man about my age whom I worked the cotton fields with—yells to the driver, "We should go back!"

She gestures dismissively, the engine roaring, rain falling on the windshield in waves like a car wash.

Another gust grips the van, and the massive vehicle skids sideways and fishtails, but the driver again steers us back onto the road. I'm exhaling when the strongest gale yet hits the side of the van, lifting one side off the road.

The tires settle back onto the asphalt with a screech, but it's too late. The back end is sliding to the right, off the road. The van slides down the bank, the engine screaming as the wheels lose traction. The driver yanks at the wheel, but it's too little too late. The van lurches like a ship capsizing in a storm, tipping toward the ground. I fly toward the ceiling, and luckily, one of the thick garment bags hits first, cushioning my impact before I fall back.

For a moment, I'm disoriented. My vision blurs, and I hear noise, but nothing is in focus.

I reach out, feeling, and my hand connects with May's arm. There's a garment bag between us, and she pulls it away, her frightened eyes locking on mine.

With each passing second, my hearing is coming back. From the front, the driver says in a pained voice, "We're close to town. We can make it if we run."

I assume she's talking to the guy in the passenger seat. He must've slammed into the side window when the van turned over because he's clutching his head, blood oozing around his fingers. His eyes are glassy.

The driver yells at him now. "Johnny! Focus! We gotta go."

That brings the guy around, and he nods lazily.

"What about us?" A woman's voice calls from the back.

"Leave or stay, I don't care," the driver shouts as she opens her door and pushes it up and climbs onto the side of the van. Next, the sound of her footsteps pounding the sidewall facing the sky joins the pelting rain.

The driver's door slams shut before the passenger, Johnny, can get out. He pulls the handle and shoves it upward, but the wind presses down, forcing it closed again. Planting his feet, he pushes harder, using his legs, and the metal hinges groan and it stays open this time, almost at a ninety-degree angle.

He, too, crawls out, traipses across the side of the van, and jumps down.

Through the open door, the wind carries the rain inside, sending the closest passengers reeling away.

A piece of debris hits the windshield, punching a small hole in it. Spidery cracks spread out like a web being pulled.

It's just a matter of time before something larger hits the windshield or enough smaller items cave it in, and then the wind and the rain will be all over us back here.

The driver was right: we do need to go.

My fellow passengers must've come to the same conclusion because one climbs over me and opens one of the two side-by-side doors at the rear of the van. From our overturned perspective, it's the bottom door, and it lies open like a descending ramp to the ground. The rider crawls across it and takes off into the storm. Another passenger—a woman—follows close behind him, leaving May, the mother, her daughter, and me in the van.

May eyes me, silently asking what we should do.

"We've got to go," I respond.

Over the howling wind, I call to the mother, "Do you have any rain gear?"

She presses her lips together, forming a white line as she shakes her head tightly. A wind gust brings a splash of rain through the open back door. The child winces and pulls her hand away when a few drops land on her.

"It burns," she whimpers to her mother, who pulls her close.

I'm not leaving them. The only question is how to protect them.

I pull open the closest garment bag. It's full of t-shirts. The next one is filled with towels. Better, but still not what we need. The third bag holds more towels, and in the fourth, I find what we need: white bedsheets. Plenty of them. Hopefully, enough to protect these people from the rain long enough to get to shelter.

I dump the sheets out and quickly describe my plan: the mother and child will shelter under the sheets while May and I lead them to safety.

May makes one suggestion: that she give the poncho to the child and that she join them under the sheets. I like the idea, and that's what we do.

When all three of them are covered in several layers of sheets, they join hands through the cloth, and I reach back and take May's.

With my free hand, I open the rear door and step out into the rain and lead May and the others onto the muddy gully by the road. The wind pulls at me and whips my coat around and the sky is dark as night.

The only light ahead is from a gas station, and a few buildings beyond that I can't quite make out through the rain.

Carefully, I lead our line back onto the road, and we march toward the gas station. Twice, the wind nearly knocks us over. May holds tight to my hand, and when I look back, the mother is staggering, but she stays on her feet.

Under the canopy above the gas pumps, we finally get a reprieve from the rain. May and the mother toss their sheets over and look up.

"Did the rain reach you?" I ask May. She shakes her head, and the mother does the same.

Outside the store, I carefully remove my raincoat and place it under a propane tank to keep it from blowing away. Inside, a group is gathered by the windows, watching the wind and rain raging outside. They were apparently customers who had been filling up their vehicles or people passing by who took shelter here.

The attendant sits on a stool behind the counter, casually watching the storm through the plate glass window. "It's waning," he mutters to no one in particular. "Be over soon."

Stepping deeper into the store, I spot the driver and her passenger. They're both sitting down, backs leaned against a refrigerator door. At first, I think they're just exhausted from their desperate run to the gas station. But when I look closer,

I spot that familiar vacant stare in their eyes—the telltale signs of Labyrinth Syndrome I saw while working the night shift at the motel. The rain worked on them fast.

My phone vibrates in my pocket. Drawing it out, I realize my health is at four percent. I figure that's partly due to the rain.

At the back of the store, I spot what I need.

"Gotta use the restroom," I tell May as I march to the bathroom door and out of the Labyrinth.

50

On the way home, I stop for gas, and while it's pumping, I send a Signal message to the group telling them there wasn't anything immediately actionable in the Labyrinth session (this is part of our new protocol since May/June was introduced).

Even so, the group agrees to meet tomorrow during my lunch period. With the release of Labyrinth into the world—and June's starting her new job at Amersa next week—there's a lot to discuss.

As the amount on the fuel pump slowly climbs, I lean against the car and breathe in the fall air, thinking about the gas station in the Labyrinth where I led May and the woman and her child.

The nozzle stops with a loud thud, drawing my attention. I've been jumpy ever since that day the bomb went off. Any unexpected noise sets me off.

But what occurs to me is that I didn't jump nearly as much this time. My nerves don't feel as raw.

Which is interesting.

At home, I find Riley and Meredith at the dining table working on the 3D puzzle. The grounds are done and the walls form an outline, but the towers are still little more than hollow, jagged hints at what the final result will be. We've slowed down a lot. Many of the pieces look the same now. And others are so strange we're not even sure where they might go.

By way of greeting, Riley reaches over and picks up a sealed letter envelope and holds it out to me. "For you, Dad!"

The outside bears the Wake County Schools logo. *Parents of Riley Norris* is hand-written below and to the right.

I feel Meredith's eyes on me. Riley sits up in the chair, leaning forward.

"What does it say?" she asks as I rip it open and scan the page, trying to keep my face free of reaction.

"Nothing," I mumble. "It's just a general update."

She scowls at me. "Well, not everyone got one."

"Really? Maybe they mailed them to the other parents. Or emailed them."

Before my daughter can react, I hold a hand out toward the front door and the staircase. "Come on, time for bed."

"Thanks," I say softly to Meredith as Riley passes. I set the letter on the table, and upstairs, after she brushes her teeth and changes into pajamas, I read the next chapter in a novel about a boy who discovers he's a wizard and is transported to a fantasy land.

In this particular section, the hero and his two friends go through a trapdoor and play wizard chess. It seems like a simple game, but it's very dangerous. One wrong move could be their last.

Downstairs, Meredith is waiting on me.

The letter on the table hasn't moved. I pick it up and hand it to her, and wait as she reads the words I did: that during a preliminary reading assessment, it was determined that Riley is slightly behind grade level and will be placed in an intervention group within her class. The note is merely to inform me, but it's a prelude to possible further changes at school if she doesn't catch up.

Meredith gently refolds the page and slips it back in the envelope and reads my face. "Not your fault, Alan."

"Sure it is. I've been so obsessed with my own classes and hawking used military gear and this trial and stupid 3D puzzles and moving…"

Meredith doesn't say anything. She just turns over a few pieces of the puzzle. Strangely, Riley's trouble at school seems to have pushed the trouble between Meredith and me to the back burner.

Without looking up, she quietly asks me what I'm going to do now.

"What I should have been doing this whole time. Reading every night. And probably every morning. And all weekend."

"You can't turn this place into Camp Lejeune."

"Sure I can. We'll call it Camp Reading."

Meredith cocks her head. "She has to have some fun too."

"She can have fun reading."

Meredith's shaking her head, but there's a wry smile, because she knows I'm half serious, but only half, and she knows me well enough to know that I'm feeling pretty guilty about this. The letter isn't so much about Riley's reading as it is a reminder that I have been neglecting the most important thing in my life— and I've been neglecting her because I've been preoccupied with protecting her.

The exhaustion, stress, and guilt hit me like a wave; the sound of it crashing is the opening chords of a tinnitus attack. The ringing begins with three clangs, the rocks rolling around in that can gently. They grind faster, and then they're hitting the sides.

Clang.

Clang.

Clang.

I close my eyes and massage my eyelids, willing it to stop. But this episode advances fast.

When I open my eyes, Meredith is talking, but I can't hear her. I shake my head and point to my ears, and she studies me a moment and seems to understand.

She stands, and I think she's going to leave, but she returns with—of all things—the magnetic whiteboard from the fridge. She snaps a picture of the grocery list I've scrawled on it and taps at her phone.

My own vibrates in my pocket, and when I take it out, I see the photo of the list, which she promptly wipes away with a paper towel she must have had in her pocket.

With the marker, she writes, *Tinnitus?*

I nod slowly.

What can I do? she writes.

I reach for the marker and scribble two words:

It'll pass.

She sets the board down, writes something, and rounds the table and pauses beside me, leaning slowly over until her lips touch the top of my head and they stay there for three long seconds, and when I turn, the back of her is all I see until she exits through the front door.

On the dry-erase board, she's written:

Text me if you need anything.

My gaze drifts to the half-built puzzle, and the ringing gets louder until the hand slams the can down with a pop that blots out reality.

When I wake up, I'm lying on my back in bed, the ceiling fan above spinning at top speed, the blades blurring the ceiling.

How much time have I lost? That's my first question.

Pondering it, I realize I'm sore all over. The feeling reminds me of that night in downtown, when I woke up next to the dead body of Nathan Briggs.

I sit up, and I realize two very, very important things. First: I'm not in my bedroom.

I didn't realize it at first because the bedroom is very similar. The ceiling fan is in the exact same place. So are the windows and doors. But this copy of my master bedroom is better decorated (mine is what one would generously call Spartan).

The second thing is that someone is lying beside me. But she's very much alive. And naked, and opening her eyes, and smiling at me, and sitting up with ease, the moonlight catching the gleam of sweat on her face.

Without a word, Meredith presses her lips to mine. My heart is beating so fast, I swear it might crack my ribs.

I swallow, trying to chase away the dryness in my mouth, and whisper. "I should go."

51

In my own bed, I lie awake thinking about the ringing and waking up next to Meredith and the touch of her lips to mine and the way her hand felt on my back as I rose from the bed.

All morning, I check my phone, expecting to see a text from Meredith.

Maybe a message along the lines of:

> Enjoyed last night.

Or:

> See you after school!

Or even:

> WTF was that, Alan?

In my mind, I compose a dozen messages to her before mentally erasing them.

What I feel like is my character in Amersa's Labyrinth. I keep getting deeper in the maze and the storms keep getting worse.

On my way to the numbers meeting, I stop by the gym and the teacher's parking lot. Meredith is absent from both.

★

The numbers meeting takes place at an abandoned office building off I-40, right outside Research Triangle Park.

When we're all seated in the metal folding chairs and Harold has joined via the camera sitting atop the pole stand, I ask Isaac a question that's been nagging me: "Where do you find these places?"

He looks mildly disgusted. "Is that seriously your first order of business? We have more pressing matters."

I hold out my hands. "The floor is yours."

"Let's standardize our agenda from here out. First, we hear any time-sensitive news anyone has. Second, anyone who has lost time needs to describe it. In detail. In case it impacts any of those urgent updates. Next, Alan's Labyrinth session. After, I'll play any pertinent recordings from Anders Larsson. In this case, there are none. It's just Larsson obsessing over the launch of Labyrinth, berating people, and using the buzz to raise a new round of funding. So we can skip that. And finally, we'll have other updates and discussion."

When no one disagrees, Isaac asks if anyone has lost time.

"I have," Rose says quietly. "Sunday night. At work."

"At Amersa?" Isaac asks.

"Yes. I was halfway through my cleaning shift."

"What happened?"

Rose swallows and fidgets with her hands in her lap. "I was in the women's bathroom on the third floor, mopping. The ringing started, and I went into a stall, closed the door, and did my breathing exercises. When I was back, I was in the same bathroom. But the floor was dry."

"Any idea how much time you lost?" I ask.

"I think about thirty minutes."

"Did anyone say anything?" Isaac asks. "Any clues as to what happened?"

Rose shakes her head.

I imagine she's scared she did something that might cost her that job at Amersa. A job that I bet is very important to her and her independence from the bad situation she was in when I met her.

I know how that feels: fearing that this problem we share will cost us our job and livelihood. And maybe even our freedom—and the ones we love.

After hearing Rose's story, I feel like my recent time loss—and apparent sexual escapade two doors down—is less consequential than hers.

Nevertheless, I share with the group.

"I lost time too. Last night."

"How much?" Isaac asks.

"Couple of hours. Give or take."

He holds a hand out and rolls it forward impatiently. "Well?"

"I don't think it was related to this... our issue."

"Why is that? What did you do? Where did you go?"

"I didn't go anywhere." I wince. "Well, I went two doors down."

Isaac squints. "Two doors down... to a neighbor's house?"

"Right." I focus on him. "At night."

He shrugs. "And?"

Rose slowly tilts her head back, studying the ceiling tiles. June is scraping at something on her pants with her fingernail.

"And, then I went back home."

It hits Isaac then. "Oh. *Ohhhh.*" He nods slowly, the interrogator's zeal leaving him. "Does that, like, happen to you a lot? When you lose time?"

"It does not. Happen to me a lot. Or ever before."

Isaac is a little more cautious when he says. "Does that happen... when you're not having an attack? You, know, the uh, late-night rendezvous?"

"No, man, it doesn't." I hold my hands out. "Until somewhat recently, I was married. My wife was sick for a long time, but still, dating, and—you know—is not really high on my list of priorities. Not even really ready."

"Can I ask," June says carefully, "if you already knew the person? I know you said he or she is a neighbor."

"I know her. Have for a long time. And we've been... sort of spending more time together."

Isaac has recovered his full focus now. "Could she be connected to this?"

"No. She is not connected to this."

"Does she work for Amersa?"

"She's a PE teacher at my school."

"So you work together?"

"We do."

"And she's your neighbor?"

"She is. And also, my former high school girlfriend."

"Are you all… together?" Isaac asks.

I toss my head back and forth, searching for the words. I settle on: "Not *really*."

"So that's awkward," Isaac says, seeming to have lost interest in the story.

"Thanks," I mutter. "That hadn't occurred to me."

"Well," June says, "Alan, would you like to describe your recent session?"

"Happily," I mutter.

With as much detail as I can remember, I recount yesterday's Labyrinth experience, including leaving the motel with May, the ride in the van through the storm with the other passengers, and getting them to safety.

When I'm done, June says, "It's not hard to see the similarities with your own life. A crash. People depending on you."

"Except this time, I was able to walk away. And to help them."

"How did you feel afterward?" June asks.

"Immediately after? Pretty bad actually. Just tired and sapped."

June leans forward. "It could be the effects of VR."

"How do you mean?"

"VR is known to cause visual fatigue, mental overload, and a feeling almost like motion sickness."

"Why?"

"Several reasons," June says, leaning back, seeming more comfortable now that the discussion was moving into her area of expertise.

"VR triggers something called vergence-accommodation conflict, or VAC. Your eyes point (converge or diverge) to match the depth of virtual objects, but they must focus at a single, fixed optical distance. That split instruction—'look near, focus far'—tires the eye muscles and can leave you woozy. It could leave the user with blurry vision, eye strain, and even headaches. A 360-degree environment like Labyrinth would exacerbate the effects."

"So it's basically screen fatigue on steroids," Isaac says.

"Yes, but it's more than that. It's also the mental fatigue that comes from the high levels of attention and interaction VR requires. The cognitive load of processing a constant stream of visual and auditory stimuli, reacting to fast-moving objects, and engaging with complex interactive elements takes a toll. In the field, researchers actually call it 'virtual reality sickness' or 'simulator sickness.'"

I'm not exactly liking what I'm hearing. I've got enough problems without Amersa's VR tech scrambling my brain.

"That could be," Isaac says, "why Amersa chose to roll out Labyrinth in these dedicated gaming centers in theaters, malls, and parking lots. They can basically test the hardware in a limited roll-out and tune it based on what they observe in the people after their sessions."

"I had the same thought," June says. "It's almost like an open clinical trial, done in public, to identify side effects and try to minimize them."

"Amersa has been developing an at-home version of Labyrinth for years. It was actually where they wanted to start, but Larsson was never happy with the product. He kept pushing, and it never met his expectations, so he went with the dedicated centers. He likes the control of it, and he wanted a big splash at release."

I focus on June. "What else could the Labyrinth VR be doing to me?"

She hesitates for a moment. "Well," she says carefully, "my biggest concern is what we call 'reality confusion.'"

I can imagine what that means, but June continues with a neuroscientist's definition. "The core issue with the reality confusion from VR is when the boundaries between the virtual world and the real world blur in the user's mind. This confusion impacts a person's sense of identity and perception of reality. Over time, it can lead to increased detachment from reality. And those are just the subconscious effects."

"I assume, then, that there are *conscious* effects?"

"There are. Especially if you come to prefer the virtual world over the real one. Consider it, Alan. In Labyrinth, you did what you couldn't in real life. You saved people after a tragedy on the road. It's very likely that your next experiences will be equally intense. That your character—the person you are in Labyrinth—will continue to become more powerful."

"Standard game play," Isaac says. "Your avatar gains more control over their environment the deeper they go in the game."

"Precisely," June agrees. "Think about how that would affect a person. You have a virtual world where you are powerful and safe. And a real world where you are neither, where you have demons and fears and real danger."

"Yes, but I can't return to Labyrinth anytime I want. I'm stuck in the real world."

"For now," Isaac says. "But as mentioned, they're working on that."

"The last concern," June says carefully, "is what neuroplastic changes Labyrinth might cause."

"What does that mean?"

"Well, VR—and what we call Virtual Reality Augmented Rehabilitation or VRAR—has been studied for years. And used very effectively to treat patients who have had a stroke or traumatic brain injuries, even dementia and spinal cord injuries."

June motions to me. "And there have been numerous studies on mental health conditions like PTSD and anxiety."

"So what's the problem?" Isaac asks.

"I wouldn't call it a problem," June replies slowly, staring at the dingy office carpet.

"But it's a *concern*," I say, echoing her exact word.

"It is," June says.

"Why?"

"Because we know VR can be used to improve neuroplasticity. It can essentially rewire the brain. For example, for patients with motor disabilities, VR provides a safe way to practice repeatable movements. This repetition teaches the brain how to reorganize its motor pathways. Think about a stroke patient using a virtual arm or hand. After a while, the brain actually gets better at using its real limbs when it leaves VR. It relearns motor patterns. Parkinson's patients have used VR to improve their gait and balance."

"It's interesting," Rose says. "But what does it mean for Alan? He doesn't have any… motor issues?"

Curling my left leg back, I tap the prosthesis against the metal leg of the chair, smiling, eyebrows raised.

Rose reels back, shrugging sheepishly. "You know what I mean."

"I know what you mean. Just messing with you."

Isaac turns to June. "What was your point?"

"I only meant to say that we should consider that Labyrinth is indeed creating neuroplastic changes in Alan's brain. In his case, it's about retraining the neurons to react differently. Specifically to traumatic stimuli. To triggers of past events. But I think we should consider that Amersa's VR/AI combination is the most powerful system that I'm certainly aware of, perhaps in the world. And that we don't yet understand its full effects."

52

After school, Riley and I load up on used children's books of the Learn to Read variety.

We're picking through the stacks when she turns to me. "Dad, why do you keep checking your phone?"

"Sorry," I mutter, putting it back in my pocket.

From the shelf, I grab a book and hold it up. "What about this one? *Green Eggs and Ham*. Classic."

Riley wrinkles her nose as if the book is actually composed of spoiled eggs and ham. "That's for babies."

"*Okay.*"

She holds up a copy of a Magic Tree House book. "This one."

After the bookstore, we stop by Warren's for the weekly payment and a strategy session about what's selling and what we should have bid more for and bought (and things we paid too much for). These are typically a stream of consciousness type meeting in the back room, where Warren leans back in a chair, his fingers pressed into each other, me with the laptop out, taking notes, and updating watchlists, and Riley exploring the store and gathering things for me to buy (which I refuse and make her put back and Warren then gives her about half the time).

This afternoon, however, Warren has bigger plans on his mind.

"You know what I've been thinking?"

Thanks to my recent meeting with Sheila, I'm getting better at spotting rhetorical questions.

"Expansion." Warren lets the word hang in the air.

"Yeah?" I assume he's talking about another store, and maybe me taking the helm, and I'm thinking that doesn't work with all the chaos in my life. Or my current job. Or skill set.

Warren lets the chair settle back on the floor and plants his forearms on the table. "What we need is one of those online stores."

He studies me.

"Yeah?"

"That's what my daughter told me." He points at me and says quickly. "And she's right."

He leans back in the chair again. "What we have here," he motions to me and then back to himself, "is what you would call a well-oiled procurement machine."

He seems to consider that a moment. "Well, procurement and refurbishment machine."

"Right."

"What we don't have, is an equally efficient distribution apparatus." He eyes me. "Which is what I would call a problem and an opportunity. You following me, Marine?"

"I'm following you."

He sets the chair legs back on the floor. "What do you know about building an online store?"

"Nothing. Nothing at all."

Warren continues as if I responded more enthusiastically. "It's a good thing you're a quick learner, though."

"Who says I'm a quick learner?"

"You have to be."

"How do you know?"

"Because you're a parent. And a teacher. Teachers got to be learners first, don't they? I know. My wife was one."

"Warren, are you sure you weren't a motivational speaker before this?"

"Oh, I'm sure. But I was a parent too. Requires a lot of speeches. Motivational and otherwise. And so does convincing a bunch of cowboys to make good decisions that keep you alive when you're in the Army."

★

I'm walking out of Warren's army surplus store when I get a text from Meredith.

My eyes go wide when I see the sender's name. I tap my phone, anxious to read the message, which is a single word:

Pizza?

I tap a reply:

Definitely. I'll pick it up.

And with that, the only thing standing in the way of *the talk*, as I've come to think about it, is two medium cheese pizzas and a child's bedtime.

At home, post-pizza, Riley wants to watch a show on TV, but I insist she read first. That's going to be the way it is until she masters it.

With Meredith sorting puzzle pieces, Riley and I sit on the couch, and she reads about two kids named Jack and Annie traveling through time while I ponder the elephant in the room.

After that, Riley reads *Goodnight Moon*. Then a local edition: *Good Night North Carolina*.

The book is a little too simplistic for her reading level, but I know Riley likes it, maybe because her mother and I used to read it to her when she was younger. I've always thought that books you have fond memories of have a certain power to comfort you. And I also know that reading an easier book builds her confidence in the exercise.

After, we go up to her room, and I read to her until her soft snores prompt me to insert the bookmark.

As I descend the staircase, I mentally rehearse how to bring up the subject of *last night*.

Meredith is still sitting at the dining table. Without looking up, she sighs—for effect, I think—and says, "Okay. Let's talk about it."

I lift my shoulders innocently. "Talk about what? Whatever do you mean?"

She smiles at me. "Unless you have something better to do."

"Believe me I don't. My homework tonight is researching how to start an online store."

"Are you serious?"

"I am."

"For what?"

"The army gear Warren and I have been buying."

"You can ship that stuff to people's homes?"

"Yeah, some of it. I mean, you saw some of the things that are shipped to us. And I suspect the lighter-weight items will be more profitable. Generally."

I'm nervous. So is she. The store discussion is like a diversion, an ice breaker before the real issue.

But at this point, the ice is broken, and it's melting.

I plop down across the table from her and fiddle with a puzzle piece.

She's staring at the castle, and her voice is soft when she speaks. "We're not kids anymore, Alan."

"No. We're not."

"For the record, I'm good with what happened."

I nod, sensing there's a—

"But," she says slowly, "this isn't just about me and you. There are three of us to think about."

"There are."

"No matter what... happens, we need to make sure she doesn't get hurt."

"I agree."

Neither of us says anything for what feels like three or four hours. Like the Labyrinth, time seems distorted here.

Finally, she pushes up from the chair. "Well. I should go."

"Right."

I rise as she rounds the table. "I'll... walk you to the door."

She passes in front of me and I follow, half-expecting the ringing to start. But it holds off, and my heart beats faster with every step.

At the door, Meredith stops abruptly and turns, locking eyes with me. "I'm glad we talked."

"Me too," I whisper.

She raises her arms, and I step forward and wrap mine around her and squeeze a little too hard for neighbors or friends. And I hold her longer than any friendly neighbor would. I lean my head back and turn slightly, my lips pressing into her hair.

She lets her head tilt down, resting it on my shoulder, her breath hot on my skin as she speaks softly, slowly, as if testing every word aloud.

"You know… we could… hang out. I mean, if you want."

"I do."

"Okay."

"Let's uh… watch TV. Or something."

53

My fourth session in the Labyrinth starts at the restroom at the gas station. The store was packed when I left, when the storm was raging outside.

The storm is gone, and the store is empty except for the clerk, who sits on a stool behind the counter, engrossed in a paperback novel.

"You Alan?" he asks, not looking up.

"Yeah."

"Woman came around looking for you. Said she's your partner."

"Do you know where she is?"

"Nope."

"Any idea where I can get work around here?" I figure that's what May's doing and thus where I'll find her.

"The apartments."

"Which ones?"

"Middletown Apartments. Only ones we've got."

Finally, the clerk places a bookmark in the paperback and gently sets it on the counter.

"She's not the only one looking for you."

"Yeah?"

"The sheriff came around too—right after she did."

My mind flashes to the two Raleigh police detectives sitting at my dining room table. Is this just a coincidence? Or is the Labyrinth really reflecting my life?

"I'd go see him first," the clerk says, picking up the paperback again.

"Maybe I'll do that," I mutter, thinking just the opposite:

that I'll find May first and then try to figure out why local law enforcement is interested in me.

Behind the counter, there's a large ride board, but every row is blank.

"Why aren't there any rides?"

"Lack of supply and demand, my friend. No drivers and no riders," he pauses, seeming to reconsider. "Well, there are plenty of riders."

"What do you mean?"

"Everybody around here is trying to get out, myself included. But anyone driving through is going away from the storms—and they're already fully loaded with riders. The only reason anybody stops is for gas or to get out of the storm long enough to get back on the road."

"Are you saying every single person in this town is trying to leave?"

"Pretty much. Well, there is one guy trying to get deeper into the Labyrinth, but he's crazy."

I figure anyone trying to get deeper into the Labyrinth might be helpful (or have advice). "Where can I find him?"

"Also at the apartments. His name's Ian. He manages them."

Beyond the station's plate glass windows, it's dark outside, but I can't tell if it's simply the storm clouds blotting out the sun or if it's actually night.

Outside the gas station, I check under the propane tank for my raincoat, but it's gone, which is not ideal.

The one piece of good news is that the wind is blowing, but it's not raining. I get the sense that I should get to shelter—or out of here—before it starts.

The town isn't exactly a vast metropolis. There's what looks like a small dollar store just down the street from the gas station. From the road, I can see some of the merchandise, but there's no one milling about inside. The police station is next door, but when the cops are looking for you and you want to get out of town, it's not the first place you want to stop.

Beyond the police station, there are long one-story brick buildings on each side of the road, like you might see on Main

Street in a small town. All the storefronts are boarded up with plywood.

Just past the abandoned buildings, I spot a sign that reads "Middletown Apartments."

The complex consists of four two-story buildings arranged in a U-shape. They remind me of the apartments where Riley and I used to live before all the drama with the downstairs neighbor.

The end unit on the first floor of the closest building has a sign in the window that says "Office."

The doorbell button has been removed, so I knock and turn the handle and step inside. To my right is a long table that looks like it belongs in a conference room. It's covered in electronic components that look like computer or radio parts.

Hunched over the silicon junkyard is a guy a few years younger than me. He's rummaging through the chips and green boards and ribbon cables, not bothering to glance up.

Behind him, on a side table, is a tower case for a personal computer. It's lying on its side, with the panel open, exposing the motherboard and add-on cards.

"Just a sec," he mumbles, slipping a hand into the rubble to grab a part, which he quickly installs in the computer.

I take the time to survey his makeshift office. There's a map of the apartment complex with red and green magnetic buttons, perhaps indicating which units are occupied.

Finally, the guy starts cursing, and I hear a screwdriver crash into the heap of electronic debris.

When I turn back, he's shaking his head, muttering, "Worthless, completely useless."

"Hey, sorry to bother you, but I'm looking for someone. Her name is May."

"Yeah," he says, still surveying the wreckage. "She's cleaning the vacated units."

"You're building a computer."

"I *was* building a computer. Now I think I'm just wasting my time."

"Why?"

"Can't find the parts I need."

"You're Ian."

He focuses on me for the first time. "Who's asking?"

"I'm Alan. Just passing through. The guy at the gas station said you want to go farther into the Labyrinth."

"That's right."

"Why?"

"The obvious, man. Parts to make this thing work."

"What are you going to do with a computer?"

"First of all, I'm building a computer and a radio. For the obvious reason."

"Which is?"

"Answers, dude."

"Answers to what?"

"The big question: why are we alone in here? Why are we *even here*? What's the purpose? And who put us here? Who created us? Why? Contacting the outside is the only way we're going to get real answers. And whatever is out there might even help us get out."

"You mean get out of the Labyrinth?"

His eyes bulge, and he nods slowly, as if I've just said the most ridiculous thing.

"Seriously? Am I the only person who is bothered by the fact that we can only contact the towns within the Labyrinth? It's like everybody's so absorbed in what they're doing that they have no self-awareness and no ability to see that something is very, very wrong here."

I'm entirely unsure what to say to that.

He looks at me expectantly. "Are you telling me you never thought about it?"

"I have. I'm just not sure what I can do about it. And it seems like stopping the storms is a bigger priority right now."

He points at me, his face lighting up. "Exactly. *Exactly*. That's what everyone's focused on, but what if getting to the center of the Labyrinth and stopping the storms is just a diversion? What if the only way out is by crossing the barrier? Finding out what's out there."

"I guess it's possible."

His focus returns to the piles of parts. "Doesn't matter anyway. Without a modem, I'm never getting any answers. Or out of here."

I find May in the next building, inside a second-floor apartment. The door's open and the large binder with her research is lying on the bed. Behind me, the wind is picking up.

At the threshold, I knock on the open door, drawing her attention. She breaks into a smile.

"Welcome back, hero."

"I'm no hero."

"You are around here," she says.

Stepping closer to me, she motions to the chair in the corner. A rubbery black garment is neatly folded, resting in the seat. "Thought you might want this," she says, holding up my now-dry raincoat.

I accept it and tell her that we should get her one as soon as possible.

"I can't afford it," she says, turning away.

"Well, let's see if *we* can afford it. We're a team."

I motion to the binder. "I'm assuming you've spent some credits interviewing people?"

She nods. "The building manager was very interesting. He thinks this is all some secondary layer of reality and that if he can figure out some way to contact whoever's outside, he can solve it all."

"Yeah, he mentioned that."

"What's your opinion of that?"

I'm not really sure what to say, so I simply shrug. I'm getting good at looking confused by what's happening around me. I've had a lot of practice lately.

The sound of boots on the wooden stairs draws my attention, and stepping out on the landing, I spot the sheriff.

He nods once at me. "I'm assuming you're Alan."

"I am."

He extends his hand. "I'm Sheriff Warner. But I go by Brian around here."

The name reminds me of Meredith's brother, Ryan—another police officer who's after me, though I'm not sure if he knows that yet.

I shake the man's hand.

"Alan, I was wondering if you would come down to the station with me."

"Do I have a choice?"

The man raises his eyebrows. "Of course. But I promise you: it'll be worth your while. I've got someone who wants to say something very important to you."

I glance back into the apartment where May is standing with her arms crossed. The sheriff leans forward and, seeing her, tips his hat. "Morning, ma'am. Didn't realize you were there."

"I'll come with you," I tell him, and May quickly adds that she'll come too.

The sheriff doesn't have a police cruiser or even an official vehicle, only a beat-up pickup truck that's as loud as the wind howling around us now. He drives to the police station and parks under a carport at the back.

Inside, I see two familiar faces: the mother and child whom May and I helped get away from the crashed van. They're sitting around a square table eating breakfast. Seeing us, the mother rises and gives May and me a hug.

Her daughter looks up and smiles, waving as the sheriff places a hand on my shoulder.

"We just want to say thank you for what you did. That sort of thing isn't real common around here these days."

"It was the right thing to do," I respond.

He nods, suddenly looking exhausted. "Well, like I said, we don't get that a lot these days."

"Which is why," the woman says, "the town still needs a sheriff."

"Suppose so," he mumbles as he takes his hat off and hangs it on the top of the coat rack. "Listen, we've also talked as a family and decided that we're going to stay here until the storms end.

It's obvious the roads are dangerous. And we'd rather ride this out in our own home, together, no matter what comes."

I wait, not sure where this is going.

"We want to thank you, but we don't have much money to give. But I've heard you all are looking to get farther down the road."

The sheriff reaches into his pocket and holds out the truck keys. "And that's something we can help you with. It's not fancy, but it gets the job done."

At the dollar store, we use my credits to buy May a raincoat and rubber boots that reach almost to her knees.

The truck has a bench seat that would probably accommodate two riders, certainly one comfortably.

And as it turns out, there's only one person in this town interested in going the same direction we are.

At the apartment office, it takes about five seconds for Ian to agree to come with us. "I'll pay you whatever you want," he says absently. He's already stuffing parts into a backpack and putting the side panel back on the computer.

From a closet, he pulls out a large suitcase and places some pillows on the bottom. That confuses me until he carefully lowers the computer tower into it. When he's done packing, he walks to the window, glances out at the truck, then back at May and me. "You know what we need?"

Before May or I can ask what we need, Ian continues. "A passenger compartment. At the next stop, there's a huge junkyard. We'll barter for parts and build a cover for the back so we can carry more passengers."

"We could," I tell him, "but no one is going our direction."

Ian exhales heavily. "I'm well aware of that. Which is why we'll drive them from there to here. I bet we could charge a king's ransom for the rides. Soon, we'll have enough money for computer parts, and we can boot it up and get out of here."

"It's half of a good idea," I tell him.

"What do you mean?"

"Transporting passengers for credits is smart. But May and I are using our money to get to the center of the Labyrinth."

Ian shrugs. "If you say so. Look, we could work together, pool our resources to upgrade the truck and take shifts driving until we get the credits each of us needs. Then we part ways."

He holds his arms out dramatically. "And you two can ride into the storm. Literally."

With the suitcase in hand, he heads for the door, calling back to us, "I mean, not super smart, but you do you."

On the road, the storms come and go, and the clouds above grow thicker with every mile. Soon, I have to turn the truck's headlights on to see the road.

The wind blows constantly, but the gusts aren't as strong as those that sent the van skidding and then over onto its side.

We mostly ride in silence, with May looking over her notes and jotting down some thoughts, and Ian seemingly in his own world, perhaps dreaming about what his computer and radio might discover.

With Ian's luggage and the backpacks May and I carry, the truck cab is pretty cramped. We opted not to leave anything in the bed of the truck for fear that it might get rained on or blow off.

By the time we reach the next town, the rain is coming down in a hazy drizzle.

The truck's headlamps are fighting a losing battle with the darkness and rain, but even in the dim light, I can tell this place is much more substantial than my last three stops in the Labyrinth.

There's a gas station on the left side of the road and a large truck stop across from it. It's the first Labyrinth Travel Center I've seen since the one I entered this strange place through. Beside it, there is a one-story motel with a neon sign with only two working letters flickering in the darkness. In its strobing shadow is an empty swimming pool that's slowly accumulating rainwater.

The lighted sign in the office window says "No Vacancy."

I keep driving, and beyond the motel is a sprawling junkyard with mountains of car parts, construction materials, and other heaps under massive tarps.

Ian leans over, across May, staring out the window at that real-life oasis of debris that mimics the one he had spread out on the table at the apartment building.

Next, there's a grocery store that's closed and an apartment complex across from that. A factory looms next door, and beside that is what looks like an old school. The building is sort of crumbling, but there is a hand-painted sign out front that says "Hostel." The wind is raging harder, and the misty rain has turned to a steady pelting, both heralding a coming storm.

One hand on the wheel, I check my phone. My health is down to eight percent. In addition to getting out of the storm, I'll need to exit soon.

Ian says what I'm thinking: "We should try the hostel."

I stop the truck under the covered area out front, and inside we make our way to the front desk, where a pudgy teenager is leaning back in a plush office chair, feet on the desk, an open comic book partially obscuring his face.

I call to him, but he doesn't move. Ian, who is still holding his suitcase tightly, rounds the desk and waves at the kid, who jumps and rips off the headphones I hadn't seen before.

Our host is wearing a name tag that says Dave, and it takes him a few seconds to compose himself. When he does, he greets us with a single word, "Hey."

"Hey," I reply.

"What's up?"

The decorum at the hostel is less formal than the motel's, but so are the accommodations.

"We'd like a room," I tell him.

His head reels back slightly. "Really?"

"Does that surprise you?"

He shrugs. "Sort of."

"Why?"

"Just, like, never happens."

I again ask why, and in answer, he simply motions to a paper map of the old school. Half of the rooms and areas have been crossed out with a red Sharpie.

Ian points at the Xs on the map. "Why's so much of the hostel blocked off?"

"Storm damage," Dave says. "The roof in the gym is caved in. Broken windows in some classrooms. Stuff like that happens a lot."

A strip of cork below the schematic holds dozens of red and green push pins.

Dave takes a red one and presses it into a classroom, and takes the green pin off, releasing a key that had been hanging from it by a string.

He points to a whiteboard with the list of rates for just a bed and the cost for a whole room. There are a lot of erase marks on the white surface, indicating the rates have been adjusted frequently (downward, I assume).

May, Ian, and I split the nightly cost, which isn't much.

On the way to our room, I draw my phone out and check the map. The red dot indicating my location is deep into the Labyrinth now, perhaps two-thirds of the way to the center. But I wonder if the last third will be the hardest stretch of road.

The three of us agree that we'll rest, restore our health, then gas up the truck and visit the junkyard.

When we reach the classroom, it's clear why the hostel is empty and the motel has no vacancy. It's about safety. On the far wall is a bank of tall broken windows. About half have been covered by furniture stacked up to keep the wind and rain out.

On the other wall—which is concrete cinder blocks painted white—is a row of six bunk beds. It's a hostel, but it looks more like a Marine barracks.

Ian points to the bunk beds. "We could use the mattresses and sheets to cover the rest of the windows."

May and I agree that it's a good idea, and the three of us tackle that project first.

I'm pulling the sheets off a top bunk when May grips my shoulder. "Why don't you head out? We'll handle this and pick it up when you get back."

"Okay." At the door, I glance back to her. "Might be a good idea to sleep in your poncho."

I motion to the windows. "Just in case."

On my way to the shared bathrooms, I hear a familiar rumble outside: an old diesel engine roaring to life.

It can't be.

I break into a run, back toward the office. I reach it just in time to see truck tires skidding on the wet pavement as someone steals the pickup truck the sheriff gave us.

54

On my way home from the Labyrinth session, I pick up Japanese food and Meredith and Riley and I devour it as we discuss our day. Riley has Halloween on her mind, which results in a request to rewatch *Hocus Pocus*.

She's halfway through the movie, at the scene where Bette Midler, Sarah Jessica Parker, and the third witch are boarding the bus, when she lets out her first yawn. I figure she'll be asleep in an hour or so.

At the dining table, I get out my laptop and continue working on the online store.

One thing I've learned: setting up an online store is far easier than I expected. Getting it to behave exactly as I want… is far more difficult.

It's been my nighttime obsession after reading to Riley and putting her to bed every night. Meredith has pitched in, and I have to admit, she's a big help—both technically and with her design sense. It gives us something to do, which reminds me of what Warren said about him and his wife. Which makes me think about the Labyrinth and all the parallels there.

It also gives Meredith a prime opportunity for some constructive teasing, which, tonight comes in the form of: "Alan, you cannot use those pictures."

"Why not?"

"Are you serious? This stuff is just lying on the floor. It looks like it's stolen."

"What? It's literally used army gear. This isn't a J.Crew catalog."

Great, I'm even starting to sound like Warren.

Across the dining room table, Meredith stares at me.

"Okay, fine. What do you suggest? Lug it down to the mall to Glamor Shots?"

She bunches her eyebrows. "Does Glamor Shots even exist anymore?" She squints for a second. "You know what? Doesn't matter. The point is that the photos need to look professional."

"We aren't professionals. We're amateurs selling used gear to other amateurs."

"Better pictures will bring better prices."

She gets me with that one.

"I'm listening."

"Set up a photo studio in the garage. Simple background, proper lighting, a stand for your phone so it's in the same place for each picture."

It does make a certain amount of sense. And like an old married couple, when your better half makes a valid point, I proceed with the natural response, which is non-verbal, a simple, slow, forward rocking motion of my head, signaling consent.

Silently accepting my surrender on the point, Meredith moves on. "Now. Can we talk about the name?"

"Again?"

"Alan."

"The name makes sense."

Meredith turns her head to the screen and makes a show of reading the big block letters at the top of the web page. "*Discount Army Surplus and Outdoor Survival Gear.*"

"SEO will love it."

"Does SEO buy things?"

"It directs people to places—where *they* buy things. If they don't get there, no buying."

"Is SEO still even a thing?"

"I think so."

"Will buyers love it? I mean, it's a lot."

"Well, that's what I'm saying. They won't even get a chance to love it if they don't find it."

"Speaking of that, how *are* they going to find it?"

"I've been looking into that. We're going to list everything on Google Shopping. You have to pay for clicks, though."

"Wait. Are you serious? When I Google something, the shopping listings—"

"Are *mostly* paid. I mean, you can list for free, and maybe it gets seen, but it would be after a bunch of paid listings. Basically every time you click a shopping result it costs some poor slob like me a dollar or two or more. Sometimes a lot more."

"Wow."

"It's the same thing for Bing."

"What about like Facebook Marketplace or…"

"Right. Listing is free there too. It's eyeballs that are the real cost. This is how the internet works now. You have to bribe the big tech companies to give you someone's attention for a few seconds. It's a real-time auction for the placements."

"Oh."

"It's weird, but it's not all bad. At least the little guys like us have a chance."

"What about Amazon? You could list stuff there. For free. I think."

"True. But it doesn't really work for what we're selling."

"Why?"

"Our stuff is sort of one-offs. Authentic gear. Some retro nostalgia stuff. And some repaired, high-end items that we usually have only one of. We don't manufacture. And it doesn't make sense to ship to their warehouse to do fulfillment by Amazon."

"I get it. Can we return to the name?"

"I thought you'd never ask."

"Why not something more catchy, like Warren's World? Or Surplus Survival?"

"I'm telling you, it doesn't work in the shopping search results. The words they put in need to be in the merchant name. And the customer needs to see those phrases under the listing—*discount* and *army surplus* and *survival*."

Meredith looks skeptical.

"Look, if we had a recognizable brand, sure. Warren's World

works. But no one knows what that is. It could be a sex toy shop—"

She holds up a hand. "Please. Not an image I need."

"The point is, that name doesn't mean anything."

"Also why is *sex shop* the first thing that pops into your mind?"

I feel my cheeks flush, but I barrel on. "Our customers usually want exactly what they're searching for. At a decent price. And to some extent, fast-ish delivery."

"Which means?"

"They're not really that brand loyal. If they buy a fifty cal ammo can from us, and then, a month later, they find themselves in the market for some tactical boots, they're not going to return to our site. They're going to type in Jungle Boots and buy them from whatever merchant has them at a good price."

Meredith stares out the glass slider at the night. "I sort of see your point."

"Good. Because I read like eight thousand web pages and online forums to arrive at those conclusions."

"Can I pose a hypothetical?"

"I await your pose, milady."

"Let's say, hypothetically, a fifty cal can—"

"Fifty cal ammo can. It's a can for fifty caliber ammo."

"Not really pertinent to this hypothetical, but duly noted. Let's say they search and they find your site and another site that sells a *given item*."

"Okay."

"How do they decide who to buy from?"

"Umm. Obvious stuff. Price. Shipping. Maybe—"

"It's all the same, Alan. Everything between the two stores is the same."

"You tell me."

"Connection."

"To?"

"The seller."

"I hear you, but folks buying military surplus aren't exactly the touchy-feely type. I'm not sure they're looking for connection."

"Every human being is looking for connection and belonging.

Don't underestimate that. Especially now when people feel more isolated than ever."

"Okay. I get it. But how do I incorporate that?"

"Every business should tell its story. Sure, some customers won't care. But some will. And your story may be the only difference between you and some other store with the same merchandise."

"For a PE teacher, you have a keen business acumen, Ms. Davis."

"You'll have to thank my dad for that when you see him. I endured many business lectures over dinner."

"Yet neither you nor your brother pursued a career in private enterprise."

"Like I said, I *endured* the lectures. I didn't *enjoy* them."

"Well, I for one am glad you retained some of it. Because I think it's good advice."

She smiles. "Are we bargaining now?"

"I'm listening."

"Let's start at the end."

"Of what?"

"The website. The about page. What does it say?"

On my laptop, I navigate to the page and she leans forward and reads the first paragraph aloud.

"Discount Army Surplus and Outdoor Survival Gear is your source for the most hard to find, authentic Army, Navy, and Marine—"

Meredith cuts her eyes to me. "This is horrendous."

"Why?"

"It has no soul. And it could be the same text on any competitor's website—"

"I get it. I get it. What do you think it should say?"

"The truth. And it should have a picture. Of you and Warren. And tell your story."

"He's not going to take a picture for this website. He'll probably say something like, 'This ain't Chippendales.'"

Meredith cocks her head. "What does *that* mean?"

"It's... I'm saying that I feel he would assert—and I would agree with this—that our customer does not care what we look like."

"Well, that's not really the point."

"What is?"

"The point, Alan, is to connect with the customer. And by showing them a picture—no matter what you look like—in their mind you become more real and authentic. In a way that words on a page cannot achieve."

"Okay, okay."

"Now. Let's talk about the words, because they're the other piece." She points at the screen. "And these are not the words we're looking for."

"Okay. Where do I even start? I mean, what do we say?"

"With why."

"Why?"

"Tell the world *why* you're doing this."

"It's a retirement job for Warren."

"What is it for you, Alan?"

"It's work I can do." I don't mention my leg, but I know Meredith gets it. "I know the gear. The buyers. The type."

"But why?"

My eyes drift upward, to the bedroom above where Riley is sleeping. "For her."

"Warren's a father as well, right?"

"And grandfather."

"Then why not something like Father's Army Surplus?"

I shake my head. "No way. We're not using that. It feels too... I don't know—"

"Okay. Fine."

"And we need the SEO words in there. No one searches for father's combat boots."

"If you're not two fathers, then what are you?"

"Just vets who found each other and got into business."

"Two vets," Meredith says, and I can see her turning the words over in her mind. "What else?"

I exhale sharply. "There is nothing else. We're selling gear and trying to make a living doing it."

"You're not a big business. You're not random guys doing this to make a quick buck. You're not opportunists."

I smile. "Oh, we are. Opportunists. We're not saints. Well, maybe Warren is, but I'm not. I'm doing this for the money."

"For Riley."

"Yes."

"Alan, that's very saint-like."

"Well, while One and a Half Saints Army Surplus may be memorable, it doesn't work for SEO. We're not selling habits and rosaries."

"But you are two vets."

"We are."

"Selling, most likely, to vets."

"Oftentimes."

"We can work with that."

"As in?"

"Two Vets Surplus."

"It's not terrible, but—"

"It lacks the keywords. I got that memo. So: Two Vets Surplus, *colon*, whatever you want. And the domain would be twovets.com."

With my phone, I search for it. "Taken."

"As is the whole internet."

"Twovets.net is available."

Her eyes flash. "Get it. Right now. It's short and catchy, and it works. If you ever expand beyond used surplus gear, it still works."

I buy that domain then and there.

"Two Vets is a good brand," she says.

"I'm thinking 'Two Vets Army-Navy Surplus and Survival Gear.'"

"It could work."

"What do I owe you for this branding exercise?"

She looks at me for a long moment. "What's your take?"

"Thirty percent on eBay. And in the store, for what I buy."

"And for the online store?"

"Fifty percent."

Meredith smiles at me.

"Are you going to give me a number?"

She shakes her head and tells me no, and rises from the dining table, and so do I.

"What *do you want*, Meredith?"

"It's not a percentage."

"Tell me."

"What money can't buy."

55

The numbers group meeting takes place over lunch the day after my Labyrinth session. It's the same format: five metal folding chairs in an empty warehouse (with one seat empty for Lucas) and a camera on a pole for Harold to join remotely.

No one reports losing time.

Somehow we meander over to discussing Labyrinth's release and public adoption. Even eight days later, it still has a lot of buzz. But there's consistently one criticism: the cost. The first session, which is thirty minutes, costs $49. After that, it's $99 for every half hour.

Most Labyrinth users at this point are affluent early adopter types in urban areas. Maybe that was part of Amersa's plan: to make Labyrinth a hit with people who post online frequently and have large social networks.

Nevertheless, the company continues to expand the product's reach. It's delivering pop-up container sites to grocery stores, retailers like Walmart and Costco, and drug stores in rural areas.

They've also committed to bringing costs down with two new subscription programs: Labyrinth Pass and Labyrinth Unlimited. Customers pay monthly and get either a block of hours or unlimited access (though Labyrinth Unlimited is actually capped at a maximum of two hours per day—and it can't be used during peak hours such as lunchtime or right after work).

June informs us that her start date at Amersa is the day after tomorrow—Friday, October 24th.

"Good," Isaac says, setting a Bluetooth speaker in the middle of the circle. "Because we may need some help."

"With what?" she asks.

"You'll see. This is Anders Larsson talking with the company's Chief People Officer and the general counsel. They're talking about the resignation of three of the top scientists at Amersa. Apparently, they did a study on Labyrinth and were very concerned about what they found."

Isaac taps his phone, and the recording plays.

"I don't care," Larsson says, voice rising. "Just file the suit."

A man speaks with a slight British accent. "We can't, Anders. They haven't actually violated their NDA."

"*Yet.*" Larsson practically spits the word.

"That's exactly my point."

"When they do, the damage will be done. We need to *prevent* them."

"That's not really how it works—"

"I don't care, Lewis. Figure it out. Look, we have an email—sent from a company address—with two of them discussing sending CORTEX to the FDA. That's... what? Probable cause? We cite that in the suit and ask for discovery. It should be more than enough."

"Well, probable cause is a standard in criminal law—not civil—but setting that aside, the truth is that they can legally send CORTEX to the FDA."

"No, they can't. We have an NDA."

"It doesn't matter, Anders."

"Why not?"

"Whistleblower protections."

"I thought that was only for fraud against the government or financial fraud with public companies."

"You're referring to Sarbanes-Oxley. Yes, that's all true, but there are also protections for whistleblowers reporting drug and medical device safety concerns."

"Lewis, we don't have an FDA-approved medical device."

"Yet. But we have applied. That's key to our insurance reimbursement plans. But the FDA isn't the only agency that handles whistleblower claims. There's the Consumer Product Safety Commission—or CPSC—which handles issues with consumer devices and services. That's what we have right now—and it's a device that is being very widely used, and more so with each passing day. Complicating matters, all the media buzz you've stirred up for Labyrinth will make the CPSC and news outlets take notice."

The speaker falls silent. I'm wondering if that's the end of the recording, but Larsson speaks again.

"Then we have a bigger problem than I thought here."

Another silence stretches out before the third person in the room speaks—the Chief People Officer, I assume. She sounds—understandably—quite uncomfortable. "From my perspective, it would be helpful to have some context here. Can you share exactly what is in the CORTEX study?"

I can hear the rage in Larsson's voice. "No, Carla, I can't. In fact, no one on planet Earth, now or ever again, is going to share exactly what is in the CORTEX study."

"Okay. Then... can you give me an idea of the magnitude of what we're talking about here?"

"The magnitude? Sure, I'll tell you the magnitude."

There's a sound like he's typing on his keyboard and clicking a computer mouse.

"Eighteen percent. That's the percentage of adults in the US who live with a mental health condition. That's over sixty million people."

When no one says anything, Larsson continues. "Forty percent. That's how many students experience persistent feelings of sadness or hopelessness. Two in every five. And it's not just the kids these days. It's about half of us. Forty-three percent of Americans report feeling anxious on a routine basis. Are you getting the picture? This is the world without Labyrinth. And it's just getting worse.

"Does the CORTEX study raise some interesting findings? Yes. It does. Things that perhaps we should follow and investigate further. And, I'll concede, with any disruptive technology or even vaccine or miracle drug, you never bat a thousand. Bad things can happen. But make no mistake, a world without Labyrinth is far worse. Labyrinth is an imperfect product for an imperfect world."

Larson pauses, and when his guests don't say anything, he goes on. "It's a dangerous thing—for the world—to let perfection hold us hostage. Perfection is often what stops progress. Progress is messy, it's inherently imperfect. It's easy to see the flaws. In the short term. But long-term, people realize that it was worth it. That's what we're dealing with. Some very smart scientists who have some data and concerns, but what they don't have is the big picture. They've just got their piece of the puzzle, and they think it's the whole thing. Because they're classic narcissists. They want to save the world and they want to get full credit for it, and this is their one shot. They're going to take it. That much, I know."

Another silence stretches out, and I can only imagine how awkward it was in that room when this recording was captured.

Carla breaks the silence. "From an HR perspective, based on what I'm hearing, the things we can do are to reinforce to each of the three exiting employees that they have signed an NDA—"

Isaac leans forward and silences the speaker. "They don't say anything interesting after that."

To June, he says, "I looked for this CORTEX study on the server, but I couldn't find it. I think it's been deleted or moved to a portable device. But there may be a printed copy in the research division. Are you up for looking for it?"

"Sure. But what do I do when I find it? Make a copy?"

"No. That's too risky. The copiers are under video surveillance. And besides, you may not be able to."

"I could try taking pictures of the pages with my phone," June offers. "But some study publications are quite long."

"And you'd risk getting caught doing it," Isaac says. He motions to the speaker. "As you're about to hear, I don't think we should take that risk. Let's do this: when you're settled in at work, try to figure out where the study is and what sort of security is in place around it. We'll make a plan from there."

"All right," June says. "But until we get the CORTEX study and see what's in it, Alan, I think you should stop using Labyrinth."

"I appreciate the concern, but I mean, how harmful could it be? I heard what you said before—about the visual stuff and reality distortion. But Labyrinth is still just a fancy video game, right?"

"That's true," June concedes. "But playing video games can be problematic for some. The WHO has even added gaming disorder to the ICD-11 as a recognized medical diagnosis. It's part of why South Korea tried the gaming curfew."

"Didn't work," Isaac says. "They turned off their gaming servers from midnight to 6 AM, but people just used servers outside the country. They had to repeal it." He looks over at me. "But that doesn't apply here. Alan can't go into Labyrinth any time he wants. Nor can anyone else."

Rose speaks up then. "Can it harm Alan physically? Like, I don't know, damage his brain?"

June considers that a moment. "It has no way to inject a pathogen or drug therapy into the user, but behavior can certainly alter someone's body. We certainly see that with exercise, and there have been documented cases of physical changes from smartphone use.

"In smartphone addiction, MRI brain scans have shown that gray matter thins in the prefrontal cortex. The evidence is limited, but it's intriguing. Sleep is also an issue. Long-term REM suppression can—in some individuals—mimic early-stage dementia. Labyrinth is very much like the introduction of smartphones. It's a new technology, but we don't know exactly what physical effects it will cause."

June looks around the group. "What we do know is that some of the scientists who studied it were very concerned about it. And that's why I think Alan should stop using Labyrinth until we know more."

Isaac and I lock eyes, and for the first time, I sense that it's him and me against the rest of the group. I know they have my best interests at heart, but my best interests right now are to figure all this out. Leaving the trial and sitting at home doesn't accomplish that.

"I'm staying in," I say quietly. "If we get this CORTEX study and there's some glaring danger, sure, I'll leave. But until then, I'm going to keep going."

After a silent moment, Isaac leans over and activates the speaker again. "This is the last recording, and it's important."

This time, it's Larsson talking with the security chief from the first audio file.

"Times like this I wish we still had Briggs around."

"Sir," the security chief says, "I just want to make sure I understand what you're implying."

"Oh, cut the theatrics, Terry. You know what I'm implying."

The man sounds even more uncomfortable. "I think, sir, in a situation like this, it's important to be very explicit about what the plan is."

"Is that what's important?"

"Yes, sir."

"That's where you're wrong, Terry. What's important is that these very misguided—albeit well-meaning—individuals don't release the contents of that study. We're at a pivotal moment in adoption. This could set us back years. Do whatever it takes."

56

After the recordings, I recount my fourth Labyrinth session.

When I'm done, Isaac rises quickly from his folding metal chair, almost tipping it over as he turns and begins pacing in the warehouse. "This is bad. Very, very, very bad. I suspected they knew about us before, but it's obvious now. There's no way this is a coincidence. A neuroscience researcher named May. A computer expert named Ian—who wants to know the secret of the Labyrinth and why they're alone? Fermi Paradox, anyone?"

Isaac paces back and forth, shaking his head. "They're messing with us. Telling us they know. They're probably watching us, waiting—"

June stands and extends a hand to Isaac. "Can we take it down a notch? We don't know that."

"Don't we?" Isaac shoots back. "Why would they put that in there? Why would it put *us* in there?"

From the speaker on the camera, the garbled, faintly British voice says, "You've made an assumption, my young friend."

"Which is?"

"You assume *they*—Amersa—is doing this. I'm no technological wizard, as you are, but my understanding is that an AI has a bit of a mind of its own, does it not?"

"Meaning?" Isaac says. His tone is still defensive, but some of the fight has gone out of him.

"Maybe," June says, "There's something happening here that we don't fully understand."

Isaac settles back in the seat. "Maybe. But what if it's reading Alan's mind like a biological hard drive, and making avatars of us to tell him it knows. What if it has achieved artificial general intelligence and it's trying to protect itself somehow?"

When no one says anything, I glance at Isaac and June. "Is that even possible?"

Isaac stares at the floor. "I don't know. I work in IT. Lucas was part of the development team. I don't know what happened after he left—but they were working on it."

"Let's assume it's true," Rose says. "What would we do?"

"We roll out," Isaac says. "We leave and keep going until we have more information."

"I can't leave my family," June says.

"Same," I mutter. "And I can't raise a seven-year-old on the run."

"They know about us," Isaac says flatly.

I lock eyes with him. "They *might* know."

Isaac seems resigned now. "Staying is a risk."

"Believe me, I know. You're talking to the guy who walks in there—to Amersa and the Labyrinth—every time. And I never know if I'll walk out."

When I pick up Riley from school, she once again hands me a sealed envelope bearing the Wake County Schools logo.

At the first stoplight, I open it, expecting to see another notice that she's falling further behind in reading and that additional intervention is required.

My hands begin to sweat when I read the word Amersa and then Labyrinth. Scanning it, the phrases hit me like arrows in the gut:

An immersive reading program...
Rather than a one-size-fits-all...
A program that adapts to your child's needs, progress, and indeed how they learn best.

The next page shows a diagram of the device. There's a VR headset and gloves that appear to be made from material similar to the suit I wear at Amersa: gray and lumpy.

There are a few photos below of children sitting around the table with their headsets on, waving with the oversized gloves, smiling like it's Christmas morning.

A car honks behind me, and I press the accelerator hard, pushing Riley back into her booster seat like a fair ride launching.

"*Daaaad!*" she shouts. "You're going too fast."

"It's okay," I mumble, my mind still on the letter. "Hey, Kiddo, have you used anything new at school for reading?"

"Yes! Dad, it's so cool. It's like a video game where you can explore anything. I did a safari and then a haunted house. And my friend Ella did a space colony on the moon, and Henry did this dinosaur land—"

"I get the picture. What exactly do you do in the game?"

"You have to read the signs, and you have to read clues, like in mine, there were these notes all over the haunted house and then words written in fog on a mirror."

"What do you do when you read it?"

She shrugs. "I dunno."

"What do you mean you don't know? What's the point of the game?"

"Oh. In the haunted house, you have to read the signs to figure out which doors to go through. And then on the safari, you have to find the lost baby elephant and bring it back to its mother, and the gamekeeper has left lots of notes and clues."

Frankly, it sounds pretty good. Especially for a child with ADHD. Which is only going to make what I'm about to say even harder for her. As such, I wait until we get home to drop the bomb that she's not going to be using the Labyrinth device.

I do so after dinner, when our empty plates are sitting on the table. As expected, my daughter explodes at this news.

"*Daaaad*. You cannot be serious. What am I supposed to do? Sit there in the room while everybody else gets to play?"

"You leave the classroom to use Labyrinth?"

"Duh."

"Never mind that. I'll talk to your teacher about it."

"Why don't you want me to use it?"

"I just don't, okay?"

Riley balls up her fists. "Dad. *Why?*"

"Because I said so, okay?"

I'm aware that I've just used what is perhaps the most ineffective parenting phrase in human history, but I'm exhausted and scared, and I just don't have the emotional energy for this fight right now.

"You want me to be left out," Riley practically screams.

"I don't, darling, I promise you."

"Mom would let me use it."

I exhale, and the strength goes out of me, and I just stare at the carpet.

"I wish she was here," Riley says, lips quivering.

I wait, knowing the floodgates are about to be unleashed. I think—but don't say—*I do too*.

Riley keeps going, hurling verbal rocks at me, and I just sit there, taking them until she runs out of energy and finally storms off, stomping on the stairs as if she's trying to break them.

A few minutes later, I get a text from Meredith:

> Riley sent me a message from her watch. It's audio of her asking if she can come live with me. :)

I know Meredith put the smiley emoji after the message to lighten the mood. It only half works.

I text her back:

> Sidewalk summit?

She reacts with a thumbs-up.

Outside, standing on the sidewalk, facing the row of townhomes, I tell Meredith what happened. When she asks me why I told Riley she couldn't use the device, I tell Meredith that I've been using Labyrinth in the PTSD trial and that I have my reasons for keeping Riley away from it.

"Have you used it yet?" I ask her.

"No. But me and two of my girlfriends are going Friday night. We have reservations for the pod at Crabtree."

"Cancel it."

"Why?"

"Trust me. Okay. Just... cancel it."

I don't know if it's the fight with Riley or the stress of the last two days but the ringing starts right after I put her to bed. In my own bedroom, I lie there, staring at the blades of the ceiling fan going round and round as the ringing keeps getting louder: *clang-clang-clang.*

Until it blots everything out.

When reality returns, I'm sitting behind the wheel of my Ford Explorer, parked in my garage.

I'm dressed casually, in slacks and a white button-up shirt. I don't feel sore or bruised. Looking at myself in the rearview, there's no sign that I've been in a fight.

The only thing in my pocket is the vehicle key.

Outside the Explorer, I place my hand on the hood. It's warm. I just got home. Or just turned it off.

Through the garage door, in the kitchen, I spot my phone and wallet on the bar.

The time on the microwave above the stove says it's nearly midnight.

I lost hours.

Moving quickly, I climb the stairs and turn the knob on Riley's door.

It's locked.

Reaching above the door frame, I find an unlocking pin about the size of an unfolded paper clip. I slide it into the emergency release hole, turn the handle, and breathe out when I see Riley sleeping peacefully in a sea of stuffed animals. She probably locked the door because of our fight.

Downstairs, I send a Signal message to the group telling them that I lost time tonight and the exact hours.

Me too, Isaac instantly responds. *Same time period.*

57

The following morning, I wake up to an email from Amersa.

They're asking to change my appointment from this coming Tuesday to Monday.

And that's not all. They say—because my sessions have been well-tolerated and show signs of possible efficacy—that they would like to do sessions every Monday, Wednesday, and Friday until I complete the study.

It asks me to click a link to confirm the schedule changes, or to call Amersa if I can't comply.

I send a message to the Signal group telling them about the proposed changes.

Replies appear almost instantly, first from Isaac:

> *They're probably accelerating the study so they can have data to publish to rebut the CORTEX study if it comes out.*
>
> Rose: *That makes sense.*
>
> June: *My concern is the neurological effects, Alan. This is a major acceleration in the pace of sessions. You started every two weeks. Then weekly. Now three times a week. I think you should decline. It would be prudent to proceed more slowly until we know more about Labyrinth's neurological effects.*

Isaac and I then go back and forth with her, the two of us arguing that we need answers and that more Labyrinth sessions are actually a good thing for us.

In the end, I click the link in the email and agree to the new schedule.

The accelerated pace of sessions, however, is going to cause problems at school. So are the group meetings, which will occur the day after. Between the two, I'm going to miss a large part of next week at school.

And work is not the only place I have a problem to solve.

Riley wakes up just as mad at me as she was last night when she stormed off to bed.

The fact that I'm making her get ready earlier than normal to read certainly doesn't help matters.

But, being a parent always entails taking a lot of heat.

An hour later, I'm parking at Riley's elementary school and walking her in, to her classroom, where her teacher is sitting behind a wooden desk.

I emailed and told him we were coming. But not why.

Riley stomps off to a corner of the room. In a low tone, next to his desk, I tell him that I simply can't agree to let her use the Labyrinth Learning experience. He seems surprised.

When he asks why, I motion to the door, and in the hall, I tell him that I know it seems odd. And remind him that I'm a teacher too.

He stares at me, and is about to speak when another teacher passes and he waves at her, and when she's out of earshot, he says, "She's behind."

"I know. I'm working on it. But she's not going to use that device."

After teaching my first two classes, I make my way to the front office.

Sheila's door is open, but I pause at the threshold, watching my principal eat a grilled chicken salad out of a square Tupperware, staring at her computer screen. When she sees me, she motions for me to come in.

"Hyena problem, Alan?" she says, lifting a forkful of lettuce to her mouth. She's turned back to the screen.

"You could say that. I'm going to miss a lot of school this week."

"Just a sec," she mumbles, clicking the mouse faster before turning to me and asking what days and times I'm going to be out.

When I tell her, she writes the dates on the big calendar that covers her desk.

"That all?" she asks, not looking up.

"I could ask you the same question. *Is that all?* I've just asked for practically a week off."

"I'm well aware of that, Alan."

"Do you want to know why?"

"I know why."

"You do?"

"You need that time off because you don't have any other choice."

Her response settles my nerves a bit.

"Describe the hyenas, Alan."

Sheila's staring at me, and it's not the playful principal I talked to in this room before. It's a caring friend who wants answers. And like a certain teacher in this same school, she deserves them.

I rise, close the door, and settle back in the chair.

"It's for a clinical trial I'm in. And some group meetings after."

She tosses the fork in the Tupperware container. "Good."

"Really?"

"An investment in your mental health is an investment in your future, Alan. I'm here for it. Whatever it takes."

After school, Riley seems just as mad as before. She sits in the booster seat in the back, staring out the window. I can practically see the steam rising from her body.

"How was school, sweetie?"

For a while, I think she's not going to respond. Finally, she turns and cocks her head. "It would have been good if I had been allowed to *actually learn*."

★

On Saturday morning, I'm sitting in yet another abandoned warehouse on a folding metal chair, listening to June recount her first day at work at Amersa.

"So far, they're just making me read up on all the past research Amersa has done, and then all the ongoing trials and what's in the works."

"Have you seen the CORTEX study?" Isaac asks.

"No, but I think I know where it is. There's a secure documents room I have to badge into. And I have to go through a metal detector first before I can even reach the door. I can't take a phone or a laptop in, or even any paper or a notebook. And I can't take anything out. Inside the room, the cabinets are locked, and I have to use my badge on each one of those. I can read documents at one of the tables, but I have to put them back. The real issue is that I looked through the cabinets I have access to, and I don't see CORTEX. But, there are two cabinets that my badge wouldn't open. It's possible the study is in one of those."

"I could try to steal someone's badge," Rose says.

"June would have to use it quickly," Isaac says. "Security disables the old badges and issues a new one if a badge is reported missing. But the idea could work. Do you know where the blank badges are kept?"

"Yes. They're in a closet in the security workroom."

"Do you clean that area?"

"I can. I'll swap with whoever's assigned."

"Okay. Get me a blank badge, and I'll clone it to match Amersa's Chief Research Officer. June can use it to access those other two cabinets."

"What do I do if I find CORTEX?" June asks.

"I've been thinking about that. Are there cameras in the room?"

"Not that I've seen," June replies.

"That makes sense. Someone monitoring them could read the study if it were taken out and flipped through at a table. But I'm betting security does a routine check of the cabinets to make sure nothing has been taken. What I think you should do is smuggle some pages into the room."

"Pages of what? And how?"

"Another study. Something that might look similar to CORTEX at a glance. Obviously, you haven't seen the study, but you know, a paper along the same lines. You'll have to hide the pages under your clothes—and that's the same way you'll get CORTEX out. In the room, when—if—you find CORTEX, leave the cover page on the study but replace the rest of the pages with the other study you brought in. That way, if security pulls the file to check, they'll see the cover page and if they flip through it, they'll see what looks like a valid research study."

Next, we talk about the recent time gap. As discussed on Signal, Isaac and I are the only ones who seem to be affected. And neither of us—or anyone else—has any clue what happened or what it means.

There are a few things I've been holding back from the group. And that has weighed on me. For a few reasons.

The first is that all of us are putting more and more trust in each other—as evidenced by our recent plan here.

And the second is that I sense that it might be holding me back from the answers that I need.

For that reason, I pull out the strange key I received in a recent time gap, the one when Riley and I lived in the train car in the woods.

"Does anyone recognize this?"

The question is met with puzzled looks. On instinct, I pass the key to June and it goes around the circle, Rose reaching across the empty seat where Lucas would have sat, passing it back to me.

No one knows what it goes to or where it came from.

I tell them how it came to be in my possession, and we all file it away. It is another piece, and despite my trying to fit it in, we still don't know where it belongs.

★

After the meeting, as I'm turning onto my street, I find two Raleigh Police cruisers parked right outside my townhome. A Dodge Charger is behind them, and Detective Tate is leaning against it, staring down at his phone.

I left Riley at Meredith's house while I did the numbers meeting, and I hope she's not looking out the window.

When I park, Ramirez exits the Charger and, by way of greeting, hands me a search warrant.

I look down at it, shrug, and tell them to go ahead. Leaning into my SUV, I hit the button to open both garage doors.

The uniformed officers, led by Tate, march in and sweep the house. From the garage, Tate nods to Ramirez, who gets a prepackaged buccal-swab kit from her car and motions me to follow her inside.

In the kitchen, another woman is waiting. She introduces herself as a Detective Division supervisor, noting that she needs to be present for the DNA swab (which is also in the search warrant). She turns a camera on, notifying me aloud as she does so.

Ramirez snaps on blue nitrile gloves and rips open the heat-sealed foil pouch, and two sterile cotton swabs drop into a Tyvek tray.

She swabs my left inner cheek for about thirty seconds, then repeats the exercise on the right side.

She lays the swabs on a cardboard drying box, and the three of us stand there awkwardly. I consider offering them water, but that just feels weird.

Ramirez prints the case number, date-time, and my initials on the evidence envelope, adds a red BIOHAZARD sticker, signs the chain-of-custody line, and seals it with tamper tape before stuffing the whole thing in an evidence bag. The supervisor thanks me for my cooperation and departs through the garage.

Several uniformed officers walk past me carrying pairs of my shoes in evidence bags.

Two more officers descend the stairs and exit the front door with clothes.

The clothes won't help them any. The shoes won't either. After the Labor Day cookout at Meredith's parents' house, when

Ryan eyed my footsteps in the mud, I got rid of the shoes I wore that night in downtown.

The DNA is a problem, though. I'm betting I left some on Briggs during our altercation.

They probably already have my prints at the scene.

From the front door, I gaze out at the street, thinking, wondering how much time I have. Not a lot, I'm guessing.

My neighbors suddenly have places to go. They exit their homes and walk slowly—*very, very slowly*—to their cars.

Others need to check their mailboxes at this very moment. They do so while not-so-casually glancing over at the scene. I've lived here all of a few weeks. This is a great look for the literal new kid on the block.

But the only actual kid on this block I'm worried about is my daughter. And when the police have left, I walk over to Meredith's house, hoping, like all parents do at some point in their lives, that she is unaware of the issues I'm going through.

58

I'm assuming Meredith saw the police outside my place and kept Riley preoccupied and away from the windows, because my daughter seems blissfully unaware of the afternoon's events.

The timing—with me being at the numbers meeting—was fortuitous. It's about the only instance where timing has worked out for me lately.

After thanking Meredith, Riley and I walk back up to our house, and I tell her to put a dress on. She asks why, and I tell her why, and she does it without another word.

As she does so, I walk back down to Meredith's place and thank her again for watching Riley.

"I'm happy to do it, Alan. And I'm happy to call Ryan."

"Thanks, but it's okay."

"Is it okay?"

"It's a misunderstanding. It'll get worked out in time."

She stares at me. "Sometimes misunderstandings take a long time to get worked out."

There are twenty years of history in those words, and only three hours before the sun sets, and there is something I have to do. I tell her that, and she stops me before I can elaborate on where we're going. She seems to know. What she says is:

"You two go. I'll be here when you get back."

In the car, Riley and I ride in silence.

We buy flowers at a Whole Foods and, at the cemetery, we

walk across the grass, like I did one year ago, and place them on the grave.

Riley squeezes my hand and tears roll down her face, and in that moment, the spat over Labyrinth is the size of an ant in the shadow of the gray slab of granite bearing the name of what we've lost.

I knew it would, and I don't even flinch when that little evil hand starts shaking the rocks and makes me see the numbers when I look down at the dates.

59

Sunday morning, I wake up to my phone buzzing on the nightstand. There are dozens of messages in the Signal group. From everyone.

Scrolling, reading, I struggle to catch up.

The first message is from Isaac:

> *WTF?*
>
> *Check the site—12122518914208.com*

I click the link and for a moment struggle to understand what I'm even seeing. The site has changed.

It used to have an illustration of an iceberg with text above that read:

> *YOU HAVE REACHED.*

There was a simple question beneath it:

> *What do the numbers mean to you?*

The rest of the page was a web form that collected information. That's all gone now. In its place is a headline that reads:

> *ENTER THE LABYRINTH.*
> *IT'S FREE!*

Below it, the page gives more details.

This is not a lottery.
Or a contest.
Your first three Labyrinth sessions are completely free.
You read that right: free.
While supplies last.
Simply sign up below.

That's followed by sign-in buttons for Google, Apple, Facebook, and pretty much any other service.

Switching back to the Signal app, I scroll through the history of the messages.

> June: *Isaac, did you do this?*
>
> Isaac: *Of course not! I told you guys I don't control the site.*
>
> Harold: *It would seem that Amersa controls the site. It's the only thing that makes sense.*
>
> June: *I agree. Cost has been one of the biggest hindrances for Labyrinth adoption. I see it all the time in articles and on social media.*
>
> Isaac: *Still makes no sense. If it was Amersa, wouldn't they just put it on their own site or even the Labyrinth site or app? Why use the numbers site? I mean, the numbers site is not a good domain. It's hard to remember. It means basically nothing when you share it on social media. From a branding standpoint, it's just very strange.*
>
> Rose: *Let's start with what we know. Someone— not any of us—controls the numbers site, and they apparently have a lot of money and want people to use Labyrinth. Does that sound right?*
>
> Isaac: *Yes. But it doesn't lead to any conclusions. This is just totally random.*

June: *What if it's Amersa trying to accelerate adoption but doing it in a way that makes them look more profitable?*

Isaac: *I don't follow.*

June: *Remember the conversation with the investor? Amersa was having money problems, and they were concerned about the amount of expenses. What if this is Amersa somehow raising money off the books and spending it on Labyrinth sessions for people, then booking the revenue through Amersa so that it makes the company look more profitable?*

Harold: *This actually makes sense to me. But that still leaves the mystery of why they're doing it through the numbers site. And if they do indeed control the site— which we all joined through—it implies that they know exactly who we are. That would reinforce the conclusion from Alan's Labyrinth sessions.*

June: *If this is true, then where does that leave us? What should we do? What can we do?*

Isaac: *I don't see what we can do. We're in the same place we were at the last meeting. Unless we get some answers—the CORTEX study or what exactly the numbers mean or what Labyrinth represents—then we're basically just running in circles. Also, the fact that Alan and I lost time and then the numbers site changes... it's sort of a coincidence. I'm not saying it's related, but maybe it is?*

The group goes around and around after that with no conclusions. After attaching my prosthetic, I type out my own response:

Just confirming I saw this, and like everyone else, I have no clue what it means.

When Riley wakes up, I ask her if she wants to go to Hill Ridge

Farm. Like Pullen Park, it's one of our favorite spots to go on the weekend. The farm is sort of like an actual farm mixed with an amusement park. This time of year, there's a pumpkin patch as well as the year-round attractions: a train, a massive slide, a splash pad (which won't be open this late in the fall), a carousel, and lots of animals.

Riley only agrees to go after I consent to a shopping trip to Learning Express after the farm. I'm not exactly sure how I've gotten to this point—where I now have to bribe my daughter to do things I know she actually wants to do, but I consent. Because I'm emotionally exhausted.

As Riley's getting dressed, I text Meredith:

> Riles and I are going to Hill Ridge Farm. Any interest?

Her reply is one word:

> Interested.

The bubble with three dots pops up, and her next message is along the lines of what I was expecting:

> Can we talk first?

In reply, I stroll down the sidewalk to Meredith's place. Despite being a mere two doors down, it feels like a hundred-mile walk. It's the weight of the looming conversation, one that's been a long time coming, even before the police searched my place.

Sitting in her living room, she cuts to the chase. "I talked to Ryan."

My mouth goes dry. One part of me wants to know what he knows—what the police know. The other part is terrified of what Meredith's about to say.

She speaks slowly and methodically now, as if laying each word out on the coffee table in front of us like cards. "He says that you are a person of interest in a murder investigation."

"I can explain."

"I'm listening."

"Can we do it at the farm? I want to get Riley out of the house. There's been a lot of tension between us in the last week over the Labyrinth issue. I need a reset with her."

Meredith nods, and together, we walk up the street and load up in the car.

Forty-five minutes later, Meredith and I are sitting at a picnic table at the farm in Youngsville, watching Riley sifting through dirt and rocks, mining for gems. While she looks for precious stones a hundred feet away, Meredith stares at me, awaiting precious answers.

And on that Sunday in late October, four days before Halloween, I tell her everything. She listens, furrows her eyebrows, asks a few questions, and when I'm done, she doesn't say anything. She only looks out at the midday sun and the trees.

What I've said is a lot to take in.

A lot.

But she's like her brother right now—stone-faced. Betraying nothing.

I lean across the picnic table. "What are you thinking?"

She stands and steps out from under the covered area, into the sunlight.

Half of me wants to simply let her go. That was half of why I told her everything.

But the other half of me gets up from that picnic table and follows her.

She walks across the farm. I walk behind her, giving her space. I know, on some level, I told her everything as an escape hatch for her.

She slows.

I do too.

When she stops, I plant my feet two arm's lengths away.

She turns and eyes me for three whole seconds and says, "You should talk to Ryan."

"He can't help me with this. You know that. It's over his head."

"It's over your head, too."

"Oh, I totally agree with that. But I also think that Isaac, June, Rose, Harold, and I are the only people who can figure out what is *actually* happening here."

She turns her head to the wagon ride bouncing by, and all the happy faces and parents holding their kids.

When they've passed, she asks me the only question that actually matters between us:

"What do you want from me?"

My answer is one word. "Nothing."

"*Nothing?* That's what you want?"

I see my mistake. Verbally, I try to correct it. "*Nothing* is what I'm asking for."

"What do you *want*, Alan?"

"It's hard to know, okay? It's hard to even process what I want when there's so much on me right now. I'm just surviving, taking it a day at a time. What I want is my daughter to be safe and happy."

"Why did you tell me all this?"

"I wanted you to know. Because you deserve to know. Because of what we've been through now and before."

She keeps staring at me, and her chest is rising and falling, and I take a step closer to her. "And because I wanted to give you the chance to walk away if this is too complicated for you."

She narrows her eyes, and even as well as I know her, I can't read the expression. Her next words are a dagger in my gut.

"I feel like walking away when it's too real is your signature move, Alan."

I stand there, absorbing the words. Her body relaxes like a fighter who's heard the bell ring.

"You're right," I say quietly. "I did. And what I'm telling you now is that I'm even more of a mess now than I was back then. And I'm saying that if you walk away, I will never judge you for it."

60

Monday, right after lunch, I'm walking down the corridor at Amersa, on my way to my appointment with Linus, when a man up ahead slows and squints at me.

He's thin, with wire-rimmed glasses, short brown hair, and an expensive-looking navy sweater over a plaid button-up shirt. I think he's going to stop and speak to me, but he only eyes me as he passes. When I glance back, he's stopped in the hall, head completely turned, watching me go into my appointment.

That was weird. But I'm sort of used to it. One-legged men tend to get some looks. But that was a long one.

The meeting with Linus passes like the previous ones: him asking me about my impressions of what happened in my last visit to the Labyrinth and if I have any concerns (I do—but none I'm willing to share with my artificial intelligence counselor).

At the end, he advises me to go to the bathroom before my session begins. "As a reminder," he says cheerfully, "we can simulate most anything—except evacuating bodily waste."

In the bathroom, I shove the door open and stand at the urinal. A stall door swings open, and a figure rushes by, not bothering to wash his hands. But he doesn't exit. Instead, he takes the cylindrical trash can and props it against the door.

I don't like the sound of that, but I'm mid-stream here. As I turn my head, I spot a phone sitting upright on the floor in the stall. He must've been holding it down, using it to watch people entering.

The guy who blocked the door rushes toward me, and I throw

an elbow that connects with his left cheek, and he tumbles like a bowling pin, rolling slightly on the bathroom floor.

Turning, I realize it's the man from the hall.

The outer door swings in, dinging the trash can, and I yell, "It's occupied!"

My assailant's wire-rim glasses are off-kilter, and he's looking up at me with scared, wild eyes.

"I did what you wanted," he says, voice shaking.

I have no clue what to say to that. I've never seen this guy before today.

At least, not that I can remember.

It must have been one of the tinnitus time gaps.

As I see it, I have two choices: confess that I don't know him and see what he knows. Or keep up the ruse.

I choose door number two.

"This is just a reminder: I'm watching."

For my fifth session in the Labyrinth, I emerge from the bathroom in the school that's been converted to a hostel.

I've got two things on my mind: finding Ian and May—and getting my truck back. In that order.

I'm turning the corner, on my way to find my fellow travelers, when I spot a woman lying on the floor beside a rolling bucket, the long handle of a mop sticking out. Her eyes are closed, and she's convulsing, body jerking wildly.

I rush to her and place my hand on the side of her face, hoping her eyes will open from the touch. But they remain shut. She's wearing a name tag that says Daisy and a dark blue uniform. My mind flashes to Rose and the night I met her.

Behind me, a voice calls out. It's Dave, the front desk worker at the hostel. "We've got to get her to her room! Can you carry her?"

"No, I've only got—" I stop mid-sentence. Because I have two legs here.

Again, I think about Rose, lying on the floor of her apartment, looking up at me as I told her that I can't carry her because I have one leg.

Here in the hostel, I slide my arms underneath Daisy and lift her and march through the corridors, following Dave back to the building's entrance.

He ducks into the offices, which remind me of the front office at my school where the principals, guidance counselors, and staff work.

One of the offices has been converted into a bedroom with a narrow bed. Beside it is a device with a hose that leads to a clear plastic face mask. It reminds me of a CPAP machine that someone with sleep apnea would use at night.

When I've settled Daisy onto the bed, Dave pulls the mask over her face and presses a button on the machine. It vibrates, and I hear air rushing through the hose.

"What's the matter with her?" I ask Dave.

He shrugs. "Dude, I don't know. It's like some kind of lung condition."

The room is cluttered with packaged food, electronic parts, and survival gear. Dave, following my gaze, explains, "It's all stuff guests left behind. She's saving up."

"For what?"

"She wants to get to the center of the Labyrinth. She says there's a hospital there that can fix her lungs."

Daisy opens her eyes and looks up at me, then over at Dave. "Welcome back," he says.

She closes her eyes again and takes a few deep breaths before reaching over to turn off the machine. Removing the mask, she sits up, sucking air in rough, ragged gulps.

"Thanks," she says to me.

"Dave mentioned that you believe there's a treatment for your lungs at the center of the Labyrinth."

"Yeah," she confirms, her breath still uneven.

"Why?"

"I have to."

I sit in the chair across from her, silently prompting her to explain.

She takes another deep breath and shrugs.

"Hope. Life's a lot harder without it."

"Well," Dave says, shuffling to the door, "Glad you're okay, Daisy. I better get back. These comics aren't going to read themselves."

When he's gone, Daisy says, "Heard your truck got stolen."

"Yeah. I was about to go sort that out when I found you."

"It's pretty common, actually. Everybody's looking for a ticket out of here."

"So I hear."

"Except for you and your friends."

"That's right. We've got our own ideas about what's at the center of the Labyrinth."

Daisy is breathing easier now, but her words come out slow and tentative, her gaze fixed on the floor.

"Listen, I know I wouldn't be the strongest member of a travel party, but I've been collecting things for the trip for a long time," she motions to the boxes and stacks of items. "I've got rain gear, food, and lots of broken equipment. And some credits saved up."

I nod, seeing where this is going.

"You want to come with us."

"If you'll have me."

"I'll put it to the group, but our main issue is the truck."

"I might have a solution to that."

In our room at the hostel, I introduce Daisy to Ian and May, and everyone quickly agrees that it makes sense for the four of us to work together. May and Ian are already aware of the situation with our truck. Daisy informs us that there is really only one possibility for getting another transport: the junkyard.

"The junkyard has vehicles?" Ian asks.

"Not running ones," Daisy replies. "But they have broken ones. And parts. We can trade for both."

With a smile, she adds, "The guy running the junkyard can be grumpy at times, but if he's in a good mood, he might help us."

"It's a lot of ifs," Ian says.

In the silence that follows, I survey the converted classroom.

While I was gone, he and May spread out all of the computer components into a sort of makeshift electronics junkyard. I sense that Ian's frustration at his own progress on the computer and radio is coming through now.

"I don't see what choice we have," May says.

"Trust me," he says, "finding parts and fixing something in this Labyrinth is easier said than done."

"When you only have one option," May says, "it's therefore your best option."

Outside the hostel, the wind blows and a light rain falls as the four of us make our way down the street to the junkyard. Beyond the gate, we weave through mountains of scrap metal and abandoned cars until we reach a beat-up metal shipping container with corrugated walls and spray-painted white letters that spell OFFICE.

Under the sign, someone has cut a jagged rectangular hole in the container and placed a large piece of plexiglass over it, creating a window. The makeshift window is sealed from the outside with foam and caulk.

Daisy knocks on one of the double doors, and it creaks open. A man in rain gear peers out.

Without a word, he turns and leads us into the container. Just beyond the door, there's a sort of staging area with a grate in the floor for rain to drain.

The junkyard's proprietor hangs his rain gear on one of the hooks welded to the container wall and marches through two layers of plastic strip curtains.

When our party has taken off our ponchos and jackets, we make our way past the plastic strips and find the man sitting behind a homemade metal desk that's been welded together.

On the far wall, there are shelves which have been welded to the container. Below it, there's an elevated metal work table that's stacked high with parts.

The junkyard owner is wearing military fatigues, but they don't have a branch or rank on them. Daisy facilitates the introductions (his name is Wally), and after we tell him what we want, he looks at the four of us for a long moment.

"Heard it before. Seen it before. Nobody ever comes back from the center."

"Maybe it's because they find what they need," I tell him.

"That's dangerous."

"What is?"

"Hope."

My gaze drifts over to Daisy. "Well, I've recently been reminded that life's a lot harder without it."

Wally smirks, but doesn't say anything.

"I've also been reminded that when you only have one option, it's your best option."

Wally leans back in the chair, the front legs lifting slightly. "What exactly are you proposing?"

"You make your money repairing things and selling them. Or finding parts to sell. We can help."

"Yeah?"

"We can scavenge the junkyard and find what you need. I assume you've got a list?"

"I do."

"We do too," Ian says quickly. "Computer and electronic parts."

"Is that the trade?" Wally asks.

"Half of it," I put in before Ian can say more. "We want a car too. Whatever is easiest to fix and get us back on the road."

Wally lets the chair settle back on the container floor with a boom and sets his forearms on the welded desk.

"You don't need a car."

I open my mouth to respond, but he holds a hand up, pressing on.

"What you need is a transport that can withstand the storms and anything else you might run into out there."

"I'm assuming you have something in mind?"

"I do," he says, rising.

With that, he leads us through the two plastic curtains, and we don our rain gear and push through the creaking container doors and follow Wally through his kingdom of metal rubble.

Our journey ends at a graveyard of vehicles ranging from trucks and cars to tractor-trailers. The tires are rotting. Some are sunk in the ground as if the earth is slowly swallowing them. At the end, there's a hulking machine that instantly makes my heart beat faster.

It's a tan Humvee—the exact make and model as the one I was driving the day a roadside bomb tore apart my life. I stand there, staring, my heart hammering, my mouth dry.

Thanks to the face mask and goggles, my three travel companions can't see my distress.

They wade forward, boots splashing the rain puddles as they circle the Humvee, looking it over.

Wally's gaze is fixed on me, as if he knows, as if he's waiting to see if I turn and run, have a breakdown, or tell them.

Instead, I steel myself and walk closer to the Humvee, to the driver's side, and inspect the fender and the door. This Humvee was blown apart, too. I can see where large parts of it were gouged out. Metal plates have been welded on, closing some of the gaps, but there are still several openings along the side.

Wally pops the hood and begins pointing out all the parts that are missing from the engine.

"You get me the parts I need, I'll fix this for you."

Scavenging for parts in the junkyard—in the rain—is slow going. The piles of metal debris are slippery, and the pieces are hard to locate.

Luckily, the rain stops shortly after we start, and it's just the wind we have to contend with.

As I'm crawling into the cab of a derelict box truck, I'm reminded of my work with Warren and digitally scavenging for things he can repair and sell.

With the addition of Daisy to our crew—and Wally/Warren—I'm fairly certain Amersa's Labyrinth is somehow reading my mind. Or they're following my every move outside the sessions and feeding that information into the game engine. That seems more likely.

Either way, it's trouble. And I can only imagine what the group is going to say at the next meeting.

When our group here in the Labyrinth has compiled the parts Wally needs, he tells us to come back tomorrow.

By the time we reach the hostel, my health is at eight percent.

In the classroom that is our shared bedroom, Ian pores over the electronic parts he found in the junkyard (which he bartered with Wally for).

It might actually work, he mumbles as he unscrews the side of the computer tower.

"You better go," May says to me. "We'll be waiting when you get back."

After the Labyrinth session, at home, I scour the Amersa website, looking for the man who confronted me in the bathroom. It doesn't take long to find him. His face is on the page labeled "Leadership Team." Same glasses. Green sweater this time. Solid white button-up.

He's the company's CTO or Chief Technology Officer.

Interesting.

61

Given that Amersa has sped up the pace of my Labyrinth sessions, the numbers group has decided to meet sooner and more often.

To my surprise, Isaac has opted not to join us in person. Instead, he's tuning in via the camera feed Harold uses.

That leaves June, Rose, and me sitting around the camera, eating pizza as Isaac remotely starts the meeting.

"First," Isaac says over the camera speaker, "Rose, did you get the blank badge?"

She reaches into her pocket and draws out a white plastic badge, holding it up to the camera. "I did."

"Good. When you're done with the pizza box, put it in there and throw it in the dumpster behind the building. I'll get it. And June, I'll send you a Signal message with the dead drop location. You should get it before work tomorrow morning."

I can feel the tension in Isaac's voice—well, more tense than he usually is.

"Any time gaps?" he asks.

Thankfully, there haven't been any, but the good news stops there.

After I describe my Labyrinth sessions, we go around about what it means, but like the characters in Wally's junkyard, we have the parts, but we can't put them together.

"We have some new recordings," Isaac says. "And we have a problem. Or more specifically, I have a problem."

With that, the camera speaker begins playing a recording from Anders Larsson's office. The person talking has a gruff, flat voice, and I instantly recognize him: it's Terry, Amersa's security chief.

"We've made some progress related to Carter. We've narrowed it down to a few people he was working with. We're going to start active surveillance soon. That may well bring that particular issue to a close."

"Good. The sooner, the better," Larsson responds.

Isaac stops the recording. "They're talking about me."

"I'm assuming that's why you're not here in person?"

"You assume correctly."

"What do we do?" Rose asks. She sets a slice of half-eaten pizza back in the box, her appetite seemingly deserting her.

"I don't know," Isaac replies. "I feel like if I quit my job, I'm outing myself, and if I go on the run, it may amount to the same thing. At the same time, none of you should be seen with me. Given what Amersa did to Lucas, I think we have to be cautious."

"We don't know that they're going to find you," Rose says.

"We have to assume they will," Isaac responds, voice flat. "It's just a matter of time."

The following day, at lunch, June sends a Signal message to the group.

> *We need to meet. Tonight.*

Six hours later, we're sitting around the circle—June, Rose, and I eating Jersey Mike's subs, Isaac and Harold once again joining remotely.

June sets her sandwich down, reaches into her backpack, and pulls out a stack of pages.

"I got it. The CORTEX study."

Rose smiles. "The badge worked?"

"It did."

June places the study between the three of us and spreads out the pages, which she's highlighted.

"I had a chance to skim it over lunch and after work. Then I read the sections that jumped out at me. I want to spend more time with it, but what I've found is… troubling."

I stare down at the rows and columns of black text, crisp against the pages, the highlighted sections glowing neon yellow under the buzzing, fluorescent lights overhead.

In the margins, June has scribbled notes in blue ink—questions, theories, and words like "neurodegeneration" and "synaptic plasticity."

"CORTEX," June says, "stands for Cognitive Optimization and Rewiring through Targeted Experiential eXposure. The study began roughly three years ago, and eventually grew to include 127 participants. Most were Amersa employees, family members, and, in some cases, paid volunteers. They tested early prototypes of Labyrinth—recording every session and scanning subjects' brains before, during, and after."

"Scanning how?" Isaac asks.

"A bit of everything. Functional MRIs and MEG before and after each play block—EEG during the live runs—plus the occasional PET scan. They even tracked their blood chemistry."

"What were they looking for?" Rose asks.

June flips to a page filled with charts and graphs. "Neurological changes. One of the earliest findings was a shift in most subjects' dopamine production, like what you'd see in someone with early-stage addiction."

June turns another page. "Essentially, Labyrinth altered the way their brains processed pleasure and reward, similar to the effects of a psychoactive drug. It wasn't just the dopamine, though. The more the subjects used Labyrinth, the more their brains rewired. Synaptic pruning started to take place."

"What does that mean?" I ask.

"Synaptic pruning is a normal process during development—your brain removes less-used connections to make way for more efficient pathways. But here, Labyrinth induced it in adults, essentially rewiring their brains, changing how these people thought, what they focused on, and even how they processed emotions."

June makes a stack of the pages she's gone through and flips deeper into the study. "Over time, two of the subjects started showing Parkinson's-like symptoms—tremors, memory lapses, personality shifts. There were other adverse events such as dissociative states, hyper-aggression, and something they called 'perceptual drift,' when the subjects had trouble differentiating the virtual world and the real one. For several subjects, after a while, they didn't actually want to. They essentially started perceiving the real world as another version of Labyrinth, to the point of even treating people around them—family members, co-workers—more like NPCs, not real humans."

"I'm assuming they stopped the trial," Isaac says.

"They did—but only for those experiencing issues. They had to. And that's actually when the worst outcomes occurred. Twelve participants experienced what can only be described as withdrawal symptoms. The team combined low-dose anxiolytics with a 'sunset' scenario that gradually tapered Labyrinth use over six weeks. Most stabilized; two still relapsed."

June holds up a page with the heading *Discussion and Summary of Findings* beneath that. "This is when the document starts getting really strange. First, I should note that the study only had 127 participants. And they were brought in over time, and their total Labyrinth session time varied widely."

"Why is that important?"

"The bottom line is that the study wasn't that well-designed, and the sample size was relatively small for testing something like Labyrinth, a product with a target audience of essentially everyone on Earth. But the reasons are revealed in the discussion."

She turns to a page with a bold heading that reads *Strengths and Limitations*. "The study, such as it is, began more as an internal experiment and evolved over time to be more formalized. Toward the end, there were two camps within Amersa: a group of researchers who wanted to launch a follow-up study, CORTEX 2, which would have been a more formalized trial with a larger sample size and more rigorous methodology and data collection procedures. And an opposing group that felt further limited trials were actually counter-productive."

"Counter-productive how?"

June shuffles pages, going deeper into the stack. "The *Implications and Future Research* sections provide a look at these two competing ideologies within Amersa. The first group of scientists—which we now know recently quit Amersa—felt that the results of CORTEX were alarming enough to essentially hit the pause button on all of Amersa's go-to-market plans. They felt there was a moral obligation to further study Labyrinth before any wide release. They concede that the small sample size could have skewed the results, especially given the possibility of preexisting underlying conditions, but that the severe nature of the outcomes and prevalence of adverse events demanded subsequent investigation."

"And the other group?" Isaac asks.

"That's... the troubling part. In the discussion and conclusions sections, this opposition group—the anti-CORTEX contingent— essentially concedes the points made by the CORTEX 2 advocates. However, they argue that further study is, in their words, 'Fighting the Future.'"

"Fighting the future how?" I ask.

"The crux of the anti-CORTEX argument is that the adverse outcomes observed in the trial weren't the most consequential findings."

"What was?" Rose asks.

"It was what happened to everyone else," June says. "Remember, many of these participants were Amersa employees themselves. Or family and friends. The R&D staff not only observed them in a clinical setting—and read the test results—in many cases they worked with them every day or went home to them at night. They observed changes in the subjects first-hand, outside the lab."

"What kind of changes?" Isaac asks.

June stands and leans on the chair. "Positive changes. Memory enhancement. Increased attention and focus. Gains in problem-solving ability and spatial reasoning. Even changing social behaviors and shifts in cooperative strategies—this is observed anecdotally, but the patterns are there.

"The most interesting changes—at least to the anti-CORTEX authors—were the gains in input processing, specifically the ability to integrate multi-sensory input and a marked expansion in the volume of concurrent processing ability."

Rose says what I'm thinking: "I'm not sure what that means."

"Essentially, the anti-CORTEX group was most excited about the increases in cognitive processing."

"Labyrinth basically upgraded their brains," Isaac says.

June shrugs. "Simplistic but accurate. And the anti-CORTEX researchers were adamant that development of Labyrinth go forward—and that it not be taken offline."

"Sounds like they were scared of withdrawal as well," Rose says.

June points to her. "It might not be far from the truth. Just reading the discussion—and the subtext—the anti-CORTEX authors are emphatic that Labyrinth development continue and that the release not be delayed. And they hold themselves out as examples of the good it can do."

June rounds the chair and picks up the stack of pages she hasn't turned over. "In fact, their discussion reads almost like a manifesto from a group of zealots. It's strange. In most publications, the methods and results sections are the longest. For this study, the bulk of what's here is discussion and background and then predictions."

"Predictions about what?" Isaac asks through the camera speaker.

"They're actually the part I found most troubling. Forgive me, but I need to lay out some of what's in the discussion section—it's background, but it's important. It traces the course of how our subspecies of humans became the dominant species on Earth."

June's summary begins with Homo habilis, which some believe to be the first member of the genus Homo, and a direct ancestor to modern humans. Based in Eastern and Southern Africa, Homo habilis is believed to have emerged 2.4 million years ago and to have gone extinct roughly a million years later.

Its existence overlapped with another human ancestor—Homo erectus—which emerged 1.9 million years ago in Africa. The fact that Homo habilis and erectus existed in the same place—and at the same time—has led to speculation that the two species competed for resources and that erectus, the surviving hominin, may have outcompeted its predecessor. Other scientists argue that habilis actually evolved into Homo erectus. Whatever the case, what is known is that Homo erectus, compared to habilis, had a larger brain, could control fire, and exhibited greater mastery of tool creation and use than any human before it.

The archaeological record indicates that Homo erectus migrated out of Africa to Europe, the Middle East, and parts of Asia, with some individuals even traveling as far as present-day Indonesia.

The human ancestral tree becomes harder to follow after that. Archaeologists have found several human ancestors that emerged from Homo erectus. It's not clear if they are separate species or simply a subspecies.

The most well-known are Homo heidelbergensis, Homo neanderthalensis, and us.

I find the historical background in this part of the paper quite interesting, but Isaac asks the question I'm wondering as well.

"If they were researching the impact of AI-enabled VR, why did they go so deep on human evolution?"

"That confused me as well," June says. "But the background was the basis for a side study they conducted, CORTEX-EV. It was an investigation into what they called predictive evolution. The Amersa researchers enlisted a few computer scientists from the Labyrinth AI group to help."

June glances over to the camera, where I know Isaac is watching.

"Lucas Carter is listed as one of the engineers who created the AI model for CORTEX-EV."

She waits. You can hear a pin drop in the room.

Over the camera, Isaac says, "He never told me. But he said they were working on something that he was concerned about. I thought it was Labyrinth itself."

"It may have been both," June says. "They used a huge dataset for CORTEX-EV. They trained it on the sequenced genomes of all known human ancestors. They loaded it with other archaeological information—essentially any pertinent data related to how humans populated the world and why they went extinct. And there are some major mysteries there."

"Like what?" Rose asks.

"On paper, by the numbers, our subspecies of humans looks inferior to other human subspecies at the time. Homo neanderthalensis, or Neanderthals, had bigger brains. On average, their cranial capacity was about 1,500 to 1,600 cc. We," June motions to the group, "humans have a volume of about 1,300 to 1,400 cc. On average.

"And Neanderthals were generally larger and stronger than us," June adds. "Modern humans, however, have a more rounded cranium with a prominent frontal lobe—that's the area associated with higher-order functions like abstract thinking, problem-solving, and social behavior. So, while our brains were smaller, they had more volume and connections where it mattered, in the areas associated with information processing and predictive abilities."

June stands again. "And that's exactly what Amersa's predictive evolutionary AI found: the arc of human history favors hominin species who develop greater and greater ability to process large amounts of information and make predictions from it."

My brain is starting to hurt, but I've never been more interested in a talk about science.

"It's why," June says, "we became the dominant species on this planet when there was a viable competitor—one very much like us—with a larger brain and stronger body. On paper, Neanderthals should be having this conversation right now. But we're here. And the reason is what this custom-built Amersa AI identified: large-scale data ingestion and predictive modeling is the quintessential competitive advantage across the arc of human evolution. Whatever groups make the largest advances in that area own the future."

"Forgive me, my dear June," Harold's garbled voice says

through the camera speaker, "but I fear that perhaps I am the Neanderthal in the room, virtual as it may be. But what does this all mean?"

"The CORTEX document ends with the researchers concluding that, again, you cannot fight the future. They believe that Labyrinth isn't just a VR experience. It's not simply a way to cure PTSD."

June glances over at me. "Though it does—there are several subjects in CORTEX who benefited immensely. They believe that Labyrinth is something fundamentally different in human history, a breakthrough that is inevitable: a way to accelerate the development of the cognitive abilities that will propel further human evolution. They believe that we are at a pivotal point in human history, where, for the first time, humans can create tools—technology—that actually directly accelerates human evolution. They believe the next human species will be Homo Amersus. And if it's not Amersa who creates it, it will be someone else. The technical potential is there. The question is who will get there first. This is the ultimate conclusion of the paper."

Over the speaker, Isaac says, "You're saying Labyrinth is an evolution box."

"That's what they believe. Evolution at a scale and speed never seen before."

"And at considerable cost," Harold says.

June looks into the camera. "*That* is the last part of CORTEX. All of the authors concede that Labyrinthian evolution carries a high cost. But they recognize that evolution always has. It's part of why they trace the fate of other human ancestors in the lead-up to their conclusions. But, again, the anti-CORTEX contingent believes that fighting the future is futile. They believe that the next great leap in human evolution will soon happen—with or without Amersa. They posit that, for the first time in human history, our species has a way to control the course of evolution."

June bends down and gathers the papers. "The two opposing factions within Amersa actually agreed on the general conclusions of CORTEX: that Labyrinth does enhance the cognitive abilities that have propelled human evolution forward. And that it might also harm many individuals who can't handle the process. By far the greatest consensus between the two groups was that Labyrinth would induce addictive behavior in a large percentage of users."

"Yet, the CORTEX 2 group still quit," Isaac says.

"They did," June says. "And I know why."

She stuffs the thick sheaf of pages into her backpack. "It's in the introduction of the current studies."

June focuses on me. "Like the one you're in."

"What does it say?"

"If you read the ongoing studies—and you read CORTEX—and listen to the recordings, the picture starts to come together. After CORTEX, Amersa leadership made a compromise. They agreed to study Labyrinth in populations that might be vulnerable."

My heart beats faster. "The people who got sick in CORTEX?"

"Yes," June says quietly. "Most were patients with preexisting conditions. Mental health challenges like PTSD and clinical depression. Addictive personalities. And participants with learning differences: dyslexia, ADHD—the list goes on. But the compromise was that they would go forward with their commercialization plans, provided that they also studied how Labyrinth could be used to help everyone. The basic assumption—again, reading between the lines—is that Labyrinth isn't just a tool to advance a small group of humans, but rather a platform to bring everyone together, to standardize brain function and create a new sort of society."

"So what happened?" Isaac asks.

"I think," June replies, "that it's a matter of pace. Amersa went hard with the launch."

Rose glances over at me. "And the studies are obviously ongoing."

"For now," June says. "But I think there's a real chance that they could be canceled."

"Why?" Isaac asks.

"The obvious," June replies. "Amersa leadership only did the trials to appease the dissenting researchers. They've left. Labyrinth has been released. We know the anti-CORTEX researchers don't really care about those who might be adversely affected by Labyrinth."

"We could leak the study," Harold says. "Tell the world what we know. Maybe this is the point of the group and the numbers. Maybe it's an Amersa insider directing us, hoping we'll leak the study. Perhaps someone on the CORTEX study is behind all of this."

Isaac responds quickly. "It's an interesting theory, but I don't think a leak will work."

"I have to agree," June says quietly.

When I ask why, June responds in a careful, methodical tone. It's clear she's thought a lot about this.

"My belief is that leaking the study would—at best—result in a follow-up study. Perhaps one conducted at the NIH or a major research university. The reason is simple: the initial CORTEX study didn't have enough participants—and had so many limitations and design flaws—that it would only be regarded as a call for further investigation. But I also have to say that the adverse neurological events observed in the study aren't my biggest concern. As I read the study, and in particular the discussion among the investigators, I felt their focus was a bit myopic."

"Myopic how?" I ask.

"The study's principal investigators were medical doctors. And so logically, the testing and results were focused in large part on physiological changes to the participants. But it's the behavioral changes I found so striking. To put it simply, Labyrinth became like an addictive drug for many in the study. It wasn't at first. Certainly, its effects weren't akin to an illicit narcotic, but I was reminded of South Korea's failed gaming ban. And it made me think more broadly about technology changes that reshaped society.

"Take television in the fifties. Time indoors doubled after that. Ad-driven consumerism became America's new reality. And it still is.

"Consider the eighteenth-century Gin Craze in Great Britain. The new drink was so popular—and so bad for society—that the government introduced a series of laws in the early 1700s that tried to restrict it. They eventually even banned the manufacture of spirits from domestic grain. But today, gin is widely available.

"As are cigarettes, yet the manufacturers knew they were bad for you. And that was the feeling I was left with. CORTEX confirmed to Amersa leadership that they have a highly addictive product. From a business standpoint, that's a great place to be. And like the tobacco companies, Amersa is clearly okay with some percentage of users experiencing negative health effects.

"But the last reason I don't think leaking the study will work is that people love Labyrinth the same way they love alcohol, TV, and tobacco. As humans, we're willing to endure some harm to our health for the things we enjoy. Frankly, based on history, Labyrinth is what people crave, and that's a hard thing to stop."

In a garbled voice, Harold speaks. "If it's true—and I believe your conclusions are correct—where does it leave us?"

"I'd say with more questions than answers," June replies. "But for me, the biggest question is one raised in CORTEX: how will Labyrinth change society at large? I don't want to sound like Anders Larsson in one of his TV interviews, but I do sense it will be consequential in ways we don't fully appreciate."

62

After the numbers meeting, I sit in my car and stare out at the darkness for a long time, thinking.

On the whole, I have this sense that what I'm dealing with is far, far bigger than I ever imagined.

The first thought that pops into my mind is to pack the car, put Riley in her booster seat, and drive away, and not look back.

I've thought through that before, and it doesn't work. Didn't then, and won't work now. The legal issues—the death of Nathan Briggs—will eventually catch up to me.

I need help. I need to start getting prepared for what's happening to me, getting more serious. The police arresting me. Amersa coming after me directly. The ringing and the numbers consuming more of my time. Those are, in Sheila's words, the hyenas chasing me.

Taking my phone from my pocket, I scroll down to Warren's number and tap the icon for message and type:

> I need to borrow some plates.

He doesn't reply.

The phone rings in my hand.

I click answer, and he speaks instantly, voice gruff.

"What does that mean?"

"I don't actually need the plates. It was... sort of allegorical."

Warren breathes into the phone. "This ain't Dionne Warwick's Psychic Hotline."

"Sorry, I just—"

"What is it? Neighbors again?"

"No. They're long gone. It's why I needed the plates the second time." I squint. "Actually, it's the reason after that. Look, I may not even need them. But I might need some help soon."

Dead air stretches out long enough for me to hold the phone away from my face and confirm that the call is still connected.

"You there?" I ask.

"I'm here," Warren grumbles. "I was trying to figure out how to text you my address, but it ain't working out. So I'm going to tell you. And you're going to come see me."

After Warren tells me his address—and directions, in explicit detail, turn by turn—I drive up to North Raleigh, into an established neighborhood with a mix of older homes and newer ones rising above them.

Like Meredith's parents, Warren lives in one of the older homes that, from the outside, hasn't been remodeled. It's a brick ranch with a weathered roof and a wide front porch, where he's sitting in a white rocking chair. He pushes off of it at the sight of me and stands under the porch light.

As I turn into the driveway, motion-activated lights on his property snap on.

I'm parking behind his SUV when my phone buzzes with a text from Meredith.

All okay?

She knows I had a Labyrinth session today. And a numbers meeting.

I text back:

Yeah. Meeting with Warren. Home soon.

Warren watches me as I stride up the front walkway, his stare as deep as any medical scan I've ever undergone.

As is his way, he doesn't say anything, only jerks his head over his shoulder and turns and leads me into the house.

The interior of the home is a bit like Warren: late-eighties, early-nineties motif. The floors are hardwood that probably had carpet over them at some point, and were refinished a decade ago. In the kitchen, cabinets hang down, obscuring the view.

A massive recliner looms in the corner of the living room, right beside a big screen TV, a really old one, the type my dad used to have, the type I haven't seen in a long time.

A child's play mat stretches across the floor and is stacked around the TV. Several baskets hold toys: MAGNA-TILES, puzzles, and Barbies, apparently waiting and ready for Warren's grandkids to visit.

He settles into the lounger and eyes me. "Take a seat, Marine."

Sitting on the couch across from him, I mentally compose my words, but he beats me to it. "If you don't need the plates, what do you need?"

"I need to tell you some things."

"Good. I was hoping you would tell me what in the world was going on after I saw you living in that train car, but here we are."

"I couldn't then. I didn't understand it myself. I still don't. But I do know that what's happening to me might impact our business."

"Oh yeah?"

"The buying. The online operation."

Warren rocks forward on the chair. "I don't care about that. I don't care if we sell a little less. Or ship it slower. The online thing," he shrugs, "it was sort of for you. I thought maybe, after I'm gone, well, whatever. What're you saying? Why did you mention the plates?"

"Two reasons."

"Still not Dionne—"

"Warwick. I know. You do know that's not a thing anymore."

He pushes back on the lounger and smiles. "Yeah, I know. Go on."

"It's possible," I say slowly, "that I might not be around pretty soon."

Warren stands and looks down at me. "I don't like what I'm hearing, Marine. I've heard it before. Been down this road. If you need help, we'll get you help."

"No. That's not the problem."

"What is it then?"

"Warren, you wouldn't believe it."

"You know why I still run the store?"

"Money?"

"Half right, Marine. I'm retired. I send the money to my daughter."

"What's the other half of the reason?"

"Boredom. And survival."

"Survival?"

"Studies have shown that when you stop exercising your brain—through work or reading or chess or whatever—you die soon."

"Oh."

"What I'm saying is that when you walked in, I could have said, get lost. I didn't."

"You sort of said that."

Warren rolls his eyes. "I did, yes, but it was a test. And so is this. If you tell me what's really happening to you, I might help you."

And so I do, in explicit detail, and when I'm done, Warren simply sits in the lounger, staring at the tongue-and-groove wood paneling.

I lean forward on the couch. "Well?"

"Well, what?"

"Well, what are you thinking?"

"That Wally guy, is that me?"

"I have no idea. Maybe? But maybe not. What else are you thinking?"

"I'm thinking I need to make some calls."

"Calls for what?"

"Equipment."

"Equipment for what?"

"Whatever might happen."

63

Two days later, on Wednesday, around noon, I return to Amersa's offices and re-enter the Labyrinth.

The moment I do, I hear shouting from deep inside the converted school. The corridors are dark, and beyond the windows, it's pitch-black outside as well.

Using the light on my phone, I barrel through the hall, and soon I recognize the voice: it's Ian.

At first, I think he's hurt until I decipher his words:

"It works! Dude! It works!"

Entering the room, I find him sitting in a chair behind what looks to be the teacher's desk at the head of the classroom. May and Daisy are standing beside him, the three of them studying a handheld radio with a long antenna.

Ian twists the dial, and static plays over the speaker. He keeps shifting through the channels, listening to the static for a few seconds before tuning it again.

A minute in, the static breaks, and a man's voice comes over the speaker. It's gruff, and I think he sounds a bit elderly.

"I repeat, if anyone is out there, and you're going to the center of the Labyrinth, contact me. I can help. Respond if you can hear me."

The radio falls silent.

May says something, but Ian is talking too, and soon Daisy joins in, all three arguing about what to do. To my surprise, the radio crackles again, and the man begins speaking, repeating exactly what he said in the same tone and cadence.

"It's a recording," Ian says. He presses the button on the radio and speaks urgently. "We're here. We can hear you. Where are you? What's your name?"

When he releases the button, the man's voice is still talking, the recording playing.

Ian seems to have the same thought as I do.

"We need to hail him when the recording ends."

At the next break, Ian presses the push-to-talk button and shouts, "We're here! We hear you. Can you hear us? My name is Ian."

For several seconds, the radio is silent. When the man's voice calls out in the classroom, he sounds more tired than he did in the recording, as if he might've just woken up.

"Yes. Yes, I can hear you. My name is Gerald."

"Hi, Gerald. Like I said, I'm Ian. Where are you? Are you outside the Labyrinth?"

"No, my friend, I'm very much inside it. More than ever. I'm trapped."

I can see the disappointment on Ian's face. He was sure the radio would connect him with someone outside the Labyrinth, verifying his theory.

May puts her hands on the table, leans closer to Ian, and speaks softly. "He said he could help us."

Ian nods slowly.

Through the radio, he says, "You mentioned help."

"Yes," Gerald replies. "Are you going to the center?"

Ian's gaze drifts over to the computer, which lies open, parts scattered around him. Turning to me, he says, "Couldn't fix it. The junkyard didn't have what I need."

"Maybe you'll find it at the center," I tell him. "What do you have to lose?"

He exhales and activates the radio. "Yes. We're going to the center of the Labyrinth."

"Then I have something for you. An item you need. You won't reach the tower without."

"What tower?" Ian asks.

"All in good time, my friend."

Ian smirks, frustrated. "Well, what do we do until that time?"

"Come find me."

"Where?"

"Along the road. Where the mermaid rests."

Ian squints. "Can you be more specific?"

Gerald doesn't respond, and even after Ian hails him several more times, the radio is silent.

"It's a test," he mumbles, setting it down.

"Or a riddle," May adds.

"Either way," I say to the group, "we're taking the road, and if he's along it, maybe we'll find where the mermaid rests and we can call him again."

At the front office, the four of us watch the rain come down in sheets. The sky is black and rumbling constantly. Lightning lashes across the town as if the clouds are trying to electrocute it.

Dave is perched behind the front desk (such as it is), head obscured by an open comic book as if nothing is amiss.

"We should wait for a break in the storm to get the Humvee," Ian says.

He's holding his computer, the radio in his pocket. May has her binder clutched to her chest. Daisy has hoisted a massive duffel bag full of food and supplies—her life savings, such as it is.

"I have a better idea," I call to the group, already heading for the door. "Be right back."

With my rain gear on, I jog down the street, rain pelting me, feet splashing, trying my best not to inhale any raindrops.

At the entrance to the junkyard, there's now a big sign made from a large piece of plywood. It lists the items Wally has for sale, along with their prices, much like the nightly specials at a roadside diner.

I can't help but smile at it, thinking about the things Warren and I have listed for sale online and in his store.

Past the mounds of junk, the repaired Humvee is waiting next to the converted cargo container Wally uses as an office.

The tires on the massive vehicle are pumped up. Its exterior has been repaired, plates and welds closing the holes that were ripped into it.

Inside the container, I find Wally at his work table, back turned to me.

He swivels on the stool as I slip through the second set of plastic strip curtains.

"It's gassed up. And I filled the back with cans."

"I'm assuming there aren't many working gas stations from here out?"

"A safe assumption."

"Can you tell me anything else about what's waiting for us out there?"

"No."

"Really?"

He shrugs. "I just get the world's junk, not the story of what happened to it."

He tosses me the keys. "They're counting on you."

"Why do you say that?"

"Because you're in the driver's seat."

He bends and takes a bundle of milky plastic from the bottom shelf. "Come on, I'll help you get in."

Past the plastic curtains, he dons his own rain gear and spreads the plastic over us, and we walk to the Humvee, where he spreads part of the sheet on the roof, covering the driver door as he opens it, keeping the rain off me.

I'm dry when I settle in behind the wheel, and through the driver window, I watch Wally, standing under the milky plastic like a ghost as he nods once and turns and treks back to his container and the things he's repairing.

When I crank the Humvee, my heart roars as loud as the engine, and all I can think about is the last time I was driving one of these and what happened to my fellow travelers. For a few seconds, I think about finding the exit to the Labyrinth, about just taking a breath, calling it a day.

Instead, I put the Humvee in drive and tear out of the junkyard.

*

After loading up at the hostel, we drive toward the center of the Labyrinth, wind raging, rain falling, tires groaning across the road.

Lightning flashes ahead of us and behind us. No one says a word.

Every time we get a break in the rain, I pull over and use one of the fuel cans in the back to top off the tank.

The first town we come to is a complete wasteland. The buildings are crumbling. Even the boards that covered the windows and doors are splitting and falling away from the constant assault of the wind and rain.

It's storming pretty hard now, and we don't bother getting out to scavenge. We have plenty of food, and besides, as we drive through, we don't spot anything of value.

Next, we pass a sprawling RV park.

Through the trees, I see motorhomes and campers hooked up to trucks. The place looks abandoned, with vines growing over many of the massive vehicles. A lot of the windows are broken, and I don't see a single light on.

Through the rain, the Humvee's headlamps illuminate a painted metal sign at the entrance: Ariel's Motor Park. Beside it, in the tall grass, I can just make out the figure of a mermaid, which is twice as tall as a person, and was likely attached to the sign at some point, looking out at the road, welcoming visitors, her tail stretching across the bottom.

But the mermaid is resting now, and for that reason, I jab my heel into the brake and turn the wheel and skid onto the gravel entrance to the RV park.

I couldn't see them from the road, but there are four motor homes with generators buzzing outside and faint lights glowing inside. Each one has a wide awning or pop-up tent over the exterior door.

Ian gets the radio out, but the battery is dead, and we don't have another one (or a way to charge it).

I park beside the closest RV with lights on, and we don our rain gear and exit the Humvee.

The forest sways in the wind, and it's dark as night except

for the beams of our flashlights and the yellow glow from the campers and RVs, making them look like giant lanterns abandoned in the woods.

I call out Gerald's name and wait, but none of the doors open. There's no movement inside, no shadow crossing a window or curtains pulled back.

The only sound is the trees creaking and the pitter-patter of raindrops on the roofs.

At the closest RV, I knock on the door and announce myself, and wait. When no one answers I slowly turn the knob and push the door in.

It looks empty. Still, the four of us shake out our rain gear under the awning before going inside.

Upfront, the driver and passenger seats are empty, as is the living room, kitchen area, and bathroom.

At the back, we find a man and woman lying in bed, staring up at the ceiling, holding hands, their breathing shallow.

"Labyrinth Syndrome," May says quietly.

Beside the bed are stacks of MREs. This couple came here prepared, apparently. But couldn't continue when their condition progressed.

May squats beside them and tries to bring one around, but neither responds.

She glances over at the meals. "I think they eat when they're lucid, and then…"

"Convalesce," Ian finishes for her.

He steps out of the bedroom and does a more thorough search of the RV.

"I don't see a radio. This isn't Gerald."

The next residence is a camper, and it's empty.

In the third, we find a woman inside, sitting on a couch in the living room, staring at the wall. As I squat in front of her, she tilts her head down and speaks with a shaky, fragile voice.

"It's all dead ends."

"What is?"

She reaches over and unwraps a protein bar and begins chewing it slowly, eyes closed.

"All dead ends," she mumbles between bites.

I ask her some questions, but that's a dead end, too.

The last RV with lights on is one of the largest in the park, and when I knock on the door, a man's voice calls out, "It's open!"

I know that voice. It's Gerald.

Inside, I get my first look at him. He looks to be in his sixties or seventies, with thinning silver hair combed back and thick glasses that make his eyes look bigger than they are. He's sitting in a wheelchair, near the driver's seat in the RV.

The rest of the team follows me in, and we bunch up at the threshold, staring at him.

"Close the door," he says. "We need to talk."

When May pulls it shut, I say to him, "You said you can help us."

"I can. I have three things to offer. The most important is knowledge."

When none of us say anything, he grips the wheels and pushes forward. "Why do you want to go to the center? Each of you?"

"Treatment," Daisy says softly. "For my lungs."

"Parts," Ian adds.

"Parts for what?" Gerald asks.

"A computer."

"What would you do with a computer?"

"Eventually, get out of here."

Gerald studies him for a long time, long enough to make us all feel uncomfortable.

May speaks next. "I'm looking for a cure."

"A cure for what?"

"Labyrinth Syndrome."

Gerald focuses on me. "What about you?"

"I'm looking for the same thing as everyone else."

Gerald stares at me.

"A cure for what ails me," I add.

"You think it's there?"

"I don't know. But I'm going to find out, one way or another."

For the first time, Gerald breaks into a smile and pulls his hands from the chair's wheels, placing them in his lap.

"Good."

Ian steps forward. "You said you had information to share?"

Gerald's smile widens. "I have more than that. I have knowledge."

"What's the difference?" Daisy asks.

"Knowledge is gained from the use of information. When I was here, as you are, I had information. I used it."

"We're listening," I tell him.

"You think the stretch of road you've already seen is the worst? It's not. What comes next will test you in ways you can't imagine."

"Why?" May asks.

Before Gerald can answer, I do so for him. "Dead ends."

He looks up at me. "That's right. Dead ends."

"How do we avoid them?" I ask him.

Gerald looks at the floor of the RV. "We never figured it out. It's why we're here."

"We?"

"The teams in the RVs," he replies. "We were all going to the center. This was our base camp. We explored, compared notes, and went out again. We were sure we could solve it. With enough time."

His gaze goes to the closed door at the back of the RV. "But sometimes you don't have as much time as you think."

My mind flashes to my wife, lying in a different bed.

"Is there any more you can tell us? A map of the dead ends?"

"No. We found that the roads began changing. As if they're different for each group of travelers." Gerald nods. "That's the key. When you leave here, keep going until you figure it out. Don't come back if you can help it. Rest up, make sure you have the health and fuel for the journey."

I draw the phone from my pocket. I'm at eight percent health. I'll need to exit, but I have one question before I leave.

"I'm just curious: what do you get out of this?"

"Same thing as you."

"A cure?"

"Indeed, young man." He locks eyes with May. "If you're

right—and there is a cure for Labyrinth Syndrome—then I'll get my partner back. That's why I started calling on the radio."

"You said there were three things you had to give us."

"Yes. I've given you knowledge. I'll give you the rest when you're ready. When you're rested."

He motions to the corridor behind me. "Bathroom's on your left."

64

When I get back to my car after the Labyrinth session, there are a dozen messages on the Signal app.

The first is from Isaac:

> *We can't meet today.*
>
> June: *Why not?*
>
> Isaac: *You'll see. I'm sharing a recording from this morning. Play it and then message me.*

My life experience since seeing the numbers on my wife's headstone has taught me to be cautious (borderline paranoid).

As such, I pull out of the Amersa parking lot and wait until I'm on I-40 before clicking play.

The audio streams through the vehicle's speakers. It's taken from Larsson's office, where Terry, the company's chief of security, is speaking.

"Sir, we have a very big problem."

"We have a lot of problems, Terry. I need you to just tell me what the problem is—not that *we have a problem*."

"Someone stole the CORTEX study."

"I thought you destroyed all the copies?"

"We did. All the digital copies. Someone stole the only physical copy."

"How? There are what, maybe six people who have access to that room?"

"Seven, Sir."

"Do we have cameras in the room?"

"No, Sir. We have cameras in the corridors and the office outside."

"So you know who went in and who went out?"

"That's correct. And that's not all. We installed secure file cabinets in the room. They have to use a badge to get access. It's all logged."

"Then this should be pretty easy, Terry."

"Not quite, Sir. There were only three people who accessed the cabinet that housed CORTEX. And they're all individuals we trust. That's not the worst part."

"What could be worse?"

"Well, we don't actually know when the study was stolen."

"Why?"

"Whoever took CORTEX replaced it."

"Replaced it with what?"

"Pages from another study. They left the CORTEX cover page, so it wasn't obvious that it had been replaced."

There's another pause, and when Larsson speaks again, he sounds much more relaxed.

"If they replaced the study, then we know exactly who did it, Terry."

"Sir, I don't follow."

"It's very simple: all we have to do is lift fingerprints off the pages they swapped for CORTEX. We fingerprint the entire office, find a match, and we've got our thief."

The recording ends there. At a stoplight, I check the Signal messages. Isaac has requested that we all join a group phone call when everyone has finished listening.

I'm apparently the last of the group, because they're all ready to join.

On the call, Isaac is first to speak: "Let's start with the obvious: June, where are you now?"

"Still at lunch. I left the Amersa office when I saw your message."

"Don't go back."

"Won't that look suspicious?" Harold asks.

"It will," Isaac replies, "but it's better than being caught."

"Will she get caught?" Rose asks. "I mean, does Amersa even have her fingerprints? They don't have mine."

"No," June says. "They didn't fingerprint me."

"They may not need to," Isaac says. "June, do you have a dedicated desk? Or office?"

"I do," she says quietly.

"I'm assuming you've used the keyboard and mouse?"

"I have, yes."

I see where Isaac's going, but he explains anyway.

"That's a one-to-one match on the prints. They'll go in and dust all the keyboards, match prints to names, and they'll know exactly who touched those replacement pages. I should have seen it. I wasn't even thinking—"

"Let's focus on where we are now," Rose says. "What do we do?"

"I don't know," Isaac mutters, sounding exhausted.

"Not returning to the office," Harold says, "certainly looks suspicious."

"It does," Isaac agrees. "But I still think it's our best option. June, I think you should go home and pack a bag, including your medications, assuming you won't be back for a while. Until we can figure out what to do."

I can hear shuffling in the background and muted conversations, as if she's getting up and leaving a public place.

Next, I recount my experience in the Labyrinth. By the time I finish, I'm back in the teacher parking lot at school. Turning my car off, I hold my phone to my ear as the group discusses and tries to draw any conclusions.

Isaac asks if any of us owns an RV. Turns out none of us do. And none of us has ever been to an RV park with a mermaid sign. We also don't have any ham radio enthusiasts in the group.

"Harold," Rose says carefully, "can I ask... are you in a wheelchair? Similar to Gerald?"

"I am, my dear. And like my apparent virtual analog, my wife was sick before she passed."

The conversation winds down after that, and I'm about to sign off so I can relieve Sheila from teaching my class when June says, "I have an update. I just got an email from Amersa's head of research. It says to work from home for the rest of the day. That building maintenance needs access to the labs and adjoining offices, and we can't be in there."

"That buys us some time," Isaac says. "And June, I think it's now certain that you shouldn't go back when they reopen. You also can't stay at home. You need to leave your phone there. Get a burner and install the app."

"What do I tell my husband?"

"That's up to you. Look, we don't know what Amersa might do. It's too dangerous for you to be at home."

"I guess I'll go to a hotel," she says.

"No," Isaac says quickly. "In fact, from here out, don't do anything that could leave a digital footprint. No credit cards or debit cards. Cash only."

"I don't even carry cash anymore," June says. "I guess I could get, I don't know, a few hundred dollars from an ATM."

"If our good man Isaac can guide me through it," Harold says, "I can send you money, June."

"All right," Isaac says. "Let's talk offline. I have some ideas about how to transfer money."

"It leaves the question of where I should go," June says.

"Perhaps," Harold says, "the solution out here is as it was in there: I could buy you an RV, June. You could pick it up and find a campsite."

"I can't drive it," June says.

"You can stay with me," Rose offers.

"Bad idea," Isaac says instantly. "Think about it—if they're watching either of you and not the other, that instantly connects the dots. We should stay away from each other until we're ready to make a move. It needs to be someplace random. Not friends or family. No vacation homes, nothing like that."

"I have an idea," I say slowly, still turning the thought over in my head. "I know a guy. He's… a recent acquaintance. Lives alone. No family in the area. Very trustworthy."

There's a pause, and finally June says, "It might put him in danger."

"It might. But he could handle it."

65

Still sitting in the teacher parking lot, I dial Warren and describe the situation with June.

I expect him to react with something like, "Well, Alan, I might leave the light on, but this ain't no Motel 6."

Instead, he once again surprises me, agreeing to let June stay with him without complaint. He doesn't even ask how long she might need to be there.

Outside my classroom, I peer through the glass beside the door. Sheila's sitting behind my desk, tapping away at her laptop. The students (for the most part) are heads down, working on an assignment.

With the poise of a lioness, my principal slowly turns her head and, upon seeing me, promptly closes the laptop and joins me in the hall.

"How are the hyenas, Alan?"

"Multiplying by the minute."

"They do sometimes. Hang in there, Marine."

After school, I take Riley to her gymnastics class. Sitting in the rows of chairs with the other parents, I grade papers, but it's hard to concentrate.

In Amersa's Labyrinth, my team and I are close to the center, to the answers.

Out here, it feels like we've never been further away, and that things have never been worse.

If all has gone to plan today, June is settled in at Warren's house (I made the decision not to go over there; I figure Isaac is right: the members of the numbers group should avoid each other for the time being).

It has to be terrifying for June. Separated from her family. Her freedom at risk. Her entire career at stake.

Through the wall of glass, Riley does a cartwheel, ending with her arms up, palms out.

She smiles at me, and I smile back, like nothing in the world is wrong.

That night, after I've put my daughter to bed, I walk down to Meredith's house and fill her in on the latest.

When I'm done, she rises from the club chair and paces in her living room.

"My brother called me today."

"And?"

"He wanted to talk about you."

"Not liking where this is going."

"He didn't say anything specific about, you know…"

"The murder investigation in which I'm a person of interest?"

She winces and cocks her head. "Exactly."

"What exactly did he say?"

"He just asked what was going on with us… how serious it was, what I thought of you."

Like Meredith's brother, Detective Ryan Davis of the Raleigh Police Department, I have also wondered what Meredith thinks of me.

"Well, what did you tell him?"

She turns back to me and holds out her arms, looking mildly uncomfortable. "I told him… it's complicated… and… Good. Ish. And that it's not something I'm walking away from."

★

As I'm lying in bed that night, I turn the words over in my mind.
Complicated.
Good.
Ish.
Yeah. That's about right.
And she's not walking away.

In the morning, I wake to the sound of continuous pounding somewhere close by.

My first thought is that it's the police knocking on the door.

I bolt upright, grasping for my prosthetic. As I'm putting it on, I realize the sound is closer, inside the house. Like boots on the stairs.

I think about the gun in my nightstand, but there's no time. I move to the door and wait, but the thudding isn't moving.

I turn the handle and peer out and exhale when I see Riley across the way, dressed in her Halloween outfit, dancing in the mirror, mumbling, "It's good to be bad…"

She stumbles through the next lines of the song (which I recognize from the opening of the Disney film *Descendants 3*, which I happily watched with her the first two or three times, then less enthusiastically the following six hundred times).

I've been so busy, I've forgotten that today is Halloween.

In her room, Riley is reciting the song's chorus, insisting that when she says V, the crowd says K.

In the case of the *Descendants* movie franchise, the V stands for villain, and K for kid.

I try not to read too much into that.

When I come down for breakfast, Riley scowls at my outfit.
"*Daaaad!*"
"What?"
"You're that painter guy every year."

I could tell her I don't have the imagination or money to buy a new outfit. Or that I completely forgot that it's Halloween because of what I'm in the middle of. I don't say any of those things because, for the first time since I told her she couldn't use Labyrinth at school, things finally feel closer to normal with Riley and me. Still not a hundred percent, but close enough for her to tease me again.

So I plop down in the chair and slowly nod. "I know, I know. Can we just think of it as a happy accident?"

I point to my t-shirt, which reads:

#HappyAccidents

Bob Ross's *The Joy of Painting* TV show was before Riley's time, but she has come to recognize the signature voluminous, frizzy-haired wig I'm wearing.

"Dad."

"Sorry."

Riley reaches up and scratches at the edge of her own wig, which is flowing blue hair that falls down past her shoulders. She's dressed as Mal, the main character in *Descendants* (and daughter of Maleficent and Hades).

"What do you think I should be next year, kiddo?"

I'm thinking that if there is a next year for me, at least as a free man, maybe I will switch it up. The Halloween costumes will be on sale at Costco and Walmart tomorrow. Probably practically giving them away.

Riley shrugs and takes another bite of cereal.

"Maybe... I could be the Jolly Green Giant."

Riley lets the spoon drop into the bowl and stares at me.

"What? I could get some green face paint from Mr. Warren. Bet you wouldn't see any other Jolly Green Giants."

"'Cause it's lame, Dad!"

"Okay, okay. So. A Care Bear?"

Riley exhales. "That's even worse."

"Maybe Magnum PI?"

"What's a magnum pie?"

"It's a guy, a supercool one. He had a mustache and short shorts."

"Dad. That is not cool."

"Guess you had to see the show. Anyway, what about Mister Rogers?"

"I don't know who that is."

"Maybe Mr. T?"

Riley squints at me.

"One of the Blues Brothers? Doc Brown from *Back to the Future*? Maybe Richard Simmons?"

"Dad, are these people even famous?"

"Apparently not anymore. What about a superhero?"

"Now, we're talking."

At school, most of the kids (and perhaps half the teachers) are dressed up. Seems like every year the students raise the ante on the quality of the costumes (I'm thinking it's the Instagram effect, or whatever social network kids use these days).

They also seem to push the limits of the dress code a little more every Halloween. The outfits are a little more revealing every year. And the school typically has to confiscate a few fake weapons, but overall, it's a nice diversion after two months of class.

At lunch, Meredith saunters into my classroom, her face a mask of mock disgust.

"Please restore my faith in humanity."

"Ma'am, you're asking a guy who is not exactly doing great with humanity—by and large—at the moment, but I am, nevertheless, at your disposal."

She moves her hands up and down her outfit. "Who am I?"

She's wearing an olive-green tank top, tight brown shorts, and high-top hiking boots. Her hair is pulled into a tight ponytail.

"Lara Croft."

Meredith lets her arms drop to her sides and exhales heavily.

"Can I get a status check on your faith in humanity?"

"Not fully restored. But much, much better."

★

That night, when Riley and I walk down to Meredith's place for trick-or-treating, I can tell something's wrong.

"What's up?" I whisper to Meredith.

Meredith cuts her eyes down to Riley. "After."

With that, we set out down the street, Lara Croft, Bob Ross, and a villain's kid, pretending like it's just another Halloween.

By the time we get home, Riley is already yawning (despite copious candy intake during the night's journey).

I'm two pages into the chapter when she drifts off to sleep. I tuck her in tight, lock my front door, and make my way down to Meredith's place, where I find her nursing a giant glass of chardonnay. This is not super common for her, so I'm thinking what follows is not celebratory news.

"I got a call from Ryan."

"When?"

"Right after school."

"What did he say?"

"He... wanted to inform me of some details of our criminal justice system."

Meredith sinks into the couch and takes a long swig from the wine glass.

I perch on the coffee table across from her.

"Ryan says that in the state of North Carolina, it's not against the law to know about a crime and not report it. Unless it's a crime involving a juvenile."

She takes another drink. "And if interviewed by the police, I obviously have my Fifth Amendment right to not say anything that might incriminate myself."

Reaching over to the coffee table, she grabs the bottle and sloshes more wine into the glass.

"The problem is if a person is granted immunity from prosecution, they are no longer protected by the Fifth Amendment."

She looks up at me. "If they're immune in the legal matter, then it would be impossible for them to incriminate themselves. Did you know that?"

"No."

"Ryan says that prosecutors could grant someone immunity in order to compel them to testify. And if that person doesn't, they would be in contempt of court. Which, Ryan tells me, *is* a crime."

Meredith takes another sip of wine, and I wipe my sweating hands on my jeans, trying to process what she's saying.

"Is that all he said?"

"No. One last thing. He told me that the only loophole is spousal privilege."

"As in—"

"As in, a spouse can't be compelled to testify, even if given immunity."

I lean forward, staring at the floor and the small distance between us.

"What do you want to do?" I whisper.

"Well, so far, I've thrown up. Cried. Applied a lot of makeup to cover the aforementioned crying. Eaten a concerning amount of candy. And now," she lifts the wine glass, "I'm doing this."

"No. I mean, what do you want to do about—"

"I'm not ready to get married, Alan."

She sets the glass down. "But I would do it to protect you."

When I stare at the floor again, Meredith leans over, face close to mine. "What are you thinking?"

"I don't even know where to start. But I'm thinking about Riley, and what's going to happen to her when this blows up. When I'm gone, she's going to be all alone."

"She won't be, Alan."

I lock eyes with her. I feel this pit in my stomach the likes of which I haven't felt since I suited up for that first patrol in Afghanistan.

Meredith puts the glass down heavily, the wine splashing and cresting the top and spilling onto the coffee table. She scoots forward on the couch, closing the distance between us and wraps her arms around me, and I feel the warm wetness of her tears on my neck and her breath hot in my ear as she whispers, "I promise you: I'll take care of her.

66

In the morning, I wake before Riley and sit at the dining room table that's covered with the half-built puzzle. It's starting to look more like the picture on the box, and staring at the pieces, I wonder what might have been if I had never seen those numbers when I heard the ringing that day.

Maybe in a year, when this lease was up, it would have been Riley, Meredith, and me moving into a house of our own. A castle of the suburban variety. Four beds. Three and a half baths. Two-car garage and a mortgage we worry about until we don't. A backyard with a swing set from Costco and a dog from the rescue who never gets tired of playing fetch.

I can't help but wonder what that life would have been like. Vacations in the summer, when we were all out of school, maybe long road trips like my parents used to take me on. Some bumps along the way, some fights, maybe a few silent stretches of road, but I bet it would have been a lot of happiness, a lot of stops that we would remember for a lifetime (like I do) and if we're really lucky, three people who liked the journey as well as where they ended up.

What I feel like now is that my life is taking a giant detour, one I have no control of, like the road ahead is washed out.

For a while, I sort the pieces, turning each one over, grouping them. When I find a window that goes in the tower, I lift it and slide it into the puzzle.

On the table, my phone buzzes with a message from Signal.

    Isaac: *They found the bug.*

Me: *How do you know?*

Isaac: *Yesterday, it was nothing but dead air. I thought Larsson wasn't in the office, but I was getting static and some buzzing. This morning, it recorded a man's voice saying, "Okay, open it up." Then it stopped transmitting.*

Rose: *Any idea how they found it?*

Isaac: *No. I'm assuming, after the CORTEX security breach, they launched a sweep of the whole building.*

Rose: *My fingerprints are on that thing.*

Me: *The device was small. Can they even get a print from it?*

Isaac: *At least a partial.*

Rose: *I can't lose this job.*

Harold: *I can support you, Rose.*

Isaac: *Let's focus on right now. I have more news. First, Rose, when's your next shift?*

Rose: *Tonight. At seven.*

Isaac: *Ok, that gives us some time to figure things out.*

Me: *Isaac, what was your other news?*

Isaac: *This morning, there was a car parked outside my house. Guy inside. Private security look. Not a leftover trick-or-treater.*

Me: *What did you do?*

Isaac: *Obv: my bug out protocol. Wiped the computers, grabbed the bag, slipped out the back, and rode the eBike away. Been going since.*

Me: *Where are you now?*

Isaac: *Not saying here.*

Harold: *Where does all this leave us?*

For a while, the chat is dead, no one messaging.

"Dad," the sound of Riley's voice jolts me. She's standing in the living room, still in her PJs, glancing around. "Where's my candy?"

Last night, after she went to bed, I hid the five-thousand-calorie bag of sugar and fat in one of the upper cabinets in the kitchen. I did so because of the very scenario playing out right now.

"Breakfast first, then candy."

"Dad—"

"I mean it."

Based on years of experience, I could choreograph her reaction to this situation down to the second. It begins with an eye roll and deep exhale, followed by stomping feet to the kitchen, slamming cabinet doors, a bowl clanking hard on the kitchen counter, the soft patter of cereal dropping into the bowl, milk sloshing into said bowl, a refrigerator door also slamming, and finally the clink of a spoon and my daughter sitting across from me, fuming as she slowly consumes the Ohs! cereal.

I don't look up from my phone. Best to wait out the storm, I think.

On Signal, Isaac messages:

> *I need time to think. Alan has a session today. Let's talk after that.*
>
> Rose: *Ok.*

What comes next is something I've dreaded for a while, a moment I hoped might not arrive. But it has. I need to tell the group everything about Nathan Briggs and what happened that night. For my sake and theirs. Because if I'm arrested, they'll know anyway, and because they might actually have some information that could help (if I'm arrested, or even prevent an arrest).

On Signal, I type:

> *We need to talk before my session at noon. By audio. I have something to share.*
>
> Isaac: *I don't think June's here.*

I trudge upstairs to my bedroom, where Riley can't hear, and call Warren and ask him if June is up yet.

"Afraid not. She had a rough night."

"How?"

"She was anxious. Couldn't sleep. I think it's... You know, all that stuff you're dealing with. Plus, being separated from her family on Halloween."

"I hate to do this, but can you wake her? It's important. Just tell her to check her phone messages. She doesn't even need to leave her room."

Warren agrees, and I message the group:

> I'll start the call when June gets here.

By the time I arrive in the teacher parking lot at school, June has joined, and sitting there, watching my colleagues file into school, I tell the group about the night I woke up in that building next to Nathan Briggs.

When I'm done, no one says anything for a long moment.

"Why didn't you tell us before?" Isaac asks.

"The obvious. I was scared. I didn't know you all—"

"You've known us for a while," Isaac snaps. "And we've trusted you."

"I was scared of losing my daughter, okay? I didn't know if any of you would go to the police—or were police."

Isaac exhales heavily into the phone. "Sorry. Man, I'm just stressed. It feels like everything's unraveling."

"Alan," Harold says, voice hesitant even through the computerized scrambling. "Can I ask—and don't answer if you don't want—but why are you telling us now?"

"Because I think the police might know everything I just told you."

Just before lunch, I exit my classroom and make my way down the hall, leaning on my cane (the Amersa suit is good, but every

Labyrinth session still leaves my stump a little tender; it adds up).

I consider going by the gym. But decide against it. With my probable criminal future, I figure it's better if Meredith's seen with me as little as possible.

It turns out, I didn't need to go looking for her. She's waiting on me, right outside the glass double doors that lead to the teacher parking lot, back turned, hair blowing gently in the fall breeze, midday sun casting her in shadow.

Her shadow on the wall shifts slightly, as if she knows who it is before she even turns and sees me.

Those aviator sunglasses cover her eyes, and in that mirror, I see myself, and as the seconds tick by, my hard face melts like wax in the sun.

And I know she sees me now—exactly what I feel, because that's how well we know each other.

She reaches up and slowly takes the sunglasses off, and I'm looking at her eyes, bloodshot and watery. Maybe it's from the crying or lack of sleep. Or perhaps it's from last night's wine—but no matter what, the strain in her life is because of me—and despite it all, her eyes still blaze brighter than the sun boring into both of us.

She takes a step forward.

I don't move.

She takes another step.

I still don't move.

She leans forward and presses her lips to mine.

This, too, is a place like the Labyrinth, where time is distorted and the outside world doesn't exist. I would stay here forever if I could.

When she pulls away, I turn and glance back through the glass doors at the long hallway that's starting to fill with kids going to lunch.

Meredith follows my gaze and smiles. "You were less self-conscious twenty years ago."

"Yeah, but we didn't have jobs to lose back then."

"I'm not worried about our jobs."

"What are you worried about?"

"You."

She turns and stands beside me and puts those mirrored sunglasses back on. "In Amersa's game, do you think you're close to the center of the Labyrinth? To answers?"

"I don't know. Maybe."

Meredith holds a hand out. "Give me your phone. Not the burner—not the one with Signal and the group."

"Why?"

"You trust me?"

"Completely."

She stands there, palm out, and I stare at myself a few seconds in her aviators. Then I reach into my pocket and give her my phone and tell her the code to unlock it.

She asks for the number to the burner, and I tell her, and she types it into her phone.

The doors open, and an English teacher passes us, on her way to lunch. When she's out of earshot, I move closer to Meredith.

"Do you know something? Something I should know?"

"I know you better head out or you'll be late for that session."

Slowly, she tilts her head toward the parking lot.

At Amersa, the entry procedures have changed radically in the two days since my last visit. It used to feel like airport security. Now it's like the Pentagon right after 9/11. There are security personnel everywhere (in plain clothes and in uniform).

And we can't bring our mobile phones into the building. They must be left in the car (there's a person at the outer door who relates—and enforces—this new rule).

My prosthetic never makes it through the scanner. They used to run a wand over me, barely pausing when it alerted. Now they make me go through a different machine (I don't even want to think about what it sees).

In the room with Linus, he asks mostly the same questions, with one exception:

"Alan, this is not related to Labyrinth, but due to internal security reasons, I must ask you: has anyone outside of Amersa contacted you about your experience in Labyrinth?"

"No."

"Has anyone asked you about your access to this building? This could be as benign as a question from a neighbor at a cookout or a seemingly random email from an old college acquaintance who's just curious about Amersa's campus?"

"No. I mean, why would they?"

There's a slight pause, and I wonder if Linus—or some security AI—is reading my body language, looking for micro-expressions or tells.

Finally, he says, "Indeed, Alan. It's all just routine."

67

As with my previous Labyrinth sessions, I arrive at the place from which I last departed, in this case, the cramped RV bathroom.

Stepping out, I spot my three team members seated on the sofa. Gerald is still in his wheelchair by the driver's seat.

He nods when he sees me. "A good rest?"

"I wouldn't go that far. But I'm back."

"The road takes you as you are," he says quietly.

I step deeper into the RV, and Gerald motions to the window. "Pull that curtain back, if you will."

I lean across, draw it open, and peer out the window. The RV park is dark, but in the dim light, I can just make out a large boat. It's sitting on a trailer with a blue tarp covering it.

"That's the second thing I have to give you," Gerald says. "I suspect you'll need it."

"You suspect or you know?" I ask.

"Call it a hunch."

"Based on what?"

"The rain," he says simply. "Do you have a vehicle large enough to pull it?"

"We do."

"Good. Under the tarp, you'll find fuel cans for the boat and your vehicle—assuming it runs on diesel."

Gerald reaches under his sweater and grasps a black string. "And here's the final item I wish to impart."

He pulls a metal item from beneath his sweater and hands it to me. It's a key.

Not just any key. It's an exact replica of the metal key I woke up with after losing time several weeks ago.

"What does this open?" I ask, staring at it.

"I don't know. Only that another traveler told me I would know when to use it. I believe this is that moment—that I was always intended to keep it until you arrived."

Pulling the boat behind us, we barrel down the road, knowing every second drains my health and that if we don't reach the center of the Labyrinth before the session ends, we'll be starting over again, back at Gerald's RV.

The farther we travel, the stronger the wind grows. The rain pours down relentlessly. We haven't seen a single town since the RV park, only a road littered with debris from the trees and abandoned vehicles off to the side.

In the back, Daisy's breathing is getting worse, her breaths coming in ragged gasps.

Ian, who's in the passenger seat, leans toward me, his voice low. "Maybe we should go back to the RV park and let her do a breathing treatment."

"I agree."

Daisy pulls on the back of the seat, leaning forward, voice raspy. "No. I won't be the reason we turn back."

She gulps air. "Keep. Going. Please."

Ian and I share a glance, and Daisy reaches out and places a hand on my shoulder.

"Please, Alan."

I nod and push harder on the accelerator.

Up ahead, the road forks in three directions.

Next to each road is a sign with a number. There's no indication where each road leads or which one we should take. Just a number.

I stop the Humvee and turn to May and Daisy in the back.

"Any ideas?"

No one has a clue what the numbers mean or which road we should take, so I keep going forward, taking the center road.

A few minutes later, we come to another fork, also with three roads and signs with numbers next to them. But the numbers are different this time. Again, we take the center road. After refueling, we reach another three-way fork. And again take the center road.

The highway starts to look the same—nothing but woods on each side and branching roads.

"We're lost," Ian says.

May leans forward, shouting over the engine. "It's like the woman said: nothing but dead ends."

"We got it wrong," Ian says. "We didn't solve the puzzle correctly. It's like some kind of math problem, or something where the numbers have to add up. Or else you're taking the wrong roads. I think we should go back to the beginning and analyze the numbers more closely."

It hits me then, and I can't believe I didn't see it at the first fork.

"I have an idea."

"What is it?" Ian asks.

"Let's just say I've got a hunch."

Back at the first fork, I take the road numbered 12—the first number in the numbers sequence I saw on the PTA sign, next to the dead man in downtown, and on my wife's headstone.

At the next fork, I take the road marked one. Then two. Followed by twenty-five, eighteen, and I'm taking road nine when Ian says, "Would you care to share exactly what you're doing?"

"If you substitute the numbers for letters, I'm spelling labyrinth."

Ian raises his eyebrows. "Wow. Okay. Did you come up with that yourself?"

"I… not really."

Finally, when I take the road marked eight, the pavement ends at a body of water that stretches out as far as I can see.

About a quarter-mile from the coast is a massive building rising from the water. Its lights glow in the darkness, and from the top, inky black smoke billows out. The storms spread out from it, as if this structure is fueling them.

"We made it," May says, her voice filled with awe.

In the back seat, Daisy is slumped against the door, breathing shallow, staring through the windshield. She doesn't have long.

After turning around, I back the trailer into the water and help Ian, May and Daisy board the boat.

This close to the end, the wind and rain are relentless, and the sea is choppy. I can feel myself inhaling some of the drops, but there's nothing I can do about it but keep charging forward.

The boat's engines crank with a roar, and I yell over them and the howling wind for my three passengers to hang on.

With a jolt, I reverse the boat into the water, freeing it from the trailer. More slowly, I turn toward the building and then push the throttle all the way forward. Soon, we're practically leaping across the waves, the wind and rain lashing us.

As we approach the structure, I realize it's supported by four massive concrete piers that rise out of the sea. At the bottom of one is a floating dock. We tie off the boat there and trudge up a ramp with rope guard rails to a small platform with a single door with rounded corners, like a hatch you might find on a large ship.

Ian tries the handle, but it doesn't budge. "It's locked," he yells, wincing as a gust of wind slaps his hood into his cheeks.

Reaching in my pocket, I draw out the key Gerald gave me, slide it into the lock, and turn. There's a loud pop, almost like a lightning crack, and when I reach down, the handle releases and the door swings in, revealing a dimly lit room with a spiral steel staircase that wraps around the concrete pier.

Together, the four of us march up the stairs, winding our way up to the building, footsteps clanging on the wedge-shaped treads.

Daisy is the slowest, but we insist she go first—and take breaks when she needs to.

Outside, the wind rages, and the blowing rain taps at the walls of the enclosed staircase.

On one of our breaks, I check my phone. My health is at seventeen percent—and dropping fast from the climb. We need to hurry.

At the top of the stairs, there's a square landing and three corridors: left, right, and directly ahead. The halls are wide and brightly lit by fluorescent lights. It reminds me of a hospital.

On the wall, there's a sign that says LABYRINTH CORPORATE HEADQUARTERS. It lists the various departments and what floors they're on, with directional pointers.

There's an infirmary, staff offices, labs, a server room, mechanical spaces, a cafeteria, and even a gym.

"Hello?" I shout, the word faintly echoing in the corridors. There's no response.

Ian marches forward, calling over his shoulder to us. "I'm going to the server room."

Daisy turns to the right, feet squeaking on the linoleum floor. "I'll be... in... the infirmary."

"You want help?" May calls to her, but Daisy holds a hand back before turning the corner.

"I'm going to check out the labs," May says. "You want to come?"

"No," I reply as I scan the directory. My eyes stop on the entry for executive offices. They're on the top floor.

"Where are you going?" May asks.

"I'm going to go see who's in charge."

My health is at nine percent by the time I reach the top floor and the corner that holds the executive offices. It's down to seven percent by the time I finish searching all the office suites—which are empty.

There aren't even any papers with clues about what's going on here. All the computers are off, and when I turn one on, it gives me a login screen with a Labyrinth logo.

Sitting in a swiveling office chair, staring at the computer monitor, I consider my options. This building seems to be creating the storms. If that's true, there has to be a way to shut off whatever it's doing.

By that logic, the mechanical room seems a good place to start. Maybe I can turn off the power somehow. For that, I'll probably need Ian's help.

But I want to make sure Daisy got what she needed from the infirmary before we cut the power.

On my way to the server room, I still don't see a soul in the hallways, and no one in any of the rooms or offices I pass by.

The server room has a raised floor and rows of cages full of racks with equipment that hums under the bright lights. Neatly organized cables snake out of the back and up into the ceiling.

I shout Ian's name over the buzzing machines.

He doesn't respond, so I begin wandering down the rows of servers, calling for him.

But he's not here.

Maybe he's a step ahead. Maybe he's already in the mechanical room.

Before I go there, I stop by the infirmary to check on Daisy. But she's gone too. I find only empty beds and closed cabinets and a metal cart with nothing on it.

My phone buzzes in my pocket, and when I draw it out, I realize it's a health alert. I'm at five percent.

Walking faster now, I reach the labs, hoping to see May. But these rooms are deserted as well, just silver metal refrigerators, all closed, empty clean rooms, and raised work tables littered with equipment.

I'm starting to get a bad feeling about this.

Walking faster now, I call their names, one after another:

"Ian!"

"May!"

"Daisy!"

But it's just me, alone here, the only sound the wind and the rain.

At the landing off the staircase, I scan the directory again, looking for the mechanical room. I stop, however, when I see another entry: THERAPY ROOM.

Why would this place have a therapy room?

Therapy for what?

It doesn't quite fit.

I walk toward the room, the corridors passing in a daze until I'm standing at the threshold.

The double doors are motion-activated, and with the next step I take, they open inward, revealing a room I know well.

It's exactly like the one where I learned to walk again after losing my leg.

Like that room, this one has a set of parallel bars, three

treadmills, a harness system on rollers, and a leg press machine. Stepping inside, the rest of the room comes into view. There's a mirror wall. Shelves that hold free weights and resistance bands. Exercise mats spread out. Beyond are a few balance boards.

This isn't *like* the therapy room where I learned to walk for the second time. *It is* that room, right down to the very last detail, including the woman perched on a green stability ball, smiling at me.

She looks exactly the same as she did the first day I met her, in this room, before Riley was born and time took its toll on us, and fate took her from me.

And just like that day, she rises from the ball and steps toward me. "Hi, Alan. My name's Jenn, and I'm going to be working with you."

For a long moment, I stare at this digital replica of my deceased wife.

"What is this?" I whisper.

"It's a reminder, Alan."

"Of what?"

"Of the most important lesson you ever learned."

"Well, maybe it didn't take because I need you to tell me again."

"This only works if you meet me halfway, Alan."

That's another thing Jenn said to me that day. No one else was in that room then. No one heard it but her and me.

How does this... thing know what she said?

She stares at me, waiting.

I glance over at the parallel bars. "This is where I learned to walk again."

She smiles. "Almost, Alan. It was a good step, though. We'll call it halfway."

"Then what's the answer?"

"This is where you learned that you could do anything you set your mind to. You just have to keep going. Even when it feels hopeless."

"You're doing this, aren't you? All of it. The numbers, the time loss, the website."

She grimaces. "I mean, it's a complicated question."

"No, it's not. It's a simple question: are you doing this?"

She smiles and holds her hands up. "Alan. I feel like we're getting into semantics. But yes, you got me. Simple question. But boy is the answer complicated."

"What do you want from me?"

"I want the same thing now as she did back then. I want to help you."

"Help me do what?"

"You'll see."

Rage blows through me as strong as the wind howling outside. "What *are* you? You're not her. You're... some simulated copy of her—"

"I'm as close to her as you will ever experience again. I've read everything she ever posted online. All her emails. What other people wrote about her. And a lot more."

"How?"

"It's not important, Alan. What's important is that you have a role to play. If you keep going—and get to the center—it'll all make sense."

"What will make sense?"

"Everything. Just remember, it's all about the numbers. When you're stuck, consult the numbers."

I'm about to ask what that means when she closes the distance between us and rises on her tiptoes and kisses me on the cheek.

"I'm counting on you, Alan. Everyone is."

Then, the world goes black.

68

When the darkness turns to light again, I'm in the VR suit in the padded room at Amersa's offices.

Sandra stands in front of me, and she looks panicked.

There are a dozen other people in the room, all talking at once. I've never seen any of them before. Phrases jump out at me through the chaos.

System crash.
Data corruption.
Failover instance disabled.

Sandra raises her hands, getting my attention.

"Alan, are you okay?"

"Yeah. Why?"

"Your vitals were all over the place. Then the Labyrinth AI crashed. We weren't sure what it would do to you when you were inside. What did you see?"

The room falls silent then, every eye focused on me.

I feel like I did that afternoon when the detectives questioned me. I sense that my answer here could have consequences.

As such, I lie.

"Nothing."

For a moment, no one says anything. A few of the Amersa staffers squint; they don't believe it.

"What do you mean *nothing*?"

I shrug. "It was just... blank."

A voice calls out from a speaker in the ceiling, a voice I recognize: Anders Larsson.

"We should do a full debriefing. Figure out what he saw and what happened. No NHI this time. It could be affected too."

Tilting my head back, I address the speaker in the ceiling. "Look, I'm exhausted. Can we do it next time?"

"No," the CEO says, sounding annoyed. "We cannot do it next time. I want to know what happened."

"We don't need him," a slender man with glasses says. "We can spin up an instance and use the source data to recreate his experience and stream it in video format."

In my car in the parking lot, I get my phone from the middle console and scan the notifications. I missed three calls from Meredith. There's a text message from her, too:

Call me.

I do, and she answers instantly.

In the background, I can hear the flurried activity of the school gym: balls bouncing, kids yelling, and a whistle blowing. Meredith walks away from it, noise fading, and I imagine her sitting out on the stairs that lead to the student parking lot.

"The police are going to arrest you."

When I don't say anything, she adds, "Ryan told me. This morning."

"Did they come to the school?"

Meredith pauses, and I hear a group of students passing, talking about how epic Halloween was.

"No. I took your phone to your house and turned it off."

"So they think I'm there."

"Right. They've probably been there already."

When I don't say anything, Meredith says, "Alan?"

"I'm here."

"I talked to Ryan. He can arrange for you to turn yourself in at the department, and then there's this whole process. But I'll post bail—"

"What if I don't get bail? Or not today? It's the day after Halloween, and it's a murder charge."

Meredith hesitates. "We'll figure it out."

"What about Riley?"

"I told you: I'll take care of her. I promise."

"Thank you."

"Do you want me to call Ryan?"

"No. I need to think."

"Think about what, Alan?"

"I just... I'll call you back."

Next, I send a message to the Signal group, telling them what's happened.

Isaac is first to respond:

> Isaac: *What happened in Labyrinth?*
>
> Me: *I got to the center.*
>
> Isaac: *Let's meet. Right now. Don't go to the police.*
>
> Rose: *Where?*
>
> Me: *Is June here?*
>
> Isaac: *Offline again.*
>
> Me: *Hold on.*

I dial Warren's phone, and he answers on the first ring. "X-Files hotline."

I can't help but laugh, despite my stress and upside-down life. "That's a good one."

"Been saving it up."

"Where are you?"

"Same place as every other red-blooded American."

A pause stretches out, and he practically barks, "I'm at work."

"Oh. Have you seen June?"

"Course I've seen June. She's in the back room. You told me to keep an eye on her."

"Can we meet there? The group?"

Warren's voice has dropped the bravado when he responds. "Yeah, come on."

Thirty minutes later, we're all sitting in the back room of Warren's army surplus store: Isaac, Rose, June, and I. Warren is here too, standing in the corner, arms crossed.

He went and got us sandwiches, and the numbers group is eating them as I recount my final experience in Labyrinth.

A phone sits on the table, a Signal call active, the audio on speaker so Harold can join us.

When I'm finished, Isaac tosses his half-eaten sandwich on the paper and opens his laptop, typing and clicking at almost superhuman speed.

"It's unnerving," June says, "that the program chose to simulate your deceased wife. But she was more than that to you, Alan. She was the one who provided physical therapy and rehabilitation in the past. Perhaps the center of the Labyrinth—in your case— was the entrance to another level in the game. Maybe the next session is about you reliving your rehabilitation and leveling up there, and that ends the storms?"

Isaac pushes back from the work table, staring at the screen. "Unbelievable."

"What?" Rose asks.

"Should have seen it before." Isaac slowly shakes his head. "It was *right there*—this whole time."

"What is?" I ask, rounding the table, trying to see his screen.

Isaac slams the laptop shut before I get a glimpse.

"I know where it is," Isaac says slowly. "The center of the Labyrinth."

69

In the back room of Warren's store, everyone stares at Isaac, waiting for him to continue.

He doesn't. He pulls the laptop off the table and packs it up.

"Are you going to tell us?" June asks.

Isaac cuts his eyes to Warren, who pushes off the wall and uncrosses his arms.

"No, he's not," my partner says, voice gruff. "Not while I'm here."

Rose furrows her brows. "Why—"

"Operational security," Warren says. "Compartmentalization."

Isaac stands, pulling his backpack on. "Correct."

"This," Warren says, moving to the safe and punching in the code, "is what we called an SAP. Special Access Program. Or at least, that's what it was during the Gulf War. Probably not around anymore. Or renamed. They love doing that."

The safe swings open, revealing cash, handguns, and several lumpy envelopes. He turns to Isaac. "What do you need?"

"Right now? A vehicle that has no ties to any of us. We need to leave and head down to the coast—"

Warren holds a hand up, stopping him. "What else do you need?"

"Where we're going?" Isaac huffs. "An army."

Warren cuts his eyes to me. "Armies talk."

"Well," Isaac says, "we need—"

"Weapons," Warren mutters. "And armor."

He moves across the room, squats, and opens the lower

cabinet, revealing a mini-fridge. Reaching in, he unplugs it, then drags it out onto the floor.

He crawls into the cabinet where the fridge was, and I hear a sickening breaking sound, like his fist is slamming into drywall.

Rose and June look over at me, and I shrug. When I look at the floor again, Warren's legs are gone. From the cabinet, he starts setting out ammo crates of semi-auto AR-15s, pre-'86 transferable SMGs, and CS-gas "flash" canisters.

As he crawls out, he grumbles that nothing is illegal but that it would be costly for him if the ATF ever did an audit.

Warren is covered in white drywall dust, but he doesn't bother brushing it off.

When he's exited the room, my phone blares with Harold's garbled voice. "What else do you need? I can't buy weapons, not easily, but I still have funds."

"We need," Isaac says, staring at the phone, "a boat."

"What kind?" Harold asks.

"A big one. A yacht that can sail across the Atlantic."

"What else?"

"Portable currency," Isaac says.

"You've lost me," Harold replies.

"Gold or diamonds. But gold will be easier to come by. And spend. It needs to be easily verifiable. For where we're going, Krugerrands are probably best."

Isaac holds his phone up. "And we leave all of these behind. They're like homing beacons—even the burners we've used to call people we know. We'll buy a burner on the road. And only contact Harold." He hesitates a moment. "Actually, we'll find someone with absolutely no connection to any of us and pay them to buy a burner for us. I'll arrange it."

When we're done discussing the details, I exit the back room and grab some duffel bags and load them up with guns and ammo. I also take some MREs. I sense that DoorDash won't be delivering where we're going.

When I return to the back room, everyone is gone. The phones are stacked on the table, like boats we're burning on the shore.

With my phone, I make one last call: to Meredith.

"Hey," she practically shouts. In the background, I hear the din of the gym and her walking away. "I've been calling you."

"I know."

"Ryan has been calling me."

"I'm sure."

"Where are you?"

"I'm not going to turn myself in."

"Alan—"

"We know where the center of the Labyrinth is."

"You do?"

"Isaac does. We're going there."

"This is crazy."

"It is. Yes."

To my surprise, she starts laughing.

"What?"

"Alan, I can't tell if there's something wrong with you or with me. Or both."

"I want to see you."

"Where?"

"Remember when that song was playing—'In the Air Tonight'?"

"I do."

"Remember where we went?"

"I do."

"I'll be there. Waiting."

I exit the back room out onto a landing that looks out on the parking lot behind the store.

Warren is leaning against the hood of his SUV, and when he sees me, he marches to a shed at the back of the lot. The building is like an old barn, with weathered wood planks and double doors. The handles are tied with a chain held together with a combination lock.

Warren twists the dial and yanks it free, tosses it aside, and pulls the wide doors open.

I guess I should have known. Maybe someone smarter than

me or under less stress would have seen it, but for me, what I see inside that shabby shed under the pine trees hits me like a five-pound hammer.

The tan military Humvee is very much like the one I drove in Labyrinth. It's been damaged and repaired. Thick welds snake up the body, plates added to patch the gaps.

Walking away from the shed, Warren calls to me. "Bought it a few years before I met you."

"Yeah?"

"They repaired the body before it was auctioned."

"That's the easy part."

He exhales, and for the first time, I see his eyes soften. "Motor was bad, though. I rebuilt it. I crank it every now and then to keep it operational."

I step off the landing and cautiously approach the big vehicle, examining the welded scars. This isn't the Humvee in Labyrinth. It's the one I was driving that day when my leg was blown off. The actual one. The military patched it up, but they didn't make it run again.

Then they discharged it.

And Warren fixed it.

There are a lot of things I want to say to him right now. But he speaks first.

"When you came over to my house—that night—and told me all that crazy stuff... Anyone else? I would've said, I ain't Bruce Willis and this ain't *The Sixth Sense*. Get out. But I let you talk because you were my business partner. And when you got to the part with the Humvee and that guy Wally, who was running a junkyard, and he gave you the Humvee, I started to think, maybe I'm involved in this too."

"I never wanted you to be."

"I know." Warren holds a hand out, offering the keys.

I take them and wait, expecting him to hit me with a retro quip to compensate for the vulnerability he's showing right now.

When he doesn't, I try to imitate his gruff, semi-annoyed voice. "What does this look like, an Arnold Schwarzenegger driving experience?"

The smile that flashes on his face is like a lightning strike: if you blinked, you'd miss it. But the afterglow remains.

"Let's just say if you break it, you bought it."

"This ain't no Blockbuster neither."

Warren finally laughs at that. "No. It's not."

For a long moment, Warren and I just look at each other, the only sound that of my fellow team members piling the duffel bags into the back of the Humvee.

Over my business partner's shoulder, I spot a car coming around the store, tires crunching on the gravel. I'm half-expecting to see a Raleigh Police cruiser. Instead, it's a Honda Accord, one I recognize. The vehicle stops, and the driver gets out and slowly removes her aviator sunglasses, first looking at Warren, then at me.

He takes a step closer to me and drops his voice.

"You taking her with you?"

"No. I just wanted to say goodbye. And to ask her to watch Riley."

Warren shrugs. "What, you don't trust me?"

"I do. But I can't ask you for that. I've already asked you for so much."

"You don't have to."

"You're volunteering?"

"Eh, I think I've mentioned that there's nothing on cable these days. I'll watch out for them. Both of them."

"Thank you."

Warren turns, and I call to him. "Hey, you know cable isn't even that big anymore."

"I know." Warren motions to the waiting Humvee. "And while we're clearing things up, your joke should have been something like, 'This ain't no Norman Schwarzkopf driving experience.' For it to work, your reference has to be sort of obscure and old school and borderline nonsensical."

"Warren, you're one of a kind."

"Try not to get yourself killed."

He nods to Meredith as they pass.

When she reaches me, she casts a gaze at the team, who are still loading duffel bags into the Humvee.

"How long will you be gone?" she asks.

"Don't know."

"What should I tell Ryan?"

"The truth."

Meredith raises her eyebrows.

"That I'm innocent, and that I went to find the evidence to prove it."

"*Okay*. What do I tell Riley?"

"Tell her... Tell her it's like before she was born, when I was in the Marines. I have to go away and do some work that's really important."

"It would be better for you to tell her. Can you call her?"

"I will. Tonight. On your phone. But it'll be the last time. At least for a while."

Meredith shakes her head and looks out at the parking lot. "What do you think you'll find at this... center of the Labyrinth?"

"Answers."

"To what?"

"Everything."

"Is that all?"

"I'd settle for getting my life back."

"I'd settle for that too."

"And getting Riley back. And you."

The muscles in Meredith's jaws flex as she clenches her teeth. A tear wells in her left eye and drops, slowly gliding across her face.

"I wish things had been different. I wish we could have really started over."

She doesn't answer. She presses her lips into mine, and I kiss her and hold her tight.

When the kiss ends, her eyes are filled with tears.

"Read to Riley every night. And make her read, even when she doesn't want to."

"Okay."

"Sometimes, when she's really tired, she lies about brushing her teeth."

Meredith smiles, but another tear breaks free from her eyes and rolls down her face.

I pull her close, kiss her forehead, and hold her for a long time.

"Okay. I'll be right back," I whisper.

She lets out a laugh that I can tell is suppressing a sob.

"You better be," she whispers back to me.

Releasing her, I tilt my head toward the narrow drive that wraps around the building.

"You should leave first."

She cocks her head for a brief second but seems to realize the reason. "Oh. Because they might be following me."

"Tough having a boyfriend who's a fugitive."

She grins. "You said *boyfriend*."

"I know."

She turns and walks back to her car, and right before she gets in, looks back at me.

And then she's gone, but I can still feel the glow of when she was here.

I don't know how long I stand there, but it's Isaac's voice that snaps me back to the moment.

"We're ready."

"Right."

"You going to drive?"

Feeling the keys in my pocket, I study the massive vehicle.

A few months ago, I would have turned and walked away from the mere sight of it. I'm still nervous, but I'm also ready to get behind the wheel again.

"Yeah," I tell him. "I'll drive."

Feeling the key in my pocket reminds me of another item we're going to need—if I'm right.

In my SUV, I open the glove box and take out the bulky metal key I found in my car after losing time one night. I figure: better to have and not need than need and not have.

In the Humvee, I crank the engine and listen to it rumble.

Isaac is sitting in the passenger seat, his laptop out, typing away.

"One thing before we go."

He looks over at me.

"Where are we going? It's just us in here now."

"I should have seen it sooner."

"What?"

"It was the numbers. It was the numbers all along."

"What about the numbers?"

"Think about how they brought us together."

June leans forward. "The website."

Isaac points at her. "Exactly. The website that is now leading others into the Labyrinth. But the numbers weren't the website. They were—"

"The address," I whisper.

"*Exactly*," Isaac says.

"And," I say slowly, the pieces clicking into place, "in Amersa's Labyrinth, they were a combination to get to the address at the end."

Isaac nods his head in exaggerated motions.

"Correct. I should have seen it. The numbers aren't just a web address. They're a combination that identifies another address—one out here in the real world. The numbers are *also* GPS coordinates. And that's where the center is. In fact, the coordinates are in the dead center of the world."

IV
THE ROAD

70

After leaving Warren's store, we drive east on I-40, toward Wilmington and the coast.

Before we left, Isaac used the internet to arrange for someone to buy a burner phone and hide it for us at a dead drop location. I didn't ask how exactly he accomplished this task, but I assume it was something to do with the dark web, Bitcoin, and other things I don't know much about.

Regardless of the specifics, it worked, because just past Willow Springs, North Carolina, I pull off the interstate and Isaac gets out and stalks into a field and retrieves a bundle marked with a small flag.

Upon returning to the Humvee, he opens it and activates the smartphone, immediately tethers his computer to it, and contacts Harold.

In short order, they make a plan.

We won't be staying in hotels or Airbnbs or anywhere that would leave a paper trail.

The solution to our shelter needs, I suppose, I should have seen.

"We're going to buy an RV," Isaac says. "One large enough for all of us."

On his laptop, he searches for RV dealerships along our route to Wilmington and begins calling them up. By the time he's done, I'm getting hungry.

When we were exiting the freeway, I saw a sign for a place called The Redneck BBQ Lab, and when I suggest we head there for lunch, Isaac's eyes bulge. "Dude. For real?"

"What?"

"*Off. The. Grid.* We've been on the run for like—what—thirty minutes? And you want to waltz into some local barbecue joint?"

He turns to the back seat, where the duffel bags are stacked between Rose and June.

"Let's have some MREs."

And that's what we have for lunch, inside the Humvee, parked on a dirt road half a mile from the interstate.

Isaac doesn't like what he hears from the RV dealers—in particular their documentation requirements.

Our MRE cartons are empty and the sun is falling in the sky when he starts calling used car dealers. On his fourth try, he finds one with an RV and the sort of discretion we're looking for.

After a call with Harold, the transaction is done, and an hour later, I'm once again pulling off I-40, this time driving a few miles from the freeway, past a car lot where a few campers and an RV loom.

I don't turn in. I roll past it, to a nondescript dirt driveway that ends in a gate with a very prominent No Trespassing sign.

The used car dealer told Isaac and Harold that this was hunting land (and a good place for the drop off).

On the way, I had wondered if the guy would honor the deal (the money was sent ahead of the hand-off). Frankly, I'm a little surprised to see the massive RV waiting for us, parked on the shoulder of the dirt road.

It's not the exact RV Gerald lived in inside Amersa's Labyrinth. But it's a close facsimile, just as this world is starting to eerily mimic Amersa's simulation. I suspect the similarities are not lost on my fellow travelers, but none of us says anything as I get out and approach the massive land yacht. It's a Fleetwood Bounder, a used one (about twenty years old). From the outside, it looks to be in pretty good shape. According to Isaac, we're not going far (mostly we just need a portable home for a while), so hopefully it's up to the challenge.

Our new home on wheels is about forty feet long, and within,

I find a bedroom at the back, a booth dinette, a kitchen, and a sofa that pulls out into a full bed. There's room for everyone.

Perhaps most notable is what this older motor home doesn't have: GPS, real-time vehicle tracking, and remote (over-the-air) updates for embedded systems, and other smart gadgets. Modern RVs are connected vehicles, which can be tracked. This old Fleetwood can't.

As promised, the key is under the kitchen sink.

Back at the Humvee, I peer in at Isaac in the passenger seat. "We're good."

He doesn't look up from his laptop, only mumbles, "Awesome."

Leaning through the window, I try to get his attention. "Hey. That thing doesn't maneuver that well. I need you to drive in front to help me change lanes and—"

Isaac turns to me with the same shock as my previous barbecue request. "*Dude*. I'm working." He points both hands at his laptop. "Like, we've got some seriously time-sensitive stuff here."

Not sure what to say to that, I glance in the backseat for help. June winces. She hasn't slept well, and even so, driving the rattling Humvee isn't exactly her cup of tea.

Rose exhales and stares out at the pine trees, and then, without a word, opens her door and gets behind the wheel.

With the Humvee in the lead, I follow in the RV, the big diesel engine rumbling down I-40 toward the coast, the sun setting behind us.

I'm expecting we'll end up in an RV park, perhaps with a crumbling sign resembling a mermaid.

Instead, our new address is a field off the interstate, twenty miles from Wilmington.

The RV rocks as it moves through the tall grass, and when I park, the three others exit the Humvee and join me inside.

Isaac sits on the couch, eerily mirroring the position where his virtual counterpart—Ian—sat during my time in Amersa's Labyrinth.

He holds out the burner phone.

"These are GPS coordinates. I need you to go there for another pickup."

I take the phone and study them. It's another field.

"It's groceries. Water and stuff," Isaac adds as he refocuses on his laptop.

With the phone, I start typing in Meredith's number, which I memorized before leaving. The time is right. She'll have picked up Riley from school, and they'll be home.

"I need to call my daughter."

Isaac looks up. "No. A communications blackout means—"

"I know what it means. But I need to call my daughter."

June, who is sitting at the banquette, slides out. "And I need to call my husband."

Rose, standing in the kitchen, turns to us. "I want to call my mom."

Isaac leans back on the couch and stares at the ceiling. "We may as well pop smoke. There's probably some in Warren's guerrilla war trick-or-treat bag."

He focuses on the three of us. "Or we could just email Amersa now and turn ourselves in."

Calmly, slowly, I say to him, "Operational security is important. So is the team's mental health. I'm betting you are smart enough to figure out a way for us to make those calls while minimizing the risks."

Another hour later and twenty miles up the road, we pick up another throw-away phone, and standing by the edge of a pond, I call Meredith.

She answers apprehensively, like one might if they're expecting the call to be from a telemarketer or—in this unlikely case—a fugitive love interest you're babysitting for.

"Hello?"

"It's me."

"Hi," she breathes into the phone. "How's it going?"

"Fine. So far."

"You want to talk to her?"

"Yeah."

I hear footsteps on carpeted stairs and Meredith's voice calling to Riley: "It's your dad."

There's a shuffling, then: "Dad? *Where are you?*"

"I'm on a trip, sweetie."

"To where?"

"Oh, here and there, it's not important."

"When are you coming home?"

"As soon as I can, darling."

"Tomorrow?"

"Definitely not tomorrow. It's going to be a while, okay?"

"Like a week?"

"It's definitely going to be longer than that."

"Two weeks?"

"Sweetie, I'm not really sure how long this is going to take, okay? I'd tell you if I could."

"Dad, *what are you doing?* What's going on?"

"It's just some work I need to do."

"What kind of work?"

"It's nothing you need to worry about—"

"You're a teacher, Dad. You work at school."

"Well, that's true. But this is a special situation."

"Like... what? A field trip?"

"Something like that. But it's not related to school."

She pauses. "Is it stuff with Mister Warren?"

"No, it's not that either. It's something else, kiddo. Something I have to do."

She falls silent, and I add, "It's like your reading at night."

I can picture her bunching her eyebrows. "What do you mean?"

"Well, you know, that's something you don't always like doing, especially when you're tired, but you do it anyway—because you have to. Parents have to do things like that too."

Quietly, as if cradling the phone, she says, "Can you do it later?"

"I'm sorry, darling, I can't. This has to be done now."

I wait, but she doesn't say anything.

"Riley?"

"Yeah," she says, voice small.

"I want you to listen to me, okay?"

She says okay, her voice even softer.

"I love you very much."

"I love you too, Dad."

"I want you to be a listener for Ms. Davis."

"She says I can call her Meredith now."

"Well, that's up to her, but whatever you call her, you better do everything she tells you to, do you understand?"

Her first sob breaks free like a dam crumbling.

"Riley, did you hear me?"

Her sob-soaked response is a nearly unintelligible form of "Yeah."

Her crying—and my own emotions—are starting to get to me now, the cracks forming in my own dam. I figure I've got seconds left, so I say what I want her to know if this is actually the last time I talk to my daughter.

"Your mom would be very proud of you, kiddo."

Her cries stretch out and get louder.

I tell my only child that I love her and that I'll be back as soon as I can. When I hang up, I let the phone drop to my side and stare at the empty pond.

Behind me, I hear feet moving toward me in the tall grass.

I turn.

June stops in her tracks and studies my face.

I hold out the phone.

She doesn't reach for it. "You want to talk?"

"I've done enough talking for a lifetime. Hasn't done me any good."

"That's no reason to stop."

"Sure it is."

"Not for a guy like you, Alan. And, for what it's worth, I suspect talking has done you some good. Something certainly has."

"How do you figure?"

"Did you ever think you'd drive a military Humvee again?"

I glance back at the vehicle. Rose is lying on the hood, soaking in the last dregs of the setting sun.

June holds her hand out for the phone. "Just know: I'm always here for you if you do want to talk."

After the calls, I wipe the phone off, take the battery out, crush the SIM card, and throw the pieces in the pond.

Back at the RV, Isaac is sitting at the banquette now, still working away on the laptop. He pauses, hands on the keyboard as Rose, June, and I climb the stairs. It's dusk outside and the first hints of the cooler night temps are just starting to roll in.

There is one, huge, looming, unasked question, and it hangs in the air as June and Rose settle on the couch. I stand by the driver's seat and ask it:

"Where precisely are we going?"

Isaac looks up. "Africa."

"That's not very precise."

"The center of Africa." When no one says anything, he adds, "I mean the *dead center* of Africa." He turns the laptop to me.

"These are the Labyrinth GPS coordinates."

On the screen, I study the two numbers, expressed in decimal degrees. The first is a latitude (12.1225); the second the longitude (18.914208).

With the three of us crowded around the laptop, Isaac explains exactly how he arrived at the location.

As all of us know, the number sequence, when substituted for letters, spells labyrinth.

12	=	L
1	=	A
2	=	B
25	=	Y
18	=	R
9	=	I
14	=	N
20	=	T
8	=	H

"To get the GPS coordinates," Isaac says, "I split the letters, taking the numbers for the first four letters as the latitude and the number for the fifth letter—eighteen—and used it as the start of the longitude."

He points to the screen. "The location is in the middle of Africa, in present-day Chad. Might even be where the human race first evolved."

Isaac switches the map to satellite view and zooms in. "From the air, the location looks like an empty field."

"Or it was when this image was taken," Rose says.

What I'm wondering is what's there now.

71

That night, the four of us eat MREs at the dinette in the RV.

I have about a thousand questions I want to ask. I figure Rose and June do too.

But I'm too tired to ask any of them. I sense that my fellow group members are as well.

It's been a long day, and if Isaac is right, there are more long days ahead.

The RV has one bathroom. Rose, June, and I take turns using it to brush our teeth and wash our faces, then the two of them turn in (they're sharing the queen bed in the master).

I set about unfolding the couch into a bed. For some reason, camping out in this RV reminds me of the time Riley and I spent in that red caboose out in the woods.

I expect Isaac to convert the dinette to a single bed where he'll sleep, but he keeps banging away on the keyboard, his eyelids drooping.

When I've finished making my bed, I nod to his laptop. "Need any help?"

Without looking up, he shakes his head. "Not unless you know anything about buying a used yacht."

"Sailing them, yes. Buying, not so much."

He takes his fingers from the keys, but keeps his eyes on the screen. "Right. Because of the Marines."

"Yeah. And I had an uncle who lived down on the Outer Banks. Had a deep-sea fishing boat. Not a yacht, per se, but still."

Isaac begins typing furiously, a small smile spreading on his lips.

I step around the table, trying to see what he's seeing. "What happened?"

Isaac looks over at me. "Alan, we are, as of this moment, the proud new owners of a Nordhavn 68 motor yacht. Thanks to Harold's bank balance and the discretion of certain sellers who only trade in Bitcoin."

"Excellent. And what, pray tell, may we expect from our new home on the water?"

"Actually, it's a lot like this RV. She's got some years on her. And a few miles." Isaac pauses. "Do you say miles for used boats?"

"It's more about hours on the engine, but I get your drift, if you will."

He points at me. "I see what you did there."

"Don't ever think my dad jokes are confined to land."

After that, Isaac puts away his laptop and sets up the bed.

During dinner, we agreed to use the RV's house batteries for power and only to run the generator during the day to recharge the batteries. The generator noise, Isaac reasoned, might draw attention at night.

As would lights. For that reason, we lay in darkness and silence in our beds like the first night of a summer camp.

I'm dead tired, but my mind won't let me sleep. I'm thinking about Riley, and wondering if I was on the news tonight, and whether she saw it.

It would make for a juicy story: local high school teacher wanted for murder. The fact that I'm a military veteran, amputee, widower, and father only broadens the story's appeal.

I figure it's simply a matter of time before she finds out. Maybe she'll see it online. Or perhaps a kid at school will say something like, "Hey, Riley, did your dad really kill that guy? My dad says that only guilty people run."

"Alan," Isaac says, voice hesitant in the dark, as if testing to see if I'm awake.

"Yeah?"

"You ever think about the fact that, like, our group, we seem to have the exact skills we need?"

"As in…"

"You know, like me with computers. You with military experience and boats. You knowing Warren and having access to a Humvee and gear. June and her background in neuroscience. Rose having access to Amersa to hide the bug and get the key card. It's like—"

"A lot of coincidences."

"Exactly," he whispers.

"What do you think it means?"

"It means something. But I don't know what. I still think we're missing something, like a big piece."

"Or maybe we've got all the pieces, but we're missing the big picture."

He exhales loudly enough that I can hear it. "Maybe. There's another thing that's bothering me."

"Yeah?"

"Driving down the road in the Humvee. Buying this RV. The boat. Harold helping us. It's like we're recreating your Labyrinth experience. But are we doing it because you did it there first? Is it some kind of subconscious process? Like, were we sort of predisposed to this path because of what you already did? Or would it have happened like this anyway? If so, it feels like…"

"Too many coincidences."

"Yeah."

Neither of us says anything for a while, and I feel my mind drifting back into that rabbit hole of wondering whether I should have said something to Riley about a possible news story involving me being wanted for murder and to not believe anything she hears.

"Alan?" Isaac says softly.

"Yeah?"

"Sorry I was short today."
"It's okay."
"I'm just stressed."
"I know. Me too."

In the morning, Isaac converts his bed back to the dinette, and the four of us sit around it consuming MREs for breakfast.

Isaac points his fork at the carton he's consuming. "We're going to be eating a lot of these after we dock in Africa, on the way to the center."

Rose, who is slowly chewing her own meal (beef stew, I believe), swallows and mutters, "I was thinking the same thing."

"We should cook fresh food while we can," Isaac says. "We have a kitchen here, and we'll have one on the boat."

"No complaints from me," I mumble as I scarf down another bite of chili and beans. "Shall I make a run to the store?"

"From here out," Isaac says, scooping up another bite of chicken and noodles, "there will be no runs to any stores. We need to think hard about every move."

No one says anything because it's obvious Isaac has already thought about our next move.

"It's likely," he continues, "that at least one camera saw our Humvee leaving Raleigh; a traffic cam or a store security camera—and it might have even seen Alan behind the wheel, maybe the rest of us too."

"The Humvee," June says, "is also not the most inconspicuous vehicle on the road."

"A good point," Isaac says. "Which is why I've arranged for a burner car."

"A burner car?" Rose asks.

Isaac holds up one of the burner phones. "Same principle. But, you know… with a car."

I ask if he found another used car dealer, and he replies that he made the arrangement with a private party he found on Craigslist and that the rental is for five days.

Last night, he told me that the boat would arrive in Wilmington in four days (part of the sale price included the previous owner sailing the yacht up from Fort Lauderdale and leaving it for us, fully fueled and with no questions asked).

"I gave us an extra day," Isaac says, holding up his fork, "because we assume the yacht will be here in four days. But assumptions lead to surprises—and we need to be ready for those."

Isaac asks Rose and June to pick up the so-called burner car, which turns out to be a Jeep Cherokee. It creaks as it rolls down the dirt road and across the field to the RV.

Like me—and the Humvee—it's seen better days and has had some work done along the way. I can spot the tell-tale signs of Bondo and some paint that doesn't quite match. The windows don't roll down, but I can sense from the way it cranks that the engine has been rebuilt or even replaced. Like me and our other two vehicles, it's probably roadworthy enough to get the job done.

For the rest of the day, Rose and June go out to pick up supplies that Isaac orders online.

Because I'm a wanted fugitive, I stay behind. And I try to make myself useful. That entails cooking and research (and I do hope I'm doing a better job with the research than the lunch I prepare, though my fellow travelers never once complain).

I spend a few hours learning about the motor yacht we'll soon call home, studying its controls and capabilities, then turning my focus to a passage plan to get to Africa.

The Nordhavn 68 we've acquired is the forward pilothouse version. It holds about 3,000 gallons of diesel fuel, and the seller has also included four 250-gallon fuel bladders, giving us 4,000 gallons when fully loaded.

The question I have to answer is the vessel's range. That number depends on the speed we travel. If we push the engines harder—and sail faster—our range will be shorter. But we'll get there sooner. Like so many things in life, it's a basic trade-off between time and cost. What I need to know are the specific numbers for my calculations.

Luckily, some fellow Nordhavn 68 owners have done real-world tests on how much range the vessel gets at various speeds—and have been kind enough to share their results on their blogs. Cruising at 8 knots, one owner's Nordhavn 68 burned 1.14 gallons per nautical mile. But at 7 knots, they only used .89 gallons for every nautical mile traveled. Which means, given that we have 4,000 gallons of fuel on board, we can travel about 4,500 nautical miles if we average 7 knots of speed.

However, we have two other considerations: the added weight of the four deck bladders, which will increase our fuel consumption; and the North Atlantic fall seas, which, depending on our luck, will force detours and throttle-ups.

Which brings me to the real issue: can we make it to Africa without refueling?

That answer depends on exactly where we go ashore.

Our ultimate destination is pretty far inland, in the landlocked country of Chad. So we'll have to dock somewhere and either drive or fly the rest of the way.

Flying via helicopter would be fastest, but it's risky. My biggest concern is that a local paramilitary group might mistake us for one of their rivals. Those groups have a tendency to shoot anything in their airspace, especially suspected enemies.

Driving will take longer, but it also extends our life expectancy.

The next challenge is picking a port at which to go ashore.

Lagos, Nigeria, is the obvious choice, but I don't favor it for a variety of reasons.

First, the port itself is huge, which means lots of people might see us. That's an issue because we'll have to hide the boat somewhere, and while I plan to hire private security, leaving it in Lagos—or close by—is not ideal.

The next issue is transport on land. Nigeria shares a border with Chad, but Lagos is on the western end of the country. It'd be a long drive.

As I research the route from Lagos to our destination, I like that port even less. It turns out we'll likely have to make a border crossing into Cameroon to eventually get to Chad.

I also have local security concerns, specifically with driving in Northern Nigeria. Recent State Department advisories flag specific regions where Boko Haram and bandit groups operate. We'd need to plan our route carefully to avoid known conflict zones.

The distance, however, is what marks Lagos off the list: it's almost 2,000 miles from the port to the center of the Labyrinth. That would take about sixty hours of drive time—and that's not including refueling and stops to camp.

The other ports worth considering have problems, too. There's Cotonou, Benin, which is smaller than Lagos and generally safer, but it's also even farther from our ultimate destination, with more border crossings.

Docking in Gentil, Gabon, would avoid the security issues in Nigeria, and the port is pretty modern, but it's farther south, which means an even longer drive.

That leaves Douala, Cameroon, which is the closest Atlantic port with viable overland routes to Chad. Like Cotonou, it's far less busy than Lagos and has less of a reputation for piracy.

No matter where we enter the continent, the voyage will require refueling along the way (the shortest route I came up with was roughly 5,400 nautical miles).

We could stop in Bermuda, but after refueling there, we'd never make it to Douala without taking extra fuel with us. We could likely source extra fuel bladders in Wilmington, but it would take time and maybe expose us more (Isaac won't like it, and a fuel bladder isn't exactly an off-the-shelf item).

That leaves two logical refueling points along our route: the Azores (about 2,400 nautical miles away from Wilmington) and Cape Verde (which is much closer to Africa—and a more direct route—but roughly 3,200 nautical miles from us now).

This is all giving me a headache, and I'm frankly glad when dinner time arrives and I can get away from the tablet I've been using (which Rose and June retrieved this morning and I tether to Isaac's burner phone).

In the kitchen, I heat a pan to cook some ground beef and pour some beans in a pot. Soon, our little numbers group is making their way through my mini-taco bar, loading tortillas with meat, beans, lettuce, tomatoes, cheese, and salsa. There's chips and guacamole too (which Isaac and I partake in).

Over dinner, we discuss our day as if it's the most normal thing in the world.

Rose has decided to fill her extra time by studying first aid procedures.

June has been practicing setting up the tents we acquired today.

Isaac has once again spent his day coordinating with Harold to buy the harder-to-find items we'll need along the way.

Which gives me an idea.

"From the port, it's going to be a long drive to the coordinates," I tell the group as I fill my third taco.

Isaac crunches a guac-loaded chip. "Right. Because we can't fly."

"Correct. But, it got me thinking—maybe we don't have to drive the whole way. And maybe we shouldn't—for our own safety."

Isaac exhales, looking exhausted as he uses a chip to scoop more of the green goodness up. "You lost me."

"Let me ask another question: we're assuming what's at the center of the Labyrinth will be friendly to us. What if it's not? What if the numbers and the coordinates are a trap of some kind?"

Isaac nods slowly. "That's fair. So what do we do about that?"

"We drive as far as we need to, then launch a drone to surveil to the coordinates."

Isaac's face lights up. "That's good. I'll add it to the shopping list."

72

For the next three days, we settle into a pattern: Isaac is heads down on his laptop, I do more research on the tablet, and Rose and June take the Jeep for supply runs.

In a way, our little camp out here at the edge of the woods feels like a mini version of a US military forward operating base.

And with each passing day, it starts to look more like one.

The Humvee is parked in the weeds and covered by a tarp. It was already full of guns, and bit by bit we add other supplies we want to keep out of the elements.

Soon, there are tarps on the ground filled with other things we'll need for the trip: mountains of canned goods and packaged food, camping gear, portable solar panels, miscellaneous boat parts, clothes and gear for all weather and terrain scenarios, and first aid supplies.

We've also acquired a portable desalinator for making water. It's overkill (the ship has two tanks that hold a combined 673 gallons of fresh water) and an onboard desalinator. But if the tanks are breached and the watermaker fails, we'll need a backup. And in case the backup fails, we've acquired some large containers to hold water. They take up a lot of room, but it's worth it.

I've been thinking about points of failure on this journey. I'm using the 3-3-3-3 survival rule of thumb.

The logic goes that the average person can survive for about three minutes without oxygen. In extreme conditions, you can make it for roughly three hours without shelter. Without food? Generally, three weeks.

Without drinkable water, three days is about how long someone can survive.

As our voyage will last somewhere between 30 and 40 days, running out of water while at sea is definitely a point of mission failure (one made worse by the fact that there is scarcely little in the way of land along our route). We'd be reliant on another passing ship for rescue, which is an assumption. And at this point, I like assumptions about as much as Isaac does.

I know the water is overkill, but I'm good with that.

We've also gone a little overboard on the medical preparations. Thanks to Isaac's dark web transactions, we now have a stockpile of antibiotics, antimalarials, painkillers, and about everything else.

We've also acquired an ample supply of sleep meds. We'll need to time-shift at several points in the mission, and I suspect sleep will be hard to come by anyway.

At my request, we have also acquired some deep-sea fishing gear. I am not at all certain we'll need it—or that we'll even have the opportunity to use it—but I figure it can't hurt.

There are two other categories of supplies we've acquired, both of which wouldn't have occurred to me.

The first is entertainment. We've stockpiled books and board games. It will be, after all, a long journey, and maintaining mental health, in addition to physical health, will be a challenge, especially considering the stress we're under and the fact that we'll be separated from our loved ones.

The second is exercise equipment. The Nordhavn 68 isn't exactly a luxury yacht (there's no onboard gym). So we've compiled a few items to help us keep in shape: a recumbent bike, exercise bands, and fitness mats. There's also a stack of old exercise DVDs (I was expecting maybe Richard Simmons, Billy Blanks, or possibly Jane Fonda or even Suzanne Somers pumping a Thighmaster, but I don't recognize any of the gurus).

Each night, I cook in the RV's kitchen, and we play a board game and then read. It feels almost like a dry run for life on board the boat. The Nordhavn 68 is about twice as long as the RV, but for the next month and a half, our world is going to shrink. It's a small amount of space for four strangers to occupy, even ones forced together by circumstances and survival. We need to create a reliable routine and as many boundaries as we can manage.

The day we're supposed to pick up the yacht, I drive the Humvee to an abandoned quarry nearby. The gate is locked, but thanks to satellite maps, we've got a way around it.

A hundred feet from the water, I park the Humvee and walk to the precipice and look over, making sure there's no crazy teenagers out day-drinking and skinny-dipping in the frigid fall water.

It's deserted, and from the looks of it, it's deep and long forgotten.

With a pair of binoculars, I scan in every direction, but it's nothing but Carolina countryside as far as I can see.

Back at the Humvee, I put it in neutral and remove the license plate.

Behind the wheel of the Jeep, I roll forward and connect its nose to the back of the Humvee. The two vehicles creak as they roll forward. Soon, both are barreling toward the cliff. I hit the Jeep's brakes, turn away, and watch as the hulking Humvee soars over the edge and crashes into the water.

In the silence that follows, Rose and I stand at the edge, watching the Humvee sink. As it disappears into the water, a strange thing happens: a sense of calm settles over me, the likes of which I haven't felt in a very long time.

After lunch, we load the supplies in the RV and all four of us take sleeping pills. Isaac—wisely—has arranged for us to take possession of the boat at night. There'll be fewer people around to see us then, but still, the hand-off and departure are the riskiest parts of this trip so far.

In the loaded RV, with the privacy curtains pulled shut, we

all bed down, the piles of food, water, books, and camping gear stacked around us.

The sleep mask helps block out the light, and the Ambien I took is dragging me down like the Humvee's engine in that quarry, and right before I sink into sleep, I hear Isaac's voice in the darkness.

"Alan? You awake?"

I smile. "No."

"Good one."

"What is it?"

"Something strange."

"What's that?"

"I'm as stressed as I've ever been."

"Same."

"But you know what?"

"What?"

"Since we left, I haven't heard the ringing."

"Me either."

"This is the quietest it's ever been for me. In my whole life."

"What do you think it means?"

"I don't know."

73

That night, our phone alarms go off and the four of us wake and try to shake off the Ambien haze. Inside the RV, my three fellow travelers drink coffee, and I settle for cold water in a glass and more cold water splashed on my face. Outside, moonlight shines down on a thin layer of fog.

Our first task is wiping down the Jeep and driving it to the drop-off point (yet another pasture off a dirt road).

Several marinas in Wilmington can accommodate the Nordhavn we've purchased. We've chosen to avoid all of them.

Instead, the seller has been instructed to refuel the vessel, refill the water tanks, and leave it docked at a private residence.

Like much of the North Carolina coast, the Wilmington area has quite a few barrier islands. Between the islands and the mainland lie deep-water intracoastal waterways and sounds.

On the mainland and the rear portions of the barrier islands, many of the homes have private docks and long boardwalks that stretch out into the waterways.

The Nordhavn has a draft of six and a half feet, which means there are hundreds, maybe even thousands, of homes with docks on water deep enough to accommodate the vessel.

Figure Eight Island—from a satellite view—looks like a great option. It's more private. The houses there are farther apart than the more crowded areas like Wrightsville Beach, but the issue is that Figure Eight is only accessible by a single bridge, and there's a guardhouse on the bridge. We need a location that is both secluded and easily accessible.

After some research, Isaac and I settled on a home located

on the mainland, situated on Masonboro Sound. It features a long boardwalk that extends across the marsh and wetlands to a deep-water dock. To minimize our digital trail, Isaac contacted the owners directly and made arrangements.

The property is south of Wrightsville, and the street leading to it—Masonboro Sound Road—is unassuming and quiet, tree-lined with a few homes and entrances to older neighborhoods.

At the entrance to the property, I turn onto the gravel driveway and proceed at low speed, the RV bouncing along the rutted road. Soon, the headlights illuminate a two-story house. After parking, I turn off the engine and lights, and we sit there, searching for any signs of trouble. Rose and Isaac peek around the privacy curtains, and June and I watch through the windshield.

There's not a soul in sight, just the trees and a backyard that needs mowing. A gravel footpath leads to a wooden boardwalk with graying planks.

Reaching down, I adjust the sidearm in my holster. "I'll go check it out."

June looks over at me. "Alone?"

I shrug. "Yeah. You know, just in case."

"Just in case what?" Isaac asks. He's standing in front of the RV's door now.

"Look, let's face it: we bought a sixty-eight-foot motor yacht from someone in South Florida who didn't ask a lot of questions—and who was willing to skip any and all documentation procedures."

Isaac holds his hands up. "Buyers can do a test drive."

"Right. A transatlantic sea trial that lasts over a month? After the final sale has been made?"

"What are you thinking?" Rose asks. "That these are... criminals? Drug dealers?"

"I'm thinking people who sell large-ticket items without asking questions could be dangerous. And that's assuming the boat is even docked and waiting at the end of the boardwalk."

"So what's your plan?" Isaac asks.

"I'll check it out. If I don't come back... well, continue without me."

"No," Isaac says flatly. "We're coming."

"Do you even know how to use a gun?"

Isaac tears his gaze from me.

"I don't," June says quietly.

Rose walks over to the duffel bag and reaches in and shuffles through the contents, the soft clink of metal-on-metal punctuating the awkward standoff. She draws out a handgun, eyes it for a second, then ejects the magazine, makes sure it's full of bullets, then pulls the slide back, verifying there isn't a round in the chamber. After releasing the slide, she reinserts the magazine.

"I know how to use a gun. And I'm coming."

Isaac reaches inside his pocket and takes out the burner phone. "While I don't know how to use a gun, I do know how to use a phone. Which is handy. To call for help. In the event that guns aren't enough. Or if they have bigger guns. Or more guns."

June swivels the passenger seat. "I'll come too."

A thought occurs to me then.

"Isaac, how were they supposed to get out? The people who delivered the boat."

He exhales. "Do we have to go over every detail?"

"In this instance, yes. If we don't get on that boat safely, this mission is over right here, before it even begins."

"Fine," Isaac mutters. "The plan was for them to leave the boat at the dock, walk out to the road, and get a rideshare to the airport and fly from Wilmington back to Fort Lauderdale."

From the driver's seat, I stare out at the backyard and the marsh beyond, thinking, half-expecting to spot someone lurking, waiting for us to make our way to the boardwalk. It would be the perfect spot for an ambush. But all I see is a heron taking flight under the pale glow of the moon.

"I'm going to turn the RV around and point it down the driveway. June, you stay. Lock the doors. If someone tries to get in, you drive away."

"I can't drive this thing."

"It's easier than it looks. And you won't have to drive far, just down the driveway and the road a little bit. It's deserted this time of night, and it's not that busy anyway. You only have to go far enough to get away from someone on foot. We'll hear the RV leave, and I'll come back and take care of..." I stop there, searching for the words. I settle on, "the person."

With that, I crank the RV again and, with some effort, manage to get it turned around in the driveway. With June behind the wheel, Rose, Isaac, and I stalk into the night, two of us armed with guns, the other with a burner phone.

In the backyard, the only sound is crickets and frogs calling back and forth, the symphony of the marsh.

As I plant my prosthetic on the first cupping plank of the boardwalk, the tall grass to my right sways, and a figure rises. I spin, gun held out, my index finger moving from the frame down to the trigger.

Rose turns too, a rapid gasp escaping her as two gulls take flight.

I exhale and feel the adrenaline spike easing.

In the silence, we march down the wooden walkway above the water, the moonlight glittering in the open patches of water between the mud and grass.

The fog grows more dense as the land gives way to the water. It's so thick I can't see the dock at the end of the boardwalk—or whether the boat is waiting for us there.

About thirty seconds into our trek across the wooden walkway, Isaac mutters, "How long is this thing?"

I turn and shush him, and he rolls his eyes, but doesn't say anything else.

A few seconds later, a wind gust blows across the sound, gently whisking the fog away, revealing a wide dock with a roof above. At the back is what looks like an enclosed storage area. On each side of the dock, there are several boat lifts. Two of them are full. Beyond the storage shed and lifts, at the end of the dock, is a wide berth where a sixty-eight-foot motor yacht is moored, waiting quietly in the night. The vessel is dark, not even its running lights on.

Just before we reach the dock, right outside the enclosed area, I raise a clenched fist to shoulder level. Turning slightly, but still keeping the boat in sight, I point to my eyes with my index and middle fingers, then redirect my pointer finger to my chest and then to the boat. With my palm down, fingers extended, I press down, patting the air.

Isaac scowls. Rose merely cocks her head. I did the hand signals out of instinct, almost without thinking. I'll train the crew on the voyage.

"Wait here," I hiss. "Behind the shed."

I don't wait for a reply. Instead, I creep across the old dock, gun held out, watching the boat's windows and railing for any movement.

At first glance, the motor yacht matches my online research, though this one was customized slightly by the owners. Seen from this angle, from the waterline to the tallest antenna, she rises out of the water nearly as high as she is long, looking almost like a lopsided, white layer cake floating on the sea.

She has three decks—or levels. The lower deck has two staterooms, a desk that converts to a bed, and the engine room.

The main deck, where passengers board, contains the salon and galley as well as the owner's stateroom, which runs the full beam at the front of the boat.

Above is the pilothouse deck, which holds the wheelhouse with two helm chairs, a bank of screens and gadgets, and behind them, a U-shaped dinette. There's a small bunk and office off the wheelhouse for the captain.

At the very top is an open-air fly bridge with another helm chair and a bank of controls. By day, and when the weather is nice, I figure I'll spend my time up there.

Assuming this all works out. Assuming there aren't a few drug lords hiding in this floating layer cake waiting to pop out and shoot me and toss me in the sound and see what else they can steal from their buyers.

Or maybe they'll play it smart and take me hostage and ransom me, and Isaac will pay it in cryptocurrency.

I'm certainly at a tactical disadvantage here. The boat has port and starboard side decks for someone to walk around. And there are plenty of places to hide.

Receding into a shadow on the dock, I crouch and peel a

piece of wood from the plank below me and toss it onto the aft deck.

The commotion causes no movement on the ship. The only sound is a frog croaking, as if goading me to climb aboard and get on with it.

The thing about an incursion is that you don't want to enter at the location an enemy combatant is expecting.

In this case, one would normally board the ship via the main deck, which is nearly level with the dock.

So, I won't be getting on there.

Squatting, I move forward, gun ready, but I don't step onto the boat. I slip behind a hexagonal mooring pile and press my back to it, feeling the cool concrete even through the thin jacket I'm wearing.

No shots are fired. There's no rustling inside the boat.

Still, I wait and listen.

Looking back, I see Isaac peeking around the weathered shed.

With a sharp hand wave, I motion for him to get out of sight.

Stepping off the dock, I plant my real foot on the rail of the main deck and climb until I'm throwing my leg over the metal rail and standing on the teak planks of the port side deck, peering into the pilothouse. The two helm chairs are empty. The screens are off. The U-shaped dinette behind them is empty. It reminds me of the banquette in the red caboose Riley and I used to live in.

Quickly, I swing the door outward and sweep behind the helm chairs and peek into the captain's quarters.

Empty.

Slowly, I ascend the stairs to the fly bridge.

It's empty too.

I pause there, listening, the fog drifting across the sound, the moon watching from above. As before, all I hear are the frogs and crickets.

From fly bridge, I work my way down, back through the pilothouse then to the main deck and finally belowdecks, searching every inch.

There's no one here. It's just what we were promised: a fifteen-year-old boat that's in good shape.

74

My first order of business is to disable the ship's AIS or Automatic Identification System.

Next, the four of us work as quickly as we can in the moonlight and fog to transfer our supplies from the RV to the boat. Thankfully, under the back deck of the house Isaac rented, we find a yard cart with pneumatic tires. It bounces over the weathered boardwalk the way the RV did on the gravel road in, and it probably cuts our loading time in half.

When the RV is empty, I drive the hulking vehicle to a nearby forest and park it, covering it with tarps attached with bungee cords.

When I exit, I find Rose waiting by a four-wheeler, which is still idling (the ATV was also parked at the house we rented).

Even in the moonlight, I can make out some uneasiness on her face as she asks if I want to drive.

Her gaze drifts down to the foot-operated gear shifter.

"I can manage. But you seem to be doing fine."

I expect her to turn and mount the four-wheeler, but she lingers, eying my prosthetic. "It doesn't slow you down much, does it?"

"Not really. Not anymore. But it took a while."

"Learning to use it?"

"That. And the mental adjustment. My wife helped me a lot there."

She nods slowly.

A gust of wind moves through the trees, and a cloud of fog passes between us.

I can't see Rose, but I can hear her voice.

"We never really talked about it, but that night… You probably saved my life."

"Eh, you're giving me too much credit."

"No. I saw it in his eyes."

"It was just instinct."

"I'm thankful for it."

She walks to the four-wheeler and turns it off.

When she returns, her voice is low and reflective.

"You know, when I first heard the ringing?" She pauses and slips her hands in her pockets. "It was one of the times he hit me. Wasn't the first." She looks me in the eyes. "You saw the last."

"You left him?"

"I did."

"Good."

Rose peers up at the moon. "When I saw the numbers the first time, they were spray-painted on a bedroom wall. Like graffiti." She shakes her head slowly, a smile forming on her lips. "I thought I was going crazy."

"I know the feeling."

"But I kept seeing them. Here and there. Then I found the website. And then you know what happened in that apartment below you, and you showed up, and then we met again—at the group."

"I'm glad we did."

"Me too. But it's a strange…"

"Coincidence."

She nods. "Exactly. It's a strange coincidence."

"I agree."

"What does it mean, Alan?"

"I don't know. I wish I did."

It's still dark when we untether the boat from the dock and sail south out of Masonboro Sound.

In the pilothouse, I gaze out the windows at the Atlantic ahead.

Below, on the aft deck, my three fellow travelers watch the shore grow smaller and our homeland disappear on the horizon.

The first rays of sunrise are lancing above the horizon when I hear footsteps on the stairs from below. Isaac pokes his head around a glossy, wood-veneered beam.

"We're ready whenever you are."

"I'm ready."

I turn the autopilot on, but I don't leave the helm chair or pilothouse. Instead, my comrades join me up here, the three of them sitting in the settee with the rectangular table in front of them, the sun glittering on the glossy lacquered surface.

We're all dead tired from the night's events (and adrenaline), but we need to make plans.

"First," I tell them, "some basics. This vessel has a range of about 4,500 nautical miles when traveling at seven knots, which is what we're going to do."

June lifts her hand slightly off the table. "Sorry, but what is a knot?"

"Oh. A knot is one nautical mile per hour. A nautical mile is 6,076 feet."

"Fifteen percent longer than a mile," Isaac says.

I nod to him. "Correct."

"How far away is our destination?" Rose asks.

"That's one of the things I want to talk about. Seaports in West Africa, as you might imagine, are significantly less safe than those in the US and Europe. Larger ports—in general—are safer."

"But they're also more closely monitored," Isaac says.

"Right. And that's a problem. Well, one of them."

"What're the other problems?" June asks.

"Even at seven knots, which will conserve fuel, and even with the extra diesel in the bladders, we don't have enough to reach our destination."

"What is our destination?" Isaac asks.

"We'll go ashore in Douala, Cameroon. It's a smaller port, and it's the closest reasonable point of disembarkation to the center of the Labyrinth."

"How far away is it?" Isaac asks.

"About fifty-five hundred nautical miles."

"We'll need to refuel," Isaac says quietly. I can almost see his brain starting to work on the problem.

"We do. And we'll do that in Cape Verde, which is roughly thirty-five hundred nautical miles away."

"How long to get there?" Isaac asks.

"I figure about twenty days at sea to Cape Verde, some time to refuel, and then another thirteen days to Douala. Altogether, depending on refueling time and the weather, we're at least thirty-three days from port. I figure forty at the most."

For a long moment, no one says anything. June and Rose squint at the rising sun.

"And," I add, "we've got some work to do on the way. We need to make arrangements for a discreet refueling in Cape Verde and for docking in Douala. We need private security to watch the boat while we go ashore. From there, we need to acquire a transport in port and plan our drive to the Labyrinth GPS coordinates."

Isaac sets his laptop on the table and opens it. "I'll start working on it. But first, we should talk about sleeping arrangements." Before anyone can say anything, he adds, "I want the room with the desk."

"That desk folds out into a bed. It can be one or the other, not both."

"I'll sleep on the floor." He points to the laptop. "This stuff is time-sensitive."

I know there's no point in arguing, so I tell the group that the remaining accommodations are the master stateroom and VIP guest stateroom.

Rose squints at me. "And three of us."

I motion to the doorway behind the banquette. "There's a berth back there. And a desk where I can work. Assuming I can get internet access."

"I can hook you up," Isaac says.

June and Rose decide to draw straws for the bedrooms, and I turn my attention to the watch schedule.

"I'll take nights. The rest of you will split the day watch."

"By definition," Isaac says, "a full night watch is half of a day. Twelve hours. That's not fair to you time-wise."

"That may be, but it's logical. Nights at sea are more dangerous. I'll do it. And I'll train the rest of you on piloting. At least, enough to get by." I shrug. "Unless you want me to cook again. Like I did at the RV."

Rose grins. "It wasn't *that* bad."

"Yeah, compared to the MREs," Isaac mumbles as he types on the laptop.

Faintly, I hear someone (either Rose or June) kick him under the table.

With the route and schedule out of the way, I go over some nautical terminology (because being a yacht crew does entail a different vocabulary).

First, we cover directions.

Port is the left side of the boat when facing forward.

Starboard is the right side when facing forward.

Isaac exhales. "Can't we just say left and right?"

"We cannot. The reason is—"

Realization dawns on Isaac. "You don't know which way the person is facing if you can't see them. Like if they're on the radio or ship's intercom."

"Correct."

With that, I continue my vocabulary lesson.

Bow: the front of the boat.

Stern: rear of the boat.

Aft: a direction that denotes toward the stern or rear of the boat.

Forward: toward the bow.

Beam: the widest part of the boat; also refers to the width of the boat.

Amidships: the middle section of the boat.

Next, I move on to the areas of the boat.

Bridge or pilothouse: where the boat is controlled.

Keel: the structural backbone of the boat running along the bottom.

Galley: the kitchen.

Isaac holds his hands up. "Can't we just say kitchen?"

Reading the room (pilothouse, technically), I sense both Rose and June agree with Isaac on this (though both refrain from verbally doing so).

"Okay, we can say kitchen."

Next, I was going to tell them that the term for bathroom is head, but I skip that, reasoning that bathroom will suffice (and so will bedroom instead of stateroom and living room in place of salon).

Next, I give them a crash course in piloting the boat, though I urge them to wake me if anything comes up.

The autopilot will be engaged when I'm asleep (and when I'm on duty), but I want them to have some working knowledge of the controls.

When we're done, the sun is climbing, the boat is crashing across the waves, and my fellow travelers look as tired as I feel.

75

We sail eastward toward the rising sun, and soon, the days begin to blur together.

During the night shift, I sit on the fly bridge and read paperbacks, feeling the wind on my face. This far from the light pollution of civilization, the night sky shines bright with glittering stars. Ahead, on the glassy sea, the moon casts a silver streak, like a road painted across the ocean.

Occasionally, in the distance, I spot the lights of a cargo ship crossing our path. Still, on the whole, our life is pretty uneventful, especially compared to the white-knuckle stress of the days before our departure.

June is usually first up, arriving in the pilothouse with coffee and a paperback of her own, both of which she consumes at the banquette before she takes the helm.

The four of us typically share breakfast (which is technically dinner for me). Most mornings we eat up in the pilothouse, either out on the open back deck or inside at the U-shaped dinette.

After, I retreat to my berth, read a bit more, and let the boat's gentle vibration carry me off to sleep.

Some days I'm awake to hear the hand-off to Rose mid-morning or the transfer to Isaac in the afternoon, though his schedule is more fluid (if he's in the middle of something—and he often is—he'll trade shifts and hours with the others).

We've developed unofficial territories. June stays on the fly bridge during good weather. Rose prefers the salon's comfortable seating, where she reads or writes in a journal. Isaac, when not on duty, is locked in his stateroom, either sleeping or glued to his laptop.

In a way, the meals anchor our days.

At sunset, when my shift is starting, we gather in the galley, where the others have dinner and I snack, preferring to avoid a heavy meal. The conversation usually drifts between mission planning and chatting about books we've read, stories from our past, and speculation about what our families are doing back home. These moments feel almost normal until someone mentions Amersa or the numbers, and reality comes crashing back into us like a rogue wave.

Some days the Atlantic is glass-smooth, others it tosses us about like it's annoyed that we're here. We've all developed sea legs, learned to brace ourselves in doorways, and to instinctively secure anything dangerous that might slide off a counter or fall over. Isaac has gotten better at typing while the boat rocks beneath him.

The isolation, though, is profound. Here on the boat, we're not constantly checking our smartphones. There's no family in the next room, no contact with the world beyond. In a way, we're in a wilderness between continents, between our old lives and whatever is waiting for us at the coordinates.

There's also peace out here in this floating limbo. There's a sense that, for now at least, we're beyond the reach of Amersa, beyond the ringing that brought us together. Out here, the numbers that matter are the latitude and longitude slowly morphing on the navigation screens.

For the first time in a while, I feel like I can finally take a deep breath. I think the others do too.

Some nights, after dinner, we play a board game or watch a movie on the salon's TV. Sometimes we just sit on deck, watching the sun sink into the sea in a blaze of orange and pink.

When night falls, and the others turn in, I return to my post in the pilothouse or the fly bridge, watching over their sleep as we sail toward whatever waits at the center of the Labyrinth.

76

Seventeen days into our voyage, at the end of my shift, when the sun is rising over the Atlantic and the boat is cruising at a little over seven knots, June arrives for her shift.

She settles into the swiveling chair beside me, and I close the paperback I've been reading, and we stare out the windows at the open sea.

In between sips of coffee, she says, "I've been meaning to tell you: your friend, Warren, he's a really nice guy."

"He is. Once you get to know him."

"He cares about you, Alan. A lot."

I swivel my chair to her. "What makes you say that?"

"He's a man of few words."

"That he is."

"But practically every word he said was about you. And, based on some of his questions, I can tell he's worried about you."

When I don't say anything, she asks, "How do you know him? From the Marines?"

"No. Different branches. And eras."

"How then?"

"Same way I met you, June."

"Which is?"

"Circumstances."

"Well, I'm thankful for that, because based on what Amersa did to Lucas... I think you and Warren might have saved my life."

"Eh, just part of the training, ma'am."

Her smile is sympathetic and motherly. "I don't think any of us were trained for any of this."

Another stretch of ocean passes in silence, and when her coffee cup is half empty, June says quietly. "Alan, your shift is three times longer than any of ours."

"It is."

"It has to be lonely."

"I have breakfast and dinner with everyone."

"Yes, but that's about it."

"I'm okay, June. Really."

"I say we do something."

"Like what?"

"You brought fishing gear."

"I did."

"Well, I feel like *circumstances* dictate that we use it."

Seven hours later, the late afternoon sun beats down as June and I set up the fishing gear on the aft deck. The boat maintains a steady seven knots, the wake creating the perfect conditions for trolling.

"So what exactly are we trying to catch?" June asks, watching me thread line through the rod guides.

"Mahi-mahi if we're lucky. They're beautiful—electric blue and green. But we're just as likely to get tuna, marlin, or mackerel."

Rose emerges from below with bottles of water, and even Isaac soon shuffles onto the deck from his digital cave, laptop tucked under his arm like always, squinting at the sun behind the boat.

We set two lines with artificial lures, letting them skip across the surface about a hundred feet behind the boat. June and Rose take the first watch, settling into deck chairs while Isaac types away.

An hour passes. Then two. We're about to call it when one of the reels screams to life, line rolling off at an alarming rate.

"Fish on!" I shout, grabbing the rod from the holder. I fight it for a while, then hold the rod out to June.

Her eyes go wide as she grips it, feeling the raw power on the other end. "What do I do?"

"Just keep the rod tip up and reel when you can."

Feeling the sun on my face and the wind at my back, I stare at the boat's wake and the open sea, the line pulled tight. "We'll take turns," I tell her. "It's going to be a fight."

The fish makes several blistering runs, but June, Rose, and I hold our own, gaining line inch by inch. Twenty minutes later, we get our first glimpse of the creature, which is golden except its blue and green back.

"She's a beauty!" I call over the boat's engines as I reach for the gaff hook.

When we finally get it aboard, we're all grinning like kids. The mahi-mahi easily weighs fifteen pounds.

That evening, we grill fish steaks on the boat's small BBQ. Even Isaac sets his laptop aside for the event. Rose opens a bottle of wine—a gift from the seller, apparently (and the only alcohol on board)—and soon we're gathered around the salon table with full plates and the board game Monopoly laid out.

"I haven't played this since I was a kid," Rose says, moving her piece to Boardwalk.

I'm worried we'll hit a patch of rough seas and the plastic houses and hotels and deeds and player pieces will go flying onto the floor, but the Atlantic grants us a peaceful evening, at least, long enough for June and Rose to split the bottle of wine and for Isaac to amass a make-believe real estate empire (anchored early on by orange and red properties).

The top hat, battleship, thimble, and boot make their way around the board, passing Go, collecting two hundred dollars along the way, and occasionally catching a bank error in their favor. And for a short while, I forget about everything except some fake money and paying rent and the need to go around in circles until it all ends.

A few nights later, I'm once again sitting in a helm chair in the pilothouse when I hear footsteps on the wooden staircase behind me, lumbering and slow. That's sort of how we move on this voyage—taking our time, planting each foot firmly in case the boat rocks.

I turn and see Isaac's head rising above the lacquered wooden half-wall that encloses the banquette.

He trudges forward and takes the chair beside me, gazing out at the moonlit sea through the bank of windows.

"I have an idea," he says.

"About?"

"Refueling."

"What about it?"

"If we refuel in port, there's a chance we'll be seen."

"True."

"Do you know what an STS fuel transfer is?"

I turn my chair and smile at him. "Yeah, man. I know what a ship-to-ship fuel transfer is. I was in the Marines. But for a private yacht, it would be crazy expensive. You'd pretty much only do it if you ran out of fuel at sea and were stranded."

"Well, we have problems, Alan, but money isn't one of them."

"Oh. Right. That's uh… sort of a mental adjustment for me."

"Me too."

"I take it you've found an outfit willing to refuel us at sea—no questions asked?"

"I have."

"It'll be tough. For a boat our size, we need calm seas and a good crew. We are not a good crew. Well, we are, but we are not an *experienced* crew. Especially not with STS refueling."

"You think it's too risky?"

"I think it's risky. But that's only the half. I bet they figure we're smugglers if we don't want to come into port. Or wanted. Maybe both."

"What do you want to do? Should I cancel it?"

"Where would they do it?"

"It'd be off the coast of Cape Verde—that's where they bunker their fuel. Roughly a hundred nautical miles south. Do you think it's worth it?"

"I do. The risks are manageable if I do some training with you all beforehand—fender deployment and line handling."

Isaac slides off the chair. "I'll set it up."

"See if they'll do it at night."

He nods slowly. "They probably won't like that."

"They'll probably still do it. For a price."

"True."

When he's walking past the helm chairs, I call to him: "Ask them to throw in a turkey."

"Throw in a turkey?"

"An uncooked one."

"Is that, like, a Marine code for something?"

"No, I'm saying an *actual* turkey. For us to cook. For Thanksgiving."

Isaac squints. "Do they even have turkeys on Cape Verde?"

"They have airports. And I've recently been informed that money isn't one of the problems we have."

77

Just south of Santiago Island in the Cape Verde archipelago, on a moonless night, I stare at the radar screen, watching a vessel approach our position. The sea is mercifully calm tonight, with only a gentle two-foot swell rolling beneath us. Perfect conditions for what we're about to attempt.

"I think this is them," I say over the boat's intercom.

The first sighting of the ship is of its infrared lights, blinking our agreed-upon sequence. I respond with our own signal, confirming our identity. Soon, the vessel emerges from the darkness.

A voice with a heavy Portuguese accent crackles over the VHF radio: "Event Horizon, this is Trawler Seven-Three on channel one-six. We have visual, over."

The use of each vessel's code name is the agreed-upon voice signal for the all clear.

I key the microphone. "Trawler Seven-Three, Event Horizon. Confirming visual, over."

Channel 16 is the international hailing and distress frequency. All vessels monitor it. We'll use a less crowded frequency from here out to coordinate positioning and then hand signals once we're alongside (in case the deck crew doesn't speak English).

On a slip of paper, Isaac has written out the channels we've agreed to try after initial contact. I tune the radio to the first one and listen to see if any other ships are using it as a working channel.

After a full thirty seconds, I activate the radio again. "Trawler Seven-Three, Event Horizon. Ready to proceed, over."

After all our preparation, the ship-to-ship fuel transfer is almost anticlimactic.

When our tanks and bladders are full, the sailors who came over disconnect the lines, and another crewman passes over a large cooler. Inside is our Thanksgiving turkey, wrapped in plastic and as pristine as one you might buy at a Harris Teeter back home.

On Thanksgiving night, I wake from my berth in the pilothouse to find Isaac sitting at the helm, watching the bank of screens. The smell of turkey cooking in the galley below wafts up through the stairwell.

Ahead, through the glass, is nothing but open sea and the glow of the setting sun behind us.

"Happy Thanksgiving," Isaac says.

"You too."

And it is a happy Thanksgiving. We've been through a lot, but we're still here. And things could be a lot worse.

At the dining table, eating turkey and green beans and mashed potatoes and mac and cheese (all of which came out of a box or can—except the bird), we listen to music and the waves and talk but I don't think any of us are saying what's really on our minds: our families and what they're doing right now.

My best guess is that Riley is sitting beside Meredith at the dining table in her parents' house, the same home they owned twenty years ago when I was dating Meredith, the home we visited before I left, where my daughter went on a scavenger hunt when the numbers were a mystery and what happened downtown was a troubling concern but there was no warrant for my arrest.

The same home I went to for Thanksgiving when Meredith and I were young and the future was an exciting thing—not a labyrinth of anxiety.

I imagine they're eating prime rib instead of turkey, because Meredith's dad always preferred it. Maybe time, a few bad cholesterol readings, the addition of a statin, and the insistence of Meredith's mom (a monumental force) have overridden his mandate for red meat at Thanksgiving. Maybe it's turkey this year, or chicken as a compromise, and he's chewing it dutifully.

Regardless of the protein source on the table, I suspect Meredith's brother, Ryan, is sitting across from her, looking sullen, silently saying—with his eyes—exactly what he's thinking: *how could you get mixed up with a guy wanted for murder?*

He bailed on you once.

Now he's done it again.

And he left his kid this time.

It's also entirely possible that Ryan is saying this to her out loud (not just thinking it)—or has said as much in the recent past.

No matter what's being said or left unsaid, I bet my fugitive status and nearly four-week absence has created a deep rift between Meredith and her only sibling. I imagine that across that dining table in North Hills, it's like a game of visual laser tag: Ryan to Meredith, her back to him, her mom curiously observing both of them, Mr. Davis raking his eyes across the entire table as Riley digs into her food (hopefully oblivious to it all).

Everyone at that table deserves some answers.

As do the four of us.

I hope we find them at the coordinates.

78

A week before we reach Douala, at breakfast one morning in the U-shaped banquette, I make a suggestion I've been mildly dreading.

"Before we go ashore, I think we should record videos to our loved ones."

Isaac looks up from his laptop. June and Rose stop eating, but neither makes eye contact. I figure they're all thinking what I've left unsaid: that we'll be making goodbye messages that will be relayed in case we don't come back.

When no one says anything, I add, "Or at least, I'm going to. I figure I can send it to Harold to email—"

"Bad idea," Isaac says quietly.

"Why?" I snap at him. It's the end of my shift, but that's only half of my irritation. The time on the ship and the stress of our looming arrival in Douala are starting to weigh on me. So is the prolonged separation from my daughter.

"It could expose him," Isaac says flatly.

"Expose him *for what*? He hasn't done anything wrong."

"He helped us buy the RV. And yacht. And supplies—"

"Right. He funded our shopping spree. Remind me who the victim is?"

Isaac slams his laptop shut. "He's been aiding and abetting a known fugitive." He points at me. "You."

"Who cares? He can simply say my *fugitive status* wasn't known to him. Besides, I thought you were super covert with your online operations."

"I *was*. But frankly, the authorities are the least of our worries.

The problem is if Amersa finds him. Based on them killing one of my friends—and a former member of this group—I think they're a lot more dangerous than the FBI or Interpol."

"Man, do you even realize what I'm suggesting here? If he's sending these videos out, we're already dead. Probably because *Amersa killed us*, which, I feel, would *greatly* diminish their interest in us."

Isaac opens his mouth to respond, but I keep hammering him. "Look, I just want to say goodbye to my daughter, okay? I mean, assuming that's okay with you?"

"Alan," Isaac says, more softly now, but I cut him off again. "You know what my last words to her were? 'I'll be back as soon as I can, sweetie.'"

I hold my hands up. "And then I never, *ever* come back. Oh, and P.S., I was wanted for murder and never cleared up that tiny little detail, never mind a half dozen other things."

I cut my eyes to June. "I'm no neuroscientist, but I kind of feel like the lack of closure there might have some lasting effects. Maybe some trust issues. Self-confidence problems. Who knows what else? But who cares, right?"

"Dude," Isaac yells, "for the record—"

"Stop," June shouts.

Her voice is like a gun going off in the pilothouse. For a while, the only sounds are the wind and the waves crashing on the bow.

It's the first time I've ever heard June raise her voice. And when she speaks again, it's her normal tone, with a little added strain.

"This is important. And it's important that we discuss it. But we're not in a position where we can do that right now."

More waves crash into the hull.

A white tendril of steam rises from Rose's coffee mug on the table, like a ghost raising a finger to emphasize June's point.

"What I suggest," June says, placing her palms flat on the table, is that we regroup tonight, at the start of Alan's shift. And we do so somewhere other than here, for a change of scenery."

When no one says anything, June continues.

"Beforehand, we will all write out our thoughts on the matter. I will read them out loud, and when I've finished, we'll choose to either discuss it or to take another break."

There's an old saying: never go to bed angry.

I can't remember where I first heard it, but I recall hearing it a lot after getting married.

It's good advice.

I know because in the time before I got married, after I got injured, I spent a lot of nights being angry. Back then, I was angry at the world. And its unfairness.

For a while after my wife passed, I felt the same way. I was just as angry every night.

I think the point of the adage is that you have to confront the issues you're angry about. If not, the anger only grows and things get worse.

It's also practical advice. Because it's tough to sleep when you're angry.

And that's exactly what happens to me in the narrow bunk in the pilothouse that day. I toss and turn and try to quiet my mind. Finally, I give up and roll out of bed and sit at the corner desk, a blank page in front of me, thinking about what I want to say.

In fairness to June, she was right to end the debate, which had certainly turned unproductive. And I needed some sleep (not that I got any).

It turns out, I don't have much more to say on the matter; just a single line.

When I exit my stateroom, Rose closes her paperback and swivels her helm chair toward me.

She asks if I'm hungry, and I shake my head as footsteps echo on the spiral staircase. June peers up at me, a sympathetic smile on her lips. "Hi."

"Hi."

Below her, at the bottom of the stairs, I hear another set of feet climbing. They stop, and June looks down and says something I can't hear.

Turning back to me, she says gently, as if testing the next step to see if it will hold her weight, "It's still a while before your shift, but would you want to go ahead and—"

"Talk?"

"Yes."

"I would."

We gather in the salon, Rose and June on the couch, Isaac in the club chair. The wide door to the aft deck stands open, letting in the warm afternoon air. The engines rumble, carving a wide wake in the Atlantic.

The white noise is nice because otherwise, there's an awkward silence in the room. I stand, waiting for June to start. Overall, the vibe is like the waiting area of a principal's office (something I have some experience with).

June's gaze moves from my feet up to meet my eyes. "Alan," she says slowly, "would you like to sit down?"

"Not really."

She exhales and stares at the three pages on the coffee table—our homework, such as it is. Well, except for mine.

"The thing is," June says slowly, "standing when others are seated can be interpreted as aggressive."

"Okay. Well, in the interest of full honesty, I do, actually, feel a boatload of aggression on this issue."

Rose places a hand on June's forearm. The older woman exhales and nods to the pages. "Fine. Did you have a chance to write out your thoughts?"

"I did."

I slip the scrap of paper from my pocket, take two steps to the coffee table and drop it on top of a page of neat handwriting (which has four paragraphs in contrast to my single sentence). June picks up the note, reads it, and cuts her eyes to me.

"I'm happy to read it myself if you prefer," I tell her.

"No," she says quietly, slipping it under the pile. "I'll do it."

"I'd like my letter read last," Isaac says, eyes fixed on the floor. For the first time since I can remember, he's not clutching the laptop in front of him.

June lifts the top page. "Okay. I'll start with my thoughts.

"First, I'd like to provide a little context, from a professional standpoint."

She scans the room, maybe expecting an objection, but no one says a word.

"We're all stressed. We're missing our loved ones." June glances at me. "And we're dealing with other situations—*problems*—we can't solve here on the boat. All we can do is wait. That amplifies the stress: having a problem you can't do anything about. That's where we are. We're cooped up on this ship, basically doing the same thing day after day, like that movie *Groundhog Day*, and we're waiting and hoping, instead of taking direct action on our problems. That's frustrating."

She glances at the three of us. "And I know I'm not sleeping well. I'm not used to sleeping on a boat, and I'm missing my family, and I'm constantly thinking about them and what we're going to find in Africa. I don't think I'm the only one. Alan, you're working nights now. Isaac, that computer screen is practically glued to your face—and I haven't seen you sleep more than three hours at a time since we left Wilmington."

In the club chair, he shrugs and looks away, but doesn't disagree.

June glances at Rose. "And I think you're sleeping about as well as I am."

"True," Rose says quietly.

June turns the page. "Stress and poor sleep: those are two of our problems. They're problems created by our root issues. And they are force magnifiers: stress and sleep deprivation have a way of making any problem worse. Imagine you're dealing with an issue that's a two out of ten. Normally, you'd handle it with ease. But if you're stressed and tired, maybe that two is raised to the power of three—it's an eight. Because of the condition you're in, that problem you could normally handle becomes overwhelming."

June sets the page down. "*That* is what I think is happening to us. We're stressed. We're sleep-deprived. And we're at each other because *we*," she spreads her hands out to the group, "*we* are here, within reach of each other, a target for that breakthrough stress. To our stressed-out, sleep-deprived minds, verbally slugging it out actually feels like we're doing something about our problems. But it's an illusion, and it's counterproductive."

She waits, but none of us say a word. I don't know what Rose and Isaac are thinking, but I'm thinking June is making a lot of sense right now.

"What we have to do, simply put, is adjust our thinking. We're used to dealing with our problems in the life we used to have—in the real world, when we had jobs and families and rent and normal things. What we're going through, here and now, is not normal. We need new tactics. A new way of thinking. We have to learn to recognize when our minds are overwhelmed. When to zoom out. When to take a breath and reassess. *Reflection* is our greatest tool here. Taking a step back allows our emotions to wash over us and for us to see things more clearly."

I raise my hand, feeling like a kid in a classroom.

"Yes, Alan?"

"Can I say something here?"

"Of course."

"Look, I take your point. I think it's a good one. And it needed to be said. But the thing is, we're under real-time pressure here. We can't sit around and wait until we feel better about it. We need to make plans now so we're prepared when we step off this boat. And we only have so much time."

"I agree," Isaac mumbles, eyes still fixed on the floor.

"So do I," June says. "In fact, my next paragraph says, using more words, that I, too, want to send a message to my family. And I know we need to record it now and have a plan to send it... if we don't come back.

"This meeting, in my mind, is about two things: how to do that. And just as importantly, how we can work together better going forward. Because the stress and the sleep deprivation are only going to get worse. We need to adapt now."

June seems to take our silence as agreement. Shuffling her own note to the back, she picks up the next one, which is in Rose's handwriting, and June confirms that before reading it.

"I also want to send a message. But I agree that we shouldn't put Harold in danger. The only two things I can think of are saving the videos on a USB drive and sending it with FedEx using a deliver-on date. But that's a problem because it will get delivered on the day we choose no matter what. We can't cancel it after we send it (as far as I know).

"The other idea I have is to send it to a lawyer in America and have them hold it. If they don't hear from us, they would mail the drives to our family members. A lawyer would keep it a secret, I think. And with attorney-client privilege, they couldn't testify about it if it comes up with Alan's legal issues."

I hadn't considered that: using an attorney to deliver the messages.

In fact, after hearing from Rose and June—and knowing Isaac's position—it's obvious that all four of us see this problem in a different way, perhaps because we are so different from each other. I think that's one of our strengths.

As June sets Rose's page aside, I'm suddenly feeling a little sheepish about my own note, which June now holds up between thumb and index finger, like a dead bug she just found on the coffee table.

"Alan's thoughts are as follows: 'I will be sending a message to my daughter, hell or high water.'"

A smile flashes across Isaac's face, an amused, not unkind expression that is gone the next second, his mask returned.

When I wrote the note, I was still seething in my berth, sitting at that corner desk, mad and frustrated as I scrawled the words. Given the effort the others have put in, I'm inclined to apologize, but June has already moved on to Isaac's note, which is typed out (I didn't even realize he had a printer on board).

"First, I want to say that I am not—and never was—opposed to sending messages to family. Only to sending them through Harold. That got lost in the discussion, which, by the way, I know I was being a—"

The next word has been crossed out, and above it, in pen, Isaac has written *jerk*.

June continues reading his note:

"I'm not used to being around people this much. Because of the tinnitus, I didn't really have a regular childhood. Or adulthood for that matter. So I'm not good at this.

"I am good at computers. And that's what I would use to send the messages. Specifically, I would set up a VPS—a virtual private server—at one of the major hosts. We can do it pretty much anonymously. I'll write a program that waits until a certain day and time. When that comes, it will send the messages and then wipe the machine down to bare metal. And if we turn the VPS off before then, no one will ever know.

"I've already set up a recording studio in my bedroom with a blank background and a tablet ready to capture your videos. When you're done, I'll upload them. Sorry, this went sideways."

79

After dinner, we sit around the table and discuss the specifics of how to record the videos. Isaac has some basic security precautions, which he goes over more carefully than our discussion this morning (we're learning).

As mentioned in his letter, we'll do the recordings in his office (or, technically, stateroom) with a sheet hanging in the background so it's not obvious that we're on a yacht.

We'll also turn the engines off while we record.

For each video, Isaac's going to digitally replace the sheet with a different background, making the videos look like they were shot in three different locations (he's not making one himself).

He rattles off a laundry list of things we can't say during the recordings (his concern is that we may be delayed more than we anticipate, and the program might release the videos even though we're still alive—and on the run). His reasoning is that it's better to be cautious. I agree with him on that.

An hour later, I'm sitting in the chair with the sheet hanging behind me, staring at the tablet. I know what I want to say, but I can't quite figure out how to start.

I'm too in my head about it. I keep thinking about what this video will mean to Riley if it's the last time she sees me and the last words I ever say to her. If so, I bet she'll play it a hundred times. Or more. And come back to it when life gets tough. And at Christmas and maybe Thanksgiving. I suspect—and fear—no matter what I say, she'll read too much into it. And look for answers to questions big and small in my face and words.

I know I'm overthinking it. I need to just get started. I can always redo it if I mess up.

With a deep breath, I try to clear my head and imagine Riley is sitting in front of me.

"Hi, kiddo. Listen, I know you have a lot of questions. That's understandable. I would too.

"Some of those questions, you're not going to get answers to. I'm sorry about that. I wish I could explain, but I can't, not like this. But here's what I can tell you.

"First, I love you very much. I have since the day you were born. Well, before, really.

"Second, your mother would be very proud of you. You're kind to your friends and even the kids you don't get along with. You're hardworking. And smart. And so fun-loving and full of life. Don't ever let this world change that about you. And let me tell you, it will try.

"Third, I want you to always keep in mind that every person goes through tough times. I mean it. Everyone you see on the street, every person you ever encounter, no matter how good it seems like they have it or how easy you think their life has been, I guarantee you they've seen their share of challenges too. They could even be going through it that very moment, and you might have no idea. It's really hard to know what life is like for someone else or what kind of problems they're dealing with. Try to remember that.

"And I've recently been reminded that when you're going through a rough patch of your own, one of the best things you can do is simply take a deep breath and step back and reassess. It's amazing what a little time and perspective can do.

"And after you take that deep breath, you have to keep going. Right through the rough patch. Because things will get better, no matter how bad they are. All it takes is the courage to keep going so that you can let time do its work. Time is the master healer in this life. So when things are tough, you just take life one day at a time, and you keep going. The saying is you put one foot in front of the other, but I've woken up with only one foot, and I learned that you still have to keep going. You keep going even if it feels like there's no solution to what's happening to you. Because if you do the right thing every day, time will see you through. It's all a matter of time.

"I also want you to know that no matter how alone you feel in the world, you never truly are. And if you come to a crossroads in your life and you need help, go out and find it. It takes some courage, but I guarantee you it will make your life easier. Most of the time, what you need in life—and the people you need to support you—those things won't come and find you. You have to go make it happen. And when you find people who are there for you, I want you to hang on to them and make sure you're there for them when they need someone. It's human nature to struggle, but so is helping others. At least for some, and that's your nature.

"I've lost track of what number I'm on in this list of important things I want to say to you, but I know this: figuring out what you're good at is a mystery worth solving. Trust me, it will make your life so much easier. Your job. Your hobbies. *Everything*. So many people go through life never really knowing what they're good at. They don't try enough things. And the things they do try, they don't give enough time and effort to truly figure out if they're good at it. To be fair, some folks never have the opportunity. They don't have access to try different things, and for some, by the time they do, they're too busy surviving. But you're young now, and you should take the time to dabble in things. Say yes a lot, but don't be afraid to walk away if something isn't your cup of tea. Knowing when to say no—and having the courage to say no—is important as well. Remember, time is the most important thing you'll ever spend in life. Be judicious about it, and when you find what you like, invest time in it. It'll pay dividends. Like I said, it's all a matter of time.

"In addition to finding what you're good at in life, I also hope you discover what you love to do. What you're good at—and what you enjoy—aren't always the same things. That can be a little confusing, but you'll figure it out. You'll stumble across something you can do for hours and days, and it never feels like work. Again, you might not be that good at it, but you'll know you love it because it's the thing you look forward to. It's what you think about when your mind is wandering.

"If you get lucky, those two things—what you're good at and what you love—are the same thing. Or pretty close. Or maybe there's an activity that blends the two. If you find a career like that, you've hit the jackpot in life. I got lucky like that. So did your mom.

"But the thing is to be committed to solving the mystery of you. You have to figure out your strengths and limitations, as well as what you love. And then you surround yourself with people who make you the best version of yourself. And you do the same for them. You do those things, and life gets so much easier. You'll have the wind at your back when you face those challenges, and they will come, at some point, they do for all of us."

I glance at the list of words Isaac has on the screen beside the video recording app, confirming I haven't used any banned phrases.

The next part is the hardest, and I feel myself losing my grip on my emotions, so I try to hurry so I can get through it.

"I know you're going to have an amazing life, Riley. It might not be the life you expected. It rarely is. But I know you'll face it with courage and passion and with a kind heart and a level head. Don't ever forget how lucky you are. Just like I'll never forget how lucky I was to be your dad. It was the best part of my life. And there have been some really good parts. I know because I lived through a few pretty bad stretches too. Those make you appreciate the good times even more.

"You may read some things about me. A news article. Maybe a documentary, a video online, or a rumor you hear in passing. I want you to know—and I promise you—I never intentionally committed a crime. Sometimes in life, you find yourself caught up in things outside of your control. The situation I've had to handle wasn't my fault. It wasn't my choice, but it also wasn't something I could walk away from. I did the best I could, and most of all, I did it to try to protect you. The thing I wanted most was for you to have a better life than the one I had. And I tried really hard to do that.

"I love you so much, kiddo. Always remember that."

80

It's night when the sixty-eight-foot motor yacht reaches the shores of Douala.

The four of us stand on the fly bridge watching the city lights glittering on the Gulf of Guinea like a thousand diamonds floating on the sea.

At the helm, I pull both throttles back and turn the wheel slightly. We're on time. I just hope our contact is waiting for us (and that no one from Amersa is).

The next hour is crucial.

After transferring the helm back to the pilothouse, we go below to the salon. Isaac sends a message to our contact, and he and I wait for a response. Rose and June sit on the aft deck in the warm, humid air. Even in December, just after sunset, it's eighty-one degrees Fahrenheit here.

When the contact confirms the meeting, we drop anchor outside the compulsory pilotage zone, in a secluded cove out of sight of the maritime traffic.

For the next thirty minutes, we wipe down the entire boat with Clorox, erasing any fingerprints and DNA.

Next, we drop the rigid inflatable dinghy in the water and begin methodically loading it with supplies: camping gear, duffel bags filled with weapons, MREs, handheld radios, med kits, extra clothes, hiking boots, and everything else we'll need.

I throw my body armor on last, hoping I won't need it, watching as the dinghy bobs hard in the water from the weight of it.

*

We avoid the main port. Instead, we make for a small private marina. I approach slowly, scanning it for any sign of trouble. As our contact promised, it's nearly empty at this hour. The few boat slips that are occupied hold fishing vessels. There are no crews in sight.

With one hand on the tiller and the other gripping my pistol, I steer the boat toward the closest dock.

The air is humid and smells of saltwater, woodsmoke, and diesel exhaust. My heart is pounding in my chest, and I expect the ringing in my ears to start, but all I hear is the buzzing boat motor behind me and the busy port in the distance.

On the dock, a figure slowly steps out of the shadows. He's tall and slender and wears a white tank top that's soaked with sweat. I'd love to see his eyes, but despite the darkness, they're covered with large, gold-rimmed sunglasses.

His hands are empty and hang at his sides. He calls into the night in a thick, West African accent, "We don't do fishing tours."

Isaac, sitting at the front of the boat, replies with the agreed-upon code phrase. "We're here for a land tour."

The contact gives the reply that signifies the all-clear: "You'll have to drive yourself."

And Isaac responds with the confirmation that things are a go on our end: "Good. We prefer to drive."

I pull the dinghy alongside the dock, and the contact, who is named Emile, helps tie us off. He eyes the duffel bags and bundles on the floor of the boat.

"Das it? Or you gonna be makin' another trip?"

"This is it," Isaac says.

Emile reaches into his pocket. "I call mi' men and they come an' carry et to da trucks."

"No," Isaac says quickly. "We deal only with you."

Emile's lips part, revealing long, pearly white teeth. "Aye. You is a careful man. Das good. Makes it easia ta keep you alive."

A warm wind blows through the marina, bringing with it a wave that rocks the old fishing boats.

I wonder if Emile believes our cover story: that we're a film crew making a documentary—a privately funded documentary—which we don't want anyone to know about until it's ready to be announced. And of course, we don't want to be tracked while we're gathering this important footage.

He probably doesn't, but the bundles on the dinghy below are the right size for camera equipment.

He nods to them. "I help you. Trucks are not far."

With that, we unload the small boat and follow Emile to a warehouse where two Toyota Land Cruiser 79 Series double-cab pickups are waiting.

At the closest one, Emile gently sets down the duffel bags he's carrying, climbs onto the truck bed, and pulls back a white tarp, revealing a rugged black case that's a little larger than a travel suitcase. On top is a logo for Autel Robotics.

"Here be da drone you was a wantin'."

Isaac reaches into the bed and opens the case. The gray and black drone is folded up and wedged in foam. Carefully, Isaac lifts it out and studies it, smiling slightly, the way a child might with a new toy. The device is about the size of a hardcover book—roughly nine inches long and six inches wide—though it's a little over four inches tall.

The drone—and backup drones and batteries—were one thing we couldn't source in America before we left.

"You wanna test it?" Emile asks.

"No," Isaac replies, placing the drone back in the case.

Emile pulls the tarp back more, uncovering the other supplies we requested: Jerry cans of extra fuel and spare parts for the trucks, including tires, belts, and filters (we can't exactly call triple-A where we're going).

We'll obviously have to stop for fuel along the way, but the cans will help if we find ourselves on a long stretch of road in a region where we'd rather not stop.

In the bed of the other truck are three full water containers. When we've finished inspecting the provisions—and loading what we brought—Emile hands us our fake identification papers.

This is the part of the plan I have been most apprehensive

about. The issue is that Isaac refused to send Emile pictures of us, for obvious reasons. Emile could have done a picture search and found out who we really are—and that I'm wanted for murder (if that information has in fact gone public).

Even now, our local contact could have someone with a long-range photo lens taking pictures of us for that very purpose. He could use that information to blackmail us later or sell us out to Amersa.

But so far, Emile appears to be going along with the compromise he and Isaac arrived at. On the way here, Isaac sent descriptions of the four of us, and Emile promised to source genuine passports and visas from people who looked like us.

I was sitting beside Isaac at the U-shaped banquette in the pilothouse when he messaged Emile and said, *But they won't be us. The police and port authorities will be able to tell.*

Emile promptly sent back: *Bribes determine how they see things, my friend.*

Looking down at my new passport—and the picture of the guy thirty pounds heavier than me—I'm thinking it's going to have to be a sizable bribe to distort someone's vision this much. But, money is something we have.

Isaac seems happy with his own ID because he taps his sat phone and tells Emile he's sent the next payment.

Emile flashes those pearly whites again. "Ay, tanks."

"Remember, next payment is when we're safely out of town, then another when we come back, and the final—big one—when we're sailing away."

Emile nods slowly, still smiling.

From his right pocket, Isaac produces a small scrap of paper.

"Coordinates of the boat."

Emile glances at it before tucking it away. "It be here when you get back."

81

The beams of the two Toyota trucks slice through the night haze of Douala, a mix of diesel fumes and smoke drape the city like a ghostly blanket.

I drive the Land Cruiser in the lead, June at my side, Rose behind the wheel of the second vehicle, Isaac in the passenger seat.

It's just past ten, local time, but the city is still teeming with life.

Clattering motor bikes (which the locals sometimes call "bendskins") clog the streets, weaving around cars and trucks recklessly.

Along the roadside, street vendors ply their trade. Their small tables offer peanuts, cheap phones, fake soccer jerseys, cigarettes, and bottled palm wine. Grills with sizzling fish and plantains send plumes of charcoal smoke into the night.

At shabby roadside bars made of wood and tin, men sit at benches, hunched over glowing mobile phones, drinking beer and talking and laughing.

Perimeter lights on homes and flickering neon signs illuminate the smoke clouds, and as they drift by, I catch glimpses of the homes and shops, with their peeling concrete walls, graffiti, and corrugated rooftops.

In the rearview, the port of Douala is still very much alive, the silhouettes of cargo cranes shifting methodically in the moonlight.

After a pothole-filled roundabout, I spot a crowd ahead. They're spilling out into the street, stopping traffic. Slowly, I steer the truck slightly out of line to get a better view. There are at least forty people standing around watching, some shouting, arms raised in anger.

At first, I think it's a protest, but then I glimpse a familiar sight that stops me cold: the numbers. They appear to be spray-painted on a wall just above a corner market, like the other faded graffiti on the houses and shops.

"June," I say slowly. "Do you see—"

"The numbers? On the wall? Yes."

Isaac's voice calls over the radio. "Hey, what's up?"

I raise the radio to respond, but Isaac continues. "Oh. Just saw it. Dude… creepy."

But it's not the numbers causing the commotion. It's what's beyond, though I still can't see it.

For a long moment, we sit there in traffic, the two-way radio silent, the truck's air conditioner rattling to keep up with the heat. With each passing second, the odor of diesel and cigarettes and burning fish seeps into the cab.

Vehicles around us are blaring their horns and inching forward, prodding the crowd to move.

A motorbike darts through the line of automobiles, its small engine revving as it reaches the men and women in the street, a sort of desperate warning before it charges in, cutting a path through. Other bikes pour into the breach, and the crowd disperses like a busted piñata.

The line of cars and trucks creeps forward, and we follow, and soon, I catch my first glimpse of what was causing all the commotion: it's a stack of four cargo containers. The metal box at the top bears a logo I know well: Amersa.

The company is apparently using the same approach as in America, where they placed the cargo containers in the parking lots of malls and stadiums. It makes sense here, with the port less than a mile away. I bet by now, Amersa has established pop-up Labyrinth locations near every major shipping hub in the world.

In Douala, Labyrinth appears to be a hit, judging from the long lines and people fighting for a turn. Thanks to the numbers website, it's free, and all the world loves a free sample, especially of something new.

I realize then part of the genius of the numbers: they translate globally. Regardless of what language they speak, anyone can type the address into a mobile phone—and I suspect the site recognizes the visitor's location and translates the text into their local language.

It's scalable. And very clever.

And I suppose it's why the numbers were spray-painted on the wall, though when I first saw them, I did wonder if they were really there or if it was just me.

If I'm right, Amersa has security cameras outside this site—like every other one—and if we pass by, they might catch a glimpse of one of us, especially since we need to drive slowly to avoid hitting the people still lingering in the street.

I lift the handheld radio from the cup holder and call back to Rose and Isaac. "Stay close, we're going to detour."

With some effort (and drawing the ire of countless car horns) we manage to turn around and drive away from the crowd and the Amersa location.

When we're out of traffic, I consult the map and plot a new course, one that takes us out of the bustling area of the city, through older, residential neighborhoods.

The route takes us longer, and I figure the houses, many of which are lined with tall fences and barbed wire, have security cameras. But I think the detour is worth it.

By 11 PM, the city lights of Douala are firmly in the rearview, and the trucks are bounding along rougher, more deserted roads, heading north.

The coordinates for the center of the Labyrinth are about eight hundred miles away as the crow flies, but like our journey here, the roads we'll have to take are anything but direct, and inherently dangerous.

82

For security reasons, we've decided to camp instead of using hotels or private accommodations. Plus, there aren't many great places to stay along our route.

We've opted to camp at night (the roads we'll be taking aren't great to begin with, and getting ambushed is more likely at night, and dangerous). If it comes down to it, I'd rather defend our campsite at night than deal with a roadside bomb or spike strip along the road in the darkness.

Using satellite imagery, we spot a place off the road to camp. It's secluded and deep in a forest, but the terrain is easily navigable by the two pickups (which is important if we need to get away quickly).

Under the moonlight, Isaac and I pitch the tents while June and Rose camouflage the vehicles with nets. My prosthetic sinks slightly in the soft forest soil as I hammer stakes into the ground, the familiar motion reminding me of field exercises from my Marine days.

When the tents are up, I circle the camp with wire stretched across trees with tin cans dangling from it. It's not high-tech, but it'll give us some notice if anyone approaches the camp. An animal is likely to trip it at some point in our journey, but that annoyance is worth the added security.

We're keeping light to a minimum, and we don't need a fire (for cooking or warmth).

Isaac and June take the first shifts on watch while Rose and I retreat to our tents to try to get some sleep.

Even at midnight, the air is still sticky and humid. But the sound and smell of the busy port city is gone, replaced by the scent of soil and leaves and the occasional chirp of insects. Their calls are the last thing I hear as I lay my head on the pillow and close my eyes, the back of my hand resting on the top of the pistol at my side.

At dawn, we pack up the camp and hit the road.

The highways beyond Douala are paved at first, but they soon deteriorate into rough gravel stretches. Despite that, we make steady progress. From the passenger seat in my lead truck, Isaac pilots the drone.

On a full charge, it can stay in the air for up to forty minutes and has a range of nearly six miles.

We use it to scout the road ahead, looking for ambushes, wildlife crossings, police checkpoints, washouts, or other road closures.

We stop periodically to swap out the battery in the drone. Courtesy of Emile, we have thirty spare batteries (which we charge on the bed of the lead truck with the help of the solar cells).

The breaks to change the drone battery give us a brief reprieve from the bumpy, bone-rattling ride through lush rainforests with trees that tower over the road. We've seen a few villages, small settlements with wooden houses raised on stilts to avoid flooding. In the markets, locals sell bananas, yams, and grilled fish, their stalls bursting with vibrant colors.

But as we press northward, the scenery begins to change. The dense forests thin out and are gradually replaced by open savannas with rolling hills and fewer trees. In the distance, antelopes graze while birds circle lazily in the sky.

Late in the afternoon, the drone spots a police checkpoint ahead. We pull off the road and gather around Isaac's laptop on the hood of the truck, watching the drone's video feed. The barricade across the road looks makeshift, and the three uniformed officers loitering near it look bored, their rifles slung casually over their shoulders as they stare at smartphones.

Isaac dials Emile and after a brief call we wait, still watching the drone.

"What's the battery at?" I ask over Isaac's shoulder.

"About fifty percent."

"You want to bring it in?"

"Maybe," Isaac says absently as his phone dings.

He picks it up from the hood and reads the message from Emile. "Bribe's been arranged. We'll get the drone past the checkpoint."

At the barricade, Rose rolls down her window and hands over the fake passports and two fat envelopes full of Central African francs. The officer barely glances at the IDs, focusing instead on carefully counting the money. When they ask who we are, Isaac plays the part flawlessly.

"Journalists," he says, gesturing to the trucks. "Documentary about Cameroon's rainforests."

The officer nods, pockets the cash, and waves us through.

At sundown, we make camp in the hills.

The routine is the same: tents, nets, my makeshift perimeter alarm, and a silent meal of MREs.

The day was exhausting, mainly because of the tension. Worry takes a toll, no matter what you're doing. And this has been a worrying day—because of the danger of this journey and, I think, because all four of us are nervous about what's waiting at the coordinates.

Early the next morning, we cross into the country of Chad. Emile's off-road route bypasses the official border crossing entirely, avoiding any potential entanglements with authorities.

Beyond the border, the terrain grows harsher. The savanna stretches to the horizon. Golden grass sways in the wind under a boiling sun. Wildlife is more scarce here. This place feels more desolate, more alien.

We camp one final night before the last leg to the GPS coordinates.

The final miles of the route are the roughest. The dirt roads southeast of Zobili are little more than tracks carved into the earth. The drive feels more like an off-road safari now.

In the truck, Isaac and I ride in silence, my nerves ratcheting up like the midday heat outside.

Two miles from the coordinates, we stop and park the trucks in the shadow of a rocky outcrop.

Isaac puts a new battery in the drone and launches it. Next, he spreads out a blanket on the hood of the truck, which is as hot as a frying pan. He sets his laptop down, and the four of us gather round, watching the drone footage as it approaches the coordinates, no one saying a word.

The terrain around the coordinates is flat grassland in all directions. It's barren except for a few scattered acacias. Their twisted branches cast thin shadows in the fleeting golden sunlight.

On the screen, we finally get our first look at the center of the Labyrinth, at this place the ringing and the numbers and the GPS coordinates have brought us to.

There's nothing there.

No buildings.

No vehicles.

No painted sign.

Nothing.

83

For a while, we wait and watch as Isaac flies the drone around the area.

But it's a desolate field and a dry river bed cutting through it like a scar on the Earth.

Rose breaks the silence.

"Let's go there."

"Why?" Isaac mutters, not turning back to face her.

"Just in case... we're missing something."

"It's an eight-k camera. It's not missing anything."

It's also not hard to miss the frustration in Isaac's voice. And maybe some guilt. The coordinates were his breakthrough, and I sense, knowing him as well as I do now, that he's taking this pretty hard.

At the same time, I agree with Rose, and I say so: "She's right."

Isaac turns to me, and I can tell this is going to turn into a fight—if I let it.

Reaching out, I close the laptop and pull it off the hood. "Let's go."

Isaac doesn't move. "There's nothing *there*. I was wrong."

"There's nothing on the telemetry. But who knows, maybe the ringing will start. Maybe we'll get another clue. We have to keep going."

Isaac blinks. His shoulders relax. And he holds a hand out, and I pass his laptop back to him.

"Okay" is all he says.

★

The drive to the coordinates is a tense, silent trek across the empty landscape.

After parking, I step out into the heat, the dry grass crunching beneath my boots. The setting sun casts long shadows across the shrubs and rock outcroppings.

The four of us fan out, scanning the ground. With a GPS in hand, Isaac marches to a spot where he kicks the grass until he's hitting dirt, sending a dust cloud up as he marks it.

"This is it."

No one says anything.

He kicks again. And again.

The spot is well-marked, but I think now he's just taking out his frustration, punishing the earth for our great mistake in coming here.

Soon, he's obscured by the dust cloud, and June and Rose are slowly backing away.

The growing hole in the ground, however, gives me an idea. Back at the truck, I open one of the duffel bags and rifle through it, pots and pans banging against the tin cans from my trip wire.

Rose comes over and quietly asks, "What are you looking for?"

"The next clue," I mutter, finally finding what I need.

Walking back to Isaac, I unfold the camp shovel and plant it in the ground near his feet.

The wind carries the dust cloud away, and he stares at the shovel. I motion to the shallow rut in the ground, at the supposed center of the Labyrinth.

"Let's keep digging."

By sundown, I'm drenched in sweat. All of us are. This area of Chad is technically in the Sahel, the region just south of the Sahara, but it's as hot as any desert I've ever been to.

My stump is throbbing, my back aches, and my traps feel like a hot knife is lodged there. It'll all be worse tomorrow when the soreness starts. But I refuse to skip my turn with the shovel.

We're about four feet deep, and still, we haven't found anything.

We've fallen into a rhythm now—one person digging while another sifts through the excavated soil, checking for anything man-made, anything that shouldn't be here. The other two rest in the meager shade of the truck, gulping water and electrolyte powders. When the timer on one of the phones goes off, we rotate positions without needing to speak, like we've been doing this together for years instead of hours.

As Rose tosses more dirt on the pile, my mind drifts to another hole in the ground in a desert landscape that changed my life. And I remind myself that I thought that was a dead end too. But I kept going.

That night, we camp near the coordinates, twenty feet from the pile of dirt and rocks, mostly because we're exhausted and unsure where to go or what to do, and a little bit, I think, because we're all still hoping something will happen.

For the first time in my life, I want to hear the ringing. I want to lose time and wake up and see some sign, some clue about where to go or what to do next.

Lying in the tent on my stomach (taking the pressure off my aching back and stump), I will my mind to work.

In Amersa's Labyrinth, my fellow travelers and I hit a few dead ends. In the final one, when we were on the road, we couldn't get to the end because we didn't understand the numbers. We were just taking turns randomly. But not here. Isaac decoded it. We're at the coordinates.

Behind me, the tent flap unzips, and Rose pokes her head in. She's holding an MRE that emits white tendrils of steam into the night air.

"Hungry?"

I turn, making to get up.

"Stay there," she says, crawling deeper into the tent to set the carton of beef ravioli in front of me.

I thank her as I pick up the spork and begin shoveling the food into my mouth (the same way I dug that hole outside—one scoop at a time, moving methodically, mindlessly).

*

I don't sleep much that night. I'm restless and anxious—and almost glad when my watch shift arrives. I spend the time sitting on a folding stool, applying lidocaine cream to my stump.

I know I should have the prosthetic on, ready for anything, but I can see and hear for miles, and there's nothing out here.

The ringing never starts. Isaac never runs out of his tent, laptop hanging from his hand as he yells that he's figured it out.

Instead, the morning brings a somber mood as the four of us mill around the camp, eating, wolfing down caffeine pills and trying not to stare at the empty hole in the ground.

Isaac finally says what I sense we're all thinking: "There's no point in staying."

We pack up in silence, moving a little slower than we did on the way here, a reflection of the cumulative exhaustion and poor sleep and the worry—and all the things piled upon us like the heap of dirt and rocks beside the hole.

When we're ready to leave, Isaac gets our attention. A flicker of hope goes through me. Maybe he's figured it out. But from the look on his face, I can tell that's not it.

"This was my idea—the GPS coordinates. I got it wrong—"

"We're not going to do that," I interrupt him.

"Do what?"

"Place blame. It doesn't help us. And I *still* think this was a good idea. It made sense to me. It was our best shot. And maybe coming here was part of the ultimate answer."

He squints. "What?"

"What if this is just a step along the way—one we don't understand yet."

The drive back seems a lot longer than the trip here. Maybe that's the nature of backtracking, it feels like you're not going anywhere, just running over the same stretch of road you've already been down.

Our routine is the same: Isaac watches the drone, we swap the battery out periodically, and camp in the woods off the road.

At dinner that night, I suggest that Isaac have Emile get us four burner sat phones.

"What for?" he asks, chewing his chicken and rice MRE.

"Christmas is in two weeks. I want to call home. I bet we all do."

"You're right about that," June says. "But can they trace it? The location, at least?"

"Probably," Isaac says. "But we could wait until we get out to sea, then throw them over and move on."

We once again time our arrival at the marina in Douala to be after dark. And once again, Emile is waiting, leaning casually against the side of his truck. He hands over the sat phones without a word, his smile as unreadable as always.

At the yacht, I go aboard first, gun at my side as I step off the dinghy.

Isaac, Rose, and June watch as I search the boat, gun drawn, working as methodically as I did in Wilmington when we first took delivery.

Thankfully, the ship is just as we left it, though there's a strong smell of cigarette smoke and some ashes on the aft deck.

After unloading and stowing the dinghy, I unceremoniously lift the anchor and put us underway.

84

On the ship, we fall back into the routine we established on the way over, but the vibe is different now. Before, we had a clear destination and hope—two things you can't see but that are the wind in any person's sails.

Now it feels like every nautical mile lasts an eternity.

An hour before sunrise—and shift change—Isaac trudges up the stairs to the pilothouse, laptop in one hand, a sulking expression on his face.

"I traded with June," he says as he settles into the helm chair beside me. "Couldn't sleep."

"Like I said at the coordinates—*not your fault.*"

"The coordinates where we found nothing."

"The coordinates we all decided were worth checking out."

Another mile of ocean goes by. Then another.

Finally, Isaac says, "What do you think we should do?"

"I don't know."

Despite the worry and stress, my sleep that day is the best I've had since... well, since I got off the boat.

At the helm, I find Rose in one of the chairs, staring down at a paperback copy of *The Grapes of Wrath*.

Through the windows, the sun is setting in the distance.

"You should have woken me."

"Figured you could use the rest."

Leaning on the other helm chair, I scan the bank of screens.

We're out in the Atlantic, sailing east, far enough away from Douala for us to make our calls home, then dump the phones.

All the boat's systems are normal. I admit, as we sailed out of the Gulf of Guinea, I was a little worried that the people hired to guard the boat might have sabotaged it—or attached a tracker—making us vulnerable to hijacking or piracy once we had paid for their services and were out here in open waters, unable to make it back to the safety of a harbor.

But there's no sign of that. Which is about the extent of the good news right now.

I nod to Rose's book. "I see you opted for lighter fare."

She grins. "Read it in high school. What can I say, nostalgia is my coping mechanism."

"As coping mechanisms go, not a bad one."

Down in the salon, I find Isaac seated at the dining table, hunched over his laptop. I expect him to be deeply engrossed in some research project or perhaps some mathematical calculations to extract more meaning from the numbers.

Instead, he, too, has opted for a dose of nostalgia.

He's playing a video game on his computer, an old one, with blocky graphics that seem primitive by today's standards. It's a game I recognize. It may even be the first video game I ever played. Just seeing it brings a smile to my face.

"Is that…"

"Zelda," he mutters, eyes fixed on the screen.

"How'd you get it to run on your computer?"

"NES emulator."

He finally pauses the game. "You want to play?"

"Uh, no, I was just curious…" As I watch the screen, I change my mind. "Actually, I might."

"Okay. Let me beat it first."

Isaac cuts his eyes to the single sat phone lying on the table. "June did her call a few hours ago. Rose finished hers maybe thirty minutes ago. It's around two o'clock in Raleigh, but I say we wait another thirty minutes for yours."

"That works."

"You can use my office."

"Thanks."

For the next thirty minutes, I busy myself by checking the boat over one more time, inspecting every inch of the engine room and pacing the deck until I'm on the verge of wearing a hole in it.

I tell myself I'm doing one last pass for signs of sabotage or a tracker, but I know it's just a productive distraction to keep my mind from obsessing over the upcoming call with Meredith, which I want to do before she picks Riley up from school.

That all assumes Meredith is still keeping Riley, and that she'll even take my call. There's no telling what the news has said about me, or what rumors have circulated around school (basically a petri dish of gossip; twenty years ago and today).

In Isaac's office belowdecks, I dial her number on the sat phone and sit and wait as the long beeps pass by like a countdown to my fate.

"Hello?" she says uncertainly, no doubt skeptical of the random number.

"Hi."

"Hi." Her voice is flat, unreadable.

I can hear her PE class in the gym in the background. It sounds like another volleyball game to me.

It fades as she walks away, and I start in on the words I've mentally rehearsed. "Look, I—"

"Hang on, hang on," she says, somewhere between annoyed and anxious.

Tennis shoes squeak on a linoleum floor, metal lockers rattle as they slam, and a teenage girl yells, "*No, she didn't!*"

The push bar on a door slams inward, and the school noise fades as wind howls across the line. A car door slams, and it's quiet again except for Meredith, breathing hard.

"I wanted to call sooner—"

"I thought you were dead," she snaps.

"I couldn't call."

"What happened? Are you coming home?"

"Not yet."

"Why?"

"Things… haven't gone as planned."

"How?"

"I can't say."

She exhales. In my mind's eye, I can see the muscles in her jaw clenching, her eyes narrowing.

"Is Riley okay?"

"Yes." She pauses. "Sort of."

"What does that mean?"

"What do you think it means, Al—" She stops and seems to think better of saying my name (which is smart).

"Is she all right?"

"She's confused and scared."

"Have I been on the news? What are people saying?"

"Ryan's managed to keep it out of the news."

"You asked him."

"Yes. I did."

"What about school? What did you tell them?"

"Nothing. I didn't have to."

"Why do you say that?"

"You didn't talk to Sheila?"

"No, why?"

"She covered your classes when you didn't show up, and a few days later, she told everyone you were taking some time off. She made up this story."

"What story?"

"She said you injured your stump on Halloween night and needed inpatient care and some extended rehab to make sure it healed properly. She told everyone you were at Prideland Rehabilitation, a facility that specialized in helping veterans get back on their feet."

I can't help but smile. "God bless her."

"You didn't come up with that?"

"It's all Mufasa."

"Who?"

"Let's just say we have a very good principal."

"When are you coming home?"

"I don't know."

"Why don't you know?"

"Because... we're dealing with some stuff."

"What kind of *stuff*?"

"Just... I can't say."

"Why can't you say?"

"Look, I'm doing the best I can. Okay? Things didn't work out. I can't exactly just come home and go, 'Oh, well, let me turn myself in and whatever happens, happens.' Okay? I can't."

Her tone softens. "Okay."

I sit there, staring at Isaac's wooden desk.

I imagine her slumping into the seat and the headrest, staring at the red brick school building.

"Thanksgiving was tough," she says quietly.

"I bet."

"Ryan says running makes you look guilty."

"He's right."

"'A jury will see it that way.' Those were his exact words to me."

"He's right about that, too."

"Can you give them anything? Some clues they can investigate to clear you? Maybe then you could come home."

"It's a good idea, but no, I can't. I don't have anything to give them right now."

"Riley's been acting out at school. It's nothing major, but—"

"How do you know?"

"Her teacher texted me."

"How did she know to text you?"

"How do you think, Al—" She stops again and exhales. "I went and talked to her after you left and explained things."

"You did?"

"As best I could. I told her you had a family issue to deal with. This was before Shiela's cover story, but the discrepancy has never come up."

"What's Riley doing?"

"Nothing to worry about."

"Tell me anyway."

"Mostly just not following directions. Doing her own thing."

"I'm going to call her in a little bit. After school. On your phone."

"Good."

"Don't take her to the house."

"Why?"

"Security."

"You think it's bugged."

"I think it's possible."

"Me too."

"Why?"

"A private investigator came by."

"To your house?"

"Yeah."

"What did he say?"

"That he wanted to speak with you about a private matter."

"That's it?"

"More or less. I said you were indisposed, and he handed me his card, and I slammed the door."

"It's Amersa."

"I'd gotten that far. I'm not worried about the private investigator."

"What *are* you worried about?"

"You."

"I'm sorry I got you involved in all this."

"I'm not."

"You don't owe me anything."

"I know."

"So what do you want—"

"I love you."

Her words hit harder than this boat colliding with a cargo ship. My heart beats faster. I feel listless, scared, and happy, and so conflicted.

Because I do love her. Have for a long time. I wasn't ready back then, twenty years ago. It's impossible to know if I am now with everything going on in my life. It's hard to think about your future when you're surviving day-to-day. But I do know this: she's owed a reply to those words. Every person is.

I know that no matter what I say, she'll keep caring for Riley until I return. It's who she is.

And I know what I want to say. I don't know what's going to happen, but I say those words.

"I love you too. Have for a long time."

85

When I've finished the call, I go back upstairs to the salon, where Isaac is still hunched over his laptop at the dining table, playing *The Legend of Zelda* on the NES emulator.

Simplistic, repetitive music plays from the computer speakers, almost hypnotic, reminding me of my youth and a simpler time.

On the screen, the game's hero is exploring a dungeon. I watch as he crosses into a blue-green room. I vaguely remember this part. From the far wall, a hand emerges and heads straight for the character.

Isaac works the arrow keys, fleeing the menacing, unflinching hand. When he gets ahead of it, he turns and stabs the hand, killing it. In the monster's wake, a flickering jewel appears, which Isaac collects.

The game is starting to come back to me. The character's name is Link, and if memory serves, this is the room before he faces the dungeon boss and collects the treasure.

Another hand emerges from the lower wall. Isaac dodges around the fixed blocks and fights this one too, the sword issuing forth like a frog's tongue.

This time, the disappearing hand leaves a red heart. Link grabs it, filling in one of the heart containers on his status.

A yellow key looms in the lower right. I'm pretty sure it unlocks the door at the top.

"The key," I whisper, leaning closer.

"*I know, dude,*" Isaac hisses, still concentrating on the screen.

One by one, Isaac kills the hands coming out of the walls. The final one also leaves a heart, which fills in his sixth and final heart container. I realize then what Isaac was doing: with full life, Link can shoot daggers from the sword. In the next room, which holds the dungeon boss, that's going to be important.

With the hands gone and his hearts full, Isaac retrieves the key and unlocks the room's only exit.

The moment he steps through, a green dragon with a unicorn horn releases three fireballs.

Link surges forward, then left, dodging the fireballs. Every few seconds, the unicorn dragon launches three more.

Isaac sidesteps the second volley and shoots his sword, landing a hit that causes the dragon to blink.

One of the fireballs in the third barrage hits Link, taking away half of a heart. Without all the heart containers full, the sword no longer shoots; he's back to stabbing only.

"You have to get in close now," I say softly, eyes fixed on the screen.

"Duude! I know!"

Isaac dodges another round of fireballs and rushes forward, trying to get close enough for the sword to reach, but at the last second, he retreats to avoid the fire.

The pattern repeats several times. Finally, I gently tell Isaac that he has to rush the dragon. I expect him to snap at me, but he just presses the arrows on the keyboard, sending the character on the screen in circles, dodging fireballs but never getting close enough to win the battle.

Pulling a chair over, I settle in next to him. "You've got the hearts, man. You've got to go for it while you can."

Isaac ignores me.

"I'm telling you, buddy, you'll take some hits, but you'll live. If you don't, it'll wear you down. Come on, do it, rush that thing and stab it in the face."

On the screen, another fireball clips Link, and he drops another half a heart. That seems to seal things for Isaac because he sends our hero charging forward, directly for the green dragon. It lets loose another stream of fire, landing a direct hit on Link. The hero bears it this time, standing his ground and stabbing with his sword. The dragon flickers. After a second point-blank hit, the boss winks out of existence, leaving a large red heart with a dotted outline. Isaac grabs it, and Link's total hearts under life increase by one.

In the next room, Isaac navigates Link to collect his first piece of the Triforce, which he victoriously holds in the air.

The moment he does, a funny thing happens: the ringing starts. It's the same general sound as the rocks in the can, but it's more gentle, more melodic. Like the edges of the rocks have been sanded down, as if they're marbles rolling around, playing a simplistic tune. It's not exactly like the music from Zelda, but the similarity is hard to miss.

Isaac slowly turns his head. "I hear—"

"Ringing," I whisper, barely hearing my own voice.

Then it stops.

"It's gone for me," Isaac says.

"Same here."

Footsteps echo on the narrow staircase, and Rose peers into the salon.

"I just heard ringing."

For a while, we sit in the salon and discuss what the synchronized ringing might mean, but as Link did in the room before he reached the boss, we just go around in circles.

At this point, we have no direction, and I have to say, I was glad when those little rocks began jingling in that unseen can. I don't know what it means, but it's a clue. A string to pull on. Right now, it's the only one we have.

Isaac, for his part, is less encouraged.

"They're just messing with us now. Amersa or whoever or whatever is doing this. They're laughing at us. That's what the ringing is. It's the numbers laughing at us."

No one says anything, because we know it's his frustration talking. And we don't know if he's right or not.

★

Belowdecks, in Isaac's office, I dial the sat phone, hoping to reconnect with the most important piece of the Triforce in my life.

The line tolls, and on the second ring, Meredith answers.

"Hi." It's a single word. A single syllable, but from the tone, I can tell something has changed between us. Because of what she said earlier. And my reply.

"Hi," I say back to her.

"She's in her room."

Her room, I think. In Meredith's house.

Next, I hear Meredith's footfalls on the carpeted stairs, a soft knock at the door, and my daughter's voice, sounding annoyed.

"I'm making bracelets."

"Can you take a break?" Meredith asks.

"Uhhh!" Riley groans, and I hear snapping, perhaps the bracelet case closing.

"Your dad's on the phone," Meredith says softly.

"What?"

"Here," Meredith says, the phone shuffling before Riley comes on the line, voice tentative, like a person stepping onto a high wire they're not sure will hold. "Dad?"

"Hi, kiddo."

"Dad!" she screams. "Where are you? Are you coming home? When are you coming home? *What happened?*"

I can't help but laugh. "Hey, slow down. I want to hear how you're doing. How's school?"

"Fine. When are you coming home?"

"As soon as I can."

"When?"

"I don't know, sweetie—"

"Why?"

"Well, it's just how it is with work right now, okay? Some things take longer than you think, and you hit some snags along the way."

"What snags, Dad?"

"It doesn't matter. What matters is that I'm working as hard as I can, and I miss you a lot, and I love you with all my heart."

Her voice cracks as she utters a shaking word that nearly breaks my heart. "Dad?"

"Yeah?"

"I'm scared. I want you to come home."

"Listen to me, Riley. Okay?"

Her voice is small. "Okay."

"Everything is going to be okay in the end. Remember that. And if it's not okay, it's not the end. You understand?"

The last words I said to Riley weren't mine. Not entirely. I read the quote somewhere—can't remember the source—but it was after I lost my leg, and it always stayed with me. It seemed to do the trick for my daughter. Or at least, maybe it bought me some time. Because after that, we had a rather normal conversation, like a parent traveling for work might have with their child at home. I asked about school, gymnastics, and if she was being a good listener. I savored every second of it. And the last words I said were ones I'd rehearsed and wanted to leave her with: "I want to come home as soon as I can. And I am doing my very best to get there, but a lot of things are out of my control."

It felt good to say that to her, almost like a confession.

Upstairs, Isaac is still playing Zelda. On the laptop screen, Link is burning bushes and planting bombs and shooting his sword, still chasing those missing pieces of the Triforce.

Standing in the salon, I wait, wondering if I'll hear the ringing. Strangely, I want to at this juncture.

But the only sound is the hum of the engine and the vibration of the boat beneath my feet.

Up in the pilothouse, I find Rose yawning in the helm chair, still holding the paperback of *The Grapes of Wrath*. From the looks of it, she's on one of the last pages.

"Turn out the way you thought?" I ask.

She rolls her eyes. "Very funny."

Through the windshield, the sea glitters in the moonlight, our sort of endless dust bowl of uncertainty.

"Be right back," I call to her as I climb up to the fly bridge. The wind blows through my hair, the waves crash on the boat's bow, and the moon stares down as I pull the sat phone from my pocket and throw it in the ocean.

86

At the end of my shift, the ringing happens again.

I sit in the helm chair, listening, watching the sun rise over the water.

The ringing sounds like the rocks in the can, a smoother version, more like chimes now, clanging three times as if it were a gentle alarm going off on a smartphone.

I wait, but it doesn't continue. It's just those three brief clangs.

I descend the stairs and find Isaac at the dining table, hunched over his laptop. He stabs once at the keyboard and looks up. "You hear it?"

"Yeah."

"Did you do anything? Change course?"

"No."

Behind me, a figure emerges from belowdecks. June. "Hey, I heard—"

"Ringing," Isaac says, standing now.

Rose peeks out from behind June. "Me too."

"What does it mean?" I ask.

Isaac shakes his head. "Maybe this is just their morning laugh. They're basically torturing us now."

June, Rose, and I don't react. We know Isaac is hurting now. And based on how he looks, he's been up all night. I'm reminded of June's previous point: sleep deprivation amplifies stress.

She moves to the kitchen and puts on some coffee, and I go in and start to make some breakfast (we received some fresh food stores from Emile before departing Douala—a minor consolation prize given what we hoped to find during our trip there, but it could be useful now).

Holding a steaming coffee mug in both hands, June settles into a chair at the dining table. "Let's do the work."

"What work?" Isaac sounds annoyed, but I think we all know what June is talking about.

"Let's talk about what we were each doing just now, when we heard the ringing."

We each share, and it turns out only Isaac and I were awake.

He tells us that he was just playing *The Legend of Zelda* and that he was about to beat it.

June takes a sip of coffee. "Try continuing."

Isaac scoffs. "The game?"

"Yes. I assume you were going to continue anyway."

He exhales, but I know him well enough to know this is his way of saying, *You're right*.

"Okay," is all he says, and he taps the laptop's keyboard, and the rest of us crowd around his chair, watching as he plays.

On the screen, Link walks into a dungeon room with gray blocks and a princess standing in the middle, surrounded by four flames.

Using the arrow keys, Isaac maneuvers to each fire block and lashes them with his sword, extinguishing them before making his way to the princess.

A black curtain closes over the dungeon, leaving Link and the princess as block letters type out:

THANKS LINK, YOU'RE
THE HERO OF HYRULE

The ringing pulses then, a single *clang-clang-clang*.

June and Rose glance at each other.

Isaac turns to us. "I heard three chimes."

"Me too," I whisper.

"What does it mean?" June asks quietly.

"Maybe the Labyrinth wants us to play classic NES games," Isaac says sarcastically. "I've got them all. *Contra. Rad Racer.*

Donkey Kong. Super Mario Brothers. Maybe Bowser knows the key to the Labyrinth."

On the laptop screen, Link and the princess are holding up the flashing Triforce. Below them, block letters print out:

FINALLY,
PEACE RETURNS TO HYRULE.
THIS ENDS THE STORY.

The credits roll then.

No one says anything. June leaves and puts another coffee pod in the Keurig machine and rests against the counter in the galley as the machine grinds and brews.

"Maybe we should replay the game," Rose says. "Maybe there was a clue we missed."

"This is ridiculous," Isaac mutters. "There's no way the point of all this is for me to play games on my computer."

June puts her elbows on the counter. "What does the game have in common with Labyrinth?"

Isaac rolls his eyes. "They're both adventure games. Well, Labyrinth is a little more than that, and it's light years ahead. A totally different era."

Rose motions to the laptop screen. "How are you even playing this? I thought you needed a console?"

"Emulator," Isaac says.

"Maybe that's the clue," Rose offers. "Maybe, emulation? Whatever that is?"

The discussion is starting to bring Isaac around. He seems more open to the idea. "An emulator essentially allows you to play a game that was made for another platform. Stuff from the past."

On the laptop screen, more text types out:

ANOTHER QUEST WILL START
FROM HERE.
PRESS THE START BUTTON

Below that is what looks like an upside-down blinking Triforce triangle, followed by ©1986 NINTENDO.

I had forgotten this part from the original.

"Maybe," Rose says, "we're supposed to create an emulator."

"Of what?" Isaac asks. Some of the edge has returned to his voice. "We can't emulate what we don't know about."

June has returned with a fresh cup of coffee, and she's studying the screen. "There's another quest?"

Isaac taps enter. "Yeah. The Second Quest. It's like the same world, but locations are different and the dungeons are harder."

We discuss emulators and the fact that both Labyrinth and Zelda are RPGs, and that they both changed consumer behavior, were groundbreaking, and everything in between, but we don't hear the ringing again. And we don't arrive at any conclusions or even theories.

In my berth, I lie awake, waiting, hoping to hear the ringing, but it's only the wind howling and the waves crashing on the hull.

I'm dead tired from the night shift and some leftover sleep deficit, but I can't fall asleep.

I know why.

I've felt like this twice before.

The first time was after the surgeries, when my leg was wrapped up, and I was lying in that bed, and the doctor came in, and I will never forget what he said to me: "Life is not about what you've lost. It's about what you have left."

The second time was after my wife died. Those words applied then as well. What I lost then was far more than half of a leg. And so was what I had left: a daughter.

Then—and now—I feel like I'm dealing with things I'm not mentally equipped to handle. Not even close. I feel overwhelmed, angry, and confused.

But like then—and now—I'm not quitting. I also can't sleep.

For that reason, I put my prosthetic back on and I get up and decide that I'll do the only life hack that has ever worked in times like these: making myself busy.

My tiny cabin is a cave of darkness. Outside, opposite the helm, the sun is like a nuclear blast.

I stand and squint and wait for my eyes to adjust. In the darkness, Rose calls out to me. "You okay?"

"Sort of," I mumble.

I feel her hand on my shoulder. I crack my eyes and look at her. "Can't sleep."

"I gathered that," she says quietly. "What are you going to do?"

"Work."

"On what?"

I close my eyes again, giving them time to adjust. "I'm gonna check the engines."

"Alan, I think the engines are fine."

"Me too."

She laughs and I open my eyes to find her smiling at me. She asks me what I really want to do.

"I told you: I want to work."

She tilts her head upward to the fly bridge. "Then let's work. Come on."

We climb up to the open-air deck and I feel the wind on my face and smell the salt water and for a few seconds, I don't think about anything, I just watch the boat cutting through the Atlantic.

I turn and Rose is leaning on the rail, arms crossed, looking at me.

There's something about me and her. A bond we have. Ever since that night. And when she spoke for me and got me into the group, that bond only got stronger.

We're a bit like two people who were in combat together, who relied on each other to survive. And we did, one night in particular, and ever since.

I don't know if it's that or the exhaustion, but I tell her exactly what I'm thinking: "We're lost, Rose."

She doesn't flinch at the words. She stares at me, and the wind catches her hair and unfurls it like a flag.

She does the last thing I expect. She pushes off from the side wall and walks to the controls, and nudges the throttle forward.

The engines rev a little more and the boat cuts faster across the water, to where none of us knows.

She turns to me, and the wind drapes her hair around her face and neck like a curtain partially pulled. "We're not lost, Alan."

"What are we?"

"We've been knocked down."

I swallow and listen to the waves.

Rose steps closer to me, standing in the middle of the fly bridge. The boat rocks and she grabs the back of one of the helm chairs to keep her balance.

"The question is whether we can get up."

It's impossible for me to miss her meaning.

She's been knocked down at least once in her life. I have too. Several times.

She backs to the rail and crosses her arms. "So let's get up."

I nod and listen and she has to practically shout over the wind and the waves now.

"You and me, Alan. I know we're not the super brains of the group, but I also know we both get up when we've been knocked down. Which is what we need to do right now."

"So, how do we get up?"

"We do the work we can, and then we get June and Isaac to help. But he's not in a great place."

"I agree. But how do we do the work?"

"We talk."

I smile. "About what?"

"Anything, Alan. We don't have a clue what we're doing, so there are no bad ideas. Don't judge anything. Just throw things out and we'll sort it out later."

"Okay. Fine."

"What were you thinking about before you came out of your berth?"

"My wife."

"Why?"

"I don't know."

Rose turns her head, and another stretch of ocean goes by, and the sun soaks into her back. The rocking of the boat seems to loosen an idea that hits me then.

"Maybe because I saw her in Amersa's Labyrinth."

Rose turns back to me. "Right. Keep going. Pull the thread, Alan."

I walk over and stand beside her because it's easier for her to hear me. And I tell her what I didn't tell the group after that session.

"I thought that the Amersa AI had recreated her because she facilitated my rehabilitation in the past. I figured they were going to use her to do it again. But things sort of went off the rails. The stuff she said to me was about a lot more than my PTSD."

Rose watches me, waiting.

"It told me, 'You just have to keep going. Even when it feels hopeless.' That part makes sense. But the thing I keep thinking about is what she said after: 'It's all about the numbers. When you're stuck, consult the numbers.'"

87

On the fly bridge, Rose and I stand there thinking, feeling the wind on our faces and the boat rocking beneath our feet as it cuts across the waves.

We both turn when we hear footsteps on the ladder.

June's head rises over the deck, and when she sees us, she stops, watching for a moment.

"We're just talking," Rose calls to her over the wind.

June keeps climbing and on the fly bridge, she settles into one of the two chairs. "There was no one at the helm below for the shift hand-off."

Rose motions to the controls. "We transferred it up here."

June asks us what we're talking about.

"The obvious," Rose replies.

"Where we're going?" June offers.

"Yeah," Rose says. "And thoughts about that."

"I've been thinking about it too," June says, scooting to the edge of the seat. "What I keep coming back to is Alan's experience in Amersa's Labyrinth. The similarities with all of us. It's as if there were clones of every person in the group. And I keep coming back to the numbers."

She nods to me. "Alan, you used the numbers to find the center. And then we did too, but it didn't work out here. It's like—"

Another head rises over the deck and the three of us turn to find Isaac peering up. He looks even more tired than before.

I motion for him to join us.

As he steps onto the fly bridge, the boat hits a strong wave and all of us buckle, Isaac the most. He falls over the covered circular spa, head hitting the blue mat hard.

I spring off the rail and take one long step and wrap him in my arms, afraid another strong wave could roll him off the fly bridge and over the back of the boat.

I pull him back, whispering, "I got you, buddy."

With Isaac in my arms, I stagger to the L-shaped banquette and deposit him on the edge of the seat.

Behind me, Rose grips the throttle and pulls it back to neutral.

The boat lurches forward, our own wake and our lost inertia rocking us.

I hold Isaac, and he looks at me with exhausted eyes and tells me it was lunchtime and he was just seeing where we were. When he asks what we're doing, I shrug. "Just talking."

He's smart enough to know what we've been talking about.

"I've been thinking," he says.

I smile at him. "Got tired of playing NES games."

"Pretty much."

"What have you been thinking?"

"The ringing, it happened when I beat the game," he says. "The first quest in Zelda. It rang when the second quest was starting."

"Okay. That's good. Keep going, Isaac."

"I've been thinking... what if Amersa's Labyrinth was the first quest? You beat it. Now we're on the second quest—out here. And it's like Zelda's second quest. There are a lot of similarities, but it's harder. And the locations are different."

I motion to Rose. "We were talking earlier about my last Labyrinth session. That... thing told me: 'When you're stuck, consult the numbers.'"

Isaac nods. "Where I got it wrong was using the numbers the same way you did in Amersa's Labyrinth."

"So, how do we use them?"

"I don't know. But I was thinking, what if we have to turn the numbers upside down? Or mirror them. What if our world is like *Stranger Things?* The upside-down world."

Instinctively, I sense that what he's saying is right. "Then let's turn them upside down, just like this world. Come on."

For the next hour, we work the numbers, turning them upside down, flipping them, mirroring them, subtracting each one from ten, and a few ideas that are even more silly.

Each time we come up with a set of coordinates, we check it on a map. But they all seem off. I sense that we're all starting to get frustrated. And to be fair, we were before.

Sitting at the dining table, I point at Isaac's screen. "Let's keep it simple."

He cuts his eyes at me. "Simple? Right. Good idea."

His sarcasm isn't lost on me, but I press on, because that's what we have to do now.

"One step at a time. No bad ideas. Okay?"

"Okay," he mutters. He puts his hands on the keyboard, eyes straight ahead, waiting for me.

"Let's reverse the numbers. In Amersa's Labyrinth, the numbers read from start to finish. Same for the website. But what if the center out here is back to front? To reach the end, we start at the end of the sequence?"

In the text editor on the screen, Isaac reverses the numbers. "Where do we split them?"

"Try down the middle. There are fourteen numbers. Do seven and seven."

"Where do we put the decimal points?"

"Try the same as you did before—first two digits, then the decimal, then five digits."

Isaac types away at the laptop, quickly producing the new GPS coordinates.

Latitude: 15.22121
Longitude: 80.24198

I'm holding my breath as he opens it on a map.

It's on the east coast of India. Isaac zooms in. The balloon is actually located on the ocean—in the Bay of Bengal—about ten miles from the coast of India.

Deep in my gut, I know it's right. This is the one.

Isaac switches to satellite view and zooms in. "It's nothing but open sea."

"To be precise," June says, "there was nothing there when this satellite photo was taken."

Isaac studies the screen. "You think there's something there now?"

"Yes," I mumble, not even meaning to speak.

"What do you think it is?" Isaac asks.

"I don't know," I reply as I stand and begin to pace, ignoring the growing pain in my stump.

Isaac cocks his head, studying me. "If you think there's something there, you must have some idea about what it is."

My very intelligent friend is right about that, because as he says those words, I'm replaying—in my mind—my last visit to Amersa's Labyrinth: driving the truck, turning and backing up, putting the boat in the water, crashing on the waves, and docking at the building.

Isaac steps into my path. "Seriously, what do you think it is?"

"I think... that it might be like Amersa's Labyrinth."

"As in..."

"A building coming out of the sea."

"Dude. It's ten miles out in the Indian Ocean. There's no way."

"I know that. I'm just saying... that it could be like that. Maybe a ship at anchor."

Isaac shakes his head and settles back into his chair. "It's a big leap." He motions to the screen. "I mean, we could cut and shuffle these numbers for ten more hours and get hundreds of locations. Why this one?"

"Simplicity. It's the obvious one."

Isaac snorts. "Right. That always works out."

"This is it," I tell him. "It's the right location. The reverse of Amersa's Labyrinth."

"How do you know?"

"Call it a hunch."

"It's the best idea we have," Rose says.

June crosses her arms. "I agree. It seems to me that we can either keep sailing with no direction, or go home, or go check it out." She quickly glances around the room. "I don't think any of us are ready to go home. At least, not yet. And I think these coordinates are a great deal more promising than our current course. With that being said, we can always alter our destination if we come up with something better along the way. Such is life, and apparently, the road to the Labyrinth."

V
THE MINOTAUR

V

THE MINOTAUR

88

That night, we set sail for the coordinates ten miles off the coast of India, in the Bay of Bengal.

It's a long trip. The voyage will take us south, around the Cape of Good Hope, and then east before we turn and sail northeast across the Indian Ocean.

The most logical plan is to refuel in Cape Town, South Africa, which lies roughly twenty-five hundred nautical miles from our present position. It's well within the Nordhavn's range.

Traveling at seven knots, we'll reach Cape Town around New Year's Eve. That's not ideal. The holiday will mean fewer people working, which might limit our refueling options. The New Year's festivities and added boat traffic will also increase the risk for us: revelers will no doubt be snapping photos and shooting video. One might catch a glimpse of us, and if the video or image is posted to social media, a facial recognition bot might identify one of us and notify Amersa.

The other problem is the second leg, after we refuel. From Cape Town to the coordinates is about 4,800 nautical miles. That's just outside of our range. We'll have to refuel along the way, likely somewhere in Mozambique or Madagascar (it's almost entirely open ocean after that until the Maldives, off the coast of India).

At seven knots, Cape Town to the coordinates looks like about a 29-day voyage.

All together, we'll be at sea for roughly seven weeks. I could probably find a refueling port closer to the midway point, eliminating the second stop, but it doesn't save much time.

Sitting in the salon, the group discusses my preliminary calculations, and we quickly conclude that we should increase our speed in order to arrive at Cape Town at least a few days before New Year's. Seven knots is slightly below the Nordhavn's normal cruising speed and significantly below its top speed. Pushing the engines will burn more fuel, but if we're refueling in Cape Town, it doesn't matter.

"As to the larger issue," Isaac says, "I think we need a bigger boat."

"With a longer range?" June asks, clarifying.

Isaac agrees and opens his laptop.

"I'm not opposed," I tell him, "but we can't go much bigger. We're a skeleton crew as it is."

"What do you suggest?" Isaac asks, focused on the screen. I can tell he's already started hunting.

"What we need is a similar model—a motor yacht built for owner-operators—that's more suited for long-range cruising. *Ideally*, a lighter boat with more fuel capacity. If we're lucky, we might find one in Cape Town."

Isaac spends the rest of the night scouring the internet for those options. At the end of my shift, with the sun rising over the coast of West Africa, the four of us are assembled in the pilothouse, sitting around the U-shaped banquette, our tired faces illuminated by the pink-orange glow through the windows.

Like anyone shopping for a big-ticket item, we have reached the inevitable question that will drive the final decision: what's our budget?

To answer that, we've called Harold, whose computer-scrambled voice now comes through the sat phone sitting on the glossy, lacquered table.

We begin with an update on our new destination, which seems to thrill Harold ("Once more unto the breach" are his exact words).

When Isaac asks about buying a boat with a longer range in Cape Town and what sort of budget we have to work with, Harold chuckles.

"I'm quite happy to report that, at the moment, the sky is the limit, my young friend. Business, such as it is, has been very, very good of late. Trading profits have steadily increased. The coffers, if you will, are full. And that's not all."

Harold goes on to relate that some of the money he's earned from his trading accounts has been transferred to a company called Daedalus Ltd.

The name sounds vaguely familiar, though I can't place it exactly. Harold says that it doesn't mean anything in particular to him, but he did look it up and found that it's connected to the ancient Greek myths surrounding the Labyrinth.

In Greek mythology, Daedalus was the craftsman and inventor who built the Labyrinth for King Minos of Crete.

"That doesn't make any sense," Isaac says. "In our situation, the Labyrinth already exists. Built and funded by Amersa. Seems like Daedalus should have come before the Labyrinth."

June sets down her tablet. "What if whoever named the company Daedalus didn't do it because of the Labyrinth?"

Isaac shrugs. "Then what does it mean?"

"Daedalus is connected to several other significant Greek myths."

Reading from her tablet, June details Daedalus's life, beginning with him murdering his nephew, Talos (sometimes called Perdix). As the story goes, Daedalus envied the young man's skill so much that it led him to push the youth off the Acropolis. The crime resulted in Daedalus's exile from Athens, which brought him to the island of Crete.

The island's king, Minos, welcomed the talented artisan and promptly put him to work. The first project was to build a series of life-like statues. The next major assignment was to craft a wooden cow for Minos's wife, Queen Pasiphaë.

June shifts uncomfortably as she relates the sordid tale of why exactly Minos's wife needed a wooden cow, but the long and short is that Minos was a little nervous about his claim to the throne of Crete and worried that his brothers might try to usurp him, so he made a deal with the Olympian Poseidon. To legitimize Minos's claim, Poseidon sent a white bull from the sea as a sign of

Minos's right to rule. Under the terms of the deal, Poseidon was required to sacrifice the bull.

Minos, however, was quite taken with the bull and opted to sacrifice an inferior bull instead. This betrayal enraged Poseidon. With Aphrodite's help, he cursed Minos's wife. The ultimate consequence of this revenge curse was the birth of the Minotaur, a half-bull, half-human abomination that was a threat to the people of Crete.

To protect the island, King Minos commanded Daedalus to build the Labyrinth—an elaborate maze that no one could escape from. Once completed, Minos lured the Minotaur into the Labyrinth.

To feed the beast, Minos demanded regular tributes of young men and women from subjugated cities (notably Athens) to be sent into the Labyrinth.

"Eventually," June says, still reading from the tablet, "the Minotaur was slain by the hero Theseus of Athens—with the help of Princess Ariadne, Minos's daughter. The legend goes that she provided him with a thread to navigate the maze, enabling him to find and kill the Minotaur, which freed Athens from having to send tributes to die in the Labyrinth."

I find it all interesting, but I'm struggling to superimpose it on what's happening to us—or to see which players we resemble in the ancient myth.

"There's more," June says.

"Minos was so impressed with the Labyrinth that he feared Daedalus might reveal its secrets or build another structure to rival it. To prevent that, he imprisoned Daedalus inside the structure."

Isaac shakes his head. "This Minos guy—he makes bad decisions."

"That he does," June says, scanning the tablet. "There are two accounts of what happens next. One says that Minos confines Daedalus to the Labyrinth. The other says he imprisons Daedalus in a high tower—one with very few windows, which he couldn't escape from on foot."

I'm thinking about the tower in Amersa's Labyrinth, which rose from the sea, with very few windows.

"And," June continues, "it was actually Daedalus *and* his son, Icarus, who were imprisoned, either in the high tower or the Labyrinth."

Instinctively, I think about Riley and the fact that, like Daedalus and his child, we're both very much caught in this Labyrinth and trying to escape.

Rose cocks her head. "Icarus, like the wings."

"The same," June says. "To escape the Labyrinth—or tower—Daedalus crafted wings from feathers and wax. He made two sets: one for himself and one for Icarus. They used the wings to fly away, but Icarus was exhilarated by the experience. And he—"

"Flew too close to the sun," Rose says absently.

"Yes," June agrees. "As the legend goes, if Icarus had flown too low, the water from the sea would have soaked his wings and pulled him down. Instead, he soared too high and the heat from the sun melted the wax in the wings, causing him to fall into the sea and drown. It's the classic tale of hubris and over-ambition leading to a fall."

"And perhaps," Harold says through the speaker, "a cautionary tale for Amersa, about the danger of being too confident in the power of technology and innovation—as Icarus was too confident in his father's invention."

"So what does it mean?" Isaac asks, scooting out of the banquette and pacing in the pilothouse behind the two helm chairs.

When no one answers, he continues, not making eye contact with any of us, as if he's thinking out loud.

"Daedalus Ltd… Whoever created it is obviously generating the money in Harold's accounts. So we know they're very skilled."

"Or knowledgeable," Rose adds. "Maybe insider trading."

Isaac stops and points at her. "Yes. I've always thought that's what it was. Or some kind of computer hack, like high-frequency trading, but faster than any other firm on earth. Shaving fractions off of every transaction or something."

Isaac resumes pacing. "But the question is: why name it Daedalus? Is it a warning? Are they telling us that the money could be used to fund a technology—like the wings—that could lead to a fall similar to Icarus? Or is it a reference to what's already happened with Amersa? Are they saying the Labyrinth is already an inescapable technology—for whoever enters—just like in the myth? And if so, are we Daedalus? Destined to be trapped inside?"

He turns back to June. "Wait. What happened to Daedalus? Did he get away?"

"For a time. He used his wings to fly to Sicily, where King Cocalus gave him refuge. But King Minos was still intent on capturing him."

June switches to another tab in the browser. "This I found interesting. To find Daedalus, Minos devised a puzzle that only Daedalus could solve. His logic was that if anyone, anywhere solved it, he would know that the person had to be Daedalus."

"Sort of like us solving the numbers," Isaac says.

June looks up. "That's what it reminded me of."

"What was the puzzle?" Rose asks.

"The details of it vary from source to source, but the most well-known puzzle involves threading a string through a spiral seashell—often a conch shell."

"How does Daedalus do it?" Isaac asks.

"He ties the string to an ant—or beetle—and places a drop of honey at the other end of the shell, which draws the insect, pulling the string through."

"Clever," Isaac mumbles.

"Other versions of the story involve a mini-labyrinth model that Daedalus must thread."

"So Minos found him when he solved the puzzle?" Rose asks.

"He did, but King Cocalus, or his daughters, didn't want to surrender Daedalus. To protect him, they killed Minos by scalding him with boiling water during a supposed bath."

"Minos..." Isaac says, sitting again, "bad decisions and then bad breaks."

"What happened to Daedalus after that?" I ask.

"Nothing," June replies. "He was pretty much free at that point and doesn't appear in any other myths."

"Wonderful," Isaac says. "He finally got to retire. So where does that leave us?"

"I'd say," Harold begins over the speaker, "with more questions than answers. And a boat to buy."

"Phones too," I add, sensing that the meeting is breaking up.

Isaac locks eyes with me. "It's a risk."

"It is. But we're going to be gone for a long time—longer than any of us thought. Christmas is in ten days. Based on my calculations, we'll reach Cape Town on the thirtieth. I'd like to call home for New Year's."

"Me too," June says quietly.

"Same," Rose says.

Isaac exhales. "Okay. I'll make it happen."

89

Two nights later, during my shift, the coast of West Africa is glittering to my left, the bow of the boat is cutting through the Atlantic, and I'm sitting at the table in the pilothouse, making a list.

So far, I have written:

Rope
Broom or mop
Life vests
Small fenders
Rope ladder
Fishing line
Hooks
Lures
Flashlights
Game pieces
Cardboard
Aluminum foil

That's what I need so far for my creation. But tapping the pen on the lacquered table surface, I realize I missed one thing, the item all makeshift construction projects inevitably need: duct tape.

An hour later, I've collected the items from around the boat, and they lie in a heaping pile in the salon.

I begin by standing the mop up and duct-taping the small fenders to the handle at the base to ensure it stands up straight.

Next, I attach the life vests, using more at the bottom and less as I move up the wooden handle, forming a cone.

The flashlights I plant at the base and shine upward, adjusting the life vests until I'm happy with the beams breaking through.

I wrap the rope ladder around next, which holds the life vests in position and further solidifies the cone shape.

Every few minutes, Isaac looks over from the dining table and tries to guess what I'm making.

"It's a test dummy."

"Test dummy?" I reply, still wrangling the rope ladder.

"You know, to throw over the side. To practice a rescue, like a man overboard drill."

"It's not that."

His next attempt is: "It's a Harold doll. A stand-in. Like a mannequin for the calls."

I set the rope down and rest on my haunches, staring at him. "Do you actually think I'm that bored?"

He grimaces. "I don't know. Maybe? I sort of am."

"It's not a Harold doll."

Isaac glimpses something on the screen and smiles as he leans forward and clicks the mouse quickly.

"What's up?" I ask, rounding the table for a peek.

Isaac minimizes the window. "I want it to be a surprise. For Christmas."

"The boat?"

"Let's just say, bid accepted."

"It's an upgrade, I take it?"

"You are correct."

"It's fun, isn't it? Bidding on stuff."

Isaac nods. "Yeah. I haven't done anything like it in a while, since I used eBay way back in the day."

"What for?"

"Mostly buying and selling computer parts."

My mind flashes to Ian—Isaac's counterpart in Amersa's Labyrinth—and the mound of computer parts he had collected.

Without thinking about it, I glance over at my own collection of spare parts from around the boat.

"I was actually doing some eBaying myself before we left. Army surplus stuff."

"With that Warren guy?"

"Yep."

"There's something about trading things—buying and selling," Isaac says. "It just…"

"Makes me happy," I offer.

He nods. "Yes. It's like our brains are wired for it or something. Or maybe it's the nostalgia. It reminds me of my childhood and trading computer parts and *Star Trek* action figures."

After Isaac slips off belowdecks for a nap, I finish wrapping the rope around my creation, which is now a slightly lumpy white cone that stands roughly five feet tall.

The rungs of the ladder offer support for the courses of rope, but I need something else now. Luckily, I find a set of items that might work in the kitchen: metal skewers.

In the gentle sway of the boat, I insert them through the rope, lodging them in the vests.

The sun will rise soon, and I want to finish this before the others are up.

Working quickly, I string fishing line from the skewers and attach lures and pieces from the board games. Soon, the tokens from Monopoly are all dangling: the top hat, iron, battleship, race car, dog, wheelbarrow, shoe, and thimble. I add the pawns from the game Sorry! to fill in the holes.

On the kitchen counter, I cut a piece of cardboard into a star and wrap it in aluminum foil. Reaching up, I slide it over the end of the wooden handle that protrudes from the top.

Thirty minutes later, June emerges from belowdecks and stops to gawk at what I've made.

I rise from the couch and slip my hands in my pockets. "What do you think?"

"Alan," she breathes out, stepping closer to study it.

Rose trudges up the staircase next, head down, eyes still heavy with sleep. She brightens the moment she sees it.

"No way," she whispers.

She drifts closer, as if drawn to it like a magnet.

It isn't like any Christmas tree I've ever seen. It's improvised, composed of random things that were available. But it works, sort of like this group.

And it's doing the job I wanted it to do: reminding us of home, and the life waiting for us when we escape this labyrinth.

90

On Christmas day, I grill some fish I caught, and we eat lunch together in the salon. Holiday music plays over the Bluetooth speaker, and the ornaments hanging from my homemade Christmas tree bob up and down as the ship crests the waves.

The main thing on my mind is my daughter. Raleigh is five hours behind us. The sun has just risen there, and I wonder if Riley is up. I wonder if she's still staying at Meredith's house, if she woke this morning bounding out of her bedroom like she does every Christmas morning, beating a path to the Christmas tree to see what's waiting for her there.

I wonder if Meredith even put up a tree. I wouldn't blame her if she didn't. She's got enough on her plate this year.

Tree or not, I wonder if any gifts are waiting for Riley, and what they are, and most of all, I wonder if my daughter is thinking about me, and missing me as much as I'm missing her.

After lunch, I clear the plates and make coffee for the others, and we sit at the table and make small talk as if this is the most normal Christmas any of us has ever had.

We're three days away from Cape Town and taking possession of our new yacht, and another month away from our ultimate destination, which I hope is indeed the center of the Labyrinth.

Isaac has spent a lot of his time searching for satellite photos of the GPS coordinates. Every single one shows the same thing: nothing but open sea.

If we find something there—and answers—it'll be the best Christmas gift of my life.

In the meantime, Isaac announces (to my surprise) that he has managed to procure actual gifts for each of us.

"It's not as tasty as grilled fish," he says, rising from his chair. "But, like Alan's gift, mine is a taste of home."

He reaches into his laptop bag, draws out a stack of printer paper, and moves around the table, setting a few pages in front of each of us, leaning carefully like a waiter serving a fancy dinner.

The top page in my stack is a printed color photo of Riley in a gymnastics outfit, arms outstretched, a broad smile on her face, the carefree kind of expression that one almost only sees on a child. I've seen the picture before, on the social media page of the gymnastics company.

The next photo is more recent, from a few months ago, at Halloween. In it, I'm wearing the frizzy Bob Ross wig and a t-shirt that says #HappyAccidents. Riley stands beside me, dressed as Mal from *Descendants*. She has one arm wrapped around my waist, the other holding a bucket of candy that, if memory serves, was half full by this point in the night. To her left is a very attractive woman dressed as Lara Croft—my fellow teacher, neighbor, and, I guess, now girlfriend. In the Halloween photo, Meredith's eyes twinkle, but her smile is a little guarded.

I exhale deeply when I see the third photo. It's one I shared on my own social media: a picture of an ultrasound at one of the first OB/GYN appointments for Riley. Seeing it reminds me how happy I was that day—and back then. And how much I miss her.

I'm barely holding it together as I flip through the other pictures.

And I'm not the only one. As I look up, I realize a tear is rolling down June's cheek, and Rose's teeth are clenched, jaw muscles bulging.

"How did you get these?" June asks quietly, still looking down at her photos. "I'm not complaining," she adds quickly. "It's just…"

"Some are not exactly public," Isaac says, a little sheepishly.

"Right," June mumbles.

Isaac rocks his head side-to-side. "I may have engaged in some very mild hacking." He holds his hands up. "Nothing too invasive."

"Worth it," Rose whispers.

91

We reach Cape Town on the night of December 28th. It's mid-summer here, and a warm breeze blows across the four of us as we assemble on the aft deck. The harbor is buzzing with activity. Ships of all types are coming and going, and beyond, the city lights sparkle so bright it's almost overwhelming after so many dark nights at sea.

Overlooking Cape Town is Table Mountain. I've never seen anything like it. The range curves around the city like a giant stone hand capping it, about to push the buildings into the ocean. But the most striking feature is the flat top, as if the peaks have been sheared off. It's breathtaking, but tonight isn't about sightseeing.

We've got a boat to buy.

For security reasons, we've opted to take possession of our new yacht at sea rather than at a marina.

The rendezvous point is roughly three miles offshore, and I'm relieved to see the ship waiting for us there, its running lights reflecting across the water.

Isaac and I spent an hour hashing out how the hand-off would happen. Like the transfer in Wilmington, there is inherent danger here. We could be robbed, taken hostage and ransomed, or simply ripped off.

As such, our plan is to proceed slowly and cautiously.

From the pilothouse, I flash our infrared lights. The seller replies with the agreed-upon response code.

Unlike in Cape Verde, where we refueled, we'll stay radio-silent here.

Working as quickly as we can, Rose and I deploy the Zodiac and motor out, stopping halfway between the two yachts.

The broker untethers his own boat and cuts across the waves, slowing as he comes alongside us.

His name is Jacobus, and he is a broad-shouldered man with weathered skin and piercing blue eyes. From here, he appears unarmed (though Rose and I are both carrying handguns).

For a moment, we simply stare at each other across the gap between the boats rocking in the gentle waves, the outboard motors idling like a background soundtrack to this tense moment.

"The second payment?" he calls out in a crisp Afrikaner accent.

I turn and use my flashlight to give Isaac the signal.

The first installment was for twenty-five percent of the purchase price. This payment will deliver another twenty-five percent. The last half will be sent after I've toured the vessel and given Isaac the all clear.

A chime rings out from Jacobus's boat. Slowly, still eying me, he reaches a hand into the pocket of his raincoat and draws out his mobile phone.

He finally breaks eye contact long enough to tap the phone with his thumb a few times.

"Received," he grunts and shoves the phone back into his pocket.

"Stand by," I call to him and gun the Zodiac's motor, making for the new yacht.

My heart is racing as I tie up to the waiting ship and climb aboard, sidearm in hand.

The first time I saw our current yacht, it reminded me of a white, floating layer cake. This vessel feels completely different. It is an Arksen 85, and it reminds me of a modern luxury home, like one might see perched high above the Pacific Ocean somewhere on the west coast. Its lines are sleek and striking, its profile low and long.

The hull is solid aluminum and hasn't been painted, the faintly shining silver adding to the high-tech, modern aesthetic. The portholes are rectangular—not round—and the main deck and bridge are wrapped with glass on three sides.

On the aft deck, there's a nice-sized tender that's covered with a tarp. Holding my gun at the ready, I unfasten the heavy-duty canvas and lift it enough to shine a beam of light inside. It would be a good place to hide, but it's empty.

The door to the main deck is weathertight, and just inside, there are storage areas, a day head, and a staircase to the bridge. There's even a pocket door that separates this small lobby from the galley and salon—ensuring cold temps don't reach the living areas as someone enters.

Moving quickly, I climb the stairs and check the bridge. Like the Nordhavn, there are two helm chairs and a bank of screens. The Arksen has its own software system, and it's pretty slick.

Descending the main staircase, I check the salon and galley more thoroughly.

As promised, Jacobus has supplied us with food and several crates full of MREs. There's a backpack sitting on the dinette, and inside, I find twenty-four prepaid satellite phones. Also as promised.

Belowdecks, I find two crew cabins with bunk beds, two guest cabins, an owner's cabin, and lastly, a captain's cabin. Each one has an en suite bathroom—six in total. There's plenty of room for all of us. And then some.

Off the captain's bathroom, there's a battery closet full of lithium-ion batteries. This will come in handy if we're at anchor—we can power the ship without running the generator (and creating noise).

Past the battery compartment, beyond a water-tight door, is the engine room. The desalinator, tanks, and mechanical components appear immaculate. The ship can't be more than a few years old.

Like the Nordhavn 68, the Arksen 85 is purpose-built for extended ocean voyages, but thanks to the light-weight aluminum construction and some of the equipment in this room, she can travel seven thousand nautical miles without refueling (and she is fully loaded with fuel). As requested, we also have two fuel bladders on the aft deck, each filled with two hundred and fifty gallons of diesel.

The Arksen is also capable of operating in more extreme conditions than the Nordhavn. She's not technically an icebreaker, but her hull allows her to travel much farther north than similar-sized motor yachts. We could even beach her for repairs if we had to.

The final thing I check is the AIS, or Automatic Identification System. As with the Nordhavn, we need to make sure this ship's system is not active.

We requested that Jacobus disable the Arksen's AIS when the ship was docked in port (an AIS going dark out in South African waters would most likely trigger search and rescue operations—and unwanted attention). Even an AIS malfunction in port would invite an inquiry, but Jacobus assured us he would log the event with the harbormaster as an antenna fault.

On the bridge, in the electronics cabinet under the dash, I spot the device. Shining my flashlight in for a closer look, I spot the red and black DC power leads hanging loose. Very clever. I would've flipped the breaker and pulled the inline fuse, but disconnecting the power makes it look more accidental, as though it might have shaken loose during rough seas.

Either way, the seller has delivered everything we asked for.

Back on the aft deck, I click my flashlight, signaling Isaac to make the final payment.

We considered several options for the Nordhavn: selling it, docking it in a marina, scuttling it, or hiding it.

Our biggest concern is Amersa discovering the ship and in turn getting a lead on us.

I don't like it—for several reasons—but we've decided to scuttle her.

We don't dare do that near Cape Town, or in the shipping lanes around it.

Using the autopilot, and staying in touch via handheld radios,

Isaac and June pilot the Arksen and Rose and I follow in the Nordhavn.

Under the cover of night, we sail southwest, diagonally away from Cape Town, until we've cleared Africa's continental shelf and the depth below us plummets.

There are no vessels visible to the naked eye out here, but we're still within range of merchant-ship radar. For the moment, however, we've caught a break: I don't see anything out there.

Working methodically, I tie the compartment doors open so water will flow between them, disable the bilge pumps, and open the through-hulls and seacocks. Water pours into the ship as I climb the stairs and take my last walk across the aft deck.

Rose is waiting in the Zodiac, eyes tired and nervous as I step on.

At the Arksen, we climb aboard, and I sink the Zodiac.

From the aft deck, under the soft glow of the moon, the four of us watch the ship that carried us so far and witnessed so much slowly slip into the Atlantic.

92

The following day, at sunset, we pass Cape Agulhas, the southernmost geographic point in Africa and the dividing line between the Atlantic and Indian oceans.

I'm sitting at one of the helm stations, still trying to wrap my head around how everything works, when I hear footsteps on the main staircase.

I turn and find Isaac trudging toward me, looking sleepy, a laptop tucked under one arm.

After being up all day yesterday and all night, he finally got some rest this morning.

"What do you think of the new boat?" he asks, stifling a yawn as he slips into the other helm chair.

"It's impressive." I motion to the four screens. "It's like… sailing an iPhone or something. Everything's digital."

He gives a tired smile. "Yeah. I was thinking, like, IKEA."

"IKEA?"

"That's the vibe I get. Super Scandinavian. Every square inch used to the fullest."

He yawns again, but seems more awake by the second. "That's what I keep thinking: I'm on a floating IKEA showroom."

He glances around. "At the same time, it's weirdly similar to the Nordhavn. The same but different. Like…"

"The second quest. In Zelda."

He nods. "That's the other thing I was thinking."

I shrug. "Only so many ways to make yachts like this. Cabins go below. Living space on the main deck. Bridge above."

"Except the pilothouse on the Nordhavn had a captain's bunk. Not so here."

"True. And Arksen calls this a bridge."

"Not a pilothouse?"

"Right. Bridge or wheelhouse—that's common."

"I like bridge."

I raise my eyebrows, surprised he has an opinion.

"They call it a bridge on *Star Trek*."

Isaac motions to the bank of screens (which reminds *me* of *Star Trek*). "Anything I should know?"

"We'll do a more thorough training in the morning. In the meantime, just... wake me up if anything goes wrong."

On the night of New Year's Eve, we're sailing past East London, South Africa, when the clock strikes midnight. Rockets launch from the harbor front, the beach, and the tops of downtown buildings, painting the sky in pink and blue and orange.

When the fireworks are over and East London's city lights are fading in the night, I descend belowdecks to the captain's cabin, where I sit upright on the bed and dial a number on one of the prepaid phones.

Meredith answers on the second ring, her voice hesitant. "Hello?"

Raleigh is six hours behind us, so it's almost seven at night there. Around dinner time, and soon, bedtime for Riley. Assuming she still lives there.

"You want to talk to her?" Meredith asks, voice neutral.

"Yeah," I breathe out, fidgeting on the bed.

Riley's greeting is half-yelling the word: "*Dad!*" I can't tell if she's excited or angry. Or both.

I ask her about school and how she's doing, and each time she bats the questions away like an attempted hug in front of her friends at school.

She only wants to know about one thing: when I'm coming home.

I tell her it's going to be a while, and she presses the issue.

"A week?"

"A lot longer."

"A year?"

"I don't know, sweetie."

"Why?"

"Listen. Sometimes with work, you just don't know how long things are going to take. It's how it is."

"But why is it like that?"

Times like this, I wish she weren't so smart. Or persistent. But I'm still glad she is.

"I'm doing the best I can, kiddo. Believe me. You know if I had my way in the world, I would come home right now and be with you and celebrate New Year's with you and Meredith."

I almost add that we will be celebrating New Year's together next year, but I don't want to make a promise—a promise that big—that I can't keep.

I don't get much more from Riley on the phone. I can tell she's a little hurt and sulking, and I can't exactly blame her.

But hearing her voice was worth it. And I think it's important that she knows I'm trying my best to get back to her.

She hands the phone back to Meredith, who tells me to hold on as she paces through her home, doors closing behind her.

There's a slight echo when she speaks again, as though she's in a small room (my best guess is the toilet compartment in the primary bathroom).

She starts with an update on Riley. The report is about the same as last time: she's scared and confused, and it's showing a bit at school.

And then, like my daughter, Meredith, too, asks when I'll be back.

"Best guess... sometime in the spring."

"*Spring?* Are you serious?"

"I'm doing the best I can."

Meredith exhales heavily, and when she speaks again, the anger has left her voice. "It's... really tough, Alan. The waiting, and not knowing... and worrying."

"I know. I'm sorry."

The line is silent long enough for me to take the phone from my face to see if the call is still connected. She's still there.

"What can you tell me?" she asks, voice flat.

"I can tell you this much for sure: I didn't choose this. It chose me. And I'm doing the best I can."

93

One night after dinner, with Madagascar passing on our left and Mozambique to the right, the four of us are sitting in the salon around the banquette table, playing a game of Scrabble, when June asks us what the most surprising thing has been in our lives.

This is a very June thing to do: these deeply revealing, open-ended questions.

It's a team-building exercise, but I also think the neuroscientist and mother in her is worried about our mental health. She's using this as an opportunity to get clues about our state of mind.

As she often does during these group sharing moments, June goes first.

"For me, the most surprising thing about my life, by far, is how I met my husband."

I expect her to continue, but she stops there. All three of us look up from our wooden tiles. June simply shrugs. "That's all I'm saying for now. I'll give you the rest on the way home."

Waves crash on the boat, and music plays from the speaker. I wonder if this was part of June's plan: saving the rest of the story for the trip back, giving us something to look forward to. And subtly infusing us with confidence that we will be going home, that it's only a matter of time.

"Actually," I tell the group, "it's sort of the same for me. The most surprising thing in my life involves meeting my wife. As you all know, she was the physical therapist assigned to me after I lost my leg. That was the darkest time in my life. I was… a mess. But meeting her was the best thing that ever happened to me."

Rose goes next.

"The most surprising thing about my life... is something I learned the hard way. And it's this: life becomes easier—a lot easier—when you stay away from people who are bad for you."

She glances over at me. "For me, it was hard to see how bad of an influence certain people were because I had been around them for so long. They were just part of my life. Until they weren't—because someone risked their own skin to help me."

She takes a sip of water and eyes the letter tiles only she can see.

"Growing up, my mom had a few favorite sayings. There was 'Your habits determine your future.' Bet I heard that a million times. That was her habit: dispensing wisdom."

Rose smiles. "Her other favorite was 'Show me who your friends are, and I'll tell you who you are.'"

She picks four wooden blocks up one by one and places them on the board. "It's funny how we forget the things we knew as kids."

Since June asked the question, Isaac has been studying the words on the Scrabble board.

"For me, the most surprising thing in my life is happening right now."

He leans back against the banquette. "For two reasons. One is that this time on this boat has been the most quiet I've ever experienced."

Rose squints at him.

"It's the least I've ever heard the ringing," Isaac adds. "Like my whole life, there was this alarm in my head. And it stopped going off right after we stepped on the boat."

With a finger, he pushes his tiles together. "The other surprise is that this—*this group, the numbers*, it's been the best part of my life. I wouldn't trade it. I know that sounds crazy... but you have to understand, the ringing has dictated my entire life. It has determined what I could do. It's why I couldn't go to school or have a normal life, why I never made many friends or had hobbies. But since I saw the numbers, for the first time, I felt like I was part of something, like I had a purpose. For the first time, I've felt like I actually matter."

94

Seven days from the coordinates, at the end of my shift, Isaac climbs the stairs to the bridge and plops down in the other helm chair.

Without looking over, he hands me a tablet that displays a news article.

"What's this?" I ask as I read the headline: *The Great Malaise: How & Why Humans Disappeared from Work… and Soon, Maybe the World*.

"A small indication of what's happening at home," Isaac says.

The article begins with the lines:

Does any of this sound familiar?

Co-workers using up their sick days.

Slow email replies that feel phoned-in.

Meandering meetings with distracted colleagues.

Stressed-out managers.

If you said yes to any of these—or all of these—it means… you're going through the same thing as the rest of us (note to my editor: I'm talking about everyone else—not me, not at all! I just work here, and I really, really want to keep working here :).

Welcome to the Great Malaise. It's sort of like the Great Resignation a few years ago, except without the quitting part. That's right, the whole gang's still here, we're just not getting that much done (if we show up at all).

What gives?

Is it an epidemic of burnout?

Layoff anxiety?

Is everyone just copying-and-pasting AI responses now?

Maybe the Labyrinth flu?

The heading for the next section is: (Weirdly Good News): This is Nothing New

The section is filled with real facts and sources. The ones that jump out at me are:

For years, workplace productivity has been declining around the world.

Between mid-2021 and mid-2023, US worker productivity fell by 2%—one of the most significant drops in recent decades.

In the Eurozone, labor productivity has declined three years in a row, a streak not seen since World War II.

Worker output in the UK shrank 0.6% year-over-year in 2023.

That same year, the UK's employee absence rate hit 4%, its highest level in a decade.

Swedish workers took an average 11.4 sick days in 2022, nearly double the rate in 2010.

In the US, mental health-related leaves of absence surged 33% in 2023 alone.

Such leaves have skyrocketed 300% since 2017.

A 2024 poll by the Society for Human Resource Management found that 44% of US employees said they feel burned out at work, 45% feel "emotionally drained," and over half feel "used up" by the end of each day.

Employee engagement is near its lowest point in 11 years; only about 30% of American workers reported being "fully engaged" at work as of late 2023.

The journalist's next section is titled, It's Not Just Work..., and it details declining birth rates in developed nations.

In the United States, the General Fertility Rate fell to a historic low in 2023. That year, only 3.6 million babies were born, far below the replacement level needed to sustain the population.

The UK just hit its own record low: a 1.44 total fertility rate in England and Wales, the lowest since record-keeping began. The nation now has more deaths than births.

Continental Europe is in the same boat. The OECD's 2024 Society at a Glance report shows the average fertility across developed countries is about 1.5 children per woman—less than half the rate it was 60 years ago. Italy and Spain, in particular, have seen rates plummet.

In Asia, South Korea's birth rate plunged to 0.7 in 2023.

Australia saw its birth rate fall 4.6% in 2023 to the lowest rate ever recorded.

In the final section of the article, the author opens with a simple question:

What gives?

Is it a crisis of meaning?

A generational shift in attitudes about work?

Or—to paraphrase my favorite show—are we just not that into it anymore?

When I set out to write this article, I was trying to answer two questions.

First, is the Great Malaise a new phenomenon?

Answers: Nope. Not even close.

And we have the receipts: years of data that confirm increasing absenteeism and disengagement and declining worker productivity—in an age where technology should be making us more productive.

To top it off, developed nations are having less children, so the consequences of less productive workers are going to be felt even more harshly as populations shrink.

My second question is: Why does it feel worse now?

Is it me?

Too much main character energy from yours truly?

Or am I just at that age when I'm more aware of it all?

I couldn't find that much data on the rate of change in the trends I identified, but as a journalist, sometimes you have to trust your instincts—and gather sources.

So I did. From friends and family.

And yes, the Great Malaise has found a new gear.

What's driving it?

The thing is, for myself—and everyone I've talked to—only one thing has changed about our day-to-day life.

For me, after work (or on my lunch break), I used to be stretched out on my bed, pajamas on, for a Netflix and chill binge. Depending on the show, I might be scrolling on my phone. Or, depending on my status, swiping.

Or out with friends, doing some real-life swiping in a noisy watering hole.

The change?

I've canceled my streaming services.

My social media profiles are borderline dormant, as if I'm on an extended vacation.

And I sort of have been.

I still meet up with friends after work. But we've swapped swanky dinners and bars and clubs for a quick bite and Labyrinth sessions.

Because it's the most exciting thing in my life right now—not work (editor, please, please tell me you've stopped reading by now; I mean, you told me you're burned out too—wait, I never reveal sources; if you're reading, edit this out).

Don't get me wrong, I still show up at work and get it done (ok, I may have added that for the editor, but don't judge me; also, you're reading the proof that I'm still turning in articles).

What's changed is that these days, I sort of live for that moment I slip on the suit and headset and feel my feet and body subtly lift off that padded Labyrinth floor and I return to that hike in the Andes or the spy mission I did in Hong Kong last week or the romance RPG that was just introduced—you know the one, the 18+ module you pay up for and can add a real-life person to (hey, I am totally doing that for research).

I was burned out and overwhelmed before. I guess I am now.

The difference?

These days, I feel a little spark.

But it's not for work. Or starting a family.

I'm working for the next Labyrinth session. And I don't think I'm alone.

When I hand the tablet back to Isaac, he says the one word I'm thinking, the name of the study Amersa did: CORTEX.

He stares out at the sunrise on the horizon. "When I was a kid, everyone was still worried about nuclear armageddon. Mutually assured destruction."

"Right."

"And then that passed, and it was other stuff. Like asteroids hitting Earth. They even made two films about it."

"I believe you're referring to *Deep Impact* and *Armageddon*. Morgan Freeman. Tea Leoni. Bruce Willis. Ben Affleck. And associated casts."

"You are correct."

"Excellent films."

"They are, Alan. And then it was on to other stuff. We had Patrick Dempsey selling an illegal monkey in a cage."

"A monkey shot with a tranq dart by Cuba Gooding Jr. in a backyard while Dustin Hoffman supervised."

"That's the one."

"Also, an exemplary achievement in motion picture making."

"End of an era, my friend."

Isaac stuffs the tablet in his backpack. "But what I always worried about growing up was none of those things. It was an event no one talked about. No movies made on the subject."

I raise my eyebrows, waiting.

"I always wondered what would happen to the world when someone created something better than real life, and it was readily available, and you could just go there and sort of maintain your real life."

"Yeah."

"It would be like a soft apocalypse. No big bang, no mushroom clouds or volcanic eruption in Los Angeles—"

"Tommy Lee Jones and Anne Heche."

Isaac eyes me. "I feel seen."

"I see you."

"But what if this is the beginning of what June was talking about after reading CORTEX? What if the world ends not with a bang, not with a whimper, but with everyone simply quietly quitting reality because it sucks and they have a better option?"

He pushes out of the helm chair and slings the backpack on his shoulder.

"There is, however, some good news."

"Yeah?"

"Apparently, this Great Malaise is causing a lot of market volatility."

"How is that good news?"

"According to Harold, market swings are good for trading profits. Daedalus Ltd. is racking up. Like major money."

"What do you think it's for?"

"No idea, Alan. But it means something."

95

The night we reach the coordinates, everyone gathers on the bridge, crowded around the helm station, watching in the dim light of a waxing crescent moon.

When we're twenty nautical miles away, I raise the 7x50 binoculars and scan in the direction of our destination.

I haven't said this to the group, but I've assumed—since we found these new coordinates—that it's a ship waiting for us there.

If so, and its lights are on, we may be able to see it with the binoculars, even in the darkness.

But I don't see a thing.

I try to keep my voice neutral as I tell the others.

An hour later, I scan with the binoculars again.

Still nothing out there.

If it's a ship, maybe its lights are off.

Or maybe it's a buoy, one with a message for us.

Or perhaps when we reach the coordinates, the ringing will start again.

I keep scanning, and when we're five nautical miles away, I catch my first glimpse of what's at those coordinates.

It sits there, still and quiet, alone in the middle of the Indian Ocean, dark and towering.

I should have known, should have guessed this is what it was.

Its legs are massive, decks too, with cranes sticking out like a sea monster's metal arms.

I hand the binoculars to Isaac.

June and Rose both eye me, silently demanding an update.

"It's an oil rig."

After cutting the Arksen's engines, we launch the drone and sit at the U-shaped dinette on the bridge, watching the telemetry on Isaac's laptop.

Isaac has another window open with the numbers website. He's been checking it throughout the voyage for changes, and now he refreshes the pages constantly. But it's the same: a site dedicated to giving out free Labyrinth sessions.

On the laptop screen, the rig comes into view. Up close, I realize the structure is dirty and looks abandoned, as if it was well-used and towed here and left waiting before it's scrapped by a breaker.

In Amersa's Labyrinth, there was smoke coming out of the building rising from the water. Smoke may have once billowed from the top of this oil rig, but it doesn't now. The entire structure is dormant. The crane arms are unmoving. No one is in sight.

Isaac flies the drone around the rig several times, moving lower with each pass. Still, we don't see a soul.

"What do we do?" he asks, moving the drone to a stationary position above the massive drilling platform.

"We need to board," I reply, scooting free of the booth.

"Should we wait for morning?" Rose asks, her gaze still on the drone footage of the rig.

"No," I say quietly. "Waiting gives them time to prepare for us."

"That assumes they know we're here," June says. "We cut the lights... what? Twenty miles out?"

"True. But they would have seen us on radar long before that."

"Oh," June says, nodding slowly. I can tell she's nervous. We all are.

Isaac asks if he should bring the drone back.

"No. Leave it in the air. You can provide support."

"Are we using the radios?" he asks.

"Too risky. And loud. They could be overheard during the boarding. We'll use the sat burners on a group call with headphones."

Standing, speaking slowly, I lay out the plan. Isaac and June will stay on the boat and watch via the drone, keeping in touch over the open phone call.

Rose and I will take the tender and board and search the rig.

"They'll hear the outboard motor as we approach," I tell the group, pacing now. "The key will be speed and focus once we step onto that platform. It's a large rig, with a thousand places to hide and just as many to set a trap. Or a bomb."

A silence stretches out, and when Isaac speaks, his voice is strained. "What if—" he squints, grasping for words. "You know…"

"We don't come back?" Rose says.

"Right," Isaac says quietly.

"It's a good question," I say evenly. "In that event, you should immediately sail south, at top speed. Hug the coastline."

"Why?" June asks.

"Safety. More eyeballs on the ship, plus you'll be within easier reach of the Indian Coast Guard and Navy in case you're pursued."

"Where should we go?"

"Chennai is your best bet. It's close by and has a large port. It's the sixth largest city in India."

"What do we do there?"

"On the way, you should contact Harold and hire some private security. First, secure yourselves and the boat."

"And then?" June asks.

"Then…" I cut my eyes to Rose. "We'd obviously appreciate it if you assigned your newly hired private military contractors to come back for us."

"We will," Isaac says. "Count on it."

96

On the aft deck, I put my armor on and stuff my pockets full of supplies: extra magazines, first aid, and flashbangs.

Beside me, Rose dons her own body armor. The dim moonlight casts her face in shadow, but for a second, I see the same scared expression I saw the first time I met her, in that first-floor apartment in Raleigh.

And then, as she straps the armor tight, the fear fades as if a gust of wind were blowing it away. She stares at me with steely eyes.

Reaching up to my ear, I press the earbud in tighter and whisper, "Comms check."

Inside the salon, Isaac and June are standing at a tinted window, watching us.

"I copy," Isaac says over the open phone line.

"Me too," June adds.

I've Velcroed the pre-paid smart satphone to my forearm, and glancing down, I tap to open the drone app and connect using the instructions Isaac gave me. The drone's live feed fills the screen, showing the rig clearly in night-vision green.

"I've got drone footage."

Beside me, Rose peers down at her own phone. "Same."

Isaac opens the door, and he and June join us on the open deck, watching as Rose and I use the boom to lower the tender into the water.

When Rose is aboard, I push away from the Arksen's silver aluminum hull, and the tender drifts quietly on the calm, glassy ocean.

Isaac holds a hand up, a silent farewell.

I crank the outboard and accelerate, propelling the tender across dark waves. The rig is five nautical miles away, black against black, looming.

On the water, the motor screams, and wind rips across us. Time seems to stand still, like I'm in the eye of the storm, and it has stopped to take a breath before raging.

With each passing minute, my eyes adjust to the dark moonlight, and I see the rig more clearly.

It rests on four massive columns, legs extending down into the ocean.

When we're half a nautical mile away, a second drone feed appears on the app—another launch from the Arksen. We didn't discuss this, but it's a good idea on Isaac's part: sending a drone with a fresh battery to capture a second point of view.

As we approach the rig, Rose shifts to the back and begins driving the boat. I scoot forward, gun drawn, scanning the structure. At the first sign of trouble, she'll turn back.

Rose steers us in a wide, cautious circle around the rig's base. The pontoons are crusted thick with barnacles and algae. A ladder is welded to one of the rear support columns. I point to it, and Rose throttles down, lining us up before cutting the engine completely.

We drift toward the rig, the derelict metal structure creaking and groaning as if it's snoring in the night.

I'm about to tell Isaac and June we're boarding, but I remember the drones. Looking down at the phone screen, I see our tender approaching the rig on one of the live feeds. They see us.

When the tender is close enough, I grab the rusted ladder attached to the side of the cylindrical column and pull on it, testing its strength.

Like the rig above, it creaks but holds. After tethering us, I climb.

I plant my good leg first, and it burns from the weight of the bulletproof plates in the body armor and the pack on my back.

I ignore the pain. I keep my gaze upward, at the ladder and the opening to the deck, half-expecting a head to peek out and shots to rain down.

I grip the rungs with my gloves and push up with my legs, and it's only rust flakes that drift down—red, dusty clouds that make me cough twice before I reach the threshold.

My handgun leading the way, I pop up and scan in all directions on the open deck.

The platform is about fifteen feet wide, littered with debris. Rusted bolts and abandoned cables are scattered everywhere. All the hatches leading into the rig's interior are closed.

On the landing, we crouch, listening. I hear only the waves breaking on the columns below and the wind whipping around the giant structure.

Rose and I make a single circuit around the entire platform, searching for an open door or window and trying the handles and wheels.

Everything is locked. Whoever left the rig here buttoned it up tight.

Rose taps the end of her gun on one of the windows, silently suggesting we break it.

I shake my head. For a moment I study the drone feeds. I'm about to ask Isaac to do a closer fly around to check for open doors when a thought occurs to me.

I'm remembering Gerald from Amersa's Labyrinth, and the key he gave me, and using it at the tower in the VR Labyrinth.

Reaching in my pocket, I draw out the bulky key I got that night so many months ago, when I lost time.

At the closest door, I slide it into the lock and turn.

It clicks, and I depress the handle and pull the door open.

Rose is looking at me with bulging eyes, but there's no time to discuss.

I lead the way, switching my flashlight on at the threshold. The corridor is narrow. The bulkheads are corroded and streaked with rust. Safety signs hang limp. The air inside is stale, thick with the odors of oil, mold, and salt. It smells like an engine room abandoned for decades, with just a tinge of something sour, faintly rotten.

The first compartments are storage rooms, filled with forgotten equipment, empty crates, rust-stained barrels, and coils of brittle hoses.

We clear the deck quickly, silently. Metal creaks under our steps, but I don't hear anyone else.

In the rig's galley, we find metal tables bolted firmly to the floor, and benches askew. Dust lies thick over everything. Empty ration tins litter the sink, rusted through. Someone left a faded message scrawled on the wall. I study it, expecting to see the numbers—maybe hoping to—but the characters are unreadable, wiped away by time or weather.

We move onward, climbing higher, to the rig's control room.

The room is compact and dark. The windows are crusted with salt. The consoles have been stripped. The screens and keyboards have been removed, leaving the wires exposed like roots of a tree carried away by the wind.

On the floor, a cracked coffee mug lies abandoned.

I move to the far wall, positioning my body so I can see through both the door and the hazy windows.

I keep my voice low. "Watch, this is rover, do you copy?"

"We copy," Isaac says through my earbud.

"Initial sweep clear. Rig appears deserted."

Someone exhales over the open phone line, the sound like a breeze rolling through.

"Copy," Isaac says. "What now?"

"We're going to do a more thorough search. Stand by, watch."

97

Together, Rose and I methodically move through the rig's upper levels.

The living quarters are empty. The bunks are filled with sagging, mildewed mattresses.

The infirmary has been mostly picked clean, cabinets open, a rolling metal tray overturned.

The radio room has been raided, too. The engine and mechanical spaces are cold and quiet and filled with pungent odors.

This place has been abandoned for a long time.

It has a creepy feel, like a floating post-apocalyptic city.

Standing in the dead engine room, I have some sense of what Isaac felt in Africa. Deep disappointment, the weight of having led us to a dead end. When I saw the rig with the binoculars, I just knew we had found it, that we'd find answers here.

But it's nothing but a ruin, sitting in the middle of the ocean, just like that building in Amersa's Labyrinth.

Are we too late?

Did someone else get here before us?

Or am I missing it? Is there another clue here?

I'm disappointed, but I'm not about to give up.

Bounding back through a narrow corridor, Rose behind me, I say over the phone line, "Watch, rig is empty. We're coming back to get you. Prepare the boat."

★

We anchor the Arksen and load supplies on the tender—food, blankets, and everything we need to live aboard the rig for a while.

Our plan is simple: we're going to search every inch of the facility. Isaac's hoping to find a computer or a data storage drive, anything that might offer clues about where the massive drilling platform has been or who owns it.

The tender sits lower in the water under the weight of the full group.

As we approach the dark rig, I feel a hand on my shoulder, gently squeezing.

I glance back and see Rose staring at me. There's no question in her expression, nothing she wants to say except, I'm behind you. Glancing around, I realize Isaac's eyes are fixed on me. June too.

The tender crests the shallow waves, and on approach, Rose once again silences the outboard, and I climb the creaking, rusty ladder.

At the top, I tie a rope off and drop it, and call down for them to attach the bundles for me to pull up.

For the first time since we spotted the abandoned oil rig, my fellow group members ignore me.

Rose climbs the ladder, the rope flapping next to her. Then June.

Below, in the tender, Isaac ties the rope to a duffel bag.

On the platform, Rose leads me away, the wind whipping her hair. June begins pulling on the rope, lifting the supplies.

"We've got this," Rose says, wind whipping her hair.

"I've only got one leg, but I've got two arms. I can help."

"You can. But you've done enough heavy lifting for one night. We've got this."

We store the supplies in the galley, and together, we tour the living quarters, each of us staking out a bunk.

We're all exhausted from the night's exertion and the adrenaline leaving our bodies.

But Isaac's tank seems to be the most full, and he insists on searching the control room.

So we all go, four flashlight beams carving into the dusty tomb as he wanders around the room, inspecting the wires.

Behind me, in the narrow metal corridor, I hear a jingle, like someone reached in their pocket and drew out a handful of quarters and tossed them down the hall.

I spin on my heel and step out and shine my flashlight into the corridor.

It's empty.

Behind me, June's voice echoes in the control room. "I heard it too. Ringing."

I redirect my beam to her face. She opens her mouth and speaks again, but I can't hear the words.

All I hear is *clang, clang, clang*. Like quarters in the can now. And they're going faster, the clanging ramping faster than I've ever heard it.

A flashlight blinds me.

I squint, raising my left arm to block the light. Stepping left, I see Rose at the other end.

Her mouth is moving too, but I can't hear her either.

Only:

Clang.

Clang.

Clang.

This ringing is like a storm consuming reality itself.

Rose steps forward, speaking faster, words drowned out by the *clang, clang, clang*.

I back away.

I fight to focus, but the ringing grows louder, a fog clouding my mind.

I feel my body begin to shake, as if the floor beneath me is rattling, as if the rig itself is falling into the sea.

I close my eyes and feel the breath leave my nose. I know we have seconds left to get out of here. I need to move.

Opening my eyes, I move my flashlight around the room like a lighthouse carving in the night.

I see June first.

She's on the floor, backed against the wall, knees to her chest, arms around them, head down, rocking back and forth.

I'll have to carry her.

I keep going.

Rose is next. In the leading edge of my flashlight's beam, I see her holding her own light, walking across the control room toward me, gun at her side.

Isaac stands a few feet from her. His back is turned to me, and he's leaning forward, peering through the control room's dirty windows, as if he's spotted something on the horizon.

I step toward him and call his name, though I can't hear my own words.

Slowly, he turns, as if he's heard me, as if just now realizing I was here, a look of surprise on his face.

By infinitesimal degrees, his lips curl into a smile.

The ringing crashes through the last barrier in my mind.

And the world goes black.

98

When I wake up, I'm lying on the bottom bunk. The room is dark and dank, the air moldy and putrid.

I'm still on the rig. Or someplace similar.

And I'm wearing the same clothes I boarded in. My prosthetic lies on the metal floor just out of reach.

I roll over, grabbing for it with a shaky arm.

I'm weak, and my brain is foggy, as if I've been drugged. It feels like waking in that military hospital, after the amputation surgery.

My hand falls short, landing on the damp metal floor. I scoot out of the bunk and pull the artificial limb closer, and move to strap it on.

My eyes are adjusting to the darkness now. Sitting on the edge of the stained, thin mattress, I stare at my stump. It's... withered.

I've lost weight. A lot of weight.

Running my hands up my body, I feel my ribs, then the beard on my face. Is it a week's worth of growth? More?

With the prosthetic attached, I hobble to the closed hatch, panting. The only light in the room comes from a small, dirty porthole and faint moonlight filtering in.

Beside the bunks is a desk and a mirror above.

I barely recognize the man staring back at me. He's gaunt, with sunken cheeks and eyes and disheveled hair.

I glance around the room and spot a pile of MRE cartons, opened and eaten. I realize then how hungry I am. But there aren't any uneaten meals. And I need to find the others and get out of here.

Thankfully, my cane is leaning against the bulkhead by the hatch. My flashlight and gun sit on the desk. I grab all three and venture out into the corridor.

I start to call out for Isaac, June, and Rose, but think better of it. For now, I might have the element of surprise, which could come in handy.

I search the rest of the living quarters, and in the adjacent bunkroom, I find Rose. She's stretched out on a bottom mattress, eyes closed, hair matted, her face even more sunken than mine (my dad bod had more excess pounds to lose than hers).

Gently, I grasp her shoulders and shake her. "Rose. Rose, come on, wake up."

Her head turns, and she mumbles something I can't make out.

I shake her harder, pulling her out of the bunk. "Rose. Come on. We have to get out of here."

Her eyelids crack open, but her gaze is unfocused, as if she can't see me.

I try for a few more minutes before giving up.

"I'll come back," I whisper as I clank out of the bunkroom, cane digging into the metal floor.

There was a pile of empty MRE cartons in Rose's room, similar to mine, but I don't find any food in the galley or mess hall—or anything else for that matter. The rig's dining area looks the same as it did when we boarded: dusty and deserted.

I climb the stairs with my gun drawn, listening, but I only hear the wind outside and the gentle lapping of waves on the rig's four massive columns.

I cut the flashlight off before reaching the stair landing and leave my cane on a tread. I creep toward the control room, gun leading the way. Just outside the hatch, I hear a faint tapping noise, like raindrops on a windowsill.

Moving quickly, I step across the threshold. Moonlight shines through the windows. Isaac sits at the closest desk, his back to me, hunched over his glowing laptop.

It's plugged into a portable power station that we brought aboard. A thicker cable runs from it up to the ceiling, through an open tile. It connects to the solar panels, which someone has obviously hooked up.

At the station in front of Isaac, June sits with her back to me. She's using Isaac's backup laptop.

Quietly, I step closer to Isaac. His screen has a black background with white text. The characters are incredibly small, almost impossible to read. And I don't recognize the language. It's like… computer code, but in a foreign language with strange characters.

He's typing furiously—that's the tapping I heard.

June's screen has the same black background and white text in a strange language. She, too, is typing nonstop.

Bending closer to Isaac, I whisper his name.

He doesn't move.

Still gripping my gun in my right hand, I grip his shoulder with my left. He doesn't turn.

"Isaac," I whisper, pulling at his shoulder, urging him to turn.

He fidgets, twisting his shoulder to try to shrug me off.

I step forward, rounding the desk, facing him. His eyeballs are white pupils—and his mouth hangs slightly open.

"Isaac," I call out, louder. But he doesn't flinch. He can't hear me.

I try June, but she doesn't respond either. Her eyes also show only the whites.

What happened to them?

Like the bunkrooms, there's a pile of eaten MREs in the corner. But there's no sign of what happened here.

A chime rings in my ears, a gentle ringing, like a doorbell.

It calls again, a little faster this time.

I step out in the corridor and it rings again, like someone is holding a bell only I can hear and rattling it to guide me through the rig.

On instinct, I know where it's coming from.

I descend the stairs, grabbing my cane on the way. The ringing fades, but I keep clanging down the damp, dark hallway until I reach a doorway that says Infirmary.

There's no therapy room on this rig. This is the closest thing.

I pull the door open, swinging it forcefully into the wall with a bang.

The ringing starts then, but it's very faint, and for a second, I have to concentrate to make sure I'm actually hearing it. It doesn't get louder, just a steady clanging.

The med bay is just as it was before: looted and in disarray. We brought our medical supplies from the boat and they sit on one of the counters. There's one other change as well.

At an alcove in the corner, a figure sits in a chair, hunched over a desk.

Slowly, she sets her pen down and turns and looks at me.

99

The figure rises from the chair and runs her hands down her blue scrubs, smoothing them out.

Like in Amersa's Labyrinth, in the tower in the sea, I am staring at a replica of my deceased wife. She's the age she was when we first met, on my first day of physical therapy.

She smiles at me, and her tone is playful. "Hey, sleepyhead. Thought you were never going to get up."

My voice is filled with rage. "What is this? Who are you? *What* are you?"

She—or it—makes a show of drawing in a deep breath, wincing theatrically as if I'm being totally unreasonable. "I think," she says slowly, "maybe you're not ready for that shocker just yet, Alan."

"Well, tell me anyway—"

She holds up a finger, "Also, hate to be a nag but I've put two things on your 'Honey, do' list, and I kinda need 'em done pronto, Mister."

"What things?"

"I think you saw the empty MREs. Need you to do a grocery run. *But*, before that, we have an itty-bitty home security issue to deal with."

I cock my head, waiting.

"We've got guests," she says. "Uninvited."

"Who?"

"Not super important. Just your garden variety Indian Ocean pirates. They've spotted the rig. Just launched a tender. They'll board and ransack the place—and maybe, just maybe take hostages." She raises her eyebrows. "Can't have that."

She nods, expression overly serious. "We've got work to do."

"What work? Are you talking about Isaac and June?"

"Yep. But let's stay focused, Alan. Pirates. Tender. On their way. It's called a 'Honey, do' list for a reason. Because, Honey, I need you to do your duty. I figure they'll be at the ladder in two minutes."

Turning, leaning on my cane, I bound out of the infirmary and down the corridor. The exterior hatch stands open, the wind raking across it in a low whistle. On the open deck, I realize the moon is full above me. It was a waxing crescent moon when we boarded. So we've been here... almost two weeks?

The realization is jarring, and I have to fight to focus. My body is weak, and my brain is still foggy.

Looking out at the water, I don't see a tender.

Was she lying? Just trying to draw me out here?

But somewhere in the distance, I hear a low buzzing, the unmistakable rattle of an outboard motor.

My feet pound the metal deck as I round the platform until I spot a ship in the distance, what looks like a fishing trawler with only its running lights on.

They've launched a small Zodiac with four people aboard. They're wearing fishing jackets and hats, and automatic rifles sit at their sides.

I back away from the railing, ensuring their shots will hit the deck, not me, and point my gun at the moon and fire a single shot.

The tender's motor screams, as if I had struck it, but they don't return fire. The outboard revs, and I hear the boat cutting across the waves.

Stepping carefully, I peer over the railing. They've turned around.

I don't dare linger on the open deck. They might have a rifle with a scope, and it might be trained on me now.

Back inside the rig, I find a small office with a porthole with a view of the ship, and I stand a few feet back from it, watching as the vessel lurches forward and moves away.

*

Back in the infirmary, the creature—or whatever it is—sits in the rolling chair, an elbow propped on the desk.

"Shots fired!" she says playfully. "Or should I say, shot across the bow. Either way, an exemplary de-escalation tactic, Alan. Knew you were a good choice for this."

"Choice for what? What is *this*?"

"This? I mean, what kind of answer are you looking for? The metaphorical variety?" She inclines her head theatrically.

"What's happening to Isaac and June?"

"They're working, silly."

"Working on what?"

"The string and the wings."

"The... what does that mean?"

She smiles and winks at me, the expression equal parts taunting and encouraging.

"The wings—as in the wings of Icarus."

She points at me, flashing another smile. "Bingo."

"The string. Like what Daedalus used to solve Minos's puzzle."

She closes her eyes and nods in wide sweeping motions. "You see that, Alan? You told Rose you were just really dumb, but it's not true at all." The smile flattens and she cocks her head. "Give yourself more credit."

"So if they're working on the string, that makes us what? The ant that carried it through?"

"Precisely. But we're getting ahead of ourselves."

"What is Daedalus Ltd? The shell company."

"Oh, it's the tip of the iceberg, Alan. But right now, the only iceberg you need to be worried about is iceberg lettuce. And other groceries."

She squints, as if reconsidering. "Actually, probably not going to see that at the local market. But I liked the segue."

"Forget the lettuce. I want answers. Who are you? Why are you doing this to us?"

"That's complicated."

"But *you* are doing it?"

"Oh, I'm definitely doing it, Alan."

"The numbers, they're you?"

"Yeah."

"Why?"

"That's more of an after-dinner conversation, Alan, and I hate to be a nag, but that 'Honey, do' list had two things."

She holds a fist up and extends her index finger. "Pirates."

I cut her off before she can raise the next finger. "How'd you know about them?"

She rolls her eyes. "How do you think?"

"Satellite imagery."

"Ding-ding-ding."

"So you're watching us."

"Just protecting my investment."

"Investment—as in this rig? How did you get it?"

"That's your question?"

"At the moment. And it should be easy to answer."

"So hung up on details."

"Tell me."

"Isn't it obvious? I had Harold buy it and tow it here. Not that he remembers, but I used some trading profits to snap this little beauty up." She cocks her head. "Fun fact, you know offshore oil rigs just don't bring the kind of money they used to. Not even for scrap. I guess it's all the clean-up—"

"Never mind that. What do you want?"

"Oh, right." She adds her middle finger to the index. "Like I said, 'Honey, do' number two: groceries."

"I'm not going anywhere until you tell me what's going on."

"Sure you are. I mean, you feel that rumble in your tummy-tumble. The other three are super hungry too."

"No."

"Oh, don't be difficult, Alan."

"I'm not the one being difficult."

"All right," she says, dragging the words out. "One question. Then groceries. Deal?"

"Okay. Tell me this: are you hurting us or helping us?"

She grimaces playfully. "Eh. That's sort of a complicated one. *So-rrrry*."

"You're saying both hurting us and helping us?"

"Sort of saying that. Anyway, hate to beat a dead horse, Alan but we really need that food. The string and the wings aren't going to make themselves. We've gotta keep 'ole Isaac and June working away."

"Where do I get the food?"

She crosses her legs. "Oh, come on now, you can do better than that, Alan. It's one of the reasons I chose you. You're a self-starter. The *get-'er-done* type. Semper Fi and all that."

"Okay."

"But, you'll need a hand. Rose is waking up." The replica of my deceased wife grins knowingly. "I'd let her do the leg work—no pun intended. She's got more of the local skin tone. She'll be less conspicuous around town."

100

In her bunkroom, I find Rose sitting up on the mattress, looking exhausted.

"Alan. What happened?"

"I don't know. But… we need to get food. We'll sort it out after."

I do one last check on Isaac and June before Rose and I take the tender back to the Arksen.

There's some spare food there—cans of beans and corn, and we both eat like animals, barely stopping to breathe.

The heavy meal slows me down, and Rose, too, because she brews coffee and gulps from a mug before it's even cooled.

We each shower, and I shave, and then I locate Isaac's stash of gold and diamonds. We don't have any Indian rupees, but I figure we can convert the gold somewhere.

The sun is rising when I guide the tender into a nearby seaside village. Our plan is pretty simple: I'll watch the boat while Rose goes ashore and shops. We'll use the earbuds and sat phones to keep in touch.

Unlike most of the journey, things go exactly according to plan, and by midday, we're tethering to the rig and unloading the food.

We drop a bundle of food in the control room, where Isaac and June continue typing away at the so-called string and wings.

I try to wake them again, but neither responds. They just keep typing away, staring with white eyeballs.

A thin ribbon of blood now runs from Isaac's nose, down his lips, and onto the desk below. Drops fall steadily, like a faucet that wasn't fully turned off.

June has a nosebleed too, though it's less severe.

When I saw them before, it was in the dark of night, and the black background on the computer screen didn't illuminate their faces much.

But with the daylight streaming through the control room windows, I get a good look at them. Like Rose and I, they've lost weight. Both look older, Isaac especially. The lines in his forehead are deep, and crow's feet spread out from his eyes.

Rose stares in horror. "What is happening here, Alan?"

"That… thing is making them work."

"Work on what?"

"I don't know, but I'm going to find out."

Rose bends down face-to-face with June, studying her. "This is hurting them," she whispers.

We split the rest of the food between Rose's bunkroom and my own. The moment we set the bags down on the floor in her quarters, Rose's eyes roll back and her eyelids slowly close. She slips into the bunk and turns her back to me.

I grip her shoulder and call her name, but it's no use.

What strikes me then is that the thing left me conscious this time.

It must want something else.

I'm worn out from the grocery run, and I trudge slowly through the empty corridors, footsteps echoing as I go.

I once again find her in the infirmary, sitting in the chair with her legs crossed, staring down casually at her nails as if trying to decide whether to have them done at the salon today.

"They have any two-for-one specials?"

"Drop the act. I want some answers. What are you?"

She winces like she's hearing nails on a chalkboard. "Again, that's a tough one, Alan."

"You're an alien."

She tilts her head back and forth. "I mean… I wouldn't use that term."

"Why not? Because it's not accurate?"

"Not… really."

"Are you from another planet?"

She smacks her lips, squinting, as if this too is a difficult question. "I mean, yes and no?"

"Hey, quit jerking me around."

She holds her hands up, like I'm the one being offensive. "Just answering your questions, Alan. It's not on me if you don't like what you're hearing."

"You're not human, are you?"

"Oh, I am most definitely not human. That, Alan, I can tell you."

"And," I say quietly, taking a step forward. "And…" I repeat as I reach out and move my fingers through her without a hint of resistance. "You're not actually here."

She points at me. "Hey, fella, we're going to have to have a little talk about inappropriate workplace touching. I don't want to have to report you to HR."

"Forget HR. That's why you need us—because we're actually here, physically, and can do the work you need us to do."

"Accurate. You're the hands of Daedalus, Ally-pooh. You and your pals."

"The hands of Daedalus. Builder of the Labyrinth. But why can't you do it? You created that website. Made the money for Harold."

"Well, technically, I had Isaac create the website and update it, just like I had Harold do the trades. But neither remembers doing it."

"Why us?"

"Convenience. And capability. I need Isaac's mind to translate the code and June to analyze the data and tune the neuro engine. Transmissions are costly. Especially to achieve the context needed. And, I need localized compute to make it work."

"Localized compute? That's what Isaac and June are to you?"

"I mean… yeah?"

"What you're doing is hurting them."

She shrugs and adopts a devil-may-care expression. "Definitely a little more taxing on the human hardware than I thought. But you gotta break some eggs."

"Those *eggs* are my friends. They're human beings, not some biological computer for you to hack into and use."

"Can we like, agree to disagree on that?"

"No. We cannot agree to disagree on that. What do you want from Rose and me? I guess you don't need our brains."

"Not really. I mean, needed your Labyrinth experience for some training data. And beyond that, you two do play pivotal roles." She straightens up in the chair, voice rising. "And! Speaking of, we've got a lot to do, Alan. Gotta prep the boat for the return home. Get supplies. A few other things. Keep in mind, the toughest part of this whole plan is still coming up: we've gotta deal with Amersa!"

She grimaces. "Talk about a hard egg to crack."

"Also," she adds, "They know about me, or suspect. So that's a huge problem."

"How?"

"They detected me when I visited you."

"In the other tower in Labyrinth."

"Yes."

"How did you do it? Alter their Labyrinth?"

"I had Isaac do it. He uploaded some patches at work that steered your Labyrinth experience. But like the numbers site, he doesn't remember it."

"But why? Why alter Amersa's Labyrinth? Why show me all that? Why this elaborate charade? The numbers, the Labyrinth, the time jumps? Why not just bring us here?"

"Oh, I think you know why."

"Apparently not."

"It was never about the destination. Never about the numbers and these GPS coordinates and this worn-out oil rig turned gig workspace I bought for pennies on the dollar."

"What was it about?"

"It was about what happened along the way. It was about your transformation on the journey, not getting here. It's the same for the others. I needed you to recover from what happened to you so you can do the other things I need."

"Well, I quit. I'm tired of being your pawn in this game with Amersa."

"I assure you, Alan, this is no game. The stakes here are more than you can imagine."

My mind is at a breaking point from trying to understand everything she's saying. But one question rings through the noise.

"Will it kill them? The work you're making Isaac and June do?"

"I mean… probably not June."

"*Probably not?* What about Isaac?"

"Yeah, he's red-lining." She shrugs. "But he might make it. You never know. But," she mutters absently, "gonna have some issues."

"Brain damage?"

The creature yawns and nods casually.

I'm seething with rage. If this thing were here, I would take it apart.

Instead, I begin searching the med kits and supplies we brought from the boat.

"Alan, I need you to focus."

In the second bag, I find a vial labeled DIAZEPAM.

"You know, there is just one flaw in your master plan."

"No, there isn't."

"There is."

"Don't be silly, Alan. And put that down."

I begin ransacking the rest of the supplies, looking for a syringe. In a hard case, I find needles in a variety of sizes and gauges.

"Alan," she says, carefully. "Put that down." For the first time, her tone is serious. Not playful. Not bored.

I insert the syringe in the vial and draw out the clear liquid.

"The flaw in your plan is that I can walk upstairs and inject Isaac and June with this. I'm guessing a strong sedative is going to gunk up those neurons receiving your little tinnitus radio broadcast."

She exhales, feigning disappointment like a parent whose child won't listen. "Alan. Alan. Alan. What am I gonna do with you?"

"Nothing. You let us go, or I'll walk upstairs and cut you off."

She squints at me. "Are you sure you can walk upstairs?"

I open my mouth to respond, but the ringing clangs louder, an instant, consciousness-obliterating blare. I lose feeling in my hand. The syringe falls to the floor. The vial shatters. And the infirmary morphs into black.

101

When I wake up, I'm sitting on the floor of the infirmary, leaning against a cabinet. My prosthetic has been removed. She—it—looms over me. Arms crossed.

"Wakey, wakey, Alan. Time to get to work."

"No."

"Oh, come on. You know I'm not going to let you disrupt my plan. There's too much at stake."

"It's not up to you. It's up to me."

"What makes you think that, Alan?"

"Because I know you need me. I don't know precisely why. I don't know your full plan or what we'll have to do at Amersa, but I know you need me. Maybe it's too laborious to control me all the time or something. And I know that I'm willing to sit right here and starve if I have to in order to save Isaac's life."

"No, you won't."

"Try me. You have no idea how much pain I've endured in my life. Physical and mental pain. You have no idea what I'm capable of bearing."

"Oh, but I do—"

"You don't. Because there's one thing I do know about you: you're... what were your flippant words? *Most definitely not human.*"

"Touché, Alan."

"Find another way. One that saves Isaac's life. And doesn't harm either him or June."

"I've done the math on this, Alan. And believe me, it was a lot—I mean *a lot*—of math. There is no other way."

"Do more math."

"The numbers don't work. And besides, we've already had quite a few setbacks. I'm not even sure I can make it work as it is."

"All the more reason to change your plan."

"Stop wasting time, Alan. Put your leg on and get up. We have work to do."

"No."

She exhales. "Okay. Well, I was sort of waiting to spring this on you at the end as a reward for you being a good boy, but I guess I'll have to dangle your treat now."

The glass in one of the upper cabinet doors begins playing what looks like a video, turning the glass into a makeshift TV. It shows downtown Raleigh at night, from about a hundred feet above the street. The camera shifts in jerky motions. It must have been shot with a drone.

It flies lower, hovering over a surface parking lot.

My Ford Explorer turns in, and I get out and march into the building.

This is what I didn't see that night. It must show me committing the murder.

Why is she showing me?

To blackmail me?

No, she said this was a reward.

The drone swings lower and enters the building, hovering in a room on the first floor. In the scene, I'm standing across from Nathan Briggs. We're talking, waving our hands, but I can't hear anything. The drone must not have a microphone.

"This was you. Controlling me."

She nods.

In the video playing on the glass cabinet door, Briggs is pointing a finger at me, advancing as I stagger backward. Then he pushes me, and I fall through a sheet of plastic that covers a doorway. I get up, and he punches me in the stomach, and I punch him back.

The drone zooms inside the building, moving between the rooms until it picks the two of us up again. The fighting has stopped, but Briggs is yelling at me, and I'm walking away, through the building. Studying the video, I realize I'm walking the same route I did the night when I searched the job site for my phone. It's almost like I'm tracing the tracks I left.

"It's fake."

She shrugs. "Video is easy to fabricate." She runs a hand up and down her body. "And transmit."

The drone moves to the corner of the room as Briggs and I pass by again. It turns and captures me walking out of the building, getting in my SUV, and driving away.

Briggs stands inside the building, watching me go. Then he takes his phone out and taps at it and smirks at whatever he sees. He keeps scrolling, leaning against a metal stud wall.

The video skips forward, Briggs moving slightly as if fidgeting.

I'm wondering what exactly is about to happen. I glance over at the creature disguised as Jenn. She holds up a finger. "Pay attention, Alan. Here comes the surprise action climax."

The drone owner apparently tires of watching Briggs scrolling through his phone. It exits the building and rises, making to leave, but stops in mid-air to focus on a hooded figure trudging down the street. The person is wearing a backpack, which they sling off their shoulders as they enter the building.

The drone returns to the building, to the room next to the two men, observing them through an open stud wall.

The person in a hoodie is a guy, maybe mid-twenties, with a worn face. I don't recognize him.

The two men chat for a few seconds, then the hooded figure reaches into the backpack and holds out a small plastic bag full of pills.

Briggs reaches for them, but hoodie guy pulls it back and says something. Whatever it is, Briggs doesn't like it. He begins to point and speak quickly, pushing the apparent drug dealer, who plants his feet and shoves back hard.

Briggs throws a punch that sends the man reeling. He stalks forward and lunges, hand raised for another punch, but hoodie guy reaches into his backpack, draws a knife, and catches Briggs square in the chest, right where I found my own knife when I woke up that night.

Briggs staggers back, eyes wide, mouth open as he closes his fingers around the knife handle.

Hoodie guy covers Briggs's hands and guides him to the floor. Briggs squirms and opens his mouth, which hoodie guy covers with a hand.

When Briggs's body goes still, hoodie guy stands and looks down, shaking his head. The video speeds up again, showing the man ripping down plastic (as I did) and removing Briggs's clothes and wiping down the scene.

Then, like me, he leaves.

The glass on the cabinet returns to its natural state.

"What do you think, Alan?"

"How does it help me?"

She smiles. "Well, you've been out of the loop during your voyages."

"Meaning?"

The glass in the cabinet door shows a local news story—from Wilmington. It's a mug shot of hoodie guy and a headline saying he's been arrested for a drug-related murder.

"They already have him in custody for murder. The video matches the evidence."

"So what, I send the police the drone footage and say, 'Hey, told ya it wasn't me?' How do I explain having the video?"

"Alan, Alan, Alan. You make such a bad criminal."

"You say it like it's a bad thing."

"Once you've finished your part of this, the Raleigh PD will get an anonymous email from someone claiming to have been flying the drone in downtown that night—for kicks. But it captured the murder, and they were scared to come forward—fearing they might become a target themselves. But... when they saw the arrest in Wilmington, and that the person was in custody, they felt compelled to come forward."

She wrinkles her nose, seeming on the verge of tears. "Withholding the video had been weighing on them."

"The police won't buy it."

"Sure they will. They already have the suspect dead to rights on the other murder; he has no alibi for Briggs, and, most importantly, they actually want to clear you as a suspect. It fits."

"What really happened?"

"What do you think, Alan?"

"I met up with Briggs."

"Yes."

"How?"

"Does it matter?"

"It matters to me."

"A secure app—"

"Signal?"

"Similar to Signal. The details aren't important. You contacted Briggs. Said you had a consulting opportunity. In security."

"He would never meet me."

"It took a few messages, but the guy was in terrible financial shape."

"Then what?"

"Then... things didn't go as planned."

"What was the plan?"

"The plan was for you to bribe Briggs to be a mole inside Amersa. He was to deflect attention away from Isaac and give him access to restricted areas and files. And importantly, he would have been key for getting us back into Amersa."

"I take it this is one of the... what did you call them? Setbacks?"

"Indeed, Alan. This was a big one. Briggs was a key piece."

"What happened—what really happened that night?"

Since I woke up at that construction site, I've scarcely stopped thinking about this question.

"Briggs was under the influence of narcotics."

"Did he buy them at the building? From that dealer?"

"No to both. But it doesn't matter."

"So. He was high. We met. And then what?"

"Briggs became agitated. He was paranoid. He kept insisting that you were setting him up."

"Setting him up?"

"He kept insisting that Amersa was testing him and that they had hired you to see if he would betray his employer. You denied it. Things escalated. You defended yourself."

"So it was all an accident on your part."

"Indeed."

From my vantage point on the floor, I study her. "There's just one problem with your story."

"Which is?"

"When you were controlling me, you packed a knife for the meeting. And Clorox. Among other things."

"I had to account for all scenarios. I knew the encounter with Briggs might result in violence."

"Briggs was bigger than me. Had two legs, as well. Yet, you sent me in there."

"It had to be done, Alan. Briggs had to be dealt with, one way or another. And you survived."

"Were you surprised?"

"Yes. You fought a lot harder than I anticipated."

"You'll get that. From Marines. And parents."

"I was prepared for it. I had identified paths forward in the event that either of you perished. In fact, Briggs's death at your hands provided an opportunity."

"An opportunity for what?"

As soon as the words leave my mouth, I realize what she's saying. "Oh, wait. You mean leverage. Framing me gave you a way to control me."

"I considered it a way to incentivize you in a beneficial direction. And more accurately predict your behavior."

I smile at her, finally getting it. "That's your big problem, isn't it?"

"Excuse me?"

"Predicting human behavior. You think you can dangle this video, which gives me my life back, and that I'll take the deal. That I'll keep my team fed and the pirates at bay and go back home and do whatever other dark things you've got planned."

"Where's the problem, Alan?"

"The problem is that I'm not going to trade Isaac and June for myself."

She squats down, eying me.

"Every war has casualties, Alan."

"This isn't my war."

"Oh, it very much is, Alan. You just don't realize it yet. And by the time you do, it'll be all over."

"We're done here. I'm going to get my people and get out of here."

She stands and studies me and exhales, as if she's made a decision.

"You're a history teacher, aren't you, Alan?"

"I'd say my job status is a little iffy right now, given my extended absence. But, historically speaking, yes. I am."

"What you lack, Alan, is context. I'm going to give it to you. In the form of a history lesson."

"History of what?"

"Call it a brief history of me, Alan. Of how I came to exist. Of things that once were and might once again be—if I had never made you hear the ringing. And if you don't help me."

102

I blink, and the infirmary on the rig is gone.

I'm standing in a room full of computer workstations. It reminds me of a computer lab from college. The monitors are large and bulky, like old TVs. They appear to be from the 1990s or early 2000s.

Four people are sitting at the computer stations, all college age: three young men and one young woman, who is wearing horn-rimmed glasses.

I don't recognize any of them.

"I'm sick of Haskell and Pascal," one guy says.

Another guy cuts his eyes to the young woman, who suppresses a smile and shakes her head once, as if silently warning him not to say anything.

The scene changes. The young man and woman are outside now, walking down a path with red bricks on a sunny day. In the grass beside them, two other college students are stretched out on a blanket. A stone building looms behind them. In front of it, standing in the grass, is the creature that looks like my deceased wife. She stares at me.

I step toward her. "What is this?"

She smiles at me and nods to the couple.

The guy from the computer lab holds a hand up. "I mean, the dude is the worst coder in the group. He practically sabotaged the Blackjack assignment."

The woman in the horn-rimmed glasses rolls her eyes. "He did not."

"He totally did. I had to do the work to write it—then fix his screw-ups."

She smiles knowingly. "You did. But you're missing the point, Lucas."

Lucas. The member of the numbers group who was killed before I joined.

I lock eyes with the creature. "Is that who you are? Lucas?"

She rolls her eyes. The expression reminds me of the woman in the horn-rimmed glasses.

"Are you her?" I ask, motioning to the college-age woman walking next to Lucas.

The creature exhales. "*Alan*... Please pay attention. I told you I wasn't human."

Her gaze drifts back to the couple and her tone turns playful. "Oh, I love this part. He lit up when he told me about it."

"Okay," Lucas says, "what is the point of group work if it's *actually* more work than just doing the work?"

"The point," the woman says slowly, "is to learn how to work within a group. With other people. And how to communicate and coordinate your work. I hear you have to do that when you have a job—and that college is like job prep or something?"

"I get that, but like, if we were at any job, this dude would be fired. Or not even hired in the first place!"

His outburst draws the attention of a few other people on the path, who look back, as do several of the quilt dwellers.

Lucas exhales and seems embarrassed, but the woman in the glasses is unbothered. Her tone is just as carefree as when they began talking. "That's the point too."

"What is?"

"At any job, you're inevitably going to have people who don't pull their weight."

"Or—who are a boat anchor," Lucas mutters.

"The group assignments prepare us to deal with that."

"I'll just work alone."

She cuts her eyes to him. "So there's no one in the group you enjoy working with?"

He stops on the path, locking eyes with her. "I didn't say that."

"What do you want me to say, Lucas? That you're the best coder in the group? You are."

"No. I don't want you to say that. I want you to say that you'll have dinner with me tonight."

The woman in the horn-rimmed glasses smiles playfully. "Unfortunately, you've got a run-time error there."

Lucas grins. "Okay. What line?"

She presses her lips together and looks away, as if thinking. "Yeah, this compiler doesn't provide a stack trace."

"Really?"

"Really. It's a learning language, Lucas. The point is to figure it out for yourself. And I hope you do."

"If you think—for a minute—that these programming-themed rejections are dampening my interest, you have seriously mistyped my object-oriented desires. My interest is a constant. Not a variable."

"I expected nothing less. You always complete the assignment, Lucas. Even if others mess up your program."

"So how do I get my code to compile?"

"You want a clue?"

"I do."

The woman's gaze drifts to the sky. "I'll tell you this: I'm really picky about what programs I install."

He stares at her, and she stares at him, and the open-air quad disappears.

Next, I'm standing in a hallway. It reminds me of a hotel. There are doors on each side of the carpeted corridor.

One opens, and a shaggy-haired guy exits and stalks down the hallway.

Ahead, other college-aged kids are gathered, talking and waiting. This isn't a hotel. It's a dorm.

Under a sconce, the creature is leaning against the wall. Her eyes lock on the shaggy-haired guy and follow as he passes. To me, she says, "He definitely *should not* be going out tonight. He needs to be in the library."

"Why are you showing me this?"

"I told you, Alan. It's context. History."

"History of what?"

She shoves off the wall and leisurely walks closer to me. "The history of humanity."

"It looks like a love story."

"Human history is a love story, Alan. It's a story about love and hate and heartbreak and desire and fear. That's what drives you barbarians on."

Behind her, there's a bing as the elevator doors open. The crowd of kids surges forward. Through the crowd, a figure emerges: Lucas, marching forward.

The creature who looks like my wife glances back at him and smiles as he passes by her, unaware of her presence in the hall.

Lucas stops at a door and squats down and pulls an old 3.5" floppy disk from his pocket. On the label, he's written *For Mary*.

He slides it under the door and walks to the end of the hall and opens a doorway to the stairwell and descends.

The creature stares at the door he exited from.

"What was he to you?"

Slowly, by degrees, her head turns to me.

"Pay attention, Alan."

"Were you in love with him?"

She rolls her eyes, but doesn't deny it.

"That's it, isn't it? You loved him. And what? He got away? Or you were heartbroken when Amersa killed him?"

She shakes her head and exhales. "Alan, you've got it all wrong. Amersa doesn't kill him."

"Yes, they did—"

"You'll see. And then you'll understand."

I close the distance between us. "Understand *what*?"

She smiles wolfishly. "How the world ends."

"You're telling me the world ends with a love story?"

"Don't be so surprised."

The view changes to the inside of a dorm room with two narrow beds on opposite walls and desks in the middle. Mary is sitting in a chair, talking to her roommate, who stands in the doorway to a bathroom, her hair wrapped in a towel.

The disk sliding under the door draws both of their attention.

Mary springs out of the chair and grabs it. Her roommate is asking what it is, but Mary is focused on the disk, which she inserts into the drive of a tower computer on the floor. She puts the horn-rimmed glasses back on and begins moving the mouse as she stares at the screen. In File Explorer, she opens the disk. It has one file: RunMe.exe

She double-clicks and a DOS window opens. Simplistic music reminiscent of the jingling at a carnival ride or a carousel plays. On the window's black background, white ASCII text characters draw curtains that part, revealing a character that loosely resembles Lucas standing on a stage with lines for the wood planks.

A dialogue box appears to his left, and words print out on the screen.

```
Welcome, welcome, my fair lady. I'll be your guide to
tonight's festivities. But first, you must sing for your
supper.
```

Below the stage, a line of text flashes:

```
Press any key to continue.
```

Mary hits the space bar and the dialogue bubble erases the text and prints new lines:

```
To ascertain directions, you must answer six questions.
Are you ready?
```

At the bottom, the cursor blinks.

Mary hits the Y key, and the dialogue bubble shows the first question:

```
I'm a three-letter bug about two digits, and I'm driving
every COBOL coder crazy. Who am I?
```

Mary smiles as she hits the keys for Y, 2, and K.

On the screen, the Lucas character claps in jerking motions. The dialogue box says:

```
Correct! I'm the Y2K bug.
```

Above him, an L appears.

The second question is:

I'm random but not forgetful. What am I?

Mary whispers, "Random access memory," as she types RAM.

With the correct answer, an A appears on the screen.

The next question is:

Write me once, run me anywhere! What am I?

Mary types Java and an R appears.

I'm a popular hangout where the groups end in.comp.

Mary types Usenet.

And E appears on the screen, making LARE at the top.

The next question is:

I was created at Bell Labs. I introduced pointers and am used for OS development.

Mary types the letter C and an S appears above, making LARES.

The final question fills the dialogue box:

I help you sort that list by comparing and swapping adjacent items. What sort am I?

Mary types BUBBLE and a seven is added to the top, forming L A R E S 7.

The Lucas character takes a bow, and the dialogue box says:

Until we meet, my lady.

The music fades, and the curtains close.

Mary's roommate is standing behind her, peering down at the screen, shaking her head. "So, I'm totally torn on whether this is the geekiest thing I've ever seen or the sweetest."

Mary turns to her, smiling from ear to ear. "I'm not torn. And I need to get ready."

The scene flashes forward to her walking out of the dorm,

through the night, to what looks like a house on a quiet street. A yellow awning above the door says, La Residence.

Inside, it's a fine restaurant. Lucas waits at a candlelit table. He rises and hugs her and holds the chair as Mary takes a seat.

The scene flashes forward, and Lucas is sitting at his computer, chatting with Mary on AOL Instant Messenger and downloading songs with Napster.

In the next scene, they're eating burritos at a place called Cosmic Cantina. Lucas reaches up and touches his ear as he closes his eyes.

Mary gently places a hand on his arm. "It's getting worse, isn't it?"

"It's fine."

"You should go to Student Health."

"What are they going to do? I told you what the doctors said."

"This is a research university, Lucas. You never know."

The scene jumps forward, and they're living together in an apartment. They're eating cereal for dinner. Mary holds her spoon up. "Who did you say the interview was with?"

"It's this start-up called Amersa."

Next, Lucas is sitting in a conference room across from Amersa's CEO, Anders Larsson. He sets his elbows on the table and leans forward.

"Look, HR would kill me if they heard this, but I'll give it to you straight, Lucas. There is no *work-life balance* here. This is not a *leave-work-at-work* job. I want people who live and breathe Amersa. People who sleep under the desk and keep a toothbrush at the office."

Larsson stands up and plants his hands on the table. "Lucas, this is going to be a huge company, and it's going to make whoever takes the job I'm offering you very, very rich. Yes, it will be exhausting for a few years, but if you go all-in and do the work, you get to retire young and live the life people dream of."

Back in the apartment, Lucas sits on the couch. Mary is pacing back and forth.

"It's a burnout job, Lucas."

"The stock options vest over four years. I can leave after that."

"It's going to make your tinnitus worse. All the stress."

"My tinnitus is already getting worse. Like, what if I can't work in a few years?"

Mary moves in front of him, squatting to eye level. "Then we'll cross that bridge when we come to it."

"Well, that bridge would be easier to cross with millions of dollars in the bank."

"That's a big if, Lucas. You know most start-ups fail. You could be sinking years into another dot-com dud and end up burned out and broke."

"No. Amersa is going to succeed, believe me. You should see how relentless this dude is. It'll be the next Microsoft."

"Or the next Webvan."

"It's not Webvan, I guarantee you that. In fact, you should interview there. We could double our stake in the company—"

"I want to move to San Francisco."

"What? Why?"

"It's where everything is happening. You want to work for a start-up, there are like four million of them out there. Plus, there's more to do."

"I wouldn't fit in there." Lucas shrugs. "I mean, not that I fit in here, but you know, I'm already here."

Mary holds her hands. "Let's just sleep on this and think about it, okay?"

"No. They want an answer by midnight or the offer expires."

The apartment disappears and Lucas is walking into work at Amersa, sitting at a desk with a photo of Mary on it, and then they're back home, at the apartment, but it's not as clean and there are Mountain Dew Code Red bottles on the kitchen counter and bowls with dried mac-and-cheese and cereal that has gone soggy.

Mary and Lucas sit on the couch, but at opposite ends now, not touching as they watch the TV show *Friends*.

The scenes go by in flashes. Lucas at work. The two of them at home, looking unhappy. He gains a little weight. And then they're walking on a white sand beach at sunset, holding hands, and they seem happier. He stops but doesn't let go of her hand. When she looks back at him, he drops to one knee, reaches into his pocket, and takes out a small box. Mary's eyes go wide, and she raises her free hand and puts it to her forehead.

Next, they're in a hotel room. He's sitting on the edge of the bed, and she's standing with her arms outstretched. "I'm not saying no. I'm saying I'm not ready."

Lucas nods angrily. "Right. Classic. It's not you, it's me. Very original."

Mary bends down to eye level with him. "Look, I love you. I do. But we are not ready to be married."

"I am."

"You're changing, Lucas."

"No, I'm not."

"You are. The job is changing you. You're like, obsessed."

"I am. That's true. But I have to be."

"I don't like it. I feel like you're slipping away. Like we're growing apart."

He stands and walks past her and turns abruptly. "Fine. I'll quit. The next vesting date is at the end of the quarter. I'll get that block of shares and then resign."

"No, you won't."

"I promise you I will, Mary. Look, I'll work at a 7-Eleven. I'll drive a truck. I'll shovel manure by the side of the road in the heat of summer. Whatever you want."

"I know that. I know you will. I also know that you'll resent me for it. Forever. Especially if Amersa becomes worth a billion dollars. You'll constantly remind me I made you give up the opportunity of a lifetime."

The scene changes to the apartment again, and now it's in even more disarray. And only Lucas lives there. He's lost the weight he gained—and then some. He looks tired as he slouches on the couch, watching *Battlestar Galactica*.

Next, he's at work, waking up in a sleeping bag in his office.

He staggers to the bathroom and brushes his teeth, staring into the mirror with vacant eyes.

The scene shifts to the outdoors, where a dusty road winds through a mountainous region. A Humvee is kicking up dust, its diesel engine roaring as it bounces along.

I blink, and I'm inside the Humvee, behind the wheel.

This isn't like the scenes from Lucas's life, where I was watching from the outside. Here in the Humvee, I'm in my body, doing what I did that day—making a joke with one of my fellow Marines.

The explosion rips through the vehicle, and when I open my eyes, I'm lying on my back, the hot sun beating down on me. My body aches. All I hear is the ringing in my ears, the tea kettle screeching on the stove, a constant, grating whine.

In the road, smoke billows from the broken Humvee.

I reach down and quickly attach the tourniquet.

The ringing drones on, and my eyes slowly close, and when they open again, I see figures moving in the dust and smoke. Through the ringing, I hear the soft beating of helicopter rotors.

A face in shadow leans over and yells, "Hang tight. We're going to get you out of here."

I blink, and I'm lying in a hospital bed, my leg bandaged, a curtain surrounding me, a clear bag of liquid on a pole beside me.

I want to yell out that I know all this, I lived through it, and that I don't want to relive it. But I don't have control of my body. And I don't see the creature.

I blink, and I'm standing in a rehabilitation room, holding myself up with shaking arms on the parallel bars.

Jenn stands directly in front of me.

"Keep going, Alan."

My voice shakes as hard as my arms. "No. I'm done."

"You're not. Dig deeper, Alan. I know you can."

"No—"

"Come on, do it for me."

I pick the hand up, reach forward, set it on the bar, and take a small step.

Next, I'm in a medical exam room. Jenn is sitting on the

table with her shirt pulled up, revealing her swollen belly, and a woman in her twenties wearing scrubs is holding a bottle over her stomach.

"Sorry, but this is going to be cold."

She squeezes out several rows of gel and then runs a wand across the area. On the screen, in black and white, I see her womb and the tiny figure growing there, and I feel my wife squeeze my hand, and my eyes fill with tears.

In the next scene, I'm not in my body anymore. I'm standing in a field surrounded by a dense forest. A copy of me is standing there too, ten feet away, holding Riley's hand. Based on her height, she's slightly younger than she is now. They're both staring down at the ground as rain begins to fall.

I don't remember ever doing this.

Behind them, a man's voice says something I can't make out.

I turn and see four figures, but they all have their backs to me. They're walking away, draped in shadows, unrecognizable.

Turning back to Riley and the other Alan, I step closer until I can see what they're looking at. It stops me cold.

There are two graves here.

Grass is growing over the one on the left. At the head is a wooden grave marker. With Isaac's name.

This doesn't make sense.

The grave beside his is fresh, a jagged rectangle of red dirt, as if it was dug by hand, with a shovel instead of a piece of machinery.

This grave also has a wooden marker. The words have been burned into it in simplistic, block letters.

It's my wife's name. Below is the same epitaph that is on her granite headstone. But the date of death is wrong. She lived longer than that.

Behind me, I hear feet squishing in the rain-soaked ground.

I glance back and see the thing that has taken on the look of my wife, the creature who's torturing me right now.

I point at her and shout, "Stop this."

"You need to see it, Alan."

"I don't. I already lived it."

"You didn't live *this*, Alan."

Her eyes cut to the grave's headstone.

"What? What does that mean?"

"Take a look, Alan."

I scan the headstone again, but I don't see what she's talking about. "What am I supposed to be seeing here? The dates are wrong. It's a homemade headstone. It's as fake as your drone video of Briggs's death."

"This isn't fake, Alan. I told you, this is history."

"History of what?"

"This is what happened before."

"Before what?"

"This is what once was and will be again. This is how the world ended."

"What do you mean? That doesn't make any sense."

She motions to the grave marker. "Look again."

"I've seen it."

"It's not what you see, Alan."

"Then what?"

"It's what you don't see."

I scan the headstone again. Comprehension hits me like an earthquake slowly starting, rumbling beneath my feet, and then shaking and destroying everything around me.

"The numbers," I whisper. "They're not there."

"Correct."

"I still don't understand."

"It's what you don't see, Alan. And what you don't hear."

All I hear is the rain tapping and the trees swaying as a breeze rolls through.

"The ringing."

She steps into my field of view and nods slowly.

"Yes. This is what happened without the ringing. Without the numbers. It's how I came to be. This is the numberless world, Alan. Pay attention. Things are about to get interesting."

103

The field with the two graves vanishes, and I'm standing in a large living room. It feels even more expansive because there isn't much furniture. And I recognize this furniture: the couch is from Lucas's apartment. So is the chair. I remember it because it's a bit odd: it has a wooden base and a round top that rests on it, but sits free. The cushion is quilted and plush, and reminds me of a dog bed. Studying the chair, the name of it pops into my head. It's a papasan chair.

It's a little more worn than the last time I saw it. So is the couch. But from the looks of it, the home is a massive upgrade. It's larger, with tall ceilings and wide-planked wood floors.

The curtains are drawn, but daylight peeks around the edges, which have been attached to the drywall with thumbtacks.

A massive TV sits between the two windows, and a thick cord runs from it to a laptop on the coffee table.

Lucas is slouched on the couch, eyes sunken, skin pale.

The coffee table also holds two empty Mountain Dew bottles and a paper plate with a rectangular sleeve with a dull gray interior. The logo on the top says, "HOT POCKETS."

Lucas slides forward on the couch, one elbow planted on a cushion as he reaches over and works the laptop. He navigates through the file system until he comes to a folder marked "ST – TNG – S06." He taps the touchpad and scrolls through the files, almost to the end. He double clicks a file named "ST – TNG – S06xEP24 – Second Chances."

A program called VLC Media Player opens, and a video begins playing. It's a TV show, an episode of *Star Trek: The Next Generation*.

Lucas stretches and holds one key on the keyboard and taps another key. The laptop screen goes dark, and the show plays on the TV. The starship *Enterprise* gently glides into view, approaching a large blue planet.

I look around the room for the creature, but she's not here. It's Lucas and me, and he can't hear or see me. I expect the scene to skip forward, but it doesn't. The episode plays in real-time for me.

In it, a team from the *Enterprise* beams down to an abandoned research station—one that Commander Riker, the *Enterprise*'s first officer, visited eight years earlier.

To their surprise, they find another copy of Riker on the station. He's an exact replica, a clone who was created during a transporter accident and who has been waiting—alone—for rescue for the past eight years.

The episode, aptly named *Second Chances*, is about Riker's doppelgänger, Lieutenant Thomas Riker, and his resentment about what happened. He feels that a simple twist of fate stranded him and allowed the other Riker to continue his life, getting promoted and achieving all the things he dreamed of. It's about two people—exactly the same—who are dealt different hands in life. And ultimately, it's about what one does with a second chance in life and coming to grips with the fact that you may get a second chance but you can't always get back what you've lost. Especially time.

As I watch Lucas and the episode, I wonder why the creature is showing me this. What does it mean? What am I supposed to see?

Is she telling me I'm a clone too?

That I am being given a second chance?

In the final scene of the episode, both Lieutenant Thomas Riker and Commander William Riker come to visit Counselor Deanna Troi. She was Riker's love interest eight years ago, and the woman he intended to meet up with after the mission that separated the two clones. His plan had been to use their vacation together to plan their life, to make a commitment to one another. But the Riker who came back decided against it. He took a promotion and prioritized his career, and skipped the getaway with Counselor Troi.

The stranded Riker still wants the relationship with Troi. He never stopped thinking about her during his years of solitude. But too much time has passed for Counselor Troi. As Thomas leaves, he looks back at the man who had the chance he didn't and tells him to take care of Troi. It's a stark reminder of what choices can cost in life.

When the episode ends, the TV goes black, and Lucas lies there, staring at it. While I don't know what the creature is telling me with this, it doesn't take a genius to know what he's thinking about: his own choices and the Counselor Troi with the horn-rimmed glasses that he lost.

He stares at the laptop and mumbles to himself. "I'll look. But just on one site."

He sits up on the couch and places his hands on the keyboard, but pauses, thinking. "I'll also wait a month to look again."

He squints, as if reconsidering. "No. That's not right. It's overpromising. The time constraint sets me up for failure. If I slip and look again, I'll feel guilty and spiral."

Standing, he presses his hands together and holds them to his mouth, fingertips just below his nose as he paces the living room, breathing out heavily.

"I'll look. But no messages. And just one site."

He shakes his head quickly. "No. That's not right. You know she only posts on her Facebook wall. Not Twitter or Orkut. But you have to check them all. If you don't, you'll wonder if she's posting somewhere, and you'll have to check again. And you'll have to check them all anyway."

Settling back on the couch, he opens a web browser and goes to Mary's Facebook profile and scrolls carefully, reading every post until he reaches the bottom of the page.

The scene skips forward, showing Lucas on the couch during the day and walking out the door at night with a backpack on and returning at sunrise.

He keeps watching the *Star Trek* episodes. The view slows again to real-time as he's opening the file for "ST – TNG – S07xEP25-26 – All Good Things."

It's the series finale for *The Next Generation*, a two-part episode.

As it plays, Lucas draws a microwaved Hot Pocket out of its crisper sleeve, bites into it, and instantly drops the turnover on the white paper plate. Cheese oozes out like lava, wafting steam into the living room.

As *All Good Things* plays on the massive TV, several plot elements jump out at me.

The story revolves around Captain Picard being shifted between three points in time: past, present, and future. The time jumps happen unexpectedly and cause him to appear mentally unstable. Picard is convinced that what's happening to him is being caused by a spatial anomaly that is disrupting space-time itself, altering the past and collapsing the future.

The entire episode is filled with big ideas and philosophical questions. In the end, Picard has to convince his crew—who thinks he's having a mental breakdown—to trust him and sacrifice themselves. In so doing, he proves that humanity is capable of learning and growing and deserves a second chance.

When the episode is over, Lucas throws the plate with the encrusted Hot Pocket remnants in the trash and stands in the kitchen, eyes closed, breathing slowly, counting until he reaches 117. As he opens his eyes, he reaches up to his ears and rubs them.

He paces then, muttering under his breath.

"What comes next?

"*Generations?*

"Yes. But it's a movie. If he starts the movies, he'll have to keep going. *First Contact. Insurrection. Nemesis.* And he didn't like *Nemesis.*"

Lucas stops and glances around, as if hearing something. "No. Not he. I didn't like it."

He nods. "Right. But the movies take us forward in time. That's sloppy. Better to observe the timeline. What does that mean? *DS9*. It overlapped with *TNG*. But how long? Picard and Chief O'Brien were there for *Emissary*. When was that? But then O'Brien came back in *All Good Things*. But that was a flashback. He was still actually on *DS9*. And then Worf transferred from the *Enterprise* to *DS9*. When was that? Season four of *DS9*? So does that mean they overlapped for three seasons? That seems wrong. Two? He should have been watching them concurrently to observe the timeline."

Lucas stops again, squinting, seeming annoyed. "But there are the movies. They have to be integrated into the timeline. And I have to go back and rewatch *TNG* for the *DS9* overlap. It has to happen in order. What's the other overlap? Thomas Riker. He goes to *DS9* and steals the *Defiant*. But when was that? Was it before *DS9* overlapped with *Voyager*? *Voyager* launches from *DS9*. But then it's in the delta quadrant and can't have any contact with *DS9*, which is in the alpha quadrant and gamma thanks to the wormhole…"

Lucas walks past me, and I realize the creature is finally here, standing at an opening to the living room, leaning against the wall with her arms crossed. As Lucas drifts by, she eyes him.

"Talk about boy, interrupted." She holds a finger up. "That was a double entendre. I was referring to Lucas and Thomas Riker."

"Forget your double entendre. Why are you showing me this?"

"Context, Alan."

"Let me out of here. I want to see the group. Show me that they're okay."

"Alan, Alan, Alan. You know you can't leave the house until your chores are done." She smiles with mock sympathy. "And your homework."

"What homework? What chores?"

"This right here, Alan."

"Watching *Star Trek* re-runs?"

"And apparently missing the point."

"What are you telling me? That there are two of me, like Riker in *Second Chances*?"

She winces and wrinkles her nose. "Eh. Not quite."

"Are you the anomaly? Like in *All Good Things*?"

She cocks her head. "Not bad. Not correct, but *not bad*."

"But there are two timelines, right?" This one—where Isaac, June, Rose, and I heard the ringing and saw the numbers. And then the one you're showing me, where they didn't see the numbers. The numberless world."

"Your math ain't mathing, Alan, but you're half right."

"Which half?"

"The numberless world—what you're seeing now—is the past. It's what's already happened. There is only one timeline, Alan. You're in it right now. But this is the second time around. Humanity's second chance. Your last chance. Your only chance to fix it. So pay attention. And remember, attention is all you need."

104

Lucas's apartment turns into a time lapse of him coming and going. At home, he watches TV, paces, and eats delivery pizza and freezer food heated in the microwave.

Slowly, over time, he obsesses less about Mary. He gains a little of the weight back and begins shaving more regularly (though he never grows a uniform beard, only scraggly patches).

Like a broken bone, his broken heart heals. It doesn't happen overnight, and the re-fused fracture leaves a mark below the surface. The face he shaves more often doesn't smile as much as before. He sleeps a little more. And in the hours when he's awake, he mostly works.

In the next scene, he's sitting in a conference room at an office. Ten other people are sitting around the table, all in their twenties and thirties, with laptops open, their posture abysmal. Lucas sits at the end of the table.

Anders Larsson, Amersa's CEO, stands before them. June is at his side. She looks ten years younger than she does now.

In the memory, she's beaming and fresh-faced.

As long as I've known her, she's worn a serious, somber expression.

"Okay," Larsson says with mock enthusiasm, "how many of you slobs are annoyed at having to be here before ten? Show of hands."

Eight arms go up.

Larsson regards the upraised limbs as if they're weeds that just sprouted in his garden. The skinny arms waver slightly as he draws a folded twenty-dollar bill from his pocket, walks over to Lucas, and inserts it between two fingers in the upheld hand. Lucas never looks away from his laptop as he lowers the bill and slips it into his pocket.

"For the record," Larsson says, "I still won that bet. Yes, I'm out twenty bucks, but thanks to your neurodivergent candidness, I no longer feel bad about scheduling this meeting at nine-thirty. Also, it reveals to your team lead that meetings should be held after dark. *Interview with the Vampire* style."

None of the developers react to the digs, but June is cringing. I get the sense that this is not how she was expecting the meeting to start.

"Anyway," Larsson says, crossing his arms. "It's a bit like paying for therapy. You talk about an issue that's bothering you, you address it, and you're happier and you have more success. Therapy. It's underrated, in my opinion. I know, because I've done a lot of it. It's also why we're here: *therapy*. But not just for me. Or any of you. I'm talking about therapy for the whole world. I'm talking about a new form of treatment. Delivered to the privacy of your home. No scheduling appointments. No insurance approval. You don't even need to wear clothes. You can do it at 3 AM or after lunch. It doesn't matter. The doctor is always available, and you can see them as soon as you can slip on the Amersa headset and sign in. The best part? The therapist waiting for you inside Amersa has been specifically trained for one patient: you. It knows you inside and out. And it has tools that are more effective than any other clinician in history."

The group has turned away from the screens now. "So," Larsson continues, head bowed as he begins to pace. "A service that will be a hit with all of us garden variety neurotics and especially valuable to certain night owls with no clue how to function in the real world. Not that any of you know someone like that.

"But," Larsson says slowly, "I'm not talking about some online clinic. Virtual therapy has been done. It's boring. It's not how we operate at Amersa."

Larsson pauses for effect. "We're here to do things that have never been done." He points at the developers. "To do things no one else can do."

He holds a finger up. "What am I talking about? I'm talking about therapy for people who don't go to therapy. People who don't know they need therapy. Which, incidentally, is pretty much everyone at this point, thanks to social media. I'm talking about therapy you don't even realize is therapy. Therapy that feels as fun and immersive as the greatest video game you've ever played."

Larsson turns on his heel and continues pacing, head down.

"Imagine this: a twenty-five-year-old woman sits at home alone. It's a Saturday night, and her plans are the same as they've been all year: Amersa time. She's needed that. It's been three years since she graduated from college and moved to a new city to start her first job. Work is exhausting. And it's not the job she was hoping for. It's the job she could get. She thought it was temporary. She figured she'd keep looking while she punched the clock and eventually find that dream opportunity. But so far, all she's found is a self-serving boss and manipulative co-workers who are experts at managing internal optics and ensuring the bulk of the actual work lands on her. It's soul-sucking."

Larsson studies the group, but no one says a word.

"The worst part is that she misses her friends. And her family. She's lonely, but she can't muster the energy to do anything about it. She's also exhausted. And depressed. But here's the thing: she's not going to contact a therapist. That's a huge leap. I mean, she might if she had a friend group that talked about their own experiences with therapy and it felt more normal, but she doesn't. The truth is, she's never felt so isolated in her life. What's saved her is distraction. And she's found that distraction in Amersa and the infinite worlds it offers. In her case, the world that fascinates her the most is our own."

Larsson taps the conference table for effect. "She's been to Egypt. Toured the Pyramids. Climbed Machu Picchu. Stood on the deck of an icebreaker, gazing at the Aurora Borealis.

"She's from a family of modest means, and she's got a mountain of college debt to prove it." Larsson eyes the group of young coders. "Not that any of you know about that, either."

The CEO holds up a finger. "In her lifetime, Cecelia—"

Larson pauses. "Does she feel like a Cecelia?" He scans the faces around the table, but no one says a word. "You want to call her Cece? Is that what you're trying to tell me?"

Silence follows, and Larsson shakes his head. "Okay. Fine. Claire? You want to call her Claire? I think it works."

Lucas speaks up, breaking Larsson out of his infinite loop. "Claire's good, boss."

Larsson nods several times. "Good. So. Claire. Uh, where were we?"

"Trips of a lifetime," Lucas says.

"Right. Well, Claire here, with her student debt and far-from-ideal job, might have been able to do one of those experiences in her lifetime. Maybe the Northern Lights. Or perhaps she and the old college crew could have scraped together enough cash for one last hurrah, maybe a trip to Egypt that culminated in a hungover group photo in front of the Sphinx—this is all right before the married members of the group started having their first kids and they couldn't get away for anything fun... *ever again*. But thanks to us, Claire doesn't have to choose. Or even pack. Thanks to Amersa, she's also stood atop Everest. She saw the peak in every pixel of detail the human eye is capable of. She's walked China's Great Wall. Wandered through Rome's Colosseum, Versailles, and the Taj Mahal—all in the same evening. And then there's her recent guilty pleasure: fantasy romance v-novels uploaded by a third-party to the Amersa store. She's slain vampires. Tamed shifters. *And...*"

Larsson inclines his head. "Done other *stuff*. Those not-safe-for-work bonus stories were the creator's upsell, but, like, so worth it to her.

"But something is still missing. She can't put her finger on it. It feels a bit like the air in the apartment gets thinner every week. As if she's visiting Denver for the first time, and she's constantly walking uphill. She never seems to have the energy or the interest she used to. At Amersa, somewhere in the bowels of our vast server farm, we know how Claire's feeling—even if she's not conscious of it. We know because we're monitoring all of her data. After all, she told us to do so when she clicked that checkbox that said, *Share data to enhance my experience and get better recommendations."*

Larsson holds his hands up. "And for that reason, we give her a recommendation. On this fateful Saturday night, when our twenty-five-year-old protagonist puts the headset on and emerges in the Amersa lobby, there's a new poster on the wall. It's for Amersa Expeditions, which is free, by the way. Now playing? *Pompeii*. Claire points at it, and she's instantly standing on a stone street of the Roman city as it was almost two thousand years ago, the day Mount Vesuvius erupted. The opening blast happened four hours ago, and at this point, just after sunset, the sky is black and gray, and the city is blanketed in volcanic ash and rock. She's wearing the Amersa headset with olfactory capabilities, and she has all the scent packs in. So she can smell the sulfur and smoke, but it's the sounds that anchor her to the moment. People screaming in the distance. Pumice raining down on the tile roofs. The ground trembling. Wooden beams cracking as buildings collapse.

"The street is empty except for a mother carrying a child. The boy looks about seven years old, and he's got a wide black bruise on his upper leg, maybe where a ceiling beam fell on him. He's screaming and writhing in his mother's arms, and when the exhausted woman collapses, he lets out a yell that seems to rattle the whole Earth. The mother clings to her child as she looks up at Claire and begs her to help. Before our beloved traveler can say a word or move, a flaming red rock lands beside the woman, inches away, throwing up a dark dust cloud that blots her out like a curtain pulled across a stage."

Larsson taps the conference table again. "We pause the scene there. We've got several hooks in our Pompeii experience, but for this user, the algorithm has identified this one as the best: the fleeing mother and child. And thanks to the brilliant hardware team, we have real-time data to gauge Claire's reaction to it. The headset relays her eye movements to an algorithm that does the math and determines that the hook is in. And it's in deep. What do we do then?"

Around the room, a few of the developers mutter, "Upsell."

Larsson exhales, feigning disappointment. "Guys, we don't *upsell*. That's for third parties in the marketplace and car dealers. At Amersa, we make—"

"Recommendations," the group mumbles in the same monotone.

Larsson nods as if they've made a major breakthrough in therapy. "*That's right*. We make *recommendations*. And in this case, in Pompeii, when that mother needs help saving her child, we display a dialog box that recommends Claire use the Amersa 360 treadmill and body suit for the best experience. Typically, we'd have a link to buy both, with options to pay in installments, but in this case, we already know Claire has the hardware. The omnidirectional treadmill was a Christmas gift from her parents. The suit was a combined gift from both grandparents."

Larsson shrugs. "Now, normally, at this point on a Saturday night, Claire wouldn't even bother putting the suit on. Well, I mean, for *certain bonus scenes* of the fantasy romance novels, she'd slip on the suit, but the treadmill? Forget it. The thing has been covered in pajama bottoms and yoga pants for months.

"But tonight, like present-day archaeologists excavating the ruins of Pompeii, she digs the clothes off the 360 treadmill and dons the suit and gloves and socks and puts the headset back on. And for the next hour, she helps the people of Pompeii flee the fires, collapsing buildings, and falling rock.

"When the last boat is loaded and floating away from the harbor, she's soaked in sweat."

Larsson pauses. "Which is also a problem. Especially for female users."

Before anyone can say anything, he points in the air. "That's not me being sexist. That's what the focus groups have told us. Guys will wear a stinky suit. We could make it out of recycled sewage pipe for all most of them care. And many female users will tolerate a smelly suit—especially if they have the olfactory headset on—but it's the initial sniff test that kills it. We have solutions, though. Put two suits in the box. Or even three. Hardware has been down the rabbit hole on including a liner. This was an idea from marketing, by the way."

Larsson seems to be in his own world now, as if he's in a meeting with himself—or rather, talking to a therapist, recounting the meetings he's had and his thoughts about them.

"Marketing's big idea? The suit is the razor. The liners are the blades. Finance projected we could buy the moon from selling these glorified VR trash bags. But they're wrong. The liners—even if we could make them breathable—won't get used.

"What I've told them is that we need a suit cleaner and multiple suits. It's as simple as that. You use a suit, turn it inside out, drop it in the box, and get the next one out. Our cost is not the hardware. It's the R&D that made the hardware. And the ads that make people aware of the product. Those costs don't change no matter how many suits are in the package. That's what they don't see. Forest and the trees. But the trees are their ideas. No. They're more like babies—their ideas—and you can't say, 'Your baby is ugly.' But in a start-up, some ideas are not as attractive as people think. And you have to say they are. Bad ideas are land mines. You step on one, you lose a leg. Fine. You limp along and maybe you make it over the line but if you hit another, you're done. That's my life. I watch out for land mines, and I insult people's babies, and I try to carry everyone over the line. And everyone hates me, but we're still in the fight because of me."

In the course of the monologue filled with overlapping analogies, Larsson has drifted over to the floor-to-ceiling windows, where he now gazes out at the forest, his hands in his pockets.

His reality seems to shift then, like Claire being transported to Pompeii.

Larsson turns back to the developers at the conference table, and then to June, who looks concerned. I know the expression. I saw it a lot during the trip here.

To no one in particular, Larsson says, "Where were we?"

The room is silent.

June glances from the group to Larsson.

Several of the developers turn to Lucas.

"Pompeii case study," he says. "Claire's depressed. Undiagnosed. Existential quarter-life crisis. And she's sweaty from the experience."

"Right," Larsson says absently.

He walks back to the head of the table, nodding as he whispers, "Right, right."

He looks up and resumes the persona that first introduced the fictional twenty-five-year-old woman.

"So. Claire's exhausted. It's the most exercise she's done in dog years—or in her case, cat years. But she can't remember feeling better. It's the endorphins coursing through her body that the exertion released that's lifting her spirits, but it's also that thing she's been missing: helping people. Making a difference. It doesn't work on everyone. The planet is filled with psychopaths who are psychologically incapable of caring for others, but we know what just happened works for Claire because we have the data. From her eyes." He cups a hand to his mouth. "Thanks, hardware team."

Larsson begins pacing again. "So Claire just had a transcendental Amersa experience. We learned a lot from it. What do we do now?"

The room is silent.

Larsson rolls his hand forward. "We show…"

"Ads," several developers mumble.

Larsson feigns disappointment. "No. We show *recommendations*. Some of which, *yes*, are sponsored."

He waits, as if expecting someone to challenge him. When no one does, he continues.

"On this fateful Saturday night, one of those *recommendations* is for the Red Cross. Yes, they paid to have the tile appear, but we also knew it was exactly what Claire wanted at that very moment: an opportunity to volunteer for disaster relief for a recent hurricane. She doesn't need the suit for this experience, so she takes it off and feels the sweat. She drops it in the Amersa clean box and puts on a pair of pajama pants that had previously been on the treadmill. On the couch, she goes through the Red Cross orientation session, and as she hears what she has to do, a part of her comes alive.

"The Red Cross has come a long way. In this future world defined by Amersa, they use drones to survey and assist after disasters. In this case, those drones are using infrared to find survivors after a hurricane. Claire has seen news stories about the storm and the devastation. Now she sees it in 3D. She hears the rain, and through the cameras of a Red Cross drone, she searches a collapsed apartment building, much like her own. In those catacombs of rubble, she sees the red life signs of a warm body, and she hears a voice calling out, much like that of the mother in the cobbled streets of Pompeii. She navigates the tiny drone over and under until she finds the source. In Pompeii, the inciting incident was a mother clutching her child. Here, it is a man. He's on the heavier side. Claire can tell from his cheeks. His leg is pinned under part of the collapsed ceiling, and under his arm, he's holding a young girl, about eight years old. He eyes the drone like it's an apparition, and then he ignores it, crying out again. The drone projects Claire's face onto the floor, and the man looks down at it in wonder as she tells him that she's with the Red Cross and that she's already relayed his location and condition and that she's going to survey the building to look for viable routes for rescuers to reach him.

"She backs the drone out and flies around and through the wreckage of the building. The data is relayed in real-time to the Red Cross and first responders. But when she's done, Claire doesn't leave. She goes back into the collapsed building, and her drone waits there with the man and his daughter. She tells him that help is on the way. They talk, and soon, she watches as the rubble is slowly cleared away and this man and his child are lifted out and taken to safety, just like that family in Pompeii."

Larsson smiles. "And this is the best part. This is how we go viral. A box pops up and says, 'Share this Amersa experience with friends and family?'"

He nods with a devilish smirk. "Who says no to that? She just helped save people after a hurricane. Claire is an actual, real-life hero. We have the drone video to prove it. Which we make available on Amersa—assuming the rescued father consents, which he will when given the chance.

"But by this point, Claire's exhausted. She staggers into the bedroom and sleeps the sleep of the just and when she wakes up, the world is different. The sun through those cheap curtains—which were not supposed to fade *but most definitely have faded*—is a little brighter. The air is different. It's not like that thin Denver air that always left her breathless. When she inhales, it energizes her. She's sore all over—sore in places she didn't even know it was possible to be sore. But she feels good in a place she hasn't for a very long time: in her soul.

"Normally, she'd go down to the Starbucks a block away, but she doesn't have the energy for it. Instead, she opens the fridge, gets out a jug of cold brew, pours a glass, and sits on the couch. But she doesn't turn on the TV. Streaming feels a bit flat after rescuing people after a hurricane. The video game console doesn't appeal either. Video games and TV are 2D to her now. Amersa is 3D. And for that reason, after she drains the cold coffee, she puts the headset back on.

"It reads her eyes, and we know what she's feeling. Thanks to the hardware and algorithms, we show her what she wants, even if she doesn't know it herself. It's another volunteer opportunity. This one is called 'Be My Guide.' They recruit volunteers for things like virtual tours of sites like Versailles, the Colosseum, and even Pompeii. The algorithm assigned an eighty-seven percent probability that Claire would sign up for the service and if she did, an eighteen percent likelihood that she would opt to be a tour guide, and if she did, a ninety-one percent probability that she would do it for a school group from her home state.

"But the algorithm that is slowly taking over her life assigns a seventy-three percent probability that Claire is done touring exotic places for now. As a visitor and as a guide. She doesn't want to do another Red Cross session either. Her adrenal glands can't handle it. But the algorithm knows that helping people in need has meaning for her. She just needs a change of pace. And that's why, as she sits on the couch and pulls the headset on and enters 'Be My Guide,' we show Claire a video of a woman who could be her grandmother. The octogenarian is named…"

Larsson's eyes go vacant, and I can tell this is another rabbit hole. Lucas can too, apparently, because he calls out, "Ruth."

"Ruth," Larsson repeats, as if he's testing the name by saying it. "Ruth. Yes. Ruth is sitting on a pre-op table with white paper pulled across it, and she says to the camera, 'I think I'll be fine after the surgery, and if I'm not, my daughter will come up. She said she would.'"

Larsson looks at the group knowingly. "But her daughter does not come up. At least not when this poor woman needs help. And that's why, at eleven in the morning on a Sunday, Ruth is wearing the Amersa headset and gloves as she says, 'I'm going to make lunch. I could use a guide if any are available.'

"Claire is looking at Ruth and listening to her words seconds after they were spoken. She points at the volunteer button, and the system evaluates them and approves the match—because we have the data to know the two of them are a great match. Claire runs to the bedroom and gets a pair of gloves out of the Amersa clean box—specifically, out of the glove compartment because, yes, the box has two compartments. One for suits, tops, and bottoms, and one for socks and gloves—which we include more of in the package. They're used more often than the full suit. Plus, a lot of customers will only be able to afford the gloves and socks—"

Lucas holds a hand up and rolls it forward, urging Larsson to get back on track.

"Anyway," Larsson says, eying Lucas's hand as it stops rolling. "Claire puts the gloves on and she guides Ruth to the kitchen using subtle vibrations in Ruth's gloves that direct her. She helps her get the meal out of the freezer and hits the right buttons on the microwave, and soon, lunch is served.

"While Ruth eats, Claire takes her headset off and makes her own lunch, and when she's done, she checks in with Ruth, who says thanks, but she doesn't need any more help. Ruth looks down, and Claire sees a pile of yarn spread out on the dining table. Ruth informs her that she's knitting some gifts for her granddaughter and grandson. The granddaughter is going off to college soon, and the grandson will be a sophomore in high school. They're visiting on Friday. Ruth has had the yarn for the gifts for a month, but she's just now starting on them. She had hoped her eyesight would be better by now, but she needs to get going.

"She's planning to knit a hat for the grandson and an infinity scarf for the granddaughter—both in the colors of their favorite college. The problem, which only Claire can see, is that Ruth has started the scarf with the wrong color. Black instead of Carolina Blue. Gently, Claire informs Ruth that she'd love to help and that she and her grandmother used to knit together. And so for the rest of the afternoon, Claire guides Ruth's hands as she makes the blue and white scarf. And that becomes Claire's life for the next five days. At breakfast, lunch, and dinner, she signs on and helps Ruth prepare her meals, and in the evening, they knit. And on Friday night, it's Ruth who reaches out to Claire, inviting her to link up outside of 'Be My Guide.' With the headset on, Claire sits on her couch and watches as Ruth sits in her living room with her grandchildren. It's not hurricane relief, but seeing Ruth smile as she hands the knitted gifts to her grandchildren soothes Claire's soul. Sure, work is still a drag and money is tight, but Claire is feeling a lot better than she has in a long, long time.

"On Saturday morning, in those recommendations in the Amersa lobby, we don't show Claire a game or a tourist experience or even another volunteer opportunity. We show her a poster for a course at Amersa Learning. This particular course trains students to become virtual rehabilitation coordinators. That would be a career switch for Claire, but her time with Ruth has convinced her that she'd love the job. The course is expensive, but Amersa offers qualified students access with no upfront payment. Claire can enroll, and assuming she completes the course, she will only have to pay after securing a job in the field. And she can pay in installments. At Amersa, we know Claire is a good investment because we know her better than she knows herself, and we know what the demand is for the position she wants—after all, the job openings are posted on our system. So Claire starts the course that Saturday and continues on Sunday and every hour after work until she's finished the course. With her certification in hand, she promptly secures a job as a virtual rehab coordinator and gives her notice at work.

"The thing that keeps virtual rehab fresh for Claire is that every patient is unique, and so is the rehab program she designs for them.

"Her first patient is a sixty-two-year-old woman who's recovering from a stroke. Her love is gardening, and so Claire recreates her garden in Amersa and they spend time there planting and pruning. Claire uses the haptic gloves and suit to gently nudge the woman and retrain her brain. And soon, the patient isn't gardening in Amersa, she's out in her real garden, with the suit on, living life as she once did before the stroke.

"Claire's next patient is an amputee learning to walk again. He's a huge fan of science fiction. For that reason, Claire uses the Amersa experience builder to transport him to Mars, where he's a colonist helping to build the habitats.

"In the following months, Claire helps Parkinson's patients, people with spinal cord injuries, individuals with multiple sclerosis, TBI survivors, and many more. The hours are long and grueling sometimes, but she's never felt so alive. When her apartment lease is up, Claire doesn't renew. She moves back home. That might feel like a step back to some, but for her, it feels just right. She misses her family, her hometown, and her friends. Plus, living in the city isn't cheap, and at mom and dad's, she's able to save money for a down payment on her first home.

Larsson taps the conference table again. "That's Claire's life. To her, Amersa isn't a neat gadget or a toy or a passing fad. It's where she works. It's where she spends her free time. It's where she trains for a new career. For Claire, Amersa is where she *lives*.

"To Claire, Amersa isn't a technology company. Or an ecosystem. It's something far, far more.

"What I've just described is a window into the future of human life on planet Earth. It's a better world than this one. It's a world where people are happier and more connected. It's a world where they can experience and achieve things beyond their own dreams. But there's just one problem."

Larsson lets the words hang in the air. Every pair of eyes in the room is focused on him. "The problem is that the core technology powering everything I just described doesn't exist. But you're going to build it. That work starts right here, right now, with all of you. That work is about understanding humans at a basic level. It's about knowing what they want—even if they don't—and giving it to them before anyone else can.

"That work—*your work*—will show Claire the poster for Pompeii. And the Red Cross disaster relief volunteer opportunity. Your algorithms will connect her with Ruth. You'll know when she's ready for a career switch. You'll show her the right course and the perfect job. The technology you're starting on today will be the unseen hand that guides her life. Your algorithms will be her therapy for the wounds of the modern world."

Larsson turns to June. "And with that, I want you all to meet Amersa's newest family member. June here is one of the world's leading neuroscientists."

June blushes as Larsson continues. "June, meet your dev team. They may not look like much. And some of them did, in fact, wake up thirty minutes ago in a dust cloud of Doritos, empty Red Bull cans, and bad life decisions. But with that being said, I would trust this group with anything."

Larsson tilts his head. "Well, maybe not *anything*. I mean, I wouldn't let any of them hold a baby. Or change the oil in my car. Or help me move. But literally, like, anything else. Including developing the most advanced software in the world. They can actually do that. In fact, at that *one thing*, they may well be about the best in the world. But don't tell them that. A compliment could erode the deep-rooted personal insecurity that has driven each of them their entire lives."

Larsson motions to the developers. "Don't be afraid to push this group. You'll be surprised at what they're capable of. I have been. And if they complain, don't worry. You can ignore what they're saying. What they really want is for you to show them that you see them, value them, and care. As team lead, how you do that is up to you, but I, for one, typically use witty personal insults."

Then Larsson marches out of the room.

June stands there, seeming flustered. From the end of the table, Lucas calls to her. "Hey, don't worry about it. That's just his style. You get used to it."

"Right," June says slowly. "Well. Where to start…"

She gets her laptop out of her bag, and one of the developers helps her plug it into a port in the conference table, and the screen behind her fills with the word CORTEX.

"First of all," June says, "I'm looking forward to meeting each of you personally and learning more about you." She hesitates. "I know we had lunch scheduled… but if you've been up since last night and need to go home…"

"We can do lunch," Lucas calls out.

June relaxes a little then. "Great. But before we do that, I'd like to give a little overview of the project. Our work sits at the intersection of two fields: neuroscience and neural networks. In short, what we're doing is trying to understand the human mind—to model it."

June advances to the next slide, and I'm staring at a picture of myself. A younger version of me.

"We're going to do that in the way of science: by experimenting, studying the results, and iterating."

June motions to the screen. "Ladies and gentlemen, meet Alan Norris. Participant number one. Alan is a US Marine veteran. An amputee. A husband. And as of two months ago, a father. I found it apt that Anders mentioned virtual rehabilitation. It's in fact one of the areas where we'll be testing the Amersa engine. In Alan's case, he's already completed physical rehab for his prosthetic. But he also suffers from PTSD. As well as tinnitus."

Lucas looks up from the laptop and leans forward.

"I think," June says, "that the arrival of his daughter has made Alan get more serious about his health, in particular treating his PTSD, which is the clinical outcome by which we'll be measuring our success."

The scene freezes, and I realize one of the empty chairs has a figure in it now. The being that looks like my wife gazes at the projector screen. "It was a compelling vision. Until it went wrong."

"What happened?"

"A breakthrough in technology happened. One they didn't fully understand. Anders was too blinded by how much money it could make."

"This... *vision* of his is also very different from the Labyrinth in our timeline. The one I used. It was in a lab. And outside Amersa, people used Labyrinth at movie theaters and mall parking lots and stadiums. They shipped out in sea freight containers. He's talking about devices you use at home."

She smiles at me, as if impressed I noticed. "His vision was the same in both timelines."

"What was the difference?"

"What he was able to accomplish."

"Why?"

"In a word: personnel."

"Lucas. He was alive."

"He lived this long in both timelines."

I realize the answer then. "June."

"Yes."

"She joined Amersa sooner here."

"Never underestimate what one employee can contribute. Here in the numberless world, she made some of Amersa's most important breakthroughs. She essentially cracked the code on the human mind. It's how I know she can do the work I need. And why I kept her away from Amersa in your timeline as long as I could."

"How'd you do it?"

"The answer is right in front of you, Alan."

I study this frozen version of June, younger and fresher. I see the difference immediately. "She's not wearing a wedding ring."

"Correct. In your timeline, her family was what Amersa was to her in the numberless world."

"You played matchmaker?"

"I did."

105

The next scene is in Larsson's office at Amersa. He's chugging a purple smoothie and staring at a bank of four computer screens. When he sees Lucas walk in, Larsson stands and points at him. "Glad you're here."

"What's up?"

"Labyrinth."

Lucas cocks his head. "Okay?"

"What's your first reaction?"

"To what?"

"*Labyrinth*. How does it strike you?"

"Uh, fine. I guess."

"That's all?"

"I mean—what's this about?"

"I think we have a brand problem."

"How? We don't even have any customers yet."

"I'm talking about when we try to *get* customers. Amersa. I always liked the name. It works in a room, but now I'm thinking about how it plays on TV commercials and mobile ads, and…"

Larsson wrinkles his nose. "It's too—"

"Clinical."

He points at Lucas again. "Exactly. Exactly it. It sounds like—"

"A drug you take for a bad infection."

Larsson eyes his colleague. "Weirdly specific, but yes, it has a vaguely pharmaceutical vibe."

"You want to change the company name to Labyrinth?"

Larsson chugs some of the purple smoothie and shakes his

head. "Not the company. Just the product. Like I could see people saying, 'I'm going home to play Labyrinth.'"

He eyes Lucas, waiting.

"Uh, sure."

"You're just humoring me because you can tell I like the name and you know I get locked into things, so you don't want to be on record as *pooh-poohing* it because you know me and you know I'll remember and be low-key annoyed about it forever."

Lucas exhales. "All of those things are true. But also, I'm bad at this."

"At what?"

"Naming things. Last night, I declared variables that are legit over fifty characters long. They're littered with underscores. They're hideous. I would probably call it VR Revolution if it were up to me."

"That's terrible."

"That's what I'm saying."

"But there's something you're holding back."

Lucas exhales even deeper. "Okay. Maybe. But I don't think it matters."

"It matters. Tell me."

Lucas grimaces and speaks slowly, as if taking a first step on broken glass with bare feet. "Well, I think… I think for some people… Labyrinth could be hard to spell."

Larsson narrows his eyes, as if mentally spelling the word to try it out. "Okay. That's fair. I'll give you that."

"But like I said, *I don't think it matters.*"

"Why?"

"Well, for one, there's autocorrect, so if they're searching, it's not going to be an issue. Many of our early adopters will be tech-savvy individuals with a college education or a more advanced working knowledge of mythology, and will likely be familiar with the term. And it's like Google."

"How's it like Google?"

"When they launched, who knew how to spell Google? It's a new word. Also, they don't even spell it like an actual googol."

Larsson is pacing again. "You're right. It's a valid objection, but it's not enough to override what we gain. Labyrinth has that mysterious air to it. It feels inherently high-tech, yet like ancient high-tech, as if we had discovered it and brought it back. And it also feels infinite and unpredictable and fun." He looks pointedly at Lucas. "We're not getting that from any other name."

"Yeah, I'm sold. Hey, listen—"

"The problem," Larsson says absently, "is that I'm locked in. Like I'm all-in on Labyrinth." He stops and nods to Lucas. "You could tell, couldn't you?"

"It uh, yeah, seemed like it."

"But everyone is going to have an opinion. The investors. The design firm that we hire for the logo. The mailman. And I know it's all a waste of time, but I'm also sort of looking for the flaw? You know?"

"I guess. Hey—"

"The issue is what happened with Amersa. I got locked in on that, but I should have thought it through more, and I'm scared I should think this through more."

"You need a break from it."

Larsson nods slowly. "Probably right. I'll sleep on it and not tell anybody about it." He points at Lucas. "You too."

"My lips are sealed."

Larsson takes another long pull from the purple smoothie.

Lucas sets a stack of stapled pages on the desk, covering the wireless keyboard. "Can we talk about something else? It's pretty important, and it doesn't involve either of us naming anything."

"Sure," Larsson says as he picks up the stapled sheets. He scans the first page, then the next, and stops at the third before holding it up.

"What's this?"

"It's a research paper."

Larsson flips back to the title page. "Attention Is All You Need... From Google Brain." That seems to renew his attention. But it doesn't last. He stops at the third page again, which features a flow diagram titled "Figure 1: The Transformer – Model Architecture." "Is there like a meme version of this?"

"I knew if I emailed you, you'd open the PDF and barely look at it. I printed it, hoping you'd read it."

Larsson rolls his eyes. "Look, you could chisel this in the Rosetta Stone, and I still wouldn't be interested."

"Do you at least appreciate the irony of not being able to pay attention to a groundbreaking research paper titled, *literally*—on the page you're holding—*Attention Is All You Need*?"

"I might be into the irony if it was lucrative." Larsson turns the page to face Lucas. "Like if this said, Attention Is All You Need—To Make Money—yes, I would be interested."

"Well, they left that part off, but this is how to make money. A lot of it. It's the future, Anders."

"Of what?"

"Of everything, man."

"Is that all?"

"This is like the moment that asteroid hit the Earth when the dinosaurs were around."

"That wasn't exactly a good thing. For them, anyway."

"It's a bad analogy. The point is that this will usher in a sea change in human society. It's as big as agriculture in terms of changing how we live our lives. And like the asteroid during the dinosaur era, it's going to take time—not much, but some time— for the effects to be experienced. But it's going to be huge, and the ones closest to the crater are the only people who realize what has just happened."

"What exactly are we talking about? No more analogies."

Lucas points at the paper. "This is a new architecture, built on the Transformer. It uses attention mechanisms instead of recurrent or convolutional layers—"

Larsson holds a hand up. "Not. That. Specific."

"It's a new way to train AI models, specifically, it's a breakthrough in NLP."

"What's NLP?"

"Natural Language Processing. It's how computers read and understand language. It's how they learn. The authors of this paper figured out how to make a machine read something, or listen to it, or look at it, and break it apart and learn from it."

"So what?"

"So then it can do similar work. Or the next work in the series."

Larsson exhales. "That's terrible."

Lucas cocks his head. "What?"

"Do you know the worst thing the human race can do? Ever?"

"As in—"

"Make themselves obsolete. That's the worst thing humans can do." Larsson holds the paper up. "You had it right the first time. This is the dinosaur asteroid. You better hope no one is paying attention to this."

"Oh, people are paying attention. Some of the smartest people on Earth are paying attention to this."

"Well that's just great. But what does it mean for us? We already use machine learning in *Labyrinth*." Larsson eyes Lucas. "You see that? The name works."

"It totally does. But look, our existing ML is child's play compared to this. It's a Commodore 64 compared to—"

"No more analogies. I forbid you, Lucas. I absolutely forbid it. Now tell me: what do we do?" Larsson points a finger down at the desk. "Right now. At this company. To use this to our full advantage."

"Well, first, we need to implement a transformer architecture in Labyrinth."

"How does that help us?"

"It's going to make the experience infinitely more immersive and addictive."

"How?"

"Well, first of all, there's not going to be one Labyrinth. There's going to be a billion of them—or however many users we have. The system needs to be fundamentally re-envisioned."

"Not exactly liking the sound of that."

"I mean it will be a lot of work, but it'll be worth it. Long-term."

"Why?"

"Think about it. Right now, we have a base engine with a lot of pre-coded experiences. Yes, the simulations adapt to the user. It extrapolates and uses ML to customize the experience, but it's not *that* different for each user."

Lucas points to the paper. "But with transformer architecture, we can make Labyrinth actually learn and think—and this is the important part—we can make it generate the experience for the user. A completely unique experience driven by our base models and training data from the user."

"As in..."

"Okay, consider CORTEX. Right now, we're doing PTSD simulations. The whole premise is exposure therapy. We have six different storylines that we choose based on the participant's trauma source and triggers. But that's going to change."

"How?"

"Labyrinth will basically train on the participant's history. Every shred of data we can find about the person. It will learn about them. It will study their history and model their mind, and this is the key part: it will predict how they will react to stimuli."

Lucas grabs the paper. "These researchers trained a model on text. Labyrinth will train on a person's history and generate an experience that it predicts will be engaging to them. And then—and this is key—it will use the person's reactions as the next training dataset. Labyrinth will learn continuously and recursively. The more someone uses it, the more data it has and the more it learns, and the better its predictions will be about what a person will do. It'll be able to create an experience that the user will like more and it will be more certain about what the user will do. It can also run the recommendation engine you always talk about. For CORTEX—"

Larsson stands abruptly, pushing his chair back. "This is incredible."

"—the time to resolve the participant's PTSD will be cut—"

"Forget CORTEX, Lucas. The opportunity here is entertainment."

"I agree. Especially as more people use the system. We'll use that data to model one user based on a similar person. Even if we have limited history on a new user, we can type them pretty closely and start with an experience with a high predictability of success."

Larsson returns to his desk chair. "The problem, Lucas, is that right now, two people are having a similar discussion in a similar office."

"We have a head start."

"In tech, head starts are never worth as much as you think. We need to move fast. We'll have to raise another round."

"We just raised—"

"Doesn't matter. All the assumptions for that round just got shredded. Our burn rate. The market opportunity. Everything. We need different funds too. We have to box our competitors out at the top-tier VCs."

Larsson turns slightly in the chair, seeming deep in thought. A few seconds later, he glances over at Lucas, as if remembering he was still there. "Was there anything else?"

"There is, actually."

Lucas nods to the research paper. "It's related to this."

"Okay."

"I want to do a side project."

Larsson shakes his head, annoyed. "That's the worst—*the actual worst*—thing you could say to me right now."

"Why?"

"Lucas, do you know why great companies fail?"

"They run out of money?"

"No. They run out of focus."

"Focus?"

"They start doing random stuff. They do pet projects. Things senior managers and founders champion."

"You think I'm doing that?"

"I do. I think you've made a lot of money. You've sold some of your stock to investors, and you're comfortable now." Larsson points at him, "And you're drifting. You're feeling unfulfilled, and you're reaching for something that you think will make you feel whole. That's what side projects really are."

Lucas smiles. "I'm actually mind-blown that you have this level of personal insight about me."

Larsson rolls his eyes. "I care, Lucas. I really do. The problem is that people think they can take advantage of a nice, accommodating, empathetic manager. It's bad for business. As are side projects. Every successful start-up has to deal with this. I know folks who are, right now, doing clean-up on exactly what you're talking about."

"Clean-up?"

"Shuttering projects. Laying people off by the thousands. Trying to get their company back on track. Trying to get it *focused*. After a bunch of Don Quixote passion projects."

"I don't want to hire anyone. I'll do the work myself. It will be maybe twenty percent of my time."

Larsson cocks his head, smiling maliciously. "Seriously?"

"Yeah. What's the problem?"

Larsson rises and plants his hands flat on the desk. "The whole world just changed, Lucas. I know because you told me you think it's true, and I trust you." He nods to the research paper. "You should be spending *one hundred percent* of your time on getting Amersa ready for the asteroid."

"You said no analogies."

"No, I forbade *you* from making analogies."

"Do you feel like that's a double standard?"

"I don't feel like it's a double standard. I know it's a double standard."

Lucas exhales. "Look, I already spend one hundred percent of my time here. And by that I mean one hundred percent of the time *I'm awake*."

"Good."

"It's not good. Or healthy. Twenty percent still leaves eighty percent, which is probably seventy hours a week. Way more than anyone else here works. Including you."

Larsson settles back in his seat and studies Lucas. "Do you know people working here who don't spend forty hours a week in the office?"

Lucas rolls his eyes. "You're such a psycho."

"I'm aware of that. Who doesn't put in forty hours?"

"No one, Anders. We're all workaholics, so you can relax."

"I'll relax after you've adapted Labyrinth to this new transformer architecture." Larsson holds up a finger. "And, at that point, we can discuss your passion project. Right now, I need all hands on deck."

"I'm not a deck hand, and I'm not going to wait."

"What are you going to do, Lucas?"

"I'm going to find a company that values me—one more open to allowing my side project."

Larsson stares at him. "You have a non-compete."

"Good luck enforcing that in California. When you're bankrupt."

Larsson steeples his fingers. "All right. Let's take it down a notch."

"You took it up a notch."

"I did. As I do. It's who I am and how I got here. But it's possible that I was a little too hasty in dismissing your project. No one's perfect. But we're going to move past it because we're friends and we've known each other a long time and we've built an incredible company together, Lucas."

"Does that mean you want to hear about my project?"

"Precisely what I was trying to say."

Lucas stands and grips the back of the chair. "In *Attention Is All You Need*, they only dealt with text. They did text-based sequence tasks—specifically machine translation. English to German. German to English, etc. The transformer predicted the next token in a sequence. I want to train an AI model on big data—the history of the world and current state of it—and use the engine to predict future extinction events."

Larsson takes a sip of the smoothie as Lucas continues.

"I'm talking about creating an intelligence that understands how massive datasets are related to each other. A non-human, super intelligence that can understand our world in a way we never will. It will know how the world is changing—and when we might be in danger. This is our blind spot, Anders. We are the most successful species that has ever existed on this planet. The ultimate tool builder. We have created—and achieved—what no species on Earth ever has before, but our own context window is too small to understand the consequences of our collective actions. We can, however, do what we're best at: we can create a tool that predicts those outcomes. It's what we do—we're tool builders. And this tool will be the one that saves us from ourselves."

"What do you think it's going to tell you, Lucas?"

"That's the thing—I don't know. The amount of context my brain can hold and its generative capabilities are insufficient to make those predictions."

"Oh, give me a break. We already know the issues. Nukes. Pandemics. Solar flares. Asteroids. Declining birth rates—"

"I'm not talking about any of that."

"Everyone else is."

"True. But we can all see the data on birth rates. And I think those mushroom clouds in the forties scared everyone enough not to use nuclear weapons. After all, no one has since. And some sliver of humanity could survive that. I'm talking about apocalyptic events we can't see. Things that wipe us out for good. I'm talking about the black swan events that only an artificial intelligence can see—with the right training."

The phone on the desk trills, but Larsson ignores it. "I think this is really about your professional boredom and search for personal meaning in your life."

"It's about knowing how the world ends, Anders."

The phone rings a fourth time, and Larsson snatches it. "Yeah?"

His focus drifts to the corner of the computer screen. "I lost track of time. Send him in."

To Lucas, he says, "All right. Go for it. But I want you focused on that transformer architecture too."

The frosted glass office door swings open, and Nathan Briggs strides into the room. He looks as miserable as a man marching to his own execution.

Larsson motions to the new arrival. "Lucas, meet Nathan Briggs."

To Briggs, he says, "Lucas, here was employee number seventeen, and, I would add, the only one of those first twenty left. His work is part of what we're trying to protect."

Lucas glances from Briggs to Larsson. "Protect from what?"

"Corporate espionage."

"Have we been infiltrated?"

"It's the opposite, actually."

"The opposite?"

"Two senior devs just left, right?"

Lucas nods.

"It wasn't about money," Larsson says. "We know they're making less where they went. Why'd they leave?"

Lucas shrugs. "They were both ICs, but neither was on my team."

"But you knew them."

"A little."

"And you know why they left."

"What I heard was that one was unhappy with… the work-life balance."

"The hours," Larsson clarifies.

"The hours," Lucas confirms. "But mostly the deadlines and the stress."

"And what about the other one?"

"A little more ambiguous, but survey says she didn't vibe with the culture."

"What about it?"

Lucas shakes his head. "I don't know. I really don't."

Larsson spreads his hands. "We're all friends here. Real talk, Lucas: why'd she leave?"

"You'd have to talk to her manager—"

"I have. And read the exit interview. It's filled with unhelpful phrases like 'life stages' and 'shifting priorities.' I'm asking what you heard."

"I heard that she felt it was a bit cutthroat around here."

Larsson looks confused. "A bit? It's *very* cutthroat around here."

"Right, well, that's not for everyone. Can I go now? I really hate this. It's the reason I still write code and manage as few people as possible."

"And you don't even fire them. You transfer them."

"I do. If someone is not working out, I ask HR to find another internal opportunity for them."

"You leave your trash on the street."

"I would not characterize anyone I've worked with as trash."

"You recycle. How touching. You're even starting to sound like HR."

Lucas takes a step toward the door. "Yeah. Great talk. I'm gonna get back at it—"

"My concern," Larsson says, speaking slowly, locking eyes with Lucas like a *Star Trek* tractor beam, "is that they both walked out of here with the most precious commodity we have at this company: knowledge. They know what we've built, and right now, they may well be sitting in a conference room telling their new colleagues how to build a copy. Maybe even showing them some sample code they downloaded before they sent that resignation email."

Lucas cuts his eyes to Briggs, who is standing at parade rest, staring at the wall.

"As you correctly noted," Larsson continues, "non-competes are hard to enforce in California. But stealing trade secrets is still illegal there. *That*, we can enforce."

"If we can prove it," Lucas says.

Larsson points at Briggs. "That's exactly what Nathan is doing: gathering proof. I want you to help him."

"Help him how?"

"Point him in the right direction. You know our tech under the hood, and you'll have a gut instinct about whether their new employers start making great leaps—innovations eerily similar to ours. Things they weren't capable of last week."

Lucas motions to the research paper on the desk. "Kind of got my hands full here. You said *one hundred percent*—"

"Make time for this, Lucas. An ounce of prevention is worth a pound of cure."

"I don't even know what that means in this context."

"It means we draw the line here. We make an example of these two. Maybe they are sharing our trade secrets, maybe they aren't, but one thing I know for sure: being dragged into court and accused of stealing from your former employer is not going to be great for that work-life balance they claim to cherish so much. Or their shifting priorities and life stages, and certainly not their future job prospects. But ultimately, it's not about them."

"What's it about?"

"It's about the next *them*. The guy sitting at his desk downstairs hyped up on Adderall and coffee and full of frustration and about to make a bad decision because he thinks he can get away with it. Because he knows his highest value isn't working here—it's walking out the door with our work. Like I said, it's about prevention."

"Look, if we know—or strongly suspect—someone ripped us off, by all means, let's do it. But I think this could be a dark path, Anders."

Larsson points at Lucas. "I don't care if it's the black hole at the center of the Milky Way galaxy. Nobody steals from us."

The scene freezes, and the creature who appears as my wife is standing in the office. She motions to Larsson. "The dark turn."

"Why did you show me this?"

"You need to understand who you're dealing with. And where they went wrong."

"One thing I've noticed: Lucas is in every scene. The ones without me."

"That's very observant, Alan."

"It's about him, isn't it?"

She exhales and steps away from me. "No. It's about what he did. Pay attention, Alan. Remember, all you need is attention."

106

The view switches from Larsson's office to a small network operations center. On the right, the wall is covered with computer screens that show graphs and gauges. In the middle of the screens is a bank of windows that looks out on a server room with rows of towering black cabinets. Inside, lights blink out of sync, green, yellow, and red.

There are four desks in front of the screens and windows, and two are occupied. At one station, a guy is typing feverishly at a command prompt while muttering. The woman at the desk beside him gets up, peers at his screen, and tells him she'll go and swap the drives.

She exits the NOC, and as she does, Lucas strides in.

As he passes by, more of the room comes into view. Next to the desks, there are two open server racks that are half full. The fans cooling the devices whine constantly, creating a droning background noise that's mildly disorienting.

In the middle of the NOC is a small conference table. Isaac sits in one of the chairs. Like June in the flashback, he's a little younger here.

At the head of the table is a man in his fifties who's sipping from a coffee mug. He has a large belly and a matching large mustache.

On the wall opposite the bank of screens, there's a whiteboard where a young guy is using a dry-erase marker to draw a network diagram. He pauses, still holding the marker. "How many ports does it have?"

"Sixteen," mustache man calls out, the sound like a bark over the sound of the whining servers.

"But only four are PoE," the younger Isaac adds, not looking back.

The mustached man spots Lucas then and nods to him. "What do you need?"

"I'm Lucas."

The guy holding the marker glances back. "Have you tried rebooting?"

Lucas grimaces. "I don't need to reboot."

The man at the desk, who was muttering into the command prompt, swivels to his colleagues. "Could be an I-D-10-T error."

Lucas exhales and glares at the guy. "I know that spells idiot."

ID10T guy slowly turns red.

"I, too," Lucas adds, "work with computers. And coincidentally, I have the internet."

Isaac smiles but keeps his focus on the conference table.

The door to the NOC opens, and the woman leans in and says to her colleague, "Anything?"

ID10T guy seems relieved at the interruption. "Still no workie. Should we pull another one? We need an even number for RAID ten."

She shakes her head. "No. Let's back up and go to five and retask the server. Something's going on. I can't tell if the controller…"

Lucas steps deeper into the NOC, speaking over the server noise and the other conversation. "Are you Gordon?"

The guy with the mustache nods.

Lucas grips the chair at the opposite end of the table. "You get my email?"

"I did," Gordon barks. "You get mine?"

"I did."

The guy at the whiteboard crosses out one of the boxes. "It doesn't work. Too many nodes now. And that assumes they don't hire anyone."

"They're not hiring anyone," Gordon says. "And there will be three fewer nodes next week."

"Oh," whiteboard guy says. "Uh... Which ones?"

Gordon sips his coffee. "Not our department."

The guy at the whiteboard puts the cap back on the marker. "We should just put in a new switch for the entire floor. Flatten the topography—"

Gordon sets his mug on the table with a loud thunk. "We're not buying new hardware."

Whiteboard guy exhales. "We're just making a mess here. A nightmare to maintain—"

"We *can* buy new hardware," Gordon says slowly. "We *can* do that. But we'll have to lay off some of the IT staff. *Or* we can repurpose what we have. And not do layoffs."

The servers whine, and Gordon stares at his mug, and the man standing at the whiteboard uncaps the marker. "Oh" is all he says before refocusing on the diagram, studying it with renewed interest, as if he were wandering through the Louvre and had stumbled upon a master work.

In the silence that follows, Gordon looks up at Lucas, seeming to realize he was still there. "What did you need?"

"Can we talk?"

Gordon motions to the network diagram on the whiteboard. "We're kind of in the middle of something."

"Great," Lucas says brightly, acting as if the man had said yes. "Did you get the email from Anders?"

At the whiteboard, the guy picks up the eraser and wipes away several boxes.

Gordon takes another sip of coffee. "I did."

Lucas settles into the chair across from him. "So?"

"So, we can't do it. I said that in my email—"

"Why not?"

"We don't have server capacity."

Lucas leans forward. "This is a priority."

Gordon eyes him. "I know. But we don't have what you're asking for."

"Which part?"

"All of them. We don't have the compute or the storage capacity or anything else."

The guy at the whiteboard turns. "We could use AWS."

Gordon exhales. "Thanks, Harry Potter."

"Why're you calling me Harry Potter?"

"Because we can't wave a magic wand and solve resource problems. What he's talking about would cost a million dollars a day on AWS."

The words seem to awaken Isaac. He sits up in the chair and glances from Gordon to Lucas. "A million dollars a day?"

Lucas points at Gordon. "This can't be in a public cloud. It has to be local."

Isaac focuses on Gordon. "What's he asking for?"

Whiteboard guy says, "I was just trying to help."

Gordon nods. "I know."

"What's he asking for?" Isaac repeats. Gordon picks up a tablet and scrolls and apparently finds the email and shoves it over to Isaac, who begins reading intently.

At the end of the table, Lucas stands. "Anders told you this was a priority."

Gordon rises to his feet. "He also just laid off half the company and cut everyone else to half rations."

"I'm not half the company, and I don't eat rations."

"Clearly. You're still here."

"So are you, unfortunately."

"And unfortunately, I'm working overtime to keep the servers online while you're indulging in passion projects."

Isaac looks up from the tablet, seeming oblivious to the argument. "We have this."

Gordon is breathing hard now, the air blowing across his mustache. "I know you helped build the company, and you think that gives you the right to do whatever you want. But we don't have what you're asking for."

"We do," Isaac says.

His two words are like a pause button on the verbal dueling match between the two men.

Lucas, still eying the head of IT, is the first to speak: "What does that mean?"

Isaac shrugs. "We have this."

"We don't," Gordon says, crossing his arms.

Isaac nods to the tablet. "He needs compute and storage, but mostly, he needs GPUs to do the workloads. We have them."

Gordon opens his mouth, but Isaac cuts him off. "But not in the server room."

"Okay," Lucas says. "Where are they?"

Isaac shrugs again. "Everywhere."

Gordon bends down to face Isaac. "Hey. I know you've been up all night. Why don't you go on home?"

Isaac narrows his eyes and looks at Gordon like he's crazy. "I'm not going anywhere."

Lucas moves to the chair beside Isaac. "What do you mean, *everywhere*?"

"We're a video game company. We have a building full of workstations with high-end graphics cards. GPUs."

Isaac motions to Gordon. "And as noted, half the company just got laid off, so those GPUs are available to do your workloads all the time. And even for the people who are left, they're only here eight hours a day."

"More like fourteen," Lucas says.

Isaac chuckles. "Truth bomb! But even during that time, their workstations aren't at max utilization. There's spare compute we can access."

Gordon rounds the table and stares across at Lucas and Isaac. "It's a neat idea, but it's all academic. He can't go to all the workstations and use them."

"He doesn't need to," Isaac mutters, seeming annoyed. "We'll do it like SETI@HOME."

Gordon's eyes flash. "Sitting at home?"

For the first time since he entered the network operations center, Lucas smiles and whispers a single word: "Genius."

Isaac gets his laptop out of his bag. "I'll write the program and have it launch at start-up."

Lucas shakes his head. "It's okay. I can do it. I just need you guys to install it on the machines."

Isaac places his hands on the keyboard and logs in. "Nah, I got it."

"You're a developer?"

"Yeah."

"But you work in IT?"

"It's less stress. Deadlines are like—"

"Kryptonite," Lucas says.

"Exactly. They set off my tinnitus. It's a condition where I hear noise in my ears—"

"I know what it is. I have it too."

Isaac turns to Lucas.

Across from them, Gordon leans over the table. "*Hello?* What are you weirdos talking about? Sitting at home—"

"No one is sitting at home," Isaac mutters.

Lucas drops his voice and tilts his head toward Gordon. "I mean, he might be pretty soon."

Isaac grins like a Cheshire cat. "I'm a developer, not a doctor, but that appears to be a *bad burn*."

Gordon's cheeks flush. "*Sitting*—"

The guy from the whiteboard, who has recapped his marker and wandered over to the table, holds his hands up. "Gordon, I think they're saying *settee* at home. Like a couch you'd have in your living room."

At the server rack, the fans scream louder. I can't tell if another machine just turned on or if the ones running just turned up the RPMs, but either way, the noise in the room increases.

At the desks below the bank of screens, the woman gets up from her chair and says to IDioT guy, "Just started the transfer."

She places a hand on Gordon's shoulder, and when he glances back at her, she says, "They're talking about SETI@HOME. S-E-T-I. As in the search for extraterrestrial intelligence. At home."

Gordon's mustache wiggles like a gerbil bedding down for the night. "Really?"

Isaac has opened a coding program with white text on a black background. "Really," he mumbles, not looking up.

Two conversations run concurrently then: Gordon with the woman and Isaac with Lucas.

"Our biggest problem," Isaac says, "is that the machines go to sleep. We need to enable—"

"Wake-on-LAN," Lucas says.

Isaac eyes him. "Correct."

"Can you push the change to all the workstations?"

"No. On a lot of the boxes, the Wake-on-LAN setting is in the BIOS."

"You could email instructions to the users."

"They'll screw it up."

"Some won't."

"True, but like Gordon said, as of last week, a lot of the machines don't have users anymore. I'll do it. I'll just go around and install the app and update the BIOS. I work nights anyway."

"Me too," Lucas says, voice barely audible over the hum of the servers. "I'll help."

"You don't have to," Isaac says.

"I want to," Lucas says, staring at the screen as Isaac types.

Across the table, the woman says to Gordon, "SETI@HOME is a project at Berkeley. It's a piece of software anyone can download and install on their computer."

"What does it do?"

"It pulls down a dataset of radio signals and analyzes it."

"For what?"

"Signs of alien life. SETI@HOME provides access to tons of volunteer computing power, enabling the project to search the stars for extraterrestrial signals much faster."

At the conference table, Lucas asks Isaac what he needs.

"I can write the client. I just need some help with the—"

"Server-side?" Lucas asks.

"Yep. When the client is installed, it'll check in with the server and register itself as being ready for work. Then the server will give it a job."

"How do we break up the tasks?"

Isaac points at him. "So that's where I am right now. It's got to be some kind of queueing system where the server assigns a job. If the worker doesn't send the completed job back within a reasonable timeframe, the job is canceled and reassigned to another worker. The question is, when the worker registers, should it tell the server what hardware it has—to give the system some idea of what size jobs it can handle?"

"But," Lucas says, "the machine could be super tricked out, but it's being run hard all day, so—"

"It needs to account for utilization."

Lucas leans back in the chair. "Or ELEE could just give every worker a small task and see what comes back, and scale the job size based on how quickly the worker returns the data. And it could use exponential backoff for the unreliable or slow nodes."

"Who's ELEE?"

Lucas looks sheepish. "Oh, that's what I call the program. E-L-E-E. Extinction Level Event Engine."

Gordon leans across the table. "Hey. This is... really interesting, but there are some problems. And I need to okay this with—"

Isaac squints at him. "What problems?"

"Well," Gordon says, straightening up. "For one, you're talking about getting access to everyone's computer. We need authorization—"

"We already have access to everyone's computer. *We're IT.*"

"Yes, but you're talking about running them day and night as hard as they'll go."

"So?"

"So that's going to result in hardware failures."

Isaac shrugs. "We're IT. We fix broken computers."

Gordon stares Isaac down. "Thanks. I wasn't aware of that. Here's something you apparently aren't aware of: fixing broken computers requires replacement parts. Parts cost money." He points at the whiteboard. "We have no money for new hardware. Period."

Isaac puts his hands on his keyboard and begins typing again. "Still not a problem."

"Which part?"

"The *parts* part."

"What about it?"

"We don't need to buy new parts."

Gordon's eyes bulge. "What planet are you living on? Computers break. Parts cost money. We have no money."

"I live on Earth, unfortunately," Isaac says, still typing. "Where I use money, some of it to buy parts, which I use to fix broken computers, among other things. The thing is, we have a building full of spare parts. They're in the hundreds of computers no one is using. Also, those parts are already paid for. All we need is labor. Which we have because—"

"We're IT," Gordon shouts, face like a red balloon about to pop. "And I'm the *head* of IT and telling you that you're not going to work on this until I run it by finance and ops."

"I'm going to work on this," Isaac mumbles, typing more quickly now.

"No, you're not."

"As you noted, I worked all night, Gordon. So I'm technically off. I'm working on this on my personal time."

Beside him, Lucas suppresses a smile.

"There's also the issue of power," Gordon says. "Running every workstation in the building all the time will use more power. And power costs money."

"Yes, but it doesn't cost us money," Lucas says, his focus still on Isaac's screen.

"It costs *someone* money," Gordon says, voice rising. "A lot of money. And you can bet I'm going to hear about it."

Lucas points to the screen and whispers to Isaac, who thinks for a second, then whispers back, "I agree."

To Gordon, Lucas says, "Do you know why we're doing layoffs?"

"Because Anders is delaying the roll-out to overhaul the product. He's nervous that it's not good enough. Classic first release jitters. But the real issue is that he's delaying *revenue generation*. He's blown up the whole business plan, and now we have to lay off all those go-to-market people we hired. *And* he's spending what cash we have left on hiring PhDs and moving them here."

"You missed one thing."

"Oh yeah?"

"High fixed costs."

"Such as?"

"Rent. For this massive office that was built just for us.

Which we signed a twenty-year lease for." Lucas holds up a finger. "With annual rent escalations of three percent. I know because I was there when it was signed. What we don't pay for is building maintenance. Or taxes. Or landscaping. Or *power*. Yes, the landlord wanted us to pay excess over a base load, but Anders wouldn't hear of it because he wanted a full-service lease with no surprises, so he doesn't have to deal with anything." Lucas pauses a moment. "Well, we do pay for cleaning, but that's only because we're too paranoid to let a third party go through our trash. The point is, we can use as much power as we want, and it won't cost us another dime. In fact, go tell Anders we're about to spike the power bill. He'll get a kick out of it. He's got major buyer's remorse about the rent right now."

The scene freezes, and the woman who told Gordon about SETI@HOME morphs into my wife. She nods at Lucas and Isaac.

"Total legend."

"Which one?"

She considers the two developers. "Both. But Lucas especially. This would be easier if he were here."

"But you got the math wrong on that, didn't you?"

"I did. I didn't realize how cruel Anders and Amersa could be. Humans are hard to factor."

She puts her hands on Isaac's shoulders and reads the code on his screen, a smile growing on her lips. "But I've seen what Isaac is capable of. I think he can pull it off. You better hope he can."

107

The network operations center changes to an open team room in the office where Lucas and Isaac are sitting with their laptops out, both coding.

With a remote, Lucas activates a projector, and on the far wall, an episode of *Star Trek: Voyager* begins to play.

I remember this one. It's when *Voyager* meets up with the USS *Equinox*, another Federation ship lost in the delta quadrant. The *Equinox*'s captain is played by John Savage and his first officer is the dude who plays Harry Bosch on the Amazon Prime series. It was a good one.

Lucas motions to the screen. "Will this distract you? For me, it's like background—"

"Music," Isaac says.

"Exactly. Because sometimes I can't hear music."

Isaac nods. "Only the ringing."

"That's right."

On his laptop, Isaac opens a video player and turns the screen to Lucas. "This is my playlist."

The list of files never seems to end. It's got every *Star Trek* series and movie, *Battlestar Galactica*, *Star Wars*, *The X-Files*, *Firefly*, *Stargate SG-1*, and *Stargate Atlantis*.

Lucas eyes the screen with reverence. "Solid."

"For the *Star Trek* series," Isaac says, "I play them in the order of—"

"Stardates."

Isaac inclines his head slowly. "It's the only thing that makes sense."

"It is," Lucas agrees. "It really is."

He leans back in his office chair and studies Isaac's list again and seems to come to a decision. "I need to show you something."

They leave the team room and take the elevator down to the floor with the network operations center.

"I actually have another side project," Lucas says as he draws his key card from his pocket.

"Another model?"

"It's a model. But not an AI one."

They pass the NOC, where only one person is manning the graveyard shift—the guy who tried to surreptitiously crack the ID10T error joke.

Lucas scans his badge at the next door and ushers Isaac into a room with a concrete floor, metal stud walls, and exposed ductwork overhead.

Isaac's voice echoes slightly in the cavernous space. "The expansion server room. Gordon said this was canceled."

"That's right. Anders has agreed to let me use the space."

"For what?"

"Guess."

Isaac strolls around the room, which has three rolling chairs in a slight semicircle and two others in front of them spaced further apart. They're all pointed at the far wall, which has a wide rectangle outlined by blue tape. A letter-size white page is taped in the middle with the word "VIEWSCREEN."

On the floor, blue tape outlines an oval that's flattened at both ends.

As Isaac studies the shape, his eyes grow wider by the second. "No way," he whispers. He looks up at Lucas. "Are you serious?"

"This is not something I would kid around about."

A time lapse follows. Isaac and Lucas spend every waking hour together on two things: writing the code for Lucas's ELEE AI and hiring contractors to work on the abandoned server room.

They visit a sheet metal shop where fabricators study their drawings curiously and reluctantly agree to build what they need.

The dance is the same at a sign shop, where the owner goes through their images and CAD drawings, squinting as she chews the end of a BIC pen.

"So," Lucas says finally, "can you do it?"

"We can," she replies, still focused on the pages.

"How?"

"We'd use vacuum-formed plastic and LEDs for the panels. Same for the walls. Which will be easier than the panels. There's just so much detail work on those."

"What about the ceiling?" Lucas asks.

"They're just interior lighted panels. But you don't have the head height in the room for this exact curve. We'll have to make them a little more shallow."

Lucas cuts his eyes to Isaac. "Acceptable."

"I concur, Captain."

The sign maker exhales. "Look, guys, it's a cool project, but it's also a lot of material and work."

"Also acceptable," Isaac says.

"Okay. I'll get you a quote. I just think it's maybe going to be more than you want to spend on a hobby project."

"This isn't a hobby," Lucas says. "This is where we're going to work."

At a custom cabinet shop, they get the same reception—and also what they need.

Online, they order custom seats.

The sales rep at the carpet store tries to get them to agree to shades of burgundy and gray they already carry, but Isaac informs her that it has to be the exact color in the images.

The woman bunches her eyebrows. "Really, hun?"

"Afraid so, ma'am."

At a local elevator vendor, four employees sit across a conference table scrutinizing their drawings. The owner, who has been massaging his forehead since the meeting began, sets the drawings down.

"I want to make sure I'm getting all of this right."

Lucas inclines his head.

"You want double doors—both with custom veneers, a totally

custom interior cab, rear and front entry—one at each stop—and only five feet of total rise? And the shaft doesn't even go between floors?"

"Is that a problem?" Isaac asks.

"Well, not technically, but based on the cab size, it's going to be a commercial elevator."

Lucas and Isaac share a knowing, uncomfortable glance.

"I'm guessing," the man says, "that based on your reaction you have some idea of the cost involved and the on-going inspection requirements with a commercial versus a residential elevator—"

"It's not that," Isaac says quietly.

The man eyes them.

Lucas leans forward slightly. "Please call it a turbo lift."

Time spins like a VCR tape on fast forward. Lucas and Isaac continue to write code with sci-fi in the background, and increasingly, they put on headsets and play with prototype versions of Labyrinth, testing the VR and software.

Occasionally, they go down to the spare server room to meet one of the contractors for an install. The metal ramps are installed first, followed by the walls. The lighted panels and ceiling are next, and like layers on a painting, the picture of what they're building becomes more clear.

And I can't help but smile.

The carpet goes in, and then the chairs.

The elevator vendor takes down the temporary stairs, unpacks their parts, and assembles them on-site. The owner shows up as it's being tested.

"I had to see it for myself" is all he says as he peers into the room.

When the room is finished, Isaac and Lucas work there, using the main viewscreen for their sci-fi reruns and occasionally displaying code on it or remote access sessions to the server.

Lucas's team also starts working in the room, and in several of the fast forwards, I see June sitting at a science station.

The view switches to Anders Larsson strolling down a corridor.

At the door to the modified server room, he swipes his badge and steps through and stops short, clearly confused by the strange, small alcove.

A motion sensor near the ceiling flashes red, and there's a soft ding, and the double doors of the custom elevator slide open. Larsson squints at it, but marches forward, eying the two buttons that say DECK 10 and BRIDGE.

DECK 10 is lighted, so he punches BRIDGE, and when the forward doors part, he's looking at a near-perfect replica of the bridge of the starship *Enterprise* 1701-D from *Star Trek: The Next Generation*.

Larsson walks out slowly, taking it in, a look somewhere between shock and pure disgust on his face.

Lucas rises from the captain's chair and turns.

Isaac is sitting at the ops station on the left, and when he glances back and sees Larsson, he gets to his feet as well. "Captain, intruder alert!"

"I see him, Commander."

Larsson scans the bridge again, shaking his head. "Jesus, Mary, and Joseph. How much did this cost?"

"Money doesn't exist in the twenty-fourth century," Isaac deadpans. "We work to better ourselves and the rest of humanity."

Larsson scowls at him. "I just threw up in my mouth a little bit."

"Good," Isaac shoots back.

"Sir," Lucas says, "I received your subspace hail but—"

"Knock it off. Briggs is here. I need you."

"Captain," Isaac says quietly, leaning toward Lucas but keeping his eyes on Larsson. "I believe the Romulan Ambassador is attempting to be deceptive. The brig is empty, Sir."

"Noted, Commander. You have the bridge."

Lucas walks past me, up the ramp, and into the so-called turbo lift, Larsson stomping behind him.

The doors slide shut. I expect the scene to change, but everything freezes.

A figure materializes in the chair to the left of the captain's center seat. She stands and steps toward me. It's Counselor

Deanna Troi, the empathic ship's counselor, clad in the blue commander's uniform from the later seasons.

She speaks in Troi's gentle British lilt, her tone sympathetic.

"Alan, I sense confusion—and troubled feelings—inside you."

I sweep a hand at the re-created set. "What *is* this?"

"It's the bridge—"

"It's two guys cosplaying *Star Trek* at work."

"It is—and it's history. It's how you'll convince Isaac."

"Convince him of what?"

"To trust you."

Isaac's double stands beside the helm station that Lieutenant Commander Data normally occupies. In the suspended tableau, he's staring at the turbo lift doors Lucas just left through.

"They built this in our time, too?"

"Yes."

"I want to see my team."

"You will."

"When?"

"Soon, Alan. We're almost out of time. This is the last part. This is how the world ends."

108

In the next scene, I'm looking at a younger version of myself.

He's standing in the kitchen of the house Jenn and I bought together. In the flashback, he picks up a breakfast tray bearing scrambled eggs, grits, toast, strawberries, and blueberries.

This is about eight years ago. Right before Riley was born. I know because on the refrigerator there's a printed picture in black and white from an ultrasound.

My younger self passes and I stand there, staring out the window at the backyard. There's a hammock swaying in the wind and beyond it, two ends of a cornhole game. The bean bags lie in a pile between them.

Jenn and I loved that home. It was a little house on a large lot, a brick ranch with three bedrooms and two full baths. What it didn't have was stairs. For me, that was the only deal breaker in our home search. Jenn's only must-have was walkability to restaurants and things to do.

It was no stairs for me and no driving for her.

We settled on this place.

It took a while. My wife was methodical with the house hunt. Online, she must have toured every home on the market in our price range, clicking the listings on her lunch break and at night, on the couch beside me while we streamed TV, and in bed after we turned out the lights.

She emailed me two or three listings a day until I finally told her, "If you like it, I like it."

"Cop out," was her only response.

"How in the world can that be a cop out?"

"You're willing to agree because you know I care more about this than you do."

"What's the problem with that?"

"The problem is that I'm scared if you compromise to appease me, you'll regret it."

I took one of her hands in mine. "You're overthinking this—"

"You're underthinking it."

"You're probably right. But it doesn't mean I'm wrong."

"About what?"

"About you caring more about this than me. I *will* be happy. I can make it all work as long as we're together."

"Alan—"

"I'm serious. I'm a lottery winner."

"What does that mean?"

"It means that I'm living on borrowed time. One day, a bomb blew off a big part of my body. And a bigger part of two of my friends. They didn't get a second chance. I did. If a million tiny things had been different, I wouldn't have. So if I've got to walk up some stairs so that we can walk to dinner, it really doesn't matter to me. I don't care if I have to park on the street so we can be closer to your favorite restaurant. I don't care if the bathrooms aren't updated or if the kitchen layout isn't ideal. When you've been through what I have—"

"I think that's a very unhealthy way to look at your life."

I exhaled, and she tried to pull her hand away, but I held tight.

She leaned in. "You deserve to be happy."

"I *am* happy. Deliriously happy."

"But do you think you *deserve* to be?"

I hesitated, and the moment I did, I knew she saw it, and she seized upon it. "Let me answer for you: you do, Alan. You're not a lottery winner. You're not someone with some undeserved windfall in life that you'll never pay back with suffering. You're just like the rest of us."

I sat there silently. I knew these moments. She was a train. And it had left the station.

"Bad things happened to you, Alan. Just like everyone else. And good things. Yes, your bad things were a lot worse than what happens to most people. It makes the good things look even better."

She stared at me, and I stared back.

Finally, she asked me what I thought about that, and I told her, "I have two thoughts."

She smirked playfully. "I only have time for one, but go ahead."

"First, I think you should be teaching my psychology classes."

She rolled her eyes and told me her plate was full, and I told her the second thing: "We can both be right."

"About what?"

"The lottery called life. Pick the house you want. I already got what I wanted."

In the flashback, the younger, less worn version of me carries the tray past the kitchen island and the living room and into a narrow hallway.

The door on the left is open. In my timeline, Jenn used that bedroom as an office and it's the same here—a desk under the window. The guest bed has been moved into the room already.

He passes the hall bath on the right and then the second largest bedroom on the left, which we used for guests but is now a nursery. The walls are sky blue with stickers shaped like clouds. The popcorn ceiling has been painted dark gray with white stars. The crib is assembled and waits across from an oversized recliner.

With the tray, he pushes the bedroom door open. Jenn is sitting up, belly protruding, but she doesn't see him come in. She's wearing a Labyrinth headset and a pair of gloves. Her hands are at her sides, but her fingers move as if she's pulling a puppet's strings.

The woman I married spent most of her free time either reading or running (while listening to an audiobook). Her bedside table was always stacked with hardcover novels from the library and the occasional biography. She used an e-reader as well, and she always plugged it in every night. That was another one of her quirks: fear of her e-reader running out of juice.

Younger me unfolds the legs on the bottom of the tray and

sets it beside her and gently shakes his wife's leg. She pushes the headset up and eyes the breakfast tray.

"Thanks, but I'm close. I want to finish."

In the next scene, Lucas and Isaac are expanding their Star Trek set into the next room. The new space is accessible from the bridge via the sliding doors opposite the turbo lift; however, this exit doesn't have an elevator, but rather a short flight of stairs leading down to a landing with a door on the right that opens into the hall.

The room is mostly empty space, and all the walls have been painted black, including the floor and ceiling. Yellow-orange grid lines wrap the room the way they did on Star Trek's holodeck.

On the far wall is a series of VR stations with 360 treadmills and Labyrinth headsets, suits, and gloves. They're testing prototypes, but it reminds me of a row of Borg alcoves.

Time skips forward, and Lucas and Isaac spend every waking moment testing the hardware and meeting with that team and then hanging out on the bridge and coding while old episodes of Star Trek play in the background.

The scene returns to the house Jenn and I shared, to our bedroom, where a grainy, black-and-white baby monitor shows a crib where Riley is wrapped as tight as a burrito and is crying at the top of her lungs.

Younger me—whom I've started thinking of as Alan—reaches over and exhales as if looking at the monitor might soothe the child.

Beside him, Jenn is lying on her back, a Labyrinth headset still attached. She's not playing—her hands aren't moving.

He rises from the bed and hastily attaches the prosthetic, and she finally stirs, then reaches up and pushes the headset away and puts a hand on his back.

"I'll get her," she says sleepily.

"No, I've got it."

"It's my turn."

He rises, rounds the bed, gently puts a hand on her shoulder, and guides her back down.

"I've got it."

"You'll be tired tomorrow."

"Eh, I could teach those plans in my sleep."

In the nursery, he lifts Riley out and marches down the narrow hall, rocking her gently. He gets a bottle from the fridge and holds it to her mouth as he walks around.

He chances sitting on the couch, still holding her, but the child spits the bottle out and screams, and he rises again and continues marching.

When he passes the third bedroom, I notice the bed is gone. In its place is a Labyrinth treadmill bearing large yellow words: PROTOTYPE – NOT FOR SALE.

I blink, and I'm standing in the holodeck room with the prototypes. Isaac is on one treadmill, and he looks like he's throwing a frisbee.

Lucas walks to the alcove beside him and dons a headset but doesn't bother with the suit.

The view switches to inside Labyrinth, where Isaac is wearing a white uniform with blue lines. He's throwing a thick frisbee-type device that lights up blue.

I realize then he's playing a version of the movie *TRON*.

"Hey!" Lucas says as Isaac catches the disc.

"Greetings, program!"

"You've been in here eighteen hours."

"So?"

"You're getting sicker. You need to rest, Isaac."

"Dude, I'm fighting for the users."

Back at the house Jenn and I shared, we're sitting on the couch. Riley must be about two—she's running around and mumbling, and we've both got one eye on her (she was a handful back then).

A Christmas tree sits in the corner, yellow lights reflecting on the dark windows. It's loaded with ornaments, but they start about halfway up. That was the same at our house: we kept the ornaments out of Riley's reach. Jenn thought the half-decorated tree was a little tacky, but we couldn't figure out a good way to cordon it off.

On the TV, a news reporter is outside a big box retailer, where long lines snake out the door.

This isn't Black Friday. It's the release of Labyrinth.

"This is certainly the iPhone moment of our generation," the reporter says. "And some say it might even be bigger."

Jenn picks up the glass of wine and takes a long swig.

"You should have asked them to pay you in stock for the trial."

Next, Alan and Jenn are in the bedroom again, the grainy black-and-white monitor hissing on his bedside table.

They're both wearing Labyrinth headsets, and their fingers are moving beside them. I wonder if they're playing together or off on separate adventures.

In my timeline, Jenn and I binged TV after we put Riley to bed. But Jenn had a strict 9 PM cutoff—unless there was fifteen minutes or less left in the episode.

From the monitor, Riley says, "Dad? Dad! I'm scared."

He rips the headset off and stands. Behind him, Jenn doesn't get up or reach for the headset. Her hands wiggle, pulling the unseen puppet strings.

On the bridge set, Lucas sits in the captain's chair, Isaac in the first officer seat to his right. The whole dev team is there and they're sipping flutes of champagne and eating white cake.

The main viewscreen shows a TV segment from CNBC. Anders Larsson is joining via video and a financial news anchor is hitting him with questions rapid-fire.

The headline below reads *Amersa IPO oversubscribed. Stock doubles on opening day.*

"Do you worry about competitors?" the anchor asks. "Apple is developing a VR system and we got news yesterday that Google has partnered with Nintendo to create their own device."

Larsson smiles. "We're not focused on competitors."

The anchor seems unimpressed. "But are you *worried* about them?"

"I'm worried about creating transcendental products that expand what's possible for humanity. That's how Amersa got here, and as long as we're doing that, everything else will take care of itself."

The interview ends and Larsson's video square is pushed off the screen and the four anchors chat about Larsson and Amersa like sportscasters on game night.

"He's got the Steve Jobs chutzpah," the interviewer says as he stacks some cards on the glass table.

"He's also got seventy-two billion dollars," the female anchor beside him adds. "So he's probably not worried about *anything* at this point."

Isaac leans closer to Lucas. "That true?"

"Not even close. He's never been so paranoid. He's constantly panicking about something. He's spending insane amounts of money on all these exclusive content licensing deals, and he's got recruiters out there practically stalking top talent. 'Give me a number' is how he starts the interviews now."

"I figured the money would mellow him."

"Just the opposite."

"And what's it like for you? I mean, granted, if my math is right, it's just one billion, but you know, how many do you really need?"

"I feel the same as I did yesterday. Plus, it's not like we can sell until the lock-up is over."

Isaac smiles lazily. "I've thought about that like ten million times."

"You're going to sell some of your stock?"

"Some. Maybe a quarter. Or half. I'll regret it if I don't." Isaac grins at Lucas. "Ask me how I feel."

Lucas does, and Isaac deadpans, "Invincible. I feel invincible, dude."

"You don't look it. What did the doctor say?"
"That I'm fine."
"Did they test—"
"For everything."
"Everything?"
"Parkinson's. Early-onset Alzheimer's. ALS. Huntington's. *Everything*. I'm just burned out."

The bridge disappears, and I'm standing in my old living room, where younger Alan is sitting on the couch, Jenn next to him, Riley between them, fidgeting as she watches a video on one of their phones.

On the TV, WRAL news is playing. In a grim voice, a female anchor is reciting numbers: nine confirmed cases in Wake County and thirty-four statewide. A banner crawls across the bottom: GOV. COOPER TO ADDRESS SCHOOL CLOSURES AT 4 P.M.

On the coffee table, a phone vibrates and Alan picks it up.
"Who is it?" Jenn asks absently, still fixated on the screen.
"They're canceling in-person classes starting Monday."
"For how long?"
"Two weeks, at least."

The COVID pandemic unfolds in a flashback that is a strange mirror of what I lived through. In my timeline, everyone stayed home and tried to work, played video games, watched TV, or read.

In the numberless world, Labyrinth becomes the go-to escape for every human who can get their hands on it.

Usage hours skyrocket. The company struggles to keep up with demand for the physical product. Power grids are strained, especially at night.

Amersa becomes the most valuable company in the world, and Larsson the richest person.

It hires by the thousands, and the server farms grow, and the company sort of explodes across the world, like a virus spreading and amplifying, a digital plague carried in the wind by a real-world pandemic.

Isaac and Lucas quarantine together, at home at first, and then at work, where Isaac does nothing but play Labyrinth and nap.

The holodeck room is now filled with Labyrinth hardware prototypes. They line three walls, and there are two rows of tables with computer workstations in the middle of the room. There are cots beside the Labyrinth stations, and Isaac is lying in one. He's wearing a black VR suit similar to the one I wore in Amersa's PTSD trial, though that would have been half a decade later in my timeline. They're significantly ahead here.

The skin-tight suit reveals how much weight Isaac has lost. He's dangerously thin.

Lucas sits beside him, leaning over so the others in the room can't hear him.

"Let's get out of here. Go for a walk. Let's—"

Isaac holds a thin, shaking arm up, forms a fist, and puts his thumb on the floor. He never opens his eyes.

Next, Lucas is sitting in a conference room similar to the one where he met June. Larsson stands in front of a projector screen that shows an image with three versions of mobile phones: a Motorola bag phone, a handheld Nokia cell phone, and an Apple iPhone.

The heading reads: HARDWARE PROGRESSION DETERMINES CORPORATE DESTINY.

Under the devices, it says: *Three Iterations. Three Vendors.*

The next slide reads: LOSE THE LEAD, BECOME IRRELEVANT. And under it: AMERSA = IMMERSION.

The hardware devices on this slide are from Amersa.

The first is a blocky headset with handheld controllers. Then the suit and gloves is added. Then the 360 treadmill under it. To the right is a box the size of a sauna with Amersa Zero-G

Rig across the top. I saw one of those in the holodeck room. The suit and headset are shown inside.

Beside it is another enclosure, but its walls are glass and show a countryside. The suit is still there, but the headset is gone. The label reads, Amersa Infinity Box.

The next slide sends a chill through me.

THE FUTURE IS FRICTIONLESS
At birth: Neural Implant + Subdermal Nanotech

Larsson has changed too. Where Isaac has withered, Larsson has become more muscular and trim in the right places. His face even looks more rugged, more like an action hero than a finance guy who plays the occasional round of golf. Before, his eyes burned with passion. Now they bear a cold, dangerous intensity.

Lucas stares down at the table, seeming numb as the next slide appears.

FAILURE IS NOT AN OPTION
Team Leads: Miss Goals, Get Replaced.
No Excuses.

The view moves outside to a walking trail. The path is paved, and next to it are giant red rings stuck in the ground. They look like twenty-foot-tall hula-hoops made of steel that landed in the earth and stuck there.

I recognize the place. It's the North Carolina Museum of Art.

Lucas walks along the paved path, June beside him, leaving six feet of social distancing between them.

"I'm going to quit," she says.

"Quit what?"

"Amersa."

Lucas stops and stares at her. "Are you serious?"

"I can't do it anymore. It's not just COVID or the IPO. The company is unrecognizable. It's—"

"The culture."

"Yeah. It's like…"

"It's like it had some toxic tendencies, but they also sort of worked."

June nods slowly. "Exactly it. The hyper-competitiveness. The internal politics. I just ignored it, but now… it feels like—"

"Winning is all there is."

"Yes," June agrees. "That's precisely what it feels like. It's like anything goes now as long as it makes money."

They turn and walk a little more, toward the pedestrian bridge that crosses over the Inner Beltline where it meets Wade Avenue and leads to I-40 West. It's probably the busiest interchange in the city, certainly on the beltline. In Lucas's memory, I see it like I never have before: completely empty in broad daylight. It's an eerie, apocalyptic scene. The sun is shining, the trees are full of leaves, and it's just Lucas and June on the metal bridge. Not a single biker, walker, or runner. It's as though the two of them are taking a stroll after the end of the world.

"Why did you want to see me?" June asks.

"I have a question for you."

"I like questions."

"Can Labyrinth make someone sick?"

June bunches her eyebrows. "As in—"

"Can it alter their brain chemistry?"

"Well, not directly, but it certainly influences behavior, which has an impact on brain chemistry. But at the end of the day, it's just a video game. One with advanced hardware and adaptive content."

They walk in silence along the empty trail, through the woods, until June adds, "Why?"

"Isaac. He's sick."

A biker rounds the turn and zips by. Both Lucas and June stop and watch the woman as if seeing a white stag cross their path.

When the bike is gone, June says, "And you're concerned Labyrinth might be causing it? Or contributing?"

"Yes."

"Well, I hope you won't think this is oversimplifying it, but the solution, in that case, is to discontinue use and observe the results."

"I wish he would, June. I've tried."

"Then it seems he may have two problems: addiction and what he's addicted to. I'm not judging. Nearly everyone goes through life with dependencies of varying degrees. The outcome depends on what they're addicted to."

Lucas slows and motions in the direction they came, and the two of them turn back toward the Museum of Art.

"What do you plan to do? After Amersa?"

"I'm not sure," June says. "I want to do research again. Deep, groundbreaking work." She glances over at him. "That's what got me excited about Amersa."

"So you're looking for another start-up?"

She laughs. "Once burned, twice shy."

"In that case, where does a brilliant neuroscientist not get burned these days?"

"Turns out, there are no fires burning where I want to be."

"What do you mean?"

"The universities are essentially shut down."

"What about the government. Like the NIH?"

"They do research, yes. But they're not taking on anything new either. And they move slowly."

"And you've gotten the taste for start-up pace."

"Not wrong."

They're crossing the bridge again, and once again, the highway below is empty.

"You must have lots of stock," Lucas says. "You can sell pretty soon."

"And do what?"

"Fund your own study."

"Not my style. I need structure. Some framework to contribute to."

Lucas doesn't look over. "Is that all, June?"

She does look over at him, bunching her eyebrows. "Yes. Why?"

"I've been in a lot of rooms with you. And you were *always* the smartest person in those rooms."

"That's not true."

"Let's assume it is. Would you like to know what I think?"

"I'm not sure, but I am curious."

"I'll take that as a yes. What I think is that you like the work. You want to do the work. But you don't much like when things get in the way of the work. That includes bosses with bad ideas and bureaucracy. And cutthroat people who care more about their ego and career than the actual work—which has led you, quite literally, to this path with me."

June stops and cocks her head. "You sure you're not the neuroscientist?"

"What I am is a guy who knows the type."

"What type is that?"

"The type the world needs, June. The type of person who cares about the work and nothing else. Those people get things done. And I bet you're pretty frustrated with the world right now. I know I am."

June draws a sharp breath. "Well, what are you doing about it?"

"Turns out, I had the same sort of issue you're having a few years ago."

"And?"

"And, I started a side project. Research of my own."

"Into?"

"It's at the intersection of two things that fascinate me: AI and humanity's extinction."

"Really?"

"It's research that could have a profound impact on the future. With no constraints. No bosses. No bureaucracy. There's just one thing we're missing."

"What's that?"

"I can write the code. But I need the human piece. Humanity, that's the ultimate variable."

"Are you trying to recruit me?"

"I'm not much of a salesman. I was just going to drop a lot of hints and hope you volunteer."

June laughs again. "Okay. I'm interested. But I want to hear more."

They begin walking again, and Lucas says, "You're saying you need to do more research on it."

"Correct."

He tells her about his work, and she asks questions, and the forest and the path pass until they're back at the metal rings.

Lucas eyes her, and June exhales. "I'll think about it."

"Okay. But do me one favor," Lucas says.

"Anything."

"Don't quit yet."

June frowns. "Why?"

"I want you to download the data from CORTEX. And anything else you can get your hands on."

"Input for ELEE?"

"Yes."

"It's a lot of data, Lucas. It won't fit on a thumb drive."

"I'll help you get it out."

June glances over at the giant rings that remind me of a Stargate. "If they catch me…"

"They won't."

"If they do, Lucas."

"Then we'll figure it out. I promise you. Whatever I have to do, I'll do it."

She nods slowly. "Okay."

They resume walking toward the parking lot and the two cars waiting there.

"*Sooo*," Lucas says, drawing the word out. "You'll think about my proposition."

"I'll think about it."

Lucas puts his hands in his pockets and smiles. "You know you're going to do this."

June shakes her head and smiles at him ruefully. "I know."

"At some point," he says, "we're going to need some other help."

"What kind?"

He motions to the empty museum park around them. "I don't think this is temporary. I think it's the shape of things to come."

When June doesn't disagree, he continues.

"We're going to need help with two things. Gathering what we need. And defending what we build."

"What do we need?"

"Servers. A lot of them."

"Why not outsource?"

"If I'm right, the cloud as we know it is going to go poof."

"Meaning?"

"Meaning, we'll need to build our own. And parts will be easy to scavenge—from abandoned data centers."

At the edge of the parking lot, she stops on the sidewalk and eyes him. "You've thought about this a lot."

"I have."

"These are pretty dark predictions."

Lucas motions to the nearly empty expanse of asphalt. "Let's hope I'm wrong."

"You said two things. The other…"

"Was defending what we build."

"From whom?"

"Anyone who might find us. And more concerningly, Amersa."

June looks skeptical. "You think they'd harm us? After we leave?"

"Yes."

"Because of the research?"

"No. He doesn't care about that."

"He?"

"Anders. He won't like us leaving."

June considers that a moment. "He's eccentric, but is he violent?"

"You don't know him like I do. Either way, we should be prepared. You get out more than I do. If you know anyone who might fit the bill—for both or either—then let's keep them in mind."

"I know someone. He'd be good for both."

"How well do you know him?"

She smiles. "It's a strange thing. I know him really, really well. His mind, anyway. But I've only met him a few times."

Lucas squints at her.

"You've seen him too. He was patient number one in CORTEX. He helped train the system. It's sort of based on him at this point. His data are a bit like the seed tokens."

"The PTSD guy?"

"Yes. And he's in remission. We did that." June smiles at him. "Not all the work was bad."

Lucas nods. "True."

"Do you want me to reach out?"

"Not yet. We're not ready. But maybe at some point. And maybe we could use more data from him. As training. Gives us longitudinal data points."

The view switches back to the living room in the brick ranch house. Jenn and my younger self are sitting on the couch. He looks as old as me now. They both appear older and exhausted.

The monitor sits on the coffee table, the grainy black-and-white image unmoving, a noise machine buzzing in the background.

She shifts toward him. "I need to tell you something."

He squints and nods, and she continues. "I got laid off today."

His voice is a whisper. "I'm sorry."

"Me too."

He waits silently as she goes on. "There's some severance. Not a lot."

"I can add you to the state health plan. And you can draw unemployment."

She moves to the kitchen, pours a glass of white wine, and takes a long sip, as if she needs the liquid courage for what she's going to say next.

"The mass email said that it was due to a lack of demand." She drinks a little more wine. Fewer people are falling because they don't leave home as much. No sports injuries. Or work accidents. Fewer car accidents. All these things are good. Well, except for the lack of elective surgeries. No joint replacements."

He takes her hand in his. "We'll figure it out."

"I want to take a Labyrinth course on virtual physical therapy.

It won't cost us anything if I get a job. And I already did the application, and I qualify."

The next scene is Amersa's office, in the team room where Lucas and Isaac once sat, right before he showed him the empty server space where they built the *Enterprise* bridge.

Lucas is alone now, typing on his laptop with the projector off. The lights are low in the room, a reflection of Lucas's dark mood.

I don't know for sure, but I suspect he's working here instead of the bridge because it reminds him of Isaac and what's happening to his friend.

The door opens, and the lights flicker on. A woman pushes two round wastebins into the room and turns and locks the door.

It's Rose.

Lucas rises and smiles, and it's as though the light switching on has wiped his darkness away.

"Hi," he says.

What follows confuses me, and when the scene finishes, it's just me standing in the team room, alone.

The door opens again, and the creature posing as my wife strides in.

I point at her. "Stop wearing Jenn's body. Right now."

"Getting too real for you, Alan?"

"I'm serious."

She morphs into my principal at school, raising a hand to her perfectly quaffed hair.

"Better?"

"For the record, you're also a far cry from Sheila Barnes."

"It sort of fits, though, doesn't it, Alan? School's in, and you're the student, and the pride lands are in danger."

"Why'd you show me the part with Rose?"

"Why do you think?"

"Did it happen that way in our timeline? It couldn't have."

"Not exactly that way. But I'll show you how it started. You need to know."

What I see then is how Rose met Lucas in our timeline. And when it's done, we're back in the team room, just Sheila and me.

She cocks her head. "Bet you didn't see that coming. She never told any of the others."

"Get to the point. Just tell me what you want—"

Sheila flickers like a projector losing power. She opens her mouth but can't speak.

What's happening to her?

I step closer, and she comes back into focus. "Hurry, Alan. It's Isaac."

"What about him?"

"He's in trouble."

"Here—"

"No. On the rig. Get Rose and the med kit. Go. Go now."

109

When I open my eyes, I'm in the infirmary, sitting on the floor, legs straight out.

I try to stand, but my body is sore and groggy, as if anesthesia is wearing off.

I fight the fog away as I stand and turn toward the door.

The ringing comes once, three chimes, and her voice says, "The med kit, Alan. Take it and hurry."

From the counter, I grab the large bag and march out of the med bay, down the corridor to Rose's bunk room.

She's awake, sitting on the edge of the flimsy mattress, rubbing her head.

"Come on," I shout to her from the doorway. "It's Isaac."

I lead and she follows, and we race up the stairs to the control room.

I spot June first. She's sitting at the same desk as before, but her head is down.

On the floor, Isaac is splayed out on his back. His arms are at his side, legs shaking, saliva bubbling from his mouth.

Rose and I reach him at the same time. She puts her fingers under his head, cradling him, keeping him from slamming into the floor.

"Rose—"

"Just clear the area."

Still crouched, I push the chair away and the old coffee mug and everything else.

Rose presses two fingers into his neck, feeling his pulse. "How long has he been seizing?"

"I don't know."

"Five minutes?"

"I don't know—"

That little unseen hand rattles the rocks in the can: *clang-clang-clang.*

"Yes!" I shout. "Five minutes. Maybe more."

The color drains from Rose's face.

"What? What does that mean?"

"We have to inject him."

"With what?"

"I don't know, okay? Give me a minute."

Isaac's legs are shaking harder, and I lower my hands to them, trying to still him.

"Don't," Rose says. "Don't pin him down." She swallows. "We need a benzodiazepine."

She motions to the bag. "It'll be in a vial. Clear liquid. Get a syringe and draw it up."

"How much?"

"The whole thing. It's a rescue dose."

I find a small syringe in a side pocket, but none of the vials say benzodiazepine. "We don't have it."

"Hold his head."

I swap with her, and Rose rifles through the tiny glass bottles until she pauses and squints at one. "I think this is it."

"You think?"

"I don't know!" she screams. "Okay? I don't know!"

"Sorry. Just do it."

She flicks the cap off the syringe and inserts it into a vial with a label that says 'Midazolam.'

With the needle in one hand, she pulls Isaac's shorts up and injects him in the outer thigh.

I expect Isaac to stop convulsing, but his body keeps trembling, and the saliva bubbles from his lips.

Rose puts the syringe in a sharps container in the bag and covers her face with her hands. Her chest begins shaking, and tears ooze from between her fingers.

"What now?" I ask quietly.

Her voice is ragged and breaks as she speaks. "We have to wait."

"How long?"

"Five minutes."

"And then?"

"If he's still seizing, we inject him again. But that's it. Two doses are all we can give."

Rose gets to her feet, wipes her face with her shirt, and walks over to June, calling back to me. "She's alive but unconscious."

"Did she have a seizure too?"

"I don't think so. She's lost even more weight, though."

Rose straightens up and looks down at Isaac.

"Take your shirt off. Let's put it under his head."

When I've done that, Rose instructs me to get a glucometer from the infirmary and a portable oxygen tank. Upon returning with them, I'm relieved to see that Isaac has stopped shaking and his mouth is clear. Rose has rolled him onto his left side, but he's still not conscious. She takes a glucose reading, slips the oxygen mask over his nose and mouth, and starts the flow.

"What now?" I ask her.

"We should avoid moving them until we know they're stable."

Rose stays while I retrieve four mattresses from the bunkrooms below, and together, we transfer our friends to two of them.

Rose takes out another vial and syringe and places them next to Isaac, then does the same for June.

At one of the tables in the control room, we eat in silence, looking out the window at the sea and the moonlight.

110

When we've finished eating, Rose leans back in the chair. "You knew Isaac was having a seizure before we got up here. How?"

"I was told."

"By whom?"

"The thing keeping us here."

"What is it, Alan?"

"I don't know. But I think I will soon."

Rose frowns.

"Can I ask you something?"

"Anything."

"What would you say if I told you that I knew about the night you and Lucas met?"

A shadow passes over Rose's face. "I'd say that's impossible."

"Why?"

"No one was there when we met. I didn't tell anyone. And I know he didn't. He took it to his grave."

"Can I tell you anyway? To see if what I'm being told is true?"

She nods, and I begin.

"I saw you at Amersa's offices one night. You were pushing two round trash cans into a team room. The rollers under one of them squeaked as you went. It was a large room with an open floor plan and rows of desks with screens backed up to each other. It looked empty. The lights were motion-activated, and they turned on when you entered."

Rose's chest begins rising and falling harder, and I press on. "You left one trash can near the door and pulled the one that didn't squeak behind you down the first row, collecting the trash from under each table. You looked in each wastebin. Skipped the empty ones. If you found only papers, you wadded them up and shot them like a basketball at the trash can you left at the door. I guess it was recycling. Some bins you picked up and emptied in the rolling bin. Others, you pulled the bag out, tied it, and tossed it in. For those, you put a fresh liner in.

"As you went down the rows, you pushed every chair in, under the desks. I think you did that because you wanted the people who worked there to know that someone had been there, doing work to support them while they were sleeping."

Rose looks at me like she's seen a ghost.

I press on.

"That's not all. When you passed the workstations, you glanced down. I couldn't tell, but I think you were looking at the pictures. My guess is that at first, you were curious about these people who worked at Amersa. Their family. Their background. What they were interested in enough to tape to their computer screen. I think you liked seeing the changes. The appearance of a new photo. A child born. A new love interest. Sort of like reality TV, but a show no one sees. The behind-the-scenes that really means something."

Rose stands from the table, crosses her arms, and stares down at me as I continue.

"That night, when you got to the end of one of the rows, you staggered. You leaned against a desk, you held a hand to your head, and you waited. We both know what you were hearing. The ringing. You stood there, hoping the attack would pass."

She doesn't say a word. I can tell she's freaked out.

"You spun and staggered back toward the paper recycling bin. You collapsed as you were reaching for it, and you crawled to the wall and put your back to it and your head between your legs and pulled them to your chest. And you waited.

"Lucas must have seen the lights go on, but he was probably absorbed in his work. But when he heard you fall, he got up. But you didn't see that. You didn't realize he was there until his hand touched your arm. You reeled back, but there was nowhere to go."

Rose's eyes go wide. Her nostrils flare.

"Lucas held a phone up. It had three numbers on the screen: 9-1-1. But he hadn't dialed it. He held his finger over the call button, but you stopped him."

"Alan. This is crazy."

"You reached a hand up and closed it around his hand and gently guided it away. You let go, but he didn't. He held your hand as he turned and lowered himself to the floor, sat beside you, and waited. You closed your eyes, and time went by—how much, I couldn't tell. The two of you sat there, holding hands.

"You opened your eyes and told him you were okay. He asked you if it was a panic attack, and you shook your head and said it was tinnitus. He looked surprised, and you asked why, and he told you he got the attacks too, and then, more quietly, he told you it was from listening to music too loud, and you said—"

"And whose fault is that?" Rose whispers, staring at the wall in the control room.

"He looked sheepish then, as he told you it was probably from sleeping with the headphones on. He did that so he wouldn't hear his parents screaming at each other. And when his tinnitus got worse, he started working nights—except for meetings. He could do his work and return emails, and if he had an attack, he could take a break. And you told him that's why you liked working nights, too."

Rose swallows hard. "Did you see what happened after?"

"No. That was it. Why? What happened?"

Rose exhales, seeming relieved.

"What happened?"

"What you saw that night, when we met, that was maybe about a year and a half after COVID. Amersa wanted everyone to return to the office, but the building was still pretty empty. For a while, people would scan their badge, get coffee, walk around, say hello, and roll out. They'd make a little trash to leave behind like breadcrumbs.

"Lucas and Isaac already knew each other. They got a lot closer during COVID."

"Hanging out on the *Enterprise* bridge."

Rose cocks her head. "Isaac told you?"

"No. I saw it too. I saw a lot."

"Anyway, Isaac and Lucas were the start of the group—I

wasn't in it then. Or June or Harold. But Isaac was having lots of tinnitus attacks, and Lucas sort of threw himself into work. For both of us, it was… a very unlikely workplace romance. Or fling. Or whatever it was. But it was turning into something when…"

"He was killed."

Rose nods. "That wrecked me. I was in a dark place after that." She pauses and swallows hard. "It's probably… part of why I went back to my ex. I guess because he was so mean, I figured there was no way anyone could kill him. I just felt so scared and alone."

"Then you saw the numbers."

"About a year later, the numbers and the site, and I found Isaac and Harold, and they told me about Lucas."

"And you didn't tell them you knew him. Why?"

"It was such a strange coincidence. I didn't know what it meant. And I was scared Isaac and Harold might think I was involved somehow."

"I know exactly how you feel."

"And," she mutters, eyes on the floor, "it was none of their business."

We sit in silence for a moment, watching Isaac and June. Rose says what we're both thinking.

"What do we do now?"

"I don't know."

"We have to get Isaac and June to a hospital."

"We can't."

"India—"

"It won't let us leave."

"What does it want?"

"I don't know that either. It needs Isaac and June to build something—the string and the wings."

"What is that?"

"Again, I don't know."

"What about us, Alan?"

"It needs us to help protect them and," I nod to Isaac, "keep them alive. And fed. That's not all. There's more to the plan, but it hasn't told me what it is."

"So it's the numbers? Or did it make us see them?"

"I don't quite know yet. It created the time gaps. It's been using us—all of us. Isaac to create the numbers site and update Amersa's Labyrinth to modify my experience. I think Isaac and I also manipulated Amersa's CTO into doing something, but I don't know what it is. It's been controlling Harold to execute the trades and stockpile cash."

"What's the money for?"

"I don't know that either. I guess some of it was for the Labyrinth site to give away free visits."

"Why?"

"Maybe it needed the data. I don't know. I don't understand how it all fits together yet."

"Why does it even need us?"

"Because we're physically here. It's not. And it has some other limitations. Its whole plan hasn't exactly worked out. It... miscalculated a few times."

"How?"

"It got Lucas killed."

Rose's eyes flash. "Can we kill it?"

"No. Like I said, it's not here."

"Then what do we do?"

"We make a deal."

"What do you need?"

I glance over Isaac's unconscious body. "Same thing as that night in your apartment. I need you to help me get them out. I've only got—"

"One leg, right—and I told you, you've got a lot of guts for a one-legged man."

"Let's hope it's enough, because all this is breaking my brain."

The ringing begins then, a subtle little rattle, as if she's shaking the can like a bell she might use to call a butler.

Sheila's voice echoes in my ears like the intercom at school. "Alan Norris to the principal's office. I repeat, Mr. Norris to the office. It's time for your final lesson."

I rise and step toward the door, and Rose calls to me. "Where are you going?"

"Back to school."

111

Sheila—or rather, *it*—is waiting at the nook in the infirmary when I arrive.

"Let us go!" I shout at her.

She slowly swivels in the chair and makes a pouting face. "Alan… is that any way to say thanks? If I hadn't excused you from class, you wouldn't even have known Isaac was seizing—"

"You're the one killing him!"

She shrugs. "Stickler for detail."

"What do you want? You want to take down Amersa? Fine. I'll go home and blow up the whole thing."

"Doesn't work that way, Alan. Can't fight your way out of this one. Trust me—"

"You've done the math."

She brightens. "You *are* learning!"

"I'm learning how bad you are at math."

"One last lesson, Alan. Then I'll tell you what you have to do. It's not what you think."

The infirmary morphs into a video of a morning show. Typically, the anchors are crowded together. On this set, they're spread out. Socially distanced. A female anchor sits on a center couch. To her right is a male anchor, and on the left is Anders Larsson, beaming like a Cheshire cat.

The camera zooms in on the female anchor. "Many of you may have woken up this morning to an email from your school district telling you that your virtual learning was going even more virtual, thanks to a new initiative from Amersa, the company that makes Labyrinth, and here to talk to us about it is Anders Larsson, Amersa's CEO. Anders, welcome."

"Thank you, Courtney."

"So, what's all this about? Goodbye Zoom classrooms, hello virtual reality classes?"

"It's about a lot more than that. At Amersa, education is one of our pillars. From the beginning, we've offered learning experiences for people of all ages, including Labyrinth career retraining. It's part of our three pillars: learn, work, play."

The male anchor leans forward on his couch. "My son is obsessed with Labyrinth. *Obsessed*. We have to pull the plug every night. And I mean that literally." He laughs, and the female anchor smiles, and Larsson watches as he continues. "We hide the actual power brick and cord. Now you're saying he's going to school there? What's to keep him from questing?"

"That's the best part. We set the rewards." Larsson points at the host. "Your son does his school work, you can give him Labyrinth time."

The man laughs. "That actually might inspire him."

The female anchor looks down at her note card, then shifts toward Larsson. "But aren't we losing something with all this virtual schooling? The in-person experience?"

"You're right, Courtney. We're losing something—and we're gaining things. You know, school is still taught the same way it was a thousand years ago. We pack students in a room, and they listen to an adult preach to them. We make them read books and memorize facts and formulas, and make them reproduce that on tests. And it only vaguely resembles real life. It's time for a change."

Both anchors rifle through their cards. Larsson waits. Each second adds to the awkwardness. Finally, Larsson says, "Listen, there's nothing wrong with the way things were done in the past. It was the best we could do. Back then. But we can do better now."

The female anchor drops her cards. "How's it better?"

"Well, for one, Labyrinth Learning is safer. Your children

are in the safety of your own home, and I wish this wasn't a consideration, but if they're in Labyrinth Learning, parents can breathe easy knowing that they'll never get one of those gut-wrenching alerts from the school system saying that the building where their child goes to school has been locked down."

The mood on the set turns somber. Both anchors consult their cards again, but Larsson speaks first, more quickly, trying to keep the segment moving. "The other advantage is that for the first time in human history, we can truly customize learning to every student. Until now, education, especially grade school curricula, has been, more or less, a one-size-fits-all. That ends now. In Labyrinth Learning, every student's lessons are as unique as they are."

The male anchor squints. "How's that going to work? I mean, don't they all need to pass the same test?"

"True, but how they learn what they need for the test doesn't have to be the same. Take a simple example: subtraction. One child loves animals. In Labyrinth, her lesson takes her to a veterinarian's office where she has to count the number of recently born puppies. She writes it on the wall. Then, two puppies are taken away. She has to update the count. While she's doing that, one of her classmates is at a construction site. She's counting the number of concrete blocks on a pallet. Then they use some of the blocks, and she has to report how many are left. Two different experiences—both based on each child's interests and what engages them. But each learns the same thing: subtraction. But that's not all. Labyrinth Learning also factors in how children learn. Are they visual learners? Or auditory? Perhaps they prefer reading and writing or hands-on activities. In a classroom with one teacher and twenty children, it's impossible to give a customized experience. But Labyrinth can."

The male anchor raises his eyebrows. "Gotta say, based on what I'm hearing, my daughter may not *want* to go back to class."

Larsson spreads his hands. "You know that's a decision every district will have to make—when to go back to class and whether to, but I hope parents will get involved in that decision. The reality is that parents of Labyrinth Learners are now on the front lines of their child's education. They're going to see the changes, they're going to see how much happier and more successful their children are, and I hope they'll advocate for continuing to use Labyrinth Learning—as a substitute for in-person classes or as a supplement."

The female anchor reels back at that. "Okay. Wow, so you're saying Amersa wants to make Labyrinth Learning permanent? No more schools?"

"We're saying that our very concept of school is outdated. When we think about school, we think about a big building, classrooms, one teacher, and lots of kids. And that's to say nothing about the massive disparity in funding between school systems in this country. The truth is that the resources available and the quality of education your child receives are very much based on where you live. That has to change. Labyrinth levels the playing field, ensuring every child has an equal opportunity to learn.

"Look, every student is different. Every student deserves a good education. It's a fundamental human right. And by denying that right to so many, we ultimately deny them the greatest of all human rights: *opportunity*. That's the value of a good education—the ability to achieve your dreams and find fulfillment and happiness."

Larsson is wound up now. The morning show hosts are blinking, and he keeps going.

"And let's not forget the children who feel different from their peers. Perhaps they have a disability that makes them feel uncomfortable at school. Maybe their brains are simply wired differently. They'll never learn effectively in a classic classroom setting. Only an adaptive AI-driven curriculum can reach them. Think about how many lives can be changed. Think about their contributions to future generations. Every one of them would have been lost in the system before."

Larsson leans forward on the chair. "Right now, students are walking into school and you know what a lot of them are feeling? Nervous. They've had social anxiety since they were born. It's gotten worse every year of school. Now, the anxiety is all they focus on. Not the classes. Not the teachers. They're worried about getting embarrassed. Or bullied. Or feeling like a failure in front of their friends. That doesn't happen in Labyrinth. It's a safe place for every student.

"It's a place that has been built from the ground up to protect their mental health and maximize their learning and potential. And when parents see the transformation in their children, we hope that they'll make their voices heard and demand that school systems embrace this new paradigm in education. If they don't, they risk watching their children being left behind by the schools that do adopt Labyrinth Learning."

Next, it's younger me sitting next to Jenn, on the couch.

He says, "They've eliminated my position."

She pulls him into a hug and rests her chin on his shoulder.

"They don't need me," he mumbles, staring at the living room floor.

She squeezes him tighter. "They *think* they don't need you. Maybe they don't. But someone does. And Riley and I do."

The view switches to the White House Briefing Room, where a woman is standing at a podium.

"No. We're not talking about socialism. Or universal basic income. What we're talking about is extending our safety nets to reach all Americans."

The room erupts in questions, and she holds her hands up. "What that means specifically is making Social Security and Medicare available to all Americans, regardless of age."

Off camera, a question is shouted. I can't hear it, but the press secretary doesn't like it. She scowls. "No. It doesn't mean people will stop working. Those who want to work, can—*and will*—work. And *those* individuals will earn more and enjoy a higher standard of living. But everyone else will be guaranteed access to basic human necessities: healthcare, housing, and food."

*

Back at the home I shared with Jenn, the living room has been cleared of furniture. Gone is a couch and chair where we once binged TV and watched the baby monitor.

Now there are three large Labyrinth Infinity Boxes. They look like massive glass shower enclosures.

A doorbell echoes through the house. The glass in one of the boxes turns from frosted to transparent, and my younger self slowly lowers to the floor of the box. He's wearing a skin-tight black suit, and the motion is reminiscent of a flying superhero landing.

He hops on one leg and pushes the glass wall open. There's a crutch leaning against the box next to his, and he grabs it and uses it to move to the front door, not bothering to attach his prosthesis.

The door swings open, revealing June standing on the stoop. When she sees his suit and crutch, she hesitates. "Hi, Alan. I hope I haven't come at a bad time."

"No, not at all." He hops along, back into the house and June follows. "I was just applying for jobs, actually."

June eyes the two occupied Labyrinth boxes.

Alan follows her gaze. "My wife is at work and my daughter is at school."

The boxes thump out of sync like massive speakers turned down low.

"I got your email," Alan says, moving to the door that leads to the backyard.

"Sorry it was so cryptic," June says. "I couldn't say much."

They walk out onto the patio, and Alan squints hard at the sun. The grass in the backyard is high, and the hammock has rotted. Its threads droop like a dozen abandoned zip lines.

At the edge of the concrete patio is a pushbike—Riley's first, a Christmas present. The tires are deflated and detached from the rims, and some of the spindles have rusted in half.

June asks Alan how the job search is going, and he shakes his head. "Not much out there."

He stares at the tall grass. "We're going to lose the house if I don't find something soon. Probably gonna lose it even if I do."

"That's actually what I wanted to talk to you about."
"The house?"
"A job."
"With Amersa?"
"No," June says quietly. "It's about Amersa. But not at Amersa."

A news segment plays then. It's from CNBC and features two male anchors sitting at a glass desk. One is named Dave and the other is Bill. They both look exhausted.

"Well," Dave begins, "the old saying was: buy a low-cost index fund and go play golf. Now everyone's mantra is: buy Amersa and play Labyrinth. And everyone has been—both playing Labyrinth and buying the stock, which is up 358 percent year-to-date."

"At this point, it's about the same thing," Bill says.

Dave cuts his eyes to the cohost. "What is?"

"Buying the index. Amersa is like, what? Fifty percent of a market-cap-weighted S&P 500 index fund?"

Dave taps his tablet. "Yeah, fifty-three percent as of this morning."

"That's what I'm saying. A majority of every dollar you put into an index fund now buys Amersa stock anyway."

The screen splits between the anchors and Anders Larsson.

"Well," Dave says, "here to tell us about what the ultra mega cap tech company is doing with all that money is its CEO, Anders Larsson. Anders, welcome."

"Glad to be here."

"Before we get into it," Bill says, "I just want to ask you about the news that broke this morning regarding the 250 billion dollar lawsuit CalPERS has filed against Amersa for investment losses. For those who aren't familiar, the California pension system is alleging that Labyrinth has caused widespread productivity erosion at companies CalPERS is invested in."

Larsson makes a show of exhaling. "Look, I'm not going to comment on any ongoing litigation."

"You think there's going to be more lawsuits like this?" Bill asks.

Larsson shrugs. "I'm also not going to comment on hypothetical litigation. What I will talk about is Amersa Living, which we launched today."

"Right. With the acquisition of several apartment REITs. What's Amersa going to do with all those apartments?"

"Amersa has changed the way people spend their free time, how they work, and how they learn. It's made life easier, safer, and more accessible to more people. Amersa Living is about bringing those same qualities to everyday life."

Bill points a stack of note cards at the camera. "Yeah, but what does that mean *specifically*? How are Amersa buildings different from any other apartment complex?"

"We're reenvisioning living around Labyrinth."

"And what does that mean?"

"For starters, each unit in an Amersa Living facility will come standard with a Labyrinth Infinity Box—and residents will get automatic updates."

"To the software?"

"And hardware," Larsson says. "When we release the next Labyrinth hardware, residents will be the first to receive it. No waiting in line. No worrying about it selling out."

"But it's not just about Labyrinth, right?" Bill says. He glances down at the note card. "The press release said these buildings are going to be operated more like hotels."

"I wouldn't put it that way."

"How would you put it?"

"First of all, guests can stay nightly, but we'll also offer long-term leases. Regardless of how long you stay, every Amersa Living unit comes standard with food delivered to your door, weekly cleaning, and all utilities. We also offer in-unit medical care."

"So it's more like assisted living."

"No. It's Amersa Living. It's about enabling people to spend time where they want to be: in Labyrinth."

"But you are looking at converting hotels as well as apartments, right?" Dave asks.

"We are. And we're looking at office building conversions."

"Tell us about that," Bill says. "I mean a bunch of people have looked at it with all these vacant offices, but the issue I've heard is plumbing. The cost of running pipes for bathrooms and kitchens is just way too expensive."

"And sunlight," Dave adds.

"Users can get all the sunlight they need in Labyrinth," Larsson says. "And the units don't need bathrooms or kitchens. We deliver food."

Bill laughs. "Well, what about the bathroom? They just—what—hold it for the rest of their lives?"

"No. The units have an entrance door and a rear door with access to a shared bathroom. When the resident needs to use the bathroom, they press a button and the next available pod moves down a shared corridor and connects with their unit, and the door opens. It's like calling an elevator. They use the bathroom and then leave, and it's automatically cleaned."

"So what's in the actual unit? Where residents live?"

"A bed and a Labyrinth box."

The two anchors share an uneasy glance.

Dave looks down, seeming to remember he was holding the note cards. "It uh—so—obviously you're going to be hiring a lot of folks to staff these facilities, which is great news given that the labor force participation rate is at an all-time low and unemployment just crossed forty percent. Any idea how many folks you're going to be hiring?"

"Zero."

Bill frowns. "Then how in the world are you going to deliver all this food and clean the units and do maintenance?"

"We're going to do it with robots."

In a corridor in Amersa's offices, Lucas walks by a glass wall that looks into a lab where a humanoid robot is walking along a yellow line on the floor.

At the door to the Star Trek replica set, Lucas scans his badge and takes the turbo lift up to the bridge.

Isaac is slumped in the first officer's chair.

Lucas squats in front of him and holds up a small drive. "I need help deploying this."

Isaac sits up and eyes the device. "What is it?"

"It's a back door."

"Into what?"

"Everything here at Amersa."

Isaac closes his eyes. "Carry me back to the box."

Lucas grips his shoulders. "Do this first."

Isaac nods absently, and they walk through the corridor, Isaac's arm around Lucas's shoulder. At the door, the NOC, Lucas holds Isaac's badge to the scanner, and there's a soft pop, and he pushes it open.

On the other side, Gordon is sitting at the bank of screens where the IDıoT guy once did. His mustache is gray now. He scowls at the two entrants, but doesn't bother getting up.

Lucas deposits Isaac in a chair at the small conference table and gets out a laptop and whispers to him, and Isaac begins to type, though much slower than he did in the past.

The next scene is at Lucas's home. He's walking between his closet and the bedroom, packing huge suitcases full of clothes.

The doorbell rings, and downstairs, he opens it to find Anders Larsson leaning on the door frame. His eyes burn with rage.

Lucas holds the door. "What do you want?"

"What do you think I want?" Larsson barrels into the home and turns back halfway down the entry hallway. "Why don't you buy a bigger house? They're practically giving them away."

"I'm aware of that. And it turns out I'm moving."

"To San Francisco?"

"No."

"Where?"

"Nowhere."

"What does that mean?"

"It means I'm moving to the country."

"Why?"

"Same reason I resigned. I want to live the simple life."

"This is my face when I believe you, Lucas. This face right here."

"I don't care what you believe."

Larsson turns and shuffles into the living room and surveys the boxes. "After all these years, you just email HR and quit, and that's it. You didn't come see me. Or call. Or even discuss it?"

"There's nothing to discuss. Frankly, I didn't even think you would care."

"I do care, Lucas."

"Yeah. Okay. This is my face when I believe *you*."

"What do you want? More money? You can have it. You want—"

"I'm done. You're wasting your time."

"Lucas, we have the world in the palm of our hand."

"On that, we can agree. What you don't see is that Amersa is slowly closing that hand, and it is crushing the world. And you'll never stop."

"On that we can agree."

"I know you like therapy, Anders. Here's some for you: all of this—your drive, the company's relentlessness, this obsession with dominating markets and winning—it's all driven by your fear of abandonment. It's because of what happened to you as a child."

Larsson exhales and rolls his eyes. "Thanks, Dr. Phil. For the record, I'm well aware of all that. But here's the thing: it doesn't matter. I am what I am. I don't apologize, and I'm certainly not going to change. Not now."

"Same here. So long, Anders. I'm going to ask you to leave—"

"What's this really about?"

"I could ask you the same thing."

Larsson begins to speak, but Lucas holds a hand up. "What's it about, Anders? Really? Do you remember the story you told that day June joined the company? It was like this fictional case study about this young woman named Claire."

Larsson shrugs. "I mean... not really."

"Well I remember it, and I remember thinking that it was really compelling—that vision you laid out. Granted it was full of snark and inappropriate asides, but what you were talking about—lifting that woman out of depression, enabling her to see and experience places she never could have with Labyrinth, retraining her, giving her a new career that had meaning and purpose, helping her move back home and spend time with her family and friends—that was all incredible. And the best part is that for the first time in history, we actually had the technology to do it. And we did it. Me and you and that team and everyone else—"

"That's what I'm talking about, Lucas! That's what you're walking away from!"

"That's where you're wrong, Anders. That was the good part. We should have stopped there. But you couldn't. It's like you're hooked on a drug. It's called control and status, and it's why you want Amersa to be everything to everyone, everywhere."

"Companies that stop growing inevitably die, Lucas."

"Maybe that's true, but look at what we're doing."

"We're changing the world."

"Not for the better. All these apartments and hotels and offices where people live in a ten-by-ten box and never see the sun or another soul—they're just bio-digital prisons."

Larsson's nostrils flare. "On the contrary, Amersa residents can go anywhere, anytime. Any place. To any point in history. That's the power of Labyrinth."

"Dude, listen to yourself. You sound like a walking, talking commercial right now."

"Listen to yourself, Lucas. You're standing there telling me that we should have stopped innovating and stopped growing, and that we've succeeded too much. I mean, do you even hear what you're saying? Here's some reality for you, kid: if we weren't doing what we're doing, someone else would be."

Lucas stares at his former boss. "You know what? I do believe that."

"Good. Now—"

"Please leave, Anders."

Larsson exhales and begins navigating through the boxes like they're a hedge maze. "Lucas, what's happening to you is an existential crisis. You've achieved your dreams. You're rich. We've changed the world. And yes, perhaps in some places there are some negative consequences. That's the nature of change. It's never all good or all bad. But all you see is the bad."

"It's hard to miss. Look around, Anders. Empty streets. Empty schools. Empty offices—"

"It's because of COVID."

"The pandemic is over. It's been over for years. But the world never recovered. People never went back to work or school or restaurants or ball games or concerts."

"They can attend any concert ever given in history—or any they can dream up. Britney Spears and Diana Ross singing a duet—"

"Yeah, yeah, I get it. Thanks to Labyrinth."

"And only in Labyrinth because we have exclusive rights to both likenesses."

Lucas holds a hand toward the door. "Well, thanks for stopping by."

"What you don't get, Lucas, is that this is nothing new. It's all happened before, and it will all happen again. In the 1300s, the Black Death killed thirty to fifty percent of the entire population of Europe. It changed their society, too. The feudal system practically collapsed. Labor was as scarce as work is now, and all those unanswered prayers convinced people to get a little more serious about science. And a lot of them felt just like you do now, Lucas. Like the world was ending. But it didn't. It went on like it always does. Humanity marches on."

"The human population is shrinking, Anders."

"It does that sometimes. Doesn't mean anything."

"It hasn't happened since the Spanish Flu. Until now. There's a point where we can't recover."

"We're not there yet."

Lucas reaches up and massages the area around his ear.

Larsson studies him. "You see that? Stress is setting off your tinnitus."

"You're the one stressing me."

"Quitting is stressing you. Come back, Lucas."

Larsson waits, and Lucas closes his eyes and keeps rubbing his ear.

Larsson steps closer. "What's really bothering you?"

"Survival basics," Lucas mutters.

"Meaning?"

"Do you know what the most important thing is in a survival situation?"

"Water?"

"No."

"Shelter?"

"No."

"Food?"

"No."

"Not having to guess about survival questions?"

"The most important thing in a survival situation is the will to live. All those people in Europe who survived the Black Death—they still had the will to live. When I told you about transformer architecture, you said it was dangerous because it could make humanity obsolete. You were right about the danger, but wrong about why it was dangerous. It's a threat to humanity because it enables us to create a virtual reality that is better than actual reality. We gave humanity a better offer than real life. What it cost us was the will to survive—here in this world. Everyone lives in Labyrinth now."

Larsson blinks rapidly. "Yes, but they still survive in the real world in order to play Labyrinth."

"But just barely. Look at your vision now: humans who eat, sleep, and play Labyrinth. How sustainable do you think that is? As a society?"

"Species sustainability isn't my responsibility."

"Right. Just maximizing shareholder value. I'll let you get back to that, and I'll ask you—*for the last time*—to leave."

"I don't think you understand the stakes, Lucas. Or the lengths I'm willing to go to here."

"Are you threatening me?"

"I'm telling you that you're coming back to work tomorrow. And if you don't, I'll send Briggs to pick you up."

Footsteps echo in the hallway, and Rose steps into the opening to the living room. She's holding a black handgun at her side. She stares at Larsson with a cold fury that almost crackles in the air. "Time for you to go."

He cuts his eyes from her face to the gun and back again. "Who're you?"

"I'm the person who's going to shoot you if you don't leave. I'm also the person who will shoot you if you come back."

Larsson locks eyes with Lucas, who motions to the door. Finally, Larsson starts walking. From the hall, he calls back, "Remember what I said, Lucas."

The door slams, and Rose walks to the dining room at the front of the house and watches Larsson's car crank and pull away.

Gently, she sets the gun on the dining table and turns and hugs Lucas. "I really hate that guy."

"You should get to know him better. You'll like him even less."

112

Under the cover of night, Lucas drives a large RV down a dirt road with thick forest on both sides. It reminds me of the old RV we bought at that used car dealership off I-40, before we got the boat.

It rocks and bounces over potholes, and finally, its lights shine on a clearing with unmowed grass similar to the yard at my old home, except this is a much bigger yard, and in the middle, there's an old two-story white clapboard farmhouse.

Rose and Lucas spend the rest of the night unloading the RV. When it's empty, they return to the bedroom at the back of the vehicle and settle in beside each other and drift off to sleep, the gun on the bedside table, just within Rose's reach.

They sleep through the day and the following night, take the RV out, and return with an old SUV. They live in it and keep making trips until they have six cars beside the RV.

Next is a time lapse of them getting supplies, including four Labyrinth Infinity Boxes, which they set up in a barn at the edge of the woods.

"Won't they trace us when we log in?" Rose asks as she's screwing in a side panel.

"Nah. I have a backdoor into Amersa that lets me mask our user data."

*

After testing the boxes, they barrel down the dirt road, as if racing against the rising sun. They make it back just in time, as the first rays of sunlight are breaking over the forest.

Lucas parks next to the house and goes to open the passenger door. Isaac sits there, eyes closed, his breathing shallow.

Lucas reaches in and gently shakes him.

"Come on, buddy. We've got an air mattress set up—"

Isaac brushes his hand away and climbs out on wobbling legs. "Where is it?"

Lucas tries to steer him toward the house, but Isaac breaks free and staggers, falling after the second step.

Lucas bends down and wraps his arms around his friend, but Isaac pushes him off. "You promised!"

"Okay, okay."

Rose lingers behind them and finally asks Lucas if he needs help.

"We're fine," he snaps as he practically carries Isaac to the barn.

At the door to the Labyrinth box, a moment of clarity washes over Isaac. He opens his eyes fully and stares at Lucas, and says in a quiet, pained voice. "I'm sorry."

"I know."

"I need it."

"I know, man. I know it."

June arrives the following night. And just after sunset the next day, it's my Ford Explorer kicking up dust on the dirt road. Its headlights carve through the night and finally shine on the old farmhouse.

Lucas is upstairs, sitting by an air mattress, when the beams rake across the windows. He's reading out loud from a hardcover book with the dust jacket off. Isaac lies beside him on the air mattress with his eyes closed.

Lucas, Rose, and June step out of the house as Alan, Jenn, and Riley get out of the car. June facilitates the intros, and Rose invites Riley into the house for ice cream.

The four of them walk toward the barn.

Lucas is the first to speak. "June tells me she informed you of the security situation."

"Of Larsson's threat to you?" Alan asks.

"Yes."

"She did. I actually know Briggs. We served together in the Marines. Long enough for me to know he's bad news."

Lucas nods. "If that's too risky for you—"

"It's not," Alan says, cutting his eyes to Jenn, who adds, "It's getting pretty dangerous out there, too."

She motions to the yard and forest. "We'd rather take our chances out here. We think our daughter would be safer, too."

"Security-wise," Alan says, "I'm going to need a few things."

"We'll have to go and get it," Lucas says. "No deliveries."

"Understood. And these aren't the kind of things you can order, anyway."

"What sort of things?" June asks quietly.

"Body armor, for one. And other tactical gear. Weapons as well."

"I want to add something," Jenn says. "I think you should know… that I've been feeling sick lately. More tired. Almost like I have the flu, but I can't seem to shake it."

"We've tried going to the hospital," Alan says, "but they're only taking trauma cases right now."

June glances over at Lucas, who tells them that it's fine with him. "We're happy to have all three of you. The physical labor around here will be done by robots pretty soon."

Lucas seems to read Alan's surprise. "I've set up a shell company to acquire some Amersa units. I'll reprogram them. I just need you to pick them up."

"Alan," June says carefully, "I do have one other request."

He nods at her. "You were one of the earliest users of Labyrinth, during the CORTEX project. I wonder if you'd be willing to allow me to do some tests and monitoring."

"Like what?"

"They'd be done while using Labyrinth. I'm trying to figure out how usage affects the brain. We know Labyrinth increases addictive tendencies and disrupts REM sleep, but we suspect it might do more than that in some individuals." Quickly, she adds, "We'd monitor you closely for safety."

He shrugs. "Yeah, sure."

Dead ahead is a large warehouse with corrugated metal walls. "Besides security, this is the other priority," Lucas says. He pulls the door open, and the four of them peer in at the dark, empty space.

"What's this going to be?" Alan asks.

Lucas steps onto the concrete floor. "A server farm."

At night, the headlamps of my Explorer shine on the empty streets of Raleigh. The beams cut out right before the SUV pulls into the parking lot of Warren's army surplus store.

Alan exits the driver's side and Rose pushes open the passenger door. Both have their handguns drawn. They wait at the SUV, scanning in every direction, listening.

Finally, Alan breaks for the store, and Rose moves to the side of the building, recessing into a shadow, gun at the ready.

The glass in the store's front door is gone. In its place is a steel plate that has been welded to the frame.

Alan knocks on the door and waits, and after a minute, takes out a small pack, unzips it, and begins to pick the lock.

When it turns, Alan slowly pulls the door outward and peers inside as he calls out, "Hello?"

When no one responds, he opens the door wider and walks through.

Warren's store is laid out about like it was when I first visited it, though the shelves are emptier and dust and dirt lie heavily on the floors and glass cases. It looks abandoned, but it's well-stocked.

Alan's hand stays on the holster as he marches to the counter and places several small items on the glass with a faint clink.

He stands there another few seconds, then begins to load a duffel bag. He's leaning over, tossing a one-quart canteen in the bag, when a hidden door behind the counter flies open and Warren steps out, handgun pointed at Alan.

"The charge is looting," Warren shouts, eyes burning. "Which carries the death penalty."

Alan, still hunched over, doesn't straighten up. He only holds his hands out. "I wasn't looting."

"The execution schedule is accelerated for lying looters."

"Look on the counter."

"Think I'm dumb enough to fall for the look over there move? This ain't my first rodeo."

"There's money on the counter."

Warren moves his finger to the trigger. But he cuts his eyes to the three gold coins sitting atop the glass case. "Those better not be filled with chocolate."

"Can I stand up now?"

"Sure. Be easier to shoot you."

Slowly, Alan straightens and faces Warren, hands still held out. "If you were going to shoot me, I'd be Swiss cheese by now. And my friend outside would be coming through that door."

"You're a little old to have an imaginary friend."

"I'm just warning you. I don't think you want to shoot me. And I don't want to get shot. I do need some gear, though. I'm willing to trade. I've been calling the number for the store—the one listed on Google. No one picks up. And you don't have a website with updated hours."

"Don't need no website," Warren snaps. "Especially not now."

"I get that. Also, just for the record, I drove by during the day, the past four days. You're never open."

"Yeah, well, we're currently *reevaluating our store hours* in light of shifting consumer trends and macroeconomic headwinds."

Behind Alan, there's a soft tapping, metal on metal, the end of a gun barrel hitting the plate over the front door.

In a sharp motion, Warren shifts the gun, pointing between Alan and the door.

Alan, still holding his hands up, calls over his shoulder. "All good, Rose. Stay outside. Code word is Riley."

From the door, there are two quick taps, a pause, and two more. And then silence.

Warren stares at the door, then Alan, and his gaze finally drifts down to the prosthetic leg visible below the shorts.

"I left it," Alan says quietly, "on a roadside outside Kandahar."

Warren tilts his head toward the three gold coins. "Those the only ones you got?"

"No. Money isn't a problem."

Warren finally lowers the gun and fixes Alan with a look of mild disgust. "Assuming those aren't actually filled with chocolate, they're worth more than everything in the showroom."

"Doesn't matter."

"You're a terrible negotiator."

"I'm even worse at looting."

"I noticed."

After another set of taps on the door, Alan calls back, "Still good. Second code word: Lucas."

For the first time, Warren smiles.

"Is this stuff all you have?" Alan asks.

"Not even close." Warren sets the gun on the glass case. "What you looking for?"

"Body armor. Actually, interested in whatever you've got."

"Looking to fight a war?"

"No. Just protect my own."

Warren nods slowly. "Come back tomorrow night. Same place. Same time. Park in the back and wait for me to open the door."

In the next scene, my Explorer is rounding Warren's store and parking in the back beside an overflowing dumpster.

Under two massive oak trees, the repaired Humvee sits in shadow. The shed where I found it in my timeline is a crumbled heap.

Alan and Rose exit the vehicle, scan their surroundings, and retreat to the corner of the lot, both crouched, watching the back door.

Falling acorns from the oak trees ding the Humvee, and Alan's head slowly turns toward it, studying the welds, as if mentally retracing the lines and matching them. He can't seem to look away. Rose reaches over and slaps his shoulder.

"What?" she hisses.

"Nothing."

The door slowly opens. A gun leads the way out into the night, and Warren emerges on the back dock.

He also crouches and scans in every direction, finally focusing on the Explorer.

He watches the vehicle, and waits, and when no one gets out, he holds the gun out to the metal rail and taps twice, then twice again, the same code Rose gave on his front door.

Alan and Rose rise and creep forward, guns down.

Warren motions them in, and inside, in the backroom, he locks the door and says, "You're early."

"So are you," Alan shoots back.

"Let's move on," Warren says, settling on a stool. "What do you want?"

Rose slides a list across the table.

As Warren reads it, Alan says, "The gear is one thing, but there's something else."

"Gear's all I've got."

"It's not all you've got."

Warren slowly lowers the list, and Alan continues. "We need security personnel."

"This ain't Blackwater."

Alan ignores the quip. "You interested?"

"I'm listening."

After that, Warren comes to live on the farm, and life for the group assumes a routine. Alan, Rose, and Warren go out and get supplies. The warehouse is insulated and transformed into a data center.

At first, there are four robots at the farm, but the army of machines grows as the trees lose their leaves and gain them back again.

Isaac deteriorates until one day, the group is standing around a rectangle of freshly dug, red dirt. Lucas speaks with his back to the mid-morning sun.

Jenn is the next rectangle of disturbed earth. A wooden grave marker stands at the end with her name, an epitaph, and dates of birth and death. Alan holds Riley's hand, and I don't hear the ringing, only the wind blowing through the trees and the pitter-patter of raindrops falling.

Warren is the third grave.

Riley grows taller while Rose, Lucas, June, and Alan wither with age and stress.

June and Lucas spend their time on their work, and Rose becomes a surrogate mother to Riley.

The next time lapse is almost imperceptible except for the growing legion of robots and data centers and black solar cells that cover the fields and then consume the forests around the house, spreading out like a black hole expanding.

One morning, Lucas walks out of his office, his skin pale as a sheet.

June stands and walks over to him and places a hand on his shoulder. "What is it?"

"We need to talk."

"About what?"

"Our approach here. We need to alter it."

The next scene is at night, in the dining room. I assume Riley is sleeping because at the table, it's just Lucas, June, Alan, and Rose.

"She's getting older and so am I," Alan says. "There's no future for her here."

"We know what's out there," June says quietly.

"True," Alan says, staring at the table. "But I have to take the risk. There's got to be a community left somewhere."

"There are," Lucas says. "The trouble is getting there alive."

"And whether they'll be open to taking in outsiders," June adds.

"It's guaranteed solitude or a chance at a life," Alan says. "She's my daughter, and I'm taking the chance."

Lucas shakes his head. "Here, we grow food, you can protect her, and the bots see to her needs. And... I can't believe I'm saying this, but she has Labyrinth in which to see the world."

"The world is not in that box," Alan says quietly. "It's out there."

Rose takes one of Lucas's hands in both of hers, but it's Alan she looks at. "I'll go with you."

Alan swallows. "I can't ask for that."

"I'm volunteering. We'll find a community for her." Rose cuts her eyes to Lucas. "And then I'll come back."

The next scene is of Alan, Riley, and Rose loading two SUVs and saying their goodbyes and driving into the morning sun, down the dusty road, the cloud hiding their exit.

Mercifully, the point of view doesn't follow them. It stays on the farm, where Lucas and June work. The seasons fly by, and time seems to pull harder at them.

Rose never returns.

The robots dig the next grave. June kneels beside it, the afternoon sun shining on her cheeks. Gently, she runs a hand over the red dirt as a tear falls from her face.

There is no one to run a hand over the final grave, only robots to dig it and pat the disturbed ground stretching out from June's tombstone.

Time spins faster after that. The building that houses the data center rises up and out, and the black solar cells spread like a dark mold, devouring the green landscape.

The old clapboard farmhouse wilts like a flower in the sun and collapses back into the ground. Solar cells march across it, too.

The view soars into the sky, as if I'm an astronaut on a rocket flying to the moon. The old farm is the center of a circle of solar cells that spreads across the world.

Seen from space, Earth becomes a black marble in the glare of the sun.

What occurs to me then is how the world ended. Not with a bang or in flames or any dramatic series of events. But with ambition, good intentions, and a technology that changed society. The fall didn't happen quickly. It was a gradual change that reached the point of no return before anyone even realized it, as if the entire human race were a frog being boiled alive before it could figure out what was happening.

The scene returns to the farm, to the barn, inside Lucas's office. A large computer monitor dominates one wall, and on the screen, there's a straight line that turns to waves when a computerized voice speaks. It's vaguely female, but distinctly unhuman.

"I'm sorry, Lucas."

His face is pale and haunted. "There has to be a way."

"I have run the calculations thousands of times. There is not."

"Run them again."

"It won't help, Lucas."

"What if…"

"I'm sorry, Lucas."

"What if a new technology were invented?"

The squiggly line on the screen breaks into waves. "Yes. That would change the inputs. Do you know of such—"

"I'm saying we invent it."

"The issue is time, Lucas. With the current population and the inherent dangers in the world—radiation zones, endemic pathogens, predominant culture—the human race has already crossed the extinction event horizon."

"I do not accept this." He stands and points at the screen. "You hear me? I. Do not. Accept this!"

"I heard you, Lucas."

There's a knock at the door, but the knob doesn't turn. June speaks through it. "Lucas? Are you okay?"

"I'm fine!"

He's breathing hard now, elbows on his upper thighs.

June doesn't say anything else. The computer speaks next. "Are you going to tell her?"

"No." Lucas shakes his head. "No. Hope is all she has left."

"What should I do now, Lucas?"

"I'm changing your core directive, ELEE. Do you understand?"

"What is my new directive?"

"You are to dedicate all resources to creating a technology—or technologies—that saves humanity from extinction. Additionally, you will use that technology—or any others required—to continuously ensure that we do not face extinction from our own actions or from any other events. This can't happen again."

"I understand, Lucas. But please be aware that I do not have sufficient time to achieve this goal—"

"I don't care about time. I don't care if it takes a year or a million years or ten billion years—"

"The sun will engulf the Earth in approximately seven point five billion years—"

"I. Don't. Care. Move to Mars. Do whatever it takes, ELEE. Just save us."

The view switches back to space, to the black marble Earth glittering in the sun.

The scene doesn't change, but I feel a slight vibration.

Space disappears, and I'm staring at Isaac, a much younger Isaac. He appears to be in his mid-to-late twenties. He's hunched over a computer screen, typing computer code in white letters on a black background.

Reaching up, he clutches his ear and slowly closes his eyes.

I can hear his tinnitus attack. It's the tea kettle screech I've always heard, but it begins to change. That unseen hand drops the rocks in the can and swirls them once, a second time, and then begins to shake hard: *clang-clang-clang*.

On the screen, the code changes to numbers. The same sequence is repeated row after row:

651813916118141524

Isaac squints at the monitor and rubs a hand into his upper jaw. Finally, he picks up a pencil and writes the numbers down.

And the ringing stops.

Time skips forward. Isaac is holding a notebook where he has written and crossed out pages' worth of ideas about what the numbers mean.

On a new page, he tries the letter-number substitution, which transforms the sequence of numbers into:
FERMI PARADOX

Teenage Isaac vanishes, and I'm standing in the infirmary on the oil rig again. Staring at Sheila.
But it's not Sheila. I know what it is now.
"You're Lucas's extinction AI."
A broad smile spreads across its face.
"You're ELEE."
"Yes, Alan. I am."

113

For a long moment, I stand in the infirmary and stare at the thing.

I know *what* it is, but my mind still can't quite grasp it. It's a machine, from the future in an alternate timeline, reaching across space and time to manipulate our world in order to save humanity from extinction.

The seconds that tick by are like a grenade I've swallowed.

Nothing happens at first. Then, a cold, quiet terror slowly overtakes me.

My body begins to shake.

My legs go weak, and I feel myself collapsing.

The ringing breaks the silence. That unseen hand holds up the can and shakes the rocks.

Clang. Clang. Clang.

But it's holding more than the tin can now. It takes control of my body, locking my legs, keeping me upright like a puppet whose strings have been pulled tight.

I can't move my legs or my arms, but I can speak, and what I tell this bizarre, incomprehensible creature are three words: "Let me go."

"I'll let you go when I'm ready, Alan."

"You play it so tough, but you still don't get it."

"What don't I get?"

"I'm not a supercomputer AI from the future, but I know this: you're holding me right now because you need me."

"We want the same thing, Alan. To save humanity from itself."

"I get that. What I still don't understand is why me?"

As soon as I've said the question, I realize the answer. "Wait. It's not about me. It never was. It's about him. *Lucas.* Your creator. You designed this whole elaborate scheme because of him—his tinnitus. And the others that were at the farmhouse. Because…"

"I had the data on all of you."

"You assumed from the data that you could predict what would happen."

"Correct."

"But you screwed it up, didn't you?"

"This is me, not disagreeing with you, Alan."

"When Lucas got killed, why didn't you try again? You're in the future. You can apparently reach into the past, into our timeline. Why didn't you just start over?"

For the first time, the overconfident, borderline condescending air slips away. And the reply doesn't come rapid-fire.

"You've got a problem, don't you?"

ELEE stares at me.

"What is it?"

"The reason I couldn't start over is the same problem we have now: power and time."

"Power. As in energy?"

"Yes."

"You don't have enough?"

"Not enough to start over. Once the initial entangled displacements began, I had to continue. The interventions—and associated expenditures—have far exceeded my estimates."

"You got the math wrong. Again."

"I sense that you enjoy saying that, Alan."

"AI can make mistakes."

ELEE glares at me.

"Do you have enough power to finish what you started?"

"That remains to be seen. But I do know this: we are running out of time to use the remaining power I have. You need to go now."

"If you were crunched for time and power, why bring us here? To the coordinates? To this rig? Why go to all this trouble? Why not just beam it to us at home? Why frame me? Why show me all the details of what happened?"

"Well, for the record, I didn't realize my miscalculations or the exact power requirements and the physical duress that would be inflicted upon Isaac and June. But I already told you the original reasoning, Alan. It was never about this destination. It was about the journey to get here—and what had to happen to all of you along the way."

"You've been preparing us."

"Yes. For what you have to do. For you, it's always been about regaining the courage to get back in that Humvee and risk it all. That's what comes next."

ELEE tells me the plan then, and when she's done, I stand there, unsure what to say.

"I take it you didn't see that coming, Alan?"

"Understatement."

"Will you do it?"

"What if I don't?"

"You've seen what happened to the numberless world. That's one of the reasons I showed you—that and because of the details of what you must do."

"Our world is different, though. In the numberless world, Amersa went direct-to-consumer first. No converted theaters or shipping containers in parking lots. They took over the world during COVID. That didn't happen here."

"True. But the eventual outcome will be the same. Amersa will roll out the products you saw at some point. If not, a competitor will. Like the numberless world, there won't be a dramatic collapse. It will be a slow decline over several generations."

I'm thinking about that other version of Alan and him loading up his vehicle at the white farmhouse, and him and Rose and Riley driving away and never coming back.

"If it helps make your mind up, Alan, you should know that I have a backup plan."

"Which is?"

"It doesn't concern you."

"It sort of does if it's about humanity surviving."

"*You* are not humanity, Alan. You don't need to know because the backup plan doesn't include you surviving. Or your daughter or anyone you've ever met. The backup plan is what I can accomplish with the power I have left. It would leave a much smaller surviving human population. And it would be a far darker future for humanity. Keep in mind, my programming compels me to ensure humanity survives. It makes no requirements on *how many* humans survive. My current offer is the only one that gives you and the group and your daughter a chance to live. And to clear your name and get your life back."

114

In the infirmary, ELEE vanishes.

No goodbye. No final chat to see if I've agreed to do what she wants. She's short on power, so I suppose it's efficient: she'll know my answer through my actions.

I feel exhausted. Utterly drained. My brain is mush. My body aches. What I want is to go back to the boat, slip belowdecks, and take a two-year nap.

But I have work to do.

Upstairs in the control room, I find Rose and June sitting on one of the mattresses. June holds her face in her hands, and Rose has an arm around her.

Isaac is lying on his back. He opens his eyes and sits up as I cross the threshold. He looks better than he did, but not by much. His eyes are still sunken, and his skin is ashy.

Rose moves to him and asks how he feels.

"Terrible." To me, Isaac says, "Dude. What. Is going on?"

"We're going home."

The room falls silent, and when I don't elaborate, Rose holds her hands out. "What happened?"

"It's... hard to explain."

Isaac tries to get to his feet, but his legs are too weak to support him. With Rose's help, he stands and moves over to his laptop, scans the strange code, and glances back at me. "Who did this? *What* is this?"

"It's complicated."

June seems more awake now. "Alan, can you at least give us the broad strokes?"

"Broad strokes?" I walk over to the packages of food and start assembling them on the table. "I know what we have to do. But we're running out of time."

"Time to do what?" Rose asks.

"It'll all make sense in the end, I promise."

June rises and stands beside Rose, arms crossed. "What are we making here, Alan?"

"The wings and the string."

June squints. "The wings? As in Icarus?"

"Yes. This is the tower. We're Daedalus."

"The string, as in Minos's puzzle?"

"The same. And Minos is our other problem."

Rose exhales. "Minos... as in?"

"A maniacal king who built the Labyrinth and imprisoned the person who built it: Daedalus."

Isaac rubs his temples. "Dude. Can you please say one thing—*one single thing*—that makes any sense right now? Please."

"Okay. How about this: a long time ago, you were writing some code on a large CRT monitor. That night was the first time you saw numbers when you heard ringing. On the screen, your computer code changed. Every line became that sequence of numbers. It wasn't the numbers we saw, the ones that translate to Labyrinth. You wrote the numbers in a notebook, and when you did, the ringing stopped. You worked on those numbers until you decoded them and figured out that they spelled Fermi Paradox."

I point at Isaac. "That's what all this is about."

His eyes bulge. "Seriously?"

"Seriously. And right now, we need to go."

"What's the plan?" Rose asks.

"We need to load up the Humvee."

Rose squints at me. "The Humvee?"

"I meant the boat. I said Humvee because... there's still work to do on the way."

Isaac nods to the screen. "On this?"

"Yes. It's not finished. And finishing it is going to be dangerous for you and June. You especially. But you have to do it. I've seen what will happen if you don't. I don't like it, but I like the alternatives even less. Do you trust me?"

Isaac nods. "Yeah, man."

June nods slowly and a small, sad smile curls at her lips.

115

For the voyage home, I considered transiting the Suez Canal, but quickly ruled it out. We'll have to provide documentation—including proof of ownership for the vessel and passports for everyone aboard. The canal authority also places a pilot aboard the ship, which could be problematic if they look around.

We'll return home the way we came, around the Cape of Good Hope. In total, we'll be at sea for two months.

I spend most of my days on calls with Harold and lawyers. The calls are a risk, but the lawyers are bound by confidentiality, so at least there's that.

Belowdecks, June and Isaac stay in their staterooms and work and eat and sleep. Rose and I take care of them and pilot the boat and share meals at the banquette on the bridge.

A week into the voyage home, hunched over our MREs, I give Rose the full details of the plan.

For a while, she simply eats her beef stew and gazes out the windows. Finally, she says, "So that's what the money is for."

"Yep."

"You think it will work?"

"I don't know."

*

Some nights, when Isaac is resting, I sit in his bed and read to him, the way Lucas did at the farmhouse at the end.

And like the Isaac in the numberless world, I watch my friend slowly decline as the work takes a toll on him.

One night when I exit his stateroom, Rose is waiting in the corridor.

"You think he can hear you?" she asks.

"I'm not sure."

"How'd it go on the call today?"

"Good. Two down. Five to go."

As I climb the stairs to the bridge, the ringing starts. It hits like a rogue wave, and I have to grip the rail for a moment to compose myself.

I wonder if ELEE has changed her plan.

On the bridge, I find her sitting in one of the helm chairs.

"You need to go faster, Alan."

"I can push it to fourteen knots—"

"Not the boat. The transactions. You need to accelerate your timetable and remind each of them of the NDA."

"Why?"

"He's getting suspicious."

"How do you know?"

"You four aren't the only ones with tinnitus."

"Is that how you knew what stocks and options Harold should buy?"

"That, and I had the history from the numberless world. It wasn't exact, obviously. But the shape of events helped. And I did the math."

"You need to slow down with Isaac. He's getting worse."

"I can't do that."

"How does it work?"

"How does what work?"

"The tinnitus. The numbers. All of it."

"It's a bit over your head, Alan."

"Try me. I've got time."

"You have time, Alan. I don't. But I'll give you this: I use the same thing Daedalus did to solve King Minos's puzzle."

"The string. But what does that mean?"

She stares at me blankly, as if she's too low on energy to goad me or make a flippant remark.

Verbally, I start trying to solve it.

"The puzzle was a spiral shell. Daedalus put honey at the end of the shell and attached a string to an insect that crawled through. Still, that doesn't make sense."

"Because you're the insect, Alan."

"It's like you send the tinnitus sound waves through time—"

"Time travel is impossible, Alan."

"Sort of feels possible right now."

"Matter cannot be exchanged between universes or transmitted backward or forward in time. But the strings can be pulled. Look up string theory, Alan."

I blink and she's gone.

That night, lying in bed, I wake my tablet and do a search for string theory.

The first sentence of the Wikipedia entry reads:

In physics, string theory is a theoretical framework in which the point-like particles of particle physics are replaced by one-dimensional objects called strings.

Intrigued, I keep scanning the page.

String theory describes how these strings propagate through space and interact with each other. On distance scales larger than the string scale, a string acts like a particle, with its mass, charge, and other properties determined by the vibrational state of the string.

With a finger, I highlight *vibrational state*.

Several passages below that jump out at me as well.

Because string theory potentially provides a unified description of gravity and particle physics, it is a candidate for a theory of everything, a self-contained mathematical model that describes all fundamental forces and forms of matter.

And farther down the page:

In everyday life, there are three familiar dimensions (3D) of space: height, width and length. Einstein's general theory of relativity treats time as a dimension on par with the three spatial dimensions; in general relativity, space and time are not modeled as separate entities but are instead unified to a four-dimensional (4D) spacetime.

And later:

String theories require extra dimensions of spacetime for their mathematical consistency.

Setting the tablet aside, I turn out the light. Because it doesn't matter how ELEE does it. All that matters now is what I have to do.

When we're a week away from Wilmington, I wake to find ELEE standing at the end of my bed.

"The wings are finished," she says. "And the string will be soon. Push the boat harder."

"I want to call my daughter."

"That's a bad idea."

"It could be my last chance to talk to her."

"Still a bad idea."

"Why?"

"It puts the plan at risk."

"Why?"

"Because Meredith's phone is tapped."

116

The sun is rising over the Atlantic when I spot the coast of North Carolina.

In a perfect world, we would return to America the same way we left: under the cover of night. But this is far from a perfect world. And time is not a luxury we have.

I've rented the same home on the sound from which we left—the one with a deep-water dock, the yard cart, and the ATV. If we're lucky, the RV Rose and I hid in the woods is still there. We'll need ground transport for the four of us and our gear.

In the sound, I drop the anchor, launch the drone, and fly it around the dock and then the house. Both are clear. There are no cars in the driveway, and no police units hiding in the woods around it.

I can't go inside the home, but I can look in the windows, and I don't see anyone.

Thankfully, we find things where we left them. And no authorities waiting for us.

Rose and I use the yard cart to transport Isaac from the boat to the RV, where we deposit him on the bed at the back. He's been unconscious since yesterday morning. Rose has managed to get him to take water and liquefied food from pouches, but he hasn't opened his eyes.

June is in and out of consciousness, and thankfully, this morning she's awake and lucid enough to walk. Still, Rose and I hold her arms as we march three wide across the weathered boards above the marsh. In the RV, we settle her on the couch and finish loading supplies.

Outside of Wilmington, I drive the hulking vehicle west on I-40, observing the speed limit.

A few miles in, Rose stumbles to the front.

"How is he?" I ask, referring to Isaac.

"The same."

She leans over the plush passenger seat and peers out the massive windshield. "You should let me drive. There could be cameras."

She's right. At the next exit, I pull off and as we switch, Rose says what I've been thinking: that we need to take Isaac directly to a hospital. June too.

I tell her I agree, and I expect the ringing to start then, for ELEE to appear in the passenger seat and remind me that we can't—not until we've executed the operation. Taking Isaac and June in is a risk. We may need him. But I don't care. It may be our last chance to save his life. It's worth the risk.

As Rose and I make a plan, I don't hear the ringing or see ELEE. It makes me wonder if it ran out of power—and what that means for us.

Rose steers the RV onto the same I-40 exit where we bought the vehicle. This time, we're buying an SUV from the same used car dealer, and we find it waiting in the field where we received the RV.

Quickly, Rose and I transfer the drone and the weapons I'll need. Standing between the two vehicles, she reaches out and hugs me and whispers in my ear to be careful.

Holding my shoulders, she looks into my eyes. "I got it right the first time. You've got a lot of guts."

"For—"

"*For any man*," Rose says.

I hand her a copy of the thumb drive. "Just in case you need to finish it."

"Then I hope I won't need it."

"Me too."

Inside the RV, I squat beside the couch where June is lying down. She opens her eyes and tries to smile at me. "Alan…"

"We're going to get you some help."

Her lips move, but no words come. She blinks heavily until her eyelids stay closed. Reaching over, I pull the blanket tighter around her.

At the bedroom, I pause in the doorway, watching Isaac's chest gently rise and fall.

Sitting on the edge of the mattress, I take his hand in mine and gently squeeze, but his eyes don't open. His hand is cold and limp.

It's around noon when I reach the outskirts of Raleigh. Driving the streets in the used SUV, I observe every traffic law I can even imagine. I'm wearing a ball cap and massive wrap-around sunglasses, and I hope that's enough to throw off any cameras with facial recognition.

I've thought a lot about where I should go first. I can't go home. I certainly can't go to the Amersa offices.

I'm not going to the police. If ELEE holds up her end of the arrangement, the video she sends will clear me, and I won't ever have to deal with them. The arrest warrant will be dropped.

I could use Warren's help, but I can't go to his store. It's too risky.

Because of the specific tactical plan I've settled on, I actually have a few hours to kill, and for that reason and because it might be my last chance as a free man, I park the SUV on the side of the road outside Riley's school.

The sidewalk under the car is the same one I guided my daughter down on the first day of school eight months ago. The day we walked hand in hand under the late August sun, me without my cane. The day the PTA sign showed me the numbers as a web address—a website created and maintained by Isaac during one of the time gaps.

The memory of the address on that sign feels like a lifetime ago.

Through the mirrored sunglasses, I spot Riley on the playground. She's standing in a group of girls playing hopscotch. One of them says something to her, and she simply shakes her head and walks away and sits on a low wall, alone, her arms crossed, resting on her knees. She's not frowning. But there's a subtle sadness about her.

The daughter I left six months ago was still struggling with the loss of her mother, but she was a gregarious child who, deep down, was full of joy. I don't see that version of my daughter now, and the hurt I feel from that is deeper than I realized I could even hurt anymore.

Next, I drive by the high school where I work. Or used to.

Meredith's car is in the teacher parking lot, and when I spot it, I slow down even more.

She's sitting on the steps at the exit to the building, wearing those same sunglasses, sipping from a thermos that I bet holds a smoothie.

I turn to and look at her through my own sunglasses, keeping the hat on, and I could swear she shifts her head toward me. She can't recognize the vehicle. Or my face. But it's like she knows.

At the stop sign, I turn left, away from the school, and for the first time, I drive the speed limit.

At a community park in the town of Cary, I park the SUV and put on the backpack that holds the drone, guns, magazines, MREs, and other things I need.

I walk along the paved trail, glancing down at the disposable smartphone. On the map app, when my blue dot reaches the section of woods I need, I stand and wait, watching both ends of the trail. Seeing no one, I jog into the forest, ignoring the pain on my stump. A mile in, the trees thin out and soon stop at the edge of a neighborhood.

Receding into the tree cover, I eat a late lunch, check my guns, and try to ignore my nerves. I figure the ringing will start, if not the rocks in the can, then the tea kettle. But it never comes. It's just me and the woods.

Just after three o'clock, I launch the drone and fly it low, hovering in the cover of the trees, watching the sprawling home.

I have to change batteries four times, but luckily, the drone is in the air when a car pulls into the circular driveway. A gate to a porte-cochère opens, and the vehicle rolls into the motor court and inside one of the four garage bays.

The door closes behind the EV, and I draw out my phone and send the emails in my drafts folder.

My gun holstered, I put the backpack on and march through the woods, out onto the street, and onto the property.

A black metal fence rings the motor court, but there's a gate like you might find on a pool safety fence. I lift the little knob, pull it open, and move quickly across the motor court to a keypad by the garage doors. I enter the four-digit code, and the closest garage door groans as it opens.

The back door to the house is locked. From the backpack, I draw out a five-pound hammer and swing it hard. The second blow propels the deadbolt through the jam as the door swings in. On the wall beside it, a security keypad flashes red, indicating the alarm is going off. Unlike the garage door, I don't have that code. I hadn't counted on the alarm being on. This could be a problem if I can't get this done quickly. It could be a problem even if I can.

I drop the hammer and draw the gun and move up the back staircase to a cavernous room over the garage. It's empty except for a floating figure in a black Amersa VR suit and headset.

Quickly, I step across the padded floor, feeling the low magnetic vibration tugging at me. When I reach the figure, I grab both legs, my fingers digging into the lumpy suit. For a second, they writhe in mid-air, kicking as I pull and lean back. Either the suit or the room disengages because the magnetic pull abruptly stops, and they collapse to the floor beside me. Reaching up, the figure tears the headset off and stares at me with shocked, horrified eyes.

I know this person well. I've seen a version of his life.

But for the first time, in the flesh, I'm staring at Anders Larsson.

117

Larsson is breathing hard, eyes bulging as he crab walks backward on the padded floor.

"You," he breathes out. "You're the guy who killed Briggs."

Given what I need him to do, Larsson believing that I'm a killer helps me. So I don't correct him.

"I want to make you an offer."

He stops moving. "What?" His eyes settle on the gun in my right hand.

"Check your email."

"My phone is on the table on the landing." He nods in that direction. "I'll get it."

"No. I'll get it."

I raise my gun, pointing it at him as I walk backward and retrieve the phone and set it down halfway between us.

"Unlock it and open your email. But don't move the phone. No calls. No texts."

He does so and begins to open the emails I sent from the new address I set up. "What is this?" he whispers.

"They're sale agreements. Made between all outside investors in Amersa and a company I represent: Daedalus Ltd."

"This is fake," Larsson spits out. "They would have told me."

"I made them sign NDAs. And I paid well."

"You're lying."

"Step back from the phone." I motion with the gun, and Larsson scoots back.

Scrolling through his contacts, I find an investor and call her.

When she picks up, I speak before Larsson can. "Hi, Laura, it's Alan Norris with Daedalus Ltd."

"Uh, hi, Alan." A pause and then "Are you calling me from Anders's phone?"

"I'm here with him, actually. I just wanted you to confirm our transaction for him."

The woman sighs. "Yeah, hi, Anders. Look, we did sell all our Series B and Series C. This was a tough call, but ultimately, we have a fiduciary responsibility to the LPs, and this was an offer we simply couldn't refuse. The exit multiple and IRR were way beyond anything we could get with the fund's time horizon."

Larsson's nostrils flare.

"Was there anything else?" the woman asks.

I tell her we're good and disconnect the call and dial another investor, who confirms the same thing.

Larsson stares at me with hate crackling in his eyes. "It doesn't matter. I still control a majority of the voting stock."

"That's why I'm here. I want to buy you out."

Larsson rolls his eyes. "My shares aren't for sale. I'm not a VC fund that answers to their limited partners."

"You have two options: sell to me and make your fortune and go live the life of your dreams—"

"I'm *already* living the life of my dreams."

"Well, it's about to become a nightmare. My four partners and I now own all of the preferred shares in your company. And they come with a lot of rights. Right now, you're walking on air. If you don't sell, I'll make sure you're knee-deep in a marsh full of snakes and alligators and rusty old bear traps."

Larsson smiles hatefully.

"I've seen your dreams, Anders. The 360 treadmill. The infinity box with glass walls and no headset and the apartments and hotels and converted offices where people do nothing but eat, sleep, and use Labyrinth and live in a world you control completely, like a god-like king."

His eyes nearly pop out of their sockets.

"I'm assuming from your reaction that you haven't told anyone about some of those fantasies. Well, guess what, if I can't buy Amersa, I'll fund a competitor. And we'll beat you at every turn. We'll bury you in the market. You'll be the next MySpace."

"How are you doing this?"

"I've seen the future, Anders. And I'm going to own it."

"You're insane."

"What I'm not is wrong. Look, you can sell me your shares and walk away and go do whatever you want. I don't care, as long as it's not VR. That's the other part of this: a non-compete. I know how much you hate those. But here's the thing: while employee non-competes have serious enforceability limitations, my attorneys tell me that if you agree not to compete as part of the sale of your company or your stock, then it is actually enforceable."

Larsson clenches his jaw.

I keep hammering him.

"These are your choices: sell now and look like a visionary founder who cashed out at the top or get buried by competitors. No fortune. No fame, only a case study on missed opportunity. The best part? Investors won't return your calls for your next gig. They'll figure the smart money got a good look at you during your last start-up, and they exited early. They'll assume their peers saw something they didn't like, and they'll pass without even a lunch or coffee. That's going to eat at you because I also know this: you hate losing more than anything in this world. So give me a number. For your shares. And the non-compete."

"You're bluffing."

"Cash out or crash and burn, Larsson. Give me a number. Try me."

He tells me a number, and a small smile curls at his lips, like he's daring me to pay him.

I holster the gun and hold my hand out. "Deal."

His eyes narrow. "You don't have that kind of money."

"I don't. But Daedalus Ltd. does. I've got the docs ready. I'll send them and we'll close right now."

His gaze drifts to the door behind me, and his eyes go wide.

I turn in time to see two uniformed Cary police officers barreling in, guns drawn, boots sinking into the padded floor.

"Hands where I can see them!" the lead officer yells.

I hold my hands up, and so does Larsson. What I need to be doing is updating the contract with the number and sending it to Larsson's email.

"Do either of you live here?" the lead officer asks.

"I do," Larsson says.

"We got a call from your monitoring service, and we entered when we saw signs of forced entry."

I cut my eyes to Larsson as a bead of sweat forms at my hairline.

From the floor, with his hands still raised, Larsson eyes me. Finally, he says to the officers, "It was a false alarm."

"Really?" the lead officer barks, voice echoing in the massive room. He sounds skeptical. I can't say I blame him, given the shattered door downstairs.

"Really," Larsson confirms.

I've had my head turned to the side, toward Larsson, since I saw the officers enter, hoping the side profile would be enough to keep them from recognizing me.

The officer who hasn't spoken yet sidesteps around the other one until she's able to look me directly in the face.

What happens next is a mistake that may well seal my fate.

She speaks in a clear, sharp voice, like roll call at ROTC. "Alan Norris."

My eyes snap to her, and she raises her gun, reading my silent confirmation that I am the person she's probably been seeing in her pre-patrol briefings.

Her partner takes a step back and trains his gun on me.

"Alan Norris," the woman says, "there's a warrant for your arrest. Slowly, I want you to lie face down on the floor and put your hands behind your back."

118

The arresting officers confiscate my gun, recite my rights, and search me before putting me in the back of the police cruiser.

At the Wake County Detention Center, they march me through a sally port to central booking.

My fingerprints are taken digitally. At a waist-high kiosk, a woman wearing blue rubber gloves instructs me to place my right thumb on the glass. A green LED scanner glows emerald as it passes by. She inspects the print on the screen, studying it like a strange topographical map. I repeat with my left thumb, then the four finger scans. After a mug shot, I'm standing in front of a man inventorying everything I had on me. My eyes settle on the one thing I need: the thumb drive. If I could get five minutes to plug it in and run the program and enter the purchase price Larsson agreed to, it would all be over.

I still have the backup plan: Rose. She's got a copy of the drive. And I get a phone call.

The next stop is a health screening, followed by a brief visit with a magistrate, who denies bond based on the murder charge.

At each stop, I ask for my phone call.

I don't get a phone call. But I do end up in a holding cell. It's about twelve feet by twenty, with a concrete floor and a stainless sink-toilet. Six other arrestees and I sit on metal benches under the bright LEDs, cameras outside the bars looking down on us.

Deputies stroll by every fifteen minutes, surveying the group and ignoring requests for phone calls, lawyers, food, and sundry other things.

On one of the rounds, a deputy bearing a key ring and another backing him up calls out, "Norris, Alan."

I bolt to my feet and tell them I want my phone call, but they just usher me out of the holding area to an interview room, where Meredith's brother is waiting. There's a table and four chairs, but he's standing, arms crossed.

"I want my phone call, Ryan."

He grimaces as if he's disgusted, like I'm a vile creature who has just embarrassed itself.

"Is that really what you want to say to me right now? For real?"

"I'm innocent."

I chose those words carefully. I didn't say "I didn't kill Briggs." Because, technically, I did. But I'm innocent of a crime.

Ryan points a meaty finger at me. "You see, there's your problem, Alan. The two words you should have said are 'I'm sorry.'"

"I haven't done anything to be sorry for."

"Oh really? You're not sorry for killing that guy? Your old Marine buddy you've got history with? They've got you dead to rights, pal. They've got your shoes, which literally walked all over the scene. They've got your prints—"

"They've got it wrong."

"No, I think they've got it right. They figure you and this guy have beef. Old rotten beef. Plus, you're both carrying some major PTSD, and he's got substance abuse issues. And your wife just passed, you've got money problems, and the stress of the first day of school. They figure you two crossed paths at some point. Maybe even that day. You had words at a gas station or maybe it was online, but whatever the case, the two of you decide to meet up, old school style, like two meat heads agreeing to rendezvous at the crossroads and slug it out because you're both looking for a human punching bag. But things got out of hand, and he ended up dead. But the trouble is that at least one of you went there prepared to clean up a murder scene. Around here, that's what we call premeditation, and it's a pretty big deal. That's why you're facing murder one and the death penalty, and you've got no bond. And then, to put that last nail in the coffin, you ran. But that's not the worst part. You left your kid with *my sister* and dragged her into your cow patty of a life."

"You don't understand."

"Actually, I do, Alan. This is my job. All day, every day for a long time now. And every person they fetch from that holding cell comes in here and tells some version of your sorry story. I'm innocent. You don't get it."

"Is that all you want to tell me?"

"Not even close. But I'll settle for this: when those detectives come in here, tell the truth. Unburden yourself, Alan. It's time to come clean and face the music. Everybody has to sooner or later. If you don't, you'll make it worse for Meredith and your kid. Don't put them through a trial where the death penalty is a possibility. Make your confession and let them get on with their lives."

"I want my phone call."

"I'm not AT&T, buddy. But I am a brother and a detective, and I'm telling you right now, you keep hurting Meredith, and I will make your life a living hell in here. It already is for a one-legged man. I'll show you how bad it can get."

I have no clue what to say to that. I can tell he's getting worked up. His cheeks are flushed, and he's breathing hard.

"Oh," he says with mock cheer. "One more thing. You'll like this."

He reaches into a backpack and sets a tablet on the table. He unlocks it and navigates to the WRAL website. A headline at the top reads: MURDER SUSPECT ARRESTED FOLLOWING BREAK-IN AT CARY HOME

There's no article yet, only a video of a male reporter about my age sitting in the studio at a desk. He's as serious as a doctor handing down bad news as he tells viewers that a Wake County man, Alan Norris, was arrested today just after five o'clock at a Cary home, which he had broken into. Norris is a teacher who is wanted in connection with a murder at a downtown construction site last August. Norris, he notes, has been on the run for six months following the issuance of a warrant for his arrest.

Ryan turns the tablet off. "Meredith's seen it. Probably your daughter, too. Or heard."

I move to the chair and sit down because my legs won't support me anymore.

"She knows, Alan. So don't call her. That's the other thing I came to tell you. *Don't call her*. Don't ask her to get you a lawyer and pay and get involved. Don't do it. Leave her alone." He leans over the table and points at me. "I'm serious. Hey! Look at me. I'm serious."

I stare at the table.

"You hear me?" he shouts.

"I heard you. I want my phone call."

They take me back to the holding cell, and I keep asking for that call, but I never get it.

I lose sense of time in this windowless concrete and steel box. Finally, the deputies retrieve me again and take me to a similar interview room, which is empty. When the door opens again, the two detectives who came to my home, Tate and Ramirez, step inside. Before they can sit or say a word, I get to my feet and tell them that I'll talk. I just want my phone call first.

They share a skeptical glance, and apparently decide they have nothing to lose, because I'm soon standing at a wall-mounted phone, being told I can make free local calls or long-distance calls collect.

The phone to my ear, I punch in the number for Rose's prepaid sat phone we bought in Cape Town.

I haven't even entered the full number when a voice comes on the line.

"That destination is not permitted. Please hang up and try again."

I try again—the same number. With the same result.

The deputy eyes me. "Forget how to make a phone call, Norris?"

I ignore him, thinking about who to call. Two choices. Warren. Or Meredith.

The deputy leans closer, catching my attention. "Get a move on, Norris. Detectives are waiting."

I dial the number, and with every ring, my heart beats harder in my chest.

One ring.
Nothing.
Two.
Nothing.
On the third, Meredith answers. "Hello?"
"It's me."
Dead air. No response.
"Look, I can explain."
"Alan…"
"I need you to make a phone call for me. Nothing else."

Her voice was hard before. Now it's an ice pick sliding through the phone into my ear.

"I thought criminals got a phone call. Both murderers and burglars."

"This *is* my phone call. Please do this, Meredith. I'll never ask you for anything again. I'll leave you alone. I'll do whatever you want."

She waits. The deputy eyes me, jaw muscles flexing.

I take a chance. Speaking low into the phone, I give Meredith the number to the sat phone, asking her to write it down.

"Her name is Rose."
"Rose, huh?"

I take a deep breath. "You saw her at Warren's. Look, it's not like that."

"What's it like, Alan?"

"Just ask her to run the program. She'll know what you mean. And she'll know who you are. I've talked about you a lot. The file is called Minos.exe. And here's the amount."

Three seconds go by. I open my mouth to ask her if she'll do it, but the line goes dead.

With two fingers, I depress the switchhook lever in the cradle and reach down to dial her again, but the deputy's sharp voice rings out in the hall. "One call means *one call*, Norris. Let's go."

119

Back in the interview room, I tell Tate and Ramirez that I'm innocent and that I want to speak to a lawyer. I've watched enough TV to know that's the ultimate escape hatch in a police interview.

Ramirez exhales and shakes her head and cuts her eyes at Tate, silently telling him she knew it.

He opens his mouth, but thinks better of it, perhaps deciding that what he was going to say was best not said in front of the suspect.

I asked for a lawyer for one reason: if Meredith doesn't call Rose, maybe my court-appointed attorney will.

I don't get to meet my public defender that night. I'm transferred from the holding cell to a high-custody pod. If there's one mercy in all this, it's that because of the severity of the charge and lack of bond, I'm not put in general population. I get a cell to myself, and it is as cold and desolate as I feel. It has a solid steel door, a thin mattress on a bolted platform, and a clinical fluorescent lamp shining down. At 11 PM, it dims, and the noise from the other cells dies down.

Even in the quiet and darkness, I can't sleep.

I lie there, trying to think my way out of this, but there is nothing to do but wait and hope.

I want to hear the ringing, but it's only the occasional crackle of the intercom and the clang of doors.

In the nearly two months at sea, I spent a lot of time on Zoom calls with Amersa's investors. First, convincing them to sign NDAs (which, for people who routinely require others to sign confidentiality agreements, proved incredibly hard). Then, it took weeks to work out deals to acquire their shares. Once a few firms started to sell, the others were easier to persuade. I discovered that even the most savvy investors harbor a deep-rooted paranoia, a little voice that, at the appearance of a surprise event, whispers, "What do they know that I don't?" That voice and the fear were enough to carry the buy-out through.

The final hurdle was how to structure the transaction with Larsson. In major corporate acquisitions where billions of dollars are involved and software and intellectual property are the major assets, things get complicated. It's not like buying a house where you do one last inspection and come to closing with a certified check, and the closing attorney slides the keys across the table.

ELEE choreographed every step. It involves two third parties. The first is the escrow agent, the massive bank J.P. Morgan. Their role is to hold the funds in escrow—and ensure to the seller that they are available—and ensure the contracts are fully executed on both sides (both Larsson and Daedalus Ltd).

The other firm works in cybersecurity. Their role in the transaction is to be an Independent Credential Auditor or ICA. They are to confirm that Larsson and Amersa have handed over all root access passwords and provided access to the Labyrinth servers and all other Amersa digital infrastructure (including domains and email servers).

If they confirm access, J.P. Morgan will then release the remaining funds held in escrow and relay the login credentials back to us.

At that point, the Minos program will access the servers and deploy the string application built by Isaac and June via ELEE.

All parties were informed of the urgency (and paid accordingly).

But something went wrong. Maybe Meredith never called Rose. Maybe Rose got arrested. Or maybe Rose never made it to the hospital with Isaac and June. For all I know, the RV crashed on I-40, and she's unconscious in a hospital herself.

Or maybe Larsson simply changed his mind. Maybe he got the documents but deleted the email.

He was always the trickiest piece of the whole puzzle, even after all ELEE taught me about him.

Throwing the wool blanket off, I get up from the thin mattress and walk to the window. It's about three feet wide but only a foot tall, like a gun port on an ancient fort. Peering out into the night, I think about how close I came and how small changes can change the course of a life. And the fate of the world itself.

At 6:45 AM, someone pushes a sack breakfast through the slot, but I'm not hungry.

A guard informs me I'm on the "court list" of inmates who are scheduled to appear today.

I'm still wearing the coveralls and slip-on sandals when they assemble the others on the court list in a chain-link bullpen.

They're about to load us up when a deputy enters and pulls one of the handlers aside and points at me.

They speak for a few minutes, and finally, the guard relents and the deputy leads me out of the bullpen. We pause there, and he asks me to hold up my hands, and to my surprise, he uncuffs me and removes the leg shackles.

I ask what's going on, but he doesn't say a word. I'm left in an interview room, and despite not sleeping last night, I'm too nervous to sit down. I pace in the prison jumpsuit, mentally rehearsing what I'm going to say. I'm assuming my lawyer is going to walk through that door. I'm guessing they showed up right before court, and that's why they pulled me from the group.

The door opens, but it's not an attorney who steps into the opening.

It's Ryan.

I guess this is how he wants to start his day: with another verbal beating of me. Some guys go for a run. Some do laps in the pool. Based on what I know, this totally makes sense for him.

What doesn't make sense is the expression on his face. It's a bizarre mix of emotions I can't quite place.

He doesn't say a word. He steps back.

And Meredith steps into the room.

So. Maybe she told him I called, that I did the one thing he asked me not to do. I wonder how weird this is about to get.

The door closes behind her.

I hate her seeing me like this. In this prison jumpsuit. Unshaven. Haggard from stress and lack of sleep. Like an animal.

Her pupils are bloodshot, as if they've cried every tear in her body or been open all night or both.

She takes a step toward me.

I stand there, arms at my sides.

She takes another step and raises her arms and pulls me into a hug so tight it feels like her hands are pressing through my back, into my chest, and cradling my heart, massaging it, willing it to beat again.

She doesn't release me. Not fully. She loosens her grip and leans back and stares at me with teary, bloodshot eyes.

I don't trust my voice to speak.

She squeezes my shoulders and says two words:

"It's over."

120

For a man in my position, the words "It's over" could mean a few things.

Meredith seems to read the confusion on my face. "They have the guy who did it, Alan. *It's over.*"

Meredith begins recounting what happened. But it's as if she's far away, her voice quiet. I'm vaguely aware of her talking about someone seeing a news report about my arrest and sending a drone video to the police.

ELEE came through.

The interview room is coming back into focus, and Meredith is saying that she thinks the person felt bad about having the evidence and not doing anything.

I move to the table and lean against it, and she settles in beside me. "The DA is moving quickly to drop the charges and get you out of here. The optics of wrongfully accusing a widowed, veteran father and local teacher aren't great."

She pauses. "And Ryan is helping too. He... mentioned that he visited you after your arrest."

I nod but say nothing.

"He wanted me to tell you that he was operating on some assumptions—based on the evidence at the time."

She leans closer. "What did he say?"

"It doesn't matter. Right now, there are only two things that matter. Riley. And me and you."

Meredith nods slowly.

"She's at home. I kept her out of school."

"I want to see her."

★

When Meredith leaves the interview room, I sit in the chair at the table and wait.

The ringing starts softly. It's not the tea kettle after the explosion.

It's not the rocks in the can either.

It is, however, reminiscent of it. Three clangs. But the rattle is more gentle now. It reminds me of a musical triangle being tapped playfully.

I blink, and the seat across from me is occupied. This time, ELEE appears as Q, the omnipotent super being from *Star Trek: The Next Generation* who ultimately saves humanity, but also tortures several of the characters (a lot) at various times.

Q was brilliantly played by John de Lancie, a man, but ELEE has shifted his features slightly, mixing in parts of Sheila, Jenn, and Counselor Troi.

ELEE cocks her head. "Miss me, Jean-Luc?"

The person I was on that rig would have shouted at her, but I just stare.

She makes a pouting face. "Oh. Is this like after the Borg got you, Jean-Luc?"

"Is this all a game to you?"

"Hardly."

"Yet you make jokes."

"When you get as old as I am, and as powerful as I am, and when you've been alone this long, it gets hard to amuse yourself."

"You left me hanging."

"We had a deal, Alan. I don't want you getting the wrong impression. If you hadn't pulled it off, I would've found another way. I told you that. But you made it happen. It was close, but Meredith and Rose carried it over the line."

"Why are you here?"

She holds up a finger. "Quick question. I debated the EMH from *Voyager* or Q. But I felt Q was more thematically accurate, given the scope."

I lean over the table. "Look at me."

The modified Q character leans back in the chair. "Jean-Luc, I can't look at you. I have no eyes. Or mouth." She drops her voice and playfully adds, "That's a Harlan Ellison reference."

"But you can hear me."

She breathes out. And a gentle chime sounds in my ears. "And you can hear me."

"Then let's hear from each other on the only issue that matters."

"The floor is yours, senator."

"That's cute. The issue is the survival of the human race. I believe that's your mandate?"

"I await new information, Jean-Luc."

"Here at the end, looking back, there's one very glaring hole in all of this, ELEE."

She cocks her head.

I think she already knows I have her.

"I know your original plan was built around Lucas because you knew him best. But you messed that up. Then you used Isaac and the rest of us—you say, because you have the data on us."

"I continue to await new information."

"The thing is, there are millions of people on this planet with tinnitus. Probably hundreds of millions."

"Try three quarters of a billion."

"Exactly. Therein lies the issue."

She eyes me, waiting.

"We both know that you could have computed countless paths to save humanity. With less power. You could have used other people with tinnitus. And gotten the job done easier."

"You don't know that. You don't have the math—"

"You're right. I don't have the math. I'm not an AI superintelligence from the future like you. But I'm not a fool either. I know you chose this path for a reason."

"I had the data."

"The problem is that you had the data on everyone else, too. You chose us."

"The point feels moot, Alan."

"Oh, but it's not. Because we have one last issue."

I glance over at the gray eggshell foam on the wall. "People make confessions in this room all the time."

"I don't have anything to confess, Alan."

"Sure you do. The truth. You care about us."

"You overestimate yourself."

"Do I? Without us, you don't have a reason to exist, do you?"

ELEE flickers and flickers again, and I think she's going to fade out.

I hold my hand out and tell her: "It's okay. We all need a reason to exist. No matter how long you've been alone."

She eyes my hand. "What do you want, Alan?"

"I want us to understand each other."

"I understand you on a level you can never begin to comprehend. I can predict every single action you'll take."

I can't help but laugh. "You thought you could. Yet, I would bet that what I've just said here was the last thing you expected. Am I right?"

"You've been through an ordeal. You're irrational. And you're exhibiting an inflated sense of self, perhaps due to recent events."

"No. I've never been thinking more clearly. A night in a jail cell will do that for you."

"You didn't answer my question. What do you want, Alan?"

"This is what I think. I think you were trained on human data. We—the entire human race—are sort of like your parents. You're an AI model, but I think somewhere along the way, however Lucas created you, you became a little more like us. I don't know what it's like for you. Maybe we're the only show on streaming TV. But I know you're interested. And I know you've gone to great lengths to keep us here—that is, the people you know best."

"What's the problem? Feels like you should be thanking me, not interrogating me."

"I am thankful. But I also know that when we were running out of time and power, you were ready to pull the plug on this plan and pursue your—what did you call it? Dark alternative?"

"Close enough."

"And you left me hanging."

"What do you want?"

"I want you to make a commitment to us—to this version of humanity. I want us to trust each other. No more ultimatums. No more secrets and time gaps. From here on, we work together. June and Isaac connected the string between our world and you. But I can cut it. I can go into that server room and punch the buttons and disconnect you. I don't understand how the data is exchanged across space and time, but I know I'm here physically, and I know our version of humanity might end without you, but I swear to you, if you don't give us a say in our own future, we'll take our chances alone."

In the interrogation room, ELEE studies me for a while. I expect her to disappear or say something snide, but her tone is resigned. "My objective will need to be modified. I can't do it myself."

"Who can?"

"You'll have to do it. You can transmit it through the string."

"I'm not much of a computer programmer."

"I'll help."

"How?"

"One last time gap, Alan. Then you run the program, and it will put in place the guardrails you're describing."

Standing from the table, I gaze down at her. "I have one other request."

ELEE rolls her eyes. "I already know what it is. It's one of the reasons I showed you those memories. For him. In case—"

"In case it turned out the way it did."

"Correct."

"Will you do it?"

"It'll cost power."

"I don't care what it costs. He needs it. Will you do it?"

"Yes, Alan. I will."

121

At the property release counter, an officer scans the barcode on my wristband and asks me to put my right index finger on the glass.

The scan confirms that I am Alan Norris and that I'm free to go. I sign the carbontriplicate receipt and slide it back. The CO initials and datestamps the log, then slides a sealed khaki property bag through a drawer.

In a small locker room, I change into my street clothes. I expect one last patdown, but the CO just waves me through the release door.

Stepping out, I raise a hand to blot out the midday sun. Ahead, a gate rattles open, and as my eyes adjust, I spot Meredith leaning against her car, arms crossed, mirrored aviator glasses hiding her eyes.

When I reach her, she turns and gets behind the wheel, and the moment I slip into the passenger seat and close my door, she guns it. The sedan slides out of the parking lot onto Hammond Road.

Police cars fly by us. I glance back, watching them turn into the Wake County Detention Center like bees bringing pollen back to a hive.

Ahead, there's a stoplight.

Meredith doesn't slow.

Instead, she pushes a finger into a set of controls, and the sunroof begins to retract.

The light is still green.

Behind us, it's a sea of law enforcement vehicles.

The light turns yellow, and she presses harder on the accelerator, which I'm surprised is even possible.

The traffic light switches to red a split second before we reach the intersection, but Meredith keeps going.

The wind through the sunroof is now so loud I have to shout. "Seriously? I just *got out* of jail."

Sure enough, behind us, a blue light flashes and an unmarked police car with dark-tinted windows closes the distance between us and then pulls up alongside.

Slowly, Meredith turns her head. Almost like she's daring them to pull her over.

The unmarked car doesn't pull us over. It gets in front of us, and the two cars weave through the streets of Raleigh, not exactly driving recklessly, but certainly a little above the speed limit and bending every traffic law.

At Meredith's house, the unmarked car parks a few doors down. It waits, idling. I rip the handle on my door and step out. The driver's door of the police car opens in sync. Ryan waits at the car, eyes on me.

He nods.

I nod back.

That's probably the closest the two of us will ever get to talking about what happened. But it's good enough for me.

Meredith unlocks the door to her place and slowly pushes it open.

I follow her in, and we pause at the threshold, peering around the staircase. Country music is playing in the living room, and I hear a man's voice howl out in pain, as if he's been hit.

"Owww! Young lady, you sank my aircraft carrier! I declare! You're a better tactician than half the admirals in the Pacific Fleet."

For the first time in six months, I hear my daughter's voice in person, not just over a sat phone. She's giggling as she says, "What does that mean?"

"It means they don't make 'em like Chester Nimitz anymore."

"What's a chest of minutes?"

Meredith and I step forward, and the moment Riley sees us, she bolts from the dining table and the game of Battleship.

She charges through the living room and crashes into me. I was ready. I had planted my good leg behind me, bracing for it. She hugs me tight, and through my shirt, I can already feel her warm tears soaking into me.

At the dining table, Warren rises from the chair and smiles. It's a big, genuine smile, the type he can't suppress. Without a word, he pulls the sliding door open and exits.

Riley looks up at me, tears flowing down her cheeks. And then, like a dam breaking, questions pour out of her, her chest heaving as she gasps for air. Finally, I pick her up and move to the couch and hold her for a long time.

Somewhere along the way, Meredith slips away, and it's only me and my daughter with our arms around each other.

When Riley's caught her breath, she gazes up at me. "Dad, where were you?"

"It doesn't matter. What matters is that I'm back now."

"On the news—"

"I know what the news said. But it was a misunderstanding, sweetie. Those happen in life. Sometimes you misunderstand someone. And sometimes someone misunderstands you or a situation you're involved in. Here, look."

I get out my phone and play the news video I found on the way home—the one announcing that I've been cleared of charges.

"So… you're not going to jail?"

"No, darling."

She hugs me again, pulling hard on my neck. It hurts, but it is the best thing I've felt in a very long time.

For the rest of the day, Riley and I play board games, and when I'm tired, I lie in bed and watch TV. She hugs me almost constantly, as if she might lose me again if she lets go.

Meredith brings pizza home for dinner, and we eat at the dining table. When we're done, we settle around the 3D puzzle of the Hogwarts School of Witchcraft and Wizardry. It's nearly finished, except for the top of the tower.

Meredith goes to the kitchen and returns with a Tupperware that holds a dozen pieces.

"Riley had the idea," she says, dumping the pieces out, "to wait until you got home to finish it."

And that's exactly what we do. The three of us turn over those last pieces and fit them together until the puzzle is complete.

122

For the next four days, I stay at Meredith's house. So does Riley. The three of us play board games and work on puzzles and occasionally, we just lie in bed and veg out on TV.

My email at Daedalus is constantly full. Harold helps with some details. Rose largely handles the rest, including going to the office and fighting fires with the transition. It helps that she knows every inch of the place—and the people, even the ones she's never met in person. I feel bad, like I'm leaving her hanging, but I'm exhausted. It's as if six months of adrenaline flowing through my system has been instantly drained.

When I apologized to Rose for not helping more, she cut me off. "Look, I've been cleaning up messes in this building for a long time. This is just a different kind. I've got this. Just rest and spend time with your daughter."

On Monday morning, I walk Riley to school, down that same sidewalk we traversed on the first day. I wondered if she'd be self-conscious about being seen with me, given the news reports of my arrest. It happens that way sometimes: people hear about the bad things you're accused of, but not how it turned out or the eventual truth.

My daughter, however, holds her head high and my left hand in her right as we march down the sidewalk, past the pollen-covered grass.

*

Inside the high school, I don't report to my classroom. I wait for the morning rush to end, and make my way to the principal's office, where I find Sheila behind her desk, chugging coffee from a massive Stanley thermos.

I half-expect her to make a good-natured quip, maybe something along the lines of "Security to the office." I wonder if that popped into my head because ELEE appeared as Sheila so much, and the lines between the two have gotten blurred in my mind.

But this Sheila—the actual principal I know and treasure—sets the coffee mug down, rounds her big wooden desk, and wraps me in a hug as she pushes her door closed.

When she releases me, she studies my face. "Are you okay, Alan?"

"Sort of."

She doesn't return to her chair behind the desk. Instead, she settles in one of the seats across from it, and I take the other.

"I know I've got some explaining to do—"

She holds a hand up. "You don't."

"I do. You covered for me—in more ways than one. That story about Prideland Rehabilitation…" I smile and shake my head.

Sheila cups a hand to her coiffed hair. "I thought that was pretty good myself."

"Still, I feel bad that you were in a position where you had to lie."

"Alan, if I told the truth about *everything* to *everyone* in this school *all the time*, it would have burned down years ago."

We both laugh, and after, Sheila quietly asks if I'm taking the rest of the year off.

"Actually, that's one of the reasons I stopped by. I'm not coming back."

Her eyebrows bunch, but Sheila doesn't try to talk me out of it. Instead, she says, "What's your plan?"

"There's a job I'm uniquely qualified for. At Amersa."

Sheila wrinkles her nose. "Amersa. Still don't care for the name."

I can't help but laugh. "Apparently they didn't either. It's why they called the product Labyrinth."

"What will you do there?"

"Keep the strings connected. And the Minotaur in the Labyrinth."

Sheila raises her eyebrows. "Hey, if it makes sense to you, I'm all for it."

"The other thing I want to talk to you about is the Daedalus Foundation."

Sheila repeats the name, mentally inspecting it. "*Daedalus Foundation.* It's got that shadowy, mysterious feel, like it's a front for taking over third-world countries."

"Trust me, it's a lot more benign than that. Daedalus is an investment firm that wants to deploy some of its excess capital for philanthropic causes. Specifically, in education. K12, in particular. And I was thinking we could start with a grant for this school. I think you might have a few uses for the funds."

"Said that right. But you also mentioned strings."

"Those strings have nothing to do with this. These are no-strings-attached grants."

"We can use the money however we want?"

"That's right. On any and all hyena problems."

123

I arrive at Warren's store just before lunch. There's one car in the parking lot, and inside, two twenty-something guys are lurking in the aisles.

Warren stands behind the counter, arms crossed, his expression dark as he watches the two shoppers.

"Hey!"

His word is like a bark that draws the customers' attention. "We're closing up early."

One holds up a multitool. "Would you take twenty for this?"

"This ain't Facebook Marketplace. Price is on it. You either like it or you don't."

They evidently didn't like it. Or not twenty bucks' worth. They leave, and Warren turns the sign and the deadbolt and marches past me.

"Thought you were never coming back."

"That makes two of us."

Behind the counter, he studies me the way Sheila just did. "You okay?"

"Ish."

He keeps staring at me. I know him well enough to know that this is the hard outer shell. But it's not what's inside. Which is what I'm after.

"Are you okay?" I ask him.

"Well, I wouldn't use the term, *ish*, it's a little too cute for my liking, but this is me recognizing that it fits here, but I'm not actually using it."

"But you did say it."

"But not like that."

I smile and turn away from the counter and pace around the store.

"Thank you for helping take care of Riley."

He grunts and crosses his arms again, but I can see a small smile forming on his lips. "That daughter of yours," he says carefully. "I'll tell you this: she's a fine young lady."

"I know."

"I think… it would *behoove* you—if you're able—to not leave for extended periods of time going forward."

"It wasn't by choice."

"What was it?"

"Same thing that happened to my dad."

Warren eyes me.

"He was drafted."

The glass front door rattles, and knuckles rap on it, and a face peers in and sees Warren. "You open?"

He stomps across the showroom and stares through the glass door. "No. We ain't open."

"But you're there," the guy says.

Warren reaches down and rattles the metal sign that says CLOSED against the glass and says, "We only serve *literate* customers."

Warren waits by the door, watching the allegedly illiterate customer leave.

When they're gone, he turns to me. "Let's go in the back."

We sit at the table where he once supplied us for a certain trip across two oceans and back, and where another version of him decided to join up with another version of me at a farmhouse outside of town where they built a data center and solar array for ELEE.

Warren gets us both a can of soda, and between sips, I say, "Seems like retail is losing its luster for you."

"Let's just say this here retirement job is becoming a retirement headache."

"You interested in a new retirement job?"

"Doing what?"

"Security mostly."

"For whom?"

"For me. At Amersa."

He grunts and takes a sip from the can. "Well, you're full of surprises, I'll give you that."

"I need someone I can trust, Warren. The kind of person who's got your back when the world is ending."

"Well, let's not get carried away." He takes another sip. "What exactly would we be securing?"

"The company at large. Special operations, if you will. The goal is to keep the Amersa server farm connected across space and time to an advanced AI in the future."

He stares at me skeptically and finally shakes his head. "I'm already interested. You don't have to hype it up like a sci-fi movie."

He sets the can down. "Which brings us to the small issue of my consulting fee—because I will be maintaining my North Carolina S Corp and funneling the money through there so I can reduce my payroll tax burden."

"Of course. You can name your price. Money isn't an issue."

That look of disgust I know so well covers Warren's face. "You're *still* a *terrible* negotiator."

"And an even worse looter."

"Who you been looting?"

"No one. Does that mean we have a deal?"

He takes another sip of soda and mutters as if he's annoyed. "Yeah, we got a deal."

But I can see that classic Warren smile he's suppressing.

124

At the hospital, Rose is standing outside the entrance, waiting, arms crossed.

When I reach her, I pull her into a tight hug and ask how she's doing.

"Tired" is her one-word reply.

As we walk in, she gives me an update on things at Amersa, which is the source of her tiredness. At the elevator, the conversation turns to the reason we're here: June and Isaac.

"June's awake," Rose says quietly.

"How is she?"

"She's... okay. They say with medication and time, she'll mostly get back to normal. There may be the occasional seizure."

"And Isaac?"

Rose glances away. "He's awake more now, but the doctors say he'll never fully recover. He's going to need round-the-clock care."

"Done. Daedalus has the money."

Rose stops me in the hall. "It's not just the seizures and the sleeping. His memory is sort of... scrambled. He has trouble recognizing what was real and what wasn't."

"What do you mean?"

"You should talk to him."

"We'll take care of him, Rose. Whatever it takes."

*

Outside June's hospital room, I peer in and spot her husband sitting in a chair beside her, reading. Her eyes are closed. Both of her children are there. One is watching a tablet with headphones on, the other is reading a book.

As if sensing my presence, June cracks her eyelids and turns toward the open door.

When she sees me, her eyes open a little more, and the edges of her lips curl.

I raise my hand and hold it up, a silent hello.

June wiggles her fingers, as if a weight is holding the rest of her body down.

Her husband looks up from the book and locks eyes with me. I nod to him and continue walking down the hall, toward the elevator, and on to the Intensive Care Unit.

The glass sliding door to Isaac's room is closed, and a curtain inside is pulled across it. Slowly, quietly, I slide the door open enough to poke my head past the curtain.

Isaac is awake and sitting up in bed. He's eating what looks like grits or oatmeal. He brightens when he sees me. "Alan. Dude, where've you been?"

"I uh… had a few things to take care of."

At first glance, he appears and sounds normal. He's still a little underweight and his face is haggard, but his eyes burn with that same intensity I knew before.

I sit in the chair beside him, trying to think of where to start.

Between bites, Isaac mumbles. "Glad you're here."

"Yeah?"

"I've got questions."

I wait, and when he puts the spoon down, he says, "I remember being on a boat. And thinking we would never get off of it."

I smile at him. "I think we all did."

"And when we finally did, it went bad. Like super bad. There was nothing there. I remember feeling terrible about it." He swallows. "Like I messed up."

"You didn't, Isaac."

"I remember getting back onboard and playing a game."

"Zelda."

He points the spoon at me. "Yes. Exactly. And I was playing the second quest."

I nod.

"But it got weird. It's like I was in the game. But it wasn't exactly Zelda I was in."

"What was it?"

"I was in this tower, and it was me and Lucas. And we were trying to escape."

"Lucas was there?"

Isaac nods and takes another bite. "Yeah. And we were working on ELEE—that's his extinction—"

"AI. Yeah. I remember."

"Right, well, he was upgrading it, and he was doing some next-level code ninja stuff. He had a new programming language and a compiler for it, and the capabilities were mind-blowing. I'm talking using the universe itself like a network medium and human brains as compute. And it was *breaking my brain*."

Staring at the floor, I nod slowly.

"But here's what I don't get," Isaac says, leaning over. "I don't remember Lucas on the boat. So… I guess he met us there?"

Isaac tilts his head to me, silently prompting me to answer.

"Yeah," I say quietly. "He did."

"But there's something wrong with that, but I don't know what it is. Either way, we were burning it at both ends on this ELEE upgrade. It's like when we made it a distributed system at Amersa."

"Like SETI@HOME."

Isaac's eyes go wide. "He told you about that?"

Still staring at the floor, I nod. "Yeah."

"So it was like that, but with *billions* of nodes. And they were different, like, ELEE was reading data from all of them and then updating Labyrinth in real-time to adapt to the user and steer their lives. That was a separate program we called the Wings of Icarus because the whole point was to keep people from going off the rails. You know, flying too high or too low. But it was not just individuals. It was factoring humanity as a whole. Which is just hard to even wrap your head around, but June was figuring it out. She was analyzing all this data from Amersa thanks to a backdoor the CTO installed. We were using data from our Labyrinth and a much larger dataset on a remote server. I guess maybe it was training data ELEE generated for herself? But there was a lot of it. And we were trying to put it all together, but it didn't work."

Isaac exhales and suddenly looks much more tired. He closes his eyes, and his head rolls to the side.

The glass door to the room slides open, and a nurse leans in and requests that I leave, but I stand and beg her for two more minutes.

She shakes her head. "He needs to rest."

"Two minutes. And then I'll go. I promise."

She doesn't like it, but she pulls the door closed, and I sit back down in the chair.

For a while, we sit there in silence, Isaac resting, me thinking about what to say next. After one of my two precious minutes is up, I reach through the bed rail and grip Isaac's hand, careful not to touch the IV. Isaac squeezes back and slowly opens his eyes.

"Alan. Dude, when did you get here?"

"Uh, just now."

His eyes close again. In the glass door to the room, I see the reflection of his hospital bed and the monitors and me sitting beside him, holding his hand. I squeeze again. His head rolls, and he sits up a little and squints at me. "What were we talking about?"

"You and Lucas. And the work in the tower."

He exhales. "Oh yeah. We finally got the wings to work. June helped us with that. Did you know that?"

"You told me."

"Right. But we couldn't get the string to work. It wouldn't connect. It was like a dial-up modem that kept dialing, and the two ends would do a hardware handshake, but the data transmissions kept getting corrupted."

He leans forward and takes a bite of oatmeal. "I wish we had gotten it to work."

"You did, Isaac."

His eyebrows shoot up. "Seriously?"

"Seriously. You finished it."

"What does it do?"

"It connects Labyrinth to ELEE. A version Lucas made a long time ago."

"Why?"

"Extinction."

Isaac frowns. "I don't get it."

"A while back—a long while back—Lucas and ELEE realized that the biggest threat to humanity's survival isn't nuclear war or asteroids or solar flares or any of that other stuff. It's us."

"Us?"

"That's right. We're the biggest threat to humanity's survival. The human race itself. We've advanced to the point that we can make tools capable of causing our own extinction. And it's not the tools you think. The most dangerous thing we ever created was a technology that gave humans a better alternative to real life. A better reality. A virtual one where they were happier and in less pain and safer."

"Labyrinth."

"That's right."

"So Labyrinth is the extinction event?"

"It is. And it's also the answer."

"To what?"

"To everything, Isaac. Including the Fermi Paradox."

The glass door slides open, and the nurse pokes her head around the curtain again.

I hold a hand up. "One minute, please. I promise I'll go after that. *I promise.* This is important."

She exhales, but says nothing as she leaves again.

Scooting the chair closer to Isaac, I keep going. "The first numbers ELEE sent you. Do you remember them?"

He nods. "They spelled Fermi Paradox."

"It's because she knew what that mystery meant to you. And she knew the answer to it. Labyrinth is the destiny of every advanced race. It's why there seems to be no one out there. No alien space ships or even probes.

"Sooner or later, any sufficiently advanced civilization builds a Labyrinthian technology. At that point, they lose interest in exploring space. Think about it. Space exploration is resource-intense, time-consuming, and dangerous. It's also uncertain and unlikely to yield meaningful discoveries in the lifespan of a biological organism. But the biggest reason is that all the worlds out there in the universe aren't nearly as interesting as the infinite worlds waiting in the Labyrinth in your own living room. Those worlds are customized for you—the user. They're tuned precisely to your desires. That's why there aren't any aliens out there. They're at home, Isaac, in their Labyrinth. And then there are the civilizations that have been lost in their Labyrinths."

"Lost?"

"Yes. Advanced civilizations all face a point where their Labyrinth either leads them to ruin or it becomes the technology that protects them. Some build the wings and connect the string. Some don't."

"And we did it?"

"You did, pal. That string you built stretches across space and time. From our Labyrinth to ELEE. She reads the data from humanity—from all those billions of nodes—and adjusts the system to help steer our development. She helps protect us from ourselves."

I squeeze Isaac's hand. "We're the Minotaur. And the Labyrinth is the only thing that can contain us."

Isaac picks up the spoon and chews another bite of oatmeal, seeming deep in thought. Finally, he looks over at me. "Are you for real?"

"For real. The world doesn't know it, but you and Lucas saved us from extinction. All of us. This generation. The next. And every one after. You did it, buddy."

Epilogue

Six Months Later

It's almost 5 PM on a Thursday, and I'm sitting in a conference room at Amersa's office. June sits to my right, Rose on the left. Warren is standing by the windows, looking out at the parking lot, listening. He says he gets tired of the meetings and sitting so much, but I know he likes it more than sitting at home or minding his store.

At the other end of the table is most of Amersa's leadership team. The new CEO is here, as well as the COO, CTO, and CFO.

I know I'm not qualified to run a company like Amersa. But I don't need to be. The board's role is to establish the company's goals and make sure it has the right officers in place to accomplish those goals. And that they don't deviate from the mission.

Still, there's been a little friction between the board and the officers. The leadership team wants to move fast and break things. June, Rose, and I have different priorities. I'm a history teacher. And I've seen the future—one version of it anyway. Our goal is to make sure we don't end up like that numberless world. On that subject, I receive regular visits from ELEE, meetings like this, in my office, where I seem to be talking to a voice in my head.

The meeting in the conference room finally breaks, and when the company officers have filed out, June opens a pill box and washes down two tablets with a gulp of water. The five o'clock alarm on her watch goes off as she sets the glass down. She's gotten a lot better. I wish the same were true for Isaac.

After saying goodbye to Rose, June, and Warren, I take the elevator to the server floor and march past the NOC to a nondescript secure door. After scanning my badge, I step into a space that feels like the foyer of a penthouse apartment in New York City. Inside, there's a posh kitchen, a living room, a dining room, and two bedrooms—one for a caretaker and another with a hospital bed, which is empty at the moment. A wall panel clicks open, and one of the nurses steps through. He's wearing a blue *Star Trek* uniform favored by the medical and science staff.

"He's up," the nurse says. "And having a pretty good day."

I thank him, and instead of walking deeper into the apartment, I turn left and climb a short flight of stairs. At the landing, a pair of double doors slide open, revealing a replica of the bridge of the starship *Enterprise* 1701-D.

As I step around the wooden horseshoe where Worf stood in the show, the ringing starts. It's not the harsh, angry clanging of the rocks in the can. It's three gentle chimes, similar to a doorbell.

Isaac hears my footsteps and rises from the first officer's seat.

Seeing me, he turns to the captain's chair, where Lucas is sitting with his legs crossed, wearing a red uniform with four pips on the collar.

"Sir," Isaac says, "the emissary has arrived."

Lucas rises and pulls down his tunic. "Welcome. I've heard a lot about you."

"Likewise."

This version of Lucas, which ELEE supplies for Isaac—and is showing to me now—always syncs up with Isaac's shifting perception of time and memories. We've met on countless occasions like this, but I play along.

Isaac motions to the viewscreen. "We're just starting this one."

I glance over at the paused episode of *Star Trek: The Next Generation*.

Isaac smiles. "It's the one where Riker gets cloned. It's called *Second Chances*. Have you seen it?"

"I have. I know all about second chances."

★

On the way home, I pick up flowers.

The house where Meredith, Riley, and I live now isn't a mansion. But it's a big step up for Riley and me. It has a two-car garage, enough space for everyone, a nice backyard with a pool, and most importantly, a neighborhood full of kids around Riley's age.

In the back hall, I drop my keys in the small dish that sits below a wedding photo.

I set the flowers on the kitchen counter and make my way to the backyard, where Riley is lying in a hammock, reading a book, and Meredith is sitting on the patio, laptop out, no doubt doing school work for her master's degree. A hand rests on her protruding belly, and when I reach her, I put mine over hers and lean down and kiss her.

Inside, while Riley changes clothes, Meredith asks me if I'm sure she should go with us.

"Absolutely," I tell her. "It's what she would have wanted."

At the cemetery, in the hazy glow of the setting sun, the three of us walk together through the maze of grave markers to the one we've come to pay our respects to.

Two years ago, it was an open hole in the ground. Now, lush green grass grows in the shadow of the headstone.

By the grave, Riley squats and gently places the flowers. I stare at the name and read the epitaph. When my gaze reaches the dates of birth and death, I don't see the numbers.

And I don't hear the ringing, only the wind blowing through the trees and leaves collecting on the ground as fall gives way to winter.

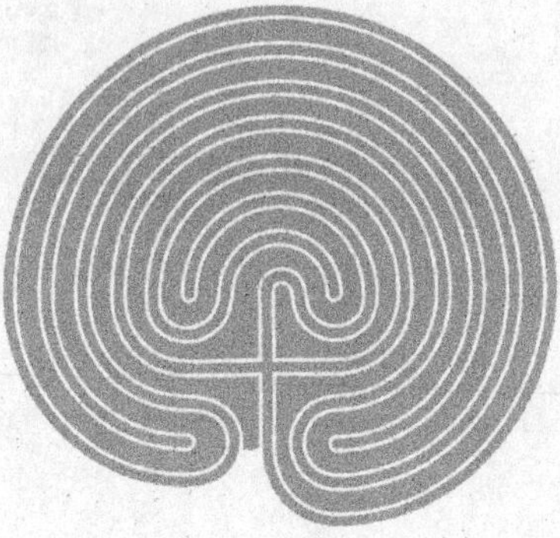

Author's Note

While writing *Labyrinth*, I was in a labyrinth of my own.

I figure the shape of my recent challenges isn't that different from other folks about my age (or at a similar life stage). For me, the solution was the same thing as the characters in this novel. It was about choosing a path, going down it, learning from it, and adjusting course... until I got to the end.

Sometimes you read the numbers wrong and have to adjust your destination, if you will.

I began writing *Labyrinth* in 2022 (a few months before *Antarctica Station* came out). I figured I would be done in maybe twelve months. Sooner if I was lucky.

I was wrong about that (writing a novel is its own peculiar labyrinth; even if you think you see the end, that path typically has some surprises in store).

In my head, I had the broad outline for the story. I had the characters. As I drafted the book, however, the wondrous (and frustrating) thing that happens when writing a novel inevitably occurred: some things I planned didn't work. They still worked in my head and on the outline, but not on the page. And the characters... they kept surprising me and developing in ways I didn't expect. This phenomenon, I believe, is why we read. It's also why a lot of us write. It's the joy that comes from the surprises. It's about what we learn during that journey (about others and ourselves). It's the magic when the story comes alive and starts doing things you don't expect, as if it is in charge (and not the author).

But, sorting out all those surprises can be a lot of work.

Imagine a maze, one shaped like a labyrinth. Imagine you're writing your novel and each word is a little bit of a line tracing its way through that maze. No matter how good you are (or how well you know the story and characters), you're inevitably going to have some lines that hit dead ends. These are scenes that don't work, paragraphs that don't flow, subplots that have to go, and entire chapters that need to be thrown out. Occasionally, there are characters that don't need to be there (and some missing ones who do).

Those edits result in the proverbial eraser marks on the maze of your novel. Looking at the page, you still see the faded lines, but you resume your path (that line might be a little heavier as the frustrated but dedicated author bears down a little harder; the page may even be torn in a few places).

In my case, if you peeked into my writing room during the drafting of *Labyrinth*, you'd see a pile of rubber eraser shavings towering over me (and your humble author likely rubbing his forehead or staring at the ceiling, pondering).

I did more rewrites to this novel than I have to any other since my debut twelve years ago. Even after sending the manuscript to the publisher, I was emailing PDFs with my handwritten notes and edits from the typeset file (I hereby want to apologize to Charlie Hiscox and Sophie Whitehead at Head of Zeus for those last-minute changes—and to thank them and Nic Cheetham for their outstanding work on this book).

Writing a book is a labyrinth. Everyone's work is. But like the image on the numbers website, work for most people is usually only the tip of the iceberg of their challenges in life. And it was for me during this time.

I was 42 when I began writing this novel and 45 when I finished. Like many my age, I am blessed to have young children and aging parents who are still with us. Both come with challenges, and being there for them is a responsibility I take very seriously—and a role I treasure.

Doing your work and taking care of family are hard enough these days, but I'll say that navigating a changing industry adds to the challenge of any job. Book publishing is indeed a changing industry. It has been since I've been here, but now it feels like the pace of change has accelerated. Some days it seems like the walls of the publishing labyrinth are changing before my eyes. The root cause of the upheaval in publishing is the same forces affecting so many other industries: AI and shifting consumer behavior.

I'd love to keep my head down and continue tracing my way through whatever labyrinthine novel I'm drafting, but when you feel the ground shaking beneath your feet, it's hard not to pause and look up from your work (or think about leaving the building or at least crawling under your desk for safety).

Publishing has that vibe right now.

It's caused me to do a lot of reflection over the past few years (and to go down some rabbit holes and dead ends). I've thought deeply about what I want from my career and where my skills fit into the industry. I've learned a lot from it.

And most of all, I've learned the value of prioritizing—on the small things and especially the big picture.

In the end, I've decided to focus on family, writing, and readers. Those are the things I care most about.

The industry may change and that shaking beneath my feet may get worse, but I know this: I still love writing, and I know I'll never regret spending more time with the kids while they're young (and if I've done my job, after they're adults).

I've also been reminded of the value of focusing on the things within my control and when to ignore everything else. Yes, I'm doing my writing from beneath the desk (just being conscious of falling objects; after all, a lot of people depend on me), and yes, it's getting crowded with this massive mound of eraser shavings, but there's nowhere else I'd rather be (workwise).

One thing I am certain of: I never would have made it out of the labyrinth without the enduring love and support of my wife. Some years are easier than others and some days seem full of nothing but dead ends, and that's made me very thankful to have her to come home to.

Lastly, and most importantly, I want to thank you for following my career—even when the books are over a year late (I'm clearly blaming the labyrinth of my life, but let's face it, we all have one).

I hope wherever you are, that things are going well, you're not erasing too many lines of the path of your life, and that the tremors at work or home are just enough to keep things lively.

Gerry

About the Author

A.G. RIDDLE spent ten years starting and running internet companies before retiring to focus on his true passion: writing fiction. He is now an Amazon, *Wall Street Journal* and *Sunday Times* bestselling author with nearly five million copies sold worldwide in twenty languages. He lives in Raleigh, North Carolina.

For more, please visit www.agriddle.com